Turbulent Skies

A Jack Coward Novel

Ronald A. Fabick

Tellwell Talent
www.tellwell.ca

ISBN
978-0-2288-0357-7 (Hardcover)
978-0-2288-0356-0 (Paperback)
978-0-2288-0358-4 (eBook)

— Chapter 1 —

Sacramento, California - September 25, 1978

The ever-brightening horizon revealed another cloudless autumn dawn, an indication of yet another mid-eighties day. Although the sun had yet to rise above the foothills, and most of Sacramento had yet to cast off its morning slumber, such was not the case in suburb where the Roshtti family lived.

Anyone looking at the split-level house at 7564 Zinfandel Drive would think they were looking at something straight out of *The Brady Bunch.* However, in place of the eternally calm, cool Mike Brady, Reza Roshtti was feverishly rushing about trying to prepare for what was promising to be the biggest presentation of his short but rocket-sharp, four-year career at California Robotics, a small but growing division of the Thompson Ramo Wooldridge (TRW) Company. TRW's work was top-secret; the company was developing state-of-the-art electronics, new technology that included computers, software and systems engineering—and one of their main clients was the United States military.

Two years earlier, in 1976, TRW had begun managing a project originally started by the United States Air Force and known as 'Project Overlook'. Project Overlook was a 'leftover' from the Vietnam War. Although the government had thrown away hundreds of lives and almost a billion dollars a month to 'win' the unwinnable Vietnam War, lack of political resolve to bring it to a victorious conclusion led to the shelving of it and many other such projects. But until government cutbacks and civil unrest had forced the Nixon administration to cancel Project Overlook, it had been a very promising reconnaissance weapon.

In June of that same year, just prior to the state primary elections, Jimmy Carter—who would soon become president—swung through California in search of political support using promises of research and development money for fledgling aerospace companies as one of his sales tactics. Wanting to benefit from this should Carter win, Reza's company, California Robotics, decided Project Overlook was a prime candidate for this program. The company knew Project Overlook had good science and planning behind it so they quickly reinvested, spending a few million dollars to upgrade the technology and streamline the plans. Now they were ready to showcase it. Reza Roshtti, one of their prime developers, was charged with taking it to the next level and he was on his way this morning to give a high-level sales pitch to the company's board of directors to encourage them to spend even more money, with a goal to sell it back to the military.

"Have you seen my briefcase?" Reza shouted downstairs to his wife Giti.

"It's in your office," Giti replied.

After a moment's pause, Reza once again shouted down to his wife, "Not that rough-looking old thing—that's the one I use every day. I was looking for the one you bought me for my birthday in November."

Upstairs, Giti could hear him frantically opening and shutting closet doors and moving piles of clothing aside. "It's where you left it the day after your birthday, where it has been gathering dust for the last eleven months—in the closet next to the shoe rack," Giti replied sarcastically.

Reza was about to respond with a similarly biting reply when the phone on top of the large roll-top, oak desk rang. In his haste to reach it, Reza banged his shin on the chair and almost plunged chin-first into the desk. Cursing under his breath, he managed to pull himself up and answer the phone on the third ring.

"Good morning, Reza." It was Tom DeSoto, his business partner. " How's the packing going? All ready for the big to-do tomorrow?"

"Almost. Just a couple more last-minute details to deal with, but I'm sure I can finish those while we're on the plane. And they really are last-minute. I was up until twelve forty-five this morning trying to iron them out!"

"Oh, sure—just you and your trusty slide rule," Tom said with a chuckle. "When are you going to start using that Texas Instruments calculator I got you?"

"I tried, but with complexity of these calculations all I got on the display was, 'Error, Error' ... something like what that robot in Star Trek is always saying." Tom laughed again and Reza concluded, "At any rate, that part is almost over. Just a few more calculations to verify our findings and the hard part is finished."

"Not quite, Reza," Tom said. "The hard part is just ahead. We've yet to convince Mr. McLennan and his board of directors that not only was the two million dollars they spent over the past two years absolutely worth it, but that a further one hundred million or more will be the ticket to take this from the blackboard and slide rule to production. That, my friend, is the hard part."

"Difficult yes," Reza agreed, "but the fact that Washington has been knocking on our door and showing genuine interest in this project should carry a lot of weight and swing the pendulum decidedly in our favour." Reza looked at his watch. "Anyway, Tom, I've got to go. We've got a plane to catch. I'll talk to you when I see you."

"Wait, wait," Tom made him halt. "I called to remind you to bring all your notes—and for God's sake, don't forget your transparencies for the overhead projector."

"Already packed and ready to go, my friend. See you soon," Reza replied.

The connection broken, Reza hurriedly placed the receiver back onto the cradle and once again returned to the task of collecting his notes. Forty-five minutes later, Giti Roshtti backed their well used, blue 1972 AMC Matador out of the driveway and headed west towards the city, her frazzled husband riding shotgun, his notes stuffed into the new briefcase, which he found right where Giti said it was.

"God I'm tired, I only had only four and a half hours of sleep," Reza complained. He glanced at his watch and said, "Honey, do you think that you can stop at the 7-11 on Folsom, so I can get a coffee? We've got a few extra minutes and, since it's early, I think we will have time."

Giti nodded and patted his thigh. "Of course," she said.

A few minutes later, coffee in hand, they traveled down Bradshaw Road, past Sacramento Mather Airport—barely four miles from their home.

"It's too bad that your seven-twenty flight doesn't leave from there," Giti casually said to Reza, "You could have had an extra half-hour of sleep. You look so tired, dear."

Looking up from the notes on top of his briefcase that he had been making some last-minute changes to, Reza responded, "Yes, that would have been a big help. Too bad Sacramento put those late-night flight restrictions on a few years ago. Oh well, once this is done maybe I can catch a few winks between here and San Diego."

"But you have to stop in Los Angeles to pick up Tom!" Giti said, confused.

Reza chuckled, "You're funny, you make it seem like the pilot is going to lower the flaps and set down a 727 for just one guy. There's going to be other people getting on the plane, you know." Then, spotting the turnoff to the airport, he said, "Oh, here comes the turnoff, Route 50 onto I-Five. It's coming up."

"I know, I see it, I'm not blind you know," snapped Giti.

"Sorry! I'm just tired that's all, I didn't mean to criticize you."

Reza released his grip on his coffee cup, slid his hand into his wife's and gave it a reassuring squeeze. His skin suddenly felt almost prickly and he noticed he'd become unusually hot and sweaty. *It's just nerves*, he thought to himself, *God, don't let me get sick now… I must be reacting to the heat.*

He remembered heat like this from an earlier, more frightening time in his life. As Giti drove, his thoughts wandered back nine years in time … across the Pacific Ocean, back to another life, when his body was drenched in sweat and his skin was prickly just like it was now—back to the jungles of South Vietnam.

His mind was relentless in its visions: specters from the past came into his sight, faces of young men, buddies who had barely got to know one another before they were brutally killed or maimed as the first mortar rounds struck inside the compound that morning.

One red-haired, freckle-faced, goofy-looking guy stood out … what was his name? Graham, Graham somebody—boy could that bastard shoot. He had Coke-bottle bottoms for glasses and everyone was surprised when he waltzed into the barracks as a new recruit in his plaid suit with flood pants, sat down on his bunk and said, "What are you losers looking at?"

Reza liked him immediately. They were both oddballs in the military; a second-generation Persian ethnic and a half-blind Canadian. They supported each other through more than a little hazing from their colleagues. But Graham sure could shoot. After passing basic training, which absolutely no one thought he could do, he proceeded to surpass all previous marksmanship records held by new recruits.

Yes, that's it … Reams, Graham Reams, Reza thought to himself. It was on all those bloody plaques and awards … Hell of a guy.

Suddenly, Reza saw orange flashes, brilliant like the sun against the emerald green foliage of the Asian jungle. The bright lights and explosions were so near he could actually feel the heat and concussive blasts … he could feel artillery fire advancing quickly toward him.

"Reza? I asked you if this is where you think I should go!" Giti asked loudly, annoyed.

Jolted back to the present, he realized he had been bedazzled by amber rays of sunlight reflecting off the mirror-glass walls of the downtown office towers. The heat he had felt was actually blasts of hot air coming through the open window.

Giti noticed him sweating. "Sorry! You can close the window if you like," she said. "But it's sure hot, considering it's only just after six o'clock in the morning. The temperature is already 78 degrees!" He didn't respond, so by way of explanation she said, "I saw it on the sign on the Mutual of Omaha building."

Reza rolled up the electric window, thinking, *that's right, one of the only really good options on this crate of a car was electric windows.*

"That's okay honey, it's just that the rush of hot air was unexpected. My mind was elsewhere." *But it should be on what we're about to do, on what we're going to accomplish, on the lives that will be saved!*

Due to a nondisclosure agreement TRW had made him sign, his wife knew very little about his work. Oh, sure, she knew the *nature* of what he was doing—she had not missed all the calls between he and Tom—and she knew *why* he was doing it (partly, at least), but she knew none of the specifics about *how* he was doing it. And she certainly didn't know the details of that time in his life that *motivated* him to do it. He could never tell her of the horror. He loved her too much. Only another vet could understand, he supposed.

But Vietnam was at the root of his work. His experiences there were seared on his soul, so after one tour of duty he spent four years at UCLA studying engineering and ultimately secured his job at California Robotics, where he quickly became a leader in circuitry design. But his heart was in national defense and so he had jumped at the chance to resurrect the project. In fact, both he and his partner Tom would almost have paid money for this break, this chance … because this was payback—payback for all the young men like him who had sacrificed their innocence; for all the Graham Reams who had sacrificed their lives. Project Overlook would be a shining light for security for the nation. Maybe it would even be a way to end the institution of war for good. The technology was impeccable. The design was sound. How could he and Tom lose? After all, they were on the side of the good guys.

He sighed. All good intentions aside, sometimes he wondered, who am I kidding? Because sometimes he wondered if what was really driving him was guilt; guilt for walking away that November morning, through the acrid smell of burning fuel and the burning rubber smell from the bombed-out Jeeps; for looking at his hands and counting his fingers while the smell of the moist earth ejected by exploding Viet Cong shells mingled with the stench of burning flesh; and most of all, for being able to walk at all and for being able to see, smell and experience the nightmares that still haunted him nightly and the visions that still came during the day. He was guilty for feeling relief— relief that it was not his mangled body lying half-in and half-out of the blackened shell of a burned-out military vehicle; it wasn't his headless torso next to a crater; and, it wasn't his body zipped into one of the dark plastic body bags that lined the edge of the tarmac, waiting for pickup and removal by the C-130 transports the day he went home.

He felt the old familiar sadness as he remembered that sight; it had been just like setting out the trash at the curb on Tuesday morning, all those bodies waiting to be picked up after their usefulness had been and gone …

"It's the next exit after Power Line Road isn't it?" Giti's question startled him.

"Yes! You take Exit Five-twenty-eight onto Airport Boulevard, then keep looking for the signs … they'll let you know where to go. And that's all you have to do on Wednesday afternoon when you pick me up; just look for the signs with the little planes on them."

"A simple yes or no would have sufficed, Reza," Giti sniffed. "After all, I've gotten us this far, haven't I?"

"Yes, you have … and again I'm sorry to be so short. Boy, I'll be glad when this is over and we can take a few weeks off together, just you and me. We can leave Sina with my brother and spend some quality time alone. Would you like that?"

He knew he was speaking out of guilt again—guilt for having practically abandoned his wife and young son to work on this project. It had turned him into a workaholic.

"Or how about a few days by ourselves then we can spend the rest of the time with Sina, all of us together?" suggested Giti. "He's getting older by the day and we—you—need to spend some time with him. Take him fishing or swimming or something. Reconnect with your son!"

Not this again, Reza thought to himself, but he said, "I know! I know! I probably haven't been spending enough time with him, but with all the pressure of this job..."

Giti wasn't buying it. "That's just an excuse and you know it. You've got to make time for him—both of us do. It is of the utmost importance to be there for him now; this is a critical time in his life. It's time for you to solidify your relationship with him. You're his father, and he will soon be a man. He needs your example to learn from. I've spent time being his mother, caring for him and raising him. But the age he is now is very special for a father and son. It's a time when their relationship changes from being that of father and son to becoming friends and men together."

He couldn't argue; he knew she was right, so he said nothing at all. His son would be a teenager in a few short years. When this project was properly launched he would be sure to spend more time with the boy.

Reza and his wife arrived at the main terminal with just a little over half an hour to spare. He retrieved his bag from the backseat and then leaned back inside the passenger door to say, "I'll see you on Wednesday afternoon; don't forget."

"I won't! I miss you already!" Giti responded and suddenly Reza remembered why he loved her. When she smiled at him, she was the beautiful Persian desert flower he had known since she was a girl. He quickly kissed and embraced her then closed the car door and walked into the terminal. If he had known this was the last moment he would share with her, he would have held her tighter.

Twenty minutes later, he'd picked up his seat assignment and boarding pass from the ticket counter, checked his one bag and was proceeding down the jet way to his aircraft. Through the windows at the gate he'd already spotted his awaiting airliner on the tarmac, all shiny and clean, with its freshly painted livery of white with stripes of pink, orange and red; its ubiquitous 'smile' under the cockpit—all letting him know that he was in the safe hands of Pacific Southwest Airlines. *Yes*, Reza thought to himself, looking up at the brilliant blue autumn sky, *it's a great day to fly*.

At the cabin door, head stewardess Ellen Campbell was almost through her greeting duties, and Reza was the last person to board the aircraft. "Good morning sir, welcome to PSA," she said as she looked at his boarding pass then directed him to his seat. "You're in seat 5A, on your right, five rows down." She had already said much the same to the other eighty-two souls who had boarded before Reza. She flashed him a smile then closed the exterior door.

After Ellen and a fellow flight attendant gave the prerequisite safety emergency evacuation speech, there was a bump to the aircraft as the tug began to push the jet back for engine start. Reza, with his bag stowed below in the baggage compartment and new briefcase tucked safely under the seat in front of him, finally started to feel excited about the presentation and what lay ahead. He checked to see that his seatbelt was buckled securely then eagerly awaited takeoff.

At precisely at 7:20 a.m., after a brief delay to get clearance for takeoff, the B727 started its roll down the runway. As the thrust from the three Pratt & Whitney turbofan engines pushed Reza and his fellow passengers farther into their seats, the aircraft accelerated, quickly reaching flying speed. The captain eased back on the control column and the airliner lifted off the ground and upwards into the blue California sky. As it climbed, it accelerated southward while Reza stared out toward the east. The gleaming, serpentine American River wound its way through his neighbourhood and though he tried, the distance was too great for him to pick out his own house. He turned his attention to the interstate below, watching the ant-like cars as they scurried along it and for one instant imagined he could see his beloved Giti in their car on her way back to Sacramento. Of course, by now she would almost be home, he realized.

Home. They lived on a quiet street lined with trees already turning their autumn colours. This was Reza's favourite time of year. He especially loved those rare evenings when, after a long day, he and Giti would walk hand-in-hand down their street, the leaves rustling and crunching under their feet, and marvel at Mother Nature's transformation of the landscape, how it morphed from the emerald green of spring and summer to the red and orange of fall. It was so different from that far-away jungle that lurked in the recesses of his mind. There, the leaves were always green and mysterious and the dense jungle that hid America's foes was always dangerous and frequently deadly, giving way only under a barrage of Agent Orange.

Maybe that was why he liked his neighbourhood so much; it was peaceful and free from crime. There, the biggest infractions included hitting a baseball through someone's window or playing Knicky-Knocky Nine Doors. In the peaceful home that he shared with Giti it was safe to raise his son. It was unlike a lot of other cities in America, which were plagued by ever-increasing crime and fueled by drugs, drugs that often originated in the home of his ancestors …

Come on, Reza, snap out of it. Get back to work!

He retrieved his briefcase from under the seat and, as he'd promised himself he would, returned to finalizing his notes and presentation. These plans were a culmination of everything he'd achieved with his education and work so far as well as a further twenty-six months of effort shared with Tom DeSoto. He puzzled over them, looking for final tweaks he could make, but, after a few fruitless moments of effort, his lack of sleep forced a premature end to anything resembling work. Exhausted, he settled down to grab some precious moments of rest.

The aircraft made a harder than usual landing at Los Angeles and the sudden jolt brought Reza out of a short but surprisingly deep sleep. As often happens when a person is awakened unexpectedly, he felt an instant of disorientation—and the unfamiliar surroundings of the plane's interior, coupled with the roar of the thrust reversers as they were applied, added to what he was starting to recognize as a general feeling of uneasiness.

A few moments later the aircraft rolled to a stop and passengers and cargo began off-loading, some to connect with other flights, others terminating their travels at Los Angeles. Reza stayed put, waiting for Tom to board. He watched Ellen Campbell capably overseeing the disembarkation of passengers and when she saw him looking, she approached.

"I'm glad you managed to get some rest," she said. "You looked like you were in desperate need of it. I would have given you a pillow but I didn't want to wake you."

"Thank you very much, I appreciate that," Reza answered, "and yes, I really needed it. I had a late night and a rather early start to my day."

Glancing past Ellen, Reza noticed Tom coming through the door and down the aisle. Ellen noticed too, and hurriedly returned to the door to resume her greeting duties. Reza rose from his seat and the two men greeted one another.

"Good morning once again, Reza. Thanks for not biting my head off this morning when I called. It wasn't until I hung up the phone that I realized what time of the day it was," Tom said. "I feel bad about that." Tom stowed his bag in the overhead compartment and settled into seat 5B beside his friend and partner.

"That's okay, Tom, but I damn near killed myself getting to the phone," Reza chuckled. "Too early to be coordinated, you know? I hit the chair and nearly landed on my head."

"Well I'm glad you didn't! Tomorrow's an absolutely huge day, so don't go dying on me. I'm depending on you to do your part," Tom said, thinking ahead to their Tuesday morning meeting at TRW. "After we're back in the air, I think you should get some rest. Tomorrow is a big day. It's what we've worked toward for so long, right Reza?"

Reza nodded. He knew what was at stake.

A short while later, with 135 passengers and crew aboard, the captain once more lined up his aluminum-skinned missile with the centerline of the runway. He released the brakes and advanced the throttles to their pre-calculated thrust settings and the PSA jetliner shot down the 8,900-foot-long ribbon of concrete toward her fate.

Within a few moments, Reza was fast asleep once more beside Tom. Tom placed some headphones in his ears, turned up the volume and began listening to the new tune by the band Exile, *Kiss You All Over.*

San Diego, California

Seventy-five miles to the south of the runway that had just launched the PSA jet, at just after 8:45 a.m., new pilot Mike Stephens and his instructor

Morgan Hill were performing a pre-flight check in preparation for Mike's morning lesson.

"Check magnetos," Morgan said, and Mike promptly switched from one magneto to the other, noting a small RPM drop each time which indicated that both were working normally and there was not a grounding fault on one side of the ignition system. A faulty magneto was something you did not want to take a chance on in flight and though there was redundancy built into the system, it was better to stay on the ground if one was not working.

Mike went about the rest of the pre-flight check, checking mixture settings, carburetor heat, ammeter, flight control surfaces and making sure that the single-engine plane was properly configured for flight.

"I want you to do a short field takeoff today, rather than a rolling takeoff like you did the last time," Morgan said as Mike continued with his pre-flight checklist. "After we're in the air and clear of local traffic, I'll have you make a couple of precautionary clearing turns to make sure we're okay, then you can put the hood on and we can practice some instrument work," Morgan added.

A knot instantly grew in Mike's stomach with that little revelation. He was comfortable enough using visual flight rules (VFR), but instrument flying was another thing. His stomach reinforced what his mind was thinking … I'm not ready for the hood! As always when in tense situations, Mike's palms got a bit sweaty and he had to keep wiping them on his pants, one hand at a time, hoping Morgan's attention was focused elsewhere and that his instructor wouldn't notice the darkening patches on his jeans.

"Roger that, Morgan," he said, trying to sound nonchalant.

The 'hood', as it's known, is not really a hood, but rather more of an oversized visor meant to restrict the pilot's vision above the instrument panel and force him or her to concentrate on the instruments rather than look out the window towards the horizon. It's not a complete shield; a pilot can still look out the windscreen, but they have to tilt their head at an awkward angle to do so. Mike wasn't sure he was ready for it, but he didn't want to admit it.

The two men saw a passenger jet far above and Mike craned his neck to look at the contrails, a little envious of the pilot. *Wonder what it feels like to fly one of those?* he thought.

Meanwhile, on the plane Tom Desoto turned his music down and focused on the sheaf of compiled notes, calculations, and cellophane transparencies that his co-worker had brought on board and laid out on top of the briefcase that rested on his lap as he slept. He did one final review of Reza's notes and calculations, found them free of errors and omissions and said a little prayer that their presentation tomorrow would be trouble-free.

Sixty-eight miles southward, at the same time that Tom was turning down the volume of the in-flight music, Mike Stevens was holding short of the runway, idling the engine on his Cessna 172 and waiting for takeoff clearance from the tower. Beside him Morgan sat patiently, quietly, only commenting when it was necessary, making notes on his ubiquitous clipboard.

"Cessna seven-seven-one-one Golf. Tower, we have an inbound 747 at five miles on final. You are cleared for immediate takeoff. No delay."

"Cessna seven-seven-one-one Golf, Roger cleared for takeoff," Mike replied, but for some inexplicable reason he sat there. Perhaps he was weighing his options—either take off now or wait several minutes for the jumbo jet to pass and land, a wait that could last several minutes.

As he hesitated, the temperature in the cockpit started quickly becoming uncomfortably hot, a combination of the outside temperature and the heat from the engine, which sat just on the other side of an eighth-of-an-inch thick firewall. Both Mike and Morgan started to perspire, but Morgan's increasing level of anxiety made it worse for him.

"Well, Mike! What's it going to be? Shit or get off the pot!" he exclaimed, clearly stressed. The urgency in his voice startled Mike. "The tower wants you to take off now, and that means now—as in *immediately*. Otherwise we can both sit here and broil in this cockpit. If you wait much longer to take off you're going to have a three-hundred-ton jumbo squashing you like a bug as it runs over your ass. So, I'm asking you Mike, what's it going to be?" Morgan asked.

His voice almost a full octave higher, Mike practically shouted out, "Alright, alright I'm going!" as he grabbed the throttle control at the lower centre of the instrument panel and slowly—too slowly—taxied the small plane onto the runway in front of the rapidly advancing jetliner. He brought the aircraft to a stop, still expecting to do the briefed, short field takeoff and was startled by Morgan's hand over his on the throttle, "Go, go, go!"

The small Cessna started its agonizingly slow roll down the runway. During the precious seconds between the time the tower had given Mike clearance and the time when he actually started his roll down the runway, the 747 had very quickly closed the gap between the two aircraft. It was only two miles distant and coming in at just over one hundred and forty knots. Two miles away the captain of United Airlines flight 329 could see the small plane coming onto the end of the runway to begin its roll out.

"Jesus, look at this idiot. I don't know if he's going to make it," he said. The small Cessna was now in the exact spot where the huge Boeing airliner was going to be in less than a minute.

The first officer had just finished doing the landing check, now he looked up and assessed the options available to his captain and asked, "How about a go-around, Skipper?" His hand was already reaching towards the flap lever. He was certain that the Federal Aviation Administration (FAA) would be incensed when they analyzed this near-miss and wondered what Air Traffic Control (ATC) was thinking to let it happen.

The captain, a 27-year veteran and senior pilot with United, had already made up his mind. He realized the small Cessna would clear the runway in time. He had also noticed his first officer's hand move towards the controls and he stopped him, saying, "Negative, but goddamn, it's going to be close. I can't believe some idiot would play chicken with a jumbo jet full of passengers. I'm sure that more than one FAA rule has been broken here."

"Either that pilot has a death wish or some idiot at ATC has screwed up big time. I'm going to find out which," said the first officer.

"Right now, we've got a plane to land. After that I'll be the one to go to the tower and talk to them about this snafu," said the captain.

At the same instant that United Flight 329 was crossing the perimeter fence at the end of the runway, the small Cessna was at 400 feet and making a hasty retreat from what truly was a near miss.

"That was a really stupid thing to do, Mike. We almost got creamed by a 747. A couple of hundred people could have been killed, including us," fumed Morgan.

"Oh, get serious. It wasn't that close." Mike still had not grasped the gravity of the situation. "And besides, what was I supposed to do with both you and the tower screaming at me?" the flustered new pilot asked. "One minute you're sitting in the co-pilot's seat not saying a fucking thing, and the next you're screaming at me to take off—so I did."

His attitude angered Morgan. "First of all, Mike, don't take that tone with me. You may be older by a few years, but I'm the instructor and you're the student. Never forget that," Morgan shot back, still not realizing how anxious his apprentice truly was, or how his badgering was only making a bad situation worse. "Right now, you've got a plane to fly, but if you're not prepared to do that I'll take us back to the barn and face the wrath of that 747 pilot and air traffic control," he added. Then, trying to hammer the point home one last time, he said "I'll be lucky if I don't lose my instructor's certificate, not to mention my pilot's license over this."

"Enough already! Let me fly the plane!" Frustrated, Mike looked at his lap, his face reddening. "I mean..." he cleared his throat, "I can fly the plane."

"Alright, Mike. Fly the rest of the lesson," said Morgan, and with that, Morgan made the second mistake of three he would make that fateful morning—the first being that he had cajoled Mike into a takeoff he should have aborted after his student's delayed taxi-out and takeoff.

In the tower, Senior Air Traffic Controller Gerry Van Der Steen was trying to discipline the controller who had given the Cessna it's takeoff clearance. "Tony, you should have had that guy hold where he was and not given clearance to take off. You more or less gave him carte blanche to do whatever he wanted, whenever he wanted to do it."

"It wasn't carte blanche," Tony defended himself. "There was enough room for that guy to safely take off. I gave him, 'no delay'. How was I to know he would piss around getting on the runway and then take his sweet time getting airborne?"

Unable to deal with his subordinate as he would have wished, Gerry relented, "Alright, we'll deal with that later, at this moment you've got planes to deal with." There was no point in making a stink; it was hard to get good air traffic controllers.

All was not well with the Air Traffic Control System. It was the late 70s, and the job had not really changed since the 50s, though the sheer volume of air traffic had grown in leaps and bounds. Air traffic controllers were required to spend long hours controlling ever-increasing numbers of flights, making the situation in the control tower unbelievably stressful and causing the number of 'incidents' to grow dramatically at every airport in the country.

Every day over 100,000 small planes took off and landed in the already crowded skies over America, adding to the stress of those in the tower. The Federal Aviation Administration's Oklahoma City training school was only putting out about 3,000 graduates per year, not nearly enough to replace retiring, sick or otherwise absent air traffic controllers.

If I piss Tony off and he quits, thought Gerry, *where would I get a replacement from?* They were already short-staffed and he needed all the warm bodies he could get manning the consoles. *They may be warm, but some of them are sure brain-dead sometimes,* he thought to himself.

After the near-miss with the 747 and a few tense moments, things began to settle down somewhat in the cockpit of the Cessna 172. Mike Stevens was focusing on the lesson at hand. He had made a complete circuit of 'Lindbergh Field', as San Diego International Airport was once called. This was the airport from which the famous Charles Lindbergh had originally departed on his solo Trans-Atlantic flight aboard the Spirit of St. Louis' in 1927.

Just to the west of the airport, at an altitude of 1,400 feet, he steered the Cessna in a north-easterly direction as instructed by Morgan and made a few 'clearing' turns to check for other traffic in the area. Mike, being in the pilot's seat, was in the best position to see the PSA jet—still some ten miles distant—but in his haste to finish his lesson and get the plane back on terra firma, his cursory inspection of the horizon failed to detect it.

"All clear here, Morgan," Mike said, not knowing that if he had continued his lookout for just a fraction of a second longer, he would have seen approaching danger.

At that precise instant, the captain of the PSA jet with Reza and Tom DeSoto on it started turning his aircraft onto the downwind leg of its approach to San Diego. A slight morning breeze blew off the Pacific, but it had little impact on the smog blanketing the San Diego area. That veil effectively camouflaged the aircraft. As the jet turned, the morning sun reflected off the fuselage, briefly illuminating it for miles, but once the PSA jet completed the turn, the reflection ceased and the brown haze hid it from view again.

In the Cessna, Morgan noted Mike's clearing maneuvers and gave him the go-ahead to carry on with the lesson. "Okay. Mike, now that you've accomplished that, it's time for you to put the hood on."

Still badly shaken after the earlier incident, Mike wiped his sweaty hands again and almost shrank away as Morgan placed the overgrown visor on his head and adjusted it.

At exactly thirty seconds before 9:00 a.m., San Diego Approach Control called PSA to warn of air traffic. A rapid exchange ensued:

San Diego Approach Control: "PSA 182, traffic twelve o'clock, one mile northbound."

PSA Crew to tower: "We're looking."

San Diego Approach Control: "PSA 182, additional traffic's, ah, twelve o'clock, three miles just north of the field northeast bound. A Cessna 172 climbing VFR out of one thousand four hundred."

PSA to tower: "Okay, we've got that other twelve."

In the cockpit, the captain, his first officer and the flight engineer relaxed a little.

San Diego Approach Control: "Cessna seven-seven-one-one Golf. San Diego departure radar contact, maintain VFR conditions at or below three thousand five hundred, fly heading zero seven zero, vector final approach course."

At the controls of the Cessna, Mike read back the clearance while maintaining intense cross-checking of his instruments. He began a turn to the new heading given by the air traffic controller, at the same time keeping his climb altitude and speed steady.

San Diego Approach Control: "PSA 182, traffic's at twelve o'clock, three miles out of one thousand seven hundred."

All three crew members on PSA 182 craned forward, peering ahead, looking for the traffic.

The first officer widened his search, shifting his gaze toward the southeast. Then he spotted it; a small aircraft several miles distant. Considering the atmospheric and lighting conditions, it wasn't clear whether this small plane was in fact the Cessna 172 or another one some miles away. It was still early in the morning and the crew of the PSA jet was looking towards the eastern horizon and the rising sun; nevertheless, the first officer called in the traffic, sounding decisive.

First Officer: "Got 'em."

PSA Crew to tower: "Traffic in sight."

San Diego Approach Control: "Okay sir, maintain visual separation, contact Lindbergh tower, one-one-eight point three, have a nice day now."

Captain: "Flaps two."

The first officer moved the flaps lever to the second detent.

Miramar Naval Station ATC: "Cessna seven-seven-one-one Golf and traffic's at six o'clock two miles eastbound PSA jet inbound to Lindbergh out of three thousand two hundred has you in sight."

The crew of PSA 182, as well as Mike and his instructor, were now all aware of each other's presence. The PSA crew informed the tower that they had visual contact with the traffic and they had been instructed by ATC to maintain visual separation—meaning it was the jet captain's responsibility not get too close.

In the Cessna, Mike was aware of the position of the PSA jet and—being in the left-hand seat—was in the best position to see it, but his vision was impaired by the visor he wore. He was also concentrating on reading his instruments instead of looking out for traffic, but even if had been flying VFR as directed, the design of the Cessna 172—with wings up above the cockpit—made it almost impossible for him to see traffic behind them.

Morgan, when he placed his student under the hood, had assumed complete responsibility for VFR; if he could not find the traffic the ATC warned him was there, he should have removed Mike's hood and instructed him to look for it. But Morgan, having fallen into a false sense of security since the ATC said the PSA jet had the Cessna in sight, did not do that. And that was a bad decision.

The PSA jet flew almost parallel to the runway as it descended.

PSA Crew to tower: "Lindbergh, PSA 182 downwind."

Lindbergh Tower: "PSA 182, Lindbergh tower, ah, traffic twelve o'clock, one mile, a Cessna."

Captain: "Is that the one we're looking at?"

First Officer: "Yeah, but I don't see him now."

PSA Crew to tower: "Okay, we had it there a minute ago."

Lindbergh Tower: "182, Roger."

PSA Crew to tower: "I think he's passed us off to our right."

Lindbergh Tower: "Yeah."

That was the single-word reply from the new approach controller trainee. Even though the PSA crew had not confirmed visual contact with the traffic, the inexperienced controller missed it. So did his training supervisor, who was at the end of his overtime shift.

Captain: "He was right over here a minute ago."

Lindbergh Tower: "How far are you going to take your downwind 182? I have company traffic waiting for departure." The captain noted that another PSA jet (company traffic) was in the queue to take off.

PSA Crew to tower: "Ah, probably about three to four miles."

Lindbergh Tower: "Okay. PSA 182, cleared to land."

The 727 was crossing over Route 103, very quickly getting to the point where the crew would turn base leg before making their final turn toward the runway.

Captain: "Gear down. Landing checklist. Flaps Five."

The captain glanced to his right and saw his first officer move the landing gear lever down, then the flap lever to the fifth detent and then look towards the south and point out another aircraft—the Cessna 401 that had been eight miles distant a few minutes earlier.

The flight engineer began reading the checklist:

Flight Engineer: "Anti-skid—five, releases. Ignition—flight start. No smoking—on. Gear—…"

Captain: "Down, in, three. Green."

Flight Engineer: "Flaps."

Captain: "Five, green light."

The flight engineer completed the final elements of the checklist.

Flight Engineer: "Hydraulics—pressure and quantity normal. Landing checklist—complete."

Both the captain and the first officer began monitoring the familiar flow of the landing checklist, totally oblivious to the small plane below them—now virtually right under the right wing of the 727. Their altitude was 2,600 feet and the Cessna was just a few feet lower and climbing, with Mike still concentrating on his instruments, oblivious to the jet.

It was Morgan who noticed a shadow pass over them. Looking out and up from the cockpit, he saw the huge bulk of the 727 looming barely ten feet above them. Before Morgan could react or shout a warning to Mike, the aerodynamic forces that occur when two aircraft are in such close proximity caused the Cessna to pull up. At that very same instant those same forces caused the wing of the Boeing 727 to dip ever so slightly.

The six-foot diameter, double-bladed propeller of the small Cessna was turning at over two thousand revolutions per minute, driven by the 110-horsepower Avro Lycoming engine. Although small, the prop sliced into the thin aluminum underside of the larger aircraft's wing. If the point of impact had been just two feet further forward or aft on the wing, the propeller would have struck a major wing spar and would have stopped almost instantly. Instead it tore open a fuel tank, disgorging the contents, which then erupted into a huge ball of fire. The loss of fuel pressure to the right engine, coupled with the loss of lift due to damage caused by the small plane, had an almost instantaneous effect, causing the right wing to dip, this time violently.

The wing essentially became a huge fly-swatter and it smashed into the smaller aircraft. Following that, the right engine of the jet struck the wing of the Cessna with so much force that the strut supporting it collapsed. With its wing buckled, not only was the Cessna completely disabled, but the buckled strut shattered the side door window and frame and the burning jet fuel—which up to that point had been trailing away into the slipstream—now rained into the cockpit. In moments, the small plane became an airborne funeral pyre as it plummeted to the earth, a half a mile below.

During the short, thirty-minute-long, final leg from Los Angeles to San Diego, Tom De Soto had remained mostly immersed in music, his eyes closed, unaware of the events happening around him. The music drowned out everything, including the alarms raised by other passengers on the plane. The maneuvers of the aircraft, though sudden, were not ones that gave him the impression anything was wrong. On the PSA jet, the impact of the small Cessna, though catastrophic for the two men aboard it, felt similar to what one would expect from the landing gear being lowered. So when the 727 started its roll to the right, Reza, who had up to this point been fast asleep was not jolted awake by the impact or by his oblivious friend, but by cries from his fellow passengers.

"Oh my God—the wing's on fire!" one passenger shouted as the orange glow outside the jet grew more intense. The aircraft continued its roll and, as it turned its belly towards the sun, the glow inside the cabin from the flames soon rivalled, and then surpassed, the morning sun.

Captain: "What have we got here?"

First Officer: "It's bad. We're hit man, we are hit!"

Captain: "Tower, we're going down, this is PSA."

Both the captain and his first officer fought to right the stricken aircraft, but burning fuel was not the only concern for those aboard. The intense heat began to soften seals on critical hydraulic lines and pumps, making the control surfaces that would counteract the roll ineffective.

Lindbergh Tower: "Okay, we'll call the equipment for you."

The captain barely acknowledged the promised deployment of emergency personnel; an impending sense of doom as the aircraft rocked around him told him their help would probably be useless.

Reza, Tom and their fellow passengers watched helplessly as the earth and sky exchanged places. The aircraft was now completely inverted; where sunlight had been entering the left-side windows, it was now coming through the right ones.

"Too late Tom, too late," Reza said, more to himself than to Tom.

As the mortally-wounded jet plummeted to the earth, Reza thought of his beloved Giti, of Sina, his son—and of his unfinished work.

"Too late …" he whispered again. The words had barely escaped his lips when the plane exploded.

— Chapter 2 —

San Diego, California

The PSA Boeing 727 and the smaller Cessna collided at an altitude of 2,600 feet. Their momentum carried them down into an area just west of Balboa Park, into a neighborhood known as North Park. Both the aircraft were relatively intact just after the collision and subsequent fall to the ground. The Cessna landed in an empty field and did very little damage upon impact, but such was not the case for the PSA jet. It weighed in at over a hundred tons and the falling jet, trailing smoke and flames, exploded and burnt upon impact, destroying or damaging twenty-two homes.

A gruesome scene met firefighter and rescue crews as they arrived on the scene; everywhere they looked they saw death and destruction. Wreckage, especially from the jet, was strewn widely. What had once been an airliner was now nothing but a twisted mass of steel and aluminum intermingled with fragments of flesh and bone.

North Park had become hell on Earth. This once-peaceful neighborhood suddenly resembled a war zone. Where cheerful, well-kept homes and their manicured lawns had once been bordered by tree-lined streets, now chaos and destruction reigned. Green lawns and gardens were now black from the fires raging everywhere and the intense heat from the flames caused fruit on the trees to sizzle and bake.

Thousands of people descended on the scene, some to assist with the rescue effort, others to give blood to local blood donor clinics for possible survivors. Still others arrived purely for selfish reasons. These vultures began looting the bodies and homes, despite local law enforcement's best efforts. The police were woefully understaffed; they called in as many off-duty officers as they could, but there was little time to monitor vandals and thieves. Most law enforcement personnel were busy with rescue attempts and locating possible survivors.

Sue Johnson, the owner of the local sandwich shop, arrived shortly after the crash with trays of sandwiches originally destined for the Monday lunchtime crowd. "I'm from the Boundary Street Deli around the corner," she said to Assistant Fire Chief, Wayne Beaucamp. "I thought you fellows might like some sandwiches and drinks."

Beaucamp was sitting on the rear step of a fire truck, taking a five-minute break, his face and body drenched in sweat. It was a hot autumn day to begin with and the heat from the burning wreckage made it seem as if he and his men were toiling in a blast furnace in the middle of the Mojave Desert. He frowned as he watched a young man emerge from the front door of a partially demolished house, carrying what appeared to be a VCR, and then gratefully took a sandwich.

"Thanks you," he said. "The boys and I can sure use some food. You're a good person. Not like those bastards!" He eyed another looter, who at least had the grace to look guilty as he ran off with a television. "Look at them," he said, "they're like vultures descending on some dying animal to peck out its eyes. I'll be glad when the National Guard gets here and can restore some kind of order. Boy, the insurance companies are going to have a field day with this one, must be over a hundred dead, maybe more …"

Suddenly a shift in the wind brought the stench of burning flesh to their nostrils. This, combined with the visual and mental signals she was receiving, was more than Sue's stomach could take. She doubled over at the rear of the firetruck and her breakfast once more saw the light of day.

Sacramento, California

Reza's trip had begun literally at the crack of dawn, but after arriving home and getting a few hours of sleep, Giti awoke feeling rejuvenated and got to work doing laundry. She already had one load hanging on the line and was doing her second load of the day. She never used a dryer, as Reza said he loved the smell of his clothes after they'd dried in the California sun.

He's almost like a child sometimes, she thought affectionately, wondering how his flight had been. It was just after noon and she was about to go downstairs to take the second load from the washer when she noticed an unfamiliar, four-door sedan pull into her driveway and stop behind the Matador. Instinctively, she knew this was not good and as she watched nervously through the window, the occupants, a man and a woman, exchanged a few words then got out and walked up the front path to her door. Suddenly, Giti was filled with a sense of foreboding.

Sina, who was home from school and playing downstairs in the rumpus room, heard the doorbell ring and came bounding up the stairs from the basement. "I'll get it," he bellowed, racing for the door.

"No, Sina, that's quite alright, I'll get it," she said, just barely heading him off when he reached the top of the stairs. He stopped running and allowed his mother to take charge.

She opened the door just as the man was about to knock. He and his professional-looking partner eyed her with surprise. His hand was raised, his knuckles at the ready. He quickly lowered his hand.

"Mrs. Roshtti," he said, "I'm Michael Sullivan and this is Janice Swift. We're from Pacific Southwest Airlines." Both of them presented their credentials, but Giti couldn't focus on them, her heart was beating so fast. Hadn't Reza been on a PSA flight?

"May we come in?" asked Michael Sullivan.

Giti's mouth was dry. She wet her lips and said, "Of course. Please come and sit down in the living room." Then she noticed Sina anxiously peering at the two strangers. "Excuse me a moment," she said and ushered her son back downstairs to the playroom while the two PSA officials sat down on the couch. A moment later she returned.

"How can I help you?" she asked nervously.

"Mrs. Roshtti, I'm afraid we have some bad news. There's been a problem with your husband's flight," Michael Sullivan began delicately, searching for the right words. But there is never an easy way to tell anyone what he had to say.

"Mrs. Roshtti ..." This time it was Janice who spoke. "I'm afraid your husband's plane has crashed. There were no survivors."

At first Giti thought she hadn't heard correctly. Then she had the odd sensation that the ground was shifting under her, leaving her standing on air, as if a magician had magically pulled the tablecloth out from under her feet and she was a teapot, waiting to crash. She felt the blood drain from her head and as the two PSA officials looked at her with concern she gasped and turned ashen. In her heart, she had been hoping that maybe the airline had simply lost Reza's luggage and that they were here to pick up some of his things … she was not prepared for this. She wasn't ready to say good-bye to the man she loved. In shock, she collapsed.

A few minutes later she awoke to find Janice applying a cold cloth to her forehead as she lay on the couch. Her mind was racing in a thousand different directions and she wanted to ask a thousand different questions, but she was afraid to hear the answers. This couldn't be true! Maybe it was just a simple case of mistaken identity! She swung her legs onto the floor and sat upright.

"Are you sure?" she managed to ask.

"Yes, Mrs. Roshtti, we are certain," said Janice. "All one hundred and thirty-five people on board were killed. There was an intense search for survivors among the wreckage, but none were found. I'm so sorry for your loss," she added.

Dumbfounded, Giti asked, "What happened? Why did it crash?"

"We don't know exactly," said Michael, "but the plane was coming into San Diego when the crash occurred."

The words of the PSA legal department were still ringing in Michael's ears as he lied. They were clear: *Don't tell the families too much.* He certainly was not allowed to reveal that the Boeing 727 had collided with a small plane, though already many of the facts about the crash were known to both PSA officials and the investigators from the National Transportation Safety Board (NTSB).

"Is there anyone we can contact who can come to be with you, some family perhaps?" Janice asked.

"Yes, please," Giti said, sinking onto the couch again, shocked. "I'll give you Reza's brother's number. Please call my brother and sister-in-law."

Then a low, guttural wail climbed its way out of the depths of her stomach as she began mourning the loss of her husband, partner … soul mate.

San Diego, California

At the crash site, the flames had been extinguished and there were now only burned-out houses and the blackened, broken shell of Flight 182's fuselage remaining. Investigators continued combing the wreckage looking for the two black boxes that would have been on the aircraft, trying to spot a flash of their bright orange colour in the soot and rubble. The orange-coloured black boxes are located at the rear of the fuselage. The flight data recorder inside them is standard on all jet aircraft. It gathers information about rudder and aileron position, air speed, and landing gear position throughout the flight, as well as other crucial information, such as what the aircraft was doing prior to the crash. The other 'black' box is the cockpit voice recorder, which records the voices and sounds inside the cockpit during a flight.

One of the NTSB investigators, John Robinson, was working alongside Assistant Fire Chief Beaucamp at the rear of the plane. The fireman was using an air-driven, cut-off saw as John explained precisely where to cut. After half an hour of meticulous cutting, the compartment that housed the two black boxes was exposed. John carefully removed the fasteners that held their cover in place then uncoupled their electrical connections.

"We've got them!" John shouted into his radio microphone. To be sure they were heard over the din of men and equipment he shouted once more, "We've got the black boxes." This time the message was relayed from the public address speakers on every fire truck.

The tired NTSB and fire crews gave out a cheer; finally, a bit of good news in a bleak day—the only good news since beginning their grisly task. What had begun mid-morning as a rescue operation had turned into a recovery operation, as it was soon apparent that all aboard, as well as many people on the ground, had perished.

Throughout the day, newspaper photographers and television crews strained against police barricades, trying to get as close as possible to the event before them, all of them searching out eyewitnesses as they took pictures in the quest for a Pulitzer Prize-winning photograph. The difficult task of recovery and cleanup continued into the evening.

One second-grader at Foster Elementary School told reporters, "We were lining up to go to class and the first-grade teacher looked up and said, 'Oh no' and pointed to the sky. All of us watched the plane that was on fire when it fell to the ground. A big ball of smoke and fire happened a few seconds later."

Another young girl told a reporter, "I was in my class at school and we heard a loud noise. I looked up towards the noise and saw a plane on fire as it fell from the sky. Johnny was scared and hid under his desk, but I was brave. I kept looking until it hit the ground. Then I saw a huge fireball."

Sacramento, California

The two PSA reps didn't leave the Roshtti household until family members arrived to console Giti; when Reza's brother Zafar and his wife Fatemah walked into the house, Giti fell into Fatemah's arms, sobbing.

"There, there," Fatemah consoled her, but Giti's pain remained sharp and insistent in her chest.

Sina had been spared the news about his father so far, but the television was on in the living room and the local news kept interrupting programming with stories about the crash. Not ready for him to know, Giti continued to try to keep her son at a distance, but he kept coming upstairs and looking in on the adults, so she couldn't be sure what he was picking up.

When she could think at all, she thought it best to wait until Zafar could take Sina aside and tell him what had happened, man to man. Sina and his Uncle Zafar were very close and Zafar had often joined Reza and Sina on outings such as going to the zoo, or to the park to watch the small boats sail past on the American River, or—Sina's favorite—to fly his remote control airplane at the school.

"This is Tony Pearson of ABC News in San Diego ..." began another report and every member of the Roshtti household except Sina, who'd been once more banished to the rumpus room, immediately had an ear cocked, listening for details about the crash.

"We have had several eyewitness reports stating that there was not one plane that crashed, but two," said Tony Pearson. "Witnesses report that what they first thought were pieces of the wing or engine of the Boeing 727 were instead pieces of a small plane that apparently collided with PSA Flight 182. We now go to Jim Saunders, our reporter at Lindbergh Field, Jim ..."

Sina came back into the room at that point and Zafar hastily sent him to his room with promises of ice cream later. Confused, he left, but, overly curious now, came back only moments later. By then, the scene had changed to a reporter standing in front of what appeared to be a radar control tower at San Diego Airport.

"Hello, Tony. I'm here at Lindbergh Field and have been so for almost eight hours, since this accident occurred at a few minutes after nine o'clock this morning. As I stand here, just a few miles from where the crash happened, you can still see smoke rising from the crash site, though it's light, almost wispy compared to the black, oily smoke that billowed up earlier today when a 727 jet crashed and burned just minutes from where I stand."

Zafar hustled Sina away again and he reluctantly left.

Tony continued. "Jim, have you been able to talk to anyone there about this accident and what went wrong?"

"Yes I have, Tony. I had a conversation earlier with an air traffic controller who did not want to appear on camera. He informed me that both the PSA and the NTSB have known almost from the beginning that a small plane collided with Flight 182 and that it was pilot error that caused this crash ..."

"That's not what they told me," Giti screamed at the television. "They told me they didn't know what happened!"

She turned to her sister-in-law. "Call the airline! I want to know what happened! I want to know what happened ..." Then she began crying again.

Sina, heard his mom's cries from the living room and again raced to see what was wrong. His aunt reached to stop him, but before she could catch him and once more get him out of earshot, his eyes became fixed on the images now filling the screen.

On the television were still shots taken by an amateur photographer as the 727 fell from the sky. The caption across the bottom of the screen read, *Flight 182 - Final Moments.*

Sina's Aunt Fatemah grabbed him and tried to turn him away from the images, but the damage had already been done. Sina recalled his dad's flight number from the tickets he'd seen lying on top of the hall table a few days ago. He immediately understood the reason his mother was so upset and why they were having such an unexpected visit from his aunt and uncle.

"That's my daddy's plane! That's my daddy's plane!" he cried as he tried to pull away, his big, brown eyes filled with tears and his face twisted into a knot of grief. He began to sob and clutch wildly at his aunt and mother, shocked and bereft. They tried to hold him and comfort him but he was inconsolable and continued to swing wildly. Finally his uncle had to grasp the boy in a bear hug. Sina could not be reached; he knew the images he'd seen of his father's plane as it plummeted to earth were the beginning of something that would change his life forever.

As the boy sobbed in his uncle's arms, the news returned to the anchor Tony Pearson.

"Our efforts to contact the airline have been unsuccessful but we are told by officials of the NTSB and PSA that a joint news conference to address the crash has been scheduled for seven o'clock."

By now it was dinnertime, but no one wanted to eat. Giti certainly wasn't able to cook. Fatemah made Sina a sandwich, but he refused to touch it. At seven o'clock, the promised press conference began. Senior NTSB Investigator Chuck Fulbright stepped up to the forest of microphones that covered the top of the podium and began to speak.

"Good evening ladies and gentlemen. As you already know, at 9:03 a.m., Pacific Standard Time, Pacific Southwest Airlines Flight 182 crashed two and a half miles northeast of San Diego International Airport, while on final approach. All 135 persons on board were killed as well as an undetermined number of persons on the ground. As of this moment we are still investigating the crash. Any questions?"

One reporter immediately jammed a mike in his face. "Mr. Fulbright," she shrieked, "We were told earlier by an air traffic controller that a Cessna or some other small plane collided with the PSA jet. Can you tell us about that? Also, can you tell us why this information was not released to us earlier?"

Giti nodded at the television in silent outrage. Then after a brief exchange with another NTSB official, Mr. Fulbright returned to the microphone to answer the question. "As I told you before, we are still investigating this tragedy, but I have no knowledge of this individual or what he is alleged to have said. It was not said in an official capacity that I, or any of my colleagues, know of."

"But sir," persisted the reporter, "That doesn't explain the crash of a small plane in virtually the same area at exactly the same time!"

After another brief exchange with the same NTSB official, Mr. Fulbright once again returned to the microphone. "As I told you before, we are still investigating this crash," he said. "We are combing the wreckage for answers and we have recovered the black boxes from the aircraft. Those are on their way to Washington where we will analyze their data. We are aware of a small plane that crashed nearby at about the same time, but whether or not the two are connected remains to be determined."

Another reporter shoved a microphone in his face. "Why can't you give us an accurate death toll?" he asked. "You said the number of people killed on the ground is—how did you put it—undetermined?"

"Look," Fullbright said, exasperated. "We've had a one hundred ton airliner crash into the middle of a residential neighborhood. That was followed by an explosion and fire. Several homes were destroyed and about a dozen more were damaged. The area is cordoned off while the investigation continues. Furthermore, with this kind of incident there are many things to consider. We need an accurate account from PSA as to how many people were onboard the aircraft. We need to contact the families of the victims on the ground to determine who was home, who was at work or school and who is still missing. The San Diego police department is doing an incredible job for us in that regard, but it does take time. This incident took place less than twelve hours ago and we are doing our very best. That's about it for now. Good night." With that, he and the other NTSB officials made a quick exit from in front the cameras. The PSA officials had been a no-show.

How strange, thought Giti. A knock on the door brought her to her feet, thought Fatemah tried to make her sit down. She looked out the window and realized that a camera crew was on her doorstep. Suddenly she was no longer as distraught as she had been earlier; in fact, now she was angry. She decided not to be afraid. She wanted to be heard. She opened the door.

"Mrs. Roshtti, I'm Pam Stevens, ABC News. We saw your husband's name on the passenger roster and were hoping we could get a local angle on the story of the jet crash. I understand if you are too upset to talk to us, but I'm hoping you can give us just a few moments of your time."

Giti's mouth was set in a hard line. She fought back tears, but pushed on, angry at the deception by PSA and hungry for the truth. She nodded her assent and Pam kicked into reporter mode.

"Mrs. Roshtti, I understand your husband was aboard Flight 182 today and that shortly afterward you had a visit from PSA officials?" Pam asked.

"Yes, and I don't think they were telling me the truth," Giti said bitterly. "They told me they didn't know very much about what had happened and now I find out that a small plane collided with my husband's plane. What else are they not telling me, not telling other families?"

Pam continued, "I noticed that PSA was absent from the joint news conference held just a few moments ago. As a victim, could you comment on that?"

"I can," Giti said firmly. "My family has been calling PSA all afternoon to get to the bottom of what went wrong, but we keep getting a recording. I want some answers as to why my husband died and I won't rest until I get them."

Al-Qa'im, Iraq

Twelve time zones away, on the opposite side of the globe, the sun had already risen on the Iraqi city of Al-Qa'im. Al-Qa'im is located on the south bank of the Euphrates River, about one hundred miles due west of Lake Tharthar, and just a dozen miles inside the border Iraq shares with Syria.

Jaffar Hamid Harraj sat watching and recording morning news from around the world. This 37-year-old Muslim—leader of one of the largest cells of the Islamic Hamas Movement, an Iraqi terrorist group—knew it was important to keep abreast of world events. A smile crossed his lips as he listened to the latest tragedy that had befallen the 'Great Satan,' the term he and his compatriots used to refer to the western world, in particular the United States. He calmly sipped his morning tea, amused by the tragedy ... until Giti Roshtti appeared on his screen. At that point he sat upright in his chair, spilling the hot liquid onto his lap.

He hardly noticed as the hot tea seeped into his robes; he sat there completely mesmerized by this beautiful American woman, who was clearly of Persian descent. "She is perfect," he said to himself. He had long wanted a foothold in the United States, and what better way than to take an American bride? Not only was Giti Roshtti stunning, widowed and vulnerable, but she would know the values of her people and not be overly crass as many of the white women were. She would know her place and she would know how to treat a man.

After the interview with Giti was over, Jaffar Harraj sat for several moments in his chair replaying it on his videocassette recorder. Then he summoned his second in command. "Abdul, come in here at once!"

Abdul Salam Al-Kubesi, Jaffar's second in command was not only entrenched in terrorist dealings with his boss, but he was also Al Qa'im's chief of police. Since Al-Qa'im was located on the route most Middle Eastern terrorist groups took to get from Syria to Iraq and Iran, Abdul's position put him in contact with a great many hard, tough men. But he could handle hard, tough men because he was one himself. And he handled them not by bringing them to justice but by recruiting them into the terrorist cell. Being chief of police—once Abdul's main source of pride—was now mainly a means to enlarge the terrorist network.

"Abdul, my dear old friend. I don't suppose you could use the resources at your disposal to find out all you can about this woman, this Giti Roshtti of Sacramento?" Jaffar indicated the frozen face of Giti on the television screen where he had paused the tape. The pleasant tone surprised Abdul; his boss was usually angry about something.

"Of course, Jaffar. I will be most pleased to do so. May I ask why?"

"No!" snapped Jaffar, more in character. "Not at this time. Maybe we can discuss it later." With that Jaffar dismissed his friend, preferring to be alone to think about this woman, this Giti.

Giti was by far the most beautiful woman he had ever laid eyes on, despite all she had obviously gone through that day. He had been with many lovely women, but this one was truly an exception, for she appeared to be both beautiful and strong—a rare combination indeed. *It must be the Americanization*, he thought. *This Giti is no shrinking flower!*

He was determined to find out all he could about her. She could be the key to establishing the Islamic Hamas Movement in America, the door to starting terrorist cells rooted in American soil. He had no doubt she could change his life; but he could not predict how much.

On Tuesday morning, the NTSB investigation was well underway; the black boxes had been recovered the previous evening and had arrived in Washington, though retrieving data from them would take at least another day.

At the crash site, the fires had all been extinguished, the grisly task of recovery was going on in earnest and the cleanup and removal of the Boeing 727 continued.

A few miles away at Lindbergh Field, the NTSB had requisitioned an empty hangar, where reconstruction of the doomed airliner would take place. Already dozens of pieces had arrived there by flatbed truck, been off-loaded and then carefully examined and photographed. Standard procedure was to photograph everything three times: first, on the scene to provide investigators a record of the landing place of every component in relation to the others; second, for the purposes of identification when each was tagged and catalogued as it was collected; and, third during reconstruction when each piece was placed as closely possible to the position would have been in an undamaged Boeing 727.

Las Vegas, Nevada

It was less than a day after the crash and two investigations were already underway—one, conducted by accredited officials focusing on the accident, the planes and all the passengers; the other, conducted by a dangerous man living in a foreign country, focusing on only one passenger and, more specifically, his widow.

Through Abdul Salam's vast global network of contacts it was not hard to find someone to get information on Giti Roshtti for Jaffar. Abdul quickly located a private investigator from Las Vegas named Jack Coward who came well-recommended.

Looking through the file that had been faxed to him by a contact in America, Mohammed Hussan, Abdul noted that Jack Coward was known to be a bit of a redneck and was also regarded as not being too fond of people from the Middle East. He was a Vietnam veteran, he drank a bit, he was single and he was an expert at hand-to-hand combat.

According to Mohammed, at first Jack Coward had been uninterested in taking the assignment. Mohammed had arrived at Jack's place of residence—a custom-made, steel-reinforced, four-wheel-drive motorhome parked on a patch of dry grass on the outskirts of Vegas—to find the man sipping a beer in the desert sun and practicing his shooting skills by knocking beer cans off an old fence.

"Not interested," Coward told Mohammed. "Let that terrorist bastard find the woman himself."

Mohammed flinched. He had not mentioned the activities of Jaffar to Jack Coward. He had only said a wealthy friend of his from the Middle East had seen this woman and become enamored. "But this is about love!" protested Mohammed, thinking of the hell he would get from Abdul if he failed to obtain the private eye's services.

"Sure it is," Coward said, letting off a shot and capably blowing a beer can to smithereens. Mohammed flinched. He wouldn't want that gun trained on him. It looked like Coward didn't often miss.

It may have been the beer that softened him, but after Mohammed waved a large wad of bills under Coward's nose and promised more when the job was done, the man finally relented. Yes! For several thousand dollars, he would certainly make an exception and work for people he clearly thought of as a bunch of terrorists.

"This woman, Giti Roshtti, you say that's spelled with two tees in the last name?" Coward asked.

"Yes! She lives in Sacramento," Mohammed said eagerly, relieved to have been successful in his mission.

"When I find you, can I reach you at this number? Will you have the rest of my money in cash?"

Mohammed nodded eagerly.

"Okay, I'll get back to you," said Jack. And just like that, Mohammed was dismissed.

Jack Coward didn't really hate people of Middle Eastern descent; he hated warmongers. He hated terrorists. He hated people who didn't treat other people properly. And he didn't care who knew it. He was the type of guy who said what he thought and did what he wanted because he knew life was short and getting shorter. He had been in Vietnam and he had seen it all. He left there knowing he was going to not waste another moment doing or being anything insincere for any reason or anybody, whatsoever. He would be his own man and owe no one anything. He especially would not ever again be indebted to the US military machine. Vietnam had left a bitter taste in his mouth.

The reason he decided to take the case was not because of the money Mohammed promised him—though, like most, he could always use more money—but because he knew from doing preliminary research that Giti's husband was a Vietnam vet and because he thought that if the man seeking her wanted to offer her a better life, then it was his duty to help his fellow veteran's family.

That's how it worked. No one left behind. The way Mohammed explained it, his boss was a very important and wealthy man and before he could woo this Giti woman, he needed to know if she was a good prospect so he could be sure his father would be pleased at the match, in the traditional way of their people. That's where Jack came in. Whatever skeletons were in her closet, he was supposed to find them.

Jack didn't really need to take the case. He wasn't rich, but he had his specially-built RV to live in and he lived simply and well. He did his private eye work more out of interest than for cash; still, he was successful at it, if success meant that people constantly sought him out and his reputation was growing more than he ever intended it to.

The name and city where Giti lived was more than enough to go on, Jack thought. He couldn't believe these people were willing to pay him that much to find the woman. Lazy asses. Had they never heard of a phone book? They could have done this investigation themselves; found her, phoned her, asked her how she was feeling. Women like Giti were generally an open book.

He sighed. Oh well, it was easy money. He'd investigated people successfully in the past with much less information and for stupider reasons.

Later that morning, after taking care of a few arrangements and ensuring the neighbour down the road would water his pet cactus, Jack Coward took whatever gear he thought he might need from his RV, packed it into his black 1976 Camaro and headed northwest, towards Sacramento.

Forty miles north on the I-95 lay the small town of Indian Springs. By the time he got there, the gas gauge was on one-quarter full and Jack was down to a couple of smokes. He spotted a Standard station just off the Interstate that looked like a promising spot to get a fair shake on a tank of gas—after all this job did not include expenses, so the more money he saved on gas, and incidentals, the more he could put in his jeans.

"Good! Only ninety-five cents a gallon," he muttered to himself. He was still longing for the days before the 1973 oil embargo, when you could buy a gallon of gas for a little more than four bits.

Jeff Green was seventeen, and pumping gas at the Standard station was his first job—that is, if you didn't count the time he worked for his dad for next-to-nothing the previous summer. He watched the Camaro pull into the gas station, thinking it was an interesting shade of light brown. Then he looked at the roof and realized it was actually black.

"Fill it up," Jack Coward said to Jeff. "Can I buy some cigarettes here?"

"Yes, sir. Inside. Do you need change for the machine?"

"No, I've got it, thanks," Jack said.

"How about a car wash?" Jeff asked. Jack just smiled.

Jeff set the gas pump to automatic and set about washing the Camaro's windows. As he did so, he glanced inside the car and, noticing the camera gear and other things, guessed incorrectly that Jack was a newspaper photographer. He also noticed the red velour interior of the car. "Gross!" he said to himself.

When Jack came back out he said, "That'll be $11.40, mister."

Jack handed Jeff twelve dollars, got into the car and headed back onto the road north. He'd been on the road about three hours and had another five or six to go, it was almost a hundred degrees in the shade and the Camaro didn't have air conditioning. This was going to be a long haul. He started rapidly rethinking his plan to drive straight through to Sacramento. The air coming through the vents was blast-furnace hot. But then he lit a cigarette and after a nice, deep inhale, he said, "Ah, fuck it," and gunned the big engine forward into the desert heat.

After another six hours of driving he was beat and his shirt was sweaty and uncomfortable. Jack wanted nothing more than a cool shower and some sleep. It was dusk, but he spotted the narrow, two-lane road he was looking for and turned right; a minute later spotted the sign that to him meant relief from the heat: *Alpine Lodge*, it read.

Alpine Lodge was on the shores of Walker Lake. The rooms were well-kept, clean, cheap and—most importantly—air-conditioned. It was a welcome relief after 300 miles of driving in the arid desert heat. Walker Lake was the remnants of a large inland lake that had covered much of western Nevada 10,000 years ago. Changing climate had caused the lake to gradually shrink until it now only covered about 60 square miles. He'd stayed here before; it was a good place to stop.

"Good evening sir. Can I help you?" Jack recognized the spectacled elderly man behind the desk from his last visit, several years ago.

"Yes! I would like a room please. Maybe one of the rooms with a lake view, like I had the last time I was here."

Five minutes later, Jack placed his duffel bag on the chair next to the desk in the cool, still room. His first task was to remove the remnants of the Great Basin Desert that coated his body and to try to expel the portion he had breathed in over the last half of the day.

Half an hour later, after a very refreshing shower, a shave and a change of clothes, Jack, sat on the deck outside the restaurant, gazing out over the lake. After giving his dinner order of fresh rainbow trout, a baked potato and a green salad to a friendly and competent waitress, his gaze once more returned to the lake. The sun had already set behind Mount Grant and the temperature had dropped noticeably. A slight breeze rippled the surface of the lake. It was peaceful. Jack pondered, for a moment, the reason he was here: to find a woman because a man thought he loved her. It was romantic and kind of sweet, he thought ruefully. It had been a long time since anything romantic and sweet had figured prominently in his own life.

Jack figured he had at least ten minutes to wait before his dinner came and he thought he might as well make good use of the time. He went back to his room so he could use the room phone to call his friend in Washington. Part of being a good P.I. was to make use of contacts, friends and associates, and doing this had saved Jack a lot of legwork over the last ten years. Donny Ziegler was Jack's go-to; a long-time friend, Donny had saved Jack a hell of a lot of legwork in the past—not to mention his life on more than one occasion.

Donny was the best researcher Jack knew and he trusted Donny with the most difficult of cases. Somehow, Donny always came through, finding those tidbits of information that were crucial to bringing cases together. Jack had called Donny before he left Las Vegas and asked him to look into Giti Roshtti. He wanted to find out if she was more than she appeared to be.

It was almost 11:00 p.m. in Washington D.C., but Jack knew Don would still be at his desk; he was rarely home before midnight, especially when he was on the hunt, tracking down leads. Jack punched in the eleven-digit phone number he knew by heart and waited until his friend answered the phone.

"Yeah?" Jack recognized the cheerful voice on the other end of the phone.

"Donny, Jack here. What have you managed to dig up for me?"

"Christ, Jack ... lots! After all I've had ... what ... half a fucking day!"

"Cut the crap! I know you. I bet I was barely packed and barely on my way to Sacramento when you'd already come up with a complete history on this Roshtti woman."

"You got that, right. I know everything about her, right down to where she buys her fucking bras and panties."

"Christ! As crude as ever," Jack said and he heard Don laugh; but he couldn't fault Donny's efficiency: he was the master of information.

"So tell me, what have you got?" Jack asked and while Don relayed his findings he began to write down some of the pertinent information. Barely five minutes later, he was back at his table with more than enough knowledge about Giti and her dead husband Reza to get him to the next stage of his investigation.

After a delicious meal, Jack stopped at the ice machine, scooped up a cupful, then returned to his room, locked the deadbolt and reached into his well-worn duffel bag. He rummaged around through his clothes until he found the almost-full bottle of Jack Daniel's whiskey he'd remembered to pack. After putting a few cubes into the glass, he poured in the amber whiskey, delighting at the sound of the ice as it fissured when the whiskey hit it. To him, that sound said, 'delicious'.

He took a sip, placed the glass on the nightstand next to the bed then reached over and switched on the bedside lamp. The glow from the forty-watt bulb was sufficient for him to review his hand-written notes he'd taken when he talked to Don. As he read them, he recalled other details Don had provided and he jotted these down as well. It was the same routine Jack Alouicious Coward had repeated many times after driving countless miles chasing one lead or another. It was a very lonely routine performed by a very lonely man.

For over a decade Jack had been doing private investigator work and mostly he liked it: the money was good, he was his own boss and he could pick and choose who he wanted to work for. Still, it was a solitary existence, and it didn't help to know that he was out here killing himself so another man could have a chance at happiness.

An hour later, Jack looked at the clock radio beside the bed to see the red numerals telling him it was 11:18 p.m. He gulped down the last swallow of what was now just watered-down whiskey, got undressed and fell down on top of the sheets. By 11:20 p.m. he was sound asleep.

Early the next morning, even before the desk had a chance to place his 6:30 a.m. wake-up call, Jack had carried his bags down to his car and was soon once again north-bound on the I-95. He wanted to take advantage of the relatively cool morning temperature and complete at least some of the remainder of his journey in comfort.

A quick stop at a truck stop for some bacon, eggs and coffee—and two Tylenol for his very slight, but noticeable hangover—and Jack was back on the road. With Carson City just a short drive from where he was, he should reach Sacramento well in front of noon … and the baking temperatures of the previous day.

Sacramento, California

Just after eleven o'clock, Jack was cruising his car slowly down Zinfandel Drive. Although he knew the exact address of the Roshtti house, there was no need to look at house numbers—the swarm of reporters gathered in front of Giti Roshtti's home made that completely unnecessary.

Jack pulled his car up to a tree-lined curb and parked. He had been casually looking towards the Roshtti house for less than a minute, when a reporter jammed a microphone through the open window and let loose a series of rapid-fire questions.

"Excuse me sir! Are you a member of the family, or are you a neighbor? What can you tell me about her? Did you know Mrs. Roshtti and her husband Reza well?"

'Raw-sh-ti' … so that's how you pronounce the name, Jack thought, just an instant before he reached up and snatched the microphone out of the surprised reporter's hand.

"Don't bother me or I'm going to bend you over and jam this microphone up your skinny little ass. I don't appreciate someone shoving a microphone in my face. Now fuck off," Jack said in a voice loud enough to terrorize the reporter, but not loud enough to draw attention.

The lightning-fast move caught the newsie completely off-guard, as did the demeanor of the car's single occupant. He didn't even bother to pick up his microphone, but jerked it up by the chord as he beat a hasty retreat back to his van. He knew the man inside the car was not to be trifled with.

Jack calmly returned to his surveillance as if nothing had happened.

A short while later the front door opened and Giti, Sina and Fatemah walked down the front steps and got into the family car, pestered by aggressive press members the whole way. Giti ignored them, but relinquished the driving duties to Fatemah. Clearly she was still shaken. Some of the assembled press started scrambling to grab their gear and pile into vehicles so they could follow.

Jack started the Camaro. Unused to the idea of being tailed, the three Roshtti family members traveled the identical route to Sacramento that Reza and Giti had driven only two days before on that fateful Sunday, completely unaware that Jack was behind them and—further away—so was the press.

Instead of going past the city, this time Giti instructed Fatemah to take the I-80 exit and headed into the downtown core. Jack followed as the blue Matador drove into a half-empty parking lot and parked. He noted with satisfaction that Fatemah had inadvertently lost the press that tried to tail them—but she hadn't lost him.

The three family members got out of the car and headed toward the front door of an adjacent, low-rise office building. Jack quickly parked and hurried into same building, just in time to see Mrs. Roshtti and her family entering the middle elevator. Not knowing if they had entered alone or with others, Jack was relieved when the illuminated numbers made a steady progression up to the fifth floor. He pressed the car call button and was rewarded when the same car arrived at the lobby without making any stops. It was empty.

He walked over to the glass-covered directory near the door and scanned the list of occupants until he saw there were only two tenants listed for that floor. Then he returned to the elevator, got in and pressed '5'. The car stopped and he got out and proceeded left down the hall. The faint outline of lettering on the olive-green door and the telltale carpet full of drywall dust told him this office had moved out. He quickly reversed direction until he reached the far side of the elevator where a masculine-looking lettered door and lights and sounds from a frosted window revealed the busy offices of McIntosh, McMillan and McIntyre Law.

Jack pulled a business card out of his shirt pocket, turned the knob and entered. The blonde receptionist looked up expectantly. "Can I help you?"

Looking down at one of his own business cards, he put on his most confused expression and asked, "Can you please tell me where Peterson and Associates is?" He used the name of the company that had moved.

"They've moved sir, they used to be down the hall until last month," the receptionist said. "Let me give you their new address." She pulled a notepad from her desk drawer and began to copy the address from a note she had taped to her desk. This gave Jack an opportunity to casually glance around the office, pretending to examine the limited edition prints that covered the walls.

"Here you are sir, good luck," she said as she handed it to him.

"Thank you, I appreciate it." Jack took the piece of paper from her and exited the office, but not before giving the lock on the door a quick examination. As he retraced his steps to the elevator and back to his car, he thought, *excellent.* It would be easy to pick.

After a short drive, he turned off the I-5 and drove down Richard Boulevard and into the Governors Inn. Once in his room, he reached for the phone to call Don. He was developing a plan for how to approach Giti Roshtti but needed some help to put it into action. Besides, he wanted his buddy to come and visit. Don was the best friend he had.

Although Jack Coward was now 33 and had been pretty much on the straight and narrow for over 10 years, such was not always the case. Jack had grown up in Sheboygan County, Wisconsin and his best friend Don Zeigler had grown up right beside him. They were, by their own admission, trouble—and though the two had managed to stay out of the local hoosegow it was by sheer luck, not good behaviour.

They deserved to be thrown in the slammer, given some of the things they did, but the closest they came to getting arrested was the night they smashed the rear window of Milner's T.V. Repair so they could steal televisions. The two of them were loading their third set into the back of Mr. Ziegler's station wagon just as the cops were making a routine patrol down the back lane.

Immediately they panicked, jumped into the car and roared down the lane with the cruiser in hot pursuit, Don driving and Jack in the back. As they sped down the narrow lane with the police in hot pursuit, a cloud of dust and debris in their wake, Jack thought it would be a good idea to start tossing televisions out the back of the car and into the path of the pursuing police vehicle.

The first bounced and struck the police car in the grille, but failed to slow it down. The second projectile was far more effective; it lodged under the front wheel, which jerked the steering wheel out of the young police officer's hands and caused the cruiser to swerve into the unyielding corner of a brick building. It put a quick end to the pursuit, much to the relief of Jack and his accomplice. The front end of the police car was crushed, the radiator jammed into the front of the engine.

Relief was short-lived, however. A few days later the police showed up on the Coward's front doorstep asking to speak to Jack's dad. After a muffled conversation on the front stoop, it was apparent the police knew Jack and Donny were involved in the break-in. The two officers had gotten a good enough look at the make and model of the getaway car create a list of owners of brand-new, 1964 Ford wagons. The number of such cars registered in the area was only a dozen or so. After searching alphabetically, they arrived at one of the last names on the list and paid a visit to the Zeigler home. Donny's dad confirmed the boys had borrowed the car earlier that week—and this confession led them to the Coward doorstep within the hour.

Jack can still recall his father closing the door and entering his room, red-faced with anger. "What the hell have you two been up to? Did you have anything to do with that B & E at the T.V. repair shop? You two are a bloody accident looking for a place to happen!" he fumed.

Denials and recriminations served little purpose; what saved the boys from jail was the intervention of their fathers. Ultimately, it was agreed that the two young men would escape prosecution if their parents' agreed to punish them as they saw fit. The next evening, the boys' parents held a meeting among themselves and, with the reluctant agreement of their spouses, both Edward Coward and Lawrence Zeigler reached the conclusion that some much-needed discipline was in order. That discipline would come by means of the United States Marines and boot camp. Both men had taken a similar, albeit voluntary route during the World War II, and it was time for Jack and Donny to grow up and do the same.

Jack wasn't sorry for his time in the military. In fact, he had exceled and learned some valuable skills that still served him well. What he was sorry for was the futility of Vietnam. It was a waste to train men to fight a war that was not based on anything rational. It was a shame to send a nation's lifeblood to die in a fight they could not win. He and Don were the lucky ones. They had each other and they didn't come back in body bags like so many others.

He didn't say much when Don picked up the phone. All he said was, "Get your ass out to Sacramento, buddy. I need you."

All Don said back was, "Okay. But you're buying."

The following Thursday, Jack arrived at Sacramento International Airport to pick up his long-time friend.

"Hey Donny, how the hell are you?" he said, giving his friend a bear-hug.

"Hey, Jack. Good to see you!"

Then the two men shook hands vigorously, both increasing pressure on the other's hand until their knuckles turned white and the blood flow diminished. It was a ritual they did when they had not seen each other for a while; a toughness test.

"Let's get something to eat, I'm starved," Donny said when they finally let go.

Jack thought back over the years he had known Donny and laughed. "What? You? Hungry? Well, that's sure unusual!" he joked.

He recalled a stint with the U.S. Marines back in 1965 when Donny had been renowned among the other men for the amount of food he could sock away. "It's a wonder that the U.S. Government didn't go broke keeping you for twenty-nine months," Jack said, tongue-in-cheek.

"What do you mean by that?" Donny countered. "Are you saying I'm the reason the country's running a deficit?" He gave a hearty laugh.

Donny Ziegler was a rather intimidating fellow: six feet two inches tall and 230 pounds—maybe a bit more if soaking wet and covered in a bath towel.

"I know just the place for a guy like you," said Jack. "Let's check out the Hungry Hunter Steak House. It's a block or so from the motel." Then, just to get in one last dig, he added wryly, "I think they have a smorgasbord."

"Pity them!" Both friends laughed.

The two of them waited for Don's bags to come down the baggage carousel. Since most of the passengers did not disembark at Sacramento, the wait was relatively short. Donny soon spotted his American Tourister bag and he leaned over and snatched it off the moving carousel before it could make its way on another circuit.

The Hungry Hunter Steakhouse must have had Don and Jack in mind when they designed their menu. The portions were huge and the prices were reasonable—cheap, in fact. The two filled their plates from a salad bar that looked almost a block long then dined on steak and king crab with baked potato. All the food was top quality and cooked to perfection.

"So what do you have in mind for us Jack?" Donny asked after he'd polished off enough food to feed a small army. "Why do you need help chasing down a little woman, a widow, no less?"

"Shut up, wise-ass," Jack said. "I don't need your help. I just wanted company."

Don grinned annoyingly. "You love me!" he said. Jack ignored him.

"First things first—I think the two of us should pay a visit to Mrs. Roshtti. How about we stake out her place for a bit, take some pictures with that nice new Olympus camera of yours? Then once it gets dark, we can pay her lawyer's office a visit. Last night I checked out the couple that cleans their fifth-floor office. They get in at seven-thirty-five and are out by a quarter of nine. You and I should be okay, if we get there at nine-thirty."

Donny nodded. He liked adventures.

After booking Donny a room and dropping his luggage off at his new accommodations, Jack and Donny parked the car a discreet distance from the Roshtti household and started watching. The throng of reporters was now almost gone, except for a few diehards. Jack did not see the reporter he'd threatened. He had gone on to greener pastures; old news is no news, as they say.

Their wait wasn't long; as Jack watched, as a red station wagon approached from behind, its image growing larger in the side view mirror, until a blur of red went past and the car turned into the Roshtti driveway. The male driver announced his arrival with two abbreviated toots of his horn and then the front door opened and Giti started down the steps followed by a small boy who could only be her son.

As the two of them got into the car Jack heard the click and whir of Donny's new camera catching the action. The station wagon pulled out and Jack and Donny did too. Keeping an unobtrusive distance behind it, they followed it as the family made their way to the local office of Pacific Southwest Airlines, conveniently located on Airport Road near the Sacramento Airport.

The two-story PSA office building sat just a few hundred yards from the runway, the company logo prominent in ten-foot-high letters on the side of the building … 'PSA' …with pink, orange and red stripes below stretching horizontally around the entire building. The PSA offices were a block away from their maintenance facility.

Having followed all the leads Donny had got for him, Jack was pretty certain it was Reza's brother Zafar driving the station wagon. He was clearly of Middle Eastern descent Giti and her son seemed inordinately comfortable with him. The man steered the station wagon into the parking lot and he and the three of them got out.

"That's her, all right," Jack muttered as Donny took more pictures. Groups of people were arriving and entering the building, huddled together as they walked, apparently consoling one another. It was clearly a gathering of those who had lost loved ones in the crash. Jack felt his heart shrink as he witnessed their sadness.

Meanwhile, just outside the building's entrance, Giti clung tightly to Zafar, glad for his support. This place and all these grief-stricken people were almost more than she could bear. Her despondency was compounded by the sound of planes taking off; every time one did, engines screaming at full throttle as they clawed their way into the sky, she looked up and soon tears began to flow.

"Come Giti, let's get inside," Zafar coaxed as he encircled her shoulder with his arm. She didn't want to go in and he almost had to pull her into the building. Her tear-filled, brown eyes were still fixed on the rapidly-climbing jet.

A hundred yards away, Jack made some notes and Donny's camera whirred and clicked as he used up yet another roll of film.

Jack did not have the advantage of a 400-millimeter telephoto lens to look through, so from three hundred feet away Giti Roshtti looked fairly ordinary, her conservative clothes giving no hint at the beauty that lay beneath and had captured a rich tycoon's imagination. Giti was generally pretty conservative in her choice of clothes as she was just not one to want to draw attention to herself; but Jack didn't know that, he assumed she was just in mourning.

It was almost four o'clock in the afternoon by the time small groups of people began to parade out of PSA's office and the Roshtti Family was among the last to leave. It was almost twenty minutes to five when Don and Jack followed them to the offices of McIntosh, McMillan & McIntyre.

Though Jack was not one to come to hasty conclusions, he had a good idea why Giti and her family were there. "They didn't like the settlement offer," he said to Donny.

"I guess not," Donny agreed.

There wasn't much point in waiting around after that. They put in another half an hour, but still the family didn't emerge so they decided to call it quits and case the lawyer's office later, as they had planned.

After a couple of burgers at a fast food joint, Jack and Donny arrived back at the lawyer's office at nine-thirty that night. It was conveniently dark, the sky cloudy and blocking the usually bright moon. Although some lights were visible on the eighth and second floors, the fifth was, as they had hoped, dark. The fact that all the offices on the fourth floor were unoccupied was a bonus; there was no one to hear their footsteps as they went from room to room.

The two men walked casually down the lane and into the small alcove outside the rear service door. Their activities were mostly shielded by a large, over-flowing dumpster, but still Jack wasted no time trying the doorknob. They were in luck; it was unlocked. He had banked on it as his surveillance a few days before had revealed that the janitors generally didn't lock the rear door while they were in the building cleaning it; they didn't want to get locked out on one of their frequent trips to the garbage.

Encountering janitors or employees who were working late was not as intimidating to Jack and Don as one would expect. As long as they didn't encounter any while entering the building—the gloves would be hard to explain—they knew it was often less of a risk than entering a completely unoccupied building. As long as the blinds were closed they could turn on lights as they went about their business and not attract undue attention.

They took the back stairs to the fifth floor. Drywall dust coated the treads and stair rail, as this was the same path Rothbury Demolition had used a few weeks back to dispose of the office walls of Pederson & Associates.

"Damn, looks like cocaine," Donny joked. Jack frowned at him.

"Here we are, fifth floor," he said quietly as he looked through the small reinforced window in the exit door into the unoccupied hallway of the fifth floor.

The lights were on but it was empty. He could see the drywall dust 'trail' in the carpet heading off around the corner to the empty office. He tried the stairwell knob. It was locked. Not a problem for Jack: he took out his lock-picking set and in almost no time had the lock picked. He quietly opened the door to the hall and a blast of cool air swept past him, bringing with it the smell of disinfectant. The cleaners had already been on this floor. *Good*, Jack thought to himself as he entered the hall with Don behind him.

They made two right-hand turns and were just passing the elevator when, from down the elevator shaft, came the rattle of a cleaning cart as it went over an obstacle.

Jack froze and Don whispered, "Don't worry Jack! That's just the cleaners below." Seconds later they heard the unmistakable sound of an elevator door shutting, followed immediately by dimming lights as the elevator's electric motor drew an initial surge of current from the building's power supply. The elevator was heading up in their direction.

"Don, let's go," Jack hissed. He was already almost at the first corner of the hallway. Don, not far behind, was surprised as he rounded the first corner to see Jack kneeling on the floor outside a doorway instead of heading for the second corner and the stairs. This wasn't the exit!

As the elevator door slid open, Jack whispered, "In here!" Jack quietly shut the door behind his friend just as the cleaning cart and a whistling janitor rounded the first left turn in the hallway.

Jack silently turned the thumb knob to lock the door and listened, his heart racing and the sound of his pulse deafening. The two men caught their breath as they heard the cart stop outside the door and the distinct sound of someone fumbling with a set of keys.

Jack was going to motion for Donny to stand on the other side of the door so they could surprise and disable the janitor, but it would have been a wasted gesture as Don was already halfway there the instant Jack's hand began to rise. It was like he could read Jack's thoughts. Jack had never been more grateful.

A key slid into the lock and both men tried to control their breathing, waiting, for they both knew what would have to happen next.

The door opened about six inches and a shaft of light sliced through the dark room, dividing the floor into two black trapezoidal shapes. Donny and Jack both braced themselves as a shadow entered the room followed by its owner. But whoever it was stopped just as soon as his or her grasping hand found the box of fluorescent tubes leaning against the wall at the far side of the door. In a clearly practiced motion, the janitor placed several loose fluorescent tubes into his cart, then shut and locked the door. He would never know that two men were just a split second from reacting to his intrusion.

As the door shut, neither Donny nor Jack was able to speak, even in a whisper, fearing the adrenaline coursing through their veins would raise the volume of their voices. They heard the cart rattle its way back over the threshold of the elevator, leaving the fifth floor in silence once again.

"That was too fucking close, Jack! Are you sure this is such a good idea?"

"It sure was close and yes, this is a good idea."

"Let's get on with it then."

The two men once again made their way around the corner, past the elevator and to the door of McIntosh, McMillan and McIntyre. This time they could only hear faint sounds coming from two or three floors down and the office seemed devoid of activity. They were both relieved. For the third time that evening, Jack put his talents to work and was rewarded by a faint click of the lock a few second later.

"I'm sure glad you haven't lost your touch, Jack!" said Don.

Jack entered the office first, followed by Donny. They both stood by the reception desk for a second, trying to get their bearings, then crossed the carpeted office. There was no need to use the small flashlights they had brought; the ambient light coming through the windows was more than sufficient for them to perform their tasks.

Donny carefully went through desk drawers and in-baskets one at a time, looking for any relevant documents pertaining to Giti or her dead husband, while Jack searched through newly-unlocked file cabinets. After today's group meeting at Pacific Southwest Airlines, they hoped to find paperwork with the PSA name or logo on it as a record of Giti's most recent activities. Twenty minutes later Donny had laid out two file folders of documents on a small table in the lawyer's office, one from the lawyer's desk and the other from the desk of the legal secretary. Jack, meanwhile, had found one relevant file in the cabinet.

"Looks like we got what we came for Donny."

"Yeah! Now let's get the hell out of here. I still haven't gotten over that bloody janitor business."

"Hold your horses. We've still got to copy this stuff and then we can leave."

"I'm sorry! I've forgotten my James Bond miniature camera … and come to think of it, I've forgotten my decoder ring too!"

Jack didn't bite. "We don't need that shit," he said. "We've got everything we need right here." He dragged Donny into a small room lined with paper and stationary but dominated by a big Xerox copy machine. He reached down and flicked the on switch, then opened the service door of the machine and shone his light inside.

On the left-hand side of the machine he found what he was looking for; the digital counter. He blew what dust he could off the electrical connector and with a tug of a single electrical plug, he made the counter inoperable. Then he closed the service door and the hum from the interior of the machine, along with the red and green lights, indicated all was well.

Donny handed Jack the file folders one at a time, so as not to get them mixed up. Having them end up back in the wrong places was not something that either of them desired as they didn't want to leave any evidence of their visit. Although none of the folder contained large amounts of documents, there was no time to sort through the material to see what they wanted so it was easier to copy the complete folder contents and sort out what was relevant back at the hotel.

In a hurry and busy copying, Jack initially failed to notice when his dusty thumb and index finger left smudges on the first three pages. But when he went to put the originals back, he saw it.

"Oh shit!"

"What's wrong, Jack?"

"I've taken the bloody trouble to disable the fucking counter, but in the process I've got two big black smudges on a couple of pages."

"Can't we just photo-copy them and put the clean ones back in the folder?"

"No, it's too easy to tell them from the originals. I'll just have to brush them off as best I can, and hope the secretary chalks it up to sloppy house-keeping. Maybe she'll think someone in the office touched a dusty bookcase or something."

While Donny returned the folders to their proper places, Jack made sure everything was as they had found it. When they were certain they'd left no evidence of their 'visit', Jack and Donny left the office and carefully made their way down the stairs and out the still-unlocked rear service door back into the lane. Except for the finger smudges, Both Donny and Jack were certain they had covered all the bases required to be discreet, but they had not.

October 2, 1978

Ms. Helen Jackson arrived at work early, as she usually did. Most Monday mornings she tidied up the things she hadn't had time to take care of the previous Friday afternoon. Generally these tasks were small and she accomplished them quickly; today, however, that was not the case. Today, because her boss, Sean, was going represent Cathy Abernathy in court in a rather important case, Helen had come in at 7:30 a.m. to make a dozen copies of his file, a task for which she had prepared last thing on Friday night.

Five minutes before closing the office, and just before switching off the Xerox, Hellen had opened and then emptied the paper tray. Then she took a fresh ream of paper, opened it, filled the paper tray and closed the door. She wanted to ensure there was enough paper in the machine to run the whole job with no interruptions.

This morning she placed the forty-page document in the document feeder and pressed the 'start' button. The Xerox 6500 began to copy and collate the pages and Helen went to make fresh coffee.

Shortly before 8:00 a.m. the machine stopped. Helen set her coffee cup down on the desk and walked over to the copier. She removed the pages from the collator and began to staple them together. Nine copies, ten copies, eleven copies, twelve copies … but almost all were missing the last five pages.

"What the hell?" Helen swore to herself quietly, though no one else had arrived in the office yet to hear her. "One, two three, four … ten, eleven, twelve …"

She was sure she had pressed the numbers 'one, two' to get twelve copies. Her weekend was not that 'good' and her math was not that 'bad' for her to make such a mistake. Puzzled, she bent down and opened the paper tray to find it empty.

"That's weird!" she exclaimed.

She took the copies back to her desk and began to go through them, thinking perhaps there might be blank pages intermingled with the printed ones; it had happened before.

"I'm glad I came in early," she muttered to herself as she flipped through 400-plus pages. Ten minutes later, it was apparent the machine had done its job perfectly—so why were there 56 pages missing? She set the originals back in the document feeder, placed more paper in the paper tray and once again pressed the big green 'start' button. Helen then went about the task of removing the staples she had put in only moments before.

Just before nine o'clock, exactly on time, Sean McMillan opened the door and entered the office. "Good morning, Helen," he said as he made his way past her desk on his way to his office.

She looked up from the piles of papers in front of her and said, "Good morning, Sean." But it had been anything but.

"Is that the Abernathy file?" he asked.

"Yes! I'll have it finished in about five minutes."

"Good, there's time for quick cup of coffee before I leave."

Right on time, Helen entered Sean's office to let him know all twelve copies were ready and on the front desk. Then she asked, "Were you in on the weekend?"

"No! Why?" Sean asked.

"You weren't? Was anyone else? Nancy, or Ryan?" she asked. She already knew Steve McIntosh was out of town.

"No, I don't think so. Again, why?"

"Well, I think someone was using our photocopier this weekend. I set it up on Friday night but this morning half the paper was gone. That's what took me so long getting the file ready."

"That's strange," said Sean.

Helen explained what she had done so far this morning. "It was missing fifty pages or so of copy paper. I checked the counter against the log that I keep in my desk and they both agree. So that means that someone was in on the weekend and they used our photocopier."

"Maybe the package of paper was short?" suggested Sean.

"Not fifty or sixty sheets. The package was the same thickness as the others in the box. One sheet, maybe two, but not fifty. That's ten percent. That's a lot."

"Call the Xerox technician to come in and check the machine and you can ask him that same question," said Sean. "Anyway, I've got to go. Let's hope you sort out this little mystery today." With that Sean gathered up his package and headed for the elevator. The door closed behind him and Helen reached for her Rolodex.

George Whitaker's pager beeped later that morning. It was Customer Service calling him to do a job. "Christ! This is turning out to be busy day," he said to himself. Usually he did three or four calls a day, but today he'd already done three. This would be his fourth call, all before lunch. He spotted a phone booth, stopped and dialed the office. After the fifth ring, a woman answered and George recognized the dispatcher's voice on the other end of the line.

"Hi, Maureen, what have you got for me … not another paper jam, I hope?"

"Nope, you're too good for that, George," she said. "This is more about disappearing paper. It's a bit of a mystery," she joked. "But it's at a lawyer's office, so you know how things can get mislaid in those places."

George chuckled, and she proceeded to give him the make and model number of the machine, along with a brief description of the problem.

"By the way, I had fun last night," she added, lowering her voice slightly. "We should do it again."

"You can count on it," George said. He didn't want to admit it, but he had also had fun on their date the previous night. She was a nice girl and he hoped to see more of her.

Shortly before noon, George arrived at the offices of McIntosh, McMillan and McIntyre, carrying his satchel of tools. The receptionist, Stacey, took him to Helen Jackson's desk. He handed over his card and she looked a bit surprised.

"That was fast, I only called you a couple of hours ago."

"We aim to please," he said cordially. "What seems to be the problem?"

She explained as she showed him the way to copy room. "Here's our machine. Let me know what you find."

"Yes, I will, thanks!" George said, watching Helen's figure as she retreated back to her desk. Nice ass, he thought to himself. Then he once again thought of Maureen and the image of her firm, sweat-covered body moving beneath him drove Helen from his mind.

He flicked the power switch of the Xerox to the 'off' position and opened its service doors. Maureen had told him that this machine was rated an 'A+', which meant the number of calls was no more than regular maintenance. Everything inside had a light coating of dust; it hadn't been looked at for a while.

It took less than fifteen seconds to notice that one connector was not only loose, but disconnected and had a lot less dust on it than the rest of the machine's parts.

"Well, look at this!" he said to himself.

He reconnected it and continued his survey of the rest of the machine. He found nothing amiss until he checked the mechanical counter, which was driven directly off the feed mechanism. The mechanical counter is strictly a backup, a way for the technician to track the number of copies a machine has made. Technicians monitor it so they can recommend service or overhaul needs at, say, 250,000 copies. That's why this machine had been rated an A+—there had been no hardware or component problems, only periodic adjustments. The mechanical counter read '213,896'.

"Not bad," George thought to himself as he noted it in his maintenance report. However, when comparing it to the digital read-out of 213,820, it was clear that there was a discrepancy of seventy-six copies. George made another note in his report then he made a dozen test copies. He wrote once more, '213,908'.

"Great," he said then he went back to speak to Helen.

"Excuse me, Miss. I'm all finished. The machine is working fine. I reconnected the digital read-out counter for you."

"Was it disconnected? That can't be! It was fine on Friday afternoon just before I left. The last thing I do to that machine every night is open the front door and record the reading for my boss!"

"Look, ma'am, all I can say is that it was disconnected and by the looks of things, on purpose. They are made not to just wiggle loose; you need to depress the center tab and pull at the same time in order for the female end to come out. I can assure you it happened recently. Would like to come and see the machine yourself?"

"Yes, yes I would," she said curtly. She was beginning to dislike this guy's attitude. *The next thing you know he's going to accuse me of pulling off that wire myself,* she thought. Both of them walked in silence back to the copy room.

George pointed to the digital counter. "Look here. This is the reading now, '213,832'. I've given you a credit for twelve copies in my report, but it doesn't agree with this counter under here." He leaned over and showed her the mechanical counter. "This one doesn't lie, since it's driven directly off the main drive mechanism. See the number, '213,908'? Now look at the plug."

George shone his flashlight on the connector. It was clearly a lot less dusty than the rest of the interior.

"Yes, I see what you mean," Helen said.

"Someone in this office pulled the connector and now you have a difference of 76 copies on the two read-outs," George concluded.

"Why would someone here do that? We charge for every phone call, every hour, every minute of time and every photocopy. That's how we make our money!" Helen was beginning to get more and more annoyed with this man.

"Yeah, so I've heard. Look, all I can say is, if it wasn't you or someone in your office, then maybe it was the cleaners. All I know for sure is that you've had visitors and that someone used this machine to make seventy-six copies. Maybe you should call the cops?" he suggested.

"That's a little extreme, don't you think? Maybe it was the cleaners. I'll make a note for our receptionist to call and ask them."

"Anything else I can do for you?"

"No, thanks. I think you've got it covered."

When Sean returned from his court appearance later that day, on his way past Hellen's desk he asked if she'd sorted out her little problem with the Xerox machine.

"Yes, I believe so."

"Good, then would you be so kind as to bring me a copy of Mrs. Roshtti's file, as well as anything else you typed up on PSA?"

"I'll do that right away."

She got up from her desk and went over to the filing cabinets and removed the appropriate folders, then took them to her boss.

"Thanks," he said.

Just as she sat down to begin some typing, Sean buzzed her desk and spoke into his speaker phone, "Helen, would come in here right away?" A second later he added, "Please?"

"Yes, Sean."

He was looking at the contents of the Roshtti file, clearly puzzled. "Just out of curiosity, can you tell me why some of the copies here have huge black smudges on them? To tell you the truth, I'm a bit surprised at this sloppiness. That's not like you."

"I'm sorry Sean, I can't explain this," she said, taken aback. "When those letters were typed on Thursday, I reviewed them myself and put them in the file. I can assure you there were no smudges on them then and as far as I know, no one has touched them since."

Sean sighed. "Can you take care of this for me please? Can you retype them or have Stacey retype them for me?"

"Of course," she said.

A few minutes later Helen sat at her typewriter, retyping the three pages. She decided to do it herself because she didn't want any more screw-ups today; two was enough.

"That's it!" She said as she hurried to finish the last few paragraphs. A few minutes later she was back in Sean's office, documents in hand. Then she detailed the events of the day to her boss.

"Maybe it was the cleaners. I've yet to hear back from Stacey on that score," she told him.

"Well if it turns out it wasn't the cleaners—or on second thought, even if it was—I would like to know. I don't like the idea of someone being sneaky about using the photocopier, cleaners or not. And I really don't like the idea that someone else might have broken into our office! Our client's files are confidential. I think I'm going to call the police … not that they will be able to do much, but at least they'll be aware of what's going on."

"Alright Sean," Helen agreed, "but I can make the call if you like. I know you're busy. I'll also make sure that Stacey talks to the cleaning company before end of the day."

It was almost quitting time before Helen called the police. In the second precinct of the Sacramento Police Department, Sgt. Pete McGarragal was working the front desk when the call came in.

"Yes, Miss Jackson, do you want us to send someone over right away?" he asked after she explained why she was calling.

"No, that won't be necessary, the office is going to close in fifteen minutes," she said.

"Well, ma'am, when would you like someone to come, then?" McGarragal asked, thinking, *God I can't believe the nerve of this woman.* In all his eighteen years on the force, this was the first time someone had scheduled an appointment for the police to come and investigate something.

"Tomorrow morning would be good, say about nine-fifteen?" Helen said.

After a brief pause to bite his tongue, McGarragal said, "Good, I'll see you then."

— Chapter 3 —

October 3, 1978

It was only eight o'clock in the morning. For the last couple of evenings, Jack and Donny had spent time not only going over the files from Giti's lawyer's office, but also her banking records and credit card statements that Donny had brought with him from Washington. It was time to put this baby to bed.

Jack took out a carefully folded piece of paper from his wallet and dialed the Las Vegas number written on it. "Mr. Hussan! Jack Coward here. I've got the information you requested."

"That's excellent news, Mr. Harraj will be most pleased. When can we meet?"

Jack stopped short when he heard that name. In an instant, the investigation changed for him. He didn't know Giti—but he was pretty sure he knew who 'Harraj' was. He knew a little about terrorist activity through some of his old-school connections in the military, but since his Vietnam years he hadn't really kept up. But he doubted there were too many men named 'Mr. Harraj' with the resources to hire a private investigator in the United States just to track down a woman.

"I'd like to some more investigating," Jack said coyly, thinking on his feet. "There are a few more things I'd like to check out. I will be back in Las Vegas on Saturday and I'll bring you my report then, as long as you have the balance of my money."

"Agreed. You know the number!" The line went dead.

All of a sudden, investigating Giti seemed like small potatoes. Now Jack was curious. If this was the man he suspected it was, what would a big-time terrorist like Jaffar Harraj want with a recently-widowed woman in America? Perhaps it wasn't her he was after at all. Perhaps his motives were more sinister.

He decided to review the photographs Donny had taken over the course of the last week. Donny had been peering through a telephoto lens, whereas Jack had been observing with the unaided eye; he needed to see more closely this woman that Jaffar was so interested in.

He pulled the photos out of their manila envelope and started looking through them; after closely peering at the eight by ten stills of the widow Roshtti, Jack could understand what Jaffar saw—at least in her physical aspects. She was gorgeous; both exotic and spirited-looking. It surprised him that long-dead feelings began to stir when he saw her soulful eyes and perfect, pursed lips. Her face was clouded with mourning for her husband and he wished he could know and comfort her.

"I'm not turning that woman over to that louse, Harraj," he muttered to himself.

"Jack, it's not good to mix business with pleasure," Donny said, coming up silently behind him. "You know that!"

"What the hell do you know, Donny? Do you think you're a bloody psychic now? You think you know what I'm thinking?"

"Look buddy, don't try to fucking fool me. I saw your face as you were looking at those bloody pictures. Don't get soft on me!"

"Bullshit!" Jack exclaimed, though he knew Donny was right.

"It's not bullshit and you know it. I've known you all my life, man. I've seen that same look in your eyes only once before—and that was when you got the hots for Michelle."

Jack looked pained. Michelle was the last woman Jack had truly been head-over-heels in love with. Donny quickly tried to change the focus of their conversation.

"Do you remember the time you asked Dawn to go out with you, when we were in grade eight? I remember what happened, do you?" A smile spread across Jack's face, as it always did at the memory of the grade eight prom.

Don continued, "Do you remember I was telling you what Shelly Campbell said to me as you ran back to ask Dawn if she'd go out with you? And I quote, 'If she says yes, I'll just die,' in a voice like some sort of girly-boy. I always wondered what the hell was wrong with you!"

Jack shot his friend a warning look.

"Remember how we were running back home so we wouldn't be late for curfew and I asked you what she said?"

"Yeah!" Jack smiled. He knew what was coming.

"Do you remember what you told me? You thought it was the best thing ever. 'She said maybe!' you said—and then you immediately fell ass over teakettle over that fucking log. You landed on your fucking face, but you didn't care because," Donny raised his voice an octave, "'She said maybe'! Jesus, Jack that still cracks me up." He started laughing.

"Okay smart ass, I know it! And I know love fucks me up every fucking time. I get your point! But if you keep telling that story over and over I'm going to fuck *you* up!" he threatened. Donny didn't' look that scared.

Donny knew Jack almost as well as he knew himself; but does any man really know another man? Within each of us is a private place rarely open to scrutiny by anyone else. All Jack knew was that he was lonely and looking at pictures of Giti made that loneliness disappear somehow, if only for a little while. *Christ, I'm already thinking of her as Giti, not Mrs. Roshtti,* thought Jack. *Maybe Donny's right; I am a sap.* Besides, by Saturday he and Donny would be back in Las Vegas and that would be the end of it—end of story.

He glanced down at his watch, "Come on Donny, let's get going," he said. They were going to get something to eat then stake out Giti Roshtti one more time.

Later that morning, full of chili dogs and coffee, the pair found themselves in what was by now familiar territory. They were parked once again a couple of hundred feet down the street from the Roshtti house. The throng of newspaper and television reporters had descended on the family once again, led by the scent of a story precipitated by an obituary that had appeared in the Sacramento Bee.

> *Reza Roshtti, born November 22, 1948, passed away on September 25, 1978, after Pacific Southwest Airlines crash in San Diego. A veteran of the Vietnam War, Reza is survived by his loving wife Giti, his son Sina, two brothers Zafar (Fatemah), Javed (Nooshin) and one sister, Sahar (Hamid). He will be missed by all who knew*

him. Services will be held at St. Nicolas Church, 9267 Gerber Road, Sacramento at 1:45 p.m., on Tuesday, October 3, 1978.

"Poor thing," Jack said to Donny as they watched the craziness unfolding outside Giti's house. "I wish they'd leave her alone."

Reza's Vietnam Years

On December 1st, 1969, just after Reza's 21st birthday the Selected Services System held its first draft 'lottery' since 1942. The military official reached into the jar to retrieve the ninth blue ball from the remaining 357. He fumbled around for a few seconds then held it up to reveal the date of 'November 22'. With that, the question of Reza's induction into the U.S. armed services instantly went from a small possibility to a certainty.

On January 9, 1970, Reza received orders to report for a physical exam. He was now classified as '1-A'. Two months later Reza received his order to report for induction into the U.S. Army. After his eight-month long basic training, Reza went onto advanced individual training at Fort Dix in New Jersey.

Before Reza was drafted, there were a number of heated discussions between him and his parents around his diminishing attendance at the mosque. Like most young men in their teens and early twenties, Reza had other priorities and was drifting further and further from his Islamic faith. His parents saw his being drafted as punishment from Allah. They were distraught.

Reza was young and didn't fully understand the implications of what was happening to him. He longed for adventure, although going to Vietnam was not exactly what he would have chosen. But at least he was getting out of the house and the old-world traditions of his family and his people.

His first combat came in early 1971. The United States and South Vietnam invaded Cambodia in the spring of 1970 in an effort to destroy communist bases as well as the supply lines that were supporting the North Vietnamese army. During this campaign, as more and more of his fellow soldiers fell around him and his visits to the bedsides of friends who been wounded became more and more frequent, Reza turned to Christianity. It was far more comforting to pray with a Chaplain at the bedside of a friend than it was to pray alone—or even worse, not at all.

For Reza, most of his life it had not been easy to make friends, but something about battle changes that. In combat, you have to rely on the men in your unit; each man's life depends on his skill and the skill of fellow soldiers.

Sadly, many friendships Reza formed during his tour of duty were cut short instantly by bullets and grenade shrapnel. Less instantaneous, but just as deadly, were the numerous and ingenious booby traps placed by the Viet Cong. These included 'punji' sticks—sharpened sticks placed in concealed pits and designed to pierce the feet and legs of enemy soldiers, often dipped in human excrement to cause infection. These, and other similar devices, did not kill large numbers; the effect was almost totally psychological. And it worked, keeping the men on edge and trigger-happy with fear and hatred.

One friendship Reza enjoyed overseas was with a hometown boy, a high school friend who came waltzing into camp to join Reza's unit one humid, damp day in April, 1971. Reza had known Rick Thompson since third grade and though they had not been best friends during their school years, present circumstances made them close. Both yearned for home. Both wished they could reclaim their innocence.

As Rick strode across the camp, trying to dodge puddles of rainwater that had collected in the freshly-cleared soil, Reza thought his eyes were playing tricks on him. He could believe a familiar face stared back in his direction.

"Thompson!" was all Reza could manage.

"Roshtti, I don't believe it!" The men embraced.

"What the hell are you doing here in this neck of the woods?" marveled Reza.

"I got here last fall but I'm heading state-side before too long. But now I find myself in this shit-hole." Thompson laughed.

For the next six weeks the men renewed their friendship, often reminiscing about their time in high school, beginning sentences with, 'remember when …' and ending them with laughter. During those moments, the years washed away both and both men forgot about the war, at least for a few precious minutes.

"Are you still seeing that girl, you know the one that you met in high school?" Thompson asked. "Giti, wasn't that her name?"

"No, we split up. It's kind of hard to keep a relationship going when you're halfway around the world, across the Pacific. Besides, you know what it was like for the two of us. My family are devoted Muslim, and hers are Christians."

"Oh yeah. It was all over the school, talk of the arguments your parents used to have with hers. Boy you sure caught nine kinds of shit over that, didn't you. Do you think it was worth it?"

"It most definitely was. She is a pretty sweet girl," he said, leering a little for effect. "But who the hell knows what will happen when I get back to the States? I don't think my parents will have much to say about it then. I might just look her up."

"That you should man, that you should," Rick replied.

A few days into June, Reza was on patrol with a squad of men and Rick was on point. Warm rain was descending so hard it was like veil in front of everyone's eyes, making seeing where your feet were going difficult.

Rick felt the toe of his boot encounter just the slightest resistance and he froze—but it was too late; just like that, a bamboo mace swung down from above and drove its foot-long spikes through his body. The force was so great that Rick was propelled twenty feet backwards, where he landed on the rain-soaked ground with a sickening thud, right at the feet of his fellow soldiers. It had happened so fast, that most of the men could only stare at the mortally wounded body of Sgt. Thompson with their mouths open. But soon the medics sprang into action.

Reza ran over to comfort his friend. "Rick, Rick just lie still," he said, his voice choking. He knew Rick's end was near; pinkish foam escaped from his mouth when Rick tried to speak.

"I was short man. I was so short!" That was all Rick could manage to say before his brain, starved for the oxygen that his punctured heart and lungs could no longer deliver, died.

Reza began to cry uncontrollably. He wanted to strike out at whoever had done this, but the men who had set this trap were long gone and there was no enemy to lash out at. All he could do was cry and clutch the vest of his friend, no longer able to keep the pain and anger inside. It was several long minutes before Reza stopped and stood up.

As he stared down at Rick's body—a vision that would haunt him all the way to his grave—Reza heard someone from his troop say, "The poor bastard had only four days to go!"

Present Day

Still observing the Roshtti house with Donny from his Camaro, Jack was glad he'd arrived early and got a parking spot. Vehicles from family members and close friends had exceeded the parking capacity of the driveway and were now overflowing onto the street which was jammed full of news trucks of all descriptions, sporting logos of almost every television station in the city.

Giti Roshtti had become a stand-out as a bereaved widow. Since taking an on-air stand against PSA, she had inadvertently become the voice of the oppressed victims. The media love a good story. They didn't want to know that those who had lost loved ones in the crash felt they were being treated fairly by the airline; they wanted to know the dirt. And they mistakenly thought Giti would provide it.

Jack's attention was focused on what appeared to be an exchange between a television reporter and Zafar Roshtti, who had stepped outside the front door.

"Would you people please leave us alone? For over a week you have been sitting out here like, like carrion eaters. I'm sorry, what's the right word? Like vultures. Yes, like vultures. Can't you please leave us alone?"

"I'm sorry sir I have a job to do. We have a job to do."

"Can't you leave my sister-in-law alone? Already she's most upset."

"I'm sorry Mr. Roshtti, but it's my job to report the news. It's in the constitution, you know, freedom of the press."

"But my relatives have no place to park! All the space has been taken over by your news trucks and cars!"

Zafar was upset about the almost constant bombardment of questions. Over the last week, the glare of camera lights in his face and the foam-covered, penis-shaped microphones that were constantly thrust at him had pushed him to the breaking point. He'd finally had enough and all of a sudden he snapped and he reached for the camera lens, trying to push it away.

"Get your hand off the lens, sir!" the cameraman shouted as he reached out and tried to physically remove Zafar's hand. He didn't make it. Donny Ziegler's hand encircled the cameraman's right wrist with vice-like force while Jack stood beside his friend, looking fierce. "Not you again," said reporter holding the microphone. He recognized Jack from their previous encounter the week before. Jack gave him a cold look.

"Yes it's me again and my message to you from the last time still stands—except this time it extends to this gentleman here," he said, indicating the cameraman. "You do recall what I told you I'd do with that microphone? Because I'll do it to your friend too."

"Yes, I do," the reporter said, then, to his partner, "Let's go, Chuck."

"No way, Roger. He just assaulted you! I'm not going to let some idiot keep me from my job. This is a clear violation of ..." But his sentence was cut short as Donny snatched the camera from his hands in one smooth, swift movement and promptly disconnected the power supply from the rear.

"I really think you gentlemen should do as my friend here asks, before something accidentally gets broken." Donny said as he gently placed the camera on the ground. "He politely asked you to leave this man and his family alone. I'm not quite as polite as him, if you catch my drift."

"Let it go, Chuck," Roger said, urging his cameraman to avoid further confrontation. Chuck relented and bent over to retrieve his camera. Donny put his foot on it to stop him.

"Not so fast my friend," Donny added. "You can come and get your camera once you've packed up all the rest of your gear and are ready to leave. And you can pass along the same message to your colleagues. There will be no more news made here today, unless you want to be part of it. Now get lost."

Zafar, who had remained completely silent during the whole exchange, thrust his hand out toward Jack and Donny to shake. "Thank you, thank you for helping me. I didn't think they would ever leave us alone. I'm sorry, I didn't get your names."

"I'm Jack, and this Donny."

"And you are neighbors?"

For reasons known only known to his sub-conscious, Jack said, "I'm a friend of Reza's." He could almost hear Donny's intake of breath at this response. But it wasn't a real risk; the only person who could dispute this claim was going to be buried later that afternoon.

"Donny and I are from Las Vegas," he said. "Our condolences to you and your family."

Zafar looked the two men up and down for a moment, noticing their attire. Jack instantly noticed and deadpanned, "We've got to go back to the hotel and change for the funeral. But we were just driving by, you know?"

"Yes, of course. My family and I thank you. Would you like to come in for a few moments?"

"No, no thanks. As I said before, we've got to go and change before the service." Jack glanced at his watch.

"Then we will see you both later?" Zafar asked.

They nodded and Zafar once again extended his hand to them then turned and walked back to the house, right past the now-departing news crews.

"Jack, are you nuts? What the hell do you think you're doing?"

"I don't know Donny. I saw that asshole shoving his microphone in that poor guy's face and I just snapped. You know, Don, that is the same newsie who did that to me the day before you got here."

"Yeah, I gathered that from his reaction. But Jack I really want to know what's going on. I mean you're Reza's friend now? How are you going to explain that, and please don't tell me we're really going to Reza's funeral service?"

"Why not? Let's go get changed. You did bring a suit with you, right?" Jack headed back to the car, taking somewhat larger steps than normal, like something inside had invigorated him.

"I don't fucking believe this," Donny said to himself, rushing to catch up. But he knew he would stick with his life-long friend like glue, no matter what. No man left behind. They were brothers.

On the way to the funeral, as he sat in the passenger seat, Donny looked over at Jack and for a moment he was transported back to a place in their past, back to June, 1965 when the two of them arrived in the Central Highlands of South Vietnam on their first 13-month-long tour of duty. It was just after Jack's twentieth birthday and both of them were relatively old for FNGs (fucking new guys); the average age of the men in the camp was nineteen.

It was their second patrol and they were about two miles from camp. During this armed trek through the jungle, each man extended his senses to the limit; eyes scanning for movement, ears searching like radar for unnatural sounds that would betray the presence of the enemy. Above, below and all around were the sounds of the jungle and the creatures that inhabited it; nerve-wracking chirps and squeaks and calls ... nature or not? So hard to tell, yet to make a mistake meant sure death. Their own footfalls were almost silent on the moist, loamy soil as they made their way through the unfamiliar forest.

Suddenly, the almost surreal calm was shattered by the unmistakable sound of distant explosions coming from the direction of the camp. Instantly the low crackle of the radioman's handset gave the orders for all patrols to return to camp and engage the enemy troops that were now firing mortar rounds at the compound. It took almost 15 minutes of quick marching through the jungle for the patrol to reach a clearing U.S. ground forces had been using as a landing zone, less than 200 yards away. This clearing was the point from which the North Vietnamese were launching their attack.

Jack's platoon stopped on the near side of the clearing and watched as approximately 60 North Vietnamese soldiers fired round after round of mortars over the swath of trees that separated them from the U.S. military base. Their aim was deadly accurate.

Reacting quickly, the platoon almost instantly split into three squads: one squad to radio position and intentions to the base; one to transmit a 'fix' on the enemy; and, one to engage the enemy in a direct assault across the 150-yard wide clearing. Two squads would retreat 20 yards or so back into the bush to circle and outflank the enemy, both acutely aware that the North Vietnamese would have men guarding their rear flank.

As Jack and his fellow marines crept forward, the sound of mortars launching their deadly salvos became clearly audible over the explosions in the distance. The circuitous route around the clearing took almost 10 agonizing minutes—10 minutes during which dozens of deadly rounds rained down on their countrymen, who had taken refuge in foxholes and bunkers.

The animated chatter of the Viet Cong became louder as they slowly advanced, now only 30 yards away. Suddenly, just 10 yards away, a lone North Vietnamese soldier emerged from behind a bush, doing up his pants. It was impossible for him to not notice the group of marines advancing on his troops. For an instant his jaw slackened in surprise, but before the nearest marine could silence him, he sounded the alarm.

"Americans, Americans!" he called frantically, followed by something unintelligible in Vietnamese."

His words were cut off by Lance Corporal Don Ziegler's left hand as it clamped across the man's mouth. Then his throat was slit ear-to-ear by the razor-sharp combat knife in Donny's right.

The limp body of the Vietnamese soldier dropped to the ground, his blood spraying all over the front of Donny's olive-green battle fatigues, turning them crimson and wet. It wasn't the first time Donny had taken another man's life; unfortunately, it wouldn't be the last.

The mortar fire momentarily slackened as the North Vietnamese Army returned fire in the general direction of their comrade's alarm. Of the dozens of soldiers on the Viet Cong's flank, two were immediately killed as the bullets from pistols and AK-47 rifles found their mark. All three squads of U.S. soldiers, coupled with support from troops from the camp, responded with fire from their M-16 rifles and M-79 grenade launchers. The Viet Cong responded by spinning all mortars that had been shelling the camp around 180 degrees to launch rounds at the surrounding U.S. troops.

He dove for cover, but the instant before Jack hit the ground a bullet struck him in his left leg, just about mid-thigh. At first, he thought maybe he had fallen on a sharp branch, but the moment he looked down to examine the wound, he knew different.

Donny inched his way back to his closest friend. "Jack, are you okay?"

"No way! My fucking leg hurts like a son of a bitch."

"Let's have a look!" Drawing his now-bloody knife, bullets racing over their heads, Donny cut away the leg of Jack's pants to expose his wound. Then he applied a field dressing from his kit and attempted to stem the bleeding.

"Do you think you can walk?" Donny asked anxiously. The firing from 'Charlie' was still very heavy, despite the Viet Cong having suffered almost 50 percent casualties. Both Jack and Donny knew they had to get out of there.

"No, but I can crawl!"

"Good, then let's get you over there, behind that fallen tree, and out of harm's way."

"That sounds like a fucking good plan. We're way too fucking exposed here."

Jack tried to crawl, but the pain forced him to stop immediately. Already blood oozed from the wound through the hastily applied bandage. It was becoming apparent that the loss of blood from Jack's leg wound would very soon become critical. Donny knew he had to do something—fast.

"Jack! We can't stay here. There's no cover. I can't even begin to control the bleeding, and the corpsman is on the far side of the clearing. I've got to move you and it's going to fucking hurt, okay? Just bear with me until I can get you somewhere safe and out of the way!"

With that, Donny picked up Jack and put him over his shoulder with one arm while he picked up their rifles with the other. Jack cried out in pain despite his friend's best efforts to avoid further injury.

"Just a few yards more, Buddy," Don coaxed.

Soon Donny had himself and Jack safely behind the fallen log, where he tried to stem the flow of blood in relative safety. As he worked he began to chuckle. "I must be rubbing off on you Jack. You know, you used the word 'fucking' in no less than two sentences in a row."

"That's because my fucking leg hurts." Both men laughed.

In less than fifteen minutes, all resistance had been taken care of. The sporadic gunfire of the last few moments stopped as the last of the Viet Cong was either captured or killed. Jack was taken back to camp where a doctor repaired the wound in his leg, a wound for which he received the first of two Purple Hearts. For his actions of the day, Donny received a Silver Star.

Later, the human cost was tallied. It was a miracle that only eight American servicemen had been killed, along with twenty-five injured. On the Viet Cong side of the ledger, fifty-two had been killed and ten injured. The remainder had fled into the bush, leaving their fallen comrades behind. That had been over thirteen years ago and both Donny and Jack had managed to put that part of their shared past behind them; had managed to lock the horror of war in the deep recesses of their minds, from which they rarely allowed it to emerge.

Such was not the case for tens of thousands of U.S. soldiers suffering from the effects of past conflicts, among them Reza Roshtti. During their mostly-happy marriage, there were things he didn't share with his wife that occasionally made him less than the ideal husband. There was affection he couldn't give sometimes—and a glint in his eye once in a while that frightened her. But he tried. And she knew that. As best he could, he expressed love to his family and they loved him back. However, at night, when he was asleep and fighting the ghosts of his dreams, Giti knew he was not the man she had met as a star-struck teenager. Her heart ached for him.

The guests attending Reza's funeral service that October morning were diverse. Among them were co-workers from California Robotics, others who had lost loved ones when the plane crashed and friends of the family, among them Jack and Donny in their hastily-pressed suits. They had been fortunate the hotel laundry was able to provide service on short notice.

The throng of reporters who'd been at the Roshtti household earlier that day were conspicuously absent—Jack wondered if his and Donny's chat with Roger and Chuck earlier in the day had sent ripples out to the rest of them, or if they'd finally got a little compassion and were leaving the Roshtti family alone.

However, one inconvenience that the absence of the reporters created was that it made taking pictures a bit more conspicuous. Donny managed to take a few by wandering away at the beginning of the service and shooting from a discreet distance. From among the nearby trees, using a telephoto lens, Donny finished his job. Then he returned the equipment to Jack's car and rejoined his friend.

Jack leaned over and asked, "Did you get some good shots?"

"Yes! I pretty much got everyone here. Thank God for that telephoto lens. It's in pretty bad taste to take pictures at a funeral, it's not like someone's wedding you know!"

"I know," said Jack. He looked over at the grieving family and a ripple of guilt washed over him. Somehow it seemed wrong to be casing them; but at least he and Donny had done some good today by ending the harassment of those reporters. "At least they can grieve in peace," he said softly.

Donny just barely caught the remark and knew what Jack meant … but he was worried about his friend. The soft side of Jack was clearly struggling to get out and it was triggered by the bereaved widow. Not that it was surprising to Donny. You'd have to be blind not to notice how gorgeous she was. But it wasn't like Jack to go all soft like that. Donny wondered if he was okay.

Jack's guilt ripple became a tsunami when he found himself in the condolence line, queued up to offer sympathy to the family. When he and Donny finally came to the front of the line, Zafar recognized them and shook hands firmly with both men.

"Thanks once again! You can't imagine how much easier you've made things for my family!"

Jack wanted to say more but he could only manage, "You're welcome."

"Of course you've met Reza's wife, my sister-in-law, Giti?"

"No! Actually we've never met," Jack managed to mumble.

Donny ably stepped in, his charm in full gear. "We never really leave Las Vegas much," he said in his most personable voice. "But if we'd known what a wonderful family Reza had, we most certainly would have made the effort to meet them. I'm so sorry for your loss, Mrs. Roshtti. Reza was a good man." He felt Jack kick him in the foot, but he warmly took both Giti's hands in his anyway and gave her a sincere, compassionate, hound-dog smile.

"Giti my dear," said Zafar, "These two gentlemen are Jack and Donny, friends of Reza's from Las Vegas. These are the men I told you about earlier."

"My condolences to you and your family," Jack said. He could see a faint smile beneath her veil. She extracted her hand from Donny's and gave it to Jack. He took it and felt his heartbeat go up a notch. It was warm and delicate and soft, the color of milky coffee. The nails were a feminine shade of subtle pink. She smelled like roses.

"Thank you," was all she said.

To her left, Jack noticed a small boy, her son, Sina, insistently tugging on his uncle's sleeve. Zafar tried to ignore him as he greeted the guests; however, when the reception line was finally over, Zafar bent down to him and said patiently, "What is it, young man?"

"That man, Jack," said Sina, "I saw him driving around behind us this week."

October 6, 1978

"Have you got the photographs, Don?" Jack asked impatiently as Don walked into his hotel room.

Don nodded. It had been a quick turnaround and the eight-by-ten enlargements had come back earlier that day. *You're always assured prompt service if you grease someone's palm with the green stuff,* Jack thought as he took the manila envelope started going through them. There were some nice shots of Giti and he wanted to linger over them but didn't because Don was watching him. Then one photo caught his eye.

"Holy shit, I don't believe it!!"

"What don't you believe?"

"I know this guy! He's the guy that hired me. Or should I say us!"

"No shit?"

"No shit. That's Mr. Hussan—Mohammed Hussan. He's the guy who handed me that wad of cash. I just talked to him the other morning to tell him we were wrapping up. That guy with him looks familiar too, but I can't place him."

"Maybe a relative?"

"No way. This guy is no relative, my friend. Look at how they're standing." He pointed to the picture and Donny scanned it. Both men stood as if ready for some sort of undefined action, with Hussan leaning almost protectively toward the other man.

"Yup, this looks like a pair of guys in cahoots. The other guy looks like partner, or maybe a big boss man," he said.

"That was a big wad of cash he gave me—I wonder if this is the source?"

"Maybe the husband hired them to off Reza?"

"Nah—when I got the call from Hussan, Reza was already dead."

"Well, it's none of our business. I think the case is closed," Donny said, "Unless there's something you're thinking and not telling me?"

"We aren't going to do anything about it right now. Today we are going to put together a package for our client," Jack responded. "We need to make duplicates of everything first, then tomorrow I'll drop you off at the airport to catch your flight home. Then I'll then meet Mr. Hussan and get the rest of our money. After that … maybe we'll deal with it."

Donny smiled. "It's that woman," he said. Jack didn't deny it.

Late the next evening, Jack got back to his RV in Las Vegas. He dropped his bags on the floor and headed immediately into the shower. After almost two weeks in a hotel, he was looking forward to sleeping in his old crate of a bed. Actually, he was pretty comfortable in the RV. He had a queen-size bed at the back and windows and a sky-light that let in the cross-breezes from the night's desert air.

Jack let the spray from the shower in his miniature bathroom cascade down his back, washing away the sweat and grime of the 14-hour drive. But despite his efforts to relax, something was picking away at the back of his mind.

I wonder who that guy at the funeral was and what he has to do with Giti? Jack thought. After drying off, he sat down on the bed and dialed Mr. Hussan's telephone number.

"Hello, Mr. Hussan. Jack Coward here. Sorry for the late hour."

"Hello, my friend. How are you?"

"Very well, thanks. I've got a package for you."

"Ah, that's great news. When can you deliver?" asked Hussan.

Jack looked at his watch. It was after nine o'clock and he was tired. "Can we meet tomorrow morning?"

"Yes! That will be fine. I'm looking forward to it!"

October 7, 1978

Jack rose early; he'd been unable to get a restful sleep. He kept trying to move on, but there was something about this case he could not let go. He'd tossed and turned, replaying the last two weeks over and over in his head. He couldn't quite put his finger on it, but perhaps it had something to do with Hussan's friend. What, he couldn't say.

After a cup of coffee, Jack headed towards the strip on Las Vegas Boulevard, south under the Oran K. Gragson Highway and past City Hall. He turned left on Fremont and miraculously found parking for the once-more 'brown' Camaro. It was only a four-block walk to the Golden Nugget Casino where he'd agreed to meet Hussan.

He arrived at exactly eleven o'clock, headed inside and he sat down at a one-armed bandit, as per Hussan's phone instructions. He put a few coins in the slot and half-heartedly pulled the lever. He had no interest in letting his hard-earned cash go to some greedy mafia boss, unlike the rest of poor, gambling-addicted slobs around him. *Look at them, the poor bastards—they're all hoping for the big pay-off,* Jack thought. *Don't they know the odds are against them?*

He felt bad for being judgmental. The odds were against him too, but here he was, alive and well and living in America. He could just as easily be nothing but bones in a jungle somewhere.

Jack noticed a familiar face approaching him from out of the crowd. "Mr. Hussan. How are you?"

"Very well my friend."

Jack wasn't sure how he felt about this sketchy guy calling him his 'friend'—and it was hard to keep his prejudice about Arabs and their ties to terrorism in check—but he kept telling himself, *the money's good.* Besides, it had been a simple assignment.

"What have you got for me," Mr. Hussan asked.

"Do you have the rest of my money?"

"Ah yes, right to the point. Here you go." He handed Jack an envelope. Jack opened it and counted the bills inside.

All there, he thought to himself and then he handed over the large manila envelope full of photos and documentation on Giti Roshtti and her family.

"Thank you," Hussan said. "It was good to see you at the funeral the other day. Clearly you have covered every base in your investigation." He watched Jack's face for some kind of reaction, though Jack wasn't sure what he expected to see. He didn't care. Jack was master of the poker-face. He gave the man nothing.

"It was good to see you as well," he said—then he went fishing. "We got some good shots of the crowd. Your friend is a handsome man." He wanted to see how this sat with Hussan and was rewarded when he saw a slight hint of surprise and … could that be fear?

"Ah, yes!" Mr. Hussan said hastily. Then he quickly rose from his seat.

Jack knew he'd struck a nerve, though he didn't understand what it was about. To Hussan, all he said was, "Keep me in mind if I can be of further service."

"Of course," Hussan responded, quickly shaking Jack's hand before beating a hasty retreat.

It was as he had expected; there was more to this than met the eye.

Jack watched as Hussan made his way through the crowded casino and when there was a large enough gap between them so he could discreetly follow, he did. It was not difficult. The casino was full of people of every size and description, but he was easy to spot. He was not tall—several inches shy of six feet—but he was undeniably round; he probably tipped the scales at over three hundred pounds and a full beard made his face look as round as a soccer ball.

Jack's pursuit did not last long. Hussan passed the gaming the tables and roulette wheels and headed straight into the Oasis Lounge. Jack watched from a discreet distance as Hussan sat down at a table, joining an Arab man who waited for him there. It was the man in the picture! Jack inched as close as he could. He didn't want to miss this discussion.

Hussan slid the envelope across the table. "Here you are, Excellency," Jack heard him say. "I hope you find it useful."

The man opened the thick manila envelope and withdrew the contents, several dozen black and white photos, as well as a hand-written report from Jack and, of course, the pages from Giti's lawyer. After a few minutes he turned to Hassan, who was clearly his subordinate, and said, "Your investigator has done a remarkable job in such a short time. We shall have to use him again."

"Yes, he's very good, but I don't like to use the same source more than once," Hassan said. "If people know my business, it can create problems."

The man thumbed through the folder's contents again and Jack heard him say, "Hmmm." Then he said, "I think you are wrong, Hussan. He may be a valuable asset. If needed, we will use this private investigator again."

"Of course, Excellency."

Later that day, Jaffar sat at the table in his hotel room. He was now able to give the contents of the envelope more than a cursory glance and he was carefully reading each page and looking at each photograph.

"Abdul, come here at once!" he called to his lieutenant. As he had many times in the past, Abdul Salam Al-Kubesi walked swiftly into the room as commanded.

"Yes, Jaffar?" he said, looking at his boss expectantly as he entered. But this time it was not the customary scowl and words of criticism on Jaffar's face that he'd grown accustomed to; instead, he saw a look not often seen by anyone, even Abdul. Jaffar's face was fixed in a broad smile as he handed Abdul the documents Donny and Jack had collected.

"Take a look at this and tell me what you think."

After several moments of studying the pages and photographs, Abdul put them down on the table, unsure of what was causing the rare smile on Jaffar's face. "Interesting, but I'm not sure what you want me to comment on," he said cautiously.

"Don't you see it Abdul? Mrs. Roshtti is going to be in for rather large legal battle with the airline and it seems that until her dead husband's insurance settles, she doesn't have the money to pay her lawyers." He looked back his friend, searching for the look of understanding in his face. There was none.

"Why does this concern you Jaffar? And what do you wish to do about it?" Abdul asked as neutrally as he could.

"Why, we are going to help her, of course. We are going to pay her legal fees, you will make all the arrangements."

Abdul waited for further explanation, but none came so he picked up the pictures again, hoping a clue to his boss's behaviour would reveal itself.

Jaffar watched him, thinking of the opportunity that might open for him if he took an American bride. He'd looked them over and been impressed with Giti Roshtti's beauty. In candid shots she was even prettier than she was on television.

Suddenly an audible gasp escaped Abdul's lips.

"What is it Abdul?" Jaffar reached across the table and took the pictures from Abdul's hand. He instantly recognized the funeral but didn't see, until Abdul's pointing finger drew his attention to it, a clear image picture of two men's faces on the left hand side of one of the shots. It was a nice picture of him. A rare one as well, for he had had taken great pains over the years to remain as inconspicuous as possible. For the most part, he'd let Abdul be the face of the day-to-day business they did. He played the part of anonymous mastermind—and he liked it that way.

He was immediately angry then went cold with betrayal. He'd considered not going to the funeral but he'd reasoned there would be many Arabs there and he would blend in. He wanted a first-hand look at his potential bride. He'd wanted to touch her hand and try to get a sense of who she was. He'd thought it unlikely anyone would take pictures! Who takes photographs at a funeral? To make it worse, this photo had been snapped when he'd taken off his hat to show respect, timed with precision, it seemed.

"Well, well," he said slowly. "It would seem Mr. Hussan was correct after all about letting business contacts become too familiar. This private investigator is just a little too good. This Jack Coward must die."

— Chapter 4 —

January 16, 1979

"Good morning. This is the BBC news for this Tuesday, January 16. The Shah of Iran has fled the country following months of increasingly violent protests against his regime," droned the Jack's small television. Jack shook his head and pulled on a pair of jeans as he listened, nearly banging his head on an overhead cupboard he'd left open. He loved his RV, but it felt small after a spacious hotel room. Besides, now that the case was over, he missed hanging with Donny and being busy and engaged. He wondered if he should get a dog. His cactus was not much of a companion.

The news from the Middle East was distressing, and Jack wondered if Giti had relatives there. He hoped not. The woman had been through enough.

The television droned on: "Shah Mohammed Reza Pahlevi and his wife, Empress Farah, left Tehran and flew to Aswan in Egypt. Their three youngest children were flown to the United States yesterday. Official reports say the Shah has left for a vacation and medical treatment. In fact he was asked to leave by the man he appointed prime minister earlier this month."

"Over the past few months there have been an increasing number of violent clashes between security forces and anti-Shah demonstrators. Opposition to the Shah has become united behind the Muslim traditionalist movement, led by Iran's spiritual leader, the Ayatollah Ruholla Khomeni, who has recently returned to the country from his exile in France."

"There was public outcry for the Ayatollah's return and the Shah's departure has been greeted with mass celebrations across Iran. British and

American ex-patriots living in Iran, regarded as symbols of westernization, have been the frequent targets of attacks. Thousands have left the country. Martial law was declared in many cities on September eighth last year, but later that month industrial action by thousands of Iranian workers culminated in mass strikes by employees in the oil industry. The strikes sparked riots and rallies across the country in support of the Ayatollah."

"Western governments, including the U.S., U.K. and West Germany, have continued to express support for the Shah. The Shah appointed a new military government in early September but it failed to stop the rising flood of support for the ayatollah. Earlier this month, the Shah appointed a new Prime Minister, Dr. Shapur Bahktiar. On January thirteenth, when the Ayatollah declared a revolutionary Islamic council to replace what he called the 'illegal government' of Iran, Dr. Bahktiar persuaded the Shah to leave."

"Saw that coming," Jack said to himself as he pulled on his socks.

Sacramento, California

Zafar and Giti arrived at the offices of McIntosh, McMillan and McIntyre at precisely ten o'clock, as instructed by the receptionist the previous Friday. Giti absent-mindedly flipped through the assortment of magazines in the reception area. A few minutes later Sean McMillan appeared and asked them to come into his office.

"Mrs. Roshtti, this is my partner Steve McIntosh. I hope you don't mind if he sits in on this. Steve has handled several cases similar to this and can offer valuable insight as to how we should proceed."

"Mr. McMillan, you remember my brother-in-law, Zafar?" Giti asked.

"Yes, of course. Thank you for coming in."

"May I ask why are we here?" Giti said, getting right to the point. "The last time we talked I explained to you that I could not afford to take my case to court. That still hasn't changed. There is still no money from Reza's insurance."

"That's precisely why I've asked you to come here," said Sean. "Last week we received a money order in the amount of twenty-five thousand dollars, to be put towards your legal fees."

Giti shook her head. "Pardon me?" she said.

The last time she had spoken to Sean, he'd made it clear that his firm did very little work on speculation; in fact, his partner Nancy McIntyre said clearly, "It's risky for us to work on speculation. We've had some pretty bad experiences. If you don't get a big payout, then where will that leave us? You do understand, I hope. We prefer money upfront."

Giti did understand, though she was saddened by the news. This was the best law firm in the city and she wanted to win her case. It was a catch-22; as always, you had to have money to make money. But now someone had paid up front. It was a mystery who, though.

"I don't understand," Giti said. "Who would do this? We have no rich relatives. No one we know could write a check for that kind of money."

"We don't know who or where it came from," Sean said, "but it seems you have an unknown benefactor." Then after a brief pause to let the news sink in Sean continued, "The thing for us to talk about now, however, is how we are going to proceed."

"It seems to me," chimed in Steve, "that both Pacific Southwest Airlines, as well as the air traffic controllers at Lindbergh Field, are to blame and should be taken to task." He continued, "Another party to look toward for compensation would be the owners of the flying school, Gibbs Flight Center. Based on the facts as we know them, that Cessna shouldn't have been in the air. Prior to hitting the PSA flight, it almost got creamed by one of United's 747s!"

"What do you mean?" Zafar asked.

"I mean that there's still the National Transportation Safety Board investigation going on, but employees in the cafeteria at the airport had a few things to say about the plane that hit your husband's flight, Mrs. Roshtti. However, this is confidential, okay? It probably will be several months before their findings are made public and until that report comes out, and blame is assigned, we can only speculate on which parties are responsible and liable for your husband's death. But we are unofficially aware of what may have happened here."

"But what will I do until then?" Giti asked, worried. "I have a household to run, a young son to feed and clothe."

"As I explained before, your mortgage had an insurance policy attached to it. I've already filled out the paperwork for you and your bank should be getting a check from First Fidelity Life to pay off your mortgage."

"But, what will I do after that? I can't work right now!"

This time it was Zafar who spoke up. "Don't worry Giti—Fatemah and I will make sure you and Sina are taken care of. The business has done rather well lately and we can let you have enough money to take of day-to-day expenses." He added, "After that, when you're feeling up to it, we'd like you to work in the store. It will be good for everyone!"

Giti was touched at his generosity. "Maybe you're right. Thank you, Zafar."

Half an hour later, on the drive home, Giti much calmer about her future, but she could not help but wonder who had sent the money.

"Maybe it was Reza's company," she said, more to herself than to Zafar.

"I'm sorry," Zafar said, trying to concentrate on the busy city traffic, "What was that?"

"Maybe it was Reza's company that sent the money," she said. But she did not hear Zafar's response, if indeed he answered at all. Instead, her mind flashed back several years, to the day she and Reza had bought their house. They only had a small down-payment to put on it—and they had scrimped and saved every cent of it, as Reza had only been with California Robotics for half a year. The $43,000 asking price had seemed like $43,000,000 … and now someone had generously given her more than half that amount—almost as much as the balance on the mortgage. But who?

March 27, 1979

Winter turned to spring and Giti tried to get on with her life. Sina was once again in school and he seemed happy enough, but was bothered frequently by nightmares. Giti had moved his room from down the hall to the one closest to hers. Most nights she could hear him thrash about the bed, often crying out at some point. Almost certainly his mind was replaying the images he had seen on the television that terrible September morning.

"Do you think I should take him to see someone?" Giti asked her family doctor. She hated to use the word 'shrink' as it implied he was crazy or unbalanced—but that's what she was thinking. "He said he doesn't want to see a … you know, special doctor …"

"I think you should play it by ear," the doctor said kindly. "Look, Giti, I remember the faces of all children I've had a hand in delivering as well as all the times I've treated them and what for. Sina talks to me with a maturity beyond his years and I can tell you without the slightest hesitation that he will pull through this—and so will you. You are a strong woman, and you've raised a strong son. If he doesn't want to go see a shrink, then let him work through it on his own. Only push him to see someone if you see him doing harmful things. Kids are resilient, both physically and emotionally. Use your judgement. You'll know if he needs extra help coming to terms with this."

"Then you think Sina will be okay?"

"I'm almost sure of it," the doctor replied.

It brought Giti some degree of comfort to be told her son might be able to work his grief out on his own. But what about her? She hadn't the nerve to tell the doctor about how she missed Reza terribly and fought a daily battle to get up from her bed and face each day alone. It was fortunate she and Reza had been blessed with Sina, for it was because of him that she did not—could not—permit feelings of self-pity to overwhelm her. Often, she felt her self-control slipping and she wondered how she would have reacted to this loss if she was childless; she was certain she would have plunged into a black, emotional abyss, perhaps out of sanity's reach forever. She could not know, of course, that the events of the last few months would pale in comparison to the emotional roller coaster her life would soon be on.

April 20, 1979

Giti awoke early on this spring day after a somewhat restless sleep. She was anxiously awaiting a call from Sean McMillan who'd told her yesterday that the National Transportation Safety Board report was going to be made public today, and since she was a victim, she would get an advance copy. "A courier is on the way with a sealed copy of the report as we speak," Sean had happily announced.

For the past three months, Giti had struggled to get her life back to some semblance of normalcy. The insurance finally came through and she paid off her mortgage, removing that burden; now she was working alongside Fatemah and Zafar in the family's textile company, as Zafar had promised. A good man, Zafar had indeed looked after his sister-in law and his nephew. His kindness had helped Giti's spirits improve and he had been a rock through this entire ordeal.

Today she was nervous. She sat in Sean's office with Zafar beside her as Sean opened the folder and began to read through the report numbered N.T.S.B.–AAR-79-05.

He read, "At 9:01:47 Pacific Standard Time, September 25, 1978, Pacific Southwest Airlines Inc., Flight 182, a Boeing 727-214, and a Cessna 172 collided in mid-air about three nautical miles northeast of Lindbergh Field, San Diego, California. The weather was clear and the visibility was ten miles."

Giti's hand reached for Zafar's and she held it tight, her fierce grip cutting the blood flow to his fingers, turning the tips a creamy white.

Sean continued, "The Cessna was under the control of San Diego Approach Control and was climbing on a northeast heading. Flight 182 was making a visual approach to runway 27 at Lindbergh Field and had been advised of the location of the Cessna by the approach controller. The flight crew told the approach controller they had the traffic in sight and were instructed to maintain visual separation from the Cessna and to contact Lindbergh Tower. Flight 182 contacted the tower on its downwind leg and was again advised of the Cessna's position. The flight crew did not have the Cessna in sight, they thought they had passed it and so they continued the approach. The two aircraft collided near twenty-six hundred feet mean sea level and fell to the ground in a residential area. Both occupants of the Cessna were killed; one hundred and thirty-five persons on the Boeing 727 were killed; seven persons on the ground were killed; and nine persons on the ground were injured. Twenty-two dwellings were damaged or destroyed."

Giti's eyes were moist with tears as Sean read the excerpt from the report and she thought about her lost love, her Reza.

Sean went on, "The National Transportation Safety Board determines that the probable cause of the accident was the failure of the flight crew of Flight 182 to comply with the provision to maintain a visual separation clearance, including the requirement to inform the controller when they no longer had the other aircraft in sight. Contributing to the accident were the air traffic control procedures that were in effect, which authorized the controllers to use visual separation when the capability was available to provide either lateral or vertical radar separation to either aircraft."

Both Giti and Zafar looked at one another and tears once again welled up in Giti's eyes. Neither of them really heard the specifics of what Sean was saying; all they heard was that it was a two-plane crash and it could have been avoided.

Such a waste of life, Giti thought absent-mindedly as she glanced down at her watch, it was 9:03 a.m. She did not realize until later that it was fortuitous that she looked at that exact moment; Reza had died 207 days prior, almost precisely to that minute.

"I know this is very difficult for you both," Sean said as he saw their reaction to his words. "However it would seem we have a strong case against the airline, as well as a possible class action suit against the Federal Aviation Administration for their failure to enforce air traffic control procedures."

As the words left his mouth, Sean imagined this very same conversation taking place in the offices of other lawyers representing the one hundred-plus victims of this accident.

"I would like to know if the two of you still want to proceed with this case, but before you answer, please understand that this will be a long and difficult process."

"We understand, and yes, we would like to go ahead with this," Zafar replied for both of them, having discussed this question with Giti many times over the last few months.

"Very well. Helen, my secretary, has copies of the petition that were already prepared earlier today. I anticipated several possible scenarios in the NTSB report and had Helen type out appropriate documents based on those scenarios. I also had her photocopy the 74-page long NTSB report. I can well imagine that many families are having their lawyers do just what we are doing right now, and the faster we file our paperwork the nearer the front of the queue we will be. I would like to have this done within the hour."

"Of course Sean … but this is just the first step of—how do you put it—the pretrial, is it not?" asked Zafar.

"No that comes later, after the defendants—being Pacific Southwest Airlines in our case—answer the statement of claim. Thirty days after that comes the discovery, where both parties exchange information. This is followed by the pretrial period, which is usually 90 days before trial."

"Ah, yes," Zafar said, recalling this explanation from an earlier conversation.

Giti only nodded. Her only experience with lawyers was limited to when she and Reza had bought their house several years before. Even then, Reza had had a far greater understanding of this sort of thing. *Thank God for Zafar,* Giti thought to herself. *I would be lost without him.*

"I'll be right back with your copy of the documents, as well as a copy of the NTSB report. After that, I must be on my way over to the courthouse," Sean said, concluding their meeting.

September 10, 1979

It was a scene reminiscent of barely a year ago, but instead of the Roshtti home being swarmed by the press, it was the Sacramento Courthouse besieged by reporters and television crews, some having arrived in the wee hours of the morning to stake out the choicest spots from which to do their jobs—the spots from which they would once again launch their assault on the families and friends of the victims of Flight 182.

Sean had been prophetic in his prediction that dozens of families would launch similar cases and that the faster the paperwork was processed, the sooner their case would be heard. What he had not predicted was the lawsuit they brought before the court in April was at the front of the queue, thrusting Giti once more into the spotlight. Now, more than ever, she had become the face of this tragedy.

This was going to be a truly ground-breaking case, as it was shaping up to be one of the biggest class action cases in American judicial history. Over the course of the last five months, the number of cases brought before the court rose steadily to finally stop at fifty-one.

Blessedly, the annoying Roger and Chuck were not reporting on this case; however the reporter du jour this time around was already in place, waiting to confront Giti or whatever other victim he could find as soon as a lone sheep left the herd.

"Good morning! This is Dagmar Madcap reporting from the Sacramento courthouse," he chirped importantly. "This could be a momentous day for the travelling public in the United States as well as those abroad. Most of you watching will remember that almost a year ago Pacific Southwest Airlines Flight 182 collided with a smaller plane near San Diego …"

In homes across America, a still shot of the doomed Boeing 727 as it fell from the sky was broadcast onto television screens, followed by a short video of the devastation in the North Park area that resulted from the crash.

"What began in April with the release of the National Transportation Safety Board report on this tragedy has now been followed by a flurry of lawsuits which have seemingly stopped at the unprecedented number of fifty-one," Dagmar said importantly.

The television screen was now split—on the left was ABC anchorman Steve Haney and on the right was Dagmar, looking intense.

"And why have no new lawsuits been filed?" Steve asked.

"Well, Steve, there's word that many of the victims' families have dropped their cases and are planning to settle settled out of court."

"What exactly does that mean for the families of the victims of flight 182," asked Steve.

"Well, Steve, it means that instead of protracted legal proceedings that many of these families can't afford either financially or in terms of their time, some have opted to settle for a standard $75,000 lump sum benefit, which is the maximum payable in such cases."

"Tell us about Giti Roshtti, Dagmar. What is it about her situation that is unique?"

"Steve, the Roshtti family has decided to go all the way. They don't want to settle and are, in fact, leading the pack with respect to seeking damages far above $75,000. If they are successful in court, it will have a huge impact on the financial viability of Pacific Southwest Airlines, especially if other victims follow suit. And based on the NTSB report, I'd have to say that the chances look good for them to win."

Al-Qa'im, Iraq

Jaffar Hamid Harraj was sitting on his large, cool covered terrace, enjoying the way the morning sun bathed the white painted houses and buildings of Al-Qa'im with its warmth, adding a golden hue to the city. Early morning was Jaffar's favorite times of day; the streets were relatively quiet and he could sit, sip his tea and watch as Al-Qa'im slowly came alive.

Suddenly Kaveh, one of Jaffar's servants, raced outside toward him bellowing, "It's that American woman! She's on the news again!"

Lost in thought as he gazed out over the city, Kaveh's sudden entrance startled Jaffar. He jumped and spilled a little tea, then cursed.

He looked at his watch, realized how late it was and quietly cursed again. He didn't like to miss the morning news and he had already missed the first few minutes. As he stepped inside, he caught only the last few words of Giti Roshtti's interview. The tirade that followed shocked Kaveh, who had served Jaffar faithfully and well for many years and was mostly immune to his temper tantrums.

"Do not let me miss the news again or I will have you dragged for miles behind a goat herder's camel!" he shrieked.

His outburst was really motivated by annoyance more than true anger; he was a little piqued, but more, he saw Kaveh's sloppiness as a golden opportunity to instill some fear into his servant. Jaffar believed in keeping control of his men and one method that was truly effective in ensuring loyal service was to make sure they were afraid of him.

Kaveh trembled. "Yes, Excellency," he stuttered then he bowed and made a hasty retreat. Silently Kaveh thanked Allah he'd recorded the show; later, when he showed it to Jaffar, it would put him on Jaffar's good side. He didn't want to be on the bad side; if he remained there it was very possible Jaffar would make good on his promise —or worse. One misstep meant that Kaveh could find himself at the wrong end of a firing squad which could conveniently be arranged by Abdul at a moment's notice.

A little over an hour later, Jaffar walked into the busy office of the chief of police—his chief of police—and made a startling request. "Abdul," he said, "I want you to pack your bags."

"But why Jaffar?" Abdul did not want to address him as 'Excellency' when there was a chance of being overheard. To most of the citizens of Al-Qa'im, their relationship to each other was strictly that of chief of police and businessman.

"Because, my friend, you and I are going to the United States on business. And you'd better change out of that clown suit you call a uniform."

"But Jaffar! You still haven't answered my question!"

Suddenly Jaffar looked sinister. Abdul blanched a little. He knew that look.

"I don't have time to argue," Jaffar said coldly. "We're to leave within the hour, please make the arrangements through the usual channels."

The usual channels, in this case, meant taking one of the dozen or so prearranged flights kept on standby for Jaffar by three travel agents that were completely loyal to him and could be trusted to remain discreet. Abdul's job was to choose one at random and change it from coach to first class. The tickets would be paid for in cash at the airport.

By ten-thirty that morning Jaffar and Abdul were boarding Royal Jordanian Airlines Flight 261, from Amman, Jordan, to New York. From there they would catch United Airline Flight 83 from Newark, New Jersey to Los Angeles. From Los Angeles they would transfer to a flight to their final destination—Sacramento, California.

After a full day of travel Jaffar and Abdul exited the taxi and entered the Hyatt Regency Sacramento on L Street. Within moments of checking into their adjoining rooms, both weary travelers were fast asleep.

September 12, 1979

At ten o'clock sharp, John Robinson from the National Transportation Safety Board was on the stand, ready to continue his testimony from the day before.

"Now Mr. Robinson, I'd like to remind you that you're still under oath," said the judge.

"Yes, your Honor," Robinson replied as he squirmed in the chair to find a more comfortable position.

The defense attorney walked over to the display easel and flipped the cover over to reveal a plan view of the Boeing 727's fuel and hydraulic schematic diagram. He turned towards the NTSB official.

"Mr. Robinson, yesterday you testified about the damage found on Flight 182's wing area. Can you tell me what specific areas of the wing were damaged and what the consequences of such damage might be?"

"Well sir, as I told you yesterday, the propeller of the Cessna 172 struck the right wing of the Boeing 727, approximately twelve and a half feet outboard of the wing root ..."

"What do you mean by the 'wing root', Mr. Robinson?"

"What I mean by the wing root is the place at which the wing connects to the fuselage of the aircraft."

"Thank you! You may continue."

"As I was saying, the propeller struck the wing in between the inboard and outboard fuel pump shut-off valves, damaging two of the four boost pump inlet lines, momentarily interrupting the flow of fuel to the number one and number two engines…"

"Why only momentarily?"

"The fuel flow was restored by the redundant fuel pump on the left wing above tank number one."

"So, the plane was still flyable!"

John Robinson had been in this position several times in the past but he was getting more and more annoyed with this attorney's interruptions.

"Well there's more to flying an aircraft than merely supplying the engines with fuel," he responded. "You also have hydraulic systems that control an aircraft's flight control surfaces, flaps, rudder, elevators, etcetera."

"What was wrong with the plane other than damaged fuel lines?"

It's an aircraft, not a plane you idiot, John thought to himself. But instead he said, "There was also damage to the hydraulic lines in the right wing as result of the impact of the Cessna's propeller, and from the fire." John used the pointer to indicate another place on chart.

"What was the damage and what caused the fire?"

"A Boeing 727's hydraulic system is provided by three independent systems—System A, System B, and a standby system …" but before he could finish, the lawyer interrupted.

"So you say that there is triple redundancy in this plane?"

"Yes sir, some systems are redundant. But if you'll let me finish, I'll answer your previous question. System A pressure is provided by engine-driven pumps on the number one and number two engines. System B pressure is provided by two electrical pumps and standby system pressure is provided by an electrically driven pump. All of them operate at about 3,000 pounds per square inch."

The lawyer remained silent so he continued.

"All flight controls are hydraulically powered. Mechanical inputs from the cockpit controls position the control valves, which determine the travel of each of the flight control surfaces." He looked toward the lawyer, half expecting another interruption, but again, surprisingly, there was none. Relieved, he went on.

"The fire resulted from the propeller severing the electrically-driven systems wiring, shorting out one or both of them, which caused the fuel to ignite. The heat from this was intense enough to melt the seals from hydraulic system A, causing it to fail, thus rendering all hydraulic systems in the right wing virtually useless."

"And this is what caused the plane to crash?"

"Yes sir, the aircraft was probably uncontrollable at this point in time."

The attorney once again walked over to the easel. He paused, turned towards the three hundred people sitting in the gallery of Courtroom 12F and flipped over to next page. A collective gasp went up from almost everyone in the courtroom, with the exception of two new faces in the back row who had arrived in town just the night before—Jaffar Hamid Harraj and Abdul Salam Al-Kubesi. It was fortunate everyone's attention had been focused on the front of the court; no one had seen their faint smiles as the shocking three-feet by five-feet photograph of Flight 182 falling out of the sky was revealed.

The courtroom was filled with murmurs and whispers as everyone took in the image of the doomed jet. For Giti, it was as if someone had unexpectedly punched her in the stomach. Visibly shaken, she gasped for breath and began to sob.

"Come my dear, let's get you out of here," Zafar said gently as he gathered up his sister-in-law and guided her by the shoulders out into the hallway.

A few minutes later Giti and Zafar were sitting on a bench around the corner and down the hall from Courtroom 12F and Giti tried to compose herself.

"This probably wasn't the best place to sit Zafar," she said quietly as the greasy, slightly-off smell from the cafeteria wafted down the hall toward them and began to make her nauseous.

"Perhaps this green tea might help soothe things a bit," said a quiet voice on her left.

Giti looked up to see a stranger, who seemed to have appeared as if by magic, holding a Styrofoam cup in his hand. He offered it to her and, surprised, she hesitated. Then she took it from him and managed to say, "Thank you very much!"

"My name is Jaffar. I hope the tea helps," he said. Then he quickly turned and walked down the hall, back towards the courtroom, leaving Giti and Zafar to stare dumbfounded at the handsome stranger in an Italian business suit as he walked away.

Abdul had been a bit surprised when Jaffar rose from his seat to follow Giti and Zafar as they left the room, but he didn't question; when Jaffar returned with a smile on his face, however, he said quietly, "That was a bit bold, wasn't it Excellency?"

Directly in front of them, heads turned to glance at them, a few with fingers to their lips trying to shush them. Abdul instantly realized his mistake as the smile on Jaffar's face was immediately replaced by an angry mask. He silently rose from his seat and made his way out of courtroom and Abdul anxiously followed. Neither man spoke during the four-minute walk back to the Hyatt.

Jaffar followed Abdul into his room and Abdul closed the door behind them then turned to face Jaffar, who gave him a vicious slap to the face. He could not remember the last time he had been on the receiving end of such a blow.

"Don't you ever speak to me in that tone! And how many times have I told you not to address me in that fashion when we are out in public? Those people in front of us overheard!"

"I'm sorry Excellency, forgive me."

Abdul's use of that term somehow infuriated Jaffar even further and he struck out once more at Abdul, hitting him squarely on the jaw even more savagely than before. Abdul staggered backwards from the blow. Since childhood only two people had hit him like that; one was Jaffar, and the other had been his father, who had beaten him regularly—right up until the moment Abdul Al-Kubesi had shoved a kitchen knife into his father's heart. Al-Kubesi Senior's last sight was the fury in his son's face which was soon replaced by blackness as the life ebbed from his body.

The same look was now on Jaffar's face. "I've had many months to think about this and the last thing I want is for someone beneath me to question my actions," he seethed. Abdul braced for another blow, but as quickly as it had come, the fury on Jaffar's face was replaced by something more benign.

"I'm going back to court. Alone!" He said. "You are to stay here until further notice."

Abdul nodded as he gingerly touched his face. That was fine with him.

For a moment Abdul thought about questioning Jaffar about the wisdom of going out alone into the crime-ridden streets of the Great Satan, but he quickly stopped himself. Instead he sat silent and watched Jaffar walk out the door, leaving Abdul in the middle of the room, alone with his thoughts, his face still smarting from the blows inflicted moments earlier.

"Maybe something will happen to you, you bastard, and I will move up in the organization," he said quietly when he was sure Jaffar was long-gone. Then he suddenly realized that this was the first time he'd ever thought such a thing about Jaffar, much less dared to speak it out loud. A rush of paranoia came over him and he spent the rest of the morning and afternoon looking for listening devices but not finding any. As he watched television and waited for Jaffar to come back, he prayed to Allah that he would be in a better mood than when he left.

It was ten minutes after four in the afternoon, four in the morning in Iraq, when Jaffar returned.

"Let's get something to eat, Abdul," he said as if nothing had happened between them, "Or would you prefer to order room service?"

To Abdul, eating out was a far better option than staying in their room, so he said, "The restaurant would be nice." In a restaurant, there was less of a chance of another outburst by Jaffar and more chance to smooth things over. Such circumstances might not present themselves otherwise.

"Let me freshen up first," Jaffar said as he unlocked the adjoining door between their rooms and went into his own. "It's almost dawn back home! I feel like I've been up for two days straight."

A short while later, downstairs in Vines and Dawson's restaurant, both men had ordered the rack of lamb from a menu upon which was written, 'Enjoy our award-winning creations from Chef Kevin Harper'. Both Jaffar and Abdul enjoyed the generous portions and finely seasoned lamb and tried to pretend the earlier confrontation had not occurred. The dinner conversation was pleasant, if somewhat strained.

"That was an excellent meal, wasn't it Abdul?" Jaffar said as he wiped the corners of his mouth with his napkin.

"It truly was, my friend," Abdul replied, deliberately avoiding use of the word 'Excellency' and emphasizing 'my friend'—for during the course of the afternoon, Abdul had come to the realization that it was only their 30-year friendship that had prevented his bullet-ridden corpse from being dumped in the Euphrates River long before this. Countless numbers of less fortunate of Jaffar's minions had died this way for providing far less offense.

Both men had barely placed their linen napkins on the table when the waiter appeared to retrieve their plates. If I didn't know better, I'd think we were being watched, thought Abdul. He decided to keep it to himself, though.

"Will that be all, gentlemen?" asked the waiter as he expertly gathered up their plates.

"No. Could I get a cup of green tea?" asked Jaffar. "And for my friend here, a cup of espresso, then the bill."

"Of course sir, just give me a moment."

A short time later both men arrived back in their rooms. The jet lag and the heavy meal had taken its toll on Abdul. His body cried out for much-needed rest and so despite it being only early in the evening, he decided to call it a night.

"I believe it is time for me to get to bed, Jaffar," he said as he tried unsuccessfully to stifle a yawn by clenching his jaw muscles tighter. "Will you be needing anything else?"

"No, not tonight. Have a restful sleep." With that both men retired to their rooms.

Within minutes Abdul had fallen fast asleep; he'd barely managed to get undressed before doing so. Such was not the case with Jaffar. Though he had reason to be much more tired than Abdul—having not slept at all on either the flight across the Atlantic or the subsequent flight from one side of America to the other—his mind refused to rest. As he lay on his bed, his thoughts raced through a whole torrent of things, jumping from the altercation with Abdul, to having actually talked to Giti Roshtti, the mystery woman from the television.

What's the problem with Abdul? The man is getting more and more insolent as times passes! He thought to himself as he tossed and turned in bed. Maybe it was time for the two of them to 'part ways'. But he had known him since they were children. It wouldn't be an easy thing to end the man's life. Jaffar tried to dismiss that most regrettable thought from his mind, replacing it instead with a vision of Giti's face looking up at him with those soulful eyes as he had handed her the cup of tea.

"What a lovely woman," he whispered before drifting off to sleep, her sweet voice echoing in his mind as she replied, "Thank you very much."

The next day Jaffar and Abdul were among the first to arrive at the courthouse, unlike the previous day when they had been the last. As before, they sat in the back but this time by choice instead of because they were late. Jaffar he could only frown as throngs of spectators raced past him to take their place in the second or third rows of the court. Angrily he sputtered, "Blood-thirsty heathens!" in a barely audible voice.

That's almost laughable, Abdul thought, recalling the hundreds, probably thousands, of people Jaffar had killed or had had a hand in killing through his terrorist activities. *You're one to talk.*

The two of them sat and watched in silence as the room quickly filled with spectators—the public, reporters and legal beagles of all kinds—who were all anxious to see what juicy tidbits would be revealed by the day's witnesses. Among the last to arrive were Giti and Zafar, who casually made their way to the front row, which was reserved for those directly involved in the case.

What followed was almost three hours of testimony from the National Transportation Safety Board which was really many different individuals saying almost the same thing over and over. It almost made Abdul nod off. At one o'clock, however, as Johan Myers, the man who had led the design team for the Boeing 727 was called to the stand, the Judge, noticing the time, adjourned the court for lunch. *Praise be to Allah*, thought Jaffar.

The courtroom began to empty, and as Giti and Zafar shuffled their way towards the exit Abdul suddenly realized why Jaffar had chosen the seats he had. Giti couldn't pass without seeing him; she looked directly at him and smiled in recognition. Although it was brief and almost imperceptible, it was a smile just the same.

October 10, 1979

The trial was now into its fifth week and almost 100 witnesses had given testimony. A few, like John Robinson from the NTSB, had spent well over a day on the stand. It seemed that everyone—right down to Jane Kennedy, the second grader from Foster Elementary School—had had their day in court.

Just before lunch Sean McMillan excused himself and headed toward the door, anxious to get to the men's room as the three cups of coffee he'd had that morning were threatening to burst his bladder. A hand reached out and grabbed his elbow.

"Mr. McMillan, I was wondering if I might have a word with you?"

"Of course you can, but only if you'll excuse me for one moment." Sean's arm shot out and pushed the door to the men's room open and he stepped in, leaving Jaffar alone in the hall with a clear understanding of the urgency of the situation.

A few minutes later Giti came around the corner and found, on one of the numerous leather-covered benches lining the hallways of the Courthouse, her lawyer Sean talking to Jaffar, her 'green tea' man. Both men noticed their approach and stood up.

"Giti, Zafar, I'd like to introduce Jaffar Harraj. Jaffar, this is Giti Roshtti and her brother-in-law Zafar."

The three shook hands as Zafar said, "We've already met, sort of!"

Sean was a bit confused as to when and where and was about to ask about it when Jaffar announced, "Here comes my 'second in command,' so to speak," and nodded toward Abdul who walked up to join them. This time it was Jaffar's turn to make the introductions. "Giti, Zafar, Sean, this is the vice president of my company, Abdul Al-Kubesi."

"My pleasure, but please just call me Abdul," he said, trying to sound Americanized.

"Would you mind if Jaffar and Abdul join us for lunch?" Sean inquired of Giti and Zafar.

Although Zafar did not wish to have company for lunch, he also did not wish to be rude. "No that would be our pleasure," he acquiesced. Soon, the five new acquaintances were strolling across the street down to the Red Lion Restaurant across from Capitol Park, within sight of the courthouse.

"Table for five please," Sean announced to the hostess.

"Would you like to be on the patio? The weather is still warm and it's quite pleasant this time of year," she said.

"That would be fine." This time it was Jaffar who answered her. They followed her serpentine route as she led them to an outdoor table. An efficient waiter quickly brought them a menu then returned shortly to take their drink and meals orders. Soon they were enjoying a light lunch and some nice wine.

As they ate, Sean decided to finish the question he'd begun to ask earlier. "You said the four of you had 'sort of' met before, Zafar. What did you mean by 'sort of'?" he asked, sounding very much like a prosecuting attorney.

"Actually it was just Giti, Jaffar and I," he said. "Jaffar brought Giti some tea one day at court when she and I were taking a break in the hallway. She was most upset with some of the pictures presented," he explained.

"You mean 'exhibits', Zafar." Giti spoke up. *She seems to be catching on*, Sean thought.

"Well, it seems that's not the first time Jaffar has come to the rescue," Sean said.

"What do you mean?" asked Zafar, taking a small bite of his baked halibut.

"Mr. Harraj told me a short time ago that it was he who sent the $25,000 for your legal fees," Sean announced proudly.

Zafar began to choke on his food; he was totally shocked by this revelation. He reached for his glass of water, took a sip and quickly recovered, but it was still several seconds before he or Giti could respond. They sat speechless as they came to terms with what had just been said. All Zafar could manage to do was extend his hand to Jaffar and whisper, "Thank you."

The four men turned to Giti, wondering if she was going to respond in kind, but her eyes told them all that was needed. They were filled with tears as she fought to control her emotions, and failed. She quickly excused herself and headed to the ladies' room, handbag and napkin in hand.

In the ensuing interval Zafar decided to get more acquainted with this extremely generous newcomer and his partner. "So may I ask what kind of business are you in, Jaffar?" he asked politely. He still couldn't believe that a complete stranger would just hand over $25,000. Who does that?

"We have some real estate investments in Nevada, but our main business has been, and still is, import and export," Jaffar said smoothly. This was true enough—if you called sponsoring terrorists and militants as they travel from one country to another 'import and export'.

"What kind of things do you export," Zafar asked courteously.

"Oh, our company is very diverse. We deal in a great many things including auto parts, luxury cars—even textiles."

"Oh yes? I'm in textiles as well. What is the name of your company? Where do you source your product?"

Jaffar didn't answer, and Zafar noted it. Instead he acted almost as if he had not heard the question and said, "With the oil embargo a few years ago, and the rising cost of fuel in America, luxury cars here are now just that. I can buy an unwanted, un-fuel-efficient Mercedes Benz here, transport it home where gas is cheap, sell it, and make a good profit—assuming, of course, that I can obtain the cars for the right price."

Before Zafar could further question him about the textile aspect of his business, Giti returned from the ladies' room, her make-up fresh, looking as though nothing had happened.

"My apologies to you all … I didn't mean to run off like that, I was just a little overwhelmed by the graciousness of your gift," she explained.

"No need to apologize Giti, we understand. Besides it gave us a chance to become better acquainted," Zafar said.

Zafar wanted to resume textile talk with Jaffar, but just then Sean looked at his watch and said, "Look at the time! It's after two o'clock, we must be getting back." A minute later the bill came, and as Zafar and Sean were in the middle of tallying up everyone's meal and drinks, Jaffar dropped two one hundred dollar bills on the table.

"No, Jaffar, that's quite alright—let us pick up the tab. You've been far too generous already," Zafar said.

"Yes! Far too generous!" This time from Giti.

Jaffar put up his hand as if to signal that he would tolerate no more discussion, making it clear that he was a man who was used to getting his way. Giti felt something more; the barest hint of attraction. She hastily stuffed it down. This man was handsome and generous—but he was not Reza and her heart and her loyalty still lay with her dead husband.

On the return walk to the courthouse Zafar asked Sean how much longer he thought the trial was going to last, the talk of textiles a thing of the past. "The way things are going, it looks like we are going to be through the list of witnesses by the end of next week and we can most likely expect a ruling by the first week of November."

"Then that could be the end of it?" Zafar asked hopefully. He looked behind him to share the news with Giti, but Giti she was suddenly gone. While Sean and Zafar had kept up a fairly brisk pace, Giti and Jaffar had lagged behind with Abdul bringing up the rear. Sean and Zafar stopped to wait for them. When they arrived, Jaffar and Giti were so engrossed in conversation they walked headlong into Zafar and Sean.

"Oh! Pardon us!" Giti said with a laugh. "We didn't see you had stopped!"

"Sean was just saying the case might be wrapped up in as little as a week and that the judge could rule by the first week of November," Zafar said, mildly annoyed for reasons he could not understand.

"Oh, that would be good, Zafar," she said, but it seemed as though she had not really heard him.

The small group continued their walk through the park, enjoying the red and gold leaves decorating the surrounding trees. The afternoon sun sparkled through the ones that stubbornly refused to release their hold on the branches and a breeze brought others fluttering to the ground. The breeze had increased since the morning, lowering the temperature. Goosebumps rose on Giti's bare shoulders.

"Brrrr! That breeze is cool," Giti said.

"Yes, it looks as though the weather is going to change!" said Zafar. Then just as he was about to give his sister-in-law his coat, Jaffar removed his and covered her shoulders. Zafar frowned. It was a little too familiar, in his opinion. But he pretended not to care.

"Do you think that you'll stay in town until the trial is over Mr. Harraj?" he asked Jaffar politely.

"No, it's unlikely at this point. I've got business in Los Angeles then I'm going to the Middle East for a while. He deliberately made it seem as though he would only be visiting there—he wasn't ready to tell them Iraq was his home.

As they entered the courtroom Giti removed Jaffar's suit jacket and returned it to him, then hurried to catch up with Zafar. All five had barely taken their seats when the court bailiff called out, "All rise!" The judge appeared from the chambers and took his seat behind the bench.

The afternoon session was short and Jaffar and Abdul were back in their hotel rooms by three-thirty. Hastily they packed what little they had brought with them into their suitcases and headed to the airport. Just before five o'clock, they were many miles from Sacramento and thousands of feet over the desert countryside. However, instead of heading to Los Angeles, they were on their way to Las Vegas. There was that nasty business with Jack Coward to take care of, among other things.

Jaffar looked out the airplane window, marveling at the desolate expanse below and at how similar it was to his own country. Soon, however, the drone of the aircraft's engines had a tranquilizing effect on Jaffar and he found himself nodding off. He was just about to fall asleep when his eyes spotted the most amazing sight. Almost two miles below he suddenly saw row upon row of immense, shiny, metal objects, spaced evenly apart, brilliant as the afternoon sun glinted off their surfaces. It was a strangely unearthly scene, so odd that Jaffar almost failed to see them for what they were.

"Most curious!" he exclaimed.

"What is that, Excellency?" Abdul asked.

"It was nothing. Nothing at all," Jaffar answered. He still wasn't sure if what he'd seen was nothing more than a trick of light, a mirage. It had looked like many, many aircraft in the middle of nowhere, but that seemed very unlikely. Unable to explain it, he let it go and in moments was fast asleep, the side of his face pressed hard against the oval shaped window. He remained that way for the rest of the flight.

Back in Sacramento, Zafar was still puzzling over the obvious flirtation between Jaffar and Giti. He wondered why it bothered him so much. Was it just because he was tired? Or because he didn't like the idea of his brother's memory being betrayed? Or was it because of that man, Jaffar. There was something about him that didn't sit right with Zafar. He wrote it off to the tedious trial. It was now in its fifth week and the emotional and physical toll it was taking on everyone was starting to show. Giti and Zafar had attended trial 22 of the 23 days it had been dragging on, missing only September 25th, the day of Reza's memorial service. That day the shop had been closed, giving Fatemah a break she badly needed, as she'd been holding down the fort while Zafar supported Giti.

That night, as they sat down to supper, sorry for her weary husband, Fatemah asked, "How did it go today?" When he didn't answer, she said, "This has been difficult on all of us, especially Giti."

Thinking about the day's events Zafar replied, "You wouldn't know it from the way that she was acting today!" Almost immediately he regretted his words.

Fatemah seized on them. "What do you mean? What was Giti doing today that would make you say such a thing?"

He wanted to change the subject, but he'd been married long enough to understand that though Fatemah asked few questions of him, when she did she was relentless until she got an answer.

Reluctantly he said, "She met someone today." He tried to sound nonchalant but from the look in his wife's eyes he knew she was on to him. "She met a man today."

"What?" She almost shouted, "What do you mean, a man?"

"Giti met the man who gave us the money for the legal fees."

Again, Zafar failed to answer satisfactorily. Fatemah put her hands on her hips and stared at him expectantly.

"What is his name, what's he like?" Her mind was racing in a thousand directions at that moment, but she knew Zafar would only answer so many questions before he tried to change the subject again.

"His name is Jaffar, Jaffar Hamid Harraj. He's from the homeland. But as to what he's like, you'll have to ask Giti." After a second he added, "As for me, I don't like him. He strikes me as some kind of a salesman. How do you say it? He's slick." He added, "Yes, slick like camel dung."

"Oh what a jealous old goat! I'm going to have to go to court with you two and not leave you alone with her, by the sounds of things," Fatemah said, only partly joking.

"What do you mean, jealous?"

"Oh, maybe that's not the right word … but she's is your sister-in-law and it has been over a year. She's been relying on you and now someone has stepped in. You're jealous. And Giti's lonely."

"You don't know what you're talking about," Zafar said, clearly miffed at his wife's cleverness. "And besides, that's not the point. The man is slimy. I just know it." But he knew Giti's loneliness *was* the point and that his wife was right. It had been over a year—a long time out of one's life to mourn for someone, especially for a young woman in the prime of her life.

The following day when Judge Villander called for recess—the first break of the day—Giti walked out of the court beside Zafar. He noticed her eyes searching the back row, looking for Jaffar, only to find strangers occupying his and Abdul's seats.

Fatemah is definitely right, he thought. *Giti is lonely. How bad would it be for her to meet a man?* He patted his sister-in-law's arm fondly and she smiled at him.

Las Vegas, Nevada

Back in Las Vegas, Jack returned to his daily routine of shooting beer cans, shooting tequila and shooting the shit with the old guy down the road, Mel. Mel was a WW II vet, so they bonded over war stories until late into the night two or three times a week. He missed Donny, but he knew Donny was busy with his own life. Unlike Jack, Donny liked to mix and mingle with people. They hadn't discussed it, but Jack assumed he had a girlfriend or two. The man had always had a way with the ladies.

He'd tried to push her out of his mind, but still, images of Giti had a way of floating into his consciousness unbidden, leaving him feeling flustered. Giti with her soulful eyes. Giti with her selfless dedication to the memory of her husband. Giti the mother, with her much-loved small son. Giti in a swimsuit, beckoning to him.

He had to wake himself up and take a shower after that one. He knew he had to let this go. But still it wouldn't leave.

And there was more. He kept wondering about this Jaffar fellow who'd hired him and his henchman Abdul. Who were these guys? There was something off about them. Jaffar, in particular, looked not only vaguely familiar, but dangerous. He hoped he hadn't inadvertently led a snake to Giti the Persian lamb. But then again, he was just doing his job. And you can't save everyone.

The next morning, over a cup of coffee, he retrieved the manila envelope he'd retained from Donny for his files, a duplicate of the one he'd given Jaffar at the casino. He opened it and dug through the photographs until he found the picture of Jaffar. He studied it. *Why do I know this character?* He put it away and got another cup of coffee. Then he got the nicest photo of Giti out of the package—the one with a hint of a soulful smile—and put it on his fridge.

It would come to him, who that guy in the picture was. It always did.

Al-Qa'im, Iraq

Jaffar and Abdul arrived back in Iraq early in the morning. Jaffar was grateful to be in the familiar surroundings of home. Before he'd left America, he'd made sure to put a little fear into Mohammed Hussan, Jaffar's point-man in the U.S.A. and the man who had found Jack Coward for him. He'd told him he was concerned about the books and that he'd review them when he was back in Iraq. He'd implied that if there was even so much as a penny missing, there would be consequences.

Usually Hussan could be counted on, but lately he'd noticed the man had developed a taste for some of the multitude of sinful pleasures the Great Satan had to offer. Jaffar knew that too much of a good thing could make a man unreliable so one of the reasons he'd gone to Vegas was to drop in unexpectedly to surprise him and keep him on his toes. And he'd insisted Hussan call him today.

The other reason he'd gone to Vegas was for business. Although he himself never gambled, Jaffar did not hesitate to invest some of Islamic Hamas's assets—albeit temporarily—in hotels in the area when the opportunity arose. Money from several terrorist-supporting countries had been funneled into Las Vegas investments over the last ten years and now Jaffar, as fund custodian, found himself the caretaker of almost a thousand rooms that were routinely 90 percent occupied. This brought in almost three-quarters of a million dollars per month to the cause. Some of these profits went back to Middle East to be put back into the coffers of the Islamic Hamas. The remainder was reinvested in more property, or discreetly funneled into Jaffar's personnel account.

Sunwest Properties was the name of the company through which Jaffar funneled the holdings of Islamic Hamas. It was Sunwest that owned 976 rooms in and around Las Vegas. But while Sunwest was technically a profit-generating exercise for Islamic Hamas, legally only one entity owned it, lock, stock and barrel: Jaffar Hamid Harraj.

Many years earlier Jaffar had decided it was not his place to die for Allah in a blaze of glory, as some of his compatriots chose to do. For Jaffar, there would be a life after terrorism. Men as clever as him did not have to die to make their mark.

With this in mind, he'd taken steps to sever himself financially while continuing to earn and keep the trust of the organization as he'd worked his way through the ranks of the Islamic Hamas Movement. He did not share his plans for the future with those under his command, though he often thought to himself, *one can't be a terrorist forever.*

The telephone beside him in the living room rang. Jaffar picked it up.

"Jaffar," asked a voice from half-way across the world.

"Mohammed Hussan, how are you today?"

"Very well, Excellency! It was good to see you in Vegas. I hope you had time for a little fun."

"I don't indulge in the type of 'fun' most others enjoy," said Jaffar dryly.

Mohammed had indeed been surprised by Abdul's Vegas visit. Luckily for him, the lack of the long distance 'echo' on the phone let Mohammed know his boss was still in the U.S., so, forewarned, he hastily cancelled his plans to meet with Veronica, one of the local call girls he was fond of, as he suspected Jaffar might drop by.

He was right. Jaffar showed up within half an hour of calling and demanded to see the most recent reports on the status of his business holdings. Luckily, Hussan had prepared them just the day before.

"Hussan, I've read the reports and have seen the ever growing-balance in the bank. This is very good …" Jaffar said.

"Thank you, Excellency," Hussan said, relieved. Hussan knew this was more than just touching base; they'd done that legwork yesterday. He took the bull by the horns and asked, "Is there anything I can do for you, Excellency?"

"Yes, Hussan, thank you for asking."

Hussan was relieved again—and glad that he had done so.

"Remember that list of properties for sale you provided me with? There is one that I like and I want you to negotiate the deal. It's time for Sunwest Properties to expand once again."

"That can be arranged. Is that all?"

"Only what we talked about."

"Of course, Excellency. The investigator. He was a little too good."

"A little," agreed Jaffar.

"What do you want me to do?" asked Mohammed.

"I want you to find him. Find out all you can about him—where he lives, what he drives—anything that will make it easier for you."

"Easier? For what Jaffar?"

Jaffar's blood boiled when he thought of that over-presumptuous private investigator. Imagine taking picture of him—Jaffar Harraj—at a funeral! What nerve. He was either dangerous or stupid. Either way, he must die.

He said, "For you to kill him, of course."

— Chapter 5 —

November 4, 1979

Jaffar sat out on his terrace, once again watching Al-Qa'im wake up. He'd slept well and woken up to find out that as of last night he was the proud new owner of Arizona Charlie's Boulder Casino Hotel. It had cost almost twice as much as he wanted to spend, but the architectural style of Arizona Charlie's had caught his eye, reminding him of his desert home. As soon as he'd seen it, he knew he had to have it. Hussan had acted as proxy and the deal had closed last night. Jaffar couldn't be more pleased.

Arizona Charlie's 132 rooms pushed his Vegas holdings to more than 1,000 rooms—and this would soon grow, as Jaffar planned to expand Arizona Charlie's to the vacant property next door.

He glanced at his watch, picked up his cup of tea, and headed inside to watch the daily news.

"It's just before midnight here in Washington but it's almost noon in Tehran," said ABC anchorman Tony Reynolds. "In breaking news, a little more than two hours ago, militant students in Iran stormed the United States Embassy in Tehran. They have taken more than 90 people hostage ..."

"Abdul, come in here. Now!" Jaffar shouted towards the next room. *This is very good news*, he thought excitedly.

"What is it, Jaffar?"

"Be quiet and listen!"

Tony continued, "The students have demanded that the Shah of Iran, who fled the country in January, be extradited from the U.S. to stand trial in Iran. We now take you to reporter Jeff Martin, who is in Tehran. Jeff, can you tell us why the Shah is here in the U.S.?"

"Yes, Tony. The report I've received indicates that the former Shah is being treated for cancer. What I don't know is what type of cancer he has, or the extent of the treatment he is receiving."

"Jeff! Can you tell us how the students were able to take over the embassy and if anyone was killed?"

"As I've said before Tony, this a developing story and it's still too early to provide any more details than that. There have been reports of gunfire, but at this point that appears to have only been sporadic, students firing their rifles into the air, celebrating a victory, that sort of thing."

"Thank you Jeff."

Jaffar let out a joyous shout, which surely could have been heard across the city. It was duplicated by one from Abdul a second later. Abdul was just about to start asking question about the startling events on television when a new story segment came on and he paused.

"In other news, the Judge's decision on the case brought against Pacific Southwest Airlines after its doomed flight 182 crashed last September killing, everyone on board, should be coming down from the Sacramento Courthouse on Monday. The Roshtti family of Sacramento brought a wrongful death suit against the airline, which also names air traffic control and the owner of the Cessna that collided with the jet as co-defendants."

"This a most glorious day, is it not, Excellency?"

"It certainly is, Abdul," said Jaffar, smiling as an image of Giti flashed onto the television. "Yes, my friend, it most certainly is. Can you tell me anything about this thing at the U.S. Embassy in Tehran?"

"No Jaffar this is the first I've anything about it, but it is most excellent news."

"Yes, it is. We'll have to learn all we can about it to see if we can use it to the advantage of Hamas," he said thoughtfully. Abdul nodded, then his boss added, "And I also want to keep up on what is going on with the Roshtti situation in Sacramento."

"Of course," said Abdul. But not for the first time he wondered why this was such a priority for him. Abdul didn't always admire or even like his boss, but he knew that the reason Jaffar was in the position he was in was because he was a ruthless man. What was happening to him? Was he losing his edge. Over a woman? It was at that moment that Abdul began to doubt Jaffar. What kind of terrorist leader would rate a court trial in the US as equal in importance to a great victory against the U.S. by Islam's followers?

November 6, 1979.

In Las Vegas, Jack was starting to get concerned. For two days, the television had been filled with an almost constant flow of news about the Tehran Embassy takeover. There had been numerous pictures of men and women wearing black hoods being led from place to place, not only within the Embassy, but within the city as well. Their changing locations were most likely a strategy to prevent a rescue attempt. The American flag was burned while thousands cheered. At one point an effigy of President Jimmy Carter was hung outside, in the city square. It was bad.

As events from abroad unfolded before him, the station switched to stateside news. The gong show that was Dagmar Madcap and Steve Haney suddenly popped up, live from Sacramento. Jack sucked in a breath, conscious that his heart had started beating a little faster. This was the outcome of Giti's lawsuit. He hoped she had won.

"Hello, Steve! I'm standing outside the Sacramento Courthouse once again, where today a decision regarding the wrongful death suit brought by the Roshtti family against Pacific Southwest Airlines was handed down."

"Dagmar, can you tell us what that verdict was?"

"Yes, Judge Villander awarded the Roshtti family one and a half million dollars in the death of Reza Roshtti. The defendants were also ordered to pay all the legal costs incurred by the Roshtti family."

"Dagmar, as I understand it, that amount is far and above the usual amount in this type of case. Do you think there will be an appeal?"

"Yes, the maximum amount in cases like this is seventy-five thousand dollars per passenger on normal or routine flight coverage. This award was twenty times that, half of which is to cover lost future earnings by Mr. Roshtti. As to the likelihood of an appeal, I don't think so, based on cautions put forward by the judge.

"What do you mean?"

"After ruling in favour of the Roshtti family, Judge Villander made it clear that evidence against the National Transportation Safety Board report was most damning and that it was his opinion that all of the defendants, not just Pacific Southwest Airlines, were at fault. He cautioned the defendants about launching an appeal and went so far as to suggest if they did so perhaps the other fifty or so cases would be settled in a similar manner. So at this point, it's probably in the best interests of the defendants to cut their losses and run."

"Thank you, Dagmar. Now back to the nation's capital where President Carter just approved a one $100 million relief fund for parts of Louisiana, Alabama and Florida to cover the costs of storm damage from September's Hurricane Noreen."

Jack was happy for Giti. She would be fine now. He wasn't sure why he cared, but he did. One of the things he hoped the money would buy her was independence. He'd been overseas enough to know that American women's libbers were the exception with regard to female roles in society. In most places across the world, women had a hard go of it and were expected to let men make all the decisions. In some places, they were little more than slaves. Jack knew Giti was Persian. Sure, she was American-Persian, but still, she would have learned how she was supposed to act from her parents. He hoped that if she ever married again, she would pick someone kind and good and never do it just for the money as many women were forced to.

Then he thought ... I wonder if she would ever pick a guy like me? He thought not. Jack was American through and through. She would probably feel way more comfortable with a man who had ties to her own culture, someone like that Jaffar character who'd been so interested in her he'd hired Jack to find her and scope her out.

I've got nothing to offer a woman like her, he thought, *and she wouldn't need me anyway—especially after the huge amount of money she's just been awarded.* Besides, even if their paths crossed again, how would he start the conversation about why he'd been at her house, at her husband's funeral? He gave his head a shake. Why was he thinking of her? She was a target. He had done his job. He'd been paid by that fat guy on behalf of that Jaffar character. It was over. It was time to let it go.

But an uncomfortable feeling went down his spine as he thought of Jaffar. That guy wasn't right. Sure, he looked amazing and he definitely had good coin ... but he seemed more the type to discreetly hire women to do his every bidding then cut the tie when he was done with them. He didn't seem the type that would want the messiness of a real relationship. So what did he want with Giti?

Al-Qa'im, Iraq

Jaffar, having seen the television broadcast about the award in the Roshtti case, quickly wrote a few lines of text on a sheet of paper and then summoned Abdul.

"Abdul! I want you to personally go down to the best florist in town that has an international connection with the USA and hand them this note. All the instructions are written down, but if they have any questions you can phone me to clarify." After a short pause he added, "Tell them not to worry about the cost, I want you to spare no expense. It must be the very best that they have."

"At once, Jaffar," said Abdul.

Al-Qa'im was an ancient city, the roads between the buildings barely wide enough for two small carts to pass each other, let alone cars and trucks. A few minutes after leaving Jaffar's, Abdul sat in his car behind three other cars in the Al-Qa'im version of rush hour traffic, all movement blocked by an ox-drawn cart. An old man fought with the uncooperative oxen as they refused to obey his commands.

Abdul calmly waited for the road to clear and, curious about his mission from Jaffar, he opened the folded piece of paper Jaffar had given him to find that this mission he was on was not to impress a business client in America as he had innocently presumed but instead it was a love note to that woman his boss had been simpering over.

Unexpectedly, his blood began to boil. *I don't believe this! Am I nothing more than an errand boy?* Feeling insulted, and with the oxen still blocking the way, he felt his blood pressure rise and his temper flare. He smashed his fist down on the padded dash of his car then thrust his palm onto the horn, as if trying to push it to the bottom of the steering column. The blaring noise startled the three drivers in front of him as well as the elderly man who was still tugging at the reins of the oxen who refused to budge, even as all four drivers opened their doors, got out and started yelling.

Abdul got out of his car, walked past the other three drivers and said to the cart-driver, "Old man! Move these smelly beasts at once!"

Mohammed Al Shazir, the oxen-driver, recognized the uniform of the Al-Qa'im Chief of Police at once, for it was the source of many a joke told by the citizens of Al-Qa'im. They liked to say that their chief of police was all adorned by ribbons for which no battles had been fought and medals for which no wars had been won. All the citizens recognized that Abdul's ribbons were for decoration and ego only and that it was a coward who hid behind them. However, the people also knew that Abdul Salam Al-Kubesi was a blood-thirsty killer, so Mohammed Al Shazir immediately tried to placate him.

"But Excellency, they do not wish to move. For ten minutes I have tried my best."

"I will not tolerate any more delays!" Abdul shouted and with that he pulled his .38 caliber revolver from its holster.

Fearing that Abdul's reputation was about to grow at his expense, Mohammed dropped the leather reigns and fled down the street. Abdul walked back a few paces toward his car, turned and fired his weapon into the air. As he predicted the oxen bolted down the street in the direction of their owner, with the wooden cart in tow, bouncing over the uneven road, spilling its entire contents as it went.

"That will teach the old fool," Abdul chuckled as he returned to his car.

Sacramento, California - November 7, 1979

Zafar and Fatemah, along with Zafar and Reza's other brother, Javed, had been planning a dinner party for many weeks, anticipating a ruling in Giti's favour. As the day of the verdict grew closer, they hoped to have a victorious conclusion to what had been a most trying period in their family's life. A favourable ruling would allow them to not only celebrate the bittersweet victory, but it would mentally free them to really celebrate Reza's life.

The day the verdict was announced, the brothers and Fatemah sprang into action and soon the Giti's home was filled to overflowing with family and close friends. Every room was crowded and the house was filled with the aroma of traditional Persian dishes such as lamb loaf with apricots and eggs, stuffed onion rolls and Fatemah's specialty, broiled chicken with oil, lemon and garlic.

"This Farareen Mashwi is delicious as always, Fatemah. I'm going to keep after you for the recipe," Javed's wife Nooshen said.

"It's never the same twice," Fatemah said proudly. "I always seem to change a bit here, add a spice there, but as I've often told you before it's basically like mother's recipe. Besides, I think my favorite is still your lamb and rice casserole."

"Why, thank you. Maybe we should just trade recipes!"

"Yes, that would be fine Nooshen. I could get a pen and some paper right now, if you like."

"Or we could get together next week for lunch and do it then!"

"That is a wonderful idea," Fatemah said. "Let's ask Giti if she would like to come."

"Of course," said Nooshen.

On the street outside, Sam Jenkins, the delivery guy for Sacramento Flowers, drove slowly down Zinfandel Drive, searching for the right address.

"Seven-five-four-eight, seven-five-six-four … that's the place," he said to himself. The only available spot was four doors down and Sam maneuvered his white Dodge panel van to park between the many vehicles lining the street.

"I hope I can get this piece of shit to start," he said as he turned the van off and it gave him an ominous death rattle. He walked around to unlock the sliding door in the passenger side and heaved out a rather large bouquet of flowers.

Inside, the noise of a dozen conversations filled the house and if not for the fact that Sina and the other children were all in the rumpus room playing 'Space Invaders,' the doorbell would never have been heard. Zafar was closest to the front door. He shouted, "I'll get it!" and opened it an instant after the second chime. All he could see from behind the wall of salal, baby's breath and four dozen long stem red roses was the top of a blond, shaggy head and a blue-uniformed arm holding a delivery slip.

"Yes?" Zafar said.

Sam announced, "This is for Giti Rashtti."

"That's Roshtti, young man."

"Sorry, but that's what it says here. Can I get your signature beside the 'x' and then can you print your name below please?"

"Of course," Zafar replied as he took the delivery slip from the courier and did as requested. Then he reached into his pants pocket and took out a ten-dollar bill which he put into the palm of the outstretched hand, along with the signed form.

"Thanks! Thanks very much," Sam said as he handed Zafar the flowers. He walked back down the concrete stairs towards the street admiring the new ten-dollar bill in his right hand. It was a good tip—almost good enough to make him forget about the temperamental van he was driving.

"Jesus, I hope the fucking thing starts." It did.

Inside the Roshtti home, conversation came to sudden stop as Zafar closed the door and turned around, his head obliterated by flowers. People had expected more family members; now they were amazed and curious about the enormous bouquet with Zafar's body beneath it as it walked by.

"Giti! This came for you," Zafar said as he placed the floral arrangement on the table. As everyone admired the flowers, he asked, "I wonder who they're from?"

Giti couldn't believe her eyes; she'd never seen such a large bouquet of flowers. She removed a small white envelope from a plastic clip that was stuck at the side of the bouquet.

"Congratulations on your victory, Giti," said the card. "Your Friend, Jaffar."

"Who are they from Giti?" asked Fatemah.

"They're from Jaffar," was all she could say. Zafar thought he saw a sparkle in her eye.

Fatemah stood beside Zafar and whispered into his ear, "Are they from that man you told me about?" Zafar nodded his head as he gave her hand a firm squeeze, signaling a quiet end to the conversation.

As Giti fussed with her flowers, people drifted back into their conversations and soon Zafar gathered all present together to pray.

"Family, friends, we are together today because one of our best was taken from our midst. Reza's departure from this earth was both unexpected and premature, as he was not even thirty years old! That is too short a life, especially for someone who showed the great potential and promise that Reza demonstrated. All of us have now had over a year to mourn his loss, but from this point forward, let's have no more tears. Let us remember all the good times that Reza shared with us and celebrate not only his life, but the way in which all our lives have been enriched by having known him. Amen!"

Later that evening after all the dishes were dried and put away and after most of the extended family members had gone home, Fatemah noticed the big black circles under Giti's eyes as she walked around the now-quiet house, straightening this, adjusting that.

"Why don't you get some sleep Giti? You've had a long day. Zafar and I will finish whatever is left to do."

"That's a good idea," Giti said. "Thank you for all that you've done. I don't think I could have managed without you! Good night."

"Good night, Giti!"

Fatemah watched her walk down the hall to her bedroom, turn on the light and close the door behind her. For the next twenty minutes she and Zafar stayed up and continued to wipe and put away the final dishes and pots, until Fatemah was satisfied that all was in order. Even the next morning's coffee was prepared, all Giti—or whoever was up first—had to do was push the 'On' button. They switched off all lights and looked down the hall toward Giti's room. They could see the sliver of light beneath her door, indicating she was still awake.

"I'm going to check on her, Zafar."

"You'll do nothing of the sort. She's probably still getting ready for bed. Today was a busy day, she'll fall asleep soon enough and we should do the same." With that they headed downstairs to Giti's guest bedroom.

As the two of them lay in bed, in a hushed voice Fatemah asked Zafar, "Now can you tell me more about the flowers and Giti's mystery man?"

"Why don't you ask her yourself? I'm sure Giti can tell you more than I, after all she spent more time with him than I did."

"I did ask her. The day after you mentioned him, in fact, and she told me there wasn't much to tell. They had had a quick chat on the way back from the restaurant."

"I guess she didn't mention the money he gave us, or more precisely, *her*, or why he gave it to us?"

"No, but you told me about this already."

"Yes, I did … and do you also recall what else I told you?"

"You said he was lower than a snake's belly!"

"No what I told you was that I thought he was slick like camel dung."

"That's a bit much, don't you think? After all you only met the man once."

"Once was enough! I will always remember what my mother told me, 'Always trust your first impression'. I will tell you this, I don't trust that guy."

"But he gave Giti all that money!"

"You don't get something for nothing. He wants something or he's up to something, I tell you. But enough of this, I don't want Giti to hear us and our voices are rising. Let's get some sleep."

"Yes, dear. Good night," Fatemah said, knowing that her husband was right. She leaned over and gave Zafar a kiss on the cheek.

Upstairs, Giti, was still a long way from sleep. During the last twenty minutes she had tossed and turned like a fish out of water, her mind still replaying the events of the day. As sleep continued to elude her, she turned on the light on top of her nightstand, picked up the small white card and read it once more:

"Congratulations on your victory, Giti," said the card. "Your Friend, Jaffar."

Giti smiled, her mind racing, full of questions. She placed the card back in the envelope, turned off the light and eventually fell asleep.

November 9, 1979

Akbal Hussan sat behind the wheel of his Ford Fairmont as the morning sky began to lighten. Today he and his brother were going to kill a man. He was just waiting for Mohammed to show up.

It had not been easy tracking down Jack Coward. Mohammed and he couldn't believe he lived in such a dumpy area—in the desert like some sort of animal—though he admired the craftsmanship of Jack's RV. The thing looked more like a military vehicle of some sort than a regular RV. He wondered where a person could get a machine like that. It looked powerful enough to crush small cars.

They had scoped out Jack's routine. He was an early riser and often he left the RV and drove to a convenience store about a quarter mile from where his RV was parked to get a coffee and a ham and egg sandwich, which he usually took back home with him. They had decided that the best way to ambush him would be to pick up the tail at the convenience store then follow him and shoot him.

He watched his brother appear of the shadows cast by the streetlight's fading illumination. The door opened and Mohammed handed him a coffee then lowered his three-hundred-pound bulk onto the undersized passenger seat.

"Do you know how far your side of the car went down when you got in, you fat slob?"

Akbal did not anticipate the vicious backhand that caught him square on his right shoulder. Unfortunately that was also the hand holding the fresh cup of hot coffee. Akbal screamed in pain as almost the entire twelve-ounce cup emptied onto his lap.

"Damn it, Mohammed! That fucking hurt like hell!!"

"I'm sorry Akbal, I didn't mean to spill your coffee in your lap, but you will show me more respect. I'm your older brother and, at this moment, I'm also the man that pays your wages." Then he asked, "Are you okay?"

"No! I'm not okay, it fucking hurts!" Akbal squirmed about in his seat, trying to alleviate the pain. He blew down toward his crotch, hoping that would help cool things. It didn't; only time would help.

Both men were almost too occupied with what was going on inside the car to notice Jack Coward's black Camaro pull in several stalls away. But while they had not seen it arrive, Akbal looked up just in time to see it pull out.

"There he goes! Quick, start the car and get after him!" Mohammed glanced at the ignition. It was inexplicably empty. "Where are the keys, Akbal?"

His younger brother fumbled to retrieve the keys from his pants pocket. He'd put them there because he'd thought he had time to get out and go to the washroom. Now they were stuck in the wet material that was plastered to his thigh. After some effort rummaging around, and massaging his parboiled skin in the process, he stabbed the key into the ignition and turned it on. The car started at once; Akbal quickly backed up and then slammed the gearshift into 'Drive'. They raced out of the parking lot after Jack.

In the semi-darkness Jack could hardly help but notice the sedan in his rearview mirror as it fish-tailed and accelerated in his direction, headlights slicing back and forth as its driver fought for control. "What the hell?" Jack said. He turned right on East Russell Road, pressed the gas pedal hard and whistled as the Camaro's V-8 engine responded with an instant rush of speed that pushed Jack flat into his seat.

Luckily, there were few people on the road at this time of the morning, so Jack could keep his pursuer in sight. He was just over half a block in front them and they were closing in. Ahead of him, Jack saw a green light—but the flashing pedestrian signal at the crosswalk gave Jack an indication that the light would soon change. He glanced into his mirror, trying to gauge the speed of the blue Ford following him, then accelerated just enough to guarantee he would make the light but his pursuers would not. His timing was perfect; the light turned to amber just as he went through the intersection.

"Hurry Akbal, he's getting away!"

"But, Mohammed! The light is changing!"

"I don't care! He mustn't get away, more gas!" Mohammed bent over and with his meaty left hand shoved his brother's leg further down on the gas. The Ford—now travelling in excess of 50 miles per hour—crossed into the intersection.

Unbeknownst to the brothers Hussan, at that moment Constable Michael Carr was travelling 100 yards in front of two other patrol cars on his way toward his precinct. He slowed down as he approached East Russell Road, but once the light changed to green he resumed his speed. He looked around to see if the other patrol cars were going to make the light, as they had plans to all stop together and pick up coffee for the staff at the precinct. In the split second that his attention was elsewhere, the blue Ford slammed into his patrol car, just behind the rear passenger door.

The impact was so severe it bent the heavy rectangular steel frame of the police car as if it was plasticine, folding it, the other car obliterating the passenger side of the Chevrolet all the way to the transmission tunnel. The trunk of the cruiser bent outward, as if to wrap itself around the crushed front end of the blue sedan that hit it. The welded seam of the gas tank bent and split under the forces imposed on it and almost the entire contents poured onto the pavement in an instant.

The impact of the collision drove the police car diagonally across the intersection and one of the two-inch-wide straps that held its gas tank in place dragged across the ground leaving a shower of sparks in its wake. The instant before both vehicles came to rest, the vapors from the spreading pool of gasoline ignited. The initial fireball was blinding in the semi-darkness and so large it momentarily engulfed both cars.

Patrolman Rob Tanner and Sergeant Richard Petrie, the two officers who had been following Constable Carr, came upon the scene almost immediately. Instantly they sprang into action and secured the area. Tanner radioed in the motor vehicle accident.

"We have an MVA at the corner of East Russell Road and Palm Street. Officer is down. I repeat, officer is down."

Then, as Petrie ran to the aid of his stricken fellow, Tanner worked on bringing the remnants of fire under control.

When Petrie reached the crumpled police car and opened Mike's door he found his friend unconscious and bleeding profusely from a large gash on his left temple. He checked his pulse and found it to be strong and steady. "That's good," he said, then he called out to Tanner, "After you get that fire out, how about you check on those people in the blue car. I've got Mike!"

"Done," Tanner called back.

Tanner finished putting out what little remained of the flames then ran over towards the Ford. As he did so he could hardly fail to notice the tell-tale, bowl-shaped bulge at the driver's side of the windshield and the thousands of cracks radiating out from the center in a star-shaped pattern.

"Uh oh," he said. He tried to open the driver's door, but it stopped at a mere six inches or so. The front fender had been pushed backward and was stopping forward movement of the door. But six inches was enough to allow Tanner a view of the interior. The top of the steering wheel was bent forward and the bulging laminations of the windscreen contained small amounts of blood and tissue. The awkward tilt of Akbal's head was clear evidence that he had broken his neck. He was clearly beyond saving.

Tanner turned his attention to the passenger, who was moaning quietly and moving slightly in his seat, still alive but in a fair degree of crisis. Both Akbal and Mohammed had, in their haste to pursue Jack Coward, failed to fasten their seatbelts. The result had been fatal for Akbal, but Mohammed was still alive, if barely.

As Petrie attended to Constable Carr in his wrecked vehicle, the wail of sirens in the distance indicated help was on the way. Tanner closed the driver's door and went to the passenger side. Though this door could open further than the driver's door had, the same problem occurred. But even if he could have opened the door, Tanner knew there was no way he could get the extremely large victim out of the car. It was fortunate his partner had been able to put out the fire; even the combined efforts of he and Petrie would not have been enough to extricate this man from the front seat.

What Bob could not figure out was why the guy was still alive. He could not know that the cause of the accident was also the reason for Mohammed's survival. Mohammed had bent over to apply more pressure to his brother's right leg in an effort to press the gas pedal all the way to floor. When the collision occurred, he was not thrown head-first into the windshield like his brother, but instead was thrown shoulder-first into the dash. His wounds were later determined to be a concussion and back and shoulder injuries but he was otherwise okay, though he was losing the battle to stay conscious.

Jack had seen the accident happen in his rearview mirror. One second the high beams of the Ford were reflecting into his eyes, the next instant they were eclipsed by the body of the police car as it passed between his vision and the blue sedan. He saw the police cruiser get thrown violently across the intersection and was temporarily blinded as the huge fireball erupted. By the time he had slowed his car down to a halt, however, he was about three hundred yards away. Without thinking twice, he got out and ran back toward the scene to offer assistance to the police.

By the time he got there, the fire was out and the police were attending to the victims. "Can I be of some help?" Jack asked. "I know first aid!"

"You sure can! Would you mind bringing me the first aid kit that's in my trunk? It's open," Petrie told him. Jack ran over to the police car as instructed and retrieved the industrial-size first aid kit.

"Here you go, Sergeant," he said, noting the insignia on the man's uniform as he handed the kit to Officer Petrie.

"Call me Rick," Petrie said as he removed antibiotics and a large piece of gauze from the kit and applied them to Constable Carr's head wound. "What's your name?"

"Jack, my name's Jack. I saw the whole thing!" Jack did not add anything further about the pursuit.

"Well, Jack, we can get a statement from you later, but for now can you take a roll of gauze and wrap it around my buddy's head so it holds this bandage in place?" As Jack did so, the sirens in the distance got closer. Help was almost here.

"Okay, Jack, I think I've got this now, but I don't think we should move him just yet. The paramedics will be here any minute. How about you go over and see if my partner can use your help."

"Right!" Jack said as he walked quickly over to blue car and around to the passenger side to find Tanner struggling to force the door open wider. "Your Sergeant said to come over and see if you need a hand."

The officer looked up and gave Jack a head-to-toe examination, instinctively sizing him up. "I think that between the two of us we should be able to get this door open," he said when he was through, "Don't you?"

"Shouldn't be a problem," Jack said. "How are the people in the car?" Jack had a pretty good idea of what to expect with the driver because he had noticed the damage to the windscreen, but he couldn't get a look at the passenger because the police officer was in the way.

At Tanner's command, Jack pulled on the doorframe from the outside while Tanner wedged his body against the door and the side of the car. Their combined efforts were enough; the door folded forward with a groan bent by their efforts.

A quick glance at the driver confirmed what he'd suspected. He'd seen enough dead bodies in Vietnam to know this one wasn't coming back to life; however when he turned his attention to the unconscious passenger—and instantly recognized him as Mohammed, the man who had hired him last year to find Giti Roshtti—he was completely taken aback and he hoped the cop beside him didn't notice as he muttered "What the hell?" to himself.

"What was that, sir?" Petrie asked.

"I said, 'bloody hell'," Jack adlibbed.

"Yeah, I know. It's very unpleasant to look at isn't it? But it's amazing what you get used to in this job."

The fire truck arrived on the scene and for the first few minutes the firemen sprayed fire retardant foam on the fuel remaining on the blacktop.

As rescue crews took over, Tanner told him, "Thanks for your assistance. I think it best you step away and wait for someone to take your statement now."

Jack nodded and stood on the sidelines, watching the emergency personnel go about their business. Petrie walked over to Jack, followed by a uniformed constable.

"Jack, you said you saw the whole thing," Petrie said, taking out a notebook and pen from his uniform pocket and passing it to the constable. "Can you tell this officer over here what happened?"

"Why can't I tell you?"

"Because I'm a witness to this accident as well and I can't allow your observations to cloud mine, in case we have different versions or perspectives on what took place here. So please give Officer Johnson here your statement."

"I understand," Jack said.

Jack gave his name and address, and as he did so he clandestinely glanced at the pad to see what was being written. Directly above his name was the name and address of Mohammed Hussan, the injured passenger—and most definitely the same man who had hired him last September.

As he answered the officer's questions, Jack began to review the morning's events. It became clear almost immediately that the men had been waiting for him in that parking lot; he had narrowly avoided an ambush. As he continued to give his version of events rescue personnel covered dead man's body with a blue tarp in an effort to shield onlookers from the gruesome sight.

At the end of the interview Jack asked, "Will the officer and the passenger of the Ford be okay?"

"Well, both probably have concussions," Johnson said, "but definitely the guy in the Ford is hurt pretty bad. From what the paramedics told me, he's likely to spend at a bit of time in the hospital."

It was mid-day before the intersection reopened. In any accident where there is a fatality, especially if it involves a police cruiser, photographs are taken, skid marks are measured and so on. It is time-consuming work.

After Jack finished with police interview, free to go, he went back to his car. After picking up some food and some beer, he retreated to his RV, opened a cold bottle of beer, sat down on the couch and dialed the phone.

When it rang in Washington D.C. and his friend picked it up he said, "Hey, Donny my friend. How are you?"

"Great Jack, what's up?"

Jack told him about the accident then said, "Guess who was in the passenger seat of that car?"

"I'll bite," said Donny, "Who?"

"Remember our fat buddy, Mohammed Hussan? The one hired by the guy stalking Giti Roshtti? It was him."

"No shit!" said Donny.

"I think I've got a problem," Jack said.

"No, my friend, we have a problem. I'll fly out first thing in the morning."

Jack had hoped for that response. But then again, he had been pretty sure of what Donny's response would be.

"That's excellent! Let me know your flight and I'll pick you up. Thanks, Buddy!"

"See you tomorrow, Jack. Good night."

November 10, 1979

Just after lunch as promised, Jack met Donny at the airport. Since he had no check-in bags on this trip there wasn't the usual wait at the baggage carousel.

"Hey Jack! Long time no see, how are you?"

"Not so bad Donny, good to see you!"

They hugged and did their usual squeeze-grip greeting. Donny winced, but Jack gave up first.

"So, what's the plan?" Donny asked, shaking out his hand to get the blood flowing again.

"Well I guess you're probably famished after, what, four hours in the air? Let's get something to eat then we can pay Mr. Hussan's place of residence a visit. I got his address off the cop's notepad. There's diner not too far from where I park the RV. Let's drop off your stuff and go there."

"Do they have all-day bacon and eggs?"

"You're in luck, this place makes the best omelets in the city."

After they ate, the two of them started out to case Mohammed Hussan's place. They headed north on Mountain Vista Avenue.

"How far is this place Jack?"

"Oh, it's only about ten or fifteen minutes from here, near Eastern."

At about four o'clock, Jack and Donny walked up the sidewalk of the Cedar Village Apartments.

"Yup, 2850. This is the place," Jack said.

At that moment a young couple came out of the building. Engrossed in conversation, they walked right past the two men without acknowledging them and Donny was able to reach for the door just before it closed.

"Good timing, Donny," said Jack.

A few minutes later they were walking down the corridor on the second floor. They stopped when they got to apartment 203. The lock would have been a piece of cake to pick, but instead Jack took out a small plastic card, about the size and thickness of a playing card, but somewhat stiffer. He bent one corner of it slightly and slid it down the space between the door and the jamb. He paused when it came in contact with the door latch and turned the door knob with his hand while applying pressure with the card. The door opened in half a second and both men stepped inside Mohammed Hussan's apartment. Jack quietly closed the door behind them and they both listened for any sign of activity in the apartment. They heard nothing. They had phoned earlier and got no response, so it was a pretty safe bet that no one was about, but it was good to make sure.

"You take the bedroom and I'll look in the kitchen and living room," Jack said.

"Right, Jack!"

After five minutes of searching every drawer and cupboard in the kitchen, Jack searched the refrigerator. Nothing there! For such a big guy, he sure doesn't eat much, he thought.

Jack then turned his attention to the living room. As he did so, he quietly asked Donny how things were going. Donny answered softly, "Not much in the bedroom except this address book."

"Let's have a look."

Donny began flipping through the small leather-bound book while Jack continued to search the living room, looking under couch cushions and opening drawers and cupboards. He even went as far as to remove the Masonite back from the RCA television in the corner.

"Jack, what was the name of that guy our friend here was working for ... Jaffy?"

"It was Jaffar. Jaffar somebody."

"Let's see Jaffar ... Jaffar." After a short pause, Donny said, "Here it is—Jaffar Hamid Harraj, 00-964-9394743, Al-Qa'im, Iraq."

"Holy shit. That must be the guy that got him to hire us. So that's the guy that wants me dead. But why? Keep looking. There must be something else around here that will tell me why."

However, after ten more minutes of searching it seemed like all they would come away with was the address book. That would do for now. Donny stood in the living room, continuing to thumb through the pages.

"Donny, are you sure you looked everywhere?"

"Yes. I've gone through everything. I even searched through all the shirt and pants pockets of his clothes. What about you?"

"Yep, looked everywhere," then Jack stopped mid-sentence and focused his attention to Donny's right. "Donny, look beside you and tell me what you see."

"I see a plant, not my idea of …"

"Exactly. It looks out of place doesn't it? And another thing … feel the leaves, they look plastic from here." Donny reached out to touch one.

"They are. How did you know?"

"My aunt used to have huge plants, just like that, big split-leaf philodendrons. She always warned me about licking my fingers after touching the leaves. Some kind of residue would make me sick."

"What about them?"

"They were in huge pots. That's what caught my eye. Look at the pot. I remember trying to move them around with my uncle, it took both of us to even budge them."

"What about it, it has dirt in it."

"Yes, but it's so small, and why put dirt in a pot for plastic plant?" Jack grabbed the plant by its base and lifted it, complete with the pot, with almost no effort. "The thing's hollow! I'd bet my life on it!"

Donny got down on his hands and knees to examine the pot more closely. "Jack hold it right there for a minute. I think that this pot has two parts, I can see a joint two thirds of the way up!" Donny put down the address book, placed his two hands around the pot and started to manipulate it in different directions. In the clockwise direction it didn't budge, but in the counter-clockwise direction the bottom portion rotated about two inches and separated neatly from the top.

"Bingo, Jack," Donny said as pulled out a journal and some photographs that were hidden inside.

As Jack set the upper part of the plant down on the floor, Donny examined the book and announced, "It's got dollar amounts, addresses and names—most of them from Las Vegas."

"Must be pretty important information for him to have gone to all that trouble to hide it in this pot. Too bad we don't have more time or the means to examine it more closely right now. Let's go back to my place and see if we can figure out what we have."

"Right, Jack. And I would suggest that once we know, we will have to pay Mr. Hussan another visit."

November 20, 1979

It was late in the day and Giti was lying in bed watching the ABC late night program *America Held Hostage*, with Ted Koppel. Finally, after what had seemed like months of daily unchanging news updates, Koppel announced, "Today thirteen hostages, all women and African Americans, were released today leaving fifty-three hostages behind, who continue to be held..."

The phone rang, startling Giti. It was unusual for someone to call her so late at night. She picked up the phone as quickly as she could, hoping it had not awakened Sina. "Hello?"

"Giti. I'm sorry for calling at this late hour. This is Jaffar!"

"Jaffar? What?" She had not expected to hear from him again. He had sent her the lovely flowers when she won her court case, but otherwise he had not contacted her. She expected that he was too busy, as she knew he traveled a lot for his work. She also knew he spent a lot of time overseas and how difficult it was to reach people long-distance, so she was surprised that he would call her from out of the blue and from so far away.

"I'm sorry, did I wake you?" Jaffar asked. "It's almost noontime where I am so I apologize again. I just wanted to be sure I reached you. I will be flying back to the U.S. for business soon and was wondering if we could get together for lunch when I get to California?"

A moment earlier, Giti had been sleepily watching the news and now as she spoke on the phone, she came wide awake and found herself unconsciously straightening her nightclothes and brushing her hair with her hand.

"Jaffar, why yes. Yes of course," she said.

"I promised you I would keep in touch," he said, "but I have not been very good at it. I have been traveling a lot and I'm not always near a phone. Some of the places I go for work are very remote. But I am calling you now!"

Flattered, Giti said, "I do understand ... and I appreciate a man who keeps his word. When do you think you'll be back in the States?"

"Probably about a week from now, depending on how things go over here."

"Well it would be lovely to see you," said Giti. "And I look forward to hearing from you then. Good night, Jaffar!"

"Good night!" Jaffar smiled. The conversation had gone even better than he had hoped.

December 7, 1979

For more than two weeks Giti had been nervously awaiting her lunch date with Jaffar. The previous evening, she'd received another call from him to inquire if Friday was okay for them to meet.

"Certainly," was her response. "You can pick me up from where I work." She gave Jaffar the name and address of Zafar and Fatemah's place of business.

On the appointed day, at five minutes to twelve, a taxi arrived outside the main entrance to the office and Jaffar got out and walked toward the door. Giti, who had been waiting impatiently, met him halfway and Jaffar shook her hand, holding it a little too long and gazing at her as if he wanted to kiss her delicate fingers. She smiled demurely, pleased at his promptness then they walked together to the waiting cab with Zafar and Fatemah watching as he opened the door for her and helped her inside.

"I would have preferred that you or I had been with her on this date," Zafar grumbled.

"Oh, Zafar be sensible. It's not as if she's a teenager that you have to worry about and wait on your doorstep for! Giti is a grown woman and Jaffar seems like a gentleman. Look at the way he opened the door for her!"

"Oh, and don't forget to remind me about the thousands of dollars he gave her, not to mention about a million flowers he sent from across the world!" Zafar did not try to hide his annoyance.

"Zafar, aren't you forgetting how lonely she's been since she lost Reza?"

"Since *we* lost Reza!"

"Yes Zafar, since *we* lost Reza. But we're talking about Giti. She needs some companionship. We don't have the right to deny her that. Except for the fact that she's your sister-in law, she can choose to do whatever she likes."

Zafar sighed. He knew she was right, but there was something about Jaffar that got under his skin. "Alright, my dear," he said, defeated for now.

The orange and black cab with Jaffar and Giti in it stopped on Folsom Boulevard, two blocks west of 59th, in front of the Espanol Restaurant, one of Sacramento's best Italian restaurants, as he had been requested to do. Jaffar got out and held the door open for Giti.

"This is one of the oldest Italian restaurants in all of Sacramento. I've been here several times before, the food is excellent," he said as he handed the cab driver a crisp, new $50 bill and told him. "Wait here, if you please."

Normally this was something that Mitch, the cabbie, was reluctant to do, but Jaffar quickly added, "There's another fifty dollars for you if you are here when we are ready to leave."

"Of course, sir. Enjoy your meal," Mitch said, happy to think that his afternoon's wages were already covered and he didn't have a thing to do but wait. He picked up his copy of the Sacramento Bee, unfolded it and turned to check the spread on next week's game against Denver. "I hope Stabler does a better job than he fucking did against Kansas City," Mitch said aloud as he tried to decide if he should put only one of fifties on the Raiders.

Inside he restaurant, Giti sat nervously in her chair as she and Jaffar waited for their lunch order to be taken. She was curious about him, and a little nervous about the kind of money he so obviously had. "So what kind of business are you in?" she began nervously.

He didn't answer because, as if on cue, the waitress appeared to take Giti's order of chicken primavera and salad. Jaffar said he would have the same.

Jaffar could sense she was nervous and he needed a moment to think about how to answer her question, so he flattered her. "The chicken is an excellent choice, Giti!" he cooed. He knew this would please her. He was good at reading people; in his business you had to be, or you might wind up instantly dead.

She smiled at the compliment which gave him just enough time to compose a plausible answer. "So, you started to ask me about my business?"

"Yes, I did. Why were you in the Middle East? From the news these days that doesn't seem to be the safest place."

"Yes, that terrible business at your U.S. Embassy in Tehran."

"Why did you say 'your' Embassy? Aren't you American?"

"No, I'm actually from Britain and my parents are from Saudi Arabia."

"But you don't have a British accent!"

"I left England when I was very young, eight years old to be precise. I grew up here in the States and my parents worked very hard to rid me of any hint of a British accent."

"They did a good job. You had me fooled," Giti admitted.

As they continued to talk about their early lives, their meals arrived. When the waitress had departed, Jaffar said, "Do you remember when we went for lunch that day at court that I said I could only give you a short explanation about why I gave you money to help you? I would now like to go into a bit more detail, if it's okay with you."

"Sure!"

"I once had friends who were in a similar position to yours, where justice was on their side, but their ability to pursue the matter was beyond their financial means. I had the means to help them, but I stood back and did nothing."

In between small bites of her chicken, Giti asked, "What happened?"

Jaffar had prepared his response weeks earlier, so the lie slid easily off his tongue. "It would only have been a small financial inconvenience for me, but as I said, I stood back and did nothing to help. Eventually they lost their home and their business, and the husband took his own life. Too late I realized my mistake and selfishness and I was ashamed. To this day I wonder how things would have been if I had stepped in sooner. Some say he was depressed anyway and my help would have made no difference, but I will never know. When your plight became known to me, when I saw you on the news, I realized this was my chance to atone for my previous lack of action. My friend's chance for justice failed, I did not want yours to fail as well."

Giti was touched. She said, "It was very kind of you to give me that money, Jaffar, and I understand why … but please be assured that I can and will pay you back every cent!"

"Don't be silly. I don't expect you to!"

"But Zafar and I have already decided that since the court is awarding me legal costs, you are going to get your money back!"

"As you wish Giti." He smiled.

Their conversation moved on to more mundane things for the reminder of their meal. The waitress returned to remove their plates and both Giti and Jaffar ordered coffee instead of dessert. Giti was almost through her coffee when she happened to glance at her watch.

"Oh my God. It's almost two-thirty! I've got to be heading back to work."

"Do you think it would be a terrible hardship for you to take the rest of the afternoon off?"

"Not a hardship so much, but I do know that Zafar is expecting me back. My God, where did the time go?" Giti started to get up to leave, "I should really get back Jaffar, I'm sorry."

"So am I, but as you wish." Jaffar paid the bill and they headed out the door. Jaffar wasn't surprised to see that the cab driver had stayed.

"Giti, can I ask you a question?"

"I believe that you just did," Giti smiled at her own cleverness and was a little deflated to see that he didn't really pick up on her small joke, so she added, "What would that be, Jaffar?"

"Why do cab companies paint their cabs such horrible colors?"

"Yes, black and orange. It looks like something from Halloween, doesn't it?' Both Giti and Jaffar laughed at that and Giti realized it had been a while since she had shared laughter with a man.

"You mean the movie?" Jaffar added, trying to make her laugh again.

He succeeded Giti laughed again. "No, not the movie, the day!"

They settled into the back seat of the cab and Jaffar instructed Mitch to drive them back to her workplace.

"That was a great meal wasn't it, Giti?"

"Yes, it most certainly was, Jaffar. Thank you!"

"I'm in town for a few more days and then I'm away again for a little while. Do you think we could have dinner before I go?"

Giti looked over at Jaffar and was about to answer in a positive way, when the image of Reza flashed into her mind and a wave of guilt swept quickly over her. With a dry mouth, she could barely manage to blurt out, "I don't know … I mean, I'm not sure." Dinner seemed so much more personal than lunch.

Jaffar was unused to this kind of response from the opposite sex. In Al-Qa'im he had no shortage of willing partners. Some were attracted to his handsome face, many were attracted by his reputation and all were seduced by the power he wielded—because all knew that the consequences for refusing Jaffar were often unpleasant.

"But why?" Jaffar asked petulantly, letting his self-control slip for a moment.

"It's too soon," was all Giti could manage.

"So, folks, how was the meal? That place gets rave reviews!" the cabbie asked jovially, unaware that theses seemingly pleasant people had hit an impasse.

"Very good," answered Jaffar curtly, and Mitch could hear the tension in his voice. *Maybe you should just keep your mouth shut, Mitch old boy, and not try to help this guy out,* Mitch said to himself, not wanting to jeopardize his chances of getting the remainder of his tip. The rest of the trip was awkward and blessedly short.

The cab stopped at the curb and Giti opened the door. As she got out she said, "I had a good time Jaffar. Thank you very much for the lunch."

"Can I call you?" he asked.

"I don't know, Jaffar!" Giti looked nervously towards the office, sure everyone was watching. Glancing at her watch, she said, "I've got to go."

"Perhaps you can call me if you change your mind?" Jaffar offered Giti his business card, which she took.

"Thank you, Jaffar." She turned and walked quickly up the sidewalk toward the front door leaving Jaffar to stare at his own reflection in the glass door of the office as it closed behind her.

"Take me back to the Hyatt Regency."

"Of course, sir."

Ten minutes later as the cabbie as watched Jaffar walk into the Hyatt, he fondled the crisp new 'Benjamin' Jaffar had given him and thought, *at least this had been a good day for one of us! Too bad for the guy though, she was pretty hot!* Then the uniformed doorman raised his hand, catching his attention, and he was back to work.

That evening Giti lay in bed attempting read the latest offering by Ken Follett, which her next door neighbor had loaned her. After reading and rereading the same page five times, she gave up and placed *The Eye of the Needle* on the bedside table. All afternoon and into the evening, ever since she'd got out of the cab, she had been unable to focus her thoughts, her mind going around and around, a whirlwind of emotions.

After lunch it became clear to Giti that work wasn't the best place for her to be, a fact not lost on Fatemah.

"You're thinking about your man, aren't you Giti?"

"Yes and no." The answer was definitely 'yes', because she had been thinking about both Reza and Jaffar.

"Is it Reza? If it is, then you and I have definitely got to talk."

"That's okay Fatemah, but thanks anyway. I've got to work this out by myself."

"Why don't you go home? Better yet why don't you let me drive you home? Zafar can pick me up later."

"I guess I'm not much good here today. Does it show that much?"

"Yes. Get your coat and I will go and tell Zafar!!" A few minutes later Fatemah was behind the wheel of Giti's old AMC Matador, heading east towards Giti's home.

"Why don't you get a new car, Giti? After all it's got what …" She looked down at the odometer "… 97,000 miles on it." Fatemah was surprised Giti continued to drive the old blue sedan. She could now afford much better.

"That's probably 297,000 miles," Giti said. "Reza and I got it used."

Fatemah tried to shift the conversation to what was really on Giti's mind. "Is that why you don't sell it and get a new car, because of Reza?"

"Well yes, sort of! Besides I know this car is reliable. We haven't spent a lot of money on it."

"You mean, *you* haven't. Reza's been gone for over a year, Giti. You've got to let go sometime."

"I don't know, Fatemah. I tried to go out with Jaffar and it didn't work out. All afternoon I've thought about Reza. I don't know what to do." Giti began to cry. Fatemah tried to comfort her sister-in-law for the rest of the trip but didn't have any luck. Both Fatemah and Giti walked up the front steps of the house on Zinfandel Drive in tears.

"I'll stay with you until Zafar comes to get me. We can have a cup of tea, maybe talk things through a bit."

"I don't know if it will help, but thanks."

"Of course it'll help, Giti. Over the last while, you and I haven't had much of a chance to talk. You've spent more time with Zafar than I have—almost to the point of me starting to get a bit jealous. Just kidding!" Both Fatemah and Giti laughed at that.

"I guess some days I have spent more time with him than you, haven't I? With court and everything …"

"Yes Giti, but you and I know that Zafar was happy to do it. Or rather, happy to be able to help you. You know what I mean!" Fatemah continued, "Did Zafar not talk to you about Reza?"

"Oh, yes, we talked about Reza often. He really misses his younger brother. But we never talked about Reza and *me*."

"I suppose that would be so. He's a man. I know he would have found it uncomfortable to talk with you about what Reza meant to you."

"Yes," Giti said. "It's nice to be able to talk with a woman about this, to get a woman's perspective on things. I miss Reza so much, sometimes more than I can stand ..." She started to cry again.

"But it's time for you to get on with your life, Giti. It's time to make a new start for you and Sina. With all the money you have now you can and you should," Fatemah said softly.

"The court case was never about the money, you know that," said Giti. "It was about fighting for Reza's memory. And now it's over and I have no reason to focus on him anymore. All I have is memories. I don't know if I can get on with my life, like people say. I don't know if it's time. I don't know if I've had enough time to mourn."

"Giti, look, Jaffar is a handsome man and apparently he's got his own money so you know he's not after yours. Let him get to know you and Sina. Let him show whether he can look after you."

"That's another thing," Giti sniffed. "What about Sina? I don't know how he'll react to me dating another man."

"I'll have Zafar talk to him. Perhaps Sina will listen to his Uncle Zafar. Perhaps Sina will never be 'good' with it, but in time he will come time to accept it."

"You really think so?"

"Yes, I do! And I'm sure Zafar and the rest of the family think so too!"

— Chapter 6 —

The next morning, during a break between loads of laundry and other housework, Giti sat outside at the back of her house on the rear patio. For early December, the day was warmer than Giti expected and the sweater she'd put on kept away any cool breeze.

That morning, Zafar had come by to take Sina for an outing. He tried very hard to fill the void Reza's absence had created in Sina's life. Today it was miniature golf. Sina seemed to be getting the hang of putting.

"He's going to be the next John Nicklaus!"

Although not an avid golfer by any stretch of the imagination, Giti was familiar with the names, "That's *Jack* Nicklaus!"

Today, if Zafar was true to his word, he was going to have a talk with Sina. Giti still had reservations about when or whether to start dating again but after her discussion with Fatemah, she was willing to at least entertain the idea. She picked up the phone and dialed the number Jaffar had written on the back of his business card. After the ninth unanswered ring she hung up, disappointed.

"I guess that was it!" she thought, but then another possibility occurred to her. In for a penny, in for a pound, she thought. Jaffar had mentioned he was staying at the Hyatt Regency. Giti went inside to get the phone book then thumbed through the hotel listings.

"Let's see … here it is, 916-443-1234." Picking up the phone once more, she dialed the number.

"Good morning, Hyatt Regency, this is Bridgette. How may I direct your call?"

"Could you put me through to Jaffar … um …" For the life of her Giti could not remember his last name. It's a good thing that she wasn't asking in person, she could feel herself turning a dozen shades of red.

"Jaffar… Do you have a last name?"

At that instant she thought to look at the front of his card. "Harraj, Jaffar Hamid Harraj!"

"I'll check for you." Giti heard a click, replaced by the soft voice of Bing Crosby singing *White Christmas*, followed by a second click, then Bridgette was on the line again. "I'm sorry ma'am. It seems as though Mr. Harraj has checked out of the hotel."

"Checked out? How can that be? I just talked to him yesterday. He gave me his card and said that he would be in town for a few more days."

"I'm sorry but he has indeed left the hotel. According to the concierge, Mr. Harraj did say that he had intended on staying for a week, but that his plans had changed."

"Is it possible to leave him a message, or get a message to him somehow?" Giti continued, "It's kind of important."

"Well ma'am that not something that we usually do, but Mr. Harraj did leave us a forwarding address and number. Unfortunately, we can't give them out, but we can forward a message for you!"

"That would be great. I'd really appreciate it!" Giti left her message with Bridgette.

At that same time, at the Scandia Family Fun Center a few miles away, as he had promised, Zafar was watching Sina as he tried repeatedly to bank his ball off the aprons at the ninth hole. Sina had announced moments before, "I can make a hole in one, Uncle Zafar!"

"If you do I'll buy you lunch!" Zafar did not mention the fact that he always bought Sina lunch when they went out together.

"I get to pick the place!" It was usually McDonald's. Zafar knew that.

"Alright."

So, for the past few minutes Sina had putted, missed and run up to get his ball, laughing all the way. Unfortunately for Sina, he may have been a budding Jack Nicklaus, but this zig-zag hole was more suited to the talents of Minnesota Fats, requiring five banks to get a hole in one.

"Sina, would you mind if I tried it now?" Zafar asked.

"I guess so," Sina said, reluctant to give up. Zafar lined up his putt, aiming for the exact spot, just to left of the knot—and intentionally coming up short.

"Oh, that was so close. I don't believe it," Zafar said.

"You could blow that one in Uncle Zafar," Sina said. "My turn!" He had watched his uncle putt and knew just where to aim his ball now. Zafar knew he would have figured it out himself eventually, but it might have taken all day.

"Just a bit harder than mine Sina!"

That last comment was unnecessary as ball speed was not Sina's problem, his aim was. He drew back his putter, struck the ball firmly and after five clunks was rewarded with a kerplunk as the ball dropped right in the center of the hole.

"Perfect, Sina!" Zafar said. He had known as soon as the ball left Sina's putter that the ball was in the hole. It had followed Zafar's previous path exactly. "That was a perfect putt!"

"Whoopee!" Sina yelled so loud that everyone in the vicinity turned their heads to look, only to see him hop and skip the 25 feet to the hole to retrieve his ball. "You have to buy me lunch, Uncle. You promised."

"Of course, Sina. Where would you like to go?" He knew what was coming.

"Can we go to McDonald's? For a Big Mac?"

"Of course, Sina," Zafar said as they moved to the last half of the course.

Zafar sat across from his nephew, eating a Filet-o-Fish sandwich. He watched Sina intently dip one French fry at a time into his Ketchup and nibble the end. Now is as good a time as any, Zafar thought to himself.

"Sina, can we talk seriously for a minute, man to man?"

"Yes, sure!" Usually when his uncle started a conversation in this manner, he was passing along a message from his mother about cleaning his room or playing on his Atari too much. This time, Sina thought, it seemed different.

"I don't know how to ask you this, Sina, so I'm going to just come straight out and ask." Sina squirmed in his chair, not knowing what to expect. "How would you feel if your mom started to see other men?"

"You mean date other men?"

"Yes, I guess that's what I mean!"

"It would be okay I guess," Sina replied. He'd had many months to think about this, ever since the first time he'd been asked the same question. For several months after his father's death he'd been unable to concentrate on his school work, sometimes reduced to tears. Talking to the school counselor had helped him to think about this as she had asked Sina the same question. At first the question had made him cry. This time it was different.

"What do you mean, I guess? This is too important to just 'guess' at, Sina. You should be sure about how you feel." Zafar continued, "That's important to your mom, your aunt, and to me too!"

Thinking back over the last several months, Sina could recall the times late at night when he'd walked down the hall to go to the bathroom and seen a light coming from under his Mom's door. "I can hear her cry sometimes at night," he confessed to his uncle.

"You can?" This was not something Zafar had anticipated. He watched as Sina took another French fry from its package. "That's because she's lonely and she doesn't know what to do. She misses your Dad."

"I do too! But I don't want my Mom to cry anymore," Sina said. His uncle could see tears start to form in Sina's eyes as he struggled with his emotions.

"It's okay Sina," he said.

"I'm fine uncle," he sniffed as he took his napkin and wiped away the tears on his cheek. "I don't want her to cry anymore!"

"Maybe you can help your mom not to cry!"

"How?" Sina asked, sniffing again as he finished his fries.

"You can tell your Mom that it's okay for her to date. Tell her just what you told me! Deal?"

"Deal!" Zafar stuck out his hand and shook his nephew's hand. He was very impressed with Sina's response.

"You are a good son, Sina," Zafar said as he watched Sina attack his Big Mac, eating one thing at a time, as he always did. The difficult part of the day out of the way, Zafar swiftly changed the subject. "So, Sina, what do you want for Christmas?"

"I want a Sony Walkman, or maybe some more Star Wars action figures like I got last year. Do you think that I could get the Millennium Falcon?"

"Have you asked your Mom?"

In between bites he answered, "Of course, Uncle Zafar!"

Al-Qa'im - February 23, 1980

It was morning in Iraq, and Jaffar was watching the news, drinking a cup of green tea.

"In a news story that has dominated our recent broadcasts, the Ayatollah Ruhollah Khomeini has declared that Iran's parliament will decide the fate of the American Embassy hostages. Today is their 111th day in captivity." The television screen split into two with the news anchor on one side and a still photograph of Iran's president on the other. "It is not known what role, if any, Abolhassin Banisadr, Iran's newly elected president will play in these events."

The scene changed back to the newsroom. "In other news, hockey fans across our nation are swelling with pride as our Olympic team has beaten the heavily favored Soviet Union to win the Gold medal in Lake Placid ..."

"Abdul, come in here at once!" yelled Jaffar.

"Yes, Jaffar what is it?"

"Have you seen the news?" Jaffar seemed to have renewed his interest in the affairs of Islamic politics of late since he had returned from America, which was good. But unfortunately, since his return in December, his mood was best described as foul by all those who were closest to him. Almost everyone avoided him, fearing repercussions. As his right-hand man, Abdul had to remain beside him, but he tried to minimize being in the same room with him.

"It would seem the Iranian Parliament is going to decide the fate of the American hostages!" Jaffer announced, clearly waiting for some kind of response from Abdul. There was none.

Then Abdul cautiously ventured, "That is excellent news, is it not, Excellency?"

"You know as well as I that the Ayatollah and his Shiite followers hold the real power in Iran, the Parliament are merely his puppets."

"But still it is good news, Jaffar?"

"It most certainly is *not*! This going to have a very detrimental effect on my holdings—I mean our holdings—in the U.S!" He did not mention to Abdul that on his solo trip to the U.S. in late November he had detected anti-Middle Eastern sentiments, some directed toward him. More than once

Jaffar had wished for Abdul's company. Instead he said, "Could you get in touch with our friend Mohammed? It's been too long since we have talked!"

Within the hour the phone rang on Jaffar's desk. "It's Mohammed, excellency. I am returning your call as ordered. It's been many weeks since we last spoke, Excellency!"

"Yes, it has." Without pause Jaffar engaged Mohammed in a discussion about the political atmosphere in the United States.

"How do you think the people are feeling? After all, you are out there among them every day," Jaffar asked. "It is hard to judge such things from just listening to the news reports. Often reporters just sensationalize news for market share, and ignore the … how do you say it? The 'grass roots' side of things."

"It's hard to say, Jaffar," Mohammed said, "but I have been the target of more angry words than usual." Mohammed thought back to the previous week when a white-haired, old man had been trying to get past him on the sidewalk with his walker and couldn't.

"Fuck you, you stupid towelhead!" the man had said. Mohammed could still hear the anger in his voice.

"And what of the situation with Jack Coward?" Jaffar asked.

"Ah, some unfortunate news, Excellency …" Mohammed said. "My brother is dead … and it is that man's fault!" Then he told Jaffar the story of the car chase and subsequent accident, with bitterness in his voice as he blamed Jack Coward for the accident. Jaffar did not react as expected.

"You idiot! Who gave you orders to chase him?"

"You did, Jaffar!" Still in the hospital recovering, Mohammed had no idea about Jaffar's state of mind and how thin the ice was upon which he was walking.

"I told you to watch him, not chase him!" Jaffar exclaimed angrily.

"But, Jaffar … if I'm to watch him, is it not true that I must follow him?"

"No! I told you to watch him, learn his movements, his schedule, when he comes and goes …" Jaffar felt angry blood rush to his face. He breathed deeply to calm himself. He couldn't believe how stupid this man was.

Mohammed continued briefing Jaffar about the accident, giving an almost second-by-second account of the brief chase. During his month of rehabilitation and physical therapy he had relived the chase and subsequent crash many times over and the result was always the same: he could hear his brother Akbar yelling "No!" as Mohammed pressed his leg harder towards the floor. He could feel the tremendous impact of the collision, followed by excruciating pain in his back and shoulders, he remembered how startled he'd been by the bright flash and the sudden warmth of the ensuing fireball. Finally, there had been blackness. Mohammed was sure that he'd died.

He'd awoken in the hospital the next day in dreadful pain, angels in white hovering above his bed. But the real pain didn't start until he found out about Akbal's death.

Jaffar, listening to the story just got angrier and angrier. When Mohammed finished his tale, he didn't acknowledge that a man had died. Instead he yelled, "You fool, you imbecile!" Then, "Have you no brains?"

"Now wait a second, Jaffar! My brother Akbal was killed in the accident!" protested Mohammed.

Having it pointed out soften Jaffar slightly. "Oh! I'm sorry to hear," he said.

For several more minutes Mohammed continued to talk to Jaffar, relating to him his long difficult convalescence as well as continuing to speak as best he could about the mood of America's citizens toward their people. Jaffar seemed to listen, so Mohammed almost forgot his earlier bad mood until Jaffar curtly asked, "Anything else you want to tell me?"

"No Jaffar, that's about it."

"Good!"

Jaffar was just about to hang up when Mohammed yelped, "Wait," into the mouthpiece. He was fighting through the four-times-a-day, doctor-prescribed 292 fog that was clouding his mind, trying to remember anything worthy of note that he could report to his boss. "There's one more thing," he said. "That Giti woman, she left you a message!"

"What? When?"

"About two months ago."

Jaffar's pulse raced. It took all he had not to scream at Mohammed, "Did you not think to call me? First you disobey my orders about the private detective, resulting in your brother's death. This could have brought our organization unwanted attention from the authorities, with serious consequences!" he said in the coldest of voices. "Second, you get a message from someone who I've gone to great expense to meet and you don't think it is necessary to call me and let me know? I would like to know the contents of Giti's message!"

Mohammed relayed Giti's message that he had received from the Hyatt Hotel in Sacramento.

Without saying good-bye, Jaffar slammed the phone down with such force that he jammed the switch hook, rendering it useless. During this conversation Abdul had been standing nearby. "What's wrong Jaffar?"

"It would seem, Abdul, that you and I have some unfinished business in the U.S.!"

"What is going on with Mohammed?"

"We can talk about that on the way to airport. Go book us a flight and pack your things."

February 27, 1980

Jaffar and Abdul arrived in Sacramento airport after flying the long, circuitous route that was becoming more and more familiar. Despite being able to take a more direct route and saving many hours, this was a much safer way for the two to travel to America.

Almost immediately Jaffar and Abdul noticed a difference in the way people treated them. The hostage crisis was hitting America hard; people with Middle Eastern features were all suspect, it seemed. While the majority of people were polite, some were quite curt and others were downright rude—particularly the cab driver at the airport. Abdul and Jaffar walked towards the cab that was at the front of the queue. Abdul opened the rear passenger door to get in and expected the driver to open the trunk and load their bags. Instead he said, "Sorry Mac! I'm off duty. Get the cab behind!"

"But your light doesn't show you as off duty," Abdul said.

The cab driver reached over and flipped a toggle switch on his dashboard. "It does now, now beat it!"

In all his adult life no one had spoken to Abdul Al-Kubesi in such a manner. It was all he could do to keep from reaching inside the cab and throttling the man. He had been cautioned by Jaffar about such actions. Jaffar had told him to blend in as much as possible and not draw any attention to them. He wished he hadn't agreed, but he had, so he simply replied, "As you wish."

Eventually they got a cab and got to their hotel where both settled in for some much-needed rest.

The next morning, Jaffar felt refreshed and ready to tackle the tasks at hand. "Today, Abdul, I want you to rent a car and drive to Las Vegas," he told his underling.

"Why Jaffar? Both you and I have had a long flight and I don't want to spend the day driving. I'd rather fly, it's faster."

"Because I pay you very handsomely for what little you do, and you'll do as I ask!"

After the briefest hesitation, Abdul replied, "Yes of course."

"I already have a problem with Mohammed. I don't want a problem with you as well Abdul!"

"You don't have to worry about me—and I will sort out the problem with Mohammed."

Less than half an hour later, just as Abdul was about to leave the room, he got last minute instructions from Jaffar. "Don't do anything without my approval!"

"Yes, Jaffar." Abdul reached for the doorknob.

"I will be here, or I will leave a number where I can be reached. Be cautious. Let me know what happens with Mohammed."

"I will!" Abdul closed the door behind him, leaving Jaffar alone with his thoughts. Abdul had probably not even reached the lobby when Jaffar dug the paper out of his bag on which he'd written Giti's work number. Several times he'd almost thrown the paper in the trash, but something had stopped him from doing so. He unfolded it now and dialed.

"Good morning. U.S. Fabrics Wholesale, Shalimar Market."

"Could I have Giti Roshtti please?"

"Hold on, please." Jaffar could hear the click as the receptionist put him on hold. He had to wait only a moment before he heard her lovely voice.

"Hello, this is Giti."

"Hello Giti, this is Jaffar."

"Jaffar! My God, I didn't think I was going to hear from you again."

"It's a long story Giti, I don't want to take you away from your work, but I will tell you later if you want." After a pause Jaffar added, "Can you have dinner with me tonight?"

"No sorry, not tonight. I've got plans with Sina."

For a moment Jaffar felt a hint a jealousy before he remembered Giti's young son was named Sina. "Oh, of course," he said, "I should not have expected you to be free on a moment's notice!"

"What about tomorrow night? I have no plans!"

"Good. I'm staying at the Hyatt Regency, the same place as last time. They have an excellent dining room, down off the lobby. It overlooks the pool!"

"That sound very nice! What time should I be there?"

"Say seven, I will send a car for you."

"No Jaffar I will bring my own car." Giti felt more secure having her own transportation there.

"Very good, I'll see you then"

February 28, 1980

Abdul awoke very early. The previous several nights of almost no sleep—combined with travelling halfway around the globe and now a long drive to Las Vegas—were taking their toll. His internal clock was completely confused.

He'd spotted the sign for Three Peaks Resort and Beach Club the evening before, turned in, signed a form and immediately fallen asleep on the bed, though it was early afternoon when he arrived. He didn't notice that the rooms were 'from $25', or that breakfast was included. He'd just traveled by car from Sacramento to South Lake Tahoe and even if he'd noticed, he would not have cared.

He'd slept for almost thirteen hours, and when he woke it was so early in the morning it was still dark, so Abdul switched on the lamp which cast a golden glow over the interior of the room. As his eyes adjusted to the light, he could see his bags were right where he'd left them, right beside the door. But now that he was less tired, he could also see the large stone fireplace that dominated one end of the room and the light pine vertical boards that covered almost all the walls.

Jaffar has a motel just like this, he thought, trying to rid his brain of cobwebs and gear up for the work he had come to do. His stomach filled with a sick-feeling knot at the thought of the unpleasant business with Mohammed that Jaffar had sent him to take care of. *Jaffar! I'm getting sick of doing his bidding. Abdul do this, Abdul do that. Abdul come in here at once!* Now he must go to Las Vegas and straighten out messes for him there as well.

Abdul went into the bathroom and turned on the shower. He looked at his face in the mirror as he waited for the water to reach the desired temperature. He definitely appeared stressed. He hoped a long hot shower would relax him. *Funny that I need relaxing, I've only been up for five minutes!* He tested the water and stepped in.

As he lathered his scalp and worked on getting rid of the previous day's dirt, he thought about Mohammed and what steps may be needed to deal with this person who was now a liability to the organization. Until recently, Jaffar had been happy with the results Mohammed had obtained for him. He wondered what had happened.

An hour later, Abdul checked out of the hotel was and soon driving on Lake Tahoe Boulevard. A large green and white sign illuminated by his headlights read, 'Welcome to the State of Nevada'. More signs indicated that U.S. Route 395 was to the right and that Las Vegas was 445 miles ahead.

Abdul did a rough calculation. "My God that's still nine hours!" he said aloud. His frustration with Jaffar and the situation Jaffar had put him in grew and continued for the remainder of the trip. Ultimately, this wouldn't be good news for Mohammed.

It was mid-afternoon when Abdul met with Mohammed in the lobby of the MGM Grand. It was one of their usual meeting places.

"Good day Abdul. How are you?" Mohammed asked. Abdul thought the man looked thinner and it definitely seemed like a spark had left him. Abdul thought it must be because his brother had died.

"Better than you it would seem," Abdul said. "I heard about your accident from Jaffar. Not good! But on the plus side, it looks like you lost some weight."

"Yes! Almost sixty pounds. Shitty hospital food and medication, I couldn't keep food down for weeks. Plus … other things ..."

"I know, your brother. I understand he died."

"Yes! I'm still very upset about that." Mohammed shook his head sadly and for a second Abdul almost felt sorry for him.

Abruptly, Abdul said, "Well, enough about that for now, I guess. Let's get down to business." He wanted to change the subject. He could see the anguish on Mohammed's face—but more, he thought of the last conversation that he'd had with Jaffar. He could not afford to feel sympathy. "I was talking to some people in town and they expect Las Vegas to almost double in size over the next 15 years!" Abdul said. "Jaffar says there are investment opportunities and has asked me to look into them. He says his connections—very well-placed individuals—say real estate is going to go crazy, even more so than it has in the last ten years."

"But Abdul, Jaffar already has real estate all over Las Vegas."

"Yes, but that's land that's already been built on—motels, hotels. He's been talking about bare land for sale."

"But what good is bare desert land? Nevada has many miles of it."

"Yes, Mohammed. But Vegas is expanding. People are going to need somewhere to build houses and to live! I've been looking at maps and information that some of Jaffar's friends have provided and I was hoping you could guide me to some of these places and that together we can advise Jaffar which are the best to invest in. Jaffar said he sent you this information as well?"

"Yes, and I have been researching them. Do you want to look at them?"

"Yes, I certainly do."

"When?"

"Right now," Abdul said. "I'll drive."

With that, they walked out through the air-conditioned MGM Grand lobby and into the hot, dry air of the Nevada Desert. It was only the end of February, but the temperature was already edging towards the 90-degree mark. As Abdul drove northwest out of the downtown strip, away from the tall buildings of Las Vegas, he caught a glimpse of dark clouds approaching the city.

"Looks like we're in for a downpour if the color of those clouds are any indication!" Mohammed said. "Is this still a good idea, Abdul? Do you know what it's like when it rains in Vegas?"

"I'm sure it will be fine, that storm still a couple of hours away, by the looks of things."

They headed northwest, passing the occasional office building surrounded by homes, which soon thinned out to just homes. In turn this thinned out to just sand and scrub brush—desolate desert.

A short distance past the last house Mohammed instructed Abdul to pull over. "This is one of the areas you asked me to take you to," he said. A sign near them read, 'Land Assembly by the Cascadia Land Corporation', but Mohammed indicated a tract of land big enough to build ten thousand houses on the other side of the sign. All that was needed was an infusion of some capital to make it happen.

"It doesn't look like much, does it Mohammed?" Abdul mused.

"Maybe not, but you can see the houses have built out this way ... it's only about a half a mile from where the water and sewer systems end."

"About three quarters of a mile," Abdul said, not as a guess, but because he'd actually checked the odometer since passing the last house, "Too close ..."

"What was that?"

"I said it's too close to those houses over there!"

"But look at that sign," Mohammed said, indicating the Cascadia sign. "It seems to indicate that they intend to build."

"Yes, but is the price worth it here? Our friends at the Cascadia Land Corporation have already driven up the land costs. Jaffar would be better off building further out, don't you think?"

"Okay, I think I've just the spot. I took a look at it a couple of days ago," Mohammed said.

The two men got back into the car and headed northwest, but only for a couple of minutes this time. The car's tires made a couple of thumps as the wheels passed over a large concrete culvert, then Abdul pulled the car over to the shoulder and stopped. He opened the door, got out, and walked around the back of the vehicle to Mohammed's side, looking around to take in his surroundings as he did so.

Mohammed opened his door and heaved himself out of the car, glancing up at the darkening skies as he did so. "We'll have to make this quick," he said.

"Yes, we certainly will!" Abdul responded, reaching behind his back and under his suit jacket towards his belt. Mohammed looked down from the skies just in time to see Abdul's arm raise up in an arc in a deadly, practiced motion.

"What the hell ...?" Unfortunately for Abdul, Mohammed had lost 60 pounds and had gained some agility in the last few months so he managed to step back enough to cause Abdul to miss his stomach, the intended target. Instead Abdul struck a glancing slash to Mohammed's forearm and a thin line of red quickly appeared where steel met flesh. This grew and spread into a crimson patch on Mohammed's clothes.

"You fucking asshole!" Mohammed yelled, reaching toward Abdul's right arm as Abdul drew it back to strike again. His adrenaline rising, he grasped Abdul's right wrist with strength he didn't know he had. Abdul struggled to break free, but Mohammed tenaciously held on. For a few seconds there was a stalemate, until Abdul managed to get his left arm loose and brought his elbow up to strike Mohammed viciously under the chin.

The blow caused Mohammed's jaw to slam shut, his upper and lower teeth shredding his tongue, which resulted in a gush of red froth pouring from between his teeth. The blow caught Mohammed completely off-guard and the pain was almost more than he could bear, but somehow he managed to hold on to Abdul's knife hand.

The sight of his opponent's blood streaming down his chin and onto his shirt seemed to spur Abdul on. Neither were in top shape and both were perspiring heavily. Mohammed's new-found agility was offset by his lack of conditioning and Abdul was used to a life spent mostly indoors. Suddenly Mohammed weakened and Abdul's right hand slipped from his grasp. Abdul quickly brought his blade up, intending to end the struggle. He aimed for the bigger man's throat but wasn't quick enough; his hesitation gave Mohammed time to react and Abdul's thrust went wide and to the right. He quickly reversed, however, and the blade tore into Mohammed's right shoulder.

Mohammed screamed in pain, his body reeling backwards. He bounced off the car door, his left arm flailing outwards, trying to fend off his attacker. Abdul smiled as Mohammed fell partially onto the front seat of the car. In an instant, without hesitation, Abdul raised his weapon and with all his strength brought his knife down, plunging it into Mohammed's chest. Mohammed's left arm still stretched outwards, trying to claw at Abdul's face. Abdul withdrew his bloodied weapon and raised it up to strike a final blow. On the downward arc, the knife glanced off the roof and door trim, but ultimately ended up embedded to the hilt in Mohammed's chest, finally killing him.

His chest heaving with exertion, Abdul stood up and looked quickly up and down the road. He was relieved to see that there was no one in sight. He waited for a few seconds to catch his breath then placed the knife on the ground and grabbed Mohammed by the ankles to drag him from the car. The sand made his task easier and within two minutes Abdul had hidden

Mohammed's corpse in the bottom of the concrete culvert they had driven over a few minutes earlier.

Abdul's shirt was now soaked in sweat. If this attack had taken place six months earlier, perhaps the larger man might have prevailed. It is certain that Abdul would not have been able to drag him the full distance to the culvert.

Abdul cleaned his knife in the sand then got back into the car. The sky was filled from horizon to horizon with ominous black clouds. *Good the rain will wash away any evidence and the desert creatures will pick his bones clean.*

He started the engine, then looked at the passenger seat and was horrified to see the huge pool of hot, sticky blood soaking into the upholstery of the rental car.

"Shit!" He struggled out of his suit jacket and hastily spread it over the stain to hide it from prying eyes. Then he removed the knife's sheath he had been wearing, put the knife in it and put them both on the floor in front of the passenger seat. He punched the gas, spun the car 180 degrees and quickly started heading back towards the beckoning lights of Las Vegas, its towers gleaming in mirrored gold and silver offset by the reflection of those ominous, dark clouds.

As he passed over the culvert, he strained his neck to see if Mohammed's body was visible in the ditch. Satisfied that it could not be seen by a casual driver, he accelerated, leaving the concrete culvert and the small sign that said 'Cold Canyon Creek Wash' behind.

In a few minutes Abdul was once again on the outskirts of Las Vegas and he quickly found the road that would take him back to Route 395 and Sacramento. As he drove up the ramp that led northward on 395, he saw he was headed into what seemed like a black curtain of clouds. It seemed fitting. He felt like he was heading into darkness. Exhausted from his life-and-death struggle with Mohammed—and the endless driving he had been forced to do for his 'master' Jaffar—his mind raced. He felt dirty and he also felt vulnerable. He hadn't disliked Mohammed, in fact they had been quite friendly; but it bothered him how easily Jaffar had Mohammed dispatched. The fact that he was the one who dispatched him seemed less important.

However, he couldn't spend time worrying about that now. He had more serious problems—like what to do about the blood stained-seat, currently camouflaged by his jacket. And that's when every other concern faded as the enormity of what he had just done suddenly struck him. He had stabbed a man he liked to death just because he had been told to do so. As if in retribution, north of Las Vegas the ominous black clouds of two storm systems—separated by only twelve miles—grew in intensity as Abdul watched. Anywhere else in the world this would not be such a huge event, but in the desert the consequences of such rain were enormous. Not since the days of Christopher Columbus would two distinct storms have such an effect on this small area of the world. Between them, in just over an hour, the clouds would disgorge almost a foot and a half of rain, most of which would fall in just twenty minutes.

The rain began to pelt the windscreen and pound on the car in machine gun-like staccato. Abdul had never experienced rain like this. *This must be what a monsoon is like,* he thought. However, within ten minutes the rain began to let off and Abdul thought the worst was over. He began to relax slightly as he left Las Vegas farther and farther in his wake.

The concrete surface of the interstate, worn smooth from countless cars and trucks traveling over it, got very slippery when it rained. Abdul looked at the road ahead as the ribbon of concrete stretched undulated, twisted and turned on its way to Sacramento. He occasionally glanced to one side or the other, taking in the scenery—something he had not done during the trip southward. A sign appeared cautioning 'Slow to 30' and Abdul applied the brakes, slowing down the car as the highway disappeared to the right around a large boulder.

The boulder was the size of a small office building, positioned by some ancient geologic event millions of years earlier. Abdul could not help but stare out the right-hand window as he passed it; it dwarfed his car. He glanced in the rearview mirror to try to get one more glimpse of this monolith and when he looked forward again, he was shocked to see the large, rounded aluminum bulk of an Airstream travel trailer filling his windshield.

Mark Trenton had been travelling northbound moments earlier in his brand new Dodge pickup, with the equally new trailer in tow. The Airstream was much bigger than his last rig and he was unused to how it would behave on the road. He had started to brake to make the sharp bend in the road and the Airstream had not slowed as expected and had instead unexpectedly swung as if attempting to pass the pickup.

Mark released the brakes halfway through the curve and accelerated as much as he dared. The truck and trailer combination cooperated somewhat—the trailer slowing its outward movement—but as the soft gravel shoulder of the highway loomed closer, he once again applied the brakes. This time the brakes on the trailer locked up and it slid sideways, pulling the back end of the truck around as well.

At this point Mark was just along for the ride, as he lacked the real estate to correct the skid. The trailer slid through a 45 degree angle, then slowly continued through 90 degrees, dragging the truck with it. It was a miracle it didn't flip. Both vehicles came to a stop across one and half lanes of highway.

Abdul could see the gravel shoulder and the right side of the pickup, with the narrow strip of pavement in between. It was fortunate he was going less than the posted speed limit and had slowed down when he approached the curve. If he'd been going just one or two miles per hour faster, his slide would have carried him right into the pickup. He stopped with just inches to spare. Abdul got out of his car and walked over to the wide-eyed owner of the truck.

"What happened?"

"I guess it got away from me. Geez! That sure was close, mister!"

Abdul looked over at the narrow gap that separating the two vehicles. "I can see that," he said. Abdul could also see that he had no chance of maneuvering past the truck and trailer. Fortunately, traffic was light, but the rain continued to fall.

"Do you think you can give me a hand getting squared away?" the truck's owner asked.

"What do you mean? Squared?"

"I mean, can you help me straighten out my trailer? You know, direct me!"

"Of course I can. I will move my car out the way!"

"You should put a jacket on while you're at it!"

"That's alright. I'm wet already." Abdul got behind the wheel and put the idling Chrysler into reverse, glancing down at the leather sheath and knife as he did so. He stopped the car about fifty feet back and reached for knife—but this time only to slide it back out of sight under the seat.

He got into position behind the rig and after about five minutes of delicate back and forth maneuvering, Mark Trenton got the trailer back where it belonged and pointed in the right direction once again. "Thanks for your help, I appreciate it."

"You're welcome!" Shaken, Abdul got back into his car and headed north, towards Scotty's Junction. A few minutes later as his second adrenaline rush of the day started to leave his body, Abdul suddenly felt very tired. He realized that he should pull over to the side of the road and get some rest, but he wanted to put as many miles between himself and Las Vegas as possible, so he drove on.

Las Vegas, Nevada

Jim Filis had been working for Clark County Regional Flood Control District for nearly 30 years. It was early afternoon when the first call came in, bad weather was on the way. This was not a good thing for the newly formed office. Even a relatively small amount of rain could have a profound effect, turning the creeks around Las Vegas into raging torrents.

Jim had risen through government ranks, starting just out of high school as a laborer. He'd had enough seniority when the posting for Water Worker Level 1 came up on the board, that the job was his—and so was the $15.12 per hour that went with it.

The main, and easy, part of his job was to monitor and record numbers from the hundreds of rain and water level gauges in and around the city. Recording rain gauge information was simple; just record the amount of rain during a given time, empty the gauge and move on to the next one. The water level gauges were a different matter. These had alarms that would sound and in turn cause an indicator to light up on a wall map. These lights were normally green, but if the water level rose, the green light would change to amber and then finally to red.

It was a quarter after three and he was almost finished for the day when the first of many alarms sounded. He looked at the map in the control room to see a sea of bright green lights, condition normal. However, as the afternoon progressed the lights on the northern outskirts of Las Vegas started to turn amber and emit small beeping alarms, like an advancing army moving southward toward the city. Later he went out into the field and Jim was in the white Clark County pickup, looking up at the ominous clouds farther north, when the first alarm went off. He knew there would be more to come.

"Jim, here's the latest weather report from the meteorological service," said his colleague, Barb, over the radio. She was about to read it to him, but he interrupted her.

"Barb, you'd better call in the afternoon shift early. Judging by the sheets of rain coming out of the clouds in the north we're in for a huge dump of rain, and I don't need a weather report to know that!"

In five minutes Jim had turned off the pavement and onto the small gravel road that ran parallel to Sawmill Wash. He could see the remote water control station that sat on its typical wooden platform over a normally-dry creek bed. Today, however, the creek had become a fast-flowing river several feet wide and over two feet deep, moving perhaps five miles an hour over the gravel bottom.

Jim got out of his truck and walked over to the station. He lifted the wooden lid to expose the digital readouts. The dials and readouts at the station were usually zero but today the flow gauge was higher than he ever seen it, seven thousand, seven hundred and eighteen gallons per second.

"Holy shit!" he said. Then he recorded the figures, shut the lid and ran back towards the truck.

As he opened the door, got in and started the truck the rain started to hit the dry ground around him, leaving small craters in the earth as it did so. By the time he made a three-point turn and had headed back to the road, the pitter patter of the rain had turned into a metallic symphony. He called dispatch.

"Barb this is Jim. I'm at remote number 2303. I've got those numbers for you. The R.L.(river level) is twenty-four-point-three and the F.R.(flow rate) is seven-seven-one-eight!" The sound of the rain on the truck body was deafening.

"Did you say seven-seven-one-eight? I can hardly hear you!"

He shouted into the microphone to be heard. "Yes! That F.R. was seven-seven-one-eight!"

"Roger that!"

"Barb, I'm on my way to station 2327."

"Keep in touch!" The rain was starting to fall harder now. Barb pulled out her calculator and punched in the number. She could have simply referred to a chart, but she preferred to do it this way first, and have the chart as a check. The turquoise digits gave her an answer she didn't want to see.

"My god, that's over 27 million gallons per hour!" She picked up the phone to call her boss. He'd better call in all the help he could, even those on holiday if they could be reached. Her next call was to be Clark County Emergency Services office.

Remote station 2327 was almost ten miles from the one at Sawmill Wash. The rain continued to pour, but for the last half of the trip, it slackened enough so Jim could at least hear himself think. As he approached the Cold Canyon Creek Wash, he could see something was terribly wrong. The water in the creek was not flowing under the road through the culvert; instead it flowed over the road in a torrent almost 60 feet wide. He stopped the truck and radioed dispatch. The day was turning into a disaster, and it was only the beginning.

"Barb, this is Jim. I'm at Cold Creek!"

"Have you got those figures for me?"

"No! I'm unable to get close enough. God, Barb, you should see the road. The water is flowing right over it!"

"You should see the board! It's lit up just like Christmas! We've had over 50 alarms. They started just after your last call in. What was that, 15 minutes ago?"

"That's bad! But Barb you should see it out here, you should hear the rain."

"Jim, I'm sure it's bad. Sawmill Wash was over 27 million per hour. I had to shut the audible alarms off, they were driving me nuts!"

"Cold Creek must be double that easily. You'd better get the highways department out here. Tell them to hurry or there won't be a bridge left when they get here!"

"Roger that, Jim. Be careful!"

Jim grabbed his rain gear from behind the seat. He couldn't remember the last time he'd had to wear it. He put his emergency four-way blinkers on and switched on the amber, revolving roof-top light. He looked at it, satisfied that it would help slow traffic enough to keep them from winding up in the creek, then he walked cautiously to the edge of the raging torrent. He could see the reason why the water was flowing up and over the road: the ends of several logs protruded from the top of the water—no doubt part of the impromptu log-jam dam that had accumulated on the metal grating covering the end of the concrete culvert.

There was no way the water could get through; even without a log jam, there was only so much that could flow through the pipe and the volume was already many times that. The overflowing water was so intense, it was starting to peel away the pavement in large pieces. The foot-square pieces of blacktop rose up at an incline, broke off then disappeared into the torrent, exposing more and more of the vulnerable roadbed underneath.

Jim stood and watched in fascination for a moment and then turned his attention toward the remote stations. He had expected to see only pilings rising above the flood waters; instead he was surprised to see an intact station, the water barely lapping at its base. If he walked a bit to the right he was sure he'd be okay to get to the remote safely to take his readings.

He walked back the 50 yards to the truck and grabbed his book. He looked at his walkie-talkie for an instant and thought, *probably wouldn't work out this far,* then dismissed the idea of bringing it along. The shoulder strap was broken anyway, and he'd need both hands free to do his job.

A minute later, he lifted the lid on the wooden enclosure. He expected the reading to be high but never dreamed the digital readout would be '9999'. The designers of this flow meter did not add a fifth digit and the county engineers never imagined that one would be needed at this location.

Jim did the math. "Jesus! That's way over the flow at oh-three! Almost 35 million gallons per hour!" A large floating tree struck the pilings below him, sending a shudder through the structure. "Time to leave!" Jim said aloud. He closed the lid and was about to turn and step off the platform, when a six-foot slice of earth and sand disappeared from around the platform, mixing instantly with the sediment-laden waters. Between Jim and dry land was now a fast-flowing river of muddy, brown water, which was getting larger by the minute. Jim could feel the platform shake from the force of the fast-flowing current. He looked down at the timber planks on which he stood and was relieved to see heavy timbers lag-bolted together. It was as sturdy as it could be.

Suddenly, he heard a loud crack over the roaring water. "Shit! What was that?" Jim looked over his shoulder and caught a glimpse of a large branch of a mesquite moving past in the waves. He wished he'd brought his walkie-talkie; he wasn't sure if his perch would hold together, especially if it took many more hits like this last one.

Barb had been desperately trying to raise Jim on the two-way radio. She gave up after ten long minutes. She knew that the highways crew would be busy with washouts, they always were when the dry desert was inundated with water. She decided to give a friend in the office a call. Maybe they could send someone out Jim's way. She dialed the number from the list on the wall. "Hey, Tom! This is Barb over in Flood Control. I was wondering if you had a crew near Cold Canyon Creek?"

"Hi, Barb. As a matter of fact, we do. Why?"

Barb explained that Jim was out of contact. Tom replied, "We're stretched pretty thin as you can imagine, but I promise I'll get someone over there as soon as we can!"

"Thanks, Tom, I appreciate it, and I know Jim will too!"

Tonopah, Nevada

The sign indicated that Tonopah was five miles ahead; Abdul had been driving for more than twelve hours. He struggled to keep his eyes open. The illuminated sign ahead advertised that the Best Western Desert Inn was just ahead.

"That would be good!" he said to himself. He took the exit onto Main Street, the tall Best Western sign acting as a beacon. He grabbed his bag from the trunk and walked towards the motel.

Kelly Clayton had been working the afternoon shift with her boss. It had been a slow night and Kevin had gone for coffee—but that was over a half an hour ago. She glanced at the large clock on the wall to see how much longer she'd have to wait until it was her turn for coffee.

"Ten thirty-seven! Only an hour and a half to go!" she said aloud. Kelly went into the adjoining office and turned on the television. The volume was not too loud, but certainly loud enough to be heard in the quiet lobby area. The ten o'clock news was on.

"And here are scenes from around Las Vegas tonight where major flooding has caused widespread damage in all parts of northern Clark County," said the reporter. The screen filled with pictures and video clips from the flooded areas. Cars and trucks were drowned in the middle of what had once been roads, houses were completely surrounded by acres by water, their former occupants now standing on the roofs.

"We have dramatic footage from earlier today at Cold Canyon Creek, where our reporter Jennifer Thiebault, is standing by." The scene changed to a young female reporter clad from head to toe in bright yellow rain gear.

"Jen, can you tell us a bit about what happened at Cold Canyon Creek today? And maybe how you happened to catch this on tape?"

"Mark, as you can see it's still raining lightly here, but this is nothing compared to what it was like late this afternoon. That's when Las Vegas was surrounded on the north side by two incredibly large storm fronts. These brought torrential rains to much of the area, causing wide-spread damage ..."

Kelly looked at the clock again. No Kevin yet. She continued to watch the small portable television set. Jill carried on with her report. "As you can see the normally dry creek bed behind me is a raging river. That's where our story takes place. As you watch the video from earlier today, you can see how a Clark County regional flood control worker was rescued."

The video showed a group of highways personnel lowering a ladder across a water-filled creek bed, much like someone would lower a draw bridge over a moat. The trapped man then gingerly walked across the rungs of the ladder to safety. "Jill can you tell the viewers how you just happened to be there?"

"All afternoon we followed a highways crew as they went into the desert north of Las Vegas, looking for washouts or flooded roads. We stopped just a few feet back from one flood and as you can see in the video, water was literally flowing right over the bridge. We saw large chunks of the road just breaking off, to be carried downstream—and the roar of the river was almost as loud as a jet taking off!"

"Jill, can you tell us about how the worker came to be rescued?"

"Yes, Mark. The road was disappearing right before our eyes and all the highways crew could do was watch. But as the water cut a swath on either side of the bridge, it flowed freely and the noise from the river dropped significantly. That was enough that the crew could hear someone yelling in the background." The camera swiveled around to the right, away from the bridge. A hundred yards or so away, a lone figure waving his arms and yelling came into view.

Kelly was absorbed in the story when the lobby doors opened and Abdul walked in. She stepped up to the front desk and said, "Good evening, sir! Welcome to the Best Western! How can I help you?"

"I'd like a room, it's just for me." Abdul said, anticipating her next question.

"And that is the story from Cold Canyon Creek," the television said in the background. Abdul recognized the name as that of where he had been earlier today.

"What's the story about on the news?" he asked

"Oh that ... Some worker got caught in the flooding today and had to be rescued by the Highways Department. That will be $27 dollars please!"

"Of course." A much-relieved Abdul opened his wallet, withdrew three damp ten-dollar bills and handed them to Kelly.

"I just came from there!" he said.

"Where, sir?"

"Las Vegas!"

"Oh!" She placed the bills in the appropriate space in the cash drawer and counted out his change. "It's definitely wet there today." She smiled. "By the way, we have an in-house laundry service if you'd like."

"What?" Abdul looked the young lady and noticed she was looking at his still-damp and now wrinkled shirt and pants. "Oh, I had some car trouble in the rain!" he explained.

"I can send someone to get your clothes and have them cleaned and pressed for the morning."

"That would be good!"

"Here's your key. Room 205, last door down the hall on the left. I will send someone up in about ten minutes."

"Thank you!"

After a much-needed hot shower, Abdul sat on the edge of the bed. A young woman from the hotel laundry had already picked up his pants and shirt for cleaning. He opened his damp wallet, removed the card from the Sacramento Hyatt and tried to read the now-blurry number he'd written on the back, so he could telephone Jaffar.

"Damn!" he said, as he could not tell if the fourth digit was a five or a sloppy eight. In frustration he turned the card over and dialed the number for the front desk which was on the front.

Sacramento, California

Giti and Jaffar were enjoying a quiet meal at the Harvard Street Grill, trying to catch up on things. "I'm really glad you called back, finally!" Giti said with just a hint of sarcasm.

"I'm very sorry, I didn't get the message for over two months and did so only because of a chance phone call to someone. That person should have given me your message in December!"

"Or you could have taken a chance and called me …" Giti said softly.

"I'm so sorry, my dear," Jaffar said equally softly, then he put his hand on hers in an intimate gesture. "I would not hurt you for all the world!"

Giti immediately softened. "I'm glad you called. I did miss you!"

"That's good, isn't it?" Jaffar asked, playing at being puzzled.

"Yes, Jaffar, I suppose it is!" Giti laughed and the meal and the conversation instantly got lighter and more close. Then suddenly Giti looked at her watch and said mysteriously, "Oh my, look at the time, ten to eleven. Only an hour to go!"

Puzzled, Jaffar asked, "An hour to go until what? Midnight?"

"An hour to go until February 29th. You know what that means!"

Legitimately confused, he said, "No …What does February 29th mean?"

"Besides being a leap year, it's sort of an early Sadie Hawkins Day," said Giti.

"Whose day?"

"You know. Li'l Abner, Sadie Hawkins?"

"No, I don't know. I do know what a leap year is, but I have no idea of who this Sadie Hawkins is!"

"February 29th is the day Sadie Hawkins chased after the town's most eligible bachelors to ask them to marry her. She was called the 'the homeliest gal in all them hills' by her dad, so he decreed that the day was Sadie Hawkins Day and assembled all the bachelors so she could chase, catch and marry one. It's a comic strip, but the idea took off."

"So, tomorrow is Sadie Hawkins Day?"

"No, that's not until November, the middle of November I think. But the tradition says that tomorrow a woman may ask a man to marry her."

"So, do you think you'll ask someone?"

"If I knew you better, I might!" Giti said to Jaffar's surprise.

"If I knew you better I'd say 'yes'," Jaffar replied. They stared at one another, each wanting to say something, but not knowing what. They were so engrossed by the moment that they failed to notice the waiter standing a few feet away. The rest of the room had momentarily faded from existence.

The waiter broke their bubble. "Excuse me Sir, but I have an urgent call for you!" He placed a new, state-of-the-art cordless phone receiver on the side of the table.

"It may have better reception if you come to the front desk to stand by the base," the waiter said.

"I'll try it here," Jaffar said. "Thanks." Then, "This is Jaffar," he said into the phone.

"It's Abdul. Mission accomplished," Abdul said discreetly.

"Oh! That's not good. I'm at dinner right now. Can we talk more in the morning, or when you get back?" After a pause, "Thank you for telling me."

"What's wrong, Jaffar?" Giti asked.

"That was Abdul. He had some disturbing news about an old friend. It seems he passed away earlier today!"

"Oh, I'm sorry to hear that!"

"It's quite alright, we had not been close for a great many years," he said. And that was as close to the truth as he could get. Giti was too smart. She would know it was more than that. Quickly, he changed the subject. "Anyway, what were we talking about? Something about Sadie Hawkins Day?"

"Oh yes, but now doesn't seem like the time to talk about such things." Giti's eyes softened a bit as she thought of Reza. She still had to wrestle with her emotions; part of her refused to let go.

"What about some dessert?" Jaffar suggested.

"Yes, Jaffar, that would be very nice. Let's ask the waiter for a dessert menu." A few minutes later the waiter returned to take their order.

"I can't decide! Why don't you order for me, Jaffar?"

"I'm a bit on the undecided side myself!"

"If I could make a suggestion, sir?" the waiter asked. "There's one thing not on our menu at this time and we only offer to special guests—it's a chocolate strawberry cheesecake. It's new here at the Hyatt."

"That sounds very good. We'll each have a serving!"

"An excellent choice," said the waiter.

He returned within minutes carrying two huge, brown, triangular wedges smothered with strawberry glaze. It's always remarkable to see how a sweet dessert has a soothing effect on people. Giti and Jaffar were no different; at almost the same instant they said to each other, "This is delicious!"

Giti laughed and relaxed somewhat. Then, mindful of the time, she said, "I have to get going soon. It's after eleven and Zafar and Fatemah are looking after Sina."

"As you wish," Jaffar replied.

Jaffar signed the bill the waiter presented then got up and helped Giti into her coat. "Do you want a taxi? I don't want you to drive all the way home at this hour."

"That would be good, thanks," Giti said. "I don't like to drive after I've had wine."

They walked to the front desk to have the concierge call a taxi for Giti.

"Can I see you tomorrow?" Jaffar asked.

"You have to—after all, I've got to come back and get my car. Luckily I'm only working half a day."

The taxi arrived outside the lobby of the Hyatt. Giti and Jaffar said their goodbyes and as Jaffar stopped and looked down at her, Giti moved closer and kissed him softly on the lips.

"Thanks for wonderful evening Jaffar!"

"It was my pleasure Giti. Good night."

"Good night Jaffar!" Giti stepped into the waiting cab and was gone.

— Chapter 7 —

Las Vegas, Nevada - February 29, 1980

Jack looked at his calendar, which was hanging on the wall next to refrigerator. This was an important calendar; not only did it feature a fine selection of pictures of Camaros posed with scantily clad women, but it was also where he penciled in appointments with clients, hours worked and places he was supposed to be. Essentially the calendar was Jack's appointment book. He'd be lost without it.

He noticed it was Sadie Hawkins Day. Sadie Hawkins Day was when the girls got to ask the guys to the dance, or—for those who took stock in such things—the day when a woman could ask a man to marry her. He wondered why he remembered that. *It was those damned school dances*, he thought, *the ones Donny always teases me about. We had a Sadie Hawkins Day dance in grade eight.* He smiled at the memory. A girl whose actual name was Sadie asked him to go to the dance with her at the last minute. He'd been so relieved. Don had had multiple offers of course. He was flypaper to women.

I don't think I have to worry about any woman asking me to marry her any time soon, Jack thought. But he couldn't help it when his thoughts turned to Giti Roshtti. *Yup, that would be okay.* "Get your mind off her, you idiot!" he said out loud. Then he laughed out loud at his thoughts and laughed even louder when he thought what Donny would say if he were here with him right now.

Looking over his calendar, he realized that it was the day he'd promised Ken Nichols that he'd call. Ken had been a good source of income for Jack over the last few months. The work was a bit spottier than Jack liked, but the pay was good as it unofficially put him on the Las Vegas city payroll.

He'd also written a note to himself to touch base with Donny to find out if he had any new information regarding Jaffar or the people he associated with. So far Jack had hit a dry well, except for the journal and ledger he and Donny had found in Mohammed's apartment. He picked up the phone and called Nichols.

"Captain Ken Nichols, please," he said. It was time to get his head back in the game.

Sacramento, California

In spite of working a full day and getting home well after midnight, Giti still found it difficult to fall asleep. She wondered if it was always going to be this way as far as Jaffar was concerned! He excited her, he made her feel feminine and alive. She replayed the events of the day over and over in her head, from the moment she left work until the taxi ride home until finally she fell asleep.

Morning came all too soon. She had hoped to sleep in a little, but was up at her usual five-thirty wakeup time and though she tried to be quiet, her activities in the kitchen woke one other person.

"Good morning Giti," yawned Fatemah. "How was your dinner date?" she asked in a whisper as she reached into the cupboard for a cup. Fatemah and Zafar had spent the night in the guest room, as that was easier for getting Sina to school in the morning.

"Oh, good morning, Fatemah. I'm sorry I woke you."

"You didn't … and you didn't answer my question, either."

"It was good! Thanks for looking after Sina for me. Did he behave?"

"He's always an angel. He gets along so well with Zafar! You know we're happy to do it anytime Giti. Now tell me about dinner! What do you mean dinner was 'good'?"

"Oh, dinner was okay!" Giti looked a little uncertain and Fatemah seized on it.

"I sense a big 'but' in there! What's wrong?" Fatemah could see the same questions, and hear the familiar hesitation in Giti's voice.

"Oh, it's nothing!" Giti continued, "Jaffar got a call from someone about a friend of his passing away yesterday."

"That's too bad. I guess it put a bad light on the rest of the evening?" Fatemah asked sympathetically.

"You mean did it put a damper on it? Yes, in a way it did."

"Look Giti, I know you still think about Reza. We all do, but as I told you before Christmas, it's time to move on. Reza would want you to! Please believe me Giti, the last person that Reza would want to be unhappy is you!"

Giti knew everything Fatemah said was true. She'd known it deep down for many months, but still she was cautious. She decided to stick to lighter thoughts. It was too early in the morning to discuss her lost love.

"You know, last night Jaffar and I talked about Sadie Hawkins Day."

"What is that, some kind of holiday?"

"No!" Giti laughed and once again gave an explanation about the L'il Abner cartoon.

"It's February 29th today! Maybe you should call him!"

"I already told him I would. I've got to go back to his hotel and get my car!"

"I can give you a ride to get your car, that way we can ride together to work, if you like."

"That would be great, but what about Sina?"

"Missing one day of school won't matter. I'm sure Zafar will be glad to have him for a couple of hours then bring him to work. The last time Sina came in with Zafar, he rode around on the forklift for hours. Zafar even let Sina work the controls!"

"I remember! Sina loved that, he talked about it for days," Giti said thoughtfully. She smiled.

"If I recall, didn't you tell me that Sina wanted to be a forklift driver!"

"Yes! That's what he said," Giti said.

"Well then?" Fatemah asked, raising one eyebrow at Giti.

Giti laughed. "Okay, you win," she said.

Fatemah drove the two of them to work and all morning Giti kept looking at the clock, wishing time would move more quickly. Her morning had been busy, but was broken into short intervals by Sina who once again got to ride the forklift in the warehouse and to work the controls. When Zafar came out of the warehouse and into the office, Sina would run in behind him, say a quick hello to his mother and sit at the desk with the electric adding machine and its seemingly endless roll of white tape. That desk belonged to his Aunt Fatemah, who came into the office to find that sales under Sina's watch had been $57,182,628.03!

Except for the frequent interruptions from Sina, the rest of the morning was uneventful for Giti—but for Sina, it was great fun. Zafar put Sina on his lap and they cruised the aisles of the warehouse, Sina taking great pleasure in leaning over and repeatedly sounding the small horn in the center of the steering wheel. Warehouse staff chuckled every time Zafar and Sina came near, the sound of the Road Runner's beep-beep reverberating in their wake.

Just before lunchtime, Giti tidied up her desk, picked up her purse and went out to find her son. He had found a pile of empty cardboard tubes and was wielding one like a light saber, pretending to be Darth Vader. As Giti approached she could hear him trying to mimic James Earl Jones, but all that came out was a croaky, "Luke! I am your father!"

"Sina, I have a lunch date and you are to stay here. I want you to be good boy for Fatemah and Zafar."

"I will, I promise!"

"Thank you, Sina. I'll see you tomorrow because hopefully you'll already be in bed and fast asleep by the time I get home. But I'll come and give you kiss on the cheek!" Giti gave Sina a big hug and then stood up to head outside.

"Okay, mom!" Sina said. Then he returned to fighting the enemy with his cardboard light saber.

The Sacramento Hyatt was short taxi ride from her work and Giti arrived just before one o'clock. She walked into the lobby and directly up to the front desk to have Jaffar paged to come down and meet her, but was interrupted halfway.

"Giti, I'm over here!" Giti turned around to see Jaffar with an almost ear-to-ear smile on his face.

"Oh, there you are!" Giti returned the smile and walked over to him.

"So what do you want to do? It's a beautiful, sunny day … perhaps we can take in the sights?"

"What do you have in mind, Jaffar?"

"Well, I talked to that young lady over there … I think her name is Bridgitte …?" Jaffar paused, a quizzical look on his face as he tried to recall, then he continued, "She suggested we take a walk over to the State Capital building or maybe see the Crocker Museum."

"Both sound good! I've never been to the Crocker Museum."

"Then, it's settled," Jaffar said extending his arm gallantly as he pointed toward the sliding door. "After you!"

The museum was only a short walk from the Hyatt and both Giti and Jaffar were pleased to find that one of the major exhibits was a collection of small, delicate paintings from Persia and China.

"This is a good sign, something from our own part of the world!" Jaffar said.

"Yes, my great-grandparents were from Persia, when it was part of the Ottoman Empire. But didn't you say you were from Saudi Arabia?" asked Giti.

"No, my parents were from Saudi Arabia, I'm from Britain," Jaffar said. But the he did add, "That makes me both British and Saudi, doesn't it?"

"I suppose it does," Giti replied. Then she heard her stomach rumble and she said, "Jaffar, would you mind if we got a quick bite to eat? I didn't have time to make my lunch this morning."

"Of course I don't mind. Perhaps I was the cause? I'm sorry for keeping you out so late, Giti."

"Don't be silly. I had a very nice time." Giti reached out her hand to his. "Thank you, Jaffar!" Her hand stayed, lightly holding Jaffar's.

"There's a sandwich shop just back there. Would that do?"

"That would be fine Jaffar. Maybe I'll just get a BLT."

Jaffar looked puzzled for moment, until Giti added, "You know—a bacon, lettuce and tomato sandwich?"

"Oh yes of course. That sounds like a winner … although I am Muslim and don't eat pork."

"Would it offend you if I did?" Giti asked.

"Of course not," said Jaffar.

Twenty minutes later they sat around a large, round, white patio table enjoying their sandwiches. Jaffar had substituted chicken for bacon and seemed to be enjoying his sandwich. Giti smiled at him.

"I always have a good time with you Jaffar!"

"Do you, Giti? That's nice to hear. I enjoy your company very much as well." He reached across the table with his left hand and was rewarded with a gentle squeeze from Giti.

"Shall we be off then? If we stay here any longer the museum will be closed!"

In the cavernous halls of the Crocker Gallery, the words of the tour guide echoed and reverberated off the walls. Janet O'Keefe had to speak loudly so that everyone in her group could hear. All day she had been shouting to be heard over a bus-load of third-graders who had invaded the normally quiet halls. She and everyone else in the group were relieved when the kids left to discover the newly-opened space exhibit in another wing.

"As I said before, the Crocker Museum is one of the oldest museums in the west, founded in 1895. But it isn't as old as that collection of dolls and paintings you just saw."

Janet and her charges headed away from the Persian exhibit just as Giti and Jaffar entered the wing housing the William and Edith Cleary Collection. The two walked hand in hand across the polished marble floor looking at showcases jammed full of hundreds of small porcelain figurines, all hand-painted. Then something caught Giti's eye. "Oh look, Jaffar, aren't these beautiful?" Giti stopped to closely examine some small, oriental paintings.

"Yes, they certainly are. But nowhere near as beautiful as you!" He put his arm around Giti's waist and gently pulled her toward him. Giti looked up at Jaffar; she'd been half-expecting this. She smiled as Jaffar bent toward her and kissed her softly on the mouth. She closed her eyes and moved closer to him. It had been a long time since she'd had such a connection with a man. She still didn't trust her feelings; maybe she felt this way because it had been so long … but perhaps it was something more.

The bliss was broken by several high-pitched giggles nearby. Jaffar and Giti opened their eyes to find four young pairs of eyes staring at them. The four girls in school uniforms had walked up to them in utter silence. This was not the case after they were discovered kissing; the girls made off in a mad dash, running and laughing as they went. "I wonder how long they were standing there?" Giti laughed.

Tonopah, Nevada

For someone who had committed murder less than 24 hours earlier, Abdul slept very well. He had a long, hot shower then called down to the front desk to get his clothes sent up to his room. Within minutes a young valet was at the door with Abdul's pants and shirt, cleaned, pressed and looking new again. He handed the young man a dollar bill; tipping was something he'd learned while traveling.

"Thank you, sir," said the valet.

Abdul shut the door. It was still a bit early to eat and he was anxious to get back on the road. Then he realized that stomach was growling, but he knew that he could not stomach a fried American breakfast. *I could have some of those pancakes, with syrup. That would be good.*

Just before heading out the door, Abdul looked around the room for his suit jacket, but it was nowhere to be found. Suddenly he remembered where his jacket was, and why it was there. Abdul walked down the hall. At the front desk he turned in his key and paid the outstanding bill for the laundering of his clothes.

"Thank you for staying at the Best Western," said the clerk.

Abdul nodded and smiled at the girl and then turned towards the front door of the lobby, purposely avoiding the restaurant. Thinking about his jacket had made him suddenly less hungry. He loaded his car and started driving. As he passed through downtown Tonopah on the way to Route 6, which would take him back to Sacramento, without warning a cat ran across the road in front of his car, pursued by a large blonde-and-black German Shepherd.

Abdul slammed on the brakes, just missing the dog's hindquarters. When stopped, he looked around to see where the dog had gone. If this was Al-Qa'im, he'd find the dog by whatever means necessary, shoot the mongrel with his pistol and have the dog's owners fined, jailed and probably shot! *Stupid animal, it's lucky I didn't run it over*, he thought. Then it occurred to him … this was the answer to his problem! *Yes! That will work!* If he said the blood on the seat of the car was animal blood, the rental company would clean it up and no one would be the wiser!

Suddenly he was hungry again, starving in fact. He stopped at the first roadside diner he could find and ordered the 'hungry man's breakfast' with three eggs, three beef sausages and three buttermilk pancakes as well as toast and coffee. He ate it all.

The nasty business with Mohammed behind him, Abdul started to feel good about most things. He had another 370 miles of driving to do, but even that didn't seem so bad now. He looked at his watch. If he left now he could be in Sacramento in about seven hours, about two o'clock. He stopped at a payphone to call Jaffar. The front desk put him through to Jaffar's room.

"Hello, this is Jaffar."

"Jaffar, this is Abdul. I'm phoning about that business from last night."

"I don't want to discuss that right now. I've got other things on my mind." Not only was Jaffar concerned about potential eavesdroppers, but he had been looking forward to another afternoon with Giti and had been expecting her to call. He thought it was Giti on the phone and was disappointed to hear Abdul's voice instead. But he did ask, "Were there any problems?"

"Yes and no!" said Abdul.

"What does that mean? Explain it to me in … uh, layman's terms."

Abdul understood and explained, "The transaction took place, but I've got problems with the car. I think I know what the problem is."

"Do you think you should take it back to the dealer?"

"Oh yes, right away! I'll probably take it to the one next to the airport!"

Jaffar understood that it was Abdul's intention to catch a plane back home as soon as he returned the rental car. Abdul seemed to have it all under control. If anyone had been listening they'd be none the wiser.

"Okay. I'll call you later," said Jaffar and he hung up the phone.

Just after two o'clock that afternoon, Abdul pulled into the Hertz Rent-a-Car location, adjacent to the airport. He got out and walked up to the front desk, where an attractive woman employee stood.

"Hello, sir, my name is Penelope. How may I help you?"

"I'd like to return a car, but I've had a small accident with it." Abdul handed her his rental agreement.

"Oh, I'm sorry to hear that. Let me just call my supervisor and we can assess the damage." Miss Penelope Davis reached for the claim forms she thought she'd need and then picked up the phone to call Greg, her supervisor. He joined them almost immediately.

"Is there much damage?" Greg asked Abdul, expecting the worst. People always said their accidents were small.

"I don't know. I don't remember seeing any. I hit a dog."

"Oh, that's different. I thought you'd had a collision with another vehicle. Let's go take a look!"

"Yes of course. It's parked right outside."

Abdul and Greg went out to look at the rental car. Greg still expected to see some damage in spite of what Abdul said, but except for a couple of small rock chips and a thin layer of road dirt, the front of the car was unmarked.

"I thought you said you'd hit a dog?"

"I did, but what I have a problem with is the front seat. You see I removed my jacket to put around the poor animal and then placed it in the car. It was hurt very badly and I'm afraid some blood soaked through and got on the seat."

"It sounds like you're an animal lover!'

"I tried to help. I drove it to the hospital."

"You mean the vet's?"

"Yes, that's right, the vet's!"

"Well, sir, I think we can take care of this. Let's go back inside and finish up the paperwork." Greg walked back inside, without even looking at the blood stain on the front seat.

"You understand that there will be an extra charge for us to shampoo the seat? It's $19.95 I think. Can I just add that to the bill?"

"Of, course!"

"That comes to a total of $109.04 for the car rental, plus the shampoo and of course all the applicable taxes for Uncle Sam."

"Who?" Then after a short pause, "Oh yes."

"How do you wish to pay?"

"Put it on my Visa card." Abdul reached for his wallet. It wasn't there. "I think I've left my wallet in my bag. I have to get it from the car. Just one moment."

Abdul hurried out to the car. He opened the trunk to retrieve his bag and on his way back he grabbed his jacket from the front seat, exposing the congealed and drying blood stain.

"Here you go!" Abdul handed over his Visa card then signed the bottom of the bill, as well as the Chargex slip.

"Thank you, sir. And thanks for choosing Hertz!" Abdul walked out the front door, past a smiling, life-sized cardboard cutout of O.J. Simpson.

"Excellent," Abdul said aloud as walked off the lot, across the street and into the Sacramento International terminal to catch a flight home. By four o'clock he was five thousand feet over the Rocky Mountains on his way to Montreal, and then home.

Car detailer Bob Williams opened the door and got into the driver's seat of the recently returned Chrysler. "What the hell?" he exclaimed. The passenger seat was stained beyond repair. This was a seat replacement, not a cleaning job!

Flipping through the work order he read, 'fill with gas', and the box beside 'shampoo interior' was also checked off. "This is utter bullshit," he said as he went inside to see his boss.

"Greg! That gold Chrysler out front that just came back and … well... I think you should see this for yourself."

"What's the problem, Bob? I thought the work order was pretty clear."

"Greg, believe me. You've got to see this for yourself!" They walked over to the car and Bob opened the door.

"What the hell?" Greg said.

"That looks like some serious blood," said Bob.

"It is! The guy said he hit a dog, a German Shepherd. He said he took it to the animal hospital and it bled all over the seat!" Greg bent down to examine the front of the car.

"Something's not right here, Bob. There's not a dent or a scratch. I don't know about you but I'm pretty sure that a dog, even a Chihuahua, would make a dent. Besides, I can't see any hair or anything else here. Just dirt and bugs!"

Bob knelt down beside the passenger side to see just how much blood he could find there. He was reaching out to touch it with his finger when Greg said, "Don't touch that! I'm going to call the cops."

"Hey man, I was just going to see if it was, you know, dry!"

"That's creepy!" Greg went inside his office, looked up the number and phoned the local precinct.

"Hello, Twelfth Precinct."

"Yes. This is Greg Johnson over at Hertz Rent-a-Car at Sacramento International. I've just had a car returned to us by a customer and there's some blood on the front seat."

"Are we talking about a lot of blood? Did your customer have an explanation for it?"

"He said he hit a dog and took it to the vet's."

"Well there you go!"

"Aren't you going to send anyone out? It looks like a lot more blood than would come out of an injured dog. I think someone should check this out."

Oh brother, Sergeant Morton, the officer on front desk duty thought to himself. He said, "Look if it will make you feel better, I'll send someone to look into it."

"When?"

"Probably not until tomorrow."

"What do you mean? Shouldn't you send someone out today?"

"Look, sir! All our investigators are working cases right now. Besides, there have been no reports of homicides in over a week and no missing person reports either. Can you just hang tight until morning?" Frustrated, he was about to hang up but added, "But don't touch or move the car until then!"

"Okay, I won't. Thanks!"

The Crocker Gallery

Giti and Jaffar explored the entire east wing of the museum together. Giti noticed a certain lightness to her step when she was in his company. And the time just flew. As they neared the end of the exhibit, she said, "You know, Jaffar I think we've looked at almost every piece in the collection.

"I'm sure we did," he agreed as the noticed one of the museum staff walking toward them.

"Excuse me," said a uniformed woman, "I thought I'd let you know that the museum is closing in ten minutes." She walked away.

Giti looked at her watch, absolutely certain the girl was mistaken; it had to be much earlier! "Oh my. How did it get so late?" she asked.

"Time flies when you're having fun," Jaffar said. "Are you having fun, Giti?"

"Yes, I am."

"Do you want to walk around and look at something else? We've got ten minutes, after all." They both laughed.

"We could walk around outside for a while. Maybe we could walk past the Capitol buildings? It's a gorgeous day."

"Let's do that," Jaffar said. They walked down the front steps of the museum and headed east, back towards the Hyatt. Some of the stores were closing for the day, their owners locking the doors, their interiors now dark. Giti browsed in some of the ones that remained open, looking through the occasional rack of dresses that caught her eye.

"Women are the same all over the world, Giti," said Jaffar as he watched her touch and assess the clothing.

"What do you mean?"

"I just meant that no matter where in the world you go, women have this fascination with clothes. Even if they have closets full of them!"

"We have to look good. Are you bored, Jaffar?"

"You do look good. And I'd like to add that I haven't been bored since I met you."

"Neither have I!" They walked down the street until they came across a small café at Ninth Street. Several tables had been set up along the sidewalk, occupied by patrons enjoying the warm afternoon.

"Let's stop Jaffar."

"That sounds good!" They sat down. The waitress promptly placed menus on the table and took their beverage order. "Are you sure you don't want something to eat?" he asked Giti when she shook her head at the waitress's request.

"No, I'm fine Jaffar, just coffee for now. Right now I need to rest these poor feet, I feel like I've been walking for hours!"

"We have!"

"Yes, I guess we have." The waitress brought them their drinks and they sat sipping coffee, in the warm, late-winter California sun.

"You know Giti, I've been waiting all day for you to ask me," Jaffar said as he got up and reached into his jacket pocket. He pulled out a small silver box and turned it around so Giti could see the contents. "Isn't Sadie Hawkins supposed to ask me something? I've been waiting all day so now it's my turn. Will you marry me?"

Flustered, Giti could only respond, "You have to do it properly, you know down on one knee." He did so.

"Will you marry me, Giti Roshtti?"

She felt her mouth go dry. Deep inside, part of her still resisted, but yet she said, "Yes, Jaffar. I will!"

He placed the ring on her finger. It was a beautiful, pear-shaped diamond, almost two full carats in size. They stood, embraced one another and kissed. For the second time that afternoon they had an audience. The other patrons at Café de Soliel applauded. Giti looked down at her new engagement ring. She couldn't remember seeing such a large diamond, except maybe on a movie star like Liz Taylor.

Giti stretched out her hand, admiring the prismatic effect of the sunlight through the fifty-seven different facets. "Where did you get such a lovely ring, Jaffar?"

"I picked it out this morning—as a matter of fact you almost caught me! I bought it from the jeweler in the hotel and I'd only sat down in lobby for minute or two when you came in. If you'd been earlier, you would have seen me in the shop!"

"You're not hiding any more secrets from me are you, Jaffar?" Giti asked with a smile.

"No! Nothing at all! Do you feel like celebrating by perhaps getting some dinner?"

"Yes that would be wonderful, but I didn't bring anything to wear! These are my work clothes," she said, indicating her attire.

"You look fine! But if you want I can buy you a dress and perhaps some different shoes?"

"Most of the stores are closed now. Besides, I remember your earlier remark about all women around the world being the same!"

"We can make it a casual dinner, nothing fancy. Whatever you want."

"I think I'm fine with casual. Besides I can't be late tonight. I promised Sina I would come in and give him a kiss good night. Oh my!"

"What's wrong?"

"Nothing, Jaffar. I just thought of Sina. I think I should wait for a while before I tell him the news. I've only just talked to him about me possibly *dating* … it's a bit too early to drop a bombshell like this!"

"Oh yes, by all means," Jaffar said, a look of concern on his face.

"Don't worry Jaffar, Sina's wise beyond his years. He actually came to me and told me it was okay to start dating!"

"I like him already."

Giti and Jaffar had a relaxing dinner on the patio of Jaffar's 15th-floor hotel suite. The view of downtown Sacramento was great, the office towers spread out below them and the dome and landscaped grounds of the State Capital awash in the glow of millions of watts of electricity. Giti was impressed.

"Do you rent this suite Jaffar? You're very lucky to have a view such as this."

"Yes! I rent it, but only by the day!" Jaffar laughed. "I guess I should think about finding more permanent accommodations! I can afford to buy something."

"Maybe a condominium, something with a view."

"Yes, something like this! That would be good!"

Later that evening, Jaffar stood alone on the balcony, looking out over the city. Giti had gone home and he was left alone to consider the course today had put him on. He pondered for a few minutes about what it would mean to have an American wife, as he'd done many times in the last few months. In terms of furthering his business interests, she was a great choice. He could easily start organizing Hamas militants on American soil ... or he could easily disassociate from the movement as well. Having Giti in his life gave him some great choices.

As a wife, she was beautiful and he couldn't wait to touch her. But she had a son, so he would never be first in her life. He would have to accept that. And would she obey him? She was Persian, but she was American-born. She might be a disobedient wife. Could he live with that?

He stepped back inside and closed the sliding door. He sat on the sofa but was restless. He turned on the television to catch the late news, something that he hadn't done in several days. The stories were all about the floods in Las Vegas.

"Yesterday we brought you the story of a dramatic rescue of a county employee from a rain-swollen creek, north of Las Vegas," announced the news anchor. "But it turns out that his rescue was only beginning of our story." The screen flashed to a young, female reporter who stood beside a large culvert where men and equipment were working. Strangely, police had cordoned it off. "What new developments do you have to report Jill?"

"Well, Tom, it's been more than 24 hours since two massive storms passed through the Las Vegas area and dropped record amounts of water on us. Water levels have dropped dramatically since then and the wash where that rescue took place yesterday is a completely different place today. The logs and debris that blocked water from flowing freely have been removed.

Yesterday, it had been flowing up and over the road." She indicated how far it had flowed with her arm.

"Yes Jill, we all saw the frightening video from last evening," the anchor commented.

"Well, Tom, today the water level dropped enough for work crews to safely clear away the debris and start repairing the road. They used a large bucket, much like a claw, to remove the debris and with its final load the body of an unidentified male was excavated."

"Has the man been identified? Has the cause of death been determined?"

"Not as yet. The police haven't been able to identify the body. They are asking for the public's help identifying this individual."

A small black and white photograph was inset into one corner of the screen. Jaffar immediately recognized the swollen, misshapen face of Mohammed.

"As for the cause of death, police are only saying the death is being treated as suspicious."

Jaffar watched the television for a while longer, but there was no more news about Mohammed's death. That was good news for him and even better news for Abdul. *There is no way for the police to link the two of us to the crime*, Jaffar thought to himself.

Then he yawned and stretched. It was time to end this most eventful of days. As he lay in bed he wondered what it would be like to have Giti's soft body lying next to his.

March 1, 1980

Jack did not have the most restful sleep. The air conditioning in the RV was on the fritz, and Las Vegas was in the middle of a mini off-season heat wave. He tossed and turned, his discomfort coupled with his inability to shut down his thoughts.

His mind kept returning to the face of Giti Roshtti, but for some unknown reason, his subconscious mind instantly switched its focus to Jaffar Harraj. Jack was sure that he'd seen his face, somewhere in the past. But where?

Disgruntled with lack of sleep, he climbed out of bed at around five o'clock. Soon he had coffee brewing, and three eggs on the boil. *I might as well wake up and get on with it,* he thought. He put two slices of bread into the toaster, and moved the lever to the on position then sliced up some bananas, for one of his favourite treats, 'smashed bananas on toast'.

He decided to give Don a call, and he picked up the phone and dialed, holding the receiver under the side of his head as he finished preparing his breakfast.

"Good morning Don," Jack said when Don answered.

"You're up early," Don commented. "It must be about five in the morning on the west coast!"

"Couldn't sleep," Jack said, "so I'm up and making breakfast. Wish you were here to eat me out of house and home."

Don laughed. "I had mine, courtesy of the Washington Grill ... the Lumberjack special!"

"Wouldn't want you to see you waste away! Christ, Don, you're going to have to stop eating like a horse."

" My metabolism can handle it. Besides I wouldn't want to be a skinny-ass like you!" Don joked.

"If I was in a better mood, I'd tell you to go pound sand, but right now I'm not in a good mood, so don't fucking bug me about my weight," Jack shot back, only half-joking.

"What's wrong?"

"I didn't sleep a whole lot. Too fucking hot here last night."

"Are you still pining away for that Giti woman?" teased Don.

"That's it," Jack deadpanned. "Donny, you're a genius."

"I always knew that."

"Okay, asshole. All kidding aside, I just remembered where I've seen that Jaffar guy before."

"Where?"

"Three or four years ago, a Middle Eastern flight blew up over Saudi Arabia. They never found the perpetrators, but they had a short list of suspects. They showed some pictures on the news!"

"I remember that," Donny said.

"I'm sure one of them was Jaffar," Jack added, "He was thinner and younger and had a scruffy looking beard, but I'm almost certain one of the pictures was him."

"I'll ask Kip!"

"Okay Don. We'll talk later." Jack hung up the phone, excited but concerned at the same time. If what he suspected was true, Jack had unknowingly introduced a terrorist to Giti Roshtti.

Later that day, Jack sat at the desk in the local library. Using micro-fiche was making him dizzy, but he was stubborn and refused to quit. Finally, after lunch had come and gone, Jack came across an article on the front page of the Las Vegas Sun, dated January 2, 1976. The article read ...

(Reuters) - Middle East Airlines Flight 438, a Boeing 720B, call sign CEDAR JET 438, was en route from Beirut, Lebanon to Abu Dhabi yesterday, when a bomb exploded in the forward cargo compartment. The aircraft broke up at an altitude of 37,100 feet and crashed, 23 miles northwest of Al Qaysumah, Saudi Arabia, killing all of its 81 passengers and crew. No one has taken credit for the bombing, but the group Islamic Hamas is rumored to be responsible, after making threats to do this very thing, just last week.

Below the article were several uncaptioned black and white photographs, one of which was a younger Jaffar Hamid Harraj.

"What have you done?" Jack asked himself as he thought of Giti Roshtti.

Sacramento, California

Inspectors Sam Jeffries and Ben Johnson were at the Hertz rental outlet just before nine o'clock in the morning. Greg Johnson led them to the gold Chrysler.

"Have you touched anything in the car?" asked Jeffries.

"Just the door handle and the steering wheel. I'm sorry! We didn't know how much blood there was until just before I called you."

"That's okay. We'll get to work and see what we can find. We may need to fingerprint you to rule you out as suspects, but for now you're free to return to your duties."

"Okay," said Greg solemnly. "Let me know if you need anything else." Greg returned to his office.

The officers peered through the windows of the car.

"Sam look at the inside of the car," said Johnson. "That's a hell of a lot of blood. Do you think an injured dog would bleed like that?"

Ben whistled and raised his eyebrows in surprise.

"Let's take a look at the front of the car," said Sam. As they examined the front of the car, he called to his partner, "Ben, do you see anything?"

"No, Sam, that's just it. I don't see anything. There's nothing to see and there should be something! Didn't the manager say that the customer hit a dog?"

"Yes! That's what the guy claimed. But if he did, don't you think there'd be hair or blood, a dent or scratch?"

"And look, even the dirt is even and consistent. No smudges! Something doesn't add up."

"Let's take a closer look at the inside of the car."

Ben reached for the handle with his gloved hand. He pulled lightly and the door opened easily. "Look at all this blood!" he exclaimed, "It's even more than it seemed at first glance!"

"Yes and it's the same story as the front of the car. No hair. You'd think a dog would shed some hair."

"For sure. That blood should be covered in hair!"

Ben placed his hand his hand above the door to keep his balance and leaned forward into the car to examine the stain more closely. "Ouch!" he yelped. "That hurts!" He stood up and looked at his hand. There was a small slice in the palm of the glove where a small trickle of blood now appeared. Ben looked up to find the source of the cut.

"Sam! Look at this door trim and the roof of the car."

"Yeah, that looks like a fresh gouge in the metal above it."

"That was probably made in the last few days. Let's see what else we have."

Ben crouched down and shone his flashlight under the front seat of the car. "Sam, take a look at this!"

"Oh shit! Let's get the lab boys over here!"

The detectives walked into Greg's office. He looked up, surprised to see them so soon. "Can I help you with anything?"

"Yes, you can. First we need to use your phone, and second, we need to impound that car."

"What do you mean, impound the car? For how long?" Greg was going to have to explain this to his boss.

"That's all I can say right now. Oh, one more thing. We'd like to see all the paperwork from this transaction—the originals, not copies. And can you tell us if the car was rented from this location?"

"No, officer. It came from our downtown location"

"Can you call them right now and have them send over all the paperwork? Or better yet we'll send someone over to pick it up. The less people who handle it, the better."

Greg picked up the phone and called the other outlet to make his request. After that was done, Greg looked up at Sam Jeffries. "Can you tell me what's going on? I've got to tell my boss something. When can we get the car back?"

"Tell your boss that the car was used in a crime and that the police are investigating," he said.

Within the hour the car was hooked up to police tow truck, wrapped in a tarp to preserve the evidence, and on the way to the forensics lab.

The Roshtti Household

Giti had already put the coffee on and was looking out the window into the backyard. The trees were bare, the buds not yet beginning to appear. She had had an amazing sleep, such as she hadn't had in many months. She heard the door of the downstairs bedroom open and close, accompanied by its mouse-like squeak.

Time for some a bit more WD-40! Giti thought. She wasn't surprised when Fatemah appeared in the kitchen. "Good morning, Fatemah," Giti said in hushed voice. It was after six, but was still too early for everyone to get up, especially on a Saturday morning.

"Good morning Giti. How are you today?"

"Great! Today I'm great!"

Fatemah thought back to their conversation a day earlier. "I can see what a difference a day makes! How was your afternoon with Jaffar?"

"We had a really nice time! Thanks so much for looking after Sina and spending the night again," she said. Sitting at the table, drinking their morning coffee, Giti told Fatemah about the museum and her walk with Jaffar around downtown afterwards.

"He likes you!" teased Fatemah.

"Yes, he does," Giti teased, then she said, "Just a minute I'll be right back!" and a moment later walked back into the kitchen with a big smile on her face.

"Fatemah you'll have to promise that you'll tell no one, not even Zafar!"

"Tell them what?"

"You have to promise!"

"Okay, I promise."

Giti took the small box from the pocket of her housecoat and opened it. Fatemah sat, slack-jawed, unable to speak. She was astonished by the sheer size of the diamond. After the initial shock she stood and gave Giti a hug that threatened to suffocate her. "Oh Giti, I'm so happy for you. But you know I was half-expecting this. So was Zafar!"

"Why?"

"All that talk about Susie Hawkins Day!"

Giti laughed. "That's *Sadie* Hawkins! Anyway, like I said, you can't tell anyone right now. At least not until I tell Sina."

"Alright, I promise, but it will be hard!"

Sacramento Police Forensics Garage

Detective Mark Rawlins had been going over the Chrysler for the past hour and a half. Although it was almost noon, there would no stopping for lunch today. Every square inch of the rental car would be examined. "Hey, Sam. Do you have the paperwork on this thing?"

"Yep, just got here. What do you need?"

"Can you tell me how many miles were on the car when it went out?"

"Yeah. Let's see, here it is … 8,974 miles."

"Now we have 10,261. What's that? About 1,300 miles out and back."

"More or less."

"So halve that, we have 650 miles. What ever happened here, took place in that radius."

They still were not certain that a murder took place. For the next two hours the detectives searched the car inside and out, looking for clues. They were waiting for the preliminary lab results that would confirm their suspicions. As if on cue, Ben Johnson opened the door and entered the garage area, carrying a manila folder in his gloved hand.

"Say Mark, I've got that blood work-up for you."

"Good. Let's take a look." Sam opened the folder and scanned the results. "The blood is definitely not canine blood, it has only 23 pairs of chromosomes, not 39 like a dog. Looks like it's human."

"So the guy was lying when he said he hit a dog?" This was from Mark.

"Probably, but lying isn't a crime, unless it becomes obstruction!"

"What about the knife?"

"No match for the prints we found on the knife, but the blood on the knife was typed. It matched the blood on the seat."

"This would be a lot easier if we had a body to go with the blood."

"Maybe we do! How far did you say the car was driven?"

"About 1,300 miles. That puts our man anywhere in a 650 mile radius. That could be as far south as San Diego or as far north as Portland. It's a lot of ground to cover."

"So! Start by checking for unsolved murders that have occurred in that radius, in say... the last 72 hours!"

"But why murders? Why not assaults?"

"Probability, fewer cases. You eliminate those first and then work your way down the list to lesser crimes."

"Okay, Sam, I'll get started. Oh, by the way, Carol in the lab wants to see you!"

"Thanks!" Sam headed for the door.

Carol Patrick had been with the crime lab for three years. She had a degree in criminology from Western Washington University. She also had a year of pre-med, but she'd changed horses mid-stream because she liked the idea of solving crimes. She looked up when Detective Jefferies entered the lab. She smiled. "Hey Sam!"

"Ben said you wanted to see me?"

"Yes, I do. I presume he showed you the test results from the blood and fingerprint evidence that you collected?"

"Yes, he sure did. Why?"

"Well, a couple of things. First you're probably looking at a murder here, judging by the amount of blood in the car, or at least aggravated assault with a deadly weapon. Second, the knife you found under the seat made the gouge in the roof and door trim that Ben cut his hand on!"

"What's three?" With Carol there were never just two things. She was always thinking.

"The driver was definitely male, and probably of Middle Eastern descent."

"That's what the girl at the Hertz car rental said."

"But here's the kicker. There was another man in the car. I've got two sets of prints that I can't account for, and at least four hair samples, two of which are from the Middle East."

"What about the other two?"

"You can probably discount them! I tell you, both the victim and perpetrator were from Iran, Iraq or somewhere around there."

"How can you be so sure?"

"I thought you'd never ask! Okay! This is so cool!"

"Tell me, for crying out loud. Tell me and I'll buy you lunch."

"Dinner!"

"Done!"

"Because both hairs were interwoven into the fabric of the seat and not just lying on it! That's what's so cool! If they had been dropped into the blood after the fact, they could never have gotten between the threads of the car seat fabric, because the viscosity of the blood would have prevented them from doing so. Kind of like trying to thread a needle with a thread covered in maple syrup … it'd be almost impossible!"

"So these Middle Eastern hairs were there *before* the blood?"

"Yes! Ninety-nine point nine-nine percent positive."

"And both the 'vic' and 'perp' were Middle Eastern?"

"Yeah!"

"That narrows it down a bit." Sam got up to go and talk to Ben.

"You owe me dinner!" she called after him.

"Yeah!"

Down the hall, Sam stood beside Ben as he typed his query into the new computer system the precinct had just installed. Many cops were uncomfortable with this new technology, but Ben loved it.

"With this new information we should be able to narrow it down a bit!" Ben said.

The terminal sending the information was hooked into similar systems in police stations in every major city across the U.S. Within minutes they had their answer. There had been 38 murders in the last 72 hours, but only one within their area of interest that matched the profile of this case. The victim was stabbed near Las Vegas, 580 miles away.

"Look Sam, the victim was Mohammed Hussan, age 29 years, of Las Vegas, Nevada. Cause of death was multiple stab wounds."

"Goddamn! Carol was bang-on!"

"What's that?"

"I said, Carol was bang-on. I owe her dinner! She told me our perpetrator and victim were most likely Middle Eastern."

"I'll call Las Vegas and get some particulars. I think we should send blood samples and photos of the knife to see if they match up to the wounds of the deceased!"

"I'll get right on it."

Las Vegas, Nevada

Jack Coward had managed to sleep in a bit. Normally he was up by seven and out of the RV on his morning jog. The occasional dig about the extra inches on his waist from Donny had persuaded him to start running again. In November, just after the run-in with Mohammed, when Donny had flown out from Washington to help Jack check out Mohammed's apartment, Donny had commented, "Nice love handles Jack!" and that stuck in Jack's mind. So now for almost four months Jack had jogged every morning.

First it was just a mile for a couple of weeks, then he worked up to two miles and now Jack was up to eleven miles. It had been more than ten years since he had been able to run that distance and he felt really good physically. He was also drinking a lot less—not that he ever drank excessively—and could almost fit in his old Marine uniform … almost.

Jack looked at the clock; it read five minutes to eight. "Almost time to check out what's happening in the world. See what those assholes in Iran are doing!"

He switched on the television and went to the kitchen to put coffee on, something else he had started drinking less of. In a few minutes, he was sitting down on the sofa, coffee in hand, just as the eight o'clock news began.

"Good morning! I'm Brad Kershaw and here's today's local news. This week's flooding cost Clark County millions of dollars. Mayor Tom Higgins is seeking state assistance to help with the costs."

The television showed now-familiar scenes from the storm and Jack was still amazed as he watched the video of familiar streets under several feet of water. He could not remember the last time Las Vegas had received that much rain in so short a time. He'd been lucky where he was. There was a slight grade up to where he parked his RV and it had been enough to keep his plot of land relatively safe from the rising water.

"And now for our top story … Police are looking for help in their investigation of the city's latest murder. Yesterday we told you about a body that was trapped in the debris of Cold Canyon Creek. This morning police released a picture of the victim along with a few details." And then a picture of Mohammed Hussan appeared on the screen.

"Holy shit!" Jack stared at the photograph. He nearly spit out his coffee.

"The man has been identified as Iraqi citizen Mohammed Hussan. Police are looking for anyone who knew the victim, or anyone who could help piece together his movements of three days ago ..."

I wonder if the cops have got to his apartment yet? If they hadn't, he needed to get there first. He picked up the phone and dialed the familiar 202 area code and phone number.

"Good morning Donny! How are you?"

"Good Jack. It's great to hear your voice. Are you still running?"

"Yep, every day."

"What's up?"

"You know my, or should I say *our*, friend from last November?" Jack didn't wait for a response. "It seems that someone didn't like him very much. He's dead."

"Probably taking driving lessons from his brother!" Donny couldn't resist the jab.

Jack laughed. "Yeah right! Anyway Don, I'm going to have to pay Mr. Hussan's apartment another visit."

"Do you want some help?" Donny was looking forward to a trip out west; he was hoping to avoid at least some of the typical cold, wet March weather in D.C.

"Not that I couldn't use it, but I've got to do this pronto. Before you know it, the cops will swarming all over his place. I'm going over there today."

"I'll get my stuff together. Do you have a case right now?"

"Nope, just finished my last one," he said. Jack's bread-and-butter cases were usually about finding dirt for jealous husbands and jealous wives to throw at each other, but lately he had been handling more and more cases from the casinos. The casinos were always on the lookout for individuals or groups who used illegal systems to beat the odds, either by counting cards or through more sophisticated methods. As well, casinos hired Jack to track down con men that hit on patrons and tried to separate them from their winnings—something that was not good for business.

"Hey Jack," Don said, "Maybe after I get there we can go fishing. I hear it's nice this time of year in Baja!"

Jack chuckled. "Sounds good! Give me a call when you get in. It's nice *any* time of year!"

Just before noon, Jack parked his car two blocks from the Cedar Village apartments where Hussan's apartment was. He didn't like working alone; it was much safer and less nerve-racking when Donny was along. Jack wished his friend lived closer but so far he'd been unsuccessful in getting Donny to move out west, though he kept trying. Don kept saying he'd think about it, to which Jack responded, "I'll believe it when I see the Goddamn moving van outside and the movers are actually unpacking your stuff."

He walked up to the intercom and buzzed 203. It rang several times and, as expected, no one answered. He hung up the phone and waited for someone to leave the building. He was in luck; the elevator door opened and an elderly man got out. He headed for the lobby doors and Jack hurriedly punched in the number to Hussan's again. Between the second and third ring the old fellow pushed open the lobby door, looked at Jack and said, "Good morning young man."

"Good morning, sir." Jack punched the button to disconnect his call. "Must be in the shower still. Thanks for opening the door for me!"

"You're welcome."

Jack walked down the second floor corridor, relieved to see it was as empty as the last time he and Donny had visited. He didn't bother to knock; he was almost certain no one was in the apartment. He entered exactly the same way as he had four months previous.

With the exception of his own breathing and the quiet hum of the refrigerator, the apartment was as quiet as a tomb and so Jack quickly went to work. Removing the bottom of the pot was a bit awkward without Donny to help him, but he managed. Then he removed the photographs and journal that had been so carefully hidden there.

He then turned his attention to the bedroom, where Donny had found the address book on their last visit. On the nightstand he found a daily journal, almost new. Beside the bed was a cloth duffel bag. Jack picked it up. *Mohammed won't be needing this,* he thought as he stuffed the journal and the contents of the flower pot into the bag. Then he headed back into the living room, set the bag down on the floor and began to reassemble the base to the philodendron plant.

The door to the elevator opened at the second floor and Jack heard it. Victor Sanchez, the manager of the building, stepped into the hallway, along with two plainclothes policemen. "I was wondering why the rent was late. Mr. Hussan always paid on time and in cash."

"Yes, sir! Now which way is his apartment?"

"This way, number 203." Victor led the trio down the hall to the left. "Dead you say? I can't believe it! Hard to find a renter like him!"

Jack heard the voices of the three men as they approached the door. He had just finished putting the bottom on the pot, when he heard the jingle of the keys outside the door.

Quickly he gathered up his loot, unlocked the sliding patio door and dropped the bag to the soft landscaping, thirteen feet below. Then he swung his leg up and over the railing, just as the hallway door opened and dropped, praying for a soft landing. It was the only option for escape.

Detective Terry Strohman entered the apartment first, followed by his partner, leaving Victor to wait in the hall as directed by the detectives. The first thing Strohman noticed was that the sliding door was open, a slight breeze blowing the curtains into the room. He rushed over to it and was just in time to see Jack drop to the ground, roll and run, his landing cushioned by a shrub. He didn't look back.

"Stop!" the detective shouted down at him, but it was wasted breath. Jack had no intention of doing so. Strohman hoped the man would look up, affording him a visual of the suspect's face—and Jack almost did; but he caught himself halfway through the motion and turned his face away just in time.

"Dave! You call it in. I'm going after him!" the Strohman said. Then he lifted himself up and over the railing and dropped down after his quarry.

Jack didn't expect that one of the benefits of his daily run would be to elude capture by the police. The noontime heat didn't bother him as he sprinted down the sidewalk towards his car; he was used to it and was barely breathing hard. He rounded the corner at the second left and spotted his black Camaro. He hadn't locked the door when he'd parked it so he opened the door, threw the bag into the back seat and quickly jumped in. He jammed the key into the ignition and turned it. Nothing happened; there was not even a click.

"Shit!" Any lead Jack had built up was surely gone. All he could do was slide as far down into his seat as possible and watch as Detective Strohman ran past, mere yards away, followed by the other detective in an unmarked police car. He was relieved to see both of them drive back towards the apartment a minute later.

Jack waited a few minutes before sitting upright in his seat. He tried the key again. Still nothing! The closest service station he could remember was three blocks away, past Cedar Village.

That is probably one of the last places the police will look, so close to the building, he thought. He decided that before getting help he'd look under the hood of the Camaro himself. He popped the hood. The first thing he checked was the battery, often the culprit when cars don't start. Wouldn't you know it, the positive cable was not sitting on the post as it should but was lying on top of the battery.

"Nah, it couldn't be that simple!" he muttered. He gave the nut a couple of turns by hand, then put the cable back on the post, rotating it as he forced it snugly downward. Then he walked around, reached in and turned the ignition. The engine turned over and roared to life. Jack shut the hood, got behind the wheel and drove home to safety.

— Chapter 8 —

March 2, 1980

Jack and Donny sat around the small but well-used kitchen table in Jack's RV. "You know Don, I was this close to getting caught red-handed!" Jack held up his hand, his thumb and index finger only an inch apart. "If I'd been in the bedroom checking Mohammed's closet or nightstand, I would never have heard those cops coming down the hall with that apartment manager."

"I guess I should have gone with you, but it might have been too late! The cops would have probably cleaned out his place, looking for clues about who killed him."

"Speaking of that, I've been looking through the address book trying to see if any names jump out at me. The only name I remember is Jaffar Hamid Harraj." Jack continued to flip through the pages. "Donny, take a look through that daily journal. See what you can see. I'll give this ledger another look!"

"Okay! But are we going fishing later?"

"Yes we can, tomorrow! But first let's have a look at this stuff and try to put some pieces together."

"Sounds good to me, Jack." Donny flipped through the pages of the journal, looking for anything that could tie the events together. "Poor bastard!"

"What's that Don?"

"Well this journal starts just after the accident last year." He continued to scan the pages. "It would seem that our late friend had conscience after all!"

"What do you mean?"

"It says here, and I quote, 'I am responsible for my brother Akbal's death. I should have stopped chasing the private detective, but instead I forced the gas pedal down, by pushing on Akbal's leg. We rushed through the intersection, causing the crash'."

"I don't believe it. That asshole!" Jack could now picture how the one brother had died and the other lived. "I wonder why he wanted to catch me so bad?"

"Maybe that journal holds some answers. Let's have another look at that."

"It's filled with addresses and cash amounts, like a ledger. When I looked at it earlier, the total was well over a hundred million dollars!"

"Jesus, Jack. That's a hell of a pile of cash! These guys must be pretty serious players to be dealing with that kind of dough!"

"That's for sure. All these places are motels or hotels around here. Look at the latest entry. Charlie's Boulder Casino Hotel. The amount, twelve million, five hundred thousand dollars. Then the date, October 22nd, 1979."

"I wonder if our man bought them or sold them?"

"Bought, most likely. I remember that place. I was driving out on Boulder Highway last fall and I remember when they put up the 'For Sale' sign up on that place." Jack continued after he thought for a minute, "No! It wasn't a 'For Sale' sign, it was a sign to redevelop the place."

"I wonder who paid that kind of cash? A hundred million bucks!" Donny tried to visualize the money. In the front of the book was a name of a company. "Sunwest Properties. I wonder who owns Sunwest Properties?" he asked.

"Let's give the people up in Carson City a call on Monday and see if we can get an answer to that. That's where the land registry office is, isn't it?"

"Yep! I'll go look up the number in the phone book, but we might have to drive up there ourselves."

"Okay, Jack! And *then* can we go fishing?"

"Yeah, sure, Don. We can go on Tuesday. I'll try to get us a couple of seats on the morning flight. That way, we can be out on the boat by two in the afternoon!"

"Sounds like a plan, Stan."

March 3, 1980

Jack and Donny were on the road early Monday morning, intent on getting to Carson City and back to Las Vegas by evening. "Jack, what's the name of this place again?"

"The Nevada Real Estate Division in Carson City. Let's hope they're cooperative. That's quite a list of properties to research!"

"It's good there are two of us. We each can take half the list. That way we'll be done by lunch." Donny was always the optimist.

"I hope so!"

It was just after lunch and Jack was only two-thirds the way down his part of the list. Donny was doing only slightly better. Jack rubbed his eyes and glanced at his notes. All the properties had been purchased in the last three years by Sunwest Properties, through a lawyer in Zurich, Switzerland.

"Look here, Don. All of these deals were signed and stamped by a lawyer, Gehringer and Associates."

"Yeah same on the stuff I'm looking at ... and look at the name on all the transactions, Bank of Lucerne."

"Why the hell would someone go to all the trouble of doing business through a Swiss bank and some Swiss lawyer?" Jack glanced down once more at the ledger that they'd brought with them. "Besides, Don, you know about Swiss banks. Client confidentiality and all! Someone didn't want to make it very easy for anyone to track down these deals."

"I bet the money went through half a dozen banks, before it even got to the Bank of Lucerne. I wonder why this didn't raise any red flags at this office?"

"That's not their job, and besides, we are talking about a dozen or so out of tens of thousands of deals during that time-frame."

"Yeah I guess, but I tell you, Jack, this smacks of something much more serious than foreign investment or money laundering. I mean these guys were after you, for Christ's sake."

"I know and I've tried to figure out why. I have no clue!"

"There was some serious intent there, Jack. The guy was so intent that he killed his brother and nearly killed himself in the process. Now just a couple of months later he turns up dead, murdered in fact! Now..."

"Hold your horses, Don!"

"Just let me finish, I'm on a roll here!" Don continued, "As I was saying … now I bet this Jaffar character is in up to his eyeballs in all of this. He either ordered those assholes to go after you, or one of his associates did."

"Still no idea why," Jack said, "Unless it has to do with Giti Roshtti."

"Oh, your crush!" Don said, "Are you still holding a flame for her?"

"Oh come on, you asshole. That was a while ago. She had no idea who I was or what I was and she didn't care."

"That's not the point," Don said. "You cared."

"Yeah, well I grew out of it," Jack said in a surly voice.

The thing was, Jack *hadn't* grown out of it, he just didn't want to be reminded of it—he had no trouble remembering Giti on his own. "Let's finish up here and head south. We can do some fishing and some thinking!"

"I've been waiting days for you to say those very words!"

"I know!" Jack laughed.

March 4, 1980

True to his word, on Tuesday morning Jack and Donny were on a Horizon flight down to La Paz, on the Baja peninsula. They had only packed a small travel bag each, travelling by the rules of the four 'S' Club: bring only essentials—shirts, shorts, sandals and sunscreen.

In Jack's bag were the two dozen or so pages of notes he and Donny had written the day before. It would have made their lives far easier, but photocopying any of the documents was not allowed.

"After the last couple of days I'll be glad to be out on the boat with my line in the water," Jack said.

"It's after the last couple of months for me, Jack. God I'm getting tired of D.C. It's so damn hot and humid in the summer and cold, wet and snowy in the winter. Sometimes it seems that both seem to last six months with no spring or fall. At least when we lived in Wisconsin, there were four seasons."

"Who's fault is that? I've been bugging you for how long to move out west? Every Goddamn time you say, 'maybe, maybe one of these days'. Every damn time! So what's it gonna be Don? Yes or no?"

"Maybe! What about all my friends in Washington, all my contacts?"

"You have friends in Washington? That's news to me! Jesus, Don, they will still be there, just a phone call away."

Donny replied, "Right!" then started flipping through the mesh pouch in the seat in front of him to see if there was anything more interesting than the brochure showing the emergency exit locations on the airplane. He spotted the stewardess coming down the aisle and raised his hand to get her attention. "Excuse me! Do you have a newspaper I could read?"

"Yes, I've got a copy of the L.A. Times."

"That would be great!" Donny watched as the flight attendant turned and walked back toward the front of the plane, hips swaying back and forth.

"Nice view, eh Jack?"

Jack laughed. "You dog," was all he said.

Jack stared out the window as they flew. Down below he could see the slender 'finger' of the Baja Peninsula pointing southward, separating the shimmering turquoise waters of the Gulf of California from the blue waters of the Pacific Ocean. The stewardess came back with the paper and this time when she walked away, Don growled.

"What was that, Don?" It took Jack a second to zero in on what had caught his friend's eye. "Oh yeah, she's a beauty!"

"I think her name is Michelle. Sorry, Jack!"

It *had* to be—out of all the women's names in the world her name *would* have to be Michelle. Michelle was a mistake in Jack's life that he had worked hard to forget. When a woman says she loves you then sleeps with your commanding officer ... well that really puts a strain on a five-year relationship. She kept the car. And the baby. Jack was pretty sure it wasn't his. No one in his family had red hair.

"It's only a name, Jack," Don said when he saw his friend's faraway expression.

"I know," he conceded. Then, trying to change the subject, he said, "Why don't you see if she likes to fish?"

"That's a hell of an idea, but you're about two hours and 90 miles too late to think of it."

"What does that mean?"

"I thought of that when we passed over the border into Mexico!" Donny and Jack both laughed. Jack could feel the plane slow as it started its descent towards La Paz, which lay at the tip of the sliver of land below.

"It's gorgeous down there," Jack said quietly, turning to Donny. But Donny was out of his seat and halfway up to the front of the plane on his way to befriend the beautiful Michelle.

"Christ! Just like a fucking bloodhound!" Jack chuckled. He couldn't blame his friend; Michelle was good-looking and had been making eye contact with Don since they sat down in their seats. Once more he turned to look out the window, thinking ahead to the 100-mile drive by car to Loreto that they would have to make.

It's too bad there's not a direct flight, he thought. Loreto had the choicest fishing spots though, and that's why he and Don always went back. A few minutes later he felt Donny lower himself into his seat. He turned to see his friend tucking a piece of paper into his shirt pocket, grinning like a Cheshire cat.

"I think I'm going to like Mexico," Don proclaimed.

"I don't believe it! Was that her phone number?"

"Yep! It's also the name of the place where she's staying. Tomorrow afternoon is her last flight for a week and she's staying at the Comfort Inn, in Cabo. She wants to lie on the beach, drink some tequila, and dip her toes in the ocean."

"And where do you want to dip your toes, or whatever...?"

"Me? I'm a perfect gentleman. You know that Jack?"

"I call bullshit on that one!"

"Jack! Instead of renting a car and driving up to Loreto, do you think we can stay in La Paz tonight? Just to see if this pans out, of course!"

"Ah-hah! You're not so damned sure of yourself, are you smart ass?"

"No! I guess not."

"But yes, we can stay put for a day or so. There's plenty of fishing charters out of La Paz."

"Thanks, Jack!"

Jack turned to look out the window once more as the plane descended rapidly on its approach to La Paz. Visible out the window was the 1,000-mile white ribbon of concrete that ran the length of the Baja, zigzagging as it linked together the small towns and villages. Jack thought it looked like a giant connect-the-dots puzzle. As they got closer to the ground, he could see many of the smaller boats scattered offshore, their owners trying to eke out a living from fishing or tourism.

In the small oval-shaped glass Jack could see his own reflection staring back at him. It somehow morphed into the image of Michelle Richards, his last girlfriend, her soft smooth face, her auburn hair … her cheating black heart. Jack hadn't thought of her for several months. "God! Why did it have to be Michelle," he said out loud.

Beside him, Don chuckled.

La Paz, Baja California Sur

Jack and Donny had checked their bags at their hotel and were walking along a floating dock, over the warm, turquoise waters of the Gulf of Mexico. The worn, sun-bleached wooden planks stretched sideways, beam to beam. Each section was supported by four, 45-gallon drums, linked together in a chain, stretching several hundred feet. Tied alongside was a collection of fishing boats ranging in size from small skiffs to large charter boats that could take a dozen or so passengers. Most of the vessels were older, but almost every one sported a fresh coat of paint, in every color of the spectrum, all lovingly applied by their owners.

Each of the boat owners eyed the Americans as they passed. When they realized they wouldn't get any business, the skippers of the small one-man boats quickly returned to their chores, mending nets or whatever. The captains of the larger boats were a different matter entirely; each one in turn implored the newcomers to come on board. Each promised a huge amount of fish would be caught, for the least amount of money. Jack and Don both smiled as they continued towards the end of the pier, politely declining the invitations with, "No thanks. Not Today." The boat they sought was the Santa Esmerelda, owned by Captain Miguel. They wanted to fish for roosterfish, and according to the man at the front desk of their hotel, Captain Miguel was the man with the right boat and equipment, especially if they were after the really big ones.

As they came to end of the pier, Jack spotted the boat owned by Captain Miguel. It was hard to miss among all the rest. Although Jack correctly judged her to be about twenty years old, she looked almost new. Every bit of hardware, every inch of bright work, gleamed in the bright tropical sun. Her deckhouse and all 30-some feet of the white hull looked as if it had been polished. Jack walked past the stern, just far enough to see name painted across the transom in black and gold letters. "This is the one Don! Hello, anyone here?"

Captain Miguel stuck his head out of the deckhouse and smiled. "Hola, Señors!"

"Hola! Are you Captain Miguel?

"Si! Yes, I am!"

"We were told at the hotel that we could charter you and your boat for a few days, perhaps a week?"

A wider than normal smile appeared on Captain Miguel's face. One-week charters were few and far between. In the slow times Miguel cleaned and polished his boat, but as his wife so often reminded him, "A clean boat doesn't pay the bills!"

"A week! Oh yes! Come aboard!"

Jack stepped onto the deck, bag in hand, followed by Don. Captain Miguel climbed down onto the stern deck and Jack reached out and shook hands with the Mexican captain.

"My name is John, but my friends call me Jack." He motioned toward Don. "This is my friend, Don."

"It's good to meet you. It will be a pleasure to take you out fishing!"

Looking out from below his Washington Redskins baseball cap, Donny's face was just like that of a five-year-old on Christmas day. He'd been anxiously waiting this. Even during the plane ride down, he'd thought that it wasn't going to happen. "Well then, let's get this gear stowed and get going!" he said.

Within minutes the skipper had expertly maneuvered his boat from the dock and past the breakwater. Jack went up the ladder to join the skipper on the flying bridge. He gripped the handhold tightly as the boat surged ahead, driven by the twin eight-cylinder Chrysler engines, their throaty growl even more pronounced as Captain Miguel advanced the throttles towards their stops.

Jack glanced down at the skipper's right hand to see that the throttles were only slightly past three-quarters of the way open. With the lack of visual reference, it was hard to tell how fast they were traveling simply by looking at the ocean rushing past—especially now that the motion had become surprisingly smooth.

After 40 minutes of dashing over the waves, Miguel cut the wheel to port and the boat sliced a graceful arc towards shore. He throttled back and reversed power, stopping the craft just yards from a narrow spit of rocks that stretched a 150 yards out from the beach. Jack eyed the nearby rocks. He had always thought you had to have a lot more water under the keel to catch a big fish. Here the water was crystal clear and you could see the bottom, the cream-colored coral sand looked close enough to touch.

"This is the best spot around," the captain said.

"I would have thought you needed to be farther out," Jack remarked. He remembered films on television of some lucky guy, miles from land, hooking a huge blue marlin as it catapulted itself out of the sea in a frenzied effort to get away.

"No! This is the best place," Miguel insisted as he lowered himself down the ladder. Miguel glanced toward shore and moved quickly to the stern. With almost no effort he picked up a concrete block and dropped it over the side. He let the rope follow without any concern. With only ten feet of line left on deck, the rope ceased to play out. Jack watched the block land on the bottom, a cloud of sand briefly rising from the impact. Miguel tied off the line to the nearest cleat.

"Looks like you've done this before," Don said, still amazed at what he saw. He looked at Jack and could almost hear Jack say, "Pretty strong for a skinny guy!" reflecting his very own thoughts.

Within minutes both Jack and Donny had their fishing rods baited with live bait and were trailing thin mono-filament lines from the stern of the boat.

"Captain Miguel can I ask you a question? You don't have to answer, if you don't want to," said Jack.

"Si, Señor Jack! Go ahead and ask me your question."

"How did you come to own a boat like this? I mean no disrespect, but it seemed so out of place at the dock in Las Paz." Jack remembered a few large boats, but they had all been imports from San Diego and Los Angeles, not locally owned.

"Oh that does not bother me to answer. I got the Santa Esmeralda from the Hurricane Lisa!"

Both Jack and Don asked almost simultaneously, "What do you mean from the hurricane?"

"At the end of September, four years ago, Hurricane Lisa came and wrecked many boats and many buildings. Many of my neighbors were killed. Many lost their homes and boats." Jack and Don both sat and listened and all three men watched the two lines, as they slowly played out into the water.

Miguel continued, "The rich American that owned her, made, how you say, a claim with the insurance and he left the boat beside the dock, in many feet of water. For days and weeks it stayed there ..." he stopped, his attention focused on the glistening ocean. Then he shouted, "Señor Jack! You have a fish!" Miguel leaped from his chair, snatched the rod from the holder and pulled hard, seating the hook firmly before passing it back to Jack, saying, "Here, señor, start to reel, very slowly and smooth, real smooth."

Jack took the rod from the skipper and started to reel in his line as instructed. He couldn't believe his eyes as he focused on the tip of the rod, which was almost bent double. "This has to be big, by the feel of it!" Jack said to Don. Jack looked at Donny and saw two ear-to-ear grins—one on Donny's face and one on his own, reflected in Donny's sun glasses.

After a few minutes of battling his fish Jack could feel the beads of sweat on his forehead turn to a trickle that ran down his nose and dripped off the end. Another river of sweat ran down his back. After ten minutes, his forearms began to ache.

"Almost there, Jack," Don said, spotting the black and silver fish darting from side to side, just below the surface of the water, mere feet away.

"God I don't know how much I've got left, Don. My left arm feels like it's on fire, and I've got a cramp in my right from reeling!"

"Just a few seconds more, Jack!" Don coached him, then added, "That's a big mother!" At that instant, Miguel stepped in between the two men and placed the net directly in the path of the fish.

"Got him, señor!" Miguel shouted. Jack reeled in the last few feet of remaining line as Miguel lifted the netted fish into the boat. Jack and Donny stood in place, jaws agape at the roosterfish as it flailed at their feet.

"Holy shit! That's a big fish," Don said.

"What do you want to do, Señor Jack? It's a big one!" Miguel asked as he looked the struggling fish over. "It's a good 75 or 80 pounds!" Then Miguel bent over and placed his gloved left hand on the fish, just behind the head, and used the pliers in his right to expertly remove the hook from the fish's mouth. His actions were smooth and effortless.

Jack and Donny were not the kind of men who would have a stuffed fish over their mantle, even if they had mantles; both were here only for the sport.

"Let it go Miguel," Jack said without hesitation. Miguel bent over, picked up the fish and lowered it as gently as possible into the sea. All three men watched as it darted back to safety, almost unharmed, ready to fight another day.

"You are not like most men, Señor Jack! Not many men would have let him go," Miguel said, his admiration obvious. He was beginning to like this gringo. He turned away to bait Jack's hook and cast it once more into the water.

"Thank you Miguel. I would never have a trophy on my wall. That fish put up a great fight. It deserved to live."

"You are right, señor!" Then all three men returned to watching their rod tips and line, doing what made up 95 percent of fishing, waiting.

"So Captain Miguel, tell us more about your boat."

"Oh yes!" Miguel continued, "For four days, my brother and I worked to lift her from the bottom." Donny and Jack sat, enthralled, as Miguel told them of all he had done to rescue and restore the Santa Esmeralda. They were fascinated by his story.

"That's amazing," Donny said clearly impressed with the ingenuity of the little Mexican. "So you saved her from a watery grave, more or less."

"Si."

"But why did you choose the name Santa Esmeralda?"

"That's my wife's name, Esmeralda. You know *Don't Let Me Be Misunderstood*?" Miguel looked at both men hoping to see a glimmer of understanding, but only saw puzzled expressions. "My wife looks very much like the woman on the cover of the record." After a moment he added, "She begged me to put the name on the boat."

Jack and Don were still puzzled.

Miguel added, "You know, the song?"

Instantly Donny said, "Yeah right, the song! You remember, Jack, the song?"

"Oh yeah, I remember," Jack said. Neither one did.

But Miguel did. He recalled how his wife always used to do a little dance just for him whenever that special song would radiate out of the portable cassette players the tourists carried, or how he would hold her in his arms and dance to it when they heard it played at one of the many discos everyone flocked to during the warm tropical nights.

The afternoon was growing late and the sun descended towards the western horizon. Jack had the only catch of the day. There had been many nibbles, but no other hits.

"We should head in, señors. I promise tomorrow will be a better day," Miguel said. He stowed the fishing gear, restarted the engines and advanced the throttles slightly then steered the boat to starboard, pivoting the craft around the anchor and staying clear of the shoal.

"Okay, Señor Jack, if you please!"

"All right, Miguel," Jack said as he started to raise the anchor off the sandy bottom. His arms protested slightly. *I'm going to have to add more weights to my routine*, he thought, *I'm out of shape*.

After the makeshift anchor had cleared the gunwales, Miguel pushed the throttles forward and steered the boat toward home. Donny turned and faced the bow, the cool breeze giving some relief from the hot sun. That and the occasional bit of spray in the face felt good. Although Donny had no luck with fishing today, he looked forward to tomorrow. Miguel promised that it would be better and he believed him. He thought about Michelle. "Yes tomorrow will be better," he smiled. Donny and the other two men had no idea what the next day would bring.

Las Vegas, Nevada - March 6, 1980

In the lounge of the Las Vegas Seventh Precinct, Detective Terry Strohman was getting his morning coffee. It was still 15 minutes until the start of his shift. A small color television sat perched on a triangular shelf. He walked over and reached up to increase the volume.

The morning news was on and beside the anchorman's head was a small inset picture of Walter Cronkite. The anchor said, "Today CBS news announced that long-time evening news anchorman, Walter Cronkite, will retire. The man many perceive as the 'most trusted' man in America is leaving broadcasting after twenty years at his CBS post."

The detective turned up the volume even more and turned to refill his coffee when the door opened and his colleague, Dave Stapleton, entered.

"Morning, Terry. What's up?"

"Not much, Dave. Want a cup?"

"Sure but only half. My bloody stomach is giving me trouble this morning. Kept me awake half the goddamn night!"

"You probably have an ulcer. I think after 17 years it's a surprise we both don't have one." He handed Dave half a cup of coffee and pointed at the television. "Did you know that Walter Cronkite is retiring? Today's his last day!"

"No shit! Boy, I wish we could retire! I still have at least five years to go before I get my pension." Terry nodded in commiseration. They both watched the television until Terry noticed the time on his watch.

"Seven fifty-eight! I guess it's that time again!" He turned the volume down on the television and the picture changed to a scene of four people on what appeared to be a pier. They were standing two on either side of a rather odd-looking fish that was about four feet long and had a huge dorsal sail fin.

"Hell of a fish," said Terry, who was a weekend warrior at the local lake. The biggest he'd ever caught was a nine-pound trout.

The co-anchor, a woman who generally got the human interest stories, said, "In other news, a local man on holiday in La Paz now shares the world record for the largest roosterfish ever caught. The previous record dates back to 1960."

The camera zoomed in on one of the men, a lean, lithe man in a ball cap as, clearly camera-shy, he turned and tried to walk out of the frame. "It wasn't me that caught it. I was just in the boat. That honor goes to Don here," the shy man said, pointing to his large, jovial-looking friend. The big guy gave a smile and patted a small Mexican man on the back. The Mexican beamed broadly and put his arm around an attractive, dark-haired woman. The three of them smiled proudly while the man with the ball cap tried to sink into the background.

"Jesus, Dave. That's the guy." Terry said excitedly, pointing at the television and spilling his coffee on the floor.

"What guy?"

"You remember last Saturday? You and I were at that dead Arab's apartment and we had that foot chase with the B&E artist?" Terry said excitedly. "I didn't get a good look at him, just a side view. But I'm sure that that's the guy."

"Did you catch a name?"

"No! But I'm sure that the television station can give it to us. Channel 13, KTNV. That's our first call of the day."

March 11, 1980 - Las Vegas, Nevada

Jack sat in his old RV reading his morning copy of the Las Vegas Sun. Minutes earlier he'd watched a taxi pull away from the curb, with Donny and Michelle in the rear seat. They were headed to the airport, where they would take separate planes home.

Jack could still see the grin on Donny's face; it had been there almost non-stop for the last week. Michelle seemed to be in the same state and they had been almost inseparable during their time down in Mexico. The fact that the trip was supposed to be a guy's fishing trip, and that Donny spent most of his time with her, didn't bother Jack. He was happy to see Don happy.

He turned his attention to the paper, trying to concentrate, but he found himself just flipping through it, scanning the pages, unable to focus on any one headline in particular. *It's been a hell of a week,* Jack thought. It had been a world record week in fact; the roosterfish was 114 pounds, almost as big as the skipper himself—but poor eating, according to Captain Miguel. The fish was destined for the local taxidermy shop and it would eventually find its way onto the lobby wall of their hotel, a small brass plate beneath it.

Jack recalled what Miguel had said, "It will bring me much business, Señor Jack!" It felt good to know that they had helped the man out. He had been so good to them during their stay.

He walked over to the answering machine to check messages for the last week. It was time for Jack to get back to work. There were several messages; a few were the usual hang-ups, with no message left, the rest were potential customers—people with problems they wanted Jack to solve. Jack jotted down their names and numbers on the pad next to the phone. There was nothing that couldn't wait.

Reluctant to get out of holiday mode, Jack headed to the bathroom to shave and shower. When he was finally ready to face the day he hopped into the Camaro and turned on the radio to find one of his favourite songs playing, *Ride Like the Wind* by Christopher Cross. He found himself tapping out the beat on the steering wheel and singing along.

The bright sunshine making him squint slightly as he left his desert quarters behind and entered the outskirts of the city. He waited for a young woman pushing a stroller to cross the road then made a right onto Mountain Vista Street, towards the bank where he had an appointment with his banker.

He continued singing, tapping in time on the wheel. Out of habit, he checked the rearview mirror for traffic as he came to a stop at a red light. He noticed a grey Ford sedan, with two men in the front seat right behind him. *Where did they come from?* Jack wondered. *I hope I didn't cut them off.*

A few changes of direction later, he checked his rearview mirror again and spotted the same grey Ford, one lane over and three cars back, trying to hide behind an orange Vega.

Christ! Not again, Jack thought, recalling last fall's tragic accident, a result of someone tailing him.

He accelerated slightly and checked his mirror once more. *Good, these guys aren't too bright,* he thought. They were completely unaware that he'd made them, so, without signaling he braked and made a hard right turn, tires squealing in protest. He pressed the gas pedal to the floor and accelerated to the next street, hoping the two men in the car wouldn't catch a glimpse of him before he had a chance to make his next turn. He was in luck. They didn't react fast enough and he made it around the corner in time.

That's good, Jack thought as he once more pushed the gas, more sedately this time. Now that he was free of them he didn't want to draw attention to himself.

The Camaro accelerated smoothly and he checked his mirror once again as he headed for the next street. He was still clear. He cut the wheel left and mashed the gas pedal. The Camaro's small-block engine responded crisply. Spotting a lane coming up on the right, he braked hard and darted down it. Commercial vehicles lined the left side of the lane, leaving a space barely wide enough for traffic to pass—but that was enough. As he made his way past the line of delivery trucks at a break-neck speed of fifteen miles per hour he checked his mirror again and could not see his pursuers. "Good!" he said out loud. About 60 feet from the end of the lane Jack stopped, not surprised to see the grey Ford as it shot by in front of him while he watched it from the safety of the lane, its occupants trying desperately to pick up his trail.

Smoothly he pulled out of the lane and headed in the opposite direction of the Ford, chuckling to himself. *I bet those two are going to be pissed,* he thought. *I wonder who they are?* Jack hoped they weren't more of Jaffar's goons.

He checked the clock on his dash, "Christ! I'm going to be late!" He sped up slightly. Jack hated to be late.

In the Ford, Detective Strohman remarked to his partner, "I can't believe you lost him, Dave."

"I can't believe it myself. That guy made us in less than a minute." He added, "Half a morning's work down the drain!"

"Wait a sec Dave," Strohman tried to calm his agitated partner. "We have his address and his license plate. We'll just pay him a visit later."

"I know Terry. It's just that I'm pissed at myself. I feel like a goddamn rookie! I can't believe the way he cut and ran."

"Oh, he just got lucky! Don't be so hard on yourself." Terry didn't believe that for a minute. *Jack Coward is no ordinary guy,* Terry thought. *No, not by a long shot!*

"Let's get back to the garage, Dave. We'll have another look at Mohammed's file."

Later that day the two detectives sat at their desks, facing one another. Terry Strohman scanned Mohammed Hussan's file but did not see anything out of the ordinary. "Last spring he was in a small scuffle at the Nugget. It seems that some other patron didn't like him sitting next to him at the slots." The detective read further. "Last fall he was in a car accident. They hit a police cruiser and his brother was killed." The report gave the name of the investigating officer. "I think we should pay a visit to Patrolman Bob Tanner."

"I believe he's over at the Ninth," Dave recalled.

"No he's not! I just saw his name downstairs, on the duty roster this morning. We can have dispatch call him in."

"Great! Let's do it!"

Within half an hour all three men were assembled in the boardroom. "Thanks for coming in so quick, Bob."

"No problem, Detective. I hope I can be of some help!"

"Did you bring your notes?"

"Yes!" The patrolman placed a stack of small, spiral-bound notepads on the desk.

"What can you tell us about last November's crash, the one where Officer Mike Carr was injured? There was a fatality." At this, the detective showed Tanner a picture of Mohammed Hussan.

The patrolman searched through his stack of notebooks in front of him until he found the appropriate one. He clearly recalled the incident and had no problem finding the right book and retrieving the information. "It happened on November ninth, last year," he said, opening the book, "Just before my transfer here to this precinct."

"Yes! What more can you tell us about it?"

Tanner scanned his notes to refresh his memory. "The driver, one Akbal Hussan, was pronounced dead at the scene. The sole passenger in the vehicle was the brother of the deceased, Mohammed Hussan. He was transported to University Medical Center by ambulance." The officer paused for a moment to scan his notes further. "There was a civilian eye-witness to the accident, one John A. Coward."

The two detectives could hardly believe their ears. "Are you sure?" This from Detective Strohman.

"Yes! He resides at here in Las Vegas, just north of the city on an acreage. He scribbled the phone number and address on a paper and handed it to the Strohman.

"Bingo!" Dave yelped, startling the young patrolman.

"What's up," Tanner asked.

"Oh you just confirmed a few facts about our friend, Mister Coward."

"He seemed like a good guy. He helped a great deal at the scene as I recall."

"I'm sure he did. Well thank you, Officer Tanner, I think we've got about all we need."

"You're welcome, sir. If I can be of any further assistance let me know."

"We will, thanks!" The door closed behind Bob Tanner as he returned to his patrol.

"Looks like Jack Coward is going to need some closer scrutiny," said Stapleton.

— Chapter 9 —

March 12, 1980

There was no watching the morning's newscast today; right after roll call Detectives Terry Strohman and Dave Stapleton entered their supervisor's office, file in hand.

"What can I do for you today, gentlemen?"

"Well, Captain, Dave and I want you to have a quick look at this case, just to keep you up to date. It's the murder that happened last week. You know, the one up near Cold Canyon Creek?"

Captain Ken Nichols took the file, shifted his bifocals from the top of his head to the bridge of his nose. "I remember the one. It was all over the news, complete with live video feed and all," he said with a look of disdain on his face. Then he said, "Funny how things work out, isn't it?"

"What do you mean?" The detectives stared at Nichols.

"What I mean is that if you two had bothered to check with me yesterday morning about this case, you wouldn't have wasted a whole fucking day investigating a case that will go absolutely nowhere."

"I'm sorry, I still don't understand what you mean," said Strohman. "Dave and I have made some progress on this case! I've—we've—got a make on the perp!" He wasn't used to being dressed down and could feel his blood pressure begin to rise.

The captain's voice rose along with it. "Bullshit! From what I hear, all you got was a quick look at the guy's face, and that from the back. Only a three-quarter view at best."

"But ...!"

"But, nothing! Yesterday you pulled Tanner off his patrol to answer a pisspot full of questions! And all that after identifying some tourist in a Hawaiian shirt on vacation down in Mexico next to a big fish on the bloody ... on television, no less!"

"Look, Captain ..."

"No! You look. Number one, I've known Jack Coward—your so-called perpetrator—for almost ten years. That was before the two you made Detective or even thought about *being* Detectives! He's as honest as the day is long."

Strohman opened his mouth to respond but thought better of it.

"He has helped us solve some major, and I do mean major, cases over the years, saving this department and the taxpayers thousands of dollars." The captain waited for his words to sink in. "Furthermore, he's an ex-marine with a chest-full of Goddamn medals. He's won the Silver Star and has two or three Purple Hearts." He looked at the two detectives, almost daring a response. There was none.

"All you had to do was bring this to me before you went off half-cocked. I am your supervisor and I get to decide what you're investigating. Besides, even if he was guilty, there's not one thing you or I or anybody else could do about it! This case is closed as far as this department is concerned."

Now it was Strohman's turn to raise his voice. "I don't believe this. I don't fucking believe this. How can you speak to us like this? I've got 19 years under my belt with this department and I'm not a complete moron. Sometimes I have to make decisions on the fly and you've never complained about it before. I've put my *own* good service into this department and I don't deserve to be treated this way."

The captain stared him down. "Before you go any further Detective, let me say that if you want to be here long enough to collect your pension, you'd better calm down, be quiet, listen, and listen good. This isn't the first time I've had to talk to you about going off half-cocked on some wild goose chase, but it better be the last!" He paused to catch his breath. "Further, in this case, the perpetrator traveled to and from the State of California during the commission of this murder. That gives the FBI jurisdiction! End of story! Now if you two will return to your desks, I've arranged a nice big pile of cases for each of you to attend to. Good day, gentlemen." He rose from his chair, crossed the room and held the door open for the two detectives.

Not one word was exchanged between the detectives during the walk back to their desks. Both Dave and Terry were mad as hell over the loud 'discussion' that had taken place in the captain's office. Nearly everyone else on the floor had heard the heated exchange as well; the walls were much too thin to provide any degree of privacy. Both men could see all eyes focused on them now. This infuriated Strohman even more, but he waited until they were back at their desks before he spoke. "If that asshole in there thinks I'm going to let this go, he can forget it!" He spoke just loud enough for Dave to hear, or so he thought.

"Forget it Terry. You heard Cappy! This case is over! Done! It's finished!"

"Not as far as I'm concerned. I know what I saw that day. It was Coward. I'll stake my reputation on it!"

"That's what you may be doing Terry, if you don't keep your voice down." Already a few heads were turned in their direction, each trying to overhear what was being said.

"I don't give shit" I'm not going to let this go! I've got friends in D.C. at the Bureau and I'm going to pursue this as far as I can!"

"The Captain will bust you, and probably me too, and I'm not going to let that happen. You may be senior Detective on this watch but I'm not going to let you get me knocked down to walking a beat somewhere. I've had it! I want a new fucking partner and I want him today!"

"You ungrateful little bastard," Strohman's voice rose about twenty decibels. "You wouldn't be where you are now without me!"

"You're Goddamn right about that. I wouldn't be in so much shit half the time," Dave fired back. "I'm going to the Captain to ask for a transfer." Dave headed back towards the captain's office.

"Not a word, Dave. Not a word!"

"You don't have to worry about that, partner. I won't say a word, I promise." He didn't have to; nearly everyone on the second floor had heard the exchange, including several other detectives who rejoiced as they felt they could use a little boost up the seniority ladder.

That evening, after a day that had started out so promising, but had turned out so badly, Terry Strohman sat in his living room. He opened his address book and looked for FBI Inspector Jim Misner's number. He dialed and a voice on the other end just said a simple, "Hello?"

"Jim? This is Terry, Detective Terry Strohman!" After a second added, "From Las Vegas."

"Oh yes, Detective. How are things?" For the life of him, Jim Misner couldn't recall this guy at all.

"First I hope I didn't catch you at bad time."

"No, it's okay. It's only nine-thirty here."

"I'm calling about a case that I've been working on." He didn't add that he was no longer working on the case. "Your bureau office in Sacramento has taken over the case."

"Is that a problem?"

"No! No problem at all." Strohman spent the next ten minutes relating the particulars of the case to the inspector.

"Is that all?"

"Yes, I think that covers it."

"Well, Detective, I'm not sure what you expect from me, but of course I'm not at liberty to discuss the case."

Suddenly Strohman felt foolish for calling. Of course the inspector wouldn't be able to discuss it; it was a regional case. "Yes, I realize that," he managed. "But I was hoping maybe you could shed some light on what's going on here."

"Well no, not really," the inspector said. "But I appreciate you taking the time to call me." He still couldn't remember this guy.

"Thanks for your time, Inspector." Strohman hung up the phone. He could tell by the tone of his voice that the inspector wasn't too interested in what he'd said. "Well no matter. Next stop, Sacramento!"

March 13, 1980

As he'd done just 24 hours earlier, Terry Strohman walked boldly up to his captain's office. He was alone this time, but he didn't care. "Captain, I'd like a few days off!"

"You're not up for vacation!"

"I know that, but I need a few days."

"Okay! You've got a few days."

"Thanks!" That was the only response given, and Strohman walked out the open door, not bothering to close it behind him.

He must be pissed that Dave asked for a transfer, the captain thought. Maybe I should talk to Dave. He waited a few minutes to be sure Terry had left the building then picked up the phone and punched extension 256 and summoned Dave to his office.

As he headed towards Captain Nichol's office, Dave was filled with trepidation. *I wonder why I'm in shit now?* It was a short walk, so he didn't have to wait long to find out.

"Come in, Dave. Sit down." The captain had a much more friendly tone than the day before.

"Captain, if this about yesterday …"

"Don't worry Dave, it's not." Dave began to relax somewhat.

"I've got a good start on some of those files," Dave tried to anticipate his superior's reason for calling him.

"No, Dave. It's not about that. It's about your soon to be ex-partner."

"Oh!" This was suddenly looking up for Dave, and not looking so good for Terry. Still, he had promised not to say anything.

"I know Terry is lead detective and that 90 percent of the time he called the shots," Cappy began, "But ..."

Uh-oh! Here it comes, Dave thought.

"But you're not some green kid we pulled off the street and pinned a Detective badge onto."

"I know, Cap. And I'm sorry. I guess I didn't use my best judgment."

"That's not why I called you in. Let's forget about that as far as you're concerned." Nichols continued, "I've got bigger fish to fry!"

Oh shit. This can't be good, the young detective thought.

"I've been hearing some rather disturbing scuttlebutt coming from around the department, and I'd like to get it straightened out. To separate fact from rumour, so to speak."

"I'll do my best to help, But I've always done my best to steer clear and mind my own business when it comes to gossip."

"Of course Dave, of course!" The captain paused, so he could carefully choose his words. "I waited until Terry had left the office. Where did he go by the way?" he asked nonchalantly, trying to catch the young detective off guard.

"I'm not sure where he went! We haven't had too much to say to each other since yesterday morning."

"No I guess not! Jim Davidson came up to me at lunch yesterday and related part of the conversation that took place at your desk!" He held up his hand, stopping Dave before he could say anything. "I also know that there is no love lost between those two. I wouldn't have called you in, but for the fact that he wasn't the only one to speak up."

"I know that Terry has pissed off a lot of people over the years, both inside and outside the department. He's stepped on a lot of toes on his way to detective rank," Dave recalled. "But other than that, I don't know how much I can tell you."

"I know you have a great deal of loyalty towards Terry, and I commend you for it, even if I feel it's misplaced."

"I always try to be fair to people."

"I know that as well, Dave. But can you answer just two questions for me? I would appreciate an honest answer."

"Yes, sir. I'll try."

"Number one. Did Terry ..." he paused for an instant. He was going to ask Dave straight out about the asshole remark. "Was Detective Terry Strohman insubordinate?"

"Yes sir, he was. He referred to you as an 'asshole'." Several people had already confirmed that.

"Number two. Do you know what he's doing now? I'm specifically referring to cases on hand or otherwise."

"No, but I can tell you that he said that this wasn't over." That should have brought a strong response from the captain, but all he did was smile.

"Thanks, for your honesty, Dave. I think that I've got I need."

"You're welcome, sir. Have a nice day."

"Thanks Dave, I will!" The captain stood smiling and shut his office door. He picked up the telex message he'd received this morning from Inspector Misner. Detective Terry Strohman had always thought his shit didn't stink. It seemed that Inspector Misner had remembered him after all—and without the fondness Terry imagined. The captain reread the paper and tucked it back into the drawer of his desk.

"I wonder what the hell he's up to?" He opened his rolodex, spun it quickly until he found the right card. He picked up the phone and dialed.

March 23, 1980

Detective Terry Strohman picked up the phone in his hotel room and asked the girl at the front desk to connect him with the Las Vegas Police Department.

"Of course, sir, what's the number?" Terry recited the number from memory, one he'd dialed countless times before.

After half a dozen rings he heard, "Hello, Seventh Precinct. How may I help you?"

The detective recognized the nasally voice on the other end of the line. It was Sharon. He smiled, thinking how much she reminded him of the wise-cracking, snorting Ernestine, Lily Tomlin's character on the comedy show, *Laugh-In*. He imagined Sharon reaching down the front of her blouse with index finger and thumb, the way Ernestine did.

"Yes, could you connect me with Captain Nichols?"

With no hesitation she said, "No, I'm sorry, the Captain is away from the office for the next two days. Can I take a message?" The exchange was the same as it had been for the last week. Detective Strohman wasn't the only one that was good with voices; Sharon knew it was Strohman and she and her fellow receptionists had standing orders not to put his calls through. "Not unless he's dead," the captain had said.

"No, thanks. I'll try again later." He placed the receiver back in its cradle and thought about what to do next.

Sacramento, California – March 26, 1980

Jaffar sat alone in the living room of his Sacramento condo, watching the morning news. It was still part of his daily ritual even though he was far-removed from his home in Al-Qa'im.

"Today is the first anniversary of the signing of the Egyptian Israeli Peace Treaty. One year ago today, Prime Minister Menachem Begin and President Anwar Sadat signed the treaty. That day President Jimmy Carter remarked, 'For 30 years Israel and Egypt have waged war, but for the last 16 months they have waged peace.'"

Jaffar watched with interest. He'd been very angry with the Arab President that day, and although some of his anger had dissipated in the year since, it still sat just below the surface. Now it came to a boil once more. "Bloody infidel. Bloody traitor," Jaffar practically spat the words at the television screen as it showed a video of Jimmy Carter and the heads of state shaking hands and posing for the camera. "Carter you fool, you weakling!" He pressed repeatedly down on the red power button, but it failed to shut the television off.

"In other news, Leonard Nimoy celebrates his 49th birthday today. Nimoy is most well-known for his role as Mr. Spock on the show 'Star Trek'."

Jaffar gave up trying to turn the television off and instead hurtled the remote in the direction of the television, shattering it and sending its electronic guts flying everywhere. The television remained on, frustrating him even more. He leapt up from his seat and went to it, where he started violently stabbing at the on/off button. The picture faded to a bright green dot in the center of the screen, the offending button broken.

He stood still a moment, trying to calm himself then went to the kitchen and poured himself a cup of hot green tea. Sitting back down in his chair, he tried not to focus on the newscast he'd just seen. He wanted to calm down. He picked up the phone and dialed; it would be late evening at the other end of the line, but he didn't care.

Abdul Salam Al-Kubesi barely heard the phone over the din of the music. His attention was focused on the three young ladies who occupied his bed. They were the latest in a long string of young women who had done so over the last several weeks. Why not? Jaffar was many thousands of miles away and didn't seem to be in any great hurry to come home. He was smitten with that American woman and planned to marry her. In his absence, Abdul was content to use Jaffar's power and influence to his *own* advantage for once. He'd put that unpleasant business with Mohammed out of his mind, mostly by spending the nights whoring and drinking—both contrary to the Koran, but what did he care?

At the moment the phone rang, one of the women—he couldn't remember her name—was down between his legs, pleasuring him orally. He reluctantly pushed her away as he leaned over another nameless lovely to answer the phone. "One of you, turn that music down," he ordered, his words slightly slurred from the effects of a couple of bottles of wine taken from Jaffar's well-stocked wine cabinet.

"Hello? Who is this?" The music was still blaring in the background.

"This is Jaffar!" Abdul snapped his fingers several times in the directions of the stereo, while trying to cover the mouthpiece with his hand in an unsuccessful effort to muffle the music.

"What the hell is going on?" Jaffar asked, annoyed.

"Oh! Excellency! So good to hear from you." It was not good to hear from him and his manhood suddenly suffered a power failure, ruining the erection the half-drunk Arab had managed. In the now-quiet room the girls laughed and pointed. Abdul glared at them in anger.

"What's going on," Jaffar demanded. "I hear women laughing."

"That's just the television." The girls took advantage of this distraction to gather up their money and clothes and make a hasty retreat back to the streets of Al-Qa'im. Jaffar thought about that for a second; he could not recall Abdul owning a television.

"You sound drunk! Have you been stealing my wine again?"

Abdul swallowed hard. "No! No, Excellency! I have not. I swear an oath to Allah." He did not realize that Jaffar was meticulous about inventorying not just his wine, but everything he possessed. He kept all of it recorded in a ledger—the better to catch unfaithful servants.

"I had better not find one bottle missing, or the consequences shall be most severe. That, I can assure you."

"I understand." Abdul said, and he did understand, all too well. He swallowed hard. He'd witnessed first-hand the consequences of crossing swords with Jaffar.

For the past few weeks Jaffar's portion of funds—automatically directed to his account in Switzerland—had diminished, ever so slightly. Jaffar had noticed and made some inquiries as to why ... another thing that had escaped Abdul's attention. For the moment, however, Jaffar had decided not to confront Abdul about where the money had gone. He would deal with that later.

"I am most disturbed to think you are taking advantage of me, my friend," was all he said.

"Of course I would never do that, Excellency," Abdul said. "And I will most gladly replace the wine," he added, good sense overcoming his guilt.

Jaffar softened a little. "I am glad you admitted to it," he said. Then Jaffar explained the news story he'd seen on the morning's broadcast and asked

Abdul to watch or record the daily news so that he wouldn't miss anything. "I need to advise Hamas on strategy. I can't miss these events," he explained.

Abdul had not watched any news broadcasts for weeks, so he was unaware of the historic event featuring the Arab leaders and the American president. In fact, the last newscast he'd watched was on the very day he and Jaffar had left for the United States; if he was more interested in international events, Abdul might have seen the results of his handiwork on the television.

"Have you talked to anyone else in our organization lately? Discussed any plans for a Jihad against the Americans or maybe the British?" Jaffar asked. He did not add, *'or have you just collected your envelopes stuffed with cash, extorted from the locals?'*

"Yes, I did. Nothing's ready to go."

"I do hope that you, or someone else, can figure out a response to this, this ...outrage," Jaffar spat. "Everyone concerned has had a year to figure out something, anything."

"Everyone's attention seems to be focused on the hostages in Tehran."

"I know. The same is true over here. This is the so-and-so day of their captivity!" Jaffar continued, "That smiling, weak excuse of a president, Jimmy Carter, appears on the television almost daily!"

"I know, I've seen him," Abdul lied.

"Well, keep me informed of any progress. Also make sure that I also get my money on time!" Jaffar did not need to add anything to further to this. He hung up, not even waiting for Abdul to answer.

"Yes, Excellency," Abdul said to dead air, as he heard the click at the end of the line.

Jaffar sat back in his chair, mentally reviewing his conversation with his subordinate. It had been bad enough to confirm his wine was being drunk without his permission. Now Jaffar was almost certain Abdul had also helped himself to some of his funds. *I think Abdul will have to be punished,* he thought. Jaffar hoped he would not have to do more. The thought of anyone stealing from him incensed him. Many men and a few women in Al-Qa'im had lost their hands for less.

Jaffar gazed in frustration out his Sacramento window. He missed his quiet terrace at home. The balcony in his condo, although it afforded him a good view, was never quiet. *The thing about the cities in this country is that they never sleep,* he thought. *There is activity all hours of the day and night, always there are people yelling and carrying on.*

He sighed. He was calmer now. It was a pleasant spring day, and the weather looked as though it was going to cooperate. *Maybe I should pick up Giti for a nice lunch on a patio somewhere,* he thought as he looked once more out the window. *Giti will probably want to talk some more about wedding plans.* He looked at his watch, it was almost ten o'clock. He made a dash to the bathroom to shower and shave.

Las Vegas, Nevada - April 2, 1980

Jack had already been for his morning jog and was now just pulling into the convenience store, as per his general routine. He reached behind his back and adjusted the leather holster he'd started to wear. He was starting to get used to the weight of the Smith and Wesson Model 66 inside. After the last car chase three or four weeks earlier he'd started to pack it on his morning jogs and it was beginning to feel more comfortable.

As got out of his car so he could go into the convenience store where he always got his morning coffee, he immediately noticed a four-door sedan in the loading zone that looked strangely clean for a service vehicle. Two men inside looked keenly at him and two others opened the door and rapidly exited the car. Jack could see one of the men mouth the words, "That's him." His mind raced instantly back to the two Hussan brothers, though he was fairly certain these two suits were not hit men. They looked more like a couple of law enforcement officers.

He stood up and shut the Camaro's door behind him.

"Mister Coward? FBI. We'd like to talk to you for a minute." Jack relaxed somewhat, trepidation replaced by curiosity. He gave the offered identification a quick glance; it looked genuine. He could spot fake I.D. a mile away. "I'm Inspector Steven Perry."

Jack was quick to ask, "Any relation to the lead singer from Journey?"

The inspector smiled politely and said, "No. Not that I know of. Is there somewhere we can go? We'd like to ask you a couple of questions."

"I guess I could spare a few minutes. We can talk right here if you like."

"Not quite what we had in mind. How about downtown?"

"Well ..." Jack was about to protest.

"Captain Nichols at the Seventh Precinct assured us that you would cooperate."

"In that case, how about down at the Seventh then? Captain Nichols could sit in. Am I going to need my lawyer?"

"Well, Mr. Coward, that remains to be seen, but you can call him if you like."

In the interrogation room of the Seventh Precinct, Jack sat across the table from the two inspectors from the FBI. A small cassette recorder was placed on the table and turned on. "Now Jack, what can you tell us about your relationship with Mr. Mohammed Hussan?"

That's right to the point, Jack thought. On the ride over he'd tried to figure out what the Fibbies wanted with him. There were several possibilities—and Jack had already guessed correctly. "He was one of my clients," he said.

"Do you know he was murdered?"

"Yes. I saw it on the news last month."

"Did you kill him," Inspector Perry asked.

"No absolutely not!" Jack looked the inspector right in the eye as he answered.

"Where were you on February 28th? And what was your relationship with Mr. Mohammed Hussan?"

"I don't know where I was. I'd have to check my daily calendar to see where I was. As to your second question, as I told you before, I'm a private investigator and he was one my clients."

"Did you murder Mr. Hussan?"

"As I told you before, the answer to that question is no! Also if you're going to ask me the same questions twice this is going to take a long time."

Inspector Perry slammed his palm down so hard on the table that the cassette recorder bounced into the air. It came down hard enough to pop open, the cassette ejecting itself on the table.

"What was your relationship with Mr. Hussan?" he demanded loudly, his face inches from Jack's, so close that Jack could smell the coffee on his breath.

Jack sat there unshaken and unimpressed. He'd been trained to resist most physical and psychological means of torture in the marines. He hadn't been really scared since that night that he and Donny had boosted those televisions. That was many years ago. Jack smiled, and once again looked Inspector Perry in the eye. "For the *third* time, he was my client."

"What business did you have? What was it he asked you to do?"

"I'm afraid that comes under the area of client privilege. I can't tell you. Do you have any other questions for me?" Jack asked.

Inspector Perry slammed his hand down on the desk, this time so hard Jack was sure he'd heard a bone snap. "Did you know that he was a member of a militant group?"

"No I did not."

"What was it he asked you to do for him?"

"As I've said before, I can't tell you."

"Your client is dead! Your client confidentiality doesn't extend past the grave!" The agent was clearly agitated now.

"Yes, as a matter of fact it does. Now, if that is all …?"

"No, that is not all!" The agent was red in the face. The other agent came to his side, took Agent Perry's arm and steered him over to the far corner of the room.

"That's enough Steve. We're not going to get anywhere with this guy."

"We will if we haul his ass down to the bureau."

"That's not going to happen! This is over." The agent turned back to the center of the room and told Jack that he could leave. The door opened from the outside and Jack came face to face with his old friend, Captain Ken Nichols.

"Hello, Ken. How are you?"

"Fine Jack, I'm just fine." As the two agents exited the interrogation room, Agent Perry pushed roughly past Jack. Jack glanced towards him, smiled calmly and then looked away.

"Jack do you think you and I could have a little chat? Off the record, of course," Nichols said. He indicated the way to his office. Jack looked towards the clock on the wall.

"Not your office, Ken. How about lunch at that tavern down the street? O'Malley's."

"Great! Let me grab my coat."

In just a few minutes, the two friends sat down at a well-worn oak table in O'Malley's, each with a beer in front of them. The waitress took their burger orders and left. The tavern was crowded with the usual lunchtime crowd; no one paid them any attention.

"Well Jack, let's have it." Nichols had watched the interview through the one-way glass. "How are you mixed up with this Mohammed fellow?"

"Well, let's see. About a year and a half ago I got a call from our friend Mr. Hussan and he asked if could do some work for him." The waitress brought the two men their burgers and Jack continued between bites all the way up to the day he had been tailed by the detectives.

Ken Nichols let out a big belly laugh, almost choking on his burger. "Jack, do you know who those two guys were?"

"No, what's so damn funny?"

"They were my two top Detectives!" The captain laughed again. "How long did it take you to make them?"

"About a block and a half."

"Christ! It's worse than I thought." Ken laughed again.

Jack left out the part about the ledger in the fake potted plant, but he did tell his friend about Mohammed's journal and even went so far as to tell Ken where and when he'd got it.

"So, the asshole was right after all."

"What does that mean," Jack asked. "What asshole?"

"Oh, just a soon to be ex-Detective. He got a look at you as you bolted from the apartment."

"I had to find out why the guy wanted to kill me."

"Yeah, I know!"

"So what kind of shit am I in, and how deep is it?"

"Christ Jack! You know me better than that. If I wanted to bust you, do you think that you and I would be having beers right now?"

"No, I suppose not." Jack smiled.

"But don't get me wrong Jack. I think you're still in deep shit!"

"Why?"

"Oh, maybe not in shit legally or criminally, but other ways."

"Explain!"

"Well let's just say that this murder has attracted a large amount of attention all the way to D.C." After a second he added, "I don't mean just the FBI, Jack."

"Ken, spit it out for Christ's sake!"

"Well let's just say that those assholes over there in Tehran who are holding those Americans hostages have raised a shit storm in Washington. You do watch the news?"

"Yeah! I watch the news. I'm sure that there's much more going on behind closed doors."

Ken reflected for a second. "There is. Of that you can be assured. But Jack, you've got to understand—the Feds are watching almost every Goddamn towelhead in the fucking country!" He paused and added, "At least it seems that way." The captain hesitated for another few seconds, pondering his next words, unsure if telling Jack could place him in even more hot water. He decided to tell him.

"We've been watching Mohammed for a long time," he said quietly. "And I know from the head of security at the Gold Nugget that the FBI confiscated videotape from the security cameras."

"That's where I met our dead friend. They don't think I offed him, do they?"

"Hell no! Whoever did this was a butcher, a Goddamned butcher. If you killed the guy it would have been quick and neat." The Captain glanced at his watch. "Jesus, where did the time go? I have to get back to work."

"Good to see you," Ken, Jack said. Then he offered, "Ken would you like to have that journal?"

"What?"

"Do you want Mohammed's journal? I'll trade it for a ride back to my RV." Jack had already made a copy. It was standard operating procedure.

"Alright, but you've got to pay for lunch."

"Do I look like I've got any money on me?"

"You drive a hard bargain Jack. I guess the department can pick up the tab for lunch. Especially after we let the Fibbies grill you."

"Yeah, you owe me," Jack laughed.

"Yeah. That's right." On the way back to the captain's car Ken asked, "By the way Jack, are you still packing?"

"Of course Ken." Jack patted his fanny pack. "I'm licensed to carry!"

The police captain let out another hoot. "I bet Emery and Perry would have shit if they'd known."

"Yeah. But if I was going to take them down, I wouldn't have needed a gun," Jack smirked.

"No! No I don't suppose you would have." Ken recalled a distant conversation he'd had with Jack's commanding officer in 1969 or 1970. He couldn't remember the man's name but he could remember how disappointed he'd been that both Jack and Donny had turned down personal invitations to be special ops. "Takes a special man for that kind of service, Lieutenant Nichols," he'd said. "Both these men could kill a man in a heartbeat with their bare hands."

But Jack and Donny had had enough of killing.

Yes, takes a special kind of man for that kind of service … after all these years, Ken Nichols could still hear those words and the words that followed … "but it takes an even better man, to know he could and refrain from doing so."

— Chapter 10 —

April 4, 1980

It was a sunny day in Washington D.C. The temperature hovered around the 60-degree mark, warm enough to melt the slush that remained from what everyone expected was the last gasp of winter. Spring had definitely arrived and it was warm enough that Donny had removed the hard top from his white, 1974 MGB. Although he knew that putting the hard top into storage was risky, in his heart he knew warm, summer weather was only weeks away. Donny did not want to waste an opportunity to feel the wind in his hair and the sun on his face.

As Donny drove from his apartment in Edgewood, he saw the streets, parks and monuments packed with sightseers, tourists and locals, all taking advantage of the sunshine. He found his way to 23rd Street, which would take him past his favorite place in Washington, the Lincoln Memorial, then over the Arlington Memorial Bridge.

"What a great day to own a convertible," he said to himself, as he enjoyed the sunlight reflecting off the waves of the Potomac when he crossed from Columbia into Virginia.

He did not want to be late today; it wasn't often a man was allowed entrance into the headquarters of America's intelligence-gathering network. He leisurely drove along the George Washington Memorial Parkway and exited onto Dolly Madison Boulevard. He took the third right, pulled up to the south gate and identified himself at the speaker box. The guard waved him forward and checked his identification. He was given a parking pass and instructed where to park.

The Central Intelligence Agency Headquarters were located on more than 250 acres of land. Donny drove unescorted, winding his way through the forest of trees that lined both sides of the road. He could see many of the bare branches had spouted buds; soon this would be a lush green forest.

Up ahead, he saw the CIA building. He parked his car and walked up the stairs to the building entrance. Inside he crossed over a large, inlaid granite seal and made his way to the guard station, where he was given a visitor's badge. He spotted his friend, Agent Kip Holmes, who was to be his escort for the duration of his visit. "Good morning, Kip."

"Good morning, Donny." Kip glanced at Donny's visitors badge, "I see security has got you all squared away. My office is on the second floor. Follow me."

"After you, Sherlock," Don said with a grin. Kip laughed, thankful the moniker assigned by Don years ago had failed to catch on at CIA.

"That's enough of that, Ziegler," he said.

The two men soon sat facing each other at Kip's desk, which was completely clear of files, save one. Don glanced past his friend, out the window. Through the trees, he could see the Potomac River. "Nice view, Kip."

"Yes, it is." Kip opened the file and scanned the first page. "I did a bit of checking on those names and the number you gave me."

"What did you come up with?"

"I can let you make some notes, but only up here." Kip pointed at his temple. "I can't let you physically touch the file."

"I know, I know—I could touch it, but then you'd have to kill me," Don joked.

"Well let's see, the name Jaffar Hamid Harraj is sure interesting. According to some, he's involved with the Islamic Hamas Movement."

"What! No way!" Don added, "Must be a different guy. This guy is a businessman, real suave."

"Could be a different guy, but I'm just going by what I've found. Harraj is a common Farsi surname."

"What about the phone number?"

"It's a simple residential number—in Iraq. It does, in fact, belong to Mr. Harraj. But he also has an American number, in Sacramento. And you could have found that yourself."

"I know," Don said. "But why would I when I can get you to do it?" Kip smiled, and Don asked, "What about the other name and number?"

"Oh yes. Abdul Salam Al-Kubesi. He actually goes by the rank of Colonel and is the Chief of Police in the town of Al-Qa'im, which is also where Mr. Harraj lives."

"What the hell! He's the Chief of Police?"

"Yep! Here's a picture of him, taken during some national holiday."

"Nice ribbons!" One could not help but notice them. Don instantly committed the face to memory.

"Yeah! This guy is a real beauty. He's responsible for several dozen prisoner deaths occurring in his jail." After reading for several seconds Kip added, "Looks like he's probably responsible for hundreds more."

"Why doesn't the government do something?"

"Like *who*? The people in charge are over there are drunk with power, corrupt beyond description. Look at Saddam Hussein, for instance. He came to power in a bloodless coup, but now that he's in power, he's killed hundreds of people, including government ministers. Even members of his own family aren't safe from him, for God's sake."

"A real charming guy," Don remarked drily.

"A real maniac is more like it."

"What else do you have, Kip?"

"Not a lot. This Harraj character has remained below the radar. Probably he's just a business man, as you say. The Chief of Police appears to be a blood-thirsty buffoon of sorts but we have nothing on him beyond that. Where did the numbers come from?"

"Just one of Jack's cases."

"Your old school pal?"

"Yes. One and the same." Donny remembered, "I told Jack that I'd ask you about the 1976 bombing of Middle East flight 438. Was Jaffar involved with that?"

"Not that I can see here. Sorry!"

Donny was a little disappointed that Kip didn't have anything better for him, but there was something else he hoped his old military buddy could tell him. "Kip, off the record, can you tell me anything about the new secret agency in Washington? The grapevine says our old commanding officer from 'Nam is involved in it."

"I've heard the same rumors. You know how things work in D.C. As to the matter of whether they are true or not, I don't know."

"I'll let you get back to work. We should get together in the next couple of weeks, before I head out west."

"Going to see Jack in Las Vegas?"

"Nope. Moving out west!"

"Really! Why so? I thought you liked D.C."

"Met someone—a stewardess, no less!. She lives out there. Besides I'm sick of the weather here. I don't think I could stand to go through another winter like this last one."

"Yes, they do seem to be getting worse." Kip picked up the file and locked it in his drawer then got up from his desk. "We can talk on the way out," he said.

"Yeah," agreed Donny.

Agent Kip Holmes shook hands with Donny then watched as his friend maneuvered the white sports car down the winding road, towards the gate. Then he went back to his office, opened his day-timer and made a couple of notes. After doing so he picked up the telephone and made a call. "Colonel Hart, please."

After a short pause a gruff man's voice said, "Colonel Hart speaking."

"Good morning, Colonel. This is Kip Holmes."

"Yes Kip, how can I help you?"

"Don Ziegler was here!"

"Thank you." The connection was broken.

Las Vegas, Nevada

It had been just over 18 months since Jack had last made his way to Sacramento, and here he was again after that same dusty drive. This time, instead of casing the lovely Giti Roshtti, he was here to dig up information on Mr. Jaffar Harraj—the man he suspected had employed him to dig up information on Giti. Just as he'd done on his previous trip, Jack stopped at the Alpine Lodge on Walker Lake. He entered the lobby and was greeted by a much younger face than expected.

"Good day, Sir. Can I help you?"

"I'd like a room, please. Just for myself."

"That'll be $21, please."

Jack handed over the bills and inquired, "What happened to the older fellow?"

"He passed away last year. Cancer, I think."

"That's too bad. I remember him from several stops I've made here over the years." He was sad to hear of the man's death. He'd been a really friendly guy. The kid at the desk remained unmoved so Jack grabbed his bag and headed for the elevator.

"Check out time is at 11 o'clock!" the clerk called after him.

Jack entered his room, put his bag down and immediately jumped into the shower. After dressing, he headed down to the small dining room for dinner, the same routine he always followed. He enjoyed a lovely dinner and the view of the lake, then topped it off with a coffee, which he nursed silently as he thought about Jaffar Harraj and Giti Roshtti. He wondered if the man had ever managed to impress her.

It was early evening when he got back to his room. He sat on the bed, turned on the small color television and casually flipped through the available channels. There was nothing that piqued his interest so he turned it off after a few moments. He opened the door to the hallway and, ice bucket in hand, wandered casually down to get some ice. Back in his room, he sat in the bed, listening, as he had done the last time he'd been here, to the ice cubes as they fissured and popped when fluid was added. This time, however, it wasn't Jack Daniels killing the ice cubes; it was plain, old water. He'd curtailed his drinking about the same time he'd started jogging and was now in peak shape, almost as good as when he was in the marines.

I guess I should call Don to see how he made out getting information on those names in Hussan's book, Jack thought. He dialed nine for an outside line and then zero.

"Hello, can I help you?"

"Yes, operator, I'd like to place a long-distance call to Washington, D.C. and I'd like to bill it to my home phone number."

After a moment he heard his friend's familiar voice, "Hello?"

"Hey, Donny. What's new?"

"Well this morning I drove into Langley to see my old pal Kip Holmes. You remember him?"

"Yes, nice guy. What did you find?"

"Not much Jack. Only that our friend Jaffar is just a Middle Eastern businessman. But his pal Abdul, that's another story."

"What do you mean?"

"Well the file Kip had wasn't all that big, just a half-a-dozen pages and some eight-by-ten glossies he barely let me look at …."

"That doesn't sound like much. Maybe there's not much too this."

"But Jack, I've not come to the best part. Jaffar's pal Abdul, he's the Chief of Police in a little Iraqi town called Al-Qa'im. As soon as I saw Kip's pictures, I remembered him from those pictures I took at the funeral."

"What?"

"Yeah! No shit! And you know what else? Someone by the name of Jaffar Hamid Harraj, is a big-wig in the Islamic Hamas Movement."

"Maybe Jaffar Harraj is like, you know, John Smith."

"That's what Kip said too."

"Let me ask you this, then. What were the Chief of Police of Al-Qa'im, Iraq and his buddy doing at a funeral in Sacramento?"

"Maybe they are family?" Don blurted out the first thing that came to mind.

"Maybe! But then why would some guy back in Iraq hire me to keep tabs on a relative?"

"Dunno. Maybe that Giti broad ran away from home."

"Yeah … maybe that's it. They like to keep tabs on their women …"

"I hear a 'but' in there somewhere."

"But why did two goons try to run me off the road last November? And why did one of those goons just happen to be the guy that hired me to follow Giti Roshtti?"

"Maybe you pissed him off?"

"Oh yeah, maybe I did. But my gut tells me there's more to this than meets the eye. And you know what else? I think the CIA have more on this than the little piece of shit file Kip stuck under your nose."

"You think they sanitized the file?"

"I wouldn't be the least bit surprised! I always follow my gut instincts."

"Yep, me too. What do you intend to do Jack?"

"Well since the only link we've got to those two guys is Sacramento and Giti Roshtti, I'm headed there."

"Unless, of course, you want to take a flight to Iraq."

"The Middle East isn't the safest place for Americans these days. I think I'll pass."

"Let me know what you find. And call me when you get back to Las Vegas."

"What are you going to do?"

"I've got a couple of things to arrange with work."

"What kind of things?"

"Oh, not much." Donny paused, "Then I've got to start packing! I'm coming your way, buddy. For what I would call an extended stay."

Jack took a moment to absorb this. Then he said, "Bullshit! Really?"

"Yeah, really! I got a job offer in Vegas, doing the same consulting stuff I'm doing here. And for more money!"

"That's great!" Jack could hardly believe his ears.

"Yeah, I think so. You know, I drove out to Langley in the MG, with the top down. It was great."

"You'll be able to do that almost all year here."

"I know ... just one of the many attractions of the west."

"I'd like to think I'm another attraction, but I think this is about Michelle, am I right?" teased Jack.

"You'd be thinking correctly," Don confirmed.

"Take care, my friend," Jack said. "I'm glad you've finally come to whatever senses you have!"

Don laughed. "I'll see you soon," he said.

Sacramento, California - April 10, 1980

For seven mornings in a row, Jack sat in his car down the block from Giti Roshtti's house. Luckily, he hadn't had to do 24-hour-a-day surveillance; Mrs. Roshtti kept a fairly strict routine, which had made Jack's job very easy, if somewhat boring. "One more day," Jack said to himself. "Just one more day."

Giti and Sina left the house at eight-fifteen as usual and either Giti drove or her sister-in law picked her up; from there the two women would drop

Sina off at school. Today, it was Giti's turn to drive. She pulled out of the driveway and headed down the street towards the house her brother-in-law shared with his wife. Nothing unusual there; Jack had been following Giti at a discreet distance all week and he fell into line as usual. He stayed far back and to date he'd been lucky that she'd been oblivious to the dusty 'brown' black Camaro.

Giti drove the short distance to pick up Fatemah in her almost-new Honda Civic wagon. It was the only luxury she'd allowed herself after receiving the court-awarded settlement from PSA and the other defendants. With the exception of the $25,000 she'd paid back to Jaffar, she placed the rest of the money into a trust fund she'd set up for Sina.

After two short beeps of the horn, Fatemah got into the passenger seat and they set off toward Sina's school. For several days Jack had followed quite far behind, observing from a distance as Giti and Fatemah drove through road construction, usually over half-inch steel plates. Today, however, the plates were gone and a flagman was guiding cars through active work. As Jack followed, Giti wound up stopped dead at the end of a traffic snake. He had no choice but to pull up and stop right behind the Honda.

Inside the car ahead, he saw Giti and Fatemah engaged in an animated conversation, using their hands freely to gesture. As the traffic delay lengthened, he started to worry that they might notice him behind him and was considering backing up and leaving but then several cars pulled up behind him leaving him with no way to get out. Trapped, he focused his attention towards the front and suddenly the small face of Sina appeared in the back window of the wagon. He stared directly at Jack, smiled and waved. Jack smiled and waved back.

The line of cars began to inch forward as the crews cleared the right lane and Sina's face disappeared from view; the boy's attention was now focused on a bright yellow backhoe. Jack watched as Giti pulled the car off the street and into the school's front parking lot to let Sina out. Except for the traffic jam, it was all the same as it had been for a week.

He continued past the school and headed into Sacramento, fairly certain he could pick her trail up at the place where she worked. He would give it one more day and then head back to Las Vegas empty-handed.

Maybe there is nothing more to this, Jack thought ... but he still had that feeling. "One more day," he said, "One more day."

April 12, 1980

It was just after seven in the morning. Giti still lay in bed, trying to coax herself from under the blankets.

"I'll sleep in tomorrow," she told herself and got up. She headed for the kitchen, poking her head into Sina's room along the way. "Still asleep! Good!" She could enjoy a cup of coffee with no distraction.

Just after seven the phone rang. She reached for it, managing to get it before the second ring. "Hello?" she said softly, not wanting to wake Sina just yet.

"Good morning Giti. I hope I didn't wake you."

"Oh no, Jaffar. I was just enjoying my morning coffee."

"Good! I was wondering if you had any plans for today?"

"Not really. It's Saturday, I usually do laundry and clean a little, and then go grocery shopping. Why?"

"I was wondering if I could take you to lunch? Then maybe we could take a walk around town?"

"I guess I could drop Sina off with his aunt and uncle when he's up and dressed," she said.

"I'll pick you up before noon."

"Could you pick me up at the office? I have some business there and I can leave Sina with Fatemah and Zafar there."

"No problem," said Jaffar.

For the eighth day, Jack parked on Giti's street. He was between two cars, half a block down. At eight o'clock he'd been there for over an hour and a half, watching, reading the morning paper, watching some more. A few cars had passed. Jack looked at the occupants, and speculated as to where they were headed. Just a bit more than 40 minutes later Giti, with Sina in tow, headed to the car.

Well it's Saturday. I don't think the young man has school today, Jack thought. I wonder where they're off to? Fifteen minutes later, Giti pulled into the parking lot of the local Safeway. Jack watched as she placed a quarter into the locking mechanism and tried to pull a buggy free; it didn't budge. She struggled with it for 30 seconds and was about to go inside to complain.

"Can I help you with that?" Giti turned, the voice had startled her, and she'd been so intent on trying to free the buggy that she hadn't heard Jack walk up behind her.

"Thanks! I put a quarter in, but this darned buggy seems to be stuck." Giti smiled at Jack.

"I have problems with these things all the time." Jack hit the mechanism hard with his open palm and the chain popped free.

"Thank you! I appreciate it. I probably would have been here all day trying to get that buggy unstuck."

"No problem. Glad I could help."

"You look familiar. Do you live around here?" Giti couldn't recall meeting Jack during Reza's funeral.

"No! I just stopped to pick up a couple of things. I'm from out of town," Jack volunteered.

Luckily Sina was still in the car, staring at a toy light sabre in his hand; he would have noticed Jack for sure.

"Oh … well, thanks again." Giti turned and wheeled her now-liberated cart into the store, leaving Jack to stare after her. He'd almost forgotten how beautiful she was. The first time he'd met her face-to-face was during a very sad occasion; before that he'd only seen her face through a telephoto lens, when she'd been grieving. She wasn't grieving today! Today, she was the complete opposite and Jack was struck by how open, genuine and warm she was.

He walked back to his car with a smile on his face. Half an hour later, as Giti lifted the rear hatch on her car to put the groceries in, he watched again. She moved so gracefully, like a dancer. He was attracted despite his efforts to remain impartial. He wanted to go over and speak to her again, but he knew he should not.

She replaced the buggy, retrieved her quarter and got into her car then headed back toward Knox Drive, but instead of turning right and heading home she turned left and headed towards downtown Sacramento. Jack was almost ready to head back to Las Vegas, but instead he instinctively turned and followed her. *In for a penny, in for a pound.* He could always go home tomorrow.

Giti eventually pulled into the parking lot of the Shalimar Market. Normally she used the lot at the far end of the building and parked in her assigned spot. Today was Saturday, however, and the offices of U.S. Fabrics Wholesale were closed, the gates locked. Only the Shalimar market was open.

Jack watched as Giti left her car and headed into the market. He watched for more than an hour, periodically reading the morning paper as he kept tabs on the vehicles that came and went. The headline on the sports page read, 'Ready to Run! After 4,000 kilometers of training, Terry Fox is eager to begin his Marathon of Hope. In addition to raising money for cancer research, Terry wants to prove to other cancer victims that any challenge can be overcome.'

"Let's hope you do it, kid," Jack said out loud. He read a bit more, glancing up periodically to make sure Giti's car was still there. 'Steve vs. Steve!' screamed a headline.

"What's this? Oh damn!" he said out loud. The headline read, 'The Giants with Steve Rogers, lost five to three to Steve Carlton and the San Diego Padres at Jack Murphy Stadium.'

"Jesus, Evans! Three fucking errors in one inning? I don't believe it," Jack said with disgust. "I wonder how Donny's Orioles did?" They hadn't done much better, he discovered; they'd lost eight to four to the Chicago White Sox.

Jack continued to scan the newspaper. Then through the partially-open driver's window, he heard the sound of tires on the pavement, growing louder by the second. Jack looked over the top of his newspaper. *Probably just another person on their way to the market.* The glare from the morning sun reflected off the windshield, making it impossible to see anything inside the car, except a dark silhouette.

The car made a right onto Northgate Boulevard and Jack could now see the driver's profile; he was handsome, Middle Eastern and appeared to be wearing an expensive suit.

Hey, he looks familiar! Jack picked up the binoculars from the passenger seat and focused on the new Buick as it approached, the orange and white Budget Rent-a-Car sticker on the bumper.

"Holy shit! I don't believe it!" he exhaled. He recognized the face from that single eight-by-ten black and white photo Donny had taken at the funeral. Jaffar Harraj walked up the steps and into the market, on his way to Giti's office. *And to think, I was about to head home!*

Jack was not one to jump to conclusions, but this unexpected turn of events filled his mind with a myriad of possible scenarios. *Clearly he used my report to find her, he thought.* A short while later, as Jack watched, Giti and Jaffar walked into the parking lot, arm-in-arm.

And it seems to be true that he was interested in her romantically, he thought as he raised his binoculars to his eyes. He found himself feeling unexpectedly jealous.

Giti and Jaffar got into separate cars, which gave Jack pause for a moment. *I know which one I'm going to follow,* he said to himself. Luckily he didn't have to choose. Jaffar turned left out of the parking lot with Giti right behind him and when it was safe to do so without being seen, he fell into line as well.

Jack scanned the traffic ahead for anything that might interfere with his tail. Then he checked the rearview as well, looking for any traffic that might overtake him—and that's when he saw the grey sedan behind him again.

"Not again!" Jack fumed. This time, he was pretty sure these were Jaffar's goons, protecting their boss. They had appeared the same time Jack had started to following the two vehicles ahead of him. However, there was nothing to be done about it now. He sighed and continued tailing Giti and Jaffar as they made their way into the city center, matching them turn for turn. The car behind Jack did the same.

"Yep still there," Jack said as he checked the mirror again. These two really knew how to tail someone and that bothered Jack. Maybe Jaffar had finally hired some professionals.

He leaned over slightly and pulled the Smith and Wesson revolver from its holster, then tucked it in right beside his thigh. Although Jack preferred this gun for what he called 'everyday use', his favorite was still the Colt 45 sidearm that had spent two tours of Vietnam on his right hip. He'd kept the Colt after he'd returned to the States, though officially it had 'gone missing' during the last few days he was over there. But while it wasn't his favored Colt, he still liked the Smith and Wesson for the weight and size and the .357 could still stop anyone; all Jack had to do was hit the mark and the person would be down—and would stay down.

The two cars ahead of him slowed down and then pulled into a parking lot. Jack slowed and drove past them. A half a block past, when traffic was clear, he made a U-turn and parked on the far side of the street facing both Giti and Jaffar, as well as the approaching gray sedan with its two occupants.

Jack watched as the sedan closed the last hundred yards or so noting that as it slowed both men looked into the lot towards Giti and Jaffar. He reached for his revolver and slid over toward the passenger door, checking to see that it was unlocked. He was ready to bail, if the situation turned bad.

As the sedan closed the last couple of yards, both men looked directly at him. *Oh shit,* Jack thought. But while they had clearly focused on Jack, as they reached the black Camaro and continued north, he noticed they also took a long gander at Giti and Jaffar, who were still in their respective vehicles.

I wonder who they work for? Clearly they weren't hired by Jaffar; they are as interested in him as they are in me! Jack watched the sedan turn right at the next street and accelerate.

Giti parked her car in the visitor's parking lot of the Monta Rosa Gardens, the address of Jaffar's condo. After locking up, she got into the passenger seat beside Jaffar, smiling, and he drove them to Kosmo's Café, a few streets away. Jack followed and watched as they sat on the terrace of Kosmo's and began to talk.

"I'm so glad you asked me out for lunch today, Jaffar."

"Oh, why is that?"

"You saved me from a pile of laundry that I had to iron and fold."

"It sounds tedious."

"Tedious, but necessary."

"Did you get your groceries?"

"Yes, they are in my trunk. Nothing's perishable. I'll leave them until later, maybe tomorrow."

"What are you going to do for the rest of the day? Do you have anything in particular that you want to do?"

"No! I told Fatemah I would call if I was going to stay with you."

"Maybe you should call!" Jaffar smiled. Giti looked at Jaffar, studying his handsome face. For an instant, his image was replaced by that of the man who had helped her with her shopping cart. There was something familiar about that man … and something reassuring as well. She couldn't put her finger on it, but she wondered if she had met him before somewhere. He was certainly kind. And handsome. Her face heated up a little; how could she think such things while having lunch with her fiancé?

"What's wrong Giti? Why are you looking at me like that?"

"What?" Back to reality, "What was that, Jaffar?"

"You looked as though you were a million miles away."

"Oh I was just thinking of my little Sina. I hope he's going to be alright with Zafar and Fatemah," she lied as she sat there questioning herself, *why do I keep thinking about that man ... he is a stranger to me!*

"He will be fine."

"Yes I'm sure!" Giti played with her salad, unable to focus all of a sudden.

"So, Giti, do you think we can get everything ready in time for the first week of July? Or do you want to run away to Las Vegas and get married?" Jaffar teased.

"No! I promised Fatemah we'd have a family wedding with all the trimmings. I told her we'd have big bouquets of flowers, lots of food and all our friends and family." She added, "And I certainly don't want to get married by Elvis!"

"Who? Oh yes, Elvis."

They sat for a while. Giti continued to pick at her food, still thinking about the strange man in the parking lot. Jaffar was talking about an interesting trip he had been on to Iraq, and how a colleague of his had been late for a meeting because of an oxen-cart blocking the street. She laughed at the right moments and suddenly thought, *oh my, all of Jaffar's family is in Iraq? How can they come to our wedding?*

"What's wrong?" Jaffar asked as she inhaled sharply.

"Jaffar, I've been so preoccupied thinking about the flowers and food for our wedding that I never asked you about your family. Who's coming from your side?"

"No one," he admitted a bit shyly. "I have no one who is close."

"I know you told me about your parents, that they died years ago. But what about Abdul?"

"No. I don't think he can come."

"Then you have no one? That's so sad!"

Jaffar thought of Abdul. He was as close to a friend as Jaffar had had for many years. He remembered the faces of his parents, his brother and sister. He thought of Akbal and Mohammed and the few others in his life who he'd even casually called friends—all were dead. Some of their faces were clear in his memory; most were distant blurry images, lost to him forever.

Jaffar was almost completely alone, a casualty of his chosen profession. He reiterated, "No one. At least no one that I want to invite."

Giti felt very sad for him. "I'm sorry."

Jaffar smiled. "I have another family, a new family. I have you and Sina. I don't need anyone else."

"Fatemah and Zafar, you have them."

"Ah yes, Fatemah and Zafar." Fatemah had always welcomed him with open arms. But Zafar, Zafar was a different story. Jaffar was a fairly good judge of men. In his line of work, he had to be. And right from the start Jaffar could feel the coldness, the contempt that radiated from Zafar. *Perhaps it is just because Giti was been married to Reza, his dead brother,* Jaffar reasoned. He'd brought up the question of how Zafar felt about his future brother-in law to Giti on a couple of occasions.

"It's all right Jaffar. I'm sure it's because he still thinks about Reza sometimes."

"I know you do sometimes too!"

"It will pass." Giti knew it probably never would. And she was okay with that because she knew she could hold her memories of him in a private place in her heart, where they belonged. What she was not okay with was how a stranger's penetrating blue eyes had pierced her heart today—during something as mundane as unsticking a shopping cart! What was wrong with her? She was not a foolish teenager anymore

Giti wasn't the only one who felt odd about the encounter. Down the street, not far away, Jack sat on a bench, casually watching Giti and Jaffar and feeding pigeons from a bag of wild bird seed he'd purchased from a vendor nearby. He was still tingling a little from the way she had looked at him, so grateful, so serene, yet with a fire underneath that was irresistible. He shouldn't be dwelling on it; Jack could see from the way Giti and Jaffar talked, the way they sat and their body language, that they were a couple. He just hoped she knew what she was getting into. He wasn't sure Jaffar was as nice as he looked.

He watched them for another hour. They finished their lunch and walked for blocks, peeking in store windows, occasionally entering and always exiting empty-handed. They were just window-shopping. *Maybe there really is nothing here.* When he'd first seen Jaffar that morning, he was sure something was up. Now, now he took one more look in the couple's direction then walked back to his car, a trail of wild bird seed marking his path behind him and a flock of pigeons tailing him.

Las Vegas, Nevada - April 13, 1980

Jack was tired; tired from the week of surveillance, tired from the 1,300 mile round trip he'd made to Sacramento ... but mostly tired from the fact that this whole thing now appeared to be a complete waste of his time—and Donny's too. Yet the fact remained that Mohammed and his brother had been chasing him ... but why? He'd never know, it seemed; now they were both dead and he couldn't ask them, and he had no proof their deaths had anything to do with Jaffar. Jaffar appeared to be quite the gentleman. As far as he could prove, the only business he'd engaged in with the man was to find Giti at Mohammed's request. That's all he knew for sure. But that's not what his gut told him.

He took a shower and dressed. Feeling somewhat refreshed, he emptied his suitcase onto the bed and placed the clean clothes back in his dresser. He would take his dirty clothes down the street to the Chinese laundry. Mrs. Chen always did a good job.

Doing these small domestic chores lifted his spirits. He felt refreshed and he almost convinced himself to go for a run, but then he decided to go jogging tomorrow. *Today you should call Donny.*

He called and there was no answer. He checked his watch. "Still a bit too early for Don to be home," he said to his pet cactus. He went to the kitchen, rummaged through the fridge and found some cold cuts and a bag of oranges. He made himself a sandwich and sliced up an orange.

During the long drive back to Las Vegas, Jack had many hours to think about what he'd seen in Sacramento. He'd seen a beautiful woman in love with a rich Middle Eastern man—and for some weird reason this was breaking his heart. He'd also seen a couple of guys in a grey sedan following him and also following her—and that Jaffar guy—which was just confusing. And he'd seen suburban life in all its glory; a dedicated mom picking up and taking her child to school, working, shopping, enjoying her life. It was something Jack had never experienced. It made him a little melancholy, as if he was missing something. And none of what he'd seen tied together in any way. He felt like his brain was stuttering, like the information was in there somewhere, but hidden somewhere behind a veil. It would come to him. It always did.

Jack returned to the living room. He hadn't bothered to check his messages when he got home and he saw he had five waiting for attention. The first was from Mrs. Chen, reminding him that he still had laundry to pick up from last time he'd dropped some off. *Damn, I forgot about that!* The second was from Donny, asking Jack to phone him when he got home. The third was from Captain Nichols. The last two were from people who hadn't bothered to leave messages.

Jack had got a run of those lately, but these two were different. He could hear breathing on the other end, as if the person was there, just listening. At first, Jack thought perhaps it was someone who had simply not known what to say … but there was usually the 'ums' and "ahs' before those kinds of callers hung up. This voiceless message had been too long, too silent. Jack sat there for a moment and tried to think of who it could have been.

— Chapter 11 —

April 14, 1980

Jack woke before six o'clock. He put his track pants on and pulled his favorite Giants baseball shirt over his head. The sun was just peaking over the trees when he left for his run. His pace had been the same for the past three months, about six and a half minute miles. Jack could step up the pace, but found he could literally run for hours at this pace, often covering fifteen or twenty miles.

He liked the solitude of running out here in the desert and was glad he'd chosen to live here. The ten acres he parked his specially-modified, custom-made, military-grade RV on was his and his alone. There weren't a bunch of cars to dodge or people to pester him while he ran. After an hour and forty minutes he'd covered fourteen miles. He jogged briskly back to his RV.

He put on coffee and took a quick shower. By eight-thirty, he sat calmly at his kitchen table, coffee in hand. Coffee was one bad habit he still allowed himself. He'd given up booze and he had no trouble going without what had been the occasional cigar—but he needed that morning coffee; that and smashed bananas on toast.

He decided to try Donny's number once again. Instead of Don or his answering machine, however, all Jack heard was, "I'm sorry. The number you have reached is not in service. Please check the number and dial again."

"What the hell?" Jack entered the ten digits once more into the phone. "I'm sorry..."

Jack sat back. For an instant all he could think was, *the stupid asshole probably forgot to pay his bill.* That was easier for Jack to accept than the possibility that Donny was actually moving out west. *I'll believe it when I see the Goddamn moving van outside and I see the movers carrying your stuff down the ramp.*

He decided to return some messages from the last week. First he dialed the Seventh Precinct. "Captain Nichols, please."

"Hello, Captain Nichols speaking."

"Ken, Jack Coward here."

"Jack, it's good to hear from you."

"You left me a message a couple of days ago. What's up?"

"I was going to ask you the same thing."

Jack could tell from the tone of Ken's voice that something was up and the call had been more than just a courtesy call. "I guess this was more than a call to say 'Hello'?"

"Jack, I don't know exactly what's going on but I've had at least two calls from that asshole Inspector Perry and another couple of calls from some other guy in Washington."

"Who was that?"

"I don't know, but they chewed me a new one before they hung up. He sounded familiar and the calls were so close together that I assumed he was from the FBI, maybe Perry's boss."

"You, for one, know better than to assume anything."

"Yes, Jack, I know. Except that before I could ask who he was, he hung up." Ken continued, "But let's forget about that. What the hell have you been up to?" Ken knew what the answer was but didn't expect his friend to say. Jack did anyway.

"I was in Sacramento." Ken had figured right.

"Trying to find out about the two dead brothers?"

"Yeah. Or at least whoever hired them to tail me." Jack paused then said, "But I got zilch. The guy just turned out to be some businessman who wanted to make it with that woman in Sacramento."

"So the two things aren't related!?"

"I don't know!" Nichols could hear the frustration in his voice. "I guess not. Probably not." Jack hesitated to tell Ken about what had gone down on his last day there. He wanted to talk with Donny first. Then maybe then he'd tell Ken—maybe.

"So, all you did was tail someone?"

"Yes! The same woman I followed a year and a half ago."

"Then why the hell have two Feds been crawling up my ass, expecting me to rein you in or something?" Nichols asked in wonder.

"What the fuck? I haven't broken any laws. I spent two hours with those clowns from the FBI less than two weeks ago!"

"I know Jack, I'm sorry. But that Goddamn FBI has even been on my back and I don't know why. Are you sure you can't shed some light on this situation?"

"Come on, Ken, you have an idea of your own. You always do." Jack knew that Ken was most likely going against orders just talking to him, but he coaxed him anyway.

"Yes, I sure do! The Feds don't want you poking your nose in this case, and they sure as hell don't want you making any more trips to Sacramento."

"It's a free country. They can't stop me!"

"Yes Jack, that's true. But they can make your life a living hell if you do."

"Okay Ken, I'll quit. Like I said the two things probably aren't related."

"Fine. I shouldn't be getting any more calls from Washington then?"

"No! I promise to behave myself."

"That's good Jack! Maybe we can do lunch soon." Captain Nichols added, "After all, I owe you one."

"Sure Ken. Maybe next week."

"Right Jack. I'll call you."

"Okay, Ken. I appreciate the heads-up!"

"You're welcome Jack. Talk to you soon." Ken Nichols knew that he had a problem on his hands. It seemed the information from Sacramento police had been correct. Jack had just verified it. Strohman had flagrantly disobeyed his direct orders, and stuck his nose once more where it shouldn't be. Well it's time to put and end to the bullshit.

It was time that Dectective Strohman and the Las Vegas police department go their separate ways. He reached for the intercom, "Sharon can you find Terry Strohman and send him to my office?"

Jack hung up the phone and leaned back in his seat. He replayed the conversation in his mind. Ken had been clear enough, relating his concerns and wishes to Jack. *I wish I could talk to Donny. Maybe there are other avenues to explore. Something or someone that can clear this up without making waves from here to Washington.* But Jack didn't know where Donny was, or even how he was.

April 18, 1980

For four days Jack went about his business and tried to put the events of the last few months behind him. He kept fairly busy resolving the problems of Mrs. Perkins, a woman who hired him to investigate her husband. The problem turned out to be that the man was living two separate lives, with two wives and even two sets of kids. Strangely, she took him back on the condition that he leave the other wife, and he accepted. She told Jack it was because she loved him. He didn't understand the power of love, he decided. He would have sucker-punched the deceitful snake. He wondered again about Giti. Her man, Jaffar, was clearly very enticing with his dark, Middle Eastern charm and his bags of money. Would he betray her? Would she love him enough to forgive him? He thought not. She looked like she had more spark than that. But again, who understood the power of love?

Friday started out much like every other day had during the last several months. Jack was up before six o'clock, as usual. He headed out for his morning run. *This will clear my head,* Jack thought. He checked his watch, adjusted his fanny pack and opened his door to see a large man looming over him in the semi-darkness.

"Good morning, Jack."

He blinked. It was Donny. And just far enough down the road that Jack hadn't heard him arrive was a bright yellow Ryder moving van. "What the hell?" Jack could hardly believe his eyes. "I don't believe it!"

"You said you wouldn't until you saw it with your own eyes." Donny gave Jack a bear hug, almost squeezing the life out of him.

Jack caught his breath and managed to say, "No! What I said was, and I quote, 'I'll believe it when I see the Goddamn moving van outside and the movers are actually unpacking your stuff.'"

"Well I'm here, two and a half thousand miles from home, so believe it."

"So that's where you've been. I thought you'd forgotten to pay your bloody phone bill."

"I had the phone disconnected. I meant to call you but I wasn't sure when you would be getting back to Vegas. I did leave you a message."

"Yeah I know. I got it." Jack looked at his watch. "Hey Donny I'm just on my way for my morning run. I'll be back at around eight o'clock. Do you want to go in and put coffee on?"

"You're just like clockwork Jack. That's why I parked out here ten minutes ago. I could use a shower, if you don't mind."

Jack took a disdainful sniff. "You sure could!" Then he handed Donny the keys from his fanny pack. "You can always come with me," he suggested, half-joking.

"Maybe tomorrow," Don laughed.

"See you in a bit." Jack turned and headed north, still shaking his head. He still couldn't quite believe it. He was almost a block away when all of a sudden he pumped his fist in the air and said, "Yes!"

Donny grabbed his gym bag out of the truck, locked its door and opened the RV. All he could think of was, "I'm here. Yes!"

Donny had showered, shaved and was on his second cup of coffee when Jack got back from his shortened run of ten miles. "I'm just going to hop in the shower. I won't be long."

The cascade of water felt especially good today. The temperature was already in the mid-eighties and over the last few weeks, the morning chill was replaced in record time by morning heat. Today would be a scorcher. Over the noise of the shower Jack could swear he heard the phone ring. He shook his head, dismissing it. Then he dried off, wrapped a towel around his waist, and headed towards the kitchen to grab a cup of coffee. "Hey Donny, did someone call?"

"Yep!" Donny said at the same instant that Jack came out of the bathroom. Jack found himself looking into the grinning faces of both Donny and Michelle.

"Jesus Christ!"

"Don't worry Jack. If I haven't seen it before I'll throw rocks at it," Michelle laughed.

Jack decided his coffee could wait and he reversed direction, back toward the bedroom, amidst a chorus of laughter. A minute later he appeared once more, more presentable this time. He pulled Michelle out of her chair and gave her a big hug. "It's good to see you."

"That's not what you thought a few minute ago."

"You caught me off guard, that's all."

"Don't blame me. It was all Donny's idea." All Donny could do was grin.

"Guilty as charged, Jack."

As he poured himself a coffee, he said to Don. "You're a jerk! Remember payback's a bitch." Donny knew Jack didn't really mean it; he also knew that if the tables were turned Jack would have done the same thing.

"So what possessed you to come here?" Jack asked, looking Michelle in the eye.

"I'm here to help my man move in."

"Where are your new digs, Don?"

"I've rented a little rancher about 20 minutes from here, up on Thousand Palms Lane ... 5190 Thousand Palms Lane."

"That's northwest Las Vegas. Past Craig Road."

"I guess so. I haven't seen it yet. It looked good in the ad. It backs onto a green belt, so it should be pretty quiet."

Jack didn't have much of anything to do on his plate today. "Well there goes my day." He laughed.

"I knew that I could count on you."

"On us, Don. On us," laughed Michelle.

"Yes, that's right, on us," Jack concurred. He offered, "If you want, I can follow you up in the Camaro. You can't drive around Vegas in a bloody moving van."

"That's alright Jack. After tomorrow my MG will be here." Jack knew that Donny would never give up his sports car. He'd had it since it was new, almost five years now. It had been garage-kept during the long Washington winters and saw the road only during the brief summers.

Nevertheless, he goaded his friend, "I thought you would have sold that long ago!"

"You know that's my pride and joy, Jack—at least until I met Michelle," he said, giving her a one-armed squeeze. "It's only got 18,000 miles on it. It's like new." Donny added, "Besides this is the place that the car deserves to be. It's sunny more than three-quarters of the year. That's the exact opposite of D.C."

"Yeah, I know. That's why I always wondered why you bought it in the first place. Anyway, enough about your car!" Jack looked at his watch, heard his stomach growl. "Let's grab some breakfast and see if we can get you moved in, Don." Jack gulped down the last of his coffee.

"Sounds like a plan, Stan."

April 25, 1980

Over the last week, Don and Michelle had transformed the modest rancher from the disaster zone it had been—piled high in every room with boxes bearing the Ryder logo—into a neat and tidy home. Everything was in its own place; they had even managed to get Donny's buffet and hutch in the small dining room. It fit, with just an inch and a half to spare. And most important of all, to Don at least, the white MGB was now in the driveway.

Donny reached for the phone. Jack would be back from his morning run. On more than one occasion he'd found himself dialing his friend long distance, as if he was still on the east coast. It would take a while to get used to the change.

"Hello?" Jack answered.

"Good morning Jack. What's up?"

"Lots. Have you listened to the news this morning?"

"Nope. We just got motivated. Michelle is heading back to L.A. later today, and I've got a new job to go see about on Tuesday. What's on the news?"

"Just turn on the television. The ABC news. I'll be over in an hour or so."

"Okay!" Don walked over to the television, switched it on and turned up the volume slightly. He then headed to join Michelle in the kitchen for a coffee.

"Was that Jack? Is he heading over today?"

"Yeah. He'll be here in an hour."

"Good. When I leave, you and Jack can hang out. He's sure is a good guy, Don."

"Yeah. Jack's the best. A real top hand. That's what my dad used to say about him."

"I like Jack. It will be good for the both of you to live so close again."

"Yeah, it's been way too long," Donny said just as the television announced the morning news with the usual orchestral introduction.

"Here is this morning's top story. A top-secret attempt by the United States military to free the American hostages, held in Tehran for the last six months, has failed. Eight soldiers were killed as a result ..."

"What? Michelle! Quick, come in here and watch this!" Both sat down on Donny's new sofa and watched as a solemn president spoke to his country.

"I ordered this rescue mission in order to safeguard American lives and protect America's national interests and to reduce the tensions in the world that have been caused among many nations as this crisis has continued," he said.

The picture changed from the grief-stricken face of President Jimmy Carter to a video feed from the National Television of Iran. The pictures showed the still-smoldering, charred wreckage of a C-130 military transport aircraft and a helicopter lying strewn about on a remote airstrip in the desert, southeast of Tehran.

"That used to be a Hercules C-130," Michelle blurted out. "Look at that, Don. They don't even look like aircraft anymore."

"No they sure don't." The two watched the drama unfold on television and all the while, Don thought, *that could have been Jack and I. And how the hell does Michelle know that was a Herc?*

"Another sad day for the country," Michelle remarked as the television announced the names of the three marines and five air force members who had lost their lives. She thought of the eight families that now must deal with their grief.

"Do you think there will be repercussions after this, or from this?"

"If what you mean is, do I think the Iranians will kill any of the hostages, then no, probably not," Donny said after a moment's thought. "The Iranian government wants to get back their $20 billion in assets that the U.S. government has frozen. A dead hostage is not much of a bargaining chip."

"No. I don't suppose so. What was it that the White House spokesman said before? 'It works out to about some $360-odd million per hostage'."

"I seem to recall that, but I don't think it was a White House official who said that, just some reporter. But any way you slice it, that's a huge amount of cash. Damn ragheads."

"Don't talk like that, Don. It's only the extremists causing problems."

"Yeah, that's why they're called extremists. They take their religious fervor or whatever, to extremes."

"But the whole country isn't like that."

"But nothing. They have to get support from somewhere."

Michelle knew when to quit. Donny was from Washington and had seen the things that went on there; the first-hand the lobbying, the power brokering and all the other things that were wrong in the nation's capital, but in spite of it was still very passionate about his country. "Okay, I give," she said. "But for the record, I don't think racial slurs are appropriate."

"Yeah, I guess," conceded Donny.

Donny still had trouble trying to figure out Michelle. He had gone to great lengths to determine what her buttons were and how to push only the good ones, but the relationship was new and sometimes he zigged when he should have zagged. He was relieved when Jack arrived a few minutes later. He could focus on something besides his verbal faux pas.

Don opened the door to look upon a rather somber face. "Good morning Jack."

"I wish it was Don. Did you watch the news?"

"Yeah we—Michelle and I—did."

"Is it still on?"

"Yeah. Come on in." Jack followed his best friend into the living room.

Jack was amazed at the transformation that had taken place over the last week. "It looks real good in here, Don. You and Michelle have done a great job."

"Thanks Jack, but I can't take much of the credit. Michelle did most of the unpacking. I was on the phone most of the time with my new job."

"How's that going by the way?"

"We can talk about that later. Let's watch." Jack sat down on the opposite end of the sofa and they watched the news about the terrible events in the Middle East. The video taken earlier that day was replayed again and as Jack and Don watched, they both had uncomfortable knots twisting away at their insides. "I watched the same clip this morning with Michelle and I could swear I heard them say the name Sergeant Dewey Johnson."

"What! They announced the names? Are you sure?"

"Yeah. They did a while ago, probably while you were on your way over here. Why would I make that up?"

"Sorry Don! I didn't mean to be so short, man."

"I know, Jack." ABC now showed the pictures of the eight men killed during the ill-fated mission.

"Jesus, Don, look at the bottom left. That's him!" The small photo showed a handsome, clean-cut marine in his dress uniform, obviously a proud young man.

"Yeah, it sure does look like him."

"It's Dewey, all right," Jack said, flinching as Dewey's name flashed on the screen. He looked over at Don to see that, like him, his buddy was shaken. The newscast changed to show President Jimmy Carter again making his announcement to the country and the rest of the world.

In the kitchen, Michelle finished rinsing out the sink. Donny was going to talk to the landlord about the malfunctioning dishwasher. The first time they had used it, it had, as Donny put it, 'pissed water all over the damn floor,' so for now they had been doing dishes manually. She heard Donny and Jack talking in the living room and thought, *I didn't know Jack was here; guess I couldn't hear the doorbell over the running water.* She was hoping Jack would take a less passionate view of things and talk a bit of sense into Don.

As Michelle approached the wall that separated the kitchen and dining room from the living room, she could hear Donny talking. "You know Jack, that could have been us instead of Dewey."

"I know. I was thinking the same thing earlier this morning, even before they announced the list of casualties."

"Are you sorry you turned down Colonel Hart after the war?"

"No Don, as I told you before, Vietnam had become a fucking joke. Congress was impotent and their policies made it impossible for us to win."

"I know, Jack. Both you and I were tired of the war, the killing." Don thought for a moment, "But it's too bad we had to look like a bunch of pussies, retreat and let the south be overrun by the communists! Christ, Jack that was a long time ago. It seems like a lifetime."

"It's only been ten years, just a third of our lives."

"Still a long time ago, Jack."

"Uh huh …"

"I heard a 'but' in there," Donny teased.

"Yeah, there's a 'but'. Sometimes I just wonder if it was all worth it. I went to Vietnam. Did that make a difference? Now I'm just a private dick, following skirt chasers who cheat on their wives. When do I actually get a life? How did I miss out on that?"

"Whoa! Jack! Where the hell is this coming from? You served your country, man."

"Did I? Did we, Don? All we did was keep our asses out of jail because we were stupid enough to boost a couple of televisions!"

"Don't forget the police car." Don added. Jack smiled; Donny knew he would, he always did. Both of them almost pissed themselves laughing when the police car crashed that night.

"We'd never have had the careers we did if it wasn't for that night," Jack mused.

"Uh huh," Don agreed. Then he poked the bear. "I do seem to recall you thinking that it would be cool to drive around all day like Cannon, that T.V. private investigator. You know, in his big-ass, white Lincoln Continental."

"Yeah, he used to spend a good 40 minutes driving around and round and about 15 minutes actually solving cases!"

"You know what I liked best about that show?" Don asked.

"What's that Don?"

"I always marvelled at when some bad ass is shooting at Cannon from up on a water tower or something, using a long gun, but still can't hit him....."

"Yeah I know, and Cannon wasn't exactly swelt."

"But the best part, was that Cannon would shoot back with his little snub-nosed 38, and wing the guy everytime." They both started to laugh.

Michelle thought this would be good time to make her entrance. She dried her hands then headed into the living room. "Jack is that you? I didn't hear the bell."

"Hi. I just got here a couple of minutes ago."

"Are you and Donny watching that awful news on T.V.?"

"Yeah!" Neither one wanted to tell Michelle about Dewey Johnson.

She was determined to shift the mood to a happy one. "Since I've been here, Mr. Ziegler, all you've had me do is work at unpacking boxes and cleaning. How would it be if Jack showed us two out-of-towners the sights?"

"What? Don't you have to go back to L.A.?"

"Yes, but I can pack up my stuff. Then we can take the cars to wherever and we can decide where to head from there."

"It's up to Jack. What about it, pal?"

"That sounds good to me. I guess that I can play the role of tour guide for a few hours. But it's not as if the two of you haven't been here before."

"Let's pretend we haven't."

"Okay, let's go."

For the next three hours Jack played the role of tour guide as the three walked the Vegas strip. Jack related the stories he'd heard over the years, of how Las Vegas had grown from almost worthless brown desert into some of the most sought after real estate in the country with the influx of each famous hotel and casino and the celebrities who stayed or played in them.

Soon it was time for Donny and Michelle to say their farewells, which they did unabashedly in front of Jack. Then she jumped in her Volkswagen Beetle and headed west towards the I-15. Donny looked at his watch, she would be home by around seven o'clock in the evening and she'd promised to call.

"You don't look too happy Don."

"Nope! I never am when she leaves."

"Do you love her Don?"

"Yeah!" He didn't even hesitate and for an unreasonable second Jack was jealous. His friend seemed so happy, yet he was alone. Once more his mind turned to the beautiful Giti. What a prize she would be! But it was an impossible dream. Jack knew he should focus elsewhere. But he found women hard to meet and even harder to talk to. Not like Don. He'd always been a charmer with the ladies.

Don waited a few minutes for the traffic to thin out. "Now Jack, let's talk about this broadcast we saw this morning. I can tell something's still up."

"It's nothing Don. I'm just really bummed out about those guys in Iran." Jack paused for a minute. "At least they were trying to make a difference."

"Yes, but this morning you tried to imply that we didn't!"

"Well, did we? The whole Vietnam War was a big fucking embarrassment for the country, and a big black eye for our military—well not so much for the military, more of a black eye for Congress. Even Jack Kennedy knew Vietnam wasn't the place for us. He was ready to pull us out of there, but some bastards murdered him before he could do it."

"Even so, Jack, you and I both signed up for a second tour. We were trying to make a difference. So the next time you start feeling bummed out and sorry for yourself, remember the Dewey Johnsons, the John Smiths and all of the other 50,000 plus guys who didn't get the chance to come home."

"Thanks for the speech, Don. I guess I needed that."

"That and a good kick in the ass. Besides I've been rehearsing all day."

Sacramento, California - July 8, 1980

Giti, Fatemah and several close friends had spent the last three weeks getting decorations ready for this day—Giti's second wedding day. In just over two hours, Giti was to exchange vows with Jaffar.

With plans in hand, the team set to work with military precision. Since early this morning they had crisscrossed Fatemah's large back yard, looping crepe onto trees and over the deck railing and hanging paper wedding bells all around the fence, creating festivity out of what was actually a pretty ordinary yard. Giti took a few moments to look over their handiwork. "It looks good, doesn't it Fatemah?"

"It really does. I think we all did a great job!"

The chairs, decorated with alternating blue and white ribbons, had been positioned in neat lines in two sections separated by a wide aisle down which the bride and groom would walk. At the end of the aisle were two podiums—one for Giti's priest and one for the Jaffar's Imam—on each side of a rose-covered trellis.

As Giti looked around and the work her friends had done with such love and care, she was almost overwhelmed. Fatemah noticed.

"Are you nervous?" she asked.

"Just a bit. Do I look it?" Mostly Giti was relieved that it was going to be over soon. She looked over the backyard once more before heading in to get showered and dressed and just for a moment thought the streamers looked a little like tentacles. She shivered then shrugged it off. It wouldn't do to get cold feet on the eve of her wedding. Besides, Jaffar was such a gentleman and treated her so well. *This is the right choice,* she told herself. But the image of tentacles remained.

July 27, 1980

The wedding had been wonderful. Giti couldn't have hoped for a better day. Her family and friends had made the day special; they accepted and welcomed her husband as if he was their own, though she could still sense some coolness toward him from Zafar. Nevertheless, he put on a good show and was polite and kind to her new husband. She knew Zafar only had her best interests at heart, but this reservation he had about him did bother her a little. However, she was certain he would grow fond of Jaffar in time.

It was Sunday morning at the newly-formed Roshtti-Harraj household. Jaffar was up, showered and dressed before Giti and Sina. He was watching the early morning news with the volume turned down when Giti awoke.

"Good morning, my love," she said, kissing him on the cheek as she walked into the kitchen to make coffee for herself and green tea for him. She brought Jaffar his drink then headed into the bathroom to take a shower.

They had decided to forgo a honeymoon for the moment. Jaffar had offered to take her on a world cruise, but she was worried about Sina's schooling, so she had asked if they could plan one for the summer and possibly take him along for part of it. "I would really like to see where you grew up in Britain," she said hopefully. "Maybe there are some long-lost friends and relatives of yours still there!" She was still a little sad that there had been no one standing up for Jaffar at their wedding.

He's smiled. "Of course," he said.

As Giti showered, on television the ABC anchor announced: "Here's today's top story. As the hostage crisis continues in Tehran, we are told that the former Shah of Iran has died in Cairo, Egypt. He passed away after a long battle with lymphatic cancer. His wife and children were at his bedside during his final hours. Egypt's President Anwar Sadat said the former head of the Iranian government will be given a state funeral in Egypt. One of the reasons for this honor is that the Shah of Iran sent two shiploads of crude oil to Egypt during the 1973 war with Israel. The former Empress Farah, the Shah's wife, and their three children will reportedly return to the United States after the funeral."

"That's excellent news!" Jaffar said quietly. He did not want Giti to hear. He was sure that the rest of the country did not share his happiness about the shah's death. He watched for a few minutes more until he heard the thump of the plumbing pipes indicating that Giti had finished showering. In a few moments she came downstairs, a towel on her head.

"That's better," she said, as she went into the kitchen to get another cup of coffee. "Did you watch your news this morning? What's happening in the world?"

"The Shah of Iran died today."

"That's terrible. He was a great ally for this country."

"Yes, he was." Jaffar bit his lip.

"What?" Giti asked, sensitive to his expression.

"Oh, nothing," said Jaffar, then changed the subject. "So, are you Fatemah still going shopping today? Is it still my day to bond with Sina?"

Giti smiled. "Yes, and I hope you have a wonderful time together. What will you do?"

"I'm not sure. There are many things we could do. It's a nice day. Perhaps I will take him to the American River. There are many miles of parks on both shores of the river."

"Or maybe you could take him up to the school. I'm sure Sina would love a chance to fly his remote control airplane. That's something that he hasn't done for a while."

"I've never flown a remote control plane before. I'm afraid I wouldn't be much help."

"You won't have to be, you're simply along for supervision. Sina knows what to do. He's even surprised Zafar with how much he knows about his planes!"

"Okay, Giti, I will give it a try."

Giti looked at the kitchen clock and gulped down what remained of her coffee. "I'd better get moving. I'll go wake him up and get myself ready to go."

Jaffar waved goodbye to Giti as she and Fatemah drove away from the house. They were on their way to the local mall, looking for summer clothes. For the first time ever, Jaffar had been left in charge of Sina. Over the last few months he'd made an effort to take over some of the responsibilities of sharing activities with Sina from Zafar. He'd tried to accompany the two of them on their weekend outings, but Jaffar found that he and Zafar always seemed to be on the verge of a confrontation, though both were exceedingly polite to one another.

Jaffar talked to Giti about it but she maintained, "He's Reza's brother and still thinks about him. He's also very protective of his nephew. Give him time." But time wasn't working; Jaffar and Zafar mixed as well as oil and water.

When Sina was ready to go, Jaffar helped him load a heavy duffel bag into the trunk of his car, grunting as he did so. "What's in here, Sina? It weighs a lot."

"Stuff for my plane," said Sina.

Later, at the park, as Jaffar got the duffel bag out again, Sina carefully lifted the red and white plane from the floor where he'd parked it between the front and back seats, as it barely fit width-wise between the doors when they were closed. As he eased the plane from the car he noticed a small puddle of gasoline had leaked onto the carpet. "Oh shit," he said under his breath. Swearing was something he'd picked up his friend Matthew during the last few months of school. Swear-words were handy and so expressive.

He took a quick sniff of the gas and hoped the smell would go away by the time they finished at the park. Sina had been around Jaffar just often enough to witness a carefully hidden temper. With a child's sensitivity, he understood that Jaffar was a man he did not want to anger.

"So you never told me what was in the bag, Sina," Jaffar said, not used to having to repeat a question.; Where he came from, such disrespect would not be tolerated. Children knew their place in Iraq.

"It's my tools, mixed gas and other stuff, Jaffar. For my plane."

That this child, his stepson, called him 'Jaffar' was again something that really grated. "I'm not used to being addressed in that manner, Sina. You will show me a little more respect."

"Yes, sir!" Sina said obediently.

For the next ten minutes Sina worked quietly and thoroughly, checking all the components of his aircraft from propeller to rudder. He filled the tank with fuel. It took only half the normal amount. Sina had neglected to empty it the last time he'd flown it.

Finally, the red-and-white model biplane came to life with a loud roar of noise. After listening for a moment, Sina was satisfied with the performance of the small motor. *Giti was certainly right about Sina and the lack of needed participation,* Jaffar thought. Then Sina took the controls in hand and transformed the formerly inanimate plane into one that, with a cacophony of noise, virtually leapt from the grass field and into the sky.

Jaffar watched for several minutes as Sina expertly guided the biplane through a series of maneuvers. The morning sun reflected off the fuselage and wings with every flick of the controls. The plane made a series of barrel rolls, loop-the-loops and even an Immelmann maneuver, an ending half-loop followed by a half-roll.

"Yippee!" Sina crowed. He flew the airplane until the engine sputtered, clearly ready for fuel. That was his cue to bring the plane down. It landed smoothly on the grass.

Twice more Sina filled the small onboard gas tank and got his craft back airborne. On the third tank, he even let Jaffar control the plane for a moment or two. Jaffar managed to complete four very jerky orbits of the field, with Sina standing close by, ready to snatch the controls from his hands should any problems arise.

It was Sina who spotted the Sacramento Police car on the street, the uniformed patrolman staring through his open driver's window, directly at them. This was the signal to pack up. No doubt a neighbor had complained about the noise of the airplane; someone usually did. Sina and Reza, and then lately Sina and Zafar, had always found it to be wise to simply pack up and go when the police arrived.

"It's time for us to leave, Jaffar." Sina nodded in the direction of the black and white parked outside of the chain-link fence.

Jaffar was about to remind Sina about his manners. Instead he looked in the direction Sina had indicated and was surprised to see the police car. Sina could see by his reaction that Jaffar was uncomfortable with the police being so close. "It's okay Jaffar. He just wants us to leave!"

"Oh! Alright, Sina." Jaffar even helped Sina collect his tools and equipment, quickly placing them in the duffel bag. Since Jaffar never offered to help Sina with much else, Sina noticed and wondered why he was being so kind. He seemed in a hurry to get away from the park, but Sina couldn't think why.

Sina carried the airplane to the car with as much care as before. Jaffar opened the trunk and placed the duffel bag inside. The police officer seemed satisfied that there was not going to be any more noise complaints today. He pulled away from the curb. Jaffar watched until he was out of sight then breathed a sigh of relief. He'd had no close encounters with any law enforcement officials since entering the United States and didn't want to start having them.

Jaffar unlocked the driver's door and got behind the wheel. He could smell the odor of gasoline wafting from the back seat. He unlocked Sina's door and Sina got in. He decided not to reprimand the boy as he was just happy to see the police leave.

"You fly your plane very well, Sina."

"You did very well too. Almost as good as Zafar and he's had much more practice," Sina fibbed.

"Thank you, Sina."

"My dad used to fly model planes too!"

"Oh. Did he fly your plane? How well did he do?"

"He did a lot better than me. He taught me to fly planes when I was just a kid." The rest of the ride home was a quiet one. *That wasn't so bad,* Sina thought. *He didn't even get mad about the spill on the carpet.* Sina was very pleased about the fact that Jaffar hadn't blown his stack about the stain. Sina could still smell the gas when he'd got in the passenger seat, and he was sure that he was going to be in trouble. Nothing happened.

Giti and Fatemah were still out when they got home, so Sina decided to show Jaffar pictures of his dad flying his plane. He managed to reach the pull chord on the attic access stair and carefully lower the folding stair. He knew exactly where the trunk was that contained the photos.

"I'll show you some pictures of my dad. Come up and see." The boy led Jaffar up the unfolded ladder. The temperature in the attic was easily over a 100 degrees, so their stay would have to be relatively short. Sina opened the trunk and reached in to retrieve the pictures. He slowly shuffled through them one at a time, explaining each picture to Jaffar.

"This is from the day when my dad and I first got my plane." A few more photos went by. "Then this is a picture of my dad at Edwards Air Force base with a plane." It showed Reza and another man, most likely the pilot, beneath the huge olive green wing of an Air Force transport.

Jaffar could feel the sweat roll down the middle of his back. It was very warm in the attic. "Come on Sina. It's too hot up here to be looking at pictures. Give them to me and I will put them back in the trunk."

"Alright!" Sina was glad to be out of the sweltering attic too. He handed Jaffar the stack of photos and headed down the ladder. Jaffar opened the lid of the trunk and placed the pictures on top of a very well-used, burgundy briefcase. Jaffar took a look over his shoulder, Sina was already gone. He released the latches on the top the case; they popped open with a loud clunk. He lifted the lid to see an old, yellowing manila file folder. It was marked, 'USAF – TOP SECRET'. His heart beat a bit faster when he saw those words, but he couldn't afford to be nosy just now. Instead, Jaffar replaced the photos and closed the trunk. Then he followed Sina down the ladder and into the hallway below, his shirt soaked with sweat, his heart still pounding in his chest.

— Chapter 12 —

July 28, 1980

Jaffar tossed and turned almost the whole night, his mind awash with questions about the contents of the file folder. This was the first time in his life the he'd actually seen with his own eyes an honest to goodness 'TOP SECRET' United States Government document. The thought of actually getting to read such a thing had never even entered his mind. Now, like a miracle from Allah, it was less than 50 feet away—though not quite in his possession as yet.

He was certain of one thing. He must be alone in the house when he read it. Before finally falling asleep, he half-convinced himself that the documents in that folder must be worthless or at the very least, out of date or obsolete.

July 29, 1980

Jaffar watched the funeral for the late Shah of Iran on the news. As he lay inside his coffin, the funeral procession traveled through the streets of Cairo with the Empress Farah and her children following the coffin on its way to the Al Rifa'I Mosque.

"The burial of the Shah in this mosque has sparked fresh rounds of protest from Islamic Fundamentalists, but the Egyptian government says the gravesite is only temporary," the news anchor said solemnly. "The Shah's body will be interned beside that of his bother-in-law, King Farouk of Egypt. Both of their tombs will be to the left of the entrance ..."

Jaffar sat on the sofa with his green tea, smiling. He thought, *I don't know which makes me happier, the death of the traitor, or the fact that today I am going to discover the secrets of the trunk.*

"The former Shah of Iran was the first Muslim leader to recognize the State of Israel," the newsman continued.

The damn traitor! The infidel! Jaffar heard the bedroom door open and close, followed by the bathroom door. He made sure to keep his face impassive, pleasant even, for his wife. But inside he was seething. Jaffar had little love for his own people and even less for the Iranians. He was at a stage now where he didn't care even about his responsibility to his terrorist overlords. Instead, almost all his efforts these days were to produce monetary gains for himself, though he did just enough business on behalf of Hamas to ensure he was not dispatched as easily as Mohammed had been. He made sure just enough checks and balances were in place to keep out of trouble and that the portion of funds he allocated to himself couldn't be traced. Then he invested the money, managed a healthy return and paid back the money he'd initially used.

"It is hoped that the Shah's remains will one day be returned to his former homeland," said the television.

"That'll happen just a few days before hell freezes over," Jaffar muttered.

"Good morning Jaffar. What did you say?"

Too late, he realized he'd slipped. He hadn't heard Giti come down the hall and he turned to see her standing there in a cream-colored bathrobe with a matching towel around her head. "Good morning Giti. I was just watching the news about the funeral. The woman from the BBC said that one day the Shah's body will be returned to Iran."

"What was that about hell freezing over?"

"I just meant that the Iranians will never let the Shah back into Iran."

"But they've wanted him to come home for months. That's the biggest reason for the hostages isn't it?"

"Well, hopefully some progress can be made and we can get those poor people back home to their families," he deadpanned.

Today was the earliest opportunity Jaffar would have to examine the contents of the trunk. For the past few days, Giti had insisted on doing family activities in an effort to encourage him to bond with Sina. Today she was taking Sina to his friend's house and she was going to the office to do some work for Zafar. He waited now, rather anxiously, for Giti and Sina to leave.

The minute the door shut behind them, Jaffar lowered the folding ladder and climbed up into the attic. Blessedly, it wasn't as hot as it had been on Sunday, but Sina wasn't there to remind Jaffar to crouch when he walked, so his forehead hit the roof with a thud, hard enough that he could see stars, and loud enough that if Giti and Sina had been home they'd have heard it.

"Damn! That bloody hurts," he said, gently touching his forehead where he felt a quickly developing 'goose egg'. He grimaced at the spot of blood on his fingertip.

He opened the trunk lid and noted the positions of the items in the trunk as he removed them. He wanted to be certain everything was left as he'd found it. He carefully lifted out the stack of pictures and set them on the wooden floor. Then he lifted out the briefcase and slid the latches to the sides. The well-used locks opened smoothly. Jaffar lifted out the manila folder and opened it. Two dozen pages or so were inside. Jaffar started to read:

United States Air Force – Operation Overlook.

Synopsis: This project is to provide the United States Air Force with an unmanned aerial vehicle system superior in capability to those available at present. This system is to be used in gathering intelligence and reconnaissance, with an emphasis on target acquisition. A future capability of enemy force interdiction would also be an asset.

History: Experimentation with unmanned aerial vehicles began during the Civil War with both Union and Confederate forces using unmanned hot air balloons, loaded with high explosives which were then flown over enemy troop formations. These were always subject to the fickleness of the prevailing winds and were for the most part ineffective …

Jaffar read for another half an hour, trying to absorb what was often quite technical information. It was a good history lesson and he was disappointed to find that the information was probably worthwhile ten or twenty years ago but was hardly earth-shattering news.

However, there was a second file in the briefcase, this bearing the logo of a company called California Robotics. In it, Jaffar found a series of diagrams, rough sketches and page after page of calculations as well as a rough draft of a speech written by Giti's former husband, Reza Roshtti. According to the title page, he was to have given the speech to the company directors and shareholders of California Robotics the day after he died! *He never told them about this,* Jaffar thought in wonder.

He read the speech and he was intrigued, This was something worth further thought; it was about unmanned aircraft! Imagine the power it would give Hamas … or better, imagine the power it would give *him*! He didn't bother to put anything away and he wasn't exactly sure how long before Giti and Sina returned, but he knew he had to protect this for himself right away. He climbed down the ladder, files in hand, grabbed the Yellow Pages from the shelf and looked under 'copying' until he found Tryman Blueprint and Graphics on Arden Way. Gathering up the files, he grabbed his keys, headed out the door and jumped into his car. He was there in about ten minutes, driving just over the speed limit and blowing two yellow lights.

At Tryman, the young clerk, Lorena Salvador, was just about to close for lunch. She flipped the sign to 'Closed', turned the hands on the little cardboard clock to '1:00 p.m.', opened the door and put her keys in the lock to lock up. In the glass the reflection of a very well-dressed gentleman standing behind her made her turn around quickly.

"Oh my, you startled me! I was about to close for lunch."

"Oh, no! Do you think that you could possibly copy a few documents for me? I'm in a bit of a hurry. Two copies is all I need. There's not much here." He waved the file at her.

Lorena looked at her watch. "Yes, I guess I could," she said a little reluctantly. She removed her keys from the lock and went back inside. Jaffar followed.

"What happened to your head? That's quite a goose egg."

"Goose egg? Oh yes, I hit my head on a bookcase."

She placed her purse and keys on the desk and Jaffar handed her the two sets of documents he'd removed from their file folders. Looking at the stack she guessed it wouldn't take more than a few minutes. "This won't take long, just have a seat," she said.

As she walked away, Jaffar observed that she was a very attractive young lady. *Yes, very attractive,* he thought as he said, "I really appreciate this. Thank you."

Copying the first set of documents took only a minute but when Lorena put the second set into the feeder it jammed. "Damn! Another paper jam. This is going to take longer than I thought," she said to herself.

Jaffar saw her bend down to fix it and he quietly walked over to the door, took a quick look outside onto the street then silently turned the thumb latch, locking the door from the inside. Then he walked quietly back into the shop as the big copy machine came to life, the paper feeding normally. The rhythmic mechanical noise of the machine masked his footsteps as he reached Lorena. She was just about to turn around and relay her progress to Jaffar when he placed his hand over her mouth to stifle any scream and viscously punched her in the right kidney. She slouched to floor in pain, unable to breathe, unable to scream. Then he turned her onto her back in front of the copier, sat on her chest and pinned her arms to her sides. She looked up at him, shocked. She noticed there was a trickle of blood running down his forehead from beneath the bandage.

Jaffar smiled as he closed his hands around the throat of the defenseless young woman, thumb directly over the hyoid bone. He squeezed with all his strength, watching her face turn red as he increased his grip. After a few more seconds, Jaffar heard the satisfying crack as her larynx was crushed. He kept the pressure on for another two full minutes, until he was certain of the result. While it had been fun to kill again, he wished Abdul were here to do this; usually he delegated such things to his subordinates.

Jaffar climbed off the limp, lifeless body and quickly gathered up his papers, stepping over the body several times as he did so, giving it no more thought than he would a dead, mongrel dog in the street.

He cautiously opened the back door to the alley. All was clear. He locked the door from the inside and closed it behind him then walked down the alley and circled the block until he was back at his car. Once in his car, he glanced around to make sure no one was watching, then turned and headed back to Giti's house. He checked the clock on the dash. Lots of time before Giti gets back, he thought.

As soon as he was safely back in the house, he returned the originals to their file folders and put them carefully back in the trunk with the stack of photos on top as they were before. Then he stashed the copies he'd had made in a secret compartment of his briefcase.

Giti and Sina arrived home just before dinner. "How was your day?" he asked.

"Sina has a bit of a tummy ache. He and his friend ate too much popcorn before they went swimming! What did you do, Jaffar?"

"Oh, I just tidied up a bit of paper work. Nothing important." Giti noticed the bandage on his head. "What did you do to your head?"

"I banged it on my desk, picking up a pen."

"So now I've got to look after both of my men!" she clucked. She took Sina by the hand. "Come on Sina, let's get you to bed."

July 30, 1980

It was just after midnight. Patrolmen Mark Harris and Ted Bachus had just started their eight-hour shift. Harris hated the graveyard shift. The beat was usually quiet and the eight hours often seemed like ten to him. Most of their arrests were drunk drivers behind of the steering wheels of their cars, endangering the public as they tried to navigate home.

He drove past a row of businesses. All were dark except one. Harris stopped the cruiser around the corner. "Dispatch this Three Adam-Two Nine. Read me Code 927 at 1759 Arden Way."

"Roger Adam Two Nine."

"Come on, Ted, let's check this out. You take the front and I'll take the rear."

"Right, Mark."

Mark Harris went north and Ted went south towards the front of the illuminated patch of sidewalk. He reached the doorway and tried the door. It was locked. He cautiously peered inside. The interior was brightly lit, but no one appeared to be there. He continued walking east, then around the block to meet up with his partner. He could hear his partner's voice on the speaker talking to dispatch.

"Dispatch this is Three Adam Two Nine. Request Code 912 on Sam Nora King Three Seven Seven!"

There was a short delay while the computer file was retrieved and relayed. "Roger, Adam Two Nine. Sam Nora King Three Seven Seven is registered to Miss Lorena Salvador, 6811 Ocean View Drive."

"Roger dispatch Code One."

"Ted! What did you find?"

"Front of the store is locked up tighter than a drum. Every light in the place is on, though. The small clock on the door indicates they will be back at 1:00. I don't know if that's one o'clock a.m. or p.m.! I don't think this is a 24-hour joint, though."

Patrolman Harris looked at his watch. "It's almost one o'clock now. We'll wait for a few minutes."

"Maybe they went for lunch and decided to take the afternoon off. The red Honda hatchback over there might belong to one of the staff. Someone named Lorena Salvador owns it. She doesn't live around here, though. Dispatch is having a unit check the registered owner's address to see if she's home. They are trying to locate the store owner as well."

"Dispatch. This is Three Adam Two Nine. Request Code Twelve our location."

"Roger, Adam Two Nine. Code Twelve."

"Now Ted, we wait."

Dean Hills walked slowly up to the two police officers who were waiting at the front of his store. It had been half an hour since the police had summoned him to his shop. It was very early in the morning, still pitch black. The lights from inside his business lit up the immediate area like a beacon. He introduced himself to Officers Harris and Bachus and stared at front of the store, "Strange I don't see any broken glass," he said. "I thought this was a break-in?"

"Can you unlock the door for us?" asked Bachus.

"Of course." Dean did as requested and started to pull the door open.

The front door chime beeped twice. While the officers at the scene had had both entrances of the store under surveillance for over an hour, as a precaution Harris said, "I'm sorry, sir, but I'm afraid you'll have to wait out here."

Upon entering the store everything appeared normal. Harris moved towards the rear of the store and spotted keys and a purse on the desk.

"Ted!" he pointed at the desk. Alarm bells went off in the heads of both officers. They moved even more slowly towards the rear of the store and at almost the same time, they spotted the body on the floor. Officer Bachus stepped towards Lorena to check for a pulse, but stopped a few feet short. It was obvious she was dead.

"Dispatch. This is Three Adam Two Nine. We have a Code 925 at this location."

Then Bachus went to the front of the store to detain the owner.

The Roshtti-Harraj Household

It was amazing that Jaffar was able to sleep so soundly. Even Abdul tossed and turned the whole night, unable to sleep, after committing murder. In addition he had nightmares for months after. Jaffar, however, slept deeply and was up early, eager to see if he could make sense of the two files in his possession. He switched on the television, volume low as usual, and sat sipping his freshly brewed tea. The six o'clock news had already started.

"Sacramento has awoken to its 27th homicide of the year. The body of a young woman was found by police early this morning at her place of business. The owner of the business has been taken into custody although no charges have been laid at this time. The woman's name has yet to be released, pending notification of the next of kin."

Jaffar sat in his chair, smiling. *They are blaming the owner. Praise be to Allah.* He could not believe his luck. In Al-Qa'im, where someone was taken into custody, more often than not they were found guilty and punished; Jaffar did not understand that in America that was not always the case.

He thought about yesterday, about how easy it had been. Americans are too trusting, he thought. He had married one and she had no idea what he was capable of. Best that he keep that to himself until he could get her back to Iraq and keep her there. One day she will see something and open her mouth to her brother-in-law—then I will not be safe.

All morning detectives had looked for clues about Lorena's murder. The red Honda had already been removed and taken to the police forensics garage. Inspectors Sam Jeffries and Ben Johnson had spent the better part of two hours trying to piece together the events leading up to the murder. They had already pulled a very clear partial print off the thumb latch on the front door. The door knob on the back door had rendered yet another good print.

"Sam. It's a good thing the air conditioning was working well."

"Yeah. The cool temperature kept the prints from turning into oily blobs."

The body had been removed by the coroner almost an hour earlier. The preliminary cause of death was determined to be strangulation. Petechial hemorrhaging was present, a strong indication of asphyxia by strangulation.

"What was she doing with the door locked, Sam?"

"Maybe the perpetrator locked it. A customer?"

"Maybe. Her purse and keys were on the desk, left untouched. That probably rules out robbery as a motive."

"Yeah and the cash drawer was also untouched."

"The Coroner said there were no signs of rape, no sign of a lengthy struggle. What the hell happened here?"

"That still leaves a customer, Ben. She was in front of the copy machine."

They worked for the rest of the morning. They carefully went over the entire store. Everything was photographed and every surface dusted for prints with the exception of one. With the body now removed, the two detectives knelt down to examine the area immediately around the machine. They noticed small drops of blood indicating two different directions of travel, along with a blank spot on the floor. They placed small flags next to each drop of blood and took additional photos. The blank area contained no blood droppings, but instead revealed something else. They both noticed a small amount of black powder in front of the machine.

"Looks like one of our boys got generous when dusting," Ben said. The trail of powder led over to a small garbage can. "Or maybe it's just a trail of toner?"

"Yeah, Sam, and some is on the front of the machine too."

Inspector Jeffries reached over and tilted the garbage can in his direction. Inside was a single, accordianed piece of paper. He removed it to examine it more closely. He grasped each end and slowly opened it to full length. The words TOP SECRET in bold letters appeared in the top right hand corner. The rest of the sheet contained a diagram of some sort of aircraft.

"Jesus! Ben, look at this!"

"That looks like it's from the United States Air Force, some sort of plane. This can't be good."

"I think we've found the motive."

"Looks like it. I bet this gets handed off to the FBI. I'll call the Captain."

"Yeah. Now all we've got to do is find the perp."

"I wouldn't pick the store owner for this one. I'll bet lunch."

"I'm with you on that. No bet."

Within an hour, four FBI inspectors came to interview the two detectives. All the evidence, with the exception of the body, was surrendered to them. Dean Hills was released a short time later.

August 6, 1980

Ever since Jaffar had accidentally discovered the files in the attic, he'd pondered what to do with them. Although he had gone the contents several times, he lacked both the technical knowledge and the imagination to figure out a use for this information. The easiest and most cost-effective thing for him to do was to sell these plans for cash. Many people would be willing to pay for such information, both in his country and the rest of the Middle East. *Maybe there is some profit in this,* he thought.

The morning news came on. "This morning in Poland more than 350,000 workers in Gdansk have threatened to quit work in protest over rising food costs, especially the cost of meat, which has risen more than 300 percent in the past year. Their leader is 37-year old electrician, Lech Walesa. In other news, the wife of the late Shah of Iran has returned to the United States. During the ten days since her husband's funeral she has been a guest of Egypt's President Anwar Sadat in Cairo.

Jaffar watched for a while longer. "Today is the 35th anniversary of the dropping of the first atomic bomb on Hiroshima, Japan. It was followed three days later by the dropping of a second bomb on Nagasaki, which led to the unconditional surrender of Japan, ending World War II ..." said the television. Then it showed video of the Los Alamos research facility in New Mexico, with the narration describing the long-abandoned laboratory.

If Hamas had an atomic bomb we could bring the United States government to its knees, thought Jaffar. *That's what I need to do! I need to do more research. There has got to be more information available than what's in these two files!* Although Jaffar knew that he was almost certainly not going to be able to lay his hands on any more TOP SECRET files, there was a huge cache of books at the library in downtown Sacramento. And none of it was secret.

August 9, 1980

Jaffar had spent the last four mornings reading books, looking at microfiche of declassified government material and making notes on foolscap paper. When he discovered the availability of this information, he was amazed again at how trusting Americans were … but his amazement was short-lived when he saw that almost every page had been heavily redacted. Sometimes whole pages were a sea of black, completely useless.

"Damn!" Jaffar thought for sure he'd hit a gold mine but it was impossible to reasonably extrapolate any sort of missing information or reach a conclusion about what the files were.

Frustrated at his lack of progress, again he thought, *maybe I should just sell the files and be done with it.* This conclusion had tempted him for almost a week.

He turned to the librarian for help, just as the sign below her desk said to do. Once more he conveyed the general topic and she directed him to a seemingly endless series of cards organized using the Dewey Decimal System. The last area Jaffar examined was the vast video library.

"Unfortunately you can't check out any of this material, with or without a valid library card. You can, however, watch them at any of the available work study stations over here." Miss. Atherton directed Jaffar to a secluded area of the library, near the checkout counter.

It was afternoon and Jaffar rubbed his tired eyes. He'd watched hours of grainy video from the First and Second World Wars, the Korean War, and, most recently, the Vietnam War. He decided that he'd very nearly reached the end of his research and he'd found nothing of value. He grabbed the first of the last two VHS tapes he planned to look at and slid it into the video machine. It stopped after just a few seconds and the machine ejected the cassette with a trail of black, half-inch-wide videotape behind it.

"Damn!" Jaffar called over the librarian and showed her the problem.

"That's all right, sir. Some of these tapes are years old. They have been viewed hundreds of times and are simply worn out."

"Okay, I'll just look at this last one, if you can give me a hand getting this tangled mess out of the machine."

"No problem." It wasn't, because Miss Atherton and her gentle hands managed to salvage the videotape and leave Jaffar watching the last video, another color documentary from the Second World War. This time the machine behaved itself and the tape wound through the rollers smoothly.

"The United States Army Air Corps had experienced very heavy losses of both trained crews and airworthy, mission-capable aircraft during the middle part of 1942 and into 1943. A new project code named 'Project Aphrodite' was conceived and brought to bear against the Nazis in the European theatre. Project Aphrodite used tired old Boeing B-17 aircraft, some which could barely fly and could not be returned to flight readiness. They were loaded with high explosives ..."

"That's it!" Jaffar shouted, drawing angry stares from those within earshot.

Miss Atherton came around the corner. "If you're not going to be quiet I am afraid that you'll have to leave."

"I'm very sorry. It won't happen again," he said contritely, barely concealing a grin.

Miss Atherton left and Jaffar watched the video several more times. The film proved to be a catalyst for a new idea for Jaffar. He suddenly realized the value of the technology he now owned and what it would mean to Hamas and to his countrymen. A new plan of attack against both the Western countries and their allies in the Middle East started germinating in his brain. Jaffar gathered up his notes, returned the stack of videos and left the library.

August 10, 1980

Giti had promised Jaffar that this year would be the last one that she would work. The settlement from the lawsuit had been sufficient for her to pay off her mortgage, set up a trust fund and a college fund for Sina and create some healthy investments for her to live off. Besides, Jaffar had enough money for the both of them. Giti was still working because of Zafar and Fatemah; they had treated her wonderfully over the years and she didn't want to leave them high and dry. They depended on her.

Over the summer, Jaffar had been looking after Sina when the boy wasn't over at his various friends' houses. That was where Sina was now, leaving Jaffar to pursue his business interests. It had been several weeks since Jaffar had called Abdul. There had been no reason to do so. Payments had resumed in their proper amounts and the men he had watching Abdul reported nothing unusual, aside from the nightly visits from the local whores. And after their talk, Abdul had even reimbursed the shortfalls of cash from the previous months. All was very quiet in Iraq, it seemed.

In spite of the time difference, Jaffar called Abdul. It was late evening and most likely he would not be home, but he answered in a surprisingly sober voice, "Hello?"

At least he's not drunk this time, Jaffar thought. "Abdul my friend. How are you?"

"I'm very well, Excellency. Is everything alright?" It usually wasn't. When Jaffar called, trouble was sure to follow.

"Everything is good. I need to come home next week. Can you make the usual arrangements?"

"Next week! When next week?"

"I've got some things to take care of here first. Make it the 16th of August."

Jaffar didn't want to get caught with the files in his possession. He drove to the post office and purchased two large airmail envelopes and a roll of packing tape. He separated the two files and placed each in its own envelope. Then he addressed them both to the Chief of Police, Colonel Abdul Al-Kubesi, Al-Qa'im, Iraq. He carefully wrapped each in tape, had the envelopes weighed and asked for first class air mail.

"That will be $19.78 please."

Jaffar handed over a twenty dollar bill and waited impatiently for his change. He was glad to have the envelopes safely on their way. The clerk assured him it would be only a week to ten days before delivery.

"That will be very good."

That evening after supper, Jaffar informed Giti that he intended to go out of the country for a few weeks. Giti was disappointed, to say the least. "But Jaffar, we've only been married for five weeks. Can't you go out of town another time?"

Jaffar hadn't even considered the fact that they were newlyweds. In Iraq, the wife would never challenge the husband about anything, but in America things were certainly different. He tried not to let it bother him and also thought once again about bringing her to Iraq so she could learn his ways.

"I have to go. This is important!"

"And Sina and I aren't?" Giti raised her voice slightly.

"I have to go, Giti. That's the end of the discussion!" he said coldly, then stalked away, leaving Giti to stare after him, speechless. This was a side of Jaffar she'd not seen, and hadn't expected.

That night Jaffar could feel the chill from the other side of the bed. Unsure of how to deal with the situation, he simply reacted the way he'd done in the past with women. Despite Giti's protests, Jaffar forced himself onto his new wife. The sex was far from gentle, almost savage. Although Jaffar could feel Giti reach her own orgasm, he also heard her cry herself to sleep.

August 16, 1980

The atmosphere in their home for the past week had been static, with heightened emotions on both sides. Jaffar was still not able to muster a much-needed apology; Giti, on the other hand, wasn't willing to accept this kind of behavior from him. She'd never had to do so with Reza, who would never have been so rough with her in the first place. But Jaffar was a far different man than she'd thought—something he'd certainly had not demonstrated previous to their marriage. Before the wedding he had been, for the most part, a considerate lover and a caring partner and Giti was not willing to let things get any further out of hand. She would never accept a subservient role in the marriage.

For the last week Jaffar hadn't presented any openings in which Giti could start any sort of dialogue and even Sina had noticed the coolness, the lack of communication between his mother and stepfather. When he asked Giti about it she said, "Jaffar and I are having a few problems right now. He's going away on business and I don't want him to go."

"Maybe you could go with him. Maybe we could both go with him."

"No, Sina. He's got to go to alone. Besides, that part of the world is very dangerous for Americans right now!"

"But Jaffar is an American isn't he?"

"No, Sina. He's English."

"But we speak English."

Trust a child to put things in terms that were so simple. "No, by English, I mean British. You know, like the Queen of England."

"Oh! That English. Will he be alright?"

"I don't know Sina. I truly don't. I hope so." Sina gave his mother the biggest hug he could manage, sensing that she needed one.

"It will be okay, Mom."

Jaffar had packed a small suitcase and an overnight bag. He tossed them in them back of his car. Giti thought this wasn't enough clothes or toiletries for the length of time Jaffar was going to be gone, but said nothing. Jaffar, of course, had kept quiet the fact that in Al-Qa'im he had a completely furnished and functional home—including a servant.

The three of them walked to his car together. "Be a good boy for your mother, Sina."

"I will."

"Take care of yourself Giti. I will see you when I get back."

Giti gave her husband a hug. "I will Jaffar. Be safe and we'll talk when you get back." She had deliberately avoided the use of the word home. Her house hadn't felt like much of a home for the past week or so. Jaffar backed out of the driveway and Giti and Sina waved as he drove away. They went back into the house, where Sina gave his mother another hug.

Al-Qa'im, Iraq - August 18, 1980

When Jaffar arrived at the small airport in Al-Qa'im, the first thing he noticed when stepping off the plane was the humidity and temperature. He had become used to the pleasant climate of Sacramento.

Abdul was waiting for him. They shook hands and gave each other the customary embrace. Abdul still wasn't sure why Jaffar had picked this particular time to come home and he wasn't happy about now having to be on the 'straight and narrow'.

Jaffar, on the other hand, was very glad to be home. He was exhausted after thirty-six hours of travel and the last week had made it abundantly clear to him that he'd have a difficult time adjusting to having his authority challenged by a wife. Life with Giti was pleasant for the most part, but he was the male of the household, and that made his word law. She would have to learn.

"Get my bags, Abdul, and take me home."

"Yes, Excellency," Abdul said as he placed Jaffar's bags in the trunk. *So it begins again …* he thought to himself. Abdul had gotten quite used to being top dog around the town during Jaffar's absence.

"Did you get those two envelopes I mailed to you?"

"Nothing yet! Maybe they will come tomorrow."

"I certainly hope so. It would make things most difficult if they have been lost." Although it hadn't been the only reason for coming home, it definitely was the most important.

August 19, 1980

Jaffar had fallen asleep the minute he got home and he slept soundly for twelve hours. He awoke refreshed. He showered, dressed and made himself a tea then called Abdul to see if his mail had arrived.

"Not yet! I checked first thing this morning."

"Damn! I hope they are not lost!" This was one of the first experiences Jaffar had had with the United States Post Office. There was a 1-800 number on the card the clerk had given him; he tried several times to dial it, with no success. He tried the second number, which was long distance, and was informed that the service was not available from outside the United States and Canada.

"I don't believe this!" He slammed the phone down in its cradle.

The rest of the day, Jaffar looked over his house for the first time in many months, enjoying the luxury and freedom he felt. It was pointless to do anything but wait; he needed the information contained in those envelopes before he could do some proper planning. For now, he could only do preliminary work and make a few phone calls. He had no idea how much the operation was going to cost, or even if it was possible. That would have to wait until the envelopes came.

August 21, 1980

For two days Jaffar had waited for his precious mail. With each day, his frustration grew along with his anger. This was just another reason for him to hate the Americans. Their postal service was inefficient and they had had more than 100 years to get it right. Judging from the mailman who had been delivering to the house in Sacramento, Jaffar was sure that all successful post office applicants had to be overweight and slow as a prerequisite. Maybe this morning would bring good news.

The telephone rang, much earlier than usual.

"Good morning, Jaffar."

"Do you have them?"

"Yes! They came yesterday, but I didn't get them until this morning."

"What! Do you mean to say they were kept overnight?"

"Yes, Excellency." Abdul knew Jaffar would be angry at that. It was clear that his time spent in the United States hadn't mellowed him. There would be severe consequences.

"Bring me the documents at once. We can discuss this other matter later."

The Chief of Police arrived ten minutes later. "Give them to me Abdul!"

Jaffar examined the exterior of the envelopes carefully, to see if they had been tampered with in any way. Satisfied that all was in order, he opened them with the sharp knife he kept in his desk—for that purpose, among others. He handed the first envelope to Abdul. "Here, read this!"

Abdul opened the first file. The words TOP SECRET jumped from the first page. "This is top secret from the Unites States government!"

"Yes! It's from their Air Force to be exact. Giti's dead husband had it in their attic, if you can believe it!" Jaffar waited a moment for Abdul to close his mouth. "Read it. I'm going to get myself some breakfast." Jaffar did not bother to ask Abdul if he wanted any.

A short while later, Jaffar returned to the room, another cup of tea in his hand. He waited for Abdul to finish reading the last few pages. Jaffar asked no question, he simply handed Abdul the second file for him to read.

When Abdul was finished, he looked at Jaffar. It was clear that he had even less comprehension than his boss had had, two weeks earlier. "What do you think Abdul?"

"I'm not sure, Excellency. There seems to be some possibilities here." Diplomatically, Abdul said, "What do you think?"

"First, I think we should call Sameed and maybe Abbas." Jaffar hadn't bothered to show Abdul the notes he'd made in the library. Those he'd save for later.

"What's the second thing, Jaffar?" There was always a second thing.

"I want you to find and punish the person responsible for holding my mail overnight!"

— Chapter 13 —

August 20, 1980

Jaffar and Abdul had gathered two of their most talented and trusted henchmen, Sameed Al-Farouk and Abbas Balochie. Both men were very familiar with the inner workings of almost any mode of transportation. They could tear down just about any engine, be it from a car, truck or airplane. They could readily diagnose any problem, then turn around and rebuild an engine so it worked flawlessly. Neither possessed a high school diploma, but they were near-geniuses when it came to machines.

Both men studied the documents placed in front of them. After an hour of reading and talking between themselves, Jaffar grew impatient. "Well my friends, do you think that it can be done?"

Both men were well-aware of both Jaffar's and Abdul's reputations. They certainly didn't want to disappoint them. Both of them nodded their heads in agreement. "Yes! But it will cost many millions."

"How much? Give me a number."

Sameed and Abbas had already made a rough guess. "Ten million dollars, maybe twenty million dollars."

"What!?" Jaffar hadn't thought it would cost nearly that much; he'd guessed at about half that amount. "Why so much?"

"Well, Jaffar, that does include the cost of the plane, the hardware and many other things! If you remember, this Reza was going to ask for many millions—hundreds of millions—of dollars."

"Yes, of course," Jaffar acknowledged, "but that was for many planes that would be accepted by the Federal Aviation Administration."

"How many planes are you needing Jaffar?"

"One. Just one!"

August 24, 1980

Jack hadn't had a particularly good day. It had been a scorcher, even by Las Vegas standards, and it had been almost more than he could bear. He'd spent all morning and part of the afternoon, sitting in his black Camaro doing Captain Nichols a favor. All his undercover officers were either busy on other cases or had just finished extended surveillance. Jack wanted to help Nichols if he could. On several occasions Ken had kept Jack out of trouble when Jack had found it necessary to 'bend' the law.

He was glad he'd had the forethought to pack a cooler with ice and bottled water. In it he'd also put a couple of cucumber sandwiches. They always seemed to cool him down on those really hot days.

Jack had been keeping an eye on a couple of sleaze balls who were apparently involved with distributing drugs that had been smuggled out of Columbia. This was the third time Ken had asked him to work this kind of detail and the fact that he wasn't a cop was an advantage; he was unknown to the local criminal element and—although he wasn't allowed to actually make an arrest—he was capable at take-down and could assist his partner. It kept him busy and paid the bills, plus it reunited him, Don and Ken.

The work with Ken had sparked one night while Donny grilled steaks and Jack and Ken made salad and baked potatoes. As Ken pulled the baked spuds out of the oven, he said to Don and Jack, "We sure could use a hand with some of our surveillance. Seems everyone's on vacation and the city's going to shit!"

Now, a few months later, Jack was sitting at the side of the road, across from a dilapidated warehouse that very likely held several million dollars' worth of cocaine. Jack enjoyed this kind of work far more than tailing some skirt-chasing, cheating husband at the behest of a wounded bride. Although that kind of work made a difference to the injured spouse, Jack usually didn't feel too great about it.

A white-over-blue, two-toned Ford Falcon came to a stop a block and a half away on the opposite side of the street. Jack recognized the car as belonging to Detective Frank McAdams, a rough-looking individual who more often than not sported several days' growth of beard. He looked like the kind of guy that would be completely at home in a biker gang. Frank's appearance was Jack's cue to finish his surveillance. Jack keyed the microphone. "I'm handing it over to you and Dan, Frank."

"Thanks, Jack."

He headed home to shower and change. He'd agreed to meet Donny at the Moose and Lamb pub. They would shoot a few games of pool, have some decent food and shoot the shit.

"Just like old times Jack," that's what Donny had said. After today's heat, he thought he might even treat himself to a beer. That would be refreshing.

Once he'd cleaned up, he headed to the pub. He'd been there for a half an hour, long enough to drink two cold bottles of water. The pub charged the same for water and beer but Jack didn't care.

There were only a few patrons scattered about the bar; some had cut out from work early, some were still there from a late liquid lunch. The small television above the bar was on but it was too far away for Jack to hear very well.

"Excuse me Miss... um, Rachel," he said, looking at the waitress's nametag, "Would it be possible to have this T.V. turned up a little?"

The waitress looked around at the near-empty bar. "Yes. I don't think that it would be a problem."

"Thanks. It's just until my friend gets here."

Rachel returned with a remote control. "Here you go. Keep the volume turned down and you can watch pretty much anything you want." She gave Jack a huge smile and walked away.

The NBC news was on. "Hurricane Cynthia brushed by the Mexican Riviera leaving thousands homeless and causing millions of dollars in damage. Miraculously only two people were killed by flying debris. And in further news, the hostage crisis continues with no end in sight. The hostages have been held for more than nine months with Tehran still demanding that all Iranian assets in the United States be unfrozen. The Islamic fundamentalists holding the hostages have refused any United Nations-sponsored negotiations."

"Also In other news from the Middle East, in the small Iraqi town of Al-Qa'im, near the Syrian border, an entire family, thirteen people including eight small children, have been found brutally murdered. Neighbors became suspicious when there had been no activity around the home for two days.

Our NBC correspondent in Iraq obtained this interview with Al-Qa'im Chief of Police …"

The scene flashed to a blond, male reporter who was on the scene in Iraq. He looked very serious as he said. He held the microphone in front of a large, overly-medaled, tough-looking Iraqi man, who said, "The murders appear to be the work of several bandits, who were probably ransacking the house. There was a struggle sometime during the robbery and the criminals turned from robbery to murder to hide their crime."

"Well I'll be damned!" Jack exclaimed under his breath when he saw the familiar face.

Abdul continued, "I tell you now, the thieves and murderers will be brought to justice!"

"That was a report from Walt Donner, our Middle East correspondent." Jack turned down the volume and focused his attention on the door, waiting for Donny to come though. He was practically busting to tell him what he had just seen. Right on time Donny came into pub from the bright outdoors. "Don!" Jack gave a quick wave and Donny spotted him.

"Hey there, Jack. You look like a happy camper. How'd your day go?"

Jack looked around to see if anyone was in earshot. "It went okay, but no one came within a block of those drugs. Ken swears that they are in that warehouse."

"What are you going to do?"

"Keep working with Ken as long as wants me. It pays better than I've been getting. But enough about that … You won't believe what I just saw on television!"

"Whoa! Let's get us some beers. By the looks of things you could use one."

"I like my water thanks, but yes I'll get a beer." Rachel came over and took their order. "Two Dos Equis, please."

"Be right back."

"Now what are you so wound up about Jack?"

"You remember that asshole with all the Goddamn medals on the front of his uniform who was tangled up with that Jaffar, the one who married Sacramento Giti?"

"Yeah. The Chief of Police."

"That's the guy! It seems a whole family got butchered in some small town in Iraq and the NBC news interviewed him."

Don gave a wry grin. "He's probably the guy that did it. You remember what Kip said?"

"Yeah, I remember. He even promised that the killers would be caught and punished."

"Right!"

Just then Rachel brought them their beer. "Can I get you some food?" she asked. Jack ordered a clubhouse and Donny ordered a double cheeseburger with fries.

"You're going to have to stop eating that crap soon, Don!"

"I know Jack, but it tastes good. Besides, my idea of a good meal doesn't involve a plate of rabbit food and a glass of water."

"Well at least you're running again. How many miles so far?"

"Five or six." Just then Donny noticed a familiar face walk into the bar. "Jesus Jack, look who it is!"

"Hey you two. Fancy meeting you here." Captain Ken Nichols sat down.

"You ass. I called you to say that Don and I would be here."

"Good to see you, Don." Rachel came back and took Ken's beer and food order. "So Jack, how did it go today? Hot?"

"You'd better believe it. I was going to weigh myself when I got home. I bet I lost five pounds."

"Anything move yet? Any sign of our boys, Ricardo and Hector?"

"Nope. How long are we going to keep this up?"

"As long as it takes."

"Hey Ken do you want to know who Jack saw on the boob tube?" Jack gave Donny's shin a tap with his shoe, along with a scowl.

"Who?"

"He spotted one of the clowns that hired him for that Sacramento job! On the news!"

Ken gave Jack a bit of a scowl, "Jack!"

"It was on the news, Ken. I remember our little talk."

"What was he doing on the news?"

"Someone in his town butchered thirteen people including eight kids. All of them in the same family."

"That's terrible! What's his connection to all that?"

"He's the fucking Chief of Police!"

Al-Qa'im, Iraq - August 25, 1980

Sameed and Abbas spent the morning reviewing the drawings and diagrams from California Robotics. They made a list of specifications for the plane that was to be modified. "According to this it has to have a Bendix Model PB-20D autopilot. FAA approved."

"Yes, but what does it mean discreet commands?"

"I don't know Abbas."

"What does it mean proportional commands?"

"Again, I don't know."

"Do you think that we should have told Jaffar that we would do the job?"

"I don't care what happens to me, I'm willing to die for Allah and the cause. But I do not want my family to be tortured and killed. You know, like those poor bastards down at the post office."

"Yes. It's best that we do our jobs. Maybe we will understand more as we become more used to the systems. Once they are built we can work out other things." But both knew they were way over their heads.

August 27, 1980

It was hot the day Jaffar arrived back in Sacramento. This trip had been the exact reverse of his trip out—another 36-plus hours of flying. Jaffar was dead-tired—too tired to drive his car home from the airport. He hired a taxi instead and within blocks he was sound asleep in the backseat. He remained so for the entire trip home, but even if he'd been awake it's unlikely he would have noticed the men in the sedan trailing him a quarter-mile back.

He arrived home to an empty house. The previous morning, Jaffar had called Giti from the Baghdad airport to let her know which flight he would be arriving on but she said she couldn't pick him up as she was taking Sina to Yosemite National park with Zafar and Fatemah the next day.

Jaffar paid the taxi and managed to get himself up the front stairs and into the house. He dropped his bags at the front door and walked down the hall to the bedroom. It was daylight outside, almost midday, but Jaffar was soon fast asleep once again.

August 28, 1980

Jaffar woke refreshed. He spotted the note on the nightstand. He'd missed it the day before:

> *Jaffar, I've gone with Sina, Fatemah and Zafar to Yosemite. Sina's friend Matthew is along to keep Sina company. Neither of the boys have ever seen a giant Redwood tree so we might go around to Redwood National Park as well. That's if the kids don't drive us three adults crazy, of course. We'll see you when we get back.*
>
> *Love Giti*
>
> *P.S. There are a couple of meals in the freezer that I prepared for you. All you have to do is follow the instructions on the note that I put on each one. Sina and I missed you.*

Jaffar had a very busy week ahead of him. He had to start shopping for a suitable piece of property in order to put his plan into action. He already knew where he could get the other major item on his list—a plane. But he had to get to Las Vegas first. He decided the best approach would be to charter a plane to Las Vegas so he could trace his path from many months before, back to the silver tubes in the middle of the desert that had glittered so brightly in the sun as he'd watched them from the air. At eight-thirty, Jaffar was in the offices of Executive Air Charter.

"Good morning Sir. How can I help you?"

"I'd like to charter a plane for a day or so."

"What is your destination?"

"Las Vegas. I'm looking for some land to buy."

"We have a Cessna Four-Fourteen. It seats six people. It leases for $500 dollars per hour."

"Of course, that would be fine." Jaffar had $17,500,000 tucked away in a newly-opened account. He intended to keep as much of this money as possible for himself after this operation was over. He opened his briefcase handed cash to the clerk. "Here's $5,000. Will that be enough?"

"Yes, of course. I'll need you to sign here." Jaffar did so and was handed a copy of his lease agreement. "If you'll wait here I'll have the crew ready the plane for departure."

Once airborne, Jaffar sat in the rear-facing seat. He made sure he was on the same side of the plane as before. He'd been on board the other plane for about an hour. He'd need approximately double that time aboard this smaller, slower aircraft. For two hours Jaffar stared out the window, looking for landmarks that would tell him where he was and if he was close to where he wanted to go. There were no familiar features. He decided to ask the pilot. "Excuse me. I'm looking for something I saw last year, when I flew over this area."

"What was that, sir?"

"I saw row after row of planes, parked in what appeared to be some sort of big parking lot."

"You mean the aircraft graveyard?"

"I'm not sure. These planes were not buried."

The pilot laughed. "Mile High Aviation is just ahead. If you'll swivel your seat 180 degrees you can see it ahead on the right side."

Jaffar smiled as the airplanes came into view. Everything looked much different from this altitude, about 15,000 feet. Previously he'd been almost three times as high. Instead of small, shiny arrows, they looked like planes.

They flew over the remote airfield and Jaffar knew that he'd found the right place. He was still amazed that such a place could exist. Jaffar couldn't even begin to guess the cost of these many hundreds planes when they were new. "Those must be worth a lot of money!"

"Yes, Sir. They're probably worth billions of dollars."

"Why are they here?"

"They are for sale mostly. Some are just in storage, until the economics are right."

"What's your name?"

"Jeff Davies."

"Well, Jeff my friend. How would you like to make some money? Say a thousand dollars?"

"Yeah sure, what do you need?"

"Can you land there for an hour or so?"

"Absolutely!" Jeff looked up the frequency. He radioed Mile High Aviation. "Mile High, this is November Bravo Yankee One One Six requesting permission to land."

"Roger November Bravo Yankee One One Six. Turn left 15 degrees and descend. You are cleared for runway eight nine. Taxi left to main building."

"Roger."

Jeff landed the Cessna and taxied up to the main building, if you could call it that. The metal siding on the outside had baked in the sun for many years. Whatever paint remained had long ago lost the ability to protect the rusting, corrugated metal beneath.

"Here you are, Jeff." Jaffar handed the pilot his $1,000. "Wait here."

"Yes Sir." Jeff watched Jaffar walk inside to talk to the manager, then he focused on the cash.

Once inside, Jaffar introduced himself to the man there. "I'm Jaffar Hodgeson. I'm the President of Sunwest Properties." He handed the manager a card.

"Pleased to meet you. I'm Fred Carlson. I run Mile High. How can I help you?"

Jaffar handed Fred a sheet of specifications typed on Sunwest letterhead. "I need a plane to meet these specifications."

Fred studied it with a frown. "Well that would be either a Boeing 707 or 720," he said. "We have several of each—actually four 720s and three 707s." He walked over to a nearby golf cart. "Hop in. I'll show them to you." Jaffar eyed the cart with apprehension. He motioned Jaffar over. "It beats walking ... unless of course you want to?"

"No! No, this will be fine."

Fred drove the golf cart down a winding gravel road. It was surprisingly smooth. There was little rain to wash the sand and small pebbles away, and the road was well compacted.

The aircraft stretched out in four rows for over a mile or so. Each plane was parked wingtip to wingtip, with just a few feet in between. Fred explained that they were on a dry lake bed, which was perfect for storage. Fred parked in front of several four-engine jet aircraft. "Here we go," he said.

"Why are they all painted gray?"

"That's not paint. It's a coating, almost like rubber. It protects the aircraft."

"What about those 747s? They are still painted."

"Those are new arrivals. Their owners are going to store them here for a while. Hanger space is very expensive. It's far cheaper to pay me to store them." He pointed to some aircraft, looking for reaction from Jaffar. "Here we are, Jaffar. Three 707s on the right and four 720s on the left."

"They look the same. How can you tell them apart?"

"The Boeing 720 is eight feet, four inches shorter and a few miles per hour faster than the Boeing 707. Other than that they are identical."

"What do such aircraft cost?"

"These 707s range in price from $2.2 million to more than $3 million."

"What about these other four?"

"They start at two and three quarters million up to four and a half million"

"That seems like a lot for a plane that's almost twenty years old."

"That's not much if you compare them to the 747s out there. The ones at the far end will sell for $27 million."

"I see what you mean."

"Also, I'd like to point out that the 720s have fewer hours on them than every one of the 707s."

"We are taking about a price difference of over a million dollars?"

"Yes," said Fred. Then he looked Jaffar in the eye. "Let me be honest with you, Mr. Hodgeson. Most people who come here to shop for an airplane bring a chief mechanic or deal with me through a broker, or perhaps both. Why did you come by yourself?"

"I prefer to do things hands-on. I usually see what I want and I get it. Right now I would like to buy a plane for my company and I am willing to pay handsomely for it."

"I'm sure we can do business, Mr. Hodgeson, but wouldn't you like to do more than just kick the tires? Wouldn't you like to at least look at the interior, the cockpit, check out the avionics?"

"No! Those things are unimportant. I intend to remodel the whole interior. New seating, everything. The outside, I will have painted in my corporate colors."

"We can do that here. I've got an FAA certified maintenance hangar."

"That's fine. So now I've got to pick which plane suits my needs. Which one would you buy if you were in my place?"

"I would pick either the ex-Federal Aviation Administration Boeing 720, or the one from Middle East Airlines, also a 720."

Jaffar wanted to stay clear of any plane from the Middle East and he was pretty sure that any plane from the FAA would be maintained properly, so the choice was easy. "I think the plane from the FAA would suit my needs, but I would like to give it some more thought."

"Of course, that's wise of you. I can give you detailed histories of all seven aircraft. You can decide which one suits the needs of you and your shareholders."

"Very well. I've got some business in Las Vegas later today. I will call you tomorrow with my decision."

"That's fair enough Mr. Hodgeson." They drove back to the main building where Jeff Davies was patiently waiting. In ten minutes Jaffar was airborne in his leased Cessna. "Jeff can you take me to Wendover, Utah?"

"I've already filed a flight plan for Las Vegas!"

"There's another thousand dollars in it for you."

"Okay. I'll call and have the desk refile for me." He switched frequencies and made the call.

Wendover Air Force Base, Utah

Tony 'Boom-Boom' Barnetson was an ex-pro-football player turned real estate agent, turned government agent. He laughed every time one of his nieces or nephews would ask him if he was a spy. "No. I'm just a plain ordinary real estate agent for Uncle Sam. That's all!" He got the name 'Boom Boom' from his team-mates in college.

"If Tony tackles somebody, all they hear are two booms. One boom when he hits them, another boom when they hit the ground. Boom! Boom!"

Tony was now a land broker for the United States military. One of his latest jobs was to arrange the sale or lease of Wendover Air Force base. During World War II, Wendover Army Air Field had been used as a training base for bombing crews before they were deployed overseas to the Pacific and European theatres.

Tony watched as the Cessna approached the runway from the east. He could see the pilot was battling a strong crosswind; the Cessna yawed slightly on its approach. At an altitude of 20 feet, the crosswind died out and Jeff straightened out the plane to land perfectly on the centerline of the runway. The plane stopped in front of the former army hangar.

Jaffar left the plane another $1,000 poorer, but this time Jeff got out, anxious to stretch his legs and use the facilities. He was also anxious to explore the old airfield and poke around for a while.

"You must be Jaffar Hodgeson. I'm Tony Barnetson. Here's my card."

Jaffar handed Barnetson his card. "That's right, Sunwest Properties. All morning I kept calling it Sunset Properties. My wife, who seems to know my business better than me, kept correcting me."

Jaffar nodded, thinking of Giti. Sometimes it seemed that she was the same way.

"Well Mr. Hodgeson, what can I do for you? When you called, you only said that you were interested in the hangar facilities and occasional use of the runway."

"That may change Mr. Barnetson. Can we have a look around the property?"

"By all means. My car is over here. Do you or your pilot need anything? Washrooms? Perhaps something to eat or drink?"

"A washroom would be nice," Jeff said shifting his weight from side to side.

"It's in that building."

"You don't mind if I looked around? I heard about this place when I was a kid."

"Go ahead. We'll be about an hour." The two men headed off down the concrete ramp that stretched for almost a mile alongside the runway. "This base was used to train bombing crews during the Second World War. It was built in 1941."

"Oh!"

"This base has had some very important roles, including being the training site for the crews that dropped the atomic bombs on Hiroshima and Nagasaki from September 1944 to August 1945. They trained on this very field."

"That's very interesting."

"There's even a swimming pool and a three-hundred bed hospital. This base has everything. Almost 20,000 people were stationed here."

"Can we see the hanger facilities, including the one that is used for aircraft maintenance?"

"Of course. That's the large building over there. You can park four Boeing 747s in there at the same time."

"That's impressive."

Tony led Jaffar into the main hangar. It was the largest building that Jaffar had ever been in, with the exception of a couple of airport terminals. It stretched over an area the size of several football fields.

"Huge, isn't it?" He needn't have asked the question; Jaffar stood motionless, mouth partially open in astonishment.

"How many acres is the base?"

"Including the bombing and gunnery range over to the southeast, there are almost three and a half million acres. Of course the bomb range could only be leased for the short-term."

"What about the rest?"

"The U.S. Government declared the field as surplus in 1976. Almost everything is up for sale. Some of the specific areas that would not be are the Enola Gay hanger, as well as the technical buildings that were used for the assembly of the atom bombs."

"It sounds like that was the most important thing this place was used for, the most historical."

"Yes certainly, though it was used for other things during the war and after. The 'Doodlebug' cruise missile, a replica of the German V-One was tested here. There was also something else that this base was used for during World War II, but I can't remember the name. It will come to me."

"So Mr. Barnetson, how much to lease or buy all of this?"

"If you wanted to lease the property to use it as an aircraft maintenance facility or something similar, you're looking at about $50,000 per month."

"What about a purchase?"

"Remember, Mr. Hodgeson, there are several limitations of ownership."

"Such as?"

"The government retains ownership of the control tower and radar site. Use of the tower would be a necessity of any maintenance operation. You could have your own qualified personnel operate it."

"What else?"

"Mineral rights below would always remain property of the United States government."

"So how much?"

"The Air Force wants about four dollars per acre. That works out to approximately $3.4 million for the land that is available." Jaffar sat across from Tony. In his mind he did some rough arithmetic. That would leave him just a shade under ten million, even if he bought the most expensive plane offered for sale. "Nine, if you include taxes," he said aloud.

"What was that?"

"Oh, nothing. Just doing a little banking in my head. My shareholders keep me on tight budget."

"Okay." The two drove around the perimeter of the airfield, the government agent pointing out different features. Jaffar could see the small town of Wendover a short distance away. He could hear a train in the distance. "That's the Western Pacific Railway. It used to stop regularly in Wendover, but in the last 15 years most folks have moved away. I guess the railroad figures there's no reason for it to do so now."

"What about the town? Can I buy gas and groceries there?"

"No, unfortunately. The nearest place for groceries is down I-80, almost 40 miles away, in Wells, Nevada."

"There's no place closer than that?"

"Nope. Except for maybe Oasis or West Wendover. I think you can still pick up a few things there."

"So it's quite secluded."

"That's why the Army built the base here in the first place. It would make a nice get-away for someone who wanted to retire. There's a real quiet beauty to this part of the country."

Jaffar looked around. "I see what you mean." Jaffar could envision the potential of this place, even after the operation he was planning in his head was over. The Islamic Hamas, who had bankrolled him in the past, had given him free reign—but they expected results for their investment. So did Jaffar.

"So what do you think?"

"I'm still not sure. I have to think about it for a while."

They had used up the hour and then some and Boom Boom said, "Let's head back. We can talk on the way." On the way, Jaffar started negotiating, using the same tactic he always used when negotiating a real estate deal. "Three and a half million is a lot of money," he said.

"Eight hundred and fifty thousand acres is a lot of land and it has an airport." Tony laughed. "How many people can say that?" Tony could see the wheels turning in Jaffar's mind. "I'll tell you what. I can give you this deal, at the same price, taxes in." The government did give him a bit of wriggle room if a deal was close.

Jaffar still kept close-lipped.

"Oh and I just remembered what else the army did here during the war," Tony said.

"What?"

"I seem to recall a project that was based here called Project Aphrodite. Yeah I'm pretty sure that was it, one of the Greek goddesses. Something to do with unmanned planes bombing the Nazis."

Jaffar smiled. He'd read about that at the library.

Jeff was waiting for them at the main building, a short walk from the Cessna when they got back. The three men walked back toward the plane. One of them was $2,000 richer. One of them was going to be several million dollars poorer. At the foot of the stairs into the small aircraft, Jaffar shook hands with Tony. "Mr. Barnetson, you've got a deal. Three million, four hundred thousand!"

"Great Mr. Hodgeson. I'll have the papers drawn up with Sunset, I mean Sunwest, Properties as the new deed holder."

"I'll have my lawyers give you a call!" Jaffar smiled as he boarded the plane. "Stage two complete. Now I've just got to decide on which plane," he said to himself.

Jeff couldn't help but notice what a good mood Jaffar was in. "Did you have a good day, Mr. Hodgeson?"

"A very good day, Jeff. A very good day indeed."

The ride back to Sacramento seemed shorter than before, though it was almost six-thirty when they landed.

Jaffar had been silent most of the flight, but when they landed he unexpectedly said to Jeff, "Jeff, if you're available I'd like to hire you. I'm going to buy one of those Boeing jets. Could you come with me?"

Jeff was surprised by the request, but cautious. However, he knew a big payday might be in store so he answered honestly, "If what you mean is a check-out ride, I sure can. But if you want me to fly it on my own, I'm not qualified. At least not yet."

"That's too bad. I'd like you to come along anyway. Here's another thousand dollars for a job well done." Jeff couldn't say no. Who didn't need cash? Gratefully, he took the money.

"Thanks," he said, "But can we keep this on the down-low? I'm not supposed to accept gratuities."

"Oh, yes. Of course," said Jaffar. After filling out the appropriate paperwork to conclude the day's flight, Jaffar said good bye to Jeff and then left for home

"Yes, it has indeed been a very good day," he said to himself with satisfaction.

— Chapter 14 —

August 29, 1980

It was early Friday morning at Mile High Aviation when the phone rang. "Good morning, Fred Carlson here."

"Good morning, Mr. Carlson. Jaffar Hodgeson here."

"Yes, of course, hello Mr. Hodgeson. How can I help you?"

"I've decided to take the ex-Federal Aviation Administration plane. I've just got one last question for you."

"What's that?"

"Because I don't presently have a qualified pilot on staff, would it be too much to ask about delivery?"

This isn't a Pizza Hut, Fred thought to himself, but he said, "Yes! I could deliver it."

"Good. Very good."

"When do you want it delivered? I'm leaving today until the day after Labor Day. It's actually a good thing you called early."

"Can I have my lawyer come over to look at the documents and make arrangements for payment?"

"That would be good. I'll see him the day after Labor Day. That's next Tuesday."

"I can have a courier deliver a bank draft today for a deposit, or I can arrange a wire transfer. How much do you require?"

"A non-refundable deposit of ten percent is required. That works out to $450,000."

"I'll call Western Union. You should have it before noon."

Fred hung up the phone, a big grin on his face. He called his wife to tell her they'd be leaving tomorrow with some extra coins in their jeans. "My commission alone is $675,000!" he told her.

September 1, 1980

It was early afternoon when Giti and Sina arrived home from their week-long vacation. Giti tooted the horn when she pulled into the driveway. Jaffar came out of the house to greet them. "Hello Giti. I missed you." He gave her a big hug and a kiss.

"What about me?" Sina asked.

"Yes, Sina. I missed you too." Jaffar helped carry in their suitcases.

"We brought you back a present, Jaffar," said Sina excitedly.

"You did? That's nice Sina. What is it?"

"Mom told me that you have to wait to get it."

Things appeared to be somewhat back to normal. Giti spent the afternoon doing laundry and getting Sina ready for the first day of school, which was the next day. Giti remarked to Jaffar, "Tomorrow he starts grade three. He's growing up so fast."

"Yes, he is. I've noticed that in the last six months."

Giti and Fatemah, over the course of their holidays, had managed to have several chats about Giti's relationship with Jaffar. She felt a little better about things, but lying in bed that night, Giti felt uncomfortable. Though she and Jaffar made love, the sex wasn't easy or giving.

"We'll just have to see where this goes. One day at a time," Fatemah had told her.

Giti had another hectic day ahead of her tomorrow and was too tired to worry about it. *Maybe Jaffar is right. Perhaps trying to balance work and family duties is just too much,* she thought. Giti turned on her side and fell asleep.

September 8, 1980

Grant McKay was Jaffar's lawyer. He'd spent the last ten days transferring money in and out of various accounts and companies that Jaffar controlled. This left a very long and confusing paper trail for anyone who was looking. In the past Grant had almost made mistakes with some of Jaffar's transactions, because the process was so convoluted. This was not one of those occasions. He'd transferred over $8,500,000 through various offshore accounts and the money was now in the hands of the respective sellers. Grant McKay was paid very well for his services; he knew discretion was of the utmost importance. The fact that Jaffar didn't want to make it easy for anyone to see where the money originated wasn't his concern. His job was to make sure no laws were broken and that Jaffar couldn't be charged with any crimes, which he did.

Jaffar drove to Executive Air. He finished the usual paperwork to lease the aircraft for another day. Jeff Davies was waiting anxiously on the ramp beside the Cessna with another pilot who would fly the Cessna back to pick them up from Wendover.

"Good morning, Jaffar. This is Al Harding. He's going to be flying the left seat instead of me. It's officially my day off."

"Good morning, gentlemen. How are you today?"

"Fine, thanks. Ready to fly." Jeff smiled.

"Shall we be off?"

They landed at Mile High at ten-fifteen, exactly on schedule. Fred Carlson had Jaffar's Boeing 720 parked on the ramp next to an auxiliary power cart.

Jaffar was amazed when he saw the plane. It didn't even look like the same aircraft! Fred had removed the orange covers from the engine intakes and the wrapping from the sensor probes. The layers of spraylat that had protected the Boeing's exterior from the ravages of sun, wind, dust and nesting animals had been peeled off, revealing the FAA livery underneath. The registration number on the rudder of the Boeing was N113.

Fred couldn't hear the Cessna as it landed because the noise from the auxiliary power cart masked the noise of the aircraft, but he spotted it as it taxied towards the hanger building.. He looked at his watch. "Right on time," Fred said to Pete, his mechanic. Fred stepped from below the wing and walked toward the Cessna.

"Good morning, gentleman."

"Good morning, Fred." Jaffar barely gave Fred the smallest of glances. Instead he looked past him at his new corporate aircraft.

"It doesn't look like the same aircraft, does it Jaffar?"

"No!" Jaffar looked over the plane, walking around, caressing the rounded surfaces of the fuselage. He stood on his toes to peer into the number two engine, just like a kid with a new toy.

Jeff walked over with Al and Fred. "These are Pratt and Whitney JT3Cs aren't they?" Jeff had done a bit of homework over the last few days.

"Yes. The later 720s came with Dees. They were much more fuel efficient. By the way Mr. Hodgeson, I've fueled her up 40,000 pounds of Jet A."

"Isn't that a lot?"

"No! We must take along a minimum reserve by FAA rules and it takes a fair bit just to take off and get to cruising altitude."

"Well, as they say … let's get this show on the road!" said Jeff.

Al walked back to the Cessna and Jeff and Jaffar climbed up the stairs to board the jet. Fred was already strapped in. Jeff did the same and then watched as Fred did the pre-flight check. Pete removed the wheel chock then Fred prepared to start the four engines as Pete carefully stowed the heavy wheel chock in the cart, a safe distance away. Fred radioed that he was about to start the number one engine. He asked Pete to take another quick look around, to make sure there was nothing that could get sucked into the spinning engine as it built up revolutions. Pete keyed his mike, "Roger Fred! All clear!" He gave the visual thumbs up to the pilot. Fred started the first Pratt and Whitney. The process was repeated three more times.

Jeff noticed that the number two engine's temperature was a bit high. He tapped the gauge and Fred was impressed by the observation. "We filled the fuel tanks with heavy oil. We use that to protect the internal engine parts during storage. The Jet A will flush out the system."

"So the temperature will return to normal?"

"I hope by the time we reach Wendover, the temperature will be back to normal."

The plane started to taxi and Fred turned the Boeing at the west end of the runway. For its length, this was one of the most seldom-used runways in the country; planes rarely took off from here, most just landed here for their final time, their fates already determined.

Like any pilot, Fred was sad when any aircraft was scrapped, never to fly again, its shell simply chopped to pieces after the engines and other useful parts had been stripped. "I'm sure glad to see this old girl get a new lease on life," he said.

"Yes, of course Fred, a new lease on life. I'll take very good care of her," said Jaffar.

The three watched the Cessna taxi onto the runway ahead of them, with Al at the controls. As the small plane rolled down the tarmac and rotated into the air, Fred waited two minutes, looking at the instruments, making sure all was well. Then he advanced the throttles towards their stops, filling the cockpit with noise as the Boeing 720 rolled down the runway. The four turbofans—with almost 70,000 pounds of thrust—literally launched the aircraft down the runway. The plane was far below its maximum takeoff weight and it leapt off the tarmac and into the air. At 2,000 feet Fred banked the plane and headed northeast to Wendover.

All three men in the cockpit could see the Cessna about five miles ahead and below them. Fred watched it pass to the left and waved at Al, even though he couldn't be seen. "So Jeff, how many hours do you have in the Cessna?"

"I've got over eleven hundred, almost twelve now."

"Obviously you have your commercial license. What else? Your single engine land?"

"Yes! I've got a single engine for sea as well. I've got almost a hundred hours on an old De Havilland Twin Otter, which my uncle owns. He used to let me take the control yoke when we went on fishing trips to Vancouver Island. I think the first time I did, my feet were a foot from the rudder pedals, and I couldn't see over the instrument panel."

"But you were hooked!"

"You bet, Fred. Hook line and sinker!"

Jaffar sat quietly as the two pilots talked for the remainder of the 45-minute trip. Jeff kept watching the gauges, noticing the engine still was running hot. "Fred, we're up around 260 on number two."

"I know. I've been watching it too. I think we can shut down both inboard engines. We'll begin our descent soon."

"Will we have to restart them later?"

"No Jeff, we've got low gross and lots of runway to play with. Almost 8,000 feet, isn't it?"

"Yeah, 8,100 feet actually."

Jaffar took note of the conversation. The pilots didn't seem too concerned about the engine temperature, so he didn't ask about it. It must be a normal occurrence.

Wendover Air Base, Utah

Abdul heard the growl of the flaps as they extended. He watched as the large aircraft approached. The airfield, now owned by Sunwest Properties, was deserted except for him, Sameed and Abbas, all of who had entered the United States less than an hour after Jaffar had taken legal ownership of the former army air field, exactly as planned. He watched as they landed on the only real functioning runway left, runway 30.

Jaffar had arranged for Tony Barnetson to meet them at the hangar and open the hangar doors. Jaffar still had not made any arrangements for appropriate help, so for now Tony was stuck doing all the grunt work. He was jovial about it. "It's nothing for one of my newest and best clients," he said to Jaffar.

The aircraft taxied to a halt on the large concrete apron in front of the hangar. Abdul, Sameed and Abbas had kept the airbase looking deserted as requested by Jaffar. He had insisted the base be kept looking as it had for the last five years and that nothing, not even lighting, be changed. Abdul hid from sight—pistol ready just in case—while Sameed and Abbas took refuge in a distant office as the plane arrived.

Tony opened one set of hangar doors and Fred taxied the jet inside. Tony stepped outside, covering his ears. The noise from the jet was deafening but Abdul had no choice but to stay put. Sameed and Abbas fared only slightly better. As the engines spooled down, the hangar became quiet once more.

Tony waited for the forward door to open on the jet and then propped an aluminum ladder against the fuselage. The three men inside climbed carefully down onto the hangar floor. Jaffar remarked, "I'll have to find something a little less makeshift so no one breaks their neck getting out of this thing."

Tony and Jaffar shook hands. "How was your flight?"

"Absolutely great! Everything worked great, didn't it Fred?"

"Yes! With the exception of the slightly higher than normal temperature on the number two engine, everything was great. I had forgotten how nice these old planes flew."

Half an hour later the four men watched the small Cessna land. Tony helped secure the hangar, then bid them farewell as Jaffar, Jeff, Fred and Al returned in the Cessna to Mile High Aviation.

As Tony drove through the main gate he stopped and got out of his pickup to close and padlock the large main gates behind him with the lock Jaffar had given him. He looked at the two new signs that had been bolted to them.

PRIVATE PROPERTY – KEEP OUT

Trespassers will be prosecuted! Sunwest Properties Limited

He shook his head and wondered, not for the first time, where all this money was coming from. "Maybe in the next life," he said to himself.

Sacramento, California

"Good morning Giti. Did you sleep well?" Jaffar asked as she wandered into the kitchen, yawning.

"Yes, Jaffar. It was one of the better sleeps that I've had for a while … except for nights I camped under the stars at Yosemite." She smiled.

"You like camping, do you?"

"Of course! So does Sina."

"How would you like to camp by the side of a pool?" he asked.

"What?" asked Giti.

"Giti, I'd like you to take a couple of days off work and come to Salt Lake City with me," he said. Jaffar remembered how upset Giti had been when he'd left her and gone to Iraq.

"I guess I could. What do you have to go to Salt Lake City for?"

"I've got some business there. It could be worth a lot of money."

"While you're doing you're business, what will I be doing?"

"Like I said, you can camp by the side of the pool—or you can shop."

"Shop?"

Jaffar had been holding his hand behind his back and now he brought forward $5,000 in cash and handed it to Giti. It was equal to what he'd paid Jeff for his two days of work, but she didn't know that. He said, "You can do whatever you want with the money."

Giti was impressed. Playfully, she said, "Are you trying to bribe me, sir?"

"No! Actually I felt bad about what happened a couple of weeks ago and I wouldn't want you to be upset again."

"So it *is* a bribe!"

"Yes! I suppose so. Please?" It was the first time since Jaffar was a child that he'd used the word 'please' in a request.

"All right. If I can arrange a sitter for Sina, I'll go with you. But you've got two days for business. That's it. Then the time is mine."

"Do you think that Fatemah and Zafar would mind doing it?"

"No I don't think so, Jaffar." She did not add, *especially since my long talk with Fatemah during our trip.*

September 10, 1980

Jaffar and Giti drove to Salt Lake City. It was early afternoon when they pulled up to the front entrance of the Salt Lake City Marriott Downtown. They walked into the lobby and checked in at the front desk.

"After we check into our rooms would it be okay if we just walk around?" Jaffar asked Giti.

"Of course, but remember, starting tomorrow, I've got my two days."

"I haven't forgotten."

That evening the newlyweds had an impromptu honeymoon—a romantic dinner at one of the best restaurants in the city and room service delivery of a bottle of champagne to their penthouse suite. They sat on the terrace and looked over the city, spread out like a jeweled carpet below them, as they drank it.

"This reminds me of when you first came to Sacramento."

"Yes, kind of like my condo, but the view is much better."

"Just a minute, Jaffar," Giti said as she got up, went inside and switched off all the interior lights in the suite. Then she came back out. "Look at the sky, Jaffar. Look how clear and bright the stars are!"

The stars were indeed much brighter than they'd been a moment earlier—and though Jaffar had seen them appear brighter in Al-Qa'im, he said softly, "I've never seen them so bright."

Jaffar and Giti spent the remainder of the evening star-gazing, sipping champagne and talking. It was exactly the kind of evening Giti had been looking forward to.

September 11, 1980

After bidding Giti a fond good-bye, Jaffar drove the 100 miles from Salt Lake City to Wendover in almost record time. He honked once to alert Abdul of his approach then unlocked the padlock and drove through the gate, locking it behind him. He parked outside the hangar and went inside, where Abdul was waiting.

The bright sunlight coming in through the windows glinted off the polished aluminum skin of the jet, the reflected light shining into the rest of the hangar, brightening some of its hidden recesses. Jaffar still found it hard to believe how easy it had been to buy a commercial airliner. For the past few weeks, his ownership had only been on paper; now it was in his possession, but he still found it unreal.

"Good morning, Excellency."

"Good morning, Abdul. How are things going?"

"Sameed and Abbas have been going over the plane. They have informed me that everything appears to be in order. It will be good when we can get power here."

"I'm going to arrange for that today. We are going to need it."

"It will be good to work with electric lights, instead of flashlights."

"What! You've been using flashlights?"

"Yes, Excellency. We've been using them to find our way around and to check out the plane."

"You fool! I told you no lights until I said so! Do you know what three men with flashlights look like?"

"No."

"Thieves, you fool! It's a good way to have someone summon the police."

"But ..."

"But nothing, Abdul. I don't want anyone poking their noses around here, making inquiries."

"You let those three pilots go the other day. We should have killed them."

"Then what? What would we do with a small plane? Police would have been here within hours, asking questions."

"They will talk, Excellency."

"No, they won't. They have been well paid." Jaffar was tired of arguing with Abdul, "That's enough! I've got things to do today and very little time to do them. I have to get back to Salt Lake City."

"When are the rest of our people coming?"

Do I have to hold your hand? Jaffar thought. "Soon," he said. "I have all this planned out. Be patient. I'm going to arrange to have the power turned on today. I want the three of you to give me a list of anything that you need. I will pick it up today and be back tomorrow."

"Alright, Excellency."

Abdul, Sameed and Abbas already had a partial list of things they required, mostly tools that they were in immediate need of. They added some items then gave the list to Jaffar.

"Some of this might take a while to get," he said with a frown.

A short while later, just before Jaffar was leaving, Jaffar, Abdul, Sameed and Abbas gathered in the hangar. They each had a glass of freshly poured wine. "A toast, my friends. To September 11th, the day we start the final battle against the Great Satan."

"Cheers!"

Jaffar went to the offices of Utah Power and Light to arrange for a new account to be set up for Sunwest Properties. Tomorrow the base would have electricity. It was just a matter of switching the account from the United States Air Force to the property developer.

Back in Salt Lake City, Jaffar spent the remainder of the day buying three sets of tools at Sears. He also bought three brand-new Chevrolet pickup trucks from the local dealer as well as an ohmmeter, an oscilloscope and other diagnostic tools.

This has been an expensive day for me, he thought. *At this rate I will have nothing left.* Then it dawned on him that everything he had purchased over the last several weeks, including the land, was in his company's name. *I own it!* Jaffar found it funny that this hadn't occurred to him before. He had essentially increased his net worth by over $3.5 million dollars in just the last few days, even if he didn't include the value of the Boeing jet.

When he'd finished his business, he made it back in time to meet Giti as planned.

"Hello, Jaffar." Giti was carrying several bags. Apparently shopping had been good.

At least my efforts to keep her happy and occupied have been successful, he thought. The last thing he wanted was to have Giti poking her nose into affairs that did not concern her. It would be most tragic to have to give certain instructions to Abdul. Jaffar surprised himself with that thought; though the idea of taking her to Iraq to teach her some manners had occurred to him several times, he hadn't given *that* scenario even a passing thought before. He shook his head. Best to let it go for now.

"I see you had a good day at the local stores. I think that you must have-single handedly, stimulated the economy!" he teased.

"Let's just call this retail therapy! You wouldn't believe the deals I got."

"Yes, I can see exactly how much you've saved," he laughed. It was apparent to him that they had each had a spending spree today—except he wasn't about to show Giti the stash of tools and equipment in the truck of his car.

"How was business today?"

"I had many problems to deal with, but I believe I got everything worked out," he said. The vaguer he was, the better. "I think that you and I should get something to eat."

"That sounds good. I should drop these things off in the suite."

September 12, 1980

Just as he'd done the day before, Jaffar drove out to Wendover Base. On both days, he'd driven as fast as he dared, but not fast enough to attract attention of the Highway Patrol. When he approached the gate, he could see the power still wasn't turned on. The power company had assured him it would be on by afternoon, but they hadn't said when.

He unlocked the gate. *I'll have to have some additional keys made,* he thought. Despite his careful planning, there were still many things he hadn't thought of.

Abdul greeted him when he arrived at the hangar. "Hello, Jaffar."

"Abdul, how are you? Do you have anything new to report?"

"No! Yesterday you restricted use of our flashlights. Progress has been slow."

"The power will be turned on later today. I've made the arrangements." Jaffar added, "Also the Chevrolet dealer will come to the gate and honk. I will let him in."

"What's he doing?"

"He's bringing us three new company trucks. When I get back to Sacramento I will have some magnetic signs made for the doors."

Sameed and Abbas joined their two superiors. "Do you all have your driving licenses with you?" Jaffar asked. All three men nodded. Their paperwork had all been prepared by the same forger that Jaffar had used in the past. The forgeries would pass most scrutiny.

"Good! I am having trucks delivered for each of you today and have also arranged for insurance and registration for these vehicles, but there are several rules for their use. They are as follows: One, only one truck at a time leaves the base unless I order it. Two, when you go to town, for whatever reason, only two of you can go. One of you is to remain here at all times. Finally, rule three. You are not to break any laws, traffic or otherwise. Potential police involvement must be avoided at all costs."

All three men understood that these instructions were to be followed to the letter. Consequences from Jaffar would be severe if local authorities were to question them in any way. Jaffar had further instruction. "Later today, Abdul, you can take Sameed and get some more food. Enough for a week or so." Abdul nodded his understanding.

They opened the large hangar doors and unloaded the trunk of Jaffar's car. Sameed and Abbas organized their new tools on the well-used workbenches inside the hangar. Abdul lifted out three one-gallon cans of paint and several paint brushes. "I want you to whitewash the inside of the exterior ground floor windows," he told Abdul. He could see Abdul start to protest so he added, "We must eliminate the chances of discovery by any curious passersby."

All three men could hear the distant but distinct sound of a large diesel truck arriving. Jaffar looked out the hangar door to see an auto transport with three brand new, wheat-land yellow colored Chevrolet pickup trucks aboard.

"Our new trucks are here. I want you two out of sight. Abdul, you come with me." He added, "No weapons!"

The auto transport stopped at the gate. The driver could see Jaffar and Abdul driving out to meet them in Jaffar's car. Jaffar stopped, got out and opened the gate.

"Are you Mr. Hodgeson?"

"Yes, that's right."

"I've got some trucks here for you. Can you sign right here?" The large man with the Southern accent indicated the line on the bottom of the form. Jaffar did as he was asked.

"Very good! I'll get them unloaded. Where do you want them?"

"Just inside the gate will be fine." Jaffar and Abdul watched as the driver carefully unloaded the three trucks, backing them slowly down the ramp.

"The paperwork for each truck is on the passenger seat. Here are the keys," he said, handing Jaffar three sets of keys.

"Thank you." The driver got back in his truck, pulled into the yard, did a U-turn and drove out again through the open gate.

Jaffar and Abdul moved the pickups next to the hangar, into the visitor parking spots. The next hour was spent putting license plates on each truck and ensuring the proper papers went with each one as well. This was all time allowed Jaffar to accomplish on the base today—aside from a few last-minute instructions to Abdul.

"Paint the windows before you turn on any lights. That's most important." With that, Jaffar got into his car and headed back to Salt Lake City.

September 13, 1980

Jaffar and Giti had a relaxing evening and another nice dinner together. They were up early, dressed and checked out. It was a long drive back to Sacramento. Before leaving, they went into the dining room for a nice breakfast.

"Everything was delicious," Giti said. Jaffar was disappointed with his tea. *If that's all he complains about, then we are doing very well,* Giti thought gratefully.

"So, my dear. Did you have a good trip?" Jaffar asked as the valet loaded their bags into the car.

"Yes! I can't wait to get home and show Fatemah my new clothes. She's going to be so jealous. What about you Jaffar? Did you get everything done that you needed to?"

"Oh yes, Giti. It was a very rewarding two days for me."

Just past eleven o'clock Jaffar and Giti were on the road, driving west along I-80, right through Wendover. Jaffar looked to the left. He could see the huge hangar in the distance. He was too far away to see any activity, but he was fairly certain the men there would obey his orders. *I will have to arrange for security to be increased. It's too bad Mohammed Hussan isn't here. He would know where to go,* Jaffar thought to himself.

September 23, 1980

It had been over a week since Jaffar had been to Wendover and it was starting to make him anxious. Today, he was up early as usual and listening to the morning news, quietly, so as not to wake Giti.

"Iraqi troops crossed over the Iranian border today and captured the Iranian oil refinery at Abadan, one of the most important in the country," the television anchor reported. "It's still unclear if this is an escalation of yesterday's clashes between the two country's air and naval forces over disputed territory, or if it is simply posturing by the Iraqi government."

"Those idiots," Jaffar said out loud. For many months there had been indications that a war between Iran and Iraq was a definite possibility. He'd hoped it could be avoided; many Muslims would die fighting each other. They should be banded together to fight the west. However, one of the advantages of this conflict was that it was focusing the attention of the United States away from the Islamic Hamas.

Jaffar needed to get back to, and had been preparing for a trip to, Wendover Base. Over the past ten days, an associate of the Hussan brothers, Hamid Fekish, had stepped up to take care of security around the base.

"Whitewash will not stop security problems," Jaffar had told Abdul, "but it will delay the curious." He made Abdul paint the windows despite the new guards.

Abdul was the one who recruited Hamid Fekish, assuring Jaffar that the man was loyal and could be trusted. Jaffar agreed and soon Hamid and his dozen men were employed by Sunwest Properties. While Abdul would normally have been in charge of this team, since Jaffar had him overseeing modifications and maintenance of the new company jet, as it was now referred to, Hamid was appointed security chief at Wendover.

During the past week, six men had been selected for the task of repairing the chain link fence around the inner perimeter. During the past 15 years, several large sections had fallen into disrepair. The outer fence, however, had been properly maintained.

When Jaffar arrived at the base he could see the repairs to the fence had been carried out. Even the grass had been mowed. "The base looks good, Abdul. I'm sure it doesn't look as good as it did back in 1944, but I do agree with you that more activity is sometimes better than little or no activity. It's less suspicious."

"Yes, Jaffar everything looks normal." Everything did look normal and Jaffar and his team had taken great pains to ensure it looked like a development corporation had moved in. Several locations around the base were now home to large plywood maps detailing many thousands of new building lots, the top of the map declaring proudly that redevelopment would commence in the 'Summer of 1981'.

"So Abdul, how are things going with the airplane?" Jaffar could see that every inspection hatch had been opened and that trouble lights and cables were leading into each.

"We are still working on things in the cockpit. They are going slowly," Abdul said.

"Why slowly? You have all the diagrams and files. What's the problem?"

"This jet is a very complicated system. All the files and most of the past projects the men have worked on were older aircraft, simpler machines from decades ago, from World War II and the Korean War. This is a modern jetliner!"

"I do not want to hear about what you can't do! I want results."

"Sameed and Abbas are working very hard. I drive them many hours. They only work, eat and sleep and they do very little of the last." Abdul was hesitant to mention the most serious problem; the number two engine wasn't quite right. He didn't want to tell Jaffar; after all, they'd been assured it wasn't a serious problem.

"Can they sort out the problems with the system? We have only six months to get all of this worked out."

"Within a few weeks we will know."

"What else do I need to know about?"

Abdul decided to spill the beans. "Sameed say that we have some problems with the number two engine. There was very little oil in it when it was checked. Sameed say that the engine may be seriously damaged from its flight here."

"What? I don't believe this! I paid for a working airplane. And I paid for delivery as well!"

"Sameed, come here at once!" Abdul called, wanting the heat removed from himself.

A small, soot-covered face poked out from inside the engine cowling. "Yes, Abdul?" Sameed ran over to them, slightly out of breath. "Yes, Abdul, what can I do for you?"

"Explain to Jaffar about the engine. Can it be fixed?"

"I don't know. Maybe if I had the parts. Maybe then it would be good enough. Maybe it will be good enough as it is."

"When will you know?"

"Tomorrow or the next day."

"See to it. The sooner the better." Jaffar walked away towards the hangar door. "I need to know about all the problems here, Abdul. This operation is crucial to the cause." Jaffar didn't add, *and crucial to my bank account.*

"I know, Jaffar. It will be done."

"Our sponsors expect results. They have given us a great deal of money and a free hand to produce those results. Let me know about the engine tomorrow."

September 25, 1980 - Sacramento

Jaffar sat on the couch in the living room. Giti was in the kitchen, making herself a cup of coffee. She had been a bit on the low-energy side today, but Jaffar had been too preoccupied with his broken airplane to ask her why. He thought she was just tired.

He called Abdul, hoping for good news. The boys should have figured something out by now. "Abdul, do you have news for me about the engine?"

"Yes, Jaffar. I regret to inform you that it cannot be repaired. Another engine is needed."

"I was afraid of that. I will call you back in one hour." Jaffar hung up and placed a second call.

The voice on the other end said, "Hello, Mile High!"

"Mr. Carlson, Jaffar Hodgeson here. I have a bit of a problem."

"What is that, Jaffar?" Fred knew what was coming. He remembered the engine issue that had become apparent when they'd flown on the 720, but he'd hoped it wasn't a serious problem.

"My Boeing 720 has a faulty engine. Can you replace it?"

"I would if I could, Jaffar, but I have no engines available."

"Can't you take one out of the other six planes?"

"No! They were sold overseas yesterday. I sold them to the Iraqi government. You know, for the war."

"Oh yes, I understand. So what are my options?"

"Well we certainly want to keep our customers happy; I can give you a refund for the engine. You may be able to find one from other sources."

"Such as?"

"I can give you a list of airplane part brokers."

Jaffar was disappointed and somewhat frustrated, but he knew he had no options, so he controlled his temper and said, "If that's all you can do for me then I guess it will have to do. I'll have one of my employees come down and pick up a check."

Hurriedly, Jaffar dialed Abdul's number but just then Giti came into the room. He looked up and smiled. She still hadn't perked up so he asked, "Why the sad look my dear?"

"I was just thinking, it's been exactly two years since Reza died in that plane crash," Giti said.

"Oh, yes." Jaffar walked over and gave Giti a big hug, trying to be understanding. "I'm sorry Giti, but it will be all right." He didn't know what else to say and he hoped she would go away and deal with it herself. He had work to do.

"Yes, I know, but I still think about him at times."

"Of course you do," he said consolingly. Then he took out his wallet, pulled out $1,000 and gave it to her.

"You know what you need? To call Fatemah and book a spa day with her! It is my treat. A massage and a nice lunch with Fatemah would take your mind off it," he said.

She smiled and took the money. “Really?” she asked.

He gave her his best benevolent look, “Of course,” he said, “I can’t stand to see you so sad!”

As she left the room he thought, *women are so easy to fool.* And then he phoned Abdul again.

— Chapter 15 —

September 26, 1980 - Sacramento

Jaffar had worked through most of the list Fred Carlson had provided to him but so far he'd had no luck finding a replacement engine. Today might be different, he hoped. Fred was refunding $250,000 to Jaffar and Abdul was going to drive down get the refund check. That should be enough to get what he needed. At noon Jaffar had reached the last name on the list. He called the head office of Pratt and Whitney in Hartford, Connecticut.

"Good afternoon, Pratt and Whitney."

"Good afternoon. Can I have your sales office please?"

After a moment a man's voice came on the line. "Hello, sales. This is Glen, how can I help you?"

"I need a replacement for a JT3C turbofan," Jaffar said, using words he had learned from Sameed and Abbas. "I would like to get one as soon as possible."

"I'm sorry, sir, I didn't get your name."

"Mr. Hodgeson."

"I'm sorry, Mr. Hodgeson, we haven't made the JT3C for over 15 years."

"What about a JT3D?"

"We're still producing them, but we have none available right now. We have eight months of back orders to be filled."

"That will be too late. What about a rebuilt unit?"

"Again, none are available," said Glen. Have you tried some of the surplus aircraft dealers in California or Arizona? Or perhaps some of the airlines? Sometimes they ..."

"Yes! I've tried all the airlines!" Jaffar was now starting to get very angry. The mention of a surplus aircraft dealer made him think of Mile High Aviation and how they'd sold him a faulty aircraft. At first it had been only mildly upsetting because he had expected that getting a replacement engine would be like going down to your local parts counter and picking one up. No fuss, no mess. Now he was beginning to see that he had a serious problem. "Where else can I try?" he asked, trying to contain his anger.

Well, you rude piece of shit, how about kiss my ass? Glen thought but said instead, "I'm sorry, sir, but the only place that you can get a new JT3D turbofan is out of an Air Force Boeing B52H or perhaps a KC135 tanker."

"Oh!" Jaffar hung up.

"What an asshole! Hey Jim! You won't believe this rude dude that was on the phone," Glen said.

Jim just laughed.

Las Vegas, Nevada

Abdul had driven down to Las Vegas after the call from Jaffar yesterday. This morning his plan was to drive to Mile High Aviation, collect the check and then return to Vegas. He thought he'd better call Jaffar first, though.

"Hello?"

"Jaffar. Good day to you."

"Abdul! I told you not to call unless it is an emergency!"

"I'm sorry, Excellency. It is not an emergency. I was wondering about any last-minute instructions for either myself or Sameed."

"No, nothing."

"Have you found a new jet engine?"

"No! No, I haven't."

"I'm sorry Excellency. I will get your money back for you."

"See that you do!"

Abdul checked out of his hotel room and three hours later he arrived at the gates of Mile High Aviation.

"Good morning. I'm Fred Carlson."

"I'm Mr. Abdul. I'm here for my boss, Mr. Hodgeson. I'm to here to pick up a check."

"I thought so." Abdul took it and verified the amount. It was a certified bank draft for the agreed amount of $250,000. "Now when can I expect the used engine in return?"

"What do you mean?"

"Well I gave you money back for a used JT3C turbofan and I expect the engine to be returned to me as soon as possible."

"Jaffar said nothing of this!"

"You can come inside and give him a call if you like."

"I don't see what difference this will make, but alright."

"Please come this way." Fred indicated the office at the corner of the hangar building. "The phone is right over there." He pointed at the desk. "I've got some paperwork I need to attend to. I'll be right back." He left the room as Abdul walked over and picked up the phone.

"Hello Jaffar. This is Abdul." He explained the situation at Mile High Aviation and that the used engine needed to be returned. Abdul looked up to see Fred Carlson stepping out of the adjoining office. Jaffar sighed; it was one problem after another.

"Please, just take care of it," said Jaffar, thinking, *surely Abdul and the boys can figure out a way to get the engine back to Fred Carlson.* He was tired of wheeling and dealing and phoning and hunting. He needed a break.

"Of course, Excellency," said Abdul and Jaffar breathed a sigh of relief.

September 27, 1980

Giti declined Fatemah's offer to go along and keep her company and give moral support, so Giti now sat alone in the waiting room of her family doctor. It was fortunate for many of Dr. Phillips' patients that he elected to open on Saturday mornings. Many of his patients, like Giti, had full time jobs Monday to Friday and had children in school during the week, so Saturday was the only option for doctor appointments, aside from taking time off work.

Several children played noisily in the corner of the room, their parents pleading with them to play more quietly. Giti watched, smiling as she did so, remembering the times she had implored Sina to do the same thing. The nurse came around the corner into the waiting room and each adult looked at her, hoping their name would be called.

"Mrs. Roshtti?" The nurse guided Giti to the examination room and placed her file in the holder on the outside of the door. "The Doctor will be with you shortly," she said before briskly walking away.

"Thank you!" Giti sat down on the chair in the corner as the nurse closed the door. The cold, molded, plastic seat made her shiver. The mostly empty, sterile room was the complete opposite of the reception area and waiting room she'd been in just a moment earlier.

Giti was alone. Normally she didn't mind coming to see her doctor, but this time it was different. *Maybe I should have let Fatemah come along*, Giti thought. The longer she sat there, the more she wanted to leave. She fumbled through the magazines that were loosely stacked on the small side table. She picked up a months-old copy of *People* and flipped through the pages. She'd already read the stories in there; frustrated, she placed it back on the pile with the others, straightening it as she did so.

She began to fidget nervously. The longer she sat, the worse her anxiety became. It was almost like when she tried to watch a scary movie by herself; one part of her could not tear herself away from the images on the screen and another part told her to get up and run away. The latter was becoming almost too strong to resist—Giti did not think that she could stay another minute but she was just beginning to rise out of her seat to leave when she heard the familiar voice of Dr. Phillips becoming louder. Before she could bolt, the smiling doctor entered the room and shut the door.

"Giti! it's good to see you!" He sat down and opened her file. "What brings you here today?"

She began to relax. His kind and gentle manner set her at ease and that is why she'd been seeing him for 20 years. "I have missed two periods in a row. I might be pregnant."

He could tell from the look on her face and her tone that this wasn't as happy an occasion as it had been when Giti was pregnant with Sina.

"Well, I'll get the nurse to get a urine sample from you and she can take it downstairs to the lab right away. While that's going on, I can check your blood pressure and we can have a chat. Okay?"

"Okay!"

"I'll be right back."

Giti hadn't wanted Fatemah to come along with her and she definitely hadn't wanted Jaffar to come—she had no idea how he would react to the news. He was a far different man than Reza had been. This morning she'd left him quietly immersed in the morning news, as was his routine. She could remember the broadcast ... "Damage from last month's Hurricane David in the Dominican Republic has reached one billion dollars. The hurricane has claimed over 600 lives."

She'd also heard of another murder, the anchor intoning as she walked into the living room with tea for Jaffar, "In other news, the owner of surplus aircraft business Mile High Aviation was found murdered last evening near Ludlow, California by one of his employees. Carlson was stabbed to death in his office. Police say robbery might have been the motive, as the office was ransacked." She'd been surprised to see him turn almost white at this news.

"Jaffar? Is something wrong?" she asked. He'd glanced up quickly at her and said, "No, just tired, that's all." Then he'd tried to smile but it had clearly been forced.

She'd left for her doctor's appointment shortly after that. As she left, she thought she heard him say, "What have you done?" and for a moment she wondered if he suspected her pregnancy. She closed the door without a word.

Washington, D.C.

In the brand new offices of the National Anti-Terrorism Agency, NATA, people were hard at work. The new headquarters of NATA were located at Number 15 DuPont Circle and N.W. P Street, in northwest D.C. The building had once been the Patterson Mansion and then more recently the Washington Club.

NATA staff were pleased to be out of the temporary offices they'd occupied since the beginning of the year and into the new offices on DuPont Circle—everything was freshly painted and smelled new. *Things* weren't new, however. The head of NATA, Colonel Robert Hart, did not spend his money on the trappings of furniture, artwork and carpets; instead he spent it on what he called his 'two most important assets'; a team of top-notch employees who were loyal to the core, and a top-of-the-line, cutting-edge computer system. The furniture was acquired from surplus.

The most recent structural renovation to the NATA offices was built in 1956—a two-story addition at the rear which included parking for a dozen cars. However, one structural expense Hart had approved was to have new windows installed. The windows looked exactly like the 1902 Patterson Mansion's original windows —but these were tripled-paned with internal vibrators to foil any laser-type listening devices. There was nothing on the exterior of the building to indicate that a secret federal agency occupied the building.

In the secure computer room on the second floor, Milt Cummings and Roger Cooper sat. These men were the two computer 'geeks' who rode herd over the fastest, most-advanced computer on the face of the planet, the Digital Input and Notifications Analysis, or 'DIANA' for short. DIANA was a hard worker—too hard, in fact. She was currently responsible for a backlog of information that threatened to bring the new agency to a grinding halt.

"I'll be sure glad when we finish writing code for the new software," Milt said.

"Yeah Milt! That fourth-generation artificial intelligence program can't come online fast enough for me. The upgrade would take over much of the heavy lifting on the analysis end of things and transform DIANA from being a huge information-gathering, collation system into something much more powerful and valuable!"

The hope was that, once upgraded, anyone with the proper clearance would actually be able to carry on a 'conversation' with DIANA and that the machine would be able to analyze information from other agencies and draw conclusions—all at nano-speed.

Colonel Hart scanned through mornings dispatches from around the globe. These dispatches were generally to do with national security and had been gathered from many sources: the Central Intelligence agency, the Federal Bureau of Investigation and the National Security Agency, to name a few. Before reaching the NATA offices, the dispatches were sorted and prioritized; this was repeated in the NATA offices.

"Michelle! Are these all of today's threat assessment files?"

Michelle Hough got up from her desk and brought Hart some additional pages. "Here's a couple more," she said. "This one probably has no significance, but the second one I would classify as moderate to high."

Colonel Hart read over the two dispatches. The second one was about the murder of a surplus aircraft parts dealer. Although he already knew the answer, he asked anyway. "Why would you classify this one in the moderate to high category? It appears to be just a burglary."

Michelle smiled. "Because a surplus aircraft dealer deals with possible export of technology. In fact, several days ago, this Fred Carlson sold six aircraft to the Iraqi Government."

"Good girl!"

It was no surprise Michelle would recall this; she was one of Hart's best agents. Hart had personally recruited all his staff, poaching from other agencies as required. Many had military service, as Michelle did. She was unique; an Air Force brat, she'd grown up around jets all her life. Her father had been an Air Force pilot and he had nurtured and encouraged her love of planes. However, even with her father's help, a woman trying to make it in the United States Air Force was unheard of—and unwelcome.

But she was tough, she took the criticism and stuck it out, earning the respect of her male peers until finally she was noticed by special ops and recruited to be part of a secret, clandestine operations unit that made it possible for her to hone her flight skills without being singled out because of her gender. Because of the secret nature of her work, she ultimately had become one of the finest pilots in the air force who no one ever heard of. And that was fine with her.

"So how are things going with Donny these days?" Hart asked her.

"Pretty good, except I haven't seen him in weeks. That and I feel really guilty about not telling him who I work for."

"I know and I'm sorry to have put you in that position. Of course, if Donny and Jack still don't want to join our little cast, then you might never have to tell him."

"I still would. I intend to keep this one around and I want to have an honest relationship with him." She added. "Besides, what if he found out by accident? Then you'd have to kill him."

"Funny, Michelle," Hart said, though the smile didn't reach his eyes. "Let's see what else we have."

"Here's a report from Iran about the Ayatollah looking for more military hardware." She handed the Colonel the dispatch. "Seems he's buying more tanks, armored personnel carriers and AK-forty-sevens from the Soviets."

"Didn't a portion of the last shipment disappear?" Hart asked.

"Yep! Kip Holmes said as much as half of the last shipment went missing on its way from the border."

"That's not good!" The Colonel stood for a moment, mulling things over and making some mental notes. "Let's get these entered into the computer and cross-referenced."

"Already done, Colonel."

He smiled. He could always count on Michelle.

Wendover, Utah - September 28, 1980

Jaffar stood toe-to-toe with Abdul, red-faced. "What the hell were you thinking? I just wanted you to collect the money!"

"But Excellency, he wanted the old motor back!"

"So what? It's useless, no good except for parts! He paid for its return!"

"Yes, but he would have talked."

"His murder talks, you imbecile! Do you think the American police don't notice a dead man? Especially one who sells airplanes? To Iraq? What the hell is wrong with you?"

"But ..."

"You've murdered how many people in the last month, fourteen? That's a record even by your standards and I would like to point out that none of those murders came on my orders."

"But ..."

"This is America, not Iraq! The murder of that family won't be questioned though everyone knows it was you who did it! In Iraq, people might be afraid of you but you aren't the Chief of Police here!"

"I'm truly sorry, Excellency."

"You may yet sabotage this operation!" Jaffar ranted. "This won't happen again. I want you to oversee Sameed and Abbas. The security, I've left to Hamid. From now on don't do anything else unless I order it!"

"I understand."

Furious—and frightened at what a liability Abdul had become—Jaffar walked out, on his way to find and talk to Hamid. He could rely on Hamid, the man had common sense. Hamid informed him, "At night Jaffar, we have manned patrols between the two fences. You asked that the large lights be turned on as well and we have done so."

"Very good, Hamid. I think this is fine for now. We don't need to make this place look like Fort Knox."

"Yes, it would attract unwanted attention." Hamid still didn't know the extent of Jaffar's plans—just that they involved the jet inside the hangar.

Cooler now, Jaffar said. "Thanks, Hamid. And now I must go back inside and talk to Abdul once more. All I seem to do is solve problems!"

Upon returning to where Abdul was working with Sameed and Abbas, Jaffar took him aside and said, "Abdul, I need you to make sure Sameed and Abbas are doing their jobs as efficiently as possible. This whole process is taking far too long. They assured me that there would be no problems doing this. Now it seems that all I have is problems!"

"Is that all, Excellency?"

"No! This base used to be a military base. Have you searched it for any items we can use?"

"Before you arrived with the plane, I looked through as many buildings as I could, but most of them were locked."

"Well, here are the keys," Jaffar said, handing them to him. "I only just received them from the realtor yesterday. Now I give them to you. I want a complete copy made and only you and I are to have them. Then I want you to look through every building, every corner, every nook and cranny and document what you find." He did not add, *make yourself useful.*

"Of course, Excellency. As you wish."

"See that you don't add to my problems, Abdul." Jaffar said. Then he looked at his watch. He must drive back to Sacramento this afternoon. This was the second time he made the round trip by car to Wendover in the past week and Giti was starting to ask questions.

October, 11, 1980

For two weeks Jaffar tried desperately to find a replacement turbofan engine; he even called back some of those on the list who'd he called previously. Someone was kind enough to direct him to the classified ads in almost a dozen Aviation magazines; the result however, was the same.

If I can't find an engine for the jet, the operation might be all for naught, Jaffar said to himself. The last JT3s had gone of the country in the Mile High deal with Iraq two weeks earlier.

Washington, D.C.

"Good morning, Colonel. Here are this morning's dispatches," Michelle said to Hart, handing him a stack of paper.

"Thanks, Michelle. Anything important?"

"The Iraqis are talking to the State Department about how they get their aircraft from Mile High that they purchased a month or so ago."

"Mile High ... oh! That's the guy who was murdered a couple of weeks back."

"One and the same."

"Any response from the State Department?"

"None. As far as I know, the planes are grounded until the investigation's finished."

"I want you to meet with the FBI agents leading the investigation out in Ludlow," Hart said. "Take Kip with you."

"I'll call Kip," Michelle said.

"I'll call the Bureau and let them know you're coming," said Hart.

Barstow, California - October 12, 1980

FBI Agents Ron Elwood and Lawrence Cameron were at the Southern California Logistics Airport to meet Kip Holmes and Michelle Hough. It was the nearest regional airport to the small town.

"Agent Holmes, this is Agent Ron Elwood and I'm Larry Cameron."

"Pleased to meet you. You can call me Kip. This is Agent Hough."

"Fine Kip, Agent Hough."

"You can call me Michelle." Cameron smiled.

They got into the car driven by Agent Elwood and headed east down Route 66 towards Ludlow, some 60 miles away.

"So how do two like it at NATA?"

"Almost all of us came from other agencies, so we're used to government work." Kip gave a non-answer, but that was enough.

"And the bureaucratic red tape?"

"There's not much of that in our outfit. Colonel Hart has had free reign to create an efficient agency. Right now we're small in size compared to the

FBI, for example, but the system we use to process and collate our data, is state-of-the-art technology."

"That's great. So what's your interest in this murder? It appears to have been a robbery gone wrong."

"Same as you," Kip answered coyly. "We think it might have international security implications."

"How so?"

"Did you know the Iraqi Government bought six Boeing 707s and Boeing 720s from Mile High?"

"No. We're still processing that murder scene. The office was a complete disaster, piles of paper scattered about the body. And we weren't called in until after almost a week's delay."

"Well keep your eyes open, okay? And we hope you're willing to share what you find," said Michelle.

"Sure thing," said Cameron. "And back at you. We don't have the man-power … I mean, person-power … to do this alone from our regional office." He turned around in the front seat to make eye contact with Michelle, pretending he was making a point, but really he was appraising her in a less than professional manner. "We would appreciate being kept apprised of what you find."

In the backseat, Kip kicked Michelle. He knew how she felt about being leered at during work hours. She understood and smiled sweetly back at Cameron.

"Of course," she said.

Ludlow, California

The four agents crossed under the yellow crime-scene tape at Mile High. They'd barely set foot on sight when an agent came running out. "Ron, I tried to call you on the radio, but I guess you were out of range."

"No, Chris," He said. "I just switched off the damn thing to get some peace and quiet. All we get is static around here."

Michelle piped up, "That's due to Twenty-Nine Palms."

"What do you mean?"

"The marine training base. Their communications and radar interfere with low-band radio signals."

"Well I'll be," said Cameron. Then he turned to his agent and said, "So what have you boys found?"

"Nothing," said his colleague, Chris. "And I mean *nothing*! The planes are gone. Some State Department wiener showed up here with the paperwork and a carload of pilots and all the planes purchased by the Iraqis were flown out of here."

"And you let them go? Jesus Christ, I don't fucking believe this!"

"I called head office and I tried to call you!"

"I bet they walked all over the place disturbing evidence."

"No! But thanks for that, Ron. I'm not that stupid. They took the service road, over there." He pointed.

"What a screw-up!" Cameron fumed. He knew he shouldn't be pissed off at Chris, though, so he apologized. "I'm sorry, Chris. This just caught me off guard. I honestly don't know what those assholes in Washington were thinking."

"Agent Cameron, do you think we could have a look at the area?" asked Kip. He nodded and they got back in the car and drove down the service road Chris had shown them, staying away from the hangar.

There was a large vacant space among the remaining aircraft. It was obvious that there had been several planes there. The four agents stepped from their vehicles. Agents Cameron and Elwood walked around the area in a casual manner, while Michelle and Kip separated and each took a different path, carefully walking, looking for evidence.

"Kip come and look at this!" Michelle called. The former CIA agent walked over and crouched down beside her. "Look at this and tell me what you see."

"I see a dark spot on the ground. In fact I see several of them."

"Yeah! Dark, cone-shaped patches! How many do you count?" Kip stood up, examining the area, shading his eyes from the glare of the sun. The patches were in groups, pointing away from a central area.

After a moment Kip said, "I count twenty-eight. Why?"

"The cone shape shows directionality and the number tells me there were seven planes here, not just six."

"How come there are dark patches?"

"Exhaust plumes from the Pratt and Whitneys."

"I'm sorry Michelle, but I'm not a fly-boy … I mean fly-girl, of course, like you. Can you put this in plain English?"

"The fuel tanks are filled with oil to protect them from corrosion. When the oil is drained and the fuel tank filled with jet fuel, residual oil in the system blows out …"

"Of course!" Kip said, catching on, "When the engines are started, the exhaust is black, because of the oil."

"Bingo!" said Michelle. "And these twelve here and those twelve over there, are fresh." She pointed then touched a dark patch of earth with the tip of her finger. "Here! Smell!"

"I see what you mean."

"Aren't you going to ask me about the last four patches?"

"I was just about to, professor." The two agents walked about 50 yards over to the last set of dark patches of earth.

"They don't look as dark as the other two dozen," commented Kip, "and this one here is darker than the other three in the group."

"Exactly! The ground has soaked up more of the oil droplets and the wind has blown a light layer of dust over them."

"So just like a cold campfire, you can tell how many hours or days ahead the bad guys are, just by feeling and smelling the ashes."

"Good analogy! But not quite right … and I don't think the bad guys left in a plane."

"Why?"

"A plane is a rather expensive get-away vehicle. I bet they came in a car or truck."

"Yeah. I think you're right. It seems we're still dealing with a robbery and murder."

"Let's go have a look at the office." They found Cameron and Elwood and the four of them drove back to the office. It was a mess, exactly as described.

"Nothing has been touched with exception of the body which was removed by the coroner. It was getting pretty ripe in the heat." Elwood said.

"You were right when you described this place as a disaster," said Michelle.

"Yes, we've been waiting for an agent from the business forensics unit to go through some of these papers. Maybe we can figure out what our perp was after."

"Have you arranged for prints to be taken?" asked Kip.

"They'd probably be oily blobs by now, with this heat. Do your best if you want to give it a shot," said Cameron.

"We'll share what we find," said Michelle, "but we'd like copies of all the paper evidence collected here and of your reports. And can you have the coroner send us a copy of the findings too?"

Cameron nodded.

"Oh and one more thing," said Michelle. "I'd really like photographs of the area around where the jet aircraft were parked."

"Of course, Agent Hough, we can do that today," Cameron said.

"Can your lab take UV and infrared photos as well?"

"Can do," Elwood said. "Anything else, Michelle?"

"No! That about covers it. Thanks!"

Back at the airport in Barstow, Kip and Michelle caught the first flight back to Las Vegas. "I wonder who took the seventh aircraft?" she wondered out loud. "The infrared pictures may tell us something—perhaps narrow the timeframe down to a couple of days. But as to who actually has the aircraft, perhaps we'll never know."

"Certainly not if the Bureau doesn't get its shit together. They've had since the twenty-seventh—almost two weeks," Kip huffed.

"To be fair, Kip, the FBI hasn't had the entire two weeks. The locals had control of the crime scene for over a week-and-a-half before they decided to make the call. Up until now everyone was sure this was simply a robbery gone bad."

"They should know better."

"You don't?"

"No way, Michelle. No way."

"Me neither," she said. "Something big is up. I can feel it."

After the short flight from Barstow, the two NATA agents walked through McCarran International Airport. "I guess I'll see you tomorrow afternoon in Washington."

"What?"

"I'm stopping off, to see Donny."

"Since when?"

"Since this morning. I've already cleared it with Colonel Hart."

"I see we will have to work on those communication skills a little bit more." He laughed. "Say hi to the big guy for me. How about using your feminine charms to get him to join us?"

She laughed. "Sure, I'll give it a try," she said. Then, "Good job today, by the way."

"Thanks! See you tomorrow."

Michelle was waiting for Donny when he got home from work. She heard the throaty growl of the MG's exhaust as Donny down-shifted at the end of the street and turned the last corner for home. She didn't even look out the window as he pulled the sports car into the driveway.

As Donny opened the front door, the aroma of Greek-style pork chops filled his nostrils. He did not even have to ask who was here. Only one person besides his mother made him his favorite food—and his mom didn't have a key to his new place. "Michelle!" Too late he saw her come out the kitchen, run toward him and almost bowl him over.

"Hi, Don. Surprised?"

"What are you doing here? I didn't expect you until next week." He inhaled deeply. "Something smells good."

"I made you one of your favorites."

"Greek style chops?"

"Yes!" She gave Donny another hug and a kiss.

They had a wonderful meal. Michelle had even thought to buy a six-pack, beer being Don's favorite drink with any meal.

After supper, however, just when Don was hoping for some cuddles, Michelle suddenly turned serious. "Donny, I really, really need to talk to you."

"Sure, babe what's up?" Donny gulped. When women started conversations like that, often they ended with the words, "I'm pregnant!"

"I was hoping to avoid all this but …"

"But what?" He was ready for this. It wasn't how he hoped things would go—at least, not yet—but he could handle it.

Michelle swallowed hard. "You remember when we met on that flight down to Los Cabos?"

"I'll never forget."

"I hate to tell you this … but Colonel Hart sent me."

"What?" For the life of him, Donny could not put this wonderful woman—who he adored—in the same mental place as his former commanding officer.

"What do you mean Colonel Hart sent you? How would a stewardess know Colonel Hart? Did he fly on one of your flights or something?" Don stuttered.

"Um, not exactly," said Michelle. "You may need to sit down for this." And as Donny's jaw fell open, Michelle explained the events leading up to last April's flight to Mexico—and that she wasn't actually a stewardess. He wasn't sure what was more interesting. The idea that she had duped him or the idea that she could probably best him in hand-to-hand combat.

October 13, 1980

Michelle walked through the front doors of NATA with a still-surprised Donny in tow. She looked at her watch. "We're running a bit late," she said.

"I'm sure the Colonel will understand. After all, we caught the first flight this morning," he reassured her. Don couldn't help but be impressed with the offices of America's newest counter-terrorism agency. Although security didn't appear to be as strict as it had been at the CIA offices in DC, he'd noticed that they'd already passed through two secured perimeter zones.

"I'm surprised by the lack of security guards."

"Don't worry Donny, this place is more secure than Fort Knox."

"I did notice a couple of cameras on the roof parapet."

"That's just for starters. But you'll hear more about that later," Michelle told him.

They got into the elevator to go up to the third floor. Michelle inserted her card into the slot of the reader, next to the control panel.

"Good morning, Agent Hough," a mechanical man's voice in the elevator said. "Please enter your personal pass code on the numerical keypad." Michelle did so and waited. "Code accepted. Push button for floor level destination."

Donny grinned. "He likes you," he said. Michelle punched his arm and he winced.

The elevator opened on the third floor, the center of operations for the agency. Donny looked around and spotted his former commanding officer across the room.

"There he is!" Don said to Michelle. Donny's first impression was that the Colonel had hardly aged over the last decade. "He still looks the same!"

"Let's go talk to him," Michelle said.

Colonel Hart had spotted the pair as they exited the elevator. This was unexpected; he had not expected Michelle to be able to wrangle Ziegler in so easily.

"Good morning, Colonel. You remember Donny?" she said politely, as if they the colonel and Don were mere acquaintances.

The colonel smiled warmly. "Lieutenant Ziegler! How are you?" He shook Donny's hand vigorously; clearly he had not lost any of his strength over the years.

"I'm fine, sir. How are you?"

"Just fine Donny, just fine." Hart made a sweeping motion with his outstretched arm, from one side of the floor to the other. "So, what do you think of my little operation?"

"It's very impressive. How many people work here?"

"Right now we have just over 60, but I'm looking to add a couple more." He glanced over at Michelle.

"I already gave him our recruitment speech last night," she sighed. "Now it's your turn."

Colonel Hart studied the young face of the former marine for signs of what was in his head. He hoped he was not angry at Michelle for posing as a stewardess to get his attention; he could tell that there was real chemistry between them.

"Did Michelle explain what we do here? "he asked. Donny had always been hard to read. Even under the stress of combat, he'd always been cool-headed and steady, no signs of fear.

"Yes, Colonel. As much as she could, I guess—after all, this is a classified operation."

"Let's talk in my office," suggested the colonel. The three entered the office overlooking DuPont Circle and Hart closed the door.

"I'm told that you're doing consulting in Las Vegas. How do you like it?"

"I like it fine, sir. It's good to be out of D.C., Colonel."

"Why is that, Donny?"

"Just tired of the weather. I sure like Las Vegas, the sunshine agrees with me. I can drive the MG every day."

"I can see that from your tan," the colonel said. Then he asked, "What about Jack? How's he doing?"

"Jack's fine, colonel. But then I guess that you would know that, seeing as how you've been keeping tabs on both of us."

"I guess I deserved that, Don. Yes, I've been keeping tabs on you because I really want you and Jack to be part of my team."

The general didn't get a response, so he continued with something he thought would be sure to elicite a response from Donny, " I've been keeping tabs on you ever since I got a call from the Sacramento police, with questions about a couple of Jack's partials."

Don never batted an eye. He remembered the incident in Giti's lawyers office. "Aren't you going to give me the speech about how my country needs me?" Don asked.

The colonel knew Donny would be a bit resentful at the fact this his girlfriend had been used as a honey-trap, but he hoped he'd get past it.

"No I'm not, son—but that doesn't change the fact that it does. Now, even more than during the Vietnam War."

Donny relaxed a bit. He knew the colonel was right, but he was still pissed off about this whole thing—mostly at Michelle. As if the colonel could read his mind he said, "Don't be mad at Michelle. I put her up to this. I found out that Jack bought tickets for the two you to go to Mexico and I put a call into the airline and got her on board as a stewardess."

"So you set us up?" Donny waved his thumb between Michelle and himself. "Not sure if I should thank you or yell at you."

"I didn't really set you up, Don. I sent Michelle after Jack. Things didn't work out as I had planned." The colonel looked very guilty, like a kid with his hand in the cookie jar. Donny looked over at Michelle and suddenly big grins appeared on both their faces and they started laughing.

"I don't see what's so damn funny."

"Colonel, Donny and I had a huge heart-to-heart talk last night. Everything is okay."

"Everything is cool, Colonel."

"So does that mean you'll join us?"

"I don't know, sir. After all, I just got out of Washington. And I've still got to talk to Jack about all this."

The colonel had anticipated this. "Would it make it easier if I told you that the two of you could join NATA and not have to live and work in Washington?"

"Would that be possible?" Even Michelle looked surprised.

"I'm the head of this outfit. I can do what I Goddamn well want."

"Give me a few days or so to think about it."

"Very good, Don. Take your time, but the sooner you can give me an answer, the better."

"Thanks, Colonel. It's been good to see you."

"You too, Donny." They shook hands and Michelle escorted Donny to the elevator.

The ride back to Dulles and the flight home took the remainder of the day. He'd been given a lot to think about by both Colonel Hart and Michelle. He was glad he and Michelle had been able to talk the previous night and he didn't care about how they'd met. The point was, they had—and he missed her already.

Las Vegas, Nevada - October 14, 1980

Donny went by Jack's RV early in the morning but did not see the black Camaro parked out front. He banged on the door, but no one answered.

"Well, he's not home," he muttered. "That leaves only one place he could be this early in the morning!"

He jumped back into the MG and headed for the industrial section of Las Vegas to see if Don was scoping out the drug house for Ken again. At the curb he spotted Jack's Camaro.

"Bingo!" he said. Then he drove past without glancing at Jack. In his rearview mirror he could see Jack's face, his eyes following the white MGB as it accelerated past. He made a right at the next street and continued out of sight.

"Frank, can you cover for few minutes?" Jack said to his partner. There had still been no activity at the warehouse for many weeks.

"Yeah, sure Jack."

"Thanks." Jack started the car and drove right past the warehouse and Frank to turn right at the next street and again at the next block. He spotted Donny's car ahead and without slowing drove right past. This was Donny's cue, He followed Jack to the local AM/PM market, several blocks away.

"Hey Don, what the hell brings you out here so early in the morning?"

"Well it's like this my friend ..." Jack was dumbfounded at the story and had a hard time reconciling the feminine Michelle with the idea of Michelle the special operations agent ... but he loosened up soon enough and even laughed when Donny told him the colonel had actually aimed Michelle at him.

"Well, I'll be damned!"

"Michelle says the Colonel really needs us."

"Bullshit, Donny. There are hundreds—thousands—of other guys he could pick from. Anyway I can't talk about this right now, I've got to get back to the warehouse."

"Right."

"Do you want to tag along? It'll only be for an hour or so, then the new kids will pick up the assignment."

Donny looked at his watch. "That puts the end of shift at oh-eight-hundred hours."

"Roger that, Donny." Don left the MG at the store and Jack drove back to the warehouse with him in the passenger seat. He parked at the curb, two blocks away. "Frank, it's Jack. I'm back on station."

"Roger that, Jack." Then for the next hour they watched and waited, watched and talked. Just before seven-thirty, the streets began to come alive. Every few minutes a car or a truck would drive by and ten minutes later the radio crackled two times and a black Lincoln appeared from around the corner, followed by a white cube van. The chain link gate opened up, obviously by remote control.

Jack keyed the mike two times: Show time. The presence of the truck indicated that the drugs would most likely be moved today.

Jack reached over and turned the knob to change radio frequencies. "Spielberg, we've got action." That was all that was needed. The radio crackled three more times, indicating that the message had been received.

Jack and Donny watched as the limousine and truck pulled into the parking lot of the warehouse. Two men got out of the cube van and the driver exited the limousine. He stopped at the rear door and opened it. It was obvious that whoever was inside was having a difficult time getting out. This was verified by the appearance of two crutches and a white cast below the bottom of the open door.

"So that's why he's been a no-show."

"Yeah. Look he's got a broken leg."

"Hey Don, are you packing?"

"No, mine's at home." Jack gave Donny one of his patented looks. "Don't give me any of that bullshit about being a boy-scout, Jack. I'm usually pretty prepared."

"There's a .357 in the glove box, along with a couple of speed loaders. That should cover you."

They watched from inside the car as the four men made their way into the warehouse. Jack could see Frank cross the street on the far side of the warehouse at the corner. He waited. Jack and Donny exited Jack's car, indicating to Frank that it was safe to advance. Frank did so, stopping on the sidewalk at the southwest corner of the warehouse. He watched Jack and Donny walk north up the sidewalk. The door at the top of the stairs opened partially. Frank held up his hand for Jack and Donny to stop immediately, half a block away. The driver of the limousine appeared at the top of the stairs, and then he took a quick look into the parking lot. He pushed the button on the remote control and watched the gate start to close. He retreated back inside the warehouse.

Jack and Donny did not advance until Frank motioned them to; now they did so in earnest, sprinting down the sidewalk toward the warehouse. All three managed to get inside the fence before the gate closed completely. They found an alcove to take cover in.

"So what's the plan, Frank?"

"Well Jack and …"

"Frank, this my friend Donny. We did two tours of duty in 'Nam."

"Pleased to meet you Donny. We've got a couple of choices. One, we wait for backup to arrive. I believe it's on the way." Jack nodded. "Two, we go in and hope that the dope is in there, and that we can avoid a firefight."

"Any other options? Do we have a search warrant?"

"Captain Nichols is bringing one. So I think that we should just wait, unless you want to let them start loading the dope?"

"Okay, Frank, we'll wait. But let's not put all our eggs in one basket." He glanced over at Donny. "We're here inside a closed perimeter; we should at least take the rear, so that if those assholes start loading the dope, we aren't all caught here."

"Right. You and Donny take the west side of the building. I'm going to stay put and wait for backup."

Frank and Donny crossed the asphalt parking lot, using the van and the limousine for cover. Jack was crouched near the front fender of the limo, watching and listening. He motioned for Donny to advance. Donny did, stopping at the driver's door. "Okay, Don, I'm heading for the far corner. Cover me."

"Right, Jack." Jack sprinted toward the corner. He got about a third of the way when he heard the sound of a forklift from inside. Almost immediately, the overhead door started to open. Jack looked to his right and could see the legs of one of the men in the truck and the legs of the man with the cast. He covered the remaining distance in seconds flat and took refuge around the corner.

Donny was still crouched behind the driver's door. Both Jack and Frank peered around the corner and saw the driver of the van walk out the door and onto the loading dock. He looked around then started coming down the concrete stairs toward them.

"Oh shit," Jack said quietly. He could see Donny crouching motionless beside the limousine as the driver walked between the rear of the limo and the front of the van. *Don't look behind you for God's sake,* Jack thought. The driver turned left and reached for the handle of the driver's door.

Then, in a move that even caught Jack by surprise, Donny launched himself toward the van, covering the distance in just a second. Before the door was even half-open, the driver was hit by the full weight of Donny's body. The force of the blow knocked the wind completely out of him and he fell to the pavement, with Donny landing on top of him.

Taking no chances, Donny clubbed him with the butt of the Smith and Wesson, knocking him unconscious. The forklift was driven out onto the dock and the driver lowered the pallet of boxes down at the edge of the loading dock, reversed the forklift, then stopped, clearly puzzled.

He took a quick look towards the gate. It was still closed. He dismounted his forklift and followed the trail his partner had taken, walking the length of the loading dock and down the stairs. Before he reached the rear of the van he could feel the muzzle of Officer Frank McAdams' gun in the small of his back.

"Not a sound my friend, not a sound. Keep walking forward around the van." He did as commanded and found himself staring into the muzzle of a second gun. Donny motioned him to kneel down on the ground, where he was hand-cuffed by Frank.

"Two down and two to go. Right, Donny?"

"Right, Frank."

The forklift sat half on the loading dock, half inside the building, its propane powered engine idling. At that moment six unmarked police cars came from both ends of the street and converged on the warehouse, all stopping outside the gate.

Captain Nichols was the first one out of his car. He looked beyond the chain link fence and could see that Frank had two suspects in custody. "Who the hell is that with him? Christ, it's Donny!" he exclaimed. He spotted Jack at the far corner of the building. Jack gave him a nod.

Out of the corner of his eye, Ken caught some movement to his right. He saw the muzzle flash of a gun, but heard no noise. His brain registered the impact, then blackness, then nothing else. The limousine driver had opened fire with an Ingram Mac-10 machine pistol, the latest weapon in the criminals' arsenal. It was on full auto.

"Oh, Christ," Jack said, bringing his Colt up and getting a bead on the gunman. But the damage was already done; the gun fell silent, its thirty-two round magazine expended in less than two seconds. The gunman turned, reaching inside his coat as he did so. "Drop it!" Jack yelled, but he did not. Instantly, Jack squeezed the trigger and a patch of crimson appeared on the man's chest. He was dead before his body hit the ground.

The man with the cast on his leg yelled form inside the warehouse, "Okay, I give up." A handgun clattered across the concrete loading dock, onto the asphalt below. Frank ordered the man to come out with his hands above his head. He did, with more than a dozen guns trained on him. He hobbled across the loading dock, trying to maintain his balance.

"Walk down the stairs slowly and lie face-down on the pavement!" yelled Frank.

"But ..."

"If you don't do exactly as I ask, we will use deadly force."

"Okay." The man managed the stairs somehow, without falling flat on his face, and positioned himself as instructed.

"Who else is in there?"

"No one. There were just the four of us." The police took no chances. An officer launched five tear gas canisters through the open door and a minute later, with white clouds of tear gas billowing out the door, the police were fairly sure the suspect was telling the truth. A plain-clothes officer used bolt cutters to open the main gate and two officers rushed in and hand-cuffed the last suspect. Then, using the tip of his boot, he kicked away the Mac-10 before kneeling down to feel for a pulse, fairly certain that there would be none. The suspect was dead.

With this part of the crime scene secure, Jack's thoughts now focused on his friend. He ran out the gate and around the front of Ken's police car. Captain Ken Nichols lay in a pool of blood and Donny was already kneeling beside him.

"Jesus, Ken!" said Jack.

"It looks bad, but I've got a pulse," Don told him.

"Has someone called for an ambulance?"

"Yes, sir, a bus is already on the way." Jack soon heard the wail of a siren in the distance, getting closer.

Later that evening, at the hospital, Jack and Donny sat in the waiting room. Captain Nichols had been in surgery for over three hours and no one had been able to give the two men an answer as to what Ken's condition was. They noticed a doctor walking down the hall toward them, his gown soaked in what appeared to be a combination of sweat and blood. He lowered his surgical mask to reveal a serious look.

"Is one of you Jack?"

"Yes, that's me. How is Ken?"

"He's lost a great deal of blood. The head wound was just a superficial wound, but the force of the bullet fractured his skull. The other three bullet wounds were more serious."

"How serious?"

"One bullet punctured his lung and then exited out his back. The second one shattered his collar bone or clavicle and then shattered his scapula. The third bullet fractured his left humerus. For now, we have stopped the bleeding and have him stabilized and I believe we have preserved function of his left arm."

"What's the prognosis Doc?"

"He will live, but as far as regaining full use of his left arm and shoulder, time will tell. It's about fifty-fifty at this point."

"Thanks Doctor! Thanks for saving our friend's life!"

"You're welcome." The doctor walked down the hall towards the nurses' station. He would follow up Captain Nichol's condition in the morning.

"So Donny, we had a hell of a day didn't we?" Jack said.

"We sure did. We bagged four bad guys, and helped the cops seize 500 kilos of cocaine."

"And, we didn't get ourselves killed in the process." He looked somber for a second. "I sure hope Ken will be okay."

"He will! You know, Jack, it was Colonel Hart that talked Ken into letting you do that stakeout detail for him."

"Why?"

"I think Ken got the impression from you, when we last sat down for some brewskies, that you didn't think being a private detective was making much of a difference in the world."

"Yeah, that sounds like my personal angst," he shrugged.

"Yeah! So what are you going to do about it, Jack?"

"I'm going to go to Washington and see an old friend! Want to come?"

"Wouldn't have it any other way."

Sacramento - October 27, 1980

For almost three weeks Jaffar had waited as patiently as possible for some good news from Wendover Base. There had been no more issues with security and there had been no more incidents with Abdul. This was, however, the only good news: Sameed and Abbas had come no closer to solving the issues with the controls of the Boeing 720 and time was ticking, which was incredibly stressful for Jaffar. If progress was not made soon, the operation would have to be revised or scrapped.

"Giti, I've got to go back to Salt Lake City, maybe for a day or two," he said, a bit guilty at all the trips he had been taking.

"Jaffar, this is your fifth trip there in five weeks. What's going on?"

"I've got business there."

"What kind of business? You said you've got a big deal going on. What kind of deal?"

"That's none of your concern!"

"It is my concern. I'm your wife, Jaffar."

"No! It's not your concern. That's the end of it!" he lashed out.

"No, it's not the end of it," she insisted. "Tell me what's going on!"

Jaffar was silent for a moment. He was very angry and a hair's breadth away from striking out. No woman had ever stood up to him and Jaffar certainly did not like it. As calmly as he could, Jaffar said, "My big deal there that looked so good a month ago is now causing me nothing but problems. I may end up losing a great deal of money."

"How much money?"

"Millions!"

"Oh," was all Giti could say.

Sacramento - October 28, 1980

This morning Jaffar had awoken earlier than usual. He found the bed beside him empty; empty and cold. He showered and got dressed; he'd packed his bag the night before. He found Giti in the kitchen in her bathrobe.

"Good morning Giti. Did you sleep well?" Jaffar knew she had not.

"Yes, okay I guess. I made your morning tea."

"Thank you." Jaffar passed beside Giti on his way to grab his favorite cup from the cupboard. He tried to give Giti a kiss, but she moved and his lips found her cheek instead.

As Jaffar poured his tea Giti asked, "What time are you going to leave today?"

"I'll wait until the morning rush is over, about nine or so."

"So you have a bit of time. I've got to get Sina and myself ready to go."

Jaffar sat down in front of the television. He still had two hours to go before he was going to leave. He made sure the VCR was recording.

"Iranian President Abolhassan Bani-Sadr has claimed that he possesses a letter from the White House stating that the U.S. has accepted conditions for the release of the American hostages. President Jimmy Carter could not reached for comment, as he is preparing for tonight's debate in Cleveland against Ronald Reagan."

"Today Boeing announced the retirement of …"

"Ahh! What a load of garbage." Jaffar switched channels on the television.

"Paul Kantner of the rock group Jefferson Starship has suffered a stroke. The 39-year-old is expected to recover …"

Jaffar switched off the television but left the Sony VCR—which was programmed to record the same news programs every day—still running.

Later that morning, just after Giti and Fatemah dropped Sina off at school, about a block from the school, Giti pulled the car off onto shoulder. "Fatemah would you mind driving?" she asked, as tears began to fall down her cheeks.

"Giti, what's wrong?" Fatemah was shocked and concerned.

In-between sobs, Giti managed to say, "It's me and Jaffar. We're fighting again."

"Oh Giti, can I help?"

"Fatemah, when you, Zafar, Sina and I went on our little holiday. I didn't tell you the whole story."

"What story? What are you trying to say Giti?"

"Jaffar raped me! And I'm pregnant from it!" Giti began to cry uncontrollably.

"He raped you? What do you mean?" Fatemah was shocked. "He is your husband, he is supposed to love you and treat you with … That bastard!"

"I couldn't believe he would treat me that way …" Giti said between sobs.

Fatemah took a deep breath, trying to control her anger at Jaffar. "I'm sorry, Giti." Fatemah said, then she held her sister-in-law while she wept. After a few minutes, she asked, "Why didn't you tell me this before?"

"I … I couldn't. I didn't want to believe it."

"Let's get you home. We'll have a nice cup of tea."

"No! I don't want to go there right now. Jaffar's still there!"

"Alright let's go to my place. Zafar will still be there. He'll know what to do."

"No, Fatemah. Please don't tell Zafar. Can't we just say that I'm sick?

"Okay Giti, we can do that. We'll just tell Zafar that you're not feeling very well, that you have the flu."

— Chapter 16 —

Wendover, Utah

It was time that Jaffar got some answers about the state of his operation and the plane on which it depended. He had been waiting for good news from Abdul for over a month. He stood next to the Boeing airliner, opposite Abdul, Abbas and Sameed. They looked a little frightened and he was glad of it.

"I want some straight answers from all three of you," he demanded.

Sameed and Abbas were nervous but Abdul had heard this kind of thing many times before. He'd been Jaffar's right hand man for a long time. He stood firm.

"I want to know what progress you have made on the engine and the controls."

Sameed and Abbas looked at one another. They had known this day would come sooner or later but it was hoped by both men that it would be much later. "The engine is ready to come out if needed. The controls and the autopilot are still causing problems," ventured Sameed.

"Can you fix them, Sameed? You two are supposed to be my best mechanics."

"We were hoping that we could work things out as we went along."

"But …"

"But we cannot. The Americans have had years with this system and spent many millions of dollars ..."

"So what you are saying is that you can't do what you told me you *could* do?" Jaffar frowned darkly, beyond frustrated.

"No, we can't," squeaked Sameed. "I'm most sorry, Excellency." Both Sameed and Abbas knew that the cost of failure would probably be the loss of their lives and that of their families. "Please Jaffar, we did the best we could. Please don't kill our families!"

"Don't worry Sameed, I won't. I still need you both here." It was clear that Jaffar would have to find someone who knew how to do the work on the jet to teach these clowns.

Sacramento, California - October 29, 1980

Jaffar came home to an empty house that evening. He was tired from the long drive, but could not sleep. He made a cup of tea and sat down in his favorite chair. He used the remote to turn on the television. He would watch the news recorded during the day.

"President Jimmy Carter could not reached for comment as he is preparing for tonight's debate in Cleveland against Ronald Reagan."

He'd heard that this morning. He fast-forwarded it to a celebration in what appeared to be an airplane hangar.

"Today Boeing announced the retirement of their chief designer, Joe Sutton. Mr. Sutton had been with Boeing since 1959, when he began work on the Boeing 737. He was transferred to the design of the Boeing 747 Jumbo jet, in 1965. During the retirement party held for Mr. Sutton, almost half the 50,000 people who worked for him during the late 1960s showed up to honor him."

The television screen portrayed a man with salt and pepper hair standing with a gracious-looking, older woman by his side.

"Mrs. Sutton, what do you think of your husband's retirement party?"

"It is amazing. I still can't get over the number of people. As you can see they had to use the main Boeing assembly plant due to the size of the party!"

"Mr. Sutton. What about you?"

"As my wife said, it's amazing. This place holds some great memories for me and my family."

"Do you have any immediate plans for your retirement?"

"My wife and I are going to spend the next few weeks with family. Our son lives just outside Las Vegas, in Boulder City. After that, we might spend some time gambling."

"This is Kathy Yamada, for KIRO 7 News in Everett."

"Thanks, Kathy. Now in other news ..."

Jaffar shut off the television and VCR. He had an idea. He picked up the phone and dialed.

"Hello?"

"Hello, Sameed. Get me Abdul."

After a moment he Abdul answered, "Hello, Jaffar."

"Abdul I want you and Hamid to go to Las Vegas. I have an important job for you," he said. Adding, "I will fill you in when I get there."

Wendover Base, Utah - October 30, 1980

The blare of an air horn bellowed nearby as Jaffar shut off the videocassette he had been playing for Abdul and Hamid. He had repeated the tape several times, until he was sure they understood what they were to do. After the third toot, the three men looked outside and saw a delivery truck at the gate. Jaffar said. "Good! Hamid see that the truck is unloaded, just outside the hangar door."

"Yes, Jaffar." Hamid drove one of the company trucks out to the gate, where the driver of the flatbed waited impatiently. He unlocked the gate and slid one side of it open.

"Where do you want this stuff, Bud?" The driver thumbed toward the back of the truck and Hamid looked to see two pallets full of white, five-gallon plastic buckets, all carefully shrink wrapped and belted down.

"Put it over there next to the main hangar building," he said. Each man got into his respective vehicle and the driver followed Hamid to the hangar then used the crane behind the cab to unload the pallets.

"Sign here, Bud." Hamid did as he was told and received the top copy of the bill of lading.

"Thanks," the trucker said. Hamid followed the truck out to the gate in his pickup then, when the trucker had departed, he closed and locked the gate once more. He was curious to see the contents of the white buckets. As he reentered the hangar building, he was surprised to see Jaffar and Abdul coming down the stairs.

"Jaffar, here's the delivery slip for those plastic buckets. What do you want me to do with them?"

"Thank you Hamid. See to it that they are bought into the hangar. Sameed and Abbas know what to do with them."

"Yes, Excellency. Anything else?"

"Abdul and I have to go to Salt Lake City to take care of some business. In the meantime, I want you to assist Sameed and Abbas. Now follow Abdul and I out to the gate and close it after us. Do not open it for anyone but us."

"I understand." After Jaffar and Abdul had left, Hamid did exactly as he was instructed. He helped Sameed and Abbas bring in the pails one at a time, until the pallets were empty, then the huge hangar door was closed.

It was the first time that Hamid had been in the hangar for a couple of days. The air was filled with dust and sound and the interior of the hangar had been transformed, the walls covered with literally acres of white plastic. The plastic stopped the dust from being disturbed and floating into the air. It also reflected the overhead lights, almost doubling the illumination inside.

He looked up to see Sameed and Abbas, one each on each wing on their hands and knees and several more men on scissor lifts on each side of the fuselage. They were all dressed in white coveralls and armed with pneumatic sanders. The Boeing was completely void of any markings, the exterior surface a patchwork of silver, gray and green, as the entire plane was being prepped for primer.

"What can I do?" he called up to Sameed.

"You will help us sand! There's a place to change and clothes and a dust mask over there." He pointed. "I have promised Jaffar to have the jet ready for primer by the end of the week and I do not want to give him another reason to displeased with me. Come, help us!"

"Okay," said Hamid.

Wendover, Utah - November 1, 1980

The day before, everyone had worked 16 hours straight to finish getting the exterior of the jet ready for primer and Hamid had slept like a dead man. The sound of a blaring horn jolted him from a deep sleep; it took him a second to realize that the blaring horn was coming from *outside* the hangar. He hastily jumped out of the army cot upon which he was sleeping, opened the door and looked out the crack to see two vehicles parked at the main gate. He recognized the first one.

Damn, that's Jaffar, he thought. He immediately started barking orders at anyone within earshot. "Wake up! Wake up and go wake up the others!"

He wondered how long Jaffar had been there. Hamid hurriedly got dressed and headed to the gate.

"Jaffar, I am pleased to see you."

"Enough of the pleasantries. What took you so long to come to the gate? You look as if you just got out of bed!"

"Yes, Excellency! The men and I worked many hours on the plane last night." Hamid unlocked the gate.

"Is it ready as I asked?"

"Yes, Excellency! It is."

"Let's go, Abdul. Hamid, shut the gate after us." Hamid did so then raced to catch up to the other two vehicles. He was surprised to see a shiny white van, the newest addition to the company fleet.

Inside the main hangar Abdul and Hamid watched Jaffar walk around the aircraft, running his hand over the fuselage many times, touching the engine nacelles. After several minutes Jaffar's audience increased by two, as Sameed and Abbas joined them in the hanger. Jaffar finally finished caressing the plane and he walked over to the four men. Abdul handed Jaffar a thick manila envelope.

"Sameed! After the plane has had two primer coats, here are the diagrams, photographs and color schemes which I want you to use in painting it. They are to be followed exactly! I will give you additional printed material once you are done."

"Yes, Excellency."

"Hamid. You will go with Abdul. He will explain the additional plans that I have for you."

"Yes, Excellency!"

"Oh, and Hamid?"

"Yes?"

"Do not make any mistakes. I am depending on this to be done!"

Sacramento, California - November 2, 1980

Giti had felt quite sick the last few days. She was slightly better today and she insisted she was well enough to go to work, but Fatemah wouldn't have it. Giti relented, but she did drive Sina to Matthew's house; it would get him out of the house for a day and give her some time to think.

For the past few days, Giti and Sina had been staying with Fatemah and Zafar. Giti had missed four days of work.

"The poor thing, she's so sick," Fatemah said to Zafar.

"Yes, dear. She looks terrible and I've heard her in the bathroom, vomiting."

"Yes, the poor thing can't keep food down."

Without thinking Zafar blurted out, "Maybe she's pregnant!" He could tell by the look on Fatemah's face that his comment had caught her totally off-guard. It was something that she had not even considered him saying.

"Don't even talk like that, Zafar. Let's hope not."

"What? Why Fatemah?"

"Nothing!"

"Fatemah my dear, you cannot fool me. I've heard her crying when she's alone. What's going on?"

Fatemah just could not keep a secret. Besides, she was frightened for her sister-in-law and very best friend. Quietly she said, "He raped her, Zafar!"

"What? Who raped her?"

"Jaffar did."

Zafar's face changed from a normal colour to a mottled purple to bright red as he understood what his wife was telling him. "That asshole! I'll kill him!" he raged.

"No, you won't!" Fatemah said, afraid that he would. "She told me this in confidence. Right now we're not going to do anything. We're going to just be there for Giti and support her. Giti doesn't know what to do, so you sure won't." Then Fatemah added, "And don't tell her that you know."

Zafar took a few deep breaths. "Alright I won't do anything for now," he said, "but do you recall what I said two years ago?

"Yes, Zafar, I remember," Fatemah admitted. He was always right when it came to the character of other men.

Boulder City, Nevada - November 8, 1980

Abdul and Hamid sat in the front seat of the brand new six-passenger Chevrolet van. They had parked facing south on California Street, on the west side of Bicentennial Park and had a clear view of the modest, two-story house on the corner of Park Place and Utah Street.

They took turns sleeping and eating. For food, they walked around the corner to eat at either the gas station or a small café down the road. Every clerk that served them was sure they were homeless and secretly they all hoped the pair would move on and find somewhere else to loiter. The inside of the van was getting ripe with the smell of anxious sweat, the new car scent probably gone forever. Both men took opportunities to sit on nearby benches to escape the smell but unfortunately it followed them like a cloud.

"Abdul! Look! I believe they are leaving." Across the park, that did seem to be the case. The husband and wife stood outside the house, on the driveway, suitcases nearby.

"Yes, Hamid, it does look that way." After seven days and nights of watching, this was a relief. Joe Sutton and his wife, Janette, waved good-bye to their son, daughter-in-law and young grandson.

"It was sure good to see my grandson," Joe said to his wife.

"*Our* grandson, and I'm afraid those two are going to have their hands full."

"Yes, he is full of energy isn't he?"

Janette Sutton could only respond with, "He sure is."

It had been a long stay, perhaps too long and they were both ready to go home. But they were sad to leave; she could read Joe like a book and knew he was thinking that it had been too long since their house was filled with children's laughter and mischievousness. However, the beauty of having grandchildren was that it wasn't a full-time job.

The couple headed west toward Las Vegas. For weeks, Joe had been looking forward to doing a bit of gambling and for weeks Janette had been reminding him that. "You can do just a bit, no more!"

Hamid followed the pair for almost ten miles. The road had been fairly good but for the past mile, the pavement had become very rough, with many potholes. Abdul and Hamid watched the car in front intently. It swerved suddenly and the front bounced wildly. As the car's motion had become more and more erratic, Joe fought for control. Abdul saw huge pieces of rubber fly from the front tire as it began to shred. Finally, the car came to a halt on the shoulder of the highway.

Hamid stopped in front of the car and put his emergency flashers on. During the last week, he'd had chance to read and reread the owner's manual for the new van, so he knew exactly what to do. Meanwhile, Abdul got out and walked back to the couple's car. "Are you two okay?"

"Yes, but I think we had a blowout. Damn lousy roads."

"Yes! My friend and I saw what happened. Can we help you?"

"No, I think I can manage. The spare's in the trunk."

"Very well." Abdul had intended to let Mr. Sutton make repairs and he would ambush them a few miles down the road but when Joe opened the trunk, he found a jack, but no spare tire.

"Dammit! I can't believe it!" He slammed the trunk lid down and as the white van started to pull away he yelled, "Wait! Wait!" Joe was relieved when he saw the brake lights go on and the van stop. He ran up to it.

"It looks like I could use a ride into town after all."

"No problem."

"I've got to get the tire off and take it for repairs because for some reason the spare for this damn rental car is missing," he said. "It will just take me a few minutes."

"All right. I will help."

"Thanks." Joe managed to jack up the car and loosen the lug nuts. The tire was almost completely gone from the rim, but the rim didn't appear to be bent. During the process, a change in wind direction brought Abdul's fragrance to the American's nostrils. Abdul noticed.

"Forgive me. My friend and I have driven a long way, almost without rest."

"Oh! That explains it." The van appeared to be new, probably a rental. Joe walked back to the front of the car to explain to Janette what he was planning to do.

"Joe don't tell me that you're going to get in that van with two strangers! You could be mugged!"

"They're tourists, Janette. He's the bloody Chief of Police in his town. He showed me his badge."

"Oh! Well you're not going to leave me here by myself in the middle of nowhere, are you?"

"Okay, you can come along. But let me warn you, Mrs. Sutton, they have been travelling a long way and you're really going to notice it ..." Both of them laughed. A few minutes later it didn't seem very funny.

"Would you mind if we opened a window or two back here?"

"No, go ahead."

Ninety minutes later they returned to the rental car. Abdul helped put the new tire back on, even tightening all the nuts for Joe. He used his fist to pound the hubcap back into place, then lowered the jack.

"My wife and I can't thank you enough! Is there anything that we can do for you?"

"Yes, as a matter of fact there is." Abdul produced a handgun from under his jacket. "We want you and your wife to get into the van."

Wendover, Utah - November 9, 1980

Sameed watched the white van travel along the airport road toward the front gate, a mid-size, rented sedan behind it. "Jaffar I think they are here."

"Yes Sameed! Go and unlock the gate and escort our new guests in."

Sameed opened the big hangar door and drove out to the gate. A few minutes later Abdul drove the van into the darkened hangar. Jaffar opened the sliding door on the passenger side. Inside on the floor he saw Mrs. Sutton, gagged, bound and very frightened.

Mr. Sutton drove his rental car into the hangar as directed by Hamid and stopped beside the van. Jaffar leaned over and opened the door. "Mr. Sutton, welcome to your new home."

"If you hurt her …! You bastards!"

"Come now, Mr. Sutton. No one has been hurt and no one will be, as long as you do what we ask."

"What do you mean? What do you want, money? I can pay you!"

"No, Mr. Sutton we do not want your money."

"Then, what do you want?"

On cue, Sameed turned on all the overhead lights, revealing the Boeing 720, in all its glory as Jaffar said, "We want you to work on that!"

— Chapter 17 —

November 9, 1980

"Hamid, you and Abdul must accompany Mrs. Sutton back to Las Vegas. I'm sure she won't cause you any trouble. She's too afraid for her husband's life," Jaffar instructed them. And so they were on the road to Vegas.

For the first two hundred miles, Mrs. Sutton lay on the floor of the van, just as she had the night before. Hamid drove the rental car, while Abdul drove the van. Up until this point Janette Sutton had absolutely no idea where her husband was and Jaffar wanted that to remain the status quo.

Just past the small town of Alamo, Hamid turned right, off of US-93, onto a narrow, winding dirt road and Abdul followed. Hamid switched seats with Abdul, and Mrs. Sutton drove the rental car, with Abdul in the passenger seat. She would drive the rest of the way into Las Vegas.

Mrs. Sutton was exhausted, having slept very little the night before. At first Jaffar did not even want her to go on this trip, but he quickly realized that whoever rented the car had to be the one who returned it or there would be unwanted questions from the authorities. Luckily for Mrs. Sutton, Abdul and Hamid had bathed the night before and the inside of the van had been cleaned; the previous evening's trip had not only left her frightened, but nauseous.

At the Budget rental center Mrs. Sutton was reminded that any attempt to alert anyone to her situation would result in not only her death, but the death of her husband and family as well.

"I understand that. I am going to cooperate completely," she assured Abdul and Hamid.

Hamid sat in a chair beside the door as she approached the counter to talk to the rental agent. Inside his jacket was a handgun and he remained within earshot so he could hear every word she said. Jaffar had been correct about Janette Sutton. There was no way she was going to start anything; she was a good person and knew that if she did, not only would she and Joe be killed, but innocent lives would be lost as well. She was certain that these dangerous men would think nothing of killing the clerk and anyone in earshot as well.

After the usual walk-around inspection—during which Hamid and Abdul made sure that one of them was with 25 feet of the woman at all times—Mrs. Sutton and the clerk returned to the front counter. The clerk commented, "I see you put a new tire on. Was there a problem?"

Mrs. Sutton wasn't going to mention the flat tire unless the clerk brought it up. She just wanted to be back with her husband. "Yes, my husband and I got a flat tire," she said.

"But this a new tire!"

"Yes that's right. There was no spare in the trunk and we had to buy a new tire. What's left of the old one is in a bag in the trunk."

"Let me talk to my manager." Hamid's hand went towards his weapon and Janette saw. She paled.

"That's not necessary!"

"It will only take a moment!" The clerk went into the back office to explain the situation. When he returned, he said, "There will be no charge for the rental, and we will refund the cost of the tire."

"Thank you!"

"It's the least we could do for your trouble." Neither the clerk or his manager had the slightest idea of the kind of trouble Mrs. Sutton and her husband were in.

Wendover, Utah

At the eastern edge of the base at Wendover were two dozen buildings that had formerly been enlisted men's quarters. After many years of neglect they had been made habitable again, but just barely; there was no heat in any of the buildings and the woodstoves had been removed decades ago. The only evidence of woodstoves ever being there were the short stubs of the flues that still projected up through the roof.

On the positive side, lights had been repaired and a new mattress was on each of the rusty bed frames. While some of the buildings were for Jaffar's men, some were for Wendover's 'guests'. To these had been added special features such as bars on the windows and heavy-duty padlocks on the doors. The buildings featured signs numbering them one through twelve but no one would guess that they were living quarters; from the outside, they looked like simple storage buildings.

After the long trip from Las Vegas back the airfield Mrs. Sutton was unceremoniously marched down to Storage Building No. 12 and pushed inside. "You will have two meals each day. There are a sink and a toilet in the small room over in the corner," said Hamid.

"What about my husband? Where is he? I want to see him!"

"He's not here. You will see him when he's done what is required of him and our job is finished here."

"But ..."

It was Abdul's turn to speak. "Mrs. Sutton, if you do not be quiet, I will be forced to use other methods to *keep* you quiet." Janette Sutton turned, quietly walked to her bed and lay down.

Joe Sutton had been working all day without rest. In fact he had been awake since the previous morning when he'd awakened at his son's home. The first thing this morning he'd been shown all the diagrams and notes from the material Jaffar had obtained, both from Reza's briefcase and from the library. He spent a couple of hours studying the material. He walked up the makeshift stairs and into the forward cabin door. He entered the cockpit—which he found in complete disarray.

"Jesus! What the hell have you people done?" Jaffar, Sameed and Abbas gathered at the doorway.

"What's the problem?" Jaffar asked.

"The problem is your men have completely butchered this aircraft and now you expect me to put it back together again. And on top of that, I have to make this passenger jet perform as it would normally, without a pilot and copilot sitting here."

"Yes! That's exactly what I what you to do. Your very life depends on you completing this task!"

"And my wife's as well! Where is she? I need to see her."

"In due time, Mr. Sutton, in due time. No harm will come to her if you do as we ask. Now stop complaining about the mess and get to work solving the problems!"

"I will need some time, maybe two or three months. I can't work like this."

"You have one month. No more!"

"It simply can't be done. It's impossible! That's simply not enough time."

"It will have to do. I have a schedule to meet."

"Why don't you just put a pilot in the cockpit, and forget all this nonsense?

"Because, Mr. Sutton, I don't trust a pilot to sit in this seat and carry out my orders." Jaffar added, "But enough of this talk. You need to get to work."

"But I need more than just a month!"

"My associate Abdul, you remember him? He followed you from your son's house. He knows where your son, daughter-in-law and new grandson live ..."

"You bastards! You animals!"

"I've been called worse Mr. Sutton, far worse. Now, what is your answer? I'm growing very tired of this discussion."

"Okay! Just don't hurt my family." Joe Sutton thought for a second, "I will need to make a list of things I will need. You will have to purchase me some equipment."

"I thought I might. Give me your list by the end of the day."

In Washington, at NATA headquarters, Michelle was going over the latest threat assessment files. One in particular, seemed more significant than the rest. A former Boeing engineer was missing, along with his wife.

Oh damn. It seems they disappeared from Vegas! I'll have to give Donny or Jack a call later, Michelle thought.

Las Vegas, Nevada - November 10, 1980

Jack was on his way to see how Ken was doing. He was listening to the news on the Camaro's radio on his way to the hospital.

"Police are asking for information regarding the whereabouts of two Seattle residents who were on vacation in the Las Vegas area, visiting family. Their rental car was returned, but they never arrived home, nor did they catch their flight back to Seattle. Joseph Sutton was last seen with his wife when they left their son and daughter's home two days ago. Janette Sutton was last seen several hours later returning their rental car, alone. Sutton had recently retired after a long engineering career with aviation giant, Boeing …"

Jack turned off the Camaro and got out. He was a little disturbed by the story of the kidnapping he had just heard. As a private investigator, his wheels naturally turned when such things happened. He let it go for the moment though. He had a friend to visit; he was really worried about Ken.

Jack nodded at the police sergeant who stood in the hallway in front of Ken Nichols' room, then quietly stepped inside. Ken lay in bed, his left arm in a cast and an intravenous drip in his other arm. A clear, plastic oxygen tube snaked its way into his nostrils.

"Hey, Ken. How are things?"

"Good Jack. I'm beginning to feel a lot better, but my shoulder hurts like hell."

"Looks as though you'll be out of the loop for a while," Jack said.

"Oh no! The Sergeant out there gives me a daily run down on what's going down in the city. Gives me something to think about, instead of feeling sorry for myself for being stuck in this fucking bed!"

"Did you hear about that missing Seattle couple?"

"Yeah! We got surveillance video and there was clearly some Arab with her, even though he was pretending *not* to be with her. They came into the car rental at the same time and left at the same time, though. And she glanced at one of them, just once. She was clearly scared. But she played it cool."

"That sounds damn suspicious."

"I'll arrange for you to look at the video, maybe you can get a couple of clear frames from that and ID the guys that were with her."

"Okay Ken, I'll give them a look. Then he said, "Speaking of looks, you look a damn sight better than the last time I saw you. Donny and I couldn't believe how many tubes were coming out of you."

"Yeah, my wife says I looked like a fucking octopus." Ken started to laugh but a spasm of pain cut it short. Jack looked at his friend with concern. "So what's up with you now that this drug bust is over?"

"Funny you should ask. Donny and I went to see Colonel Hart."

"Oh!" Ken figured Jack might be pissed at him for his role in helping Hart to find him.

"'Oh'! Is that all you have to say?"

Jack laughed. "Rest easy, Ken. Donny and I start training next week."

"Back to boot camp?"

"Something like that, though not as bad. Anyway, my friend, it's okay. Everything is going to work out just great." Jack could see Ken was beginning to tire; he was fighting to keep his eyes open.

"I should get going. I've got to get a lot of stuff done before Sunday," Jack said. "Work on getting better, okay?"

"Okay, Jack. Thanks for coming in for a visit."

"No sweat, Ken. No man left behind, right?" Jack turned to go then quickly turned back. "Oh Ken. I forgot to tell you. You know who works for Colonel Hart?"

"No, who?"

"Donny's girl, Michelle."

"Well, I'll be damned," Ken said quietly.

"I'll come and see you before I go to Washington. Get some rest." Jack needn't have bothered saying that as Ken was already fast asleep.

"Good drugs," Jack said to himself as he walked out of the room, past the guard and down the hall to the nurse's station.

That afternoon, Jack and Donny sat in Don's living room, watching Sunday NFL football. The game between the Buffalo Bills and the Jets was in the last quarter. Earlier they had watched Donny's Washington Redskins lose to the Bears.

"I really thought that Kruczek would do it this time," Don said.

"You know Don, I bet they win less than seven games this year."

"Bullshit! Twenty bucks!"

"You're on! Now watch the bloody game. It might be one of the last ones we get to see for a while."

Between games Jack and Donny had a dinner of barbecue chicken wings and a couple of beers. It would be their last crap food dinner for a while. While sipping a beer, Jack said, "I went to see Ken today."

"How's he doing?"

"Well, you know Ken. He thinks he's doing pretty good, but I talked to the doctor and he said Ken's progress is slower than he would like. The arm and shoulder are going to take a very long time to heal. I cut out early. Ken was tired."

"I hear a 'but' in there somewhere."

"The Doctor says he still doesn't know how much use he'll have of his arm and shoulder. His shoulder got busted up pretty bad. All we can do is keep our fingers crossed."

"Did the doctor say anything else," asked Don.

"He did say that no matter the outcome, he's going to recommend that Ken retires. I understand thet he's already spoken to the Chief of Police about it, when the Chief dropped in for a visit to see Ken in the hospital."

"That sucks big time!"

"Oh I don't know about that. Ken's got his twenty years in, and since he was hurt on the job, I'd expect that he would make out like a bandit. Full pension at the very least!"

"Maybe a lot more."

After dinner, Jack and Donny watched the rest of the football game. Jim Plunkett and his Oakland Raiders ended up defeating Cincinnati 28-17.

The phone rang and Jack picked it up. "Don, it's for you," he said in his best girly voice. He grinned as he handed his friend the telephone. It was Michelle on the line.

Sacramento, California - November 17, 1980

Giti finally returned home after almost a week at Fatemah and Zafar's. Fatemah had pleaded with her to stay longer, but Giti insisted on leaving.

"Sina is starting to ask questions, some that I can't answer. It's better at home," she said.

"He's a bright boy, Giti, very sensitive to other's feelings. Much like his mother."

In spite of herself, Giti smiled. "Thanks Fatemah, but we'll be fine. I'm going to spend the rest of the day catching up on housework and just keeping myself busy."

Giti dropped Sina off at his school then went home. It was kind of like coming home after a week's vacation. The first thing she did was make herself a pot of fresh coffee. While the coffee was brewing she made herself a grocery list. By noon the laundry was almost under control and Giti had even managed to dust every room except one; she had yet to tackle Jaffar's office. Usually the job wasn't too bad, but one look inside his office told her that she would be quite a while in there. Every surface looked as if it was covered by a light white film.

Jaffar hated it when Giti dusted. Having his things moved around annoyed him; everything had to be just so. Giti took care of the bookshelves first, then the blinds. As she extended her arm to reach the far side of the blind, her toe kicked the wastebasket and spilled the contents across the floor.

"Oh, Damn!" Giti knelt down to pick up the papers and return them to the wastebasket but when she glanced under the desk she could clearly see a burgundy briefcase.

"Funny! That looks familiar." Giti set aside the trash and reached under the desk. She pulled out the briefcase. There were no initials on the top, but now that it was out in the light she recognized it. Even after two years Giti could tell by the scuffs and gouges that it was Reza's.

What's this doing here? I thought Zafar put this in the attic!

She blew the dust off the top edge of the case and placed it on top of the desk. She tried the thumb latches. The locks snapped open, Giti lifted the lid. The papers were right on top, just as she'd left them. *What is this doing Jaffar's office? It was upstairs in the attic, in the trunk.* Giti closed the briefcase and took it into the hall. *I'll put it back upstairs later.*

Wendover, Utah - November 27, 1980

With Joe Sutton at work and in charge of fixing the Boeing, the main hanger looked completely different than it had just two weeks earlier. The large poly sheets were gone. Everything, every surface, was as dust-free as possible. Joe Sutton had insisted on that. At the Boeing plant in Everett, Washington, he'd worked in almost sterile conditions. Nothing was dirty, nothing was out of place and for him to do his best work, this place would be no different. The hangar looked better than it had for many years, perhaps better than it ever had, even when new.

Jaffar didn't care what Joe did or what Joe needed, as long as progress was being made—and it was. So far the work had continued without a hitch. The remote station had been fabricated and assembled. Today the remote station was going to be tested—but Joe Sutton still had his doubts about its viability. Two hours later his doubts were realized.

Abdul entered the hangar and crossed the polished concrete floor in the direction of raised voices. Joe stood facing Sameed and Abbas, with the newly constructed remote station in between them. "I've been telling you for almost two weeks that this wasn't going to work properly!" Joe shouted angrily.

"Yes, you have. But we have been working on it for many weeks before you, American."

"Yes, I can see that. You two fucking idiots have butchered this poor aircraft so badly that if it flies again anytime soon it will be a damn miracle!"

"Why you ... you have no right to speak to us in this manner!" Abbas reached for his knife, He was tired of taking orders from this American, this non-believer, even if he did know practically everything there was to know about this jet. Joe Sutton stepped back, realizing that he'd crossed the line.

Abdul reached the three men too late. Abbas slashed out with his knife in a wide arc from left to right. The blade tore through the fabric of Joe's shirt and a crimson stain appeared across his chest.

"What the hell?" Abdul was too late to stop the initial attack. He smashed his fist into the side of Abbas' face, knocking him to the floor. The pain of the blow caused Abbas to drop the knife. He looked around to see who had punched him. At first he thought it was Sameed, but was surprised to see it was Abdul.

"Why did you ...?" Abdul kicked Abbas in the ribs, knocking the wind out of him. Abbas went limp and his head struck the floor. Abdul picked the knife up off of the floor, ending the confrontation, but the damage was done. Abdul looked at Joe. His face was pale and the front of his shirt was bright crimson, the blood starting to soak through the material. He glanced up at Sameed. He looked shocked by the attack.

"Sameed! Go and get Jaffar and then bring me the medicine kit from the office. Hurry!"

Sameed took off, running in the direction of the corner office. His haste made him careless and he spun around slightly as his thigh struck the corner of the bench. He gathered himself up and once more headed in the direction of Jaffar's office, this time slightly slower and with a noticeable limp. Abdul watched him disappear through the door.

"Imbecile!" It was a word he'd learned from Jaffar.

He turned his attention to Joe, who was lying on the concrete floor. The stain now covered him from his neck to his waist. Abdul looked for some rags to cover the wound and stem the flow of blood. He grabbed some clean rags off the stack and pressed them onto the wound. He knew that Joe was the only chance they had to get this airplane off the ground; he wasn't looking forward to what Jaffar would say when he saw how badly Joe had been hurt.

The sound of hurried footfalls echoed across the hangar. Abdul looked up to see Jaffar and Sameed running toward him.

"What's going on? How bad is he?" Jaffar demanded.

"I do not know, Excellency? There is so much blood!"

"Tear his shirt! I must see." Abdul released pressure on the wound and grabbed both collars of Joe's shirt. Button flew in all directions and Joe's torso was exposed. A wound over a foot long arced across his chest, oozing blood.

"It's still bleeding, but not as bad as a moment ago," Abdul said.

"What happened? All Sameed told me was that Sutton was hurt."

"There was an argument. Abbas cut him with his knife."

"The idiot!" Jaffar struck out with his boot, kicking the unconscious Abbas in the ribs. Both Abdul and Sameed winced as he did so, hearing several ribs crack from the impact. Jaffar could suddenly see his well-planned operation falling apart before his eyes. He was furious.

"Abdul, tend to Mr. Sutton's injuries."

"Yes, Excellency!"

"Keep pressure on the wound. Sameed, you help him."

"As you wish."

"I'm going to find Hamid. I will return shortly. Keep trying to stop the bleeding."

A short while later Jaffar returned with Hamid. Abdul and Sameed were still tending to Joe, with some success. They had managed to stem the flow of blood as the clotting factors in his blood started to work. However, every time Joe breathed in and out, the wound would reopen and more blood would ooze out.

"How's he doing?" asked Jaffar.

"The bleeding is less but I don't know if we can stop it. Maybe we should take him to a doctor," suggested Abdul.

Although it was last on Jaffar's list of options, it was becoming apparent that he would have no choice. "I have already thought of that." Jaffar said looking down at Joe Sutton, his life fluid flowing slowly out of his body. "Use every gauze pad in that kit and then wrap his chest with that tensor bandage. That should hold things in place, for a while at least." The two men did so and the flow of blood seemed to stop for a moment. "Bring him to the van and lay him down on the bench seat."

Jaffar gathered up what remained of the first aid kit. "Hamid, gather up as many of the clean rags as you can and place them in the back of the van."

"Yes, Jaffar." Hamid could hear the desperation in Jaffar's voice. It was the first time in all their history that he could recall that happening. It was clear that Jaffar did not want the American to die.

Hamid placed two stacks of clean rags in the van, within easy reach of Abdul and Sameed. "Anything else, Excellency?"

"Yes, Hamid." Jaffar pointed at Abbas. "After we leave, I want you tie up this imbecile and then put a guard on him, 24 hours a day. Put him in the shed farthest away from Mrs. Sutton."

Hamid knew what that meant. On one of the trips to the city he had picked up a load of building supplies and then Hamid and his security team had spent days making the shed in question almost soundproof. Only he, Abdul, Jaffar knew why this was done: it was in case one of Wendover's reluctant guests became uncooperative.

"Yes, Excellency. Anything else?"

"Yes Hamid! Pray that the American does not die!"

Hamid's eyes opened wide with surprise. "Yes, Excellency."

Salt Lake City, Utah - November 27, 1980

During more than a dozen trips into Salt lake City, Abdul and Jaffar had passed through several small towns repeatedly, but neither could recall seeing any signs for a hospital along I-85. Jaffar thought their best chance to remain anonymous was in Salt Lake City itself, where they could blend into the crowds. In a small town, the doctor would be more likely to ask questions—ones Jaffar could not, would not like to answer.

However, Jaffar had noticed a walk-in clinic during one of his shopping trips around town. It was on Union Boulevard, but he was having difficulty remembering the cross street. Abdul and Sameed had taken turns on the floor in front of the bench seat tending to their wounded captive while Jaffar drove around looking for it.

"Where the hell is it?" Jaffar hissed as he drove east from Union Park Street. "It was up this way, as I recall—maybe five or six blocks."

"There it is! Rocky Mountain Medical." Jaffar pulled the van over to the curb, right in front of the emergency entrance. Abdul got out and, with Jaffar's help, got Mr. Sutton through the doors. Thankfully it wasn't busy, but even if it had been the admitting nurse took one look at Mr. Sutton and called for a doctor right away.

"Let's get him in right away." She helped seat the injured man in a wheelchair then another nurse whisked him away down the hall.

"Abdul you go with him in case he needs anything! I will take care of the paperwork with this young lady." Jaffar smiled at the nurse, she smiled back. He looked at the sign on her desk, Leslie Chandler, R.N.

"Now, sir, I will need some information on the patient. What is his name?"

"Joe Sutton. I don't know his age, fifty-nine I think." Nurse Chandler gave Jaffar a strange look. "Look, miss all that information is back at the office."

"What's the name of your company?"

"Sunwest Properties! Look, miss, ah… Leslie. I don't want to get in trouble with labour standards. Is there any way I can reduce the amount of paperwork?" He didn't need to add, *and questions.*

The young nurse smiled. It wasn't the first time this had been asked. "Well let's see how the Doctor makes out first, shall we? Have a seat over there." About two hours later, Doctor Murray walked out of the emergency room and into reception. He looked around at the people waiting.

"Which of you is Mr. Sutton's boss?"

"I am. Is he okay?"

"Yes. He's been given two pints of Ringers Lactate. I've stitched up rather large laceration on his chest and I've also stitched up a large laceration on his scalp. He may have a slight concussion. Finally, I gave him a tetanus shot."

"Thank you."

"How did he receive the injuries by the way? The other gentleman didn't know much about what happened." During the long trip from Wendover to Salt Lake City, Jaffar had thought about this very question. He'd had sufficient time to come up with what he thought was a credible response. "I was told he fell through a chain link fence the men were working on."

"Oh, that explains it!" Doctor Murray knew Jaffar was lying. A man who fell through a chain link fence would have had several wounds and not nearly as deep, more like gouges. A knife, the doctor knew, was closer to the truth.

"Can he be released?"

"Yes, I don't see why not! I would like him to be off work for at least a week or two, so he can get some rest."

"Of course!"

"Let me get my nurse to finish the paperwork. How will you be paying for this?"

"Cash."

"Excellent!"

Jaffar was glad to see the skyline of Salt Lake City receding in the rearview mirror. Mr. Sutton sat in the backseat, next to Abdul. He was still groggy, but he was alive. During the trip back to Wendover, Joe seemed to come more alert and aware of his surroundings. Jaffar noticed Joe's hand go to his chest, and a groan of pain escaped his lips. "I see you're still with us, Mr. Sutton."

"Yes! I guess I am."

"That's good. Is there anything we can do for you?"

"I'm tired. I'd like to rest for a while. Where's Janette?" Joe was obviously still a little bit foggy.

"You can rest now. Perhaps Abdul can give you some of your medication so that you sleep."

"Alright." The three, 25-milligram tablets of Pregabalin put Joe to sleep in just a few minutes, helping with his healing while ensuring he didn't see where they were going.

Thank Allah he didn't die, thought Jaffar.

Wendover, Utah - November 28, 1980

"Well Abdul, let's go in and see how our patient is doing today." Jaffar and Abdul walked past the row of offices along the south side of the hanger and into one which had been converted into a secure hospital room for Joe Sutton. It was far warmer in the hanger than in the storage buildings.

Abdul unlocked the door and switched on the light. Joe Sutton lay in bed, secured by several restraints. The medication he'd been given the previous evening had yet to wear off and he was still fast asleep.

"I am going to see Hamid and I want you to stay here, in case Mr. Sutton wakes up," Jaffar said.

"Yes, Excellency."

Jaffar went back to the hangar to find Hamid. As he walked into the vast open space of the hanger, his footsteps echoed loudly. Work on the Boeing was at a standstill and Jaffar wondered how long it would be before it commenced once again.

"Hamid! Hamid where are you?"

There was no answer. Jaffar looked over to the bench where the newly constructed remote station sat; the congealed puddle of Joe's blood was still on the floor next to it. *Where the fuck is Hamid?* Jaffar opened the emergency exit door and, outside standing next to one of the pickups, Hamid was talking to Sameed. The conversation stopped abruptly when they saw Jaffar approach.

"Hamid, I've been calling you."

"Sorry, Excellency. I was here with Sameed."

"I want you to accompany me to storage building number one."

"You want to see Abbas?"

"Yes, I do."

"Do you think that's wise?

"What do you mean?"

"You may need Abbas to help Mr. Sutton complete the work. He already has several damaged ribs."

"He's lucky that's all I did to him."

"My point exactly."

"I see what you mean. Maybe I should wait until Mr. Sutton recovers."

"That might be best, Excellency."

"Perhaps, to speed his recovery, Mrs. Sutton should be allowed to see her husband. Maybe tomorrow or the next day?"

"Won't she be angry when she sees what has happened?"

"No one will tell her. I was able to convince that foolish, greedy American Doctor. I can do the same with her."

November 29, 1980

For almost three weeks, Janette Sutton had been kept prisoner in storage building number twelve. Her only contact with the outside was when Hamid or one of his men brought her twice-a-day meals. She'd had no contact with her husband, despite her daily requests.

The two-room cell she was in had only a toilet, sink and a bed. While a chimney fixture indicated that a woodstove had once been in the room, it was long since gone and the November chill at night was almost unbearable. The two thin blankets she'd been given barely helped to keep the cold at bay and the cold water from the tap that she used to wash herself only made the frigid air more difficult to bear. Now, in spite of her best efforts, Mrs. Sutton was almost as fragrant as Abdul and Hamid had been on the trip from Las Vegas to Wendover.

Daylight was filtering in through the small, barred windows when the sound of keys at the door jarred Janette awake. The door opened. "Good morning, Mrs. Sutton."

All she could see was a shadowy silhouette standing in the bright doorway. "What is it? Who's there?"

"We are taking you to see your husband." There it was. Not a question or a request, just a declaration, as always.

"What? To see Joe?" she said groggily. Jaffar thought this news would bring a better response. It was obvious that Mrs. Sutton was still not quite awake.

"We will leave in five minutes. Wash yourself and get ready to go." Jaffar closed the door. Just a couple of minutes later, the door opened and a visibly refreshed Mrs. Sutton practically jumped down the steps.

"Okay, I'm ready!" She slid onto the bench seat next to Abdul. Jaffar got in and closed the passenger door. Abdul shifted the truck into gear and drove slowly back toward the hangar.

"Mrs. Sutton, I'm afraid your husband has had an accident. He was trying to escape from the compound and injured himself in the process." The two men witnessed an almost instant reversal of moods. As high as Janette Sutton had been a moment earlier, she was now equally low. The news took the wind from her sails.

"What! What's wrong with Joe?"

"He's going to be alright, but he's lost a lot of blood. Right now he's in the first aid room, resting. He needs a few more days of rest, but the doctor assured us he would recover."

"This is all your fault! You're keeping us here against our will!" she cried.

Jaffar felt himself tense up at her words. She was not in the position to be talking back to him. However, he understood she was stressed so all he said was, "As soon as your husband has done his job, you both can go home. You can go back to your family in Boulder City."

Her eyes went wide in surprise. "What? No! Please don't hurt my family. Please!" Mrs. Sutton began to sob.

"Stop crying! You don't want your husband to see you weak!" Jaffar said firmly and then marveled as Mrs. Sutton gathered herself together and the tears subsided. Many men would have broken under the treatment she'd had been given; beneath the grubby, soiled clothing, Mrs. Janette Sutton was a strong woman. Jaffar had a new-found respect for her.

They stopped at the front of the hangar. Mrs. Sutton was led down the hallway to the room where Joe was recovering. Abdul unlocked and opened the door. Joe lay on the bed, gauze bandages on his head. The restraints had been removed and hidden from view. Joe was still asleep, thanks to the twice-daily medication Jaffar had been administering.

Janette ran to the side of the bed. "Oh Joseph, what have you done?" She sat down on the chair by the side of the bed and gathered Joe's hand in hers. She stayed like that for more than an hour, as long as Jaffar would permit her, but Joe did not stir.

"Mrs. Sutton, it's time for you to go." She looked at Jaffar and her face hardened. Then she placed Joe's hand under the sheets and reluctantly let go of it. She walked backwards out the door, as if she was afraid this was the last time she would see her beloved husband. Abdul closed Joe's door behind her and she turned and headed back towards the exit.

"Abdul, give Mrs. Sutton her suitcase," Jaffar said.

Janette stopped. "What?" Abdul handed her the small suitcase. It had already been searched, on more than one occasion. There was nothing inside that could be used as a weapon, or as a means to escape. Even her nail file had been confiscated.

"I think it would be good if we let you have a shower and allowed you to freshen up a bit and change your clothes. Follow Abdul down the hall. He will show you which room to use."

"Why are you doing this?"

"A woman should look presentable while visiting her husband. You will see him again tomorrow."

"Thank you."

After noon, Jaffar went into Joe's room to check on him. Abdul had already replaced the restraints. They would, of course, be removed before Janette Sutton's next visit. Joe was awake, but just barely. The sleeping pills were beginning to wear off. Jaffar checked his wounds. His scalp and chest were healing very well, though some of the surrounding tissue looked very red. The bandages could probably come off in a couple of days. Joe looked up at Jaffar, trying to focus.

"Your wounds are healing very well."

"Where am I? What happened?"

"You had an accident."

Joe tried to get up but the straps across his chest pressed against the wound, straining the new stitches. Joe stopped instantly, a wave of pain reflected in his face.

"Do not move, Mr. Sutton! You don't want to tear out your stitches."

Joe relaxed immediately. "That hurt like hell!"

"I'm sure it did. You have over a hundred stitches on your chest and about a dozen on your head." Joe was suddenly aware of the pain at the back of his head. He reached up to feel the wound. His fingers gently probed until a sudden jolt of pain stopped him. When he pulled them away, crusty blood coated his fingertips.

"What happened? You said I had an accident."

"What's the last thing you remember?"

"I was in the hangar working on the Boeing."

"Yes, that's right! You fell. But you're going to be okay. You need to get some rest. We can talk about it later." Joe tried to rise once again, but a wave of pain stopped him.

"Christ, that hurts!"

"The wound will heal soon and then we can let you get up and walk around. Until then, rest." Jaffar added, "Do you need anything?"

"Yes! I wanted something. I can't remember. I wanted something for the Boeing 720, but I can't remember."

"Rest. We can talk later," Jaffar repeated and then he and Abdul left. Out of earshot, Jaffar said, "I want someone with him 24 hours a day. Pick at least five of Hamid's men. They should all be able to understand English."

"But Excellency! That's a lot of men!"

"Abdul, I don't want to argue about this. You know full well how critical Sutton is to this operation. He must be given everything he needs to achieve that end."

"Yes."

"Good. Now go back in there and guard him. And take notes. Write down anything he says."

"Yes, Excellency."

"Hamid and I have to pay a visit to Abbas. I will see to it that Hamid sends you the men you need." Jaffar turned and walked away.

Twenty minutes later Jaffar and Hamid stood outside the door of storage building number one. There was no sound from inside. Hamid quietly slid the key into the lock and the door unlocked with a click. Jaffar opened the door and flipped on the light. Abbas lay on the bed in fetal position. It was clear he had not heard the door unlatch. He sat up painfully, wide-eyed like a frightened animal. For three days and nights Abbas had been locked in the shed. He'd not been given any food or medical treatment during that time. He'd been able to drink from the faucet.

Abbas watched in fear as Jaffar and Hamid crossed the room towards him. "Please! Please don't kill me!"

"Don't worry Abbas we are just here to talk to you."

"No! You're going to kill me and then have my family killed. That's why you brought Hamid with you."

"Hamid is just here for protection, both yours and mine. I'm just here to talk to you." Hamid closed the door to the soundproof shed.

— Chapter 18 —

December 3, 1980

Joe Sutton made remarkable progress. As each day passed, the puffy redness around the chest wound steadily decreased thanks to antibiotics and he slept soundly thanks to sleeping pills.

Outside, the temperature had hovered just around freezing for several days. Today there was a light dusting of snow on the ground. When Abdul and Jaffar went to escort Mrs. Sutton from her accommodations, they could see the effect the cold was beginning to have on her. It was obvious Janette Sutton was losing weight; her body was using what fat reserves it had just to keep her warm.

"Good morning Mrs. Sutton," said Jaffar.

"Good morning." They got into the pickup in their usual seating arrangement. During the ride to hangar, Mrs. Sutton moved her feet as close as possible to the heater. But not once did she complain. Not to Abdul, not to Jaffar, not even to Joe during her daily visits.

They were met at the hangar by Hamid and the four of them walked down the hallway to Joe Sutton's room. Abdul unlocked the door. Janette Sutton was surprised to see her husband sitting upright in bed.

"Mrs. Sutton, you have two hours," Jaffar said as he looked at his watch. Abdul accompanied her into the room and closed the door behind them. He sat down in the chair next to the door.

"Hamid, I have a couple of jobs for you and Sameed," Jaffar said once he was outside the room.

Hamid's men had found a pallet full of the old cast iron woodstoves that had once been in the enlisted men's quarters during the building-to-building search Jaffar had ordered many weeks earlier.

"I want you to install a stove in Mrs. Sutton's room," he told Hamid.

Just over three hours later Abdul and Jaffar drove Mrs. Sutton back to building number twelve. A light snow had started once again and the snow blew across the concrete runway, in filamentous ribbons of white. Abdul stopped the truck. A frigid blast of cold air struck the three of them in their faces as they got out of the truck. As they walked toward the building, the wind blew from behind, mercifully sparing them from most of the cold. The light powder swirled in the wind, blowing toward the airfield, carrying the odor of burning wood away from Mrs. Sutton. She did not look up and see the smoke. Jaffar found himself delighted to be creating a surprise for her.

As Mrs. Sutton reluctantly opened her door, a blast of warm air came from the interior of building number twelve. Inside the illuminated interior of the building Mrs. Sutton could see an old woodstoves occupying its former place in the corner. A brand new section of shiny vertical flue connected the stove to a stub that went through the roof. On top of the stove was a small kettle. Behind the door was a small stack of firewood. Jaffar smiled with satisfaction. Finally a job had been done right.

"Over there on the shelf you will find a cup and a supply of tea and some packaged hot chocolate and soup. Hopefully it will make things more comfortable."

"Thank you Jaffar, but why?"

Jaffar did not respond to the question. He only smiled. "See you tomorrow, Mrs. Sutton."

Abdul locked the door and replaced the padlock through the hasp. He returned to the Chevy, as surprised as Mrs. Sutton had been. "Why did you do this Jaffar?"

"It was obvious to me this morning that as time went by Mrs. Sutton's condition was deteriorating, even while Mr. Sutton's condition was improving. Soon it would be apparent to him that his wife's condition was failing. And as I've said to you before. I need him. *We* need him."

"But ..."

"But nothing, Abdul. I want Mrs. Sutton to be given three meals a day from now on instead of just two. Poor treatment only works so far."

"Yes, Excellency."

"Has Mr. Sutton said anything worthy of note to you or Hamid's men?

"Just some mumbling during his sleep, a couple of nights ago."

"What did he say?"

"He just said something about the plane and the autopilot."

"Good. Now I want to stop by and see Abbas. Maybe it's time that he rejoined the flock."

December 5, 1980

Mrs. Sutton had just finished visiting her husband. Both of them had made huge improvements during the last 48 hours. Yesterday, with the assistance of his wife and accompanied by Abdul, Joe had been permitted to take a walk down the hallway as far as the hangar and back. Today, they managed to do the same thing, with Joe lingering for a time to stare at the freshly painted Boeing.

Jaffar sat with Joe in his room for a while after Mrs. Sutton had been escorted out by Abdul and Hamid. "Do you require anything Mr. Sutton?"

"I've been trying to think … the other day, something was on the tip of my tongue."

"Maybe when Abdul gets back we can take you down to the hangar to see if anything jogs your memory." Several days earlier, the hangar floor had been cleaned, all evidence of the fight between Abbas and Joe had been erased.

Joe Sutton still did not seem to have any recollection of the fight with Abbas or exactly how he had been injured. Jaffar hoped there was no permanent memory loss—at least not as far as the project was concerned.

When Abdul returned with Hamid, the three men escorted Joe down the hallway to the hangar. Mr. Sutton walked, unaided, to the fuselage of the aircraft. As he ran his hand lovingly over the new paint, it was clear he was passionate about his work.

Joe walked slowly around the fuselage, not too fast, taking his time—still wary about the stitches across his chest. He was breathing hard when he reached the bench with the remote control unit on top. He slowly turned the rheostat and flipped the power switch to the 'on' position. The red indicator light next to it glowed brightly.

"The other day you mentioned the Bendix Corporation. They are in Indiana, right?" asked Jaffar.

"Yes, I think so. At least they used to be. They make the autopilot and avionics for a variety of Boeing aircraft."

"Yes ..." Jaffar waited anxiously for Joe to complete the sentence.

"Including the Boeing 720. That's it, Jaffar! That's what I've been trying to remember. I think I made some notes about the one on this plane."

"Where are they?"

"Over there on the bench, in that green binder." Jaffar handed the binder to Joe. The older man flipped through it to the last few pages and read them through. He was having trouble catching his breath and Jaffar wasn't sure if it was from the walk around the aircraft, or from the excitement of the conversation. But he didn't want to take any chances with Joe's health.

"Come, Mr. Sutton. It's time for you to get back to bed."

"But, I should stay here and work for a bit."

Jaffar didn't want Joe to collapse and set the time table back even more. They'd lost almost ten days as it was.

"Abdul will get your notes for you. Once you have rested for a while, you can review them. Hamid! Come and assist Mr. Sutton." They got Joe back into bed and gave him some more medication to help him rest. Jaffar was anxious for him to get back to work, but tomorrow would be soon enough.

December 6, 1980

Jaffar had been true to his word. He'd allowed daily visits for Mrs. Sutton—but today's visit had been almost as hard for her as the first one. Lately Joe had been improving, but she could see that he was exhausted. She also noticed the green binder on the small table next to his bed. Aside from being tired, it was clear that Joe was distracted, as if on autopilot. He responded to her questions, but didn't really answer them. This wasn't the first time she'd seen this happen to Joe; when he was working, often she would call him at the Boeing plant and get the same kind of disconnected conversation. It was clear that Joe was thinking about work—this work, the work their captors had imprisoned them for.

She cut off her visit. "I guess I will be going and let you get some rest." Janette Sutton said fretfully. She didn't think her husband would listen.

Fort Bragg, North Carolina - December 7, 1980

Today was a special day for enlisted men all over the United States. It was Sunday, the 39th anniversary of the day Japan launched the sneak attack on Pearl Harbor; the day that officially brought the United States into the Second World War.

It was also a special day for Jack and Donny. Today was their last day at Fort Bragg. They were halfway through their special forces training. Tomorrow, their 14-man unit, would be transferred to Camp Pendleton, near San Diego. They and the 12 other recruits had been handpicked by Colonel Hart from hundreds of prospects. All came from the various branches of the United States military—Army, Navy, Air Force and Marines.

Donny was forever grateful Jack had convinced him to start running again. The rucksack marches during their time at Fort Bragg had started out at just over 11 miles. Today's nature hike was the last and longest of them, at over 30 miles.

Four hours earlier the unit had been split into seven pairs and had rappelled from twin helicopters, Hueys. As part of their land navigation exercise, they'd been spread out west of Fort Bragg, from Highway 690 in the north to Interstate 401 in the south. Now frigid Arctic air from the Canadian prairies had come together with a cold front from off the Atlantic and wind howled and whipped the snow in almost horizontal lines, seemingly coming from every direction at once. Visibility was no more than 30 feet.

Donny matched his best friend's pace as they found their way back to Bragg. He yelled ahead to Jack, "I moved to Las Vegas to get away from this shit!"

"Yeah, Don but let's not forget who got us into this, remember?"

"Yes, Jack. I remember!"

Jack laughed and kept marching. "Only seven and a half miles to go, Don."

Wendover, Utah

Joe sat upright in bed, his binder on his lap and a pad of lined paper beside him. Abdul was closely watching the retired Boeing engineer. Several times that morning Joe put the binder down, and made notes on the pad for ten or fifteen minutes. Then he would then scan through the binder once more.

Joe got up to use the bathroom only once through the morning and Abdul took the opportunity to look over what he'd written. The pad was filled with notes and diagrams that made no sense to Abdul. He only recognized a few words here and there. He heard the toilet flush and quickly returned to his seat.

Joe came out of the bathroom, climbed back into bed and continued to work. At two o'clock, he tore off a sheet of paper from the pad. "Abdul, could you go and get Jaffar for me?"

"Yes!" Abdul got up and went down to hall to where he knew Jaffar had been sitting and going over some bills. He returned to Joe's room. "He will be here shortly."

"Thank you." A short time later Jaffar entered the room and walked toward Joe's bed.

"How are you today Mr. Sutton? You look well."

"I feel good today. More to the point I feel very well and I've got some news about your ailing aircraft out in the hangar."

Obviously Joe still did not, or could not, recall the incident with Abbas in the hangar. Jaffar had confirmed with Doctor Murray last week that Joe might suffer some memory loss due to his head injury.

"What is it?" Jaffar was hoping for the best, but prepared for the worst.

"Over the course of the last few weeks, I have been making notes on all of the aircraft systems, especially the Bendix autopilot and the flight control systems."

"Yes."

"I've made a list of all damaged components that will be needed to make the remote system work properly." Joe handed the list to Jaffar.

"This is quite a list!"

"Yes, Jaffar, and it will not be cheap."

"So far nothing about this has been cheap. Can I not buy any of these things used?"

"Perhaps, but they are often inferior to new. After all, you want the aircraft to perform properly with the remote station, do you not?"

"Of course, I do!"

"I've indicated suppliers where the items can be obtained, but you had better act quickly. Most of these companies close during the Christmas holidays."

"With these things everything will work properly?"

"I guarantee it," Joe said confidently.

Jaffar smiled and started to walk towards the door, "Thank you, Mr. Sutton."

"You're welcome. Oh, one last thing, Jaffar. Have you given thought to the problem of the faulty number two engine? A substitute should be installed or all this work will be for nothing."

"Yes, Mr. Sutton. I have given the matter a great deal of thought. I believe I have a solution."

Jaffar had spent many frustrating hours on the telephone searching for a new engine for his airplane, with no luck. But a possible solution had literally dropped into his lap when he was deciding on the new paint scheme for the Boeing. He had to plan carefully, though, as his idea was risky. It was so risky he hadn't discussed it with anyone yet, not even Abdul, and of course he said nothing to Joe; instead he just looked at the list once more and headed towards the door. It was time that he returned to Sacramento. But first he had to talk to Abdul and Hamid. Outside Joe's room, he called them over.

"Abdul, I want you and Sameed to look after things around here while I return to Sacramento."

"Yes, Excellency."

"That includes looking after Mr. and Mrs. Sutton. I've got to order the parts Mr. Sutton has requested and I can do that best from home. Until those parts get here, there's not much for me to do. I will get these parts and return—and it is my plan to have this plane operational by the end of December. The Suttons are crucial to my plan. Treat them well."

"Yes, Excellency."

"Our guests are not allowed outside, except for when you are escorting Mrs. Sutton back and forth to her quarters. And there is more than enough money to look after the needs of the men while I am away."

Jaffar looked at his watch. He would not get back to Sacramento until late in the evening, provided the roads were not too bad. He hoped Giti would not be too angry at him for his long absence. He'd noticed her giving him the cold shoulder as of late. Sometimes he wondered if it had been a mistake, marrying her. She was beautiful but quite demanding. American women were so entitled. He didn't think he could stand it much longer. But he did enjoy the privilege having an American wife afforded him. It made it so easy for him to operate on American soil.

He sighed. He would go home and face the music. She could only stay angry for so long.

Sacramento, California

Giti was up late watching the news when she noticed the headlights from Jaffar's car in the driveway. She looked out through the blinds and saw him get out of the car with his briefcase and overnight bag. A knot tightened in her stomach. During the last month Giti had put on some weight as her body changed shape. She still wasn't too big, but to her the change was very apparent.

But beyond than that, in her heart she had still not forgiven Jaffar for what he had done. A child should be created in love, but this child had been created through domination. It was not right. She knew she would love and care for any child she brought into the world. But would he? Sometimes he was so loving ... but other times he was so cold. Her marriage was not what she had expected it to be and it troubled her.

Jaffar unlocked the front door and entered the living room. "Hello, Giti. I'm surprised to see you still awake!" He put his bags down on the floor and crossed the room to give his wife a kiss and a hug.

"Hello, Jaffar. I'm happy to see you." She held him as close to her as she dared and turned her head, redirecting his kiss onto her cheek. "I couldn't sleep. I'm not feeling very well. I think I might have the flu," she told in explanation of why she would not meet his lips.

"Oh I hope not," Jaffar said. "You need to get lots of rest if you are sick! I think you should go to bed. I will sleep in the spare room downstairs."

"That might be best. I've got to work in the morning."

"I'm going to have a shower before going to bed." Jaffar gave Giti another kiss on the cheek. "Good night."

Giti lay in bed a few minutes later. She could hear Jaffar shuffling around in the bathroom, and when he turned on the shower. His arrival home wasn't totally unexpected. During the week, he had called to say that he might be home in the next couple of days. What surprised her was that his arrival was unwelcome.

She rolled over and thought about what she had expected their marriage to be. She wondered if she had been blind. Zafar tried to tell her that Jaffar was not as sweet as he seemed—but he had been sweet to *her*—now he was often indifferent and preoccupied with business. She felt he was keeping secrets from her and he generally got very angry when she asked him about his day-to-day activities. It felt like he was living a completely different life than she was and that he was coming home only to shower, change and pretend he loved her.

She sighed and rolled over. Unexpectedly, she remembered the man who had helped her get her shopping cart unstuck so long ago. He had such a nice smile. He seemed kind. Jaffar had seemed that way for so long. What had happened? Now he seemed haunted and angry most of the time. In truth, she was a little frightened of him.

Slowly, despite her heightened anxiety, she drifted off to sleep.

December 8, 1980

Giti awoke early after a very restless night. No one else was awake yet. She quickly showered and dressed, picking an outfit that would best hide her fuller figure. She would have to tell Jaffar about her pregnancy this week, while he was home—something of a rarity lately.

He came into the kitchen as she and Sina were leaving. "What, leaving me so soon?" he asked.

"I have to work and Sina has school," she said hastily as she quickly kissed his cheek.

Truthfully, Jaffar was glad to be left alone to take care of business. He'd already called the Bendix Corporation in Indiana, along with several others on the list Joe Sutton had given him the previous day. He received assurances from all that the orders would be filled and shipped before the Christmas break, with delivery before year's end.

It was obvious that work on the jet would take the better part of December. However, to meet this deadline Jaffar would have to make more progress on getting the engine replacement. He opened his briefcase again, found his address book and quickly dialed.

"Hello. This is the Embassy of the Islamic Republic of Iran," said a voice in English.

"Yes, could you please connect me with the media affairs office, extension two-two-five?"

"One moment, please."

"Hello, this is media affairs. Behrouz Kholm speaking. How can I help you?"

"Behrouz? Jaffar Hamid Harraj here."

"Yes, Jaffar."

"It's been a while since I talked to you. Can you give me any more information on the matter we talked about?"

"There's nothing new at the moment. I will, of course, call if anything develops. Can I reach you at the same number?"

"No! You can call me at home."

"Of course, Excellency."

Camp Pendleton, California

Just after ten o'clock in the morning, the wheels of a Lockheed C-130 screeched to a halt as the behemoth settled onto the runway of Munn Field at the United States Marine Corps air facility, where Jack, Donny and the other twelve men would spend the remainder of their training—guests of the United States Marine Corps.

Jack walked down the ramp at the rear of the aircraft. He looked up at the blue sky and the mountains that surrounded the base and inhaled deeply. He could smell the scent of the ocean, carried inland off the Pacific.

"Look at the color of that sky, Don." It had been almost 15 years since they were last here.

"Yeah, blue sky, not the shitty gray I'm used to!" The unit walked toward the truck that would first take them to meet the base commander and then to their barracks, where they would be billeted for the duration of their stay.

Part of their task at Pendleton was to work alongside marine security, where they would oversee security measures for the base. Their squad, along with the marines, would then be instructed regarding how to enhance regular security features when external threats exceeded the base's security capability.

That afternoon, in conditions that were completely opposite of those of the previous day, the squad walked along a ridge line trail, between Talega

Creek and San Mateo Creek, near the northern boundary of the base. Camp Pendleton was slightly smaller than Fort Bragg and the geography varied from oceanfront to bush-covered hills. It was ideal for every kind of training—from sea-to-shore maneuvers, to mountain warfare and special forces operations.

Sergeant Joseph Riggs, a big ex-marine and an eight-year veteran was point on today's march. During his training, he had been stationed at Camp Pendleton and he knew the place well.

Jack yelled ahead to the Sergeant, "Hey, Riggs!"

"Yo!"

"How does your little song go?"

Joe had been waiting for someone to ask that very question. In fact he was surprised it had taken this long. He started singing *'Surfer Joe'* at the top of his lungs. Startled, a pair of quail noisily took to the air, flying across the trail directly in front the squad. Joe never missed a beat, and continued singing.

The whole squad joined in with the chorus, in time with the cadence of their march. Jack was sure that they could be heard all the way down the hill to Oceanside.

Three hours later they marched past O'Neill Lake on their left and approached the base. They had made it through almost two dozen renditions of the *'Ballad of the Green Berets'* and *'Surfer Joe'*.

Sacramento, California

Fatemah and Zafar came to pick up Sina, so that he could have a sleep-over.

"Why do I have to have a sleep-over during the week?"

Zafar looked over at his wife and smiled. "We want to leave your mom and Jaffar alone. They haven't been able to see much of each other lately, and they need to spend some time alone together."

In a moment right out of the Art Linkletter Show, Sina asked, "Do they want to do the wild thing?" Although they didn't want to encourage their nephew, both Zafar and Fatemah laughed until they had tears in their eyes.

Zafar wiped his face, "Where did you hear that from?"

"From Matthew. He was talking about where babies come from."

"Oh!" Fatemah looked at Zafar, who was carefully studying Sina in the rearview mirror. "What made you talk to Matthew about this?"

"I told him about my mom."

"Oh! What did you say about your mom?"

"I told Matthew that my mom might be pregnant. She's been barfing a lot and getting big. Just like Miss Cassidy did last year."

"Well Sina, that's something that some women don't want to talk about."

"Why?"

"Because they are very sensitive about it."

"Is that why Mrs. Cassidy didn't tell us?"

"Probably. That's also part of the reason why your mom and Jaffar have to talk."

"Yeah. He's sure been away a lot."

Zafar shook his head. "That is something for another day." He tried to change the subject. "What do you want for Christmas?" he asked. "I remember last year that you wanted the Millennium Falcon or a light sabre."

"Yeah. I'll write out my list for you tonight."

Giti had made reservations for the Espanol Restaurant, the first dine-in restaurant Jaffar had taken her to—the place where they had lunch a year ago.

Since Zafar and Fatemah had come to get Sina an hour ago, Giti had spent the time getting ready for dinner. She put on her earrings and called out, "Jaffar, I'll be five more minutes."

"Alright! I'm ready." Jaffar had been ready for over half an hour and now he impatiently waited. He had difficulty understanding why Giti had such a problem being ready on time. All the women in Al-Qa'im Jaffar had been with dared not be late the way she did!

Jaffar drove while Giti cheerily gave directions— something else Jaffar didn't approve of. He knew the way and did not need to be told. Yet she told him anyway. It was a woman's place to be silent. He tried not to let it bother him. American women were different. He knew that.

"Did you say Zafar and Fatemah were going to take Sina directly to school?" he asked as pleasantly as he could.

"Yes, as a bonus I've got tomorrow off!" She was happy to think that perhaps she and Jaffar could use the time to reconnect and that all her worrying about her marriage had been for nothing.

"Zafar has treated you well, hasn't he?" Jaffar mused. She nodded. Jaffar did not see the reason for Giti to work. Both her financial situation, as well as his, had continued to improve over the past year. Even with her payout socked away, he had more than enough for both of them. He would have to correct this as soon as he had launched his plane! She was too independent. It was not comely in a woman.

Jaffar parked the car and as Giti and he walked around the corner to the restaurant, Jaffar recognized the establishment. "This is where I took you for lunch so long ago!"

"Surprise!" Giti said. She looked at the clock as they stepped inside the front vestibule. "And with six minutes to spare."

The hostess who greeted them, "Do you have a reservation?"

"Yes! Under Harraj." Giti looked over at Jaffar. He was surprised. Giti had originally made the reservation under the name of Roshtti, but corrected it, remembering how much aggravation it caused Jaffar that she had not yet changed her surname. *No point in upsetting him*, she thought. *Tonight will be difficult enough as it is!*

Jaffar smiled at the hostess, who showed them the way to their table. "Would you like anything to drink?"

"Nothing for me thanks. Just water," said Giti.

"And for you, Sir?"

Jaffar quickly scanned the wine list from the table. "I'll have a liter of the Hunter Estates Amarone." Giti thought, *that's good! Jaffar is usually in a much more amicable mood when he's had a bit of wine.*

The waitress came to the table, filled their glasses with ice water and then took their dinner order. Both Giti and Jaffar ordered the Chicken Parmigiana.

During dinner, Giti could tell the wine was having the desired effect. Jaffar was not used to alcohol and he started slurring his words slightly. She was tempted to order another half-liter of wine, but thought better of it. She didn't think she could manage to carry him up the front steps of the house.

"Jaffar, I noticed when we entered the restaurant you seemed surprised that I made the reservations under the name of Harraj."

"Yes, I was a bit surprised. No! I was more than a bit surprised."

"I know you have always been disappointed that I haven't changed my last name. I've explained that I wanted to wait until Sina finishes school."

"I know—you explained it before. But it seems wrong for a man's wife to bear a different man's name." He took a big swallow of wine.

She took his hand and smiled at him. "Harrij is a wonderful name," she said, "and that is a good surname for your new son or daughter, don't you think? What surname would you like for your new son or daughter?"

Some nearby patrons caught wind of the conversation between Giti and Jaffar and most of the talk in the vicinity suddenly ceased.

"What?" Jaffar said, his eyes wide.

Giti was sure Jaffar could hear her, especially in the now-quiet dining room. She repeated herself just the same. "I said, what surname would you like for your new son or daughter?"

"Are you going to have a baby?"

"Yes!"

Jaffar smiled widely. "That's excellent news!" he said as he got up and unsteadily walked around the table so he could hug his wife. "When?"

Giti was still stunned by his joy. She had agonized for weeks about what about how to tell him and what he would say. He had been so distant—both physically and emotionally—that she was certain he would see a baby as an intrusion in his life and be angry.

"When is the child due?" he demanded excitedly. "When will I meet my child?"

"Doctor Phillips told me in May, around the twenty-fourth."

"It will be spring. A good time for a male to be born!"

"You sound so sure that it will be a boy!"

"Of course!" he said. "All children born to my family in the spring are male."

Giti smiled, relieved. "We'll see when the time comes. I'm sure Sina would like a baby brother to play with."

"As you say, we'll see."

He hugged her again.

December 9, 1980

It was good Giti had been allowed the day off. She awoke dog-tired though she'd had a restful sleep. It was certainly due to the late night the evening before, coupled with her being four months along in her pregnancy.

With Sina, Giti had been very sick early on but felt better the closer the due date got. She hoped that this would be the case again.

Today, she was sure she felt much better than Jaffar. During dinner, despite her protests, Jaffar had managed to drink an additional bottle of Amarone as the nice couple at the table beside them insisted on buying them a second bottle. Giti had smiled politely as they insisted, knowing the consequences. She could still hear Jaffar saying to them, "Oh, why thank you very mush."

As if on cue, she heard Jaffar slowly climb the stairs from the downstairs guest room. He poked his head around the corner. "Good morning Jaffar. How do you feel?" She looked closer through tired eyes and realized she need not have asked the question … Jaffar, in the current vernacular, looked like shit.

"I don't feel that well."

"You shouldn't feel that well. You had not one, but two bottles of wine!" Giti didn't really blame him for celebrating a little bit. "Why don't you go have a shower and get dressed? I will put on some tea and fix you some breakfast."

Jaffar rubbed his stomach through his robe. "No, no breakfast for me. I don't think my stomach could take it."

"Oh! So you are human after all!" Jaffar withdrew to the bathroom, knowing he wasn't in any condition to spar with his wife.

Sacramento, California - December 18, 1980

"Giti, I've got to go back to Salt Lake City for a few more days."

"But, Jaffar you were just there for almost a month!" she protested.

"Don't worry. I will be home to spend Christmas with you and Sina. When is his last day of school?"

"He's off school on next Tuesday. At noon!"

"The 23rd of December? That's late, isn't it?"

"He has some extracurricular activities he will wrap up with his model airplane club, as well as some end-of-term celebrations." Then she said, "Oh, Jaffar, do you have to go?" For the past ten days things had been almost normal around the house and all the doubts Giti had experienced over the past several months had disappeared.

"Giti, it's only for a few days. The work there is almost done."

"And then you're finished?"

"Yes, I'm going to retire. I told you that the other day." The Jaffar added, "And so will you!"

Wendover, Utah - December 19, 1980

When Jaffar arrived at Wendover, he found Joe Sutton working with Abdul and Sameed to remove the plastic wrap and tie-down straps from a skid of boxes that had just arrived.

"Is this the last of them, Abdul?"

"No, Excellency. The driver is returning to Salt Lake City to pick up the last pallet. He said he didn't have room when he loaded, but insisted we'd have it by the end of the day."

"They told me it would all fit when I ordered it—they better get it to us on time. How's everything else going, Mr. Sutton?"

"With Sameed's help, I've managed to install most of the components that arrived yesterday morning. However, I must wait for the last shipment before going any father with the reassembly."

Jaffar was frustrated with the delay but could say nothing to Joe. He pulled Abdul aside. "How's it really going?"

"Sameed said everything is going well. As Sutton has said, everything fits like a glove."

"That's good news. I won't stand for any more delays. After the airplane is put back together it must be tested."

"Sameed told me this won't be any trouble. With the progress made during the last day or two, the plane will be ready to go by New Year's Day. What about the engine?"

"I'm working on it!"

"Sutton told me you have a new engine for us. Is this true?" Abdul was upset that Jaffar had not bothered to tell him, but had instead confided in the American, the infidel, the enemy.

"Yes! I'm still working on it. I've got some more details to work out."

"I should have ..." Abdul hesitated, "I could have been told."

"I do not need to discuss every detail of this operation with you," Jaffar said sharply. "I still have to finalize many details. You will be told when and where I feel the time is right."

"Yes, Excellency." Abdul watched Jaffar walk away toward his office, angry that once again he was being treated so poorly by Jaffar. This had been going on for many years, but seemed to be getting worse since he'd decided to meet and marry an American. It was like he no longer cared as much about the cause. Was it possible Jaffar wanted to put down roots here? Was it possible he actually loved that woman? Abdul thought it unlikely; after all, Jaffar could have any woman he wanted back home. Yet it seemed he had been distancing himself from home and from Abdul. Jaffar has been robbing Abdul of responsibility lately, assigning security duties to Hamid and his men was one example.

Abdul was bitter. It was becoming increasingly apparent that he was nothing more than a glorified errand boy to Jaffar.

— Chapter 19 —

December 30, 1980

Abdul called Jaffar's Sacramento number. As the phone rang on the other end he looked at his watch; it was very early in the morning, but he'd waited as long as he dared. He was certain Jaffar would want this news as soon as possible—as a matter of fact Jaffar had insisted this be the case. After about 20 rings, Abdul gave up. He would try again a little later. There was little he could do for now except wait and make certain that all was well with the aircraft.

"Sutton, are you sure everything is ready with the plane?"

"Of course. With the exception of an in-flight test, the aircraft flight controls are ready to go. I just made the last few, small modifications on the cockpit instruments this morning."

"So, there is nothing more to do?"

"Oh, yes! There's much to do. The most urgent item is the procurement of a proper functioning turbo fan for the aircraft."

"What? Oh, you mean getting a new engine."

"Oh yes, Jaffar and I have already discussed this."

"I know." Abdul turned and walked away. He recalled his conversation with Jaffar a few days earlier. Except for his daily trips to escort Mrs. Sutton to and from the hangar, Abdul had barely ventured outside, preferring to stay inside the offices that served as living quarters for himself, Jaffar, Hamid and of course Mr. Sutton.

Whenever Abdul ventured outside, the cold wind seemed to pass right through him, no matter how many layers of clothing he wore. He was anxious to have all this nonsense over with so he and Jaffar could return home. This was the longest Abdul had been away from Al-Qa'im and, while he didn't miss the dusty little town and wasn't homesick, he did miss the familiarity of Al-Qa'im. There, he and everyone else knew his role; he was chief of police, he was an important man. Here in the high desert of Utah, not only was it cold and the ways of world unfamiliar, but he was just a flunky for Jaffar, not his right-hand man. At the thought of his unfair treatment, an unwelcome shiver passed through him.

Abdul sat in Jaffar's office for almost an hour until it was once more time to call his boss. This time Jaffar answered after just a few rings. "Hello?"

"Jaffar, I have good news for you."

"Abdul! Have you looked at your watch?"

Instantly Abdul looked about the hangar for cameras, wondering how Jaffar knew he'd done just that. "Yes, I have looked at my watch. Why!"

"Because if you had, then you'd know it was six o'clock in the fucking morning! Giti is sleeping and she can't be disturbed!"

"I'm sorry Jaffar, but I have good news for you."

"Could this not wait? I have had a very long, sleepless night—in the hospital."

"Oh!" This caused Abdul to hesitate for a moment. "I hope everything is good."

"Giti was unwell last night and asked me to take her to the hospital. There was blood. We thought the baby was coming early."

"It was wise to go to the hospital, Jaffar." Abdul said.

"Anyway Abdul, what is this good news that you have for me that couldn't wait?"

He sounds frustrated. Perhaps he needs this good news, Abdul thought. "You asked me to call you, to let you know when the plane was ready."

"And is it?"

"Yes, Excellency. Sutton …"

"Abdul!!" Jaffar yelled into the receiver, cutting him off mid-sentence. "I will call you later today." He slammed the phone down. "What a fool," he said out loud. He was very tired. Abdul had been right to call about the jet. The timing was just a bit difficult. Jaffar went upstairs to check on Giti. She was sound asleep.

Earlier, they had rushed to the hospital because Giti had been spotting. Jaffar had been terrified at the thought of losing his son, his strong and perfect son. An ultrasound revealed no problems; the fetal heartbeat was strong and normal. The doctor prescribed rest and a follow-up visit in the morning.

Jaffar was pleased to hear about the jet and, as tired as he was, he knew he had to get to work. Giti was sound asleep so Jaffar went into his office to make the long-awaited phone call. It would be after nine in the morning in Ottawa, Canada.

"Behrouz Kholm. How can I help you?"

"Behrouz. Jaffar Harraj speaking."

"Yes, Jaffar. What can I do for you?"

"Is everything ready for us?"

"Yes! As I told you last week I have several qualified men who will be at your disposal. When do you want them ready?"

"They are to be ready today! We will go tomorrow, just before New Year's Eve. They can meet my men at the main entrance."

"Farouk and his men will be there."

"You serve Allah well."

"Thank you, Excellency."

Jaffar had just two more calls to make then he could get some sleep. First, he called Abdul back.

"Abdul," he said when the man answered. "I'm going to make this call as brief as possible. I want you to go to my desk and open the bottom, right-hand drawer. I want you to read the contents of the large brown folder that is in there very carefully. I will call you back in 20 minutes to answer any questions you have."

When Jaffar hung up, as instructed, Abdul opened the folder and read through it once and then started to read through it a second time. The phone rang, "Yes?" he said.

"Do you have any questions?"

"Yes, Jaffar, two or three."

"What are they?"

"Where do I meet the Iranians?"

"At the entrance to the motel."

"Which gate do we go in?"

"They will know which one!"

"Who shall I take with me?"

"Take only Hamid. Is that all?"

"When do you want us to leave?"

"The two of you have to leave within the hour. I have made all the arrangements with Behrouz. This has to be done by tomorrow night at midnight. It's New Year's Eve and the security will be lacking. The Americans like their alcohol far too much to pay the attention to that."

"Yes, Excellency." Abdul hung up the phone. He summoned Hamid and handed the folder to him. He watched Hamid scan the contents and began to feel the true gravity of this situation. The consequences of failure could be most grave.

Passing through the gates of Wendover and leaving the safety of the airfield behind, Hamid and Abdul first headed west into Nevada and then southwest towards California. As Hamid drove along the snowy, windswept interstate, Abdul once again read through the material from Jaffar, information that he'd been ignorant of just a few hours earlier. As he did so, some of the more subtle aspects of Jaffar's plan became quite clear. "Very good, Excellency, very good."

Hamid quickly looked over at Abdul, "What?"

"It's nothing, Hamid. Pay attention to your driving. You don't want to be killed in an accident and be meeting Allah this day, do you?"

At about the halfway point in their trip, Hamid pulled off to the shoulder to let Abdul drive. For almost four hours Abdul and Hamid travelled south towards Las Vegas until a small, white sign on the shoulder indicated that they were crossing into Clark County.

"Abdul, the left turn is in about four miles."

"I know Hamid, I see the sign. It's hard to miss in this God-forsaken land." Abdul still harbored resentment for his passenger, but in light of the fact that both of them would have to work together closely on this next part of the project, Abdul decided it would be best if these feelings were set aside for the time being. It was likely they would have to depend on each other's abilities, perhaps even for their very lives.

Abdul turned left on Route 168, towards Moapa River and Interstate 15. After another ten minutes a Motel 6 came into view. Abdul glanced at his watch. Right on time.

The parking lot was full and the neon sign indicated there were no vacancies. This puzzled Abdul until he realized they were only 50 miles or so from Las Vegas. Close enough to the bright lights, but far enough for room rates to be still reasonable. Abdul pulled the pickup over to shoulder and stopped. He looked over at Hamid who was busy scanning the lot for a van that matched the description Jaffar had given him. "Do you see it?"

"No, Abdul, I do not. Wait! There it is." Hamid looked to see if there was anyone inside the van then noticed a sliding door open. A man got out and walked in the direction of the road, but Hamid was still uncertain if this was their contact.

The man was dressed in denim jeans and a plaid shirt. As he got closer one could see his face had the appearance of darkened, old leather. On his feet he wore an old pair of cowboy boots. Only one thing looked out of place; the gleaming silver tip on the pointed toe of each boot.

Hamid watched the man walk onto the road past their white truck. The man appeared to be nothing more than one of the locals, perhaps from the Indian reservation nearby—but then suddenly the driver's door opened and the man said clearly in Arabic, "Move over. I'll drive."

Startled, Abdul just sat there. "Quickly!" the man said, and this time Abdul obliged and the stranger slid onto the seat. He started the truck and drove south, silently. Hamid watched in the side mirror as the old Dodge van pulled out of the parking lot and took up a position a few hundred yards behind.

They turned right onto Hidden Valley Road. Every ten seconds the driver would check his rear- and side-view mirrors nervously. Once they were on the Interstate, Abdul saw the man relax; he checked his surroundings much less frequently.

"I am Abdul and this in Hamid." For several more minutes the man drove on silently.

"I am Farouk Aziz." The stranger said shattering the awkward silence. "I'm sorry I could not talk earlier but I was concentrating. I had to make certain we were not being followed. We can't be careful enough. Now, everywhere the Americans see people from the Middle East, they see Iranians, very dangerous."

"Are you a friend of Jaffar?"

"No and also yes. Anyone who is an enemy of the Americans is our friend."

"Where are we going?"

"Relax, my friend. My men have had the targets under watch for many days. We will meet them later at the safe house."

"When are we going to begin the operation?"

"You ask many questions, Abdul. Sit back and enjoy the ride. All your answers will come later. Relax like your friend, Hamid."

Abdul could tell that Farouk wasn't willing to engage in any more conversation. He looked once more at the folder from Jaffar, but after a minute closed it again and did as Farouk suggested. He just looked out the window at the scenery.

As they approached Las Vegas, Abdul could see several airplanes take off from the left side of the freeway. "What are those?" he asked, indicating the grey-colored ones that were quickly climbing away.

"They are jets from Nellis Air Force base."

After a few minutes Abdul could see the high rises of Las Vegas looming in the distance. They continued into Vegas and through the city center, but as the two vehicles travelled south towards the outskirts of the city, Farouk once again became vigilant looking at the road behind, checking for signs of being tailed.

The two vehicles each took one of the last two exits within the city limits and circled the block in a practiced maneuver. Then they each re-entered the interstate a minute later and resumed their respective positions.

They continued into the most southern portion of the state of Nevada. Just shy of the California border, Farouk took the exit onto Route 53 and then onto a small, two-lane road. He further veered onto a single-lane dirt road that snaked over and around several small hills, with the van close behind.

Abdul spotted an ancient-looking tractor in the distance and the shape of a man standing next to it. As they got closer, Abdul noticed the man held a Kalashnikov assault rifle, with its distinctive curved magazine underneath, in his hands. Farouk gave him a wave as the pickup passed.

"There's our safe house for the night," Farouk said, indicating a small house near the end of the road. Abdul now understood that the dirt road was a private, mile-long driveway.

The house looked to be about the same vintage as the Massey Ferguson tractor in the field; the siding was weathered to silver-grey, with rust streaks trailing from the nails that held the boards them to the framing beneath. The large barn at the terminus of the driveway was in a similar state of neglect.

"When will we get to the airfield?" Abdul asked.

"We will stay here tonight. Tomorrow we travel to the targets … but enough questions for now. We will discuss this later. Go into the house." Abdul and Hamid got out and Farouk drove past the house and into the barn. After his passengers had disembarked, the driver of the van did the same.

Camp Pendleton, California - December 30, 1980

It was another warm, sunny afternoon in Southern California. In less than three weeks, President Elect Ronald Reagan was to be sworn in. There was much optimism around the base and indeed around the country as a whole; the coming year would surely be better than the last.

The camp commander, Lieutenant General Gary Roy, had requested that both Jack and Donny be in his office at precisely 0800 hours. They were sitting outside his office at ten minutes to eight. A pretty blonde corporal sat at her desk typing—or at least trying to type.

Jack quietly stared at the general's closed office door, waiting for it to open. Donny sat next to him. Jack noticed the young corporal smiling at Donny. He gently tapped the side of Donny's boot with his toe and grinned at him. As usual, the chicks seem to gravitate toward Donny. Donny had an unquantifiable quality that drew women toward him like a magnet. It was a source of wonder for Jack. It wasn't because Don was extremely handsome; many men were more handsome … but they didn't have what Don had. In a room full of men, women would gravitate toward him, completely ignoring other men—sometimes including their own dates—just like moths to a flame. Perhaps it was pheromones, but whatever it was, Donny had it.

At precisely eight o'clock, the door to the general's office opened. Jack and Donny quickly rose to their feet and stood at attention. The general stood in his doorway. "Come in, gentlemen."

"Yes, sir." The pair followed Lieutenant General Roy into his office. Both trainees were surprised to see Colonel Hart off to one side of the office. Jack and Donny saluted their commanding officer. Colonel Hart had instructed all his men that such formalities were unnecessary under normal circumstances. However in cases such as this, military decorum demanded it. Colonel Hart returned their salute.

"Good morning, gentlemen. Have a seat." All four men did so.

"Gentlemen! I called you here because you are entering the last three weeks of your training. I want you to work closely with Colonel Hart for the duration."

"Yes, sir."

"This morning the Colonel and I have been discussing some of the items that still need to be addressed. Colonel Hart, they are all yours."

"Thank you, General." Colonel Hart handed Jack and Donny a brief that covered their training. He gave the two of them a few minutes to read the 12-page document.

"On page three you can see the objectives for this week." Both men flipped to the proper page. "Jack, you and Donny are most familiar with the personnel who have been training with you. Can you give us some additional ideas regarding this week's training?"

Both Jack and Donny pondered the question for a few minutes. Then Jack turned over the handout and wrote down a brief description of the exercises he thought would be of the most use to the unit along with an equipment list. Don took the paper from him, read what Jack had written and added his own notes. Then he handed it to the colonel.

Colonel Hart read over the paper, his left eyebrow arched, but said nothing. He simply handed it to the general. By the reaction of the general, it was clear both senior officers were surprised by the content of Jack's and Donny's suggestions, not to mention pleased. After about a half hour of discussion the three officers from NATA and the marine base commander came to a consensus regarding the logistics of the new training regime.

"Put things in motion, Lieutenant. The Colonel and I will make the necessary arrangements on our end. That will be all, gentlemen, dismissed!"

"Yes, sir." Jack and Donny saluted and left.

"Well Colonel you are definitely correct about Lieutenant Coward. I can see why you fought so hard to recruit him into your organization. He's got a very keen mind."

Colonel Hart reflected back over the years and remembered the often frustrating attempts, to lure Jack out of private life. He smiled, knowing he had won a huge victory. "Both those men will be an enormous asset to both NATA and their country," he said.

Southwest Nevada - December 31, 1980

As the evening wore on, it became apparent to Abdul and Hamid that Jaffar and Farouk had spent many weeks putting this operation together; the planning on the part of the Iranians was nearly perfect. It was unfortunate that Jaffar was forced to use the Iranians and not his own resources, but they had gathered more intelligence and were obviously much more familiar with the targets. The discussion about the operation lasted until the wee hours of the morning. Abdul and Hamid dropped into their cots, exhausted.

Before the sun had a chance to rise above the nearby hills, Abdul heard voices outside the house, near the barn. It was hard to believe someone was actually awake at this hour. He recognized the voice of Farouk, but was unsure who he was talking to.

Abdul listened for several more minutes. A vehicle started and he heard the sound of tires on gravel beside the house. He assumed this was the van that had tailed them the day before, since he'd seen only two vehicles on the property. The van idled quietly down the driveway towards the road, leaving only silence in its wake. Abdul closed his eyes to try and get some more sleep. Today was going to be a long day, certainly much longer than the previous one.

Camp Pendleton

Along with Sergeant Riggs, Private Sam Jacobson was assigned to guard the San Luiz Rey gate. Having the big ex-marine with him made the duty a lot less stressful. It wasn't just that the sergeant was sure to intimidate any intruders with his massive size and intimidating presence, but he also had a great sense of humor and an easy-going nature. Besides, it was New

Year's Eve day and the mood around the Camp was relaxed, so Jacobson was happy with his shift.

The mood of the occupants inside the van traveling northbound on I-5, however, was very tense and few words were exchanged. The van turned onto State Highway 76. It was just a few miles until the turn onto College Boulevard. They were certain that with the hours of planning they had put in, the execution of their plan would be smooth and their goals would be achieved.

Private Jacobson watched the van approach on Vandegrift Boulevard. He glanced towards Riggs, who was just calling in his quarter-hourly check-in. He'd just reported all was quiet.

The van looked quite ordinary. It was equipped with front and rear spoilers, fender flares and wide, after-market tires. It looked as though it could use a wash and Jacobson noticed a wisp of steam escaping from the front grill.

The van stopped at the steel barrier. The young marine walked confidently toward the vehicle, his right hand resting on his holstered sidearm. He looked at the driver and passenger—a man and a woman—who were both wearing brightly-colored Hawaiian shirts. They looked harmless and lost.

The driver was deeply-tanned and wore a baseball cap and sunglasses. His blond, equally-tanned female companion wore sunglasses but no hat. She smiled winningly at Jacobson. At first glance there didn't appear to be passengers in the rear, but as he got closer he saw the silhouette of at least one more person.

"Can I help you, Sir?" Jacobson asked.

"Yes, I think I'm lost. I was going south on the highway towards South Carlsbad Beach. I passed it, I think."

Jacobson looked over his shoulder, "Sergeant Riggs! These folks are looking for South Carlsbad Beach."

Riggs came over and appraised the van and its occupants.

"You've got to go back to the Interstate and go south about seven miles," he said.

"Can I turn around here?" the driver asked.

"No, sir. You've got to back up and turn around over there," Riggs said, pointing to a wide area on the other side of the road.

"Thanks," the driver said as he shifted the van into reverse and began to inch back. A silenced pistol suddenly appeared in the right hand of the passenger and all anyone nearby heard were two quiet puffs. A crimson patch appeared on the chests of both Private Jacobson and Sergeant Riggs followed by a brief look of surprise as both men fell to the ground and were still.

The passenger opened the door and ran inside the gatehouse to activate the button that opened the gate and the bodies of both guards were dragged inside, out of sight. Once the passenger was safely back inside the van, the driver accelerated towards the camp headquarters and the airfield.

Las Vegas, Nevada

At the southeast side of McCarran International Airport, Abdul and two of Farouk's men waited inside a stolen United Parcel Services van, observing the action around them. Their job was to observe movements in and out of the American Airlines Corporation hangar. The hangar, almost a mile distant, dwarfed almost every other building within many miles. The hangar was one target of a two-pronged plan concocted by Jaffar and his Iranian friends. It was still twilight and it would be at least a couple of hours before action would be needed. As the evening darkened, a rotating amber light on each side of the hangar door began to flash. Then the huge right hand door started to slide open, revealing several passenger jets gleaming under the wash of overhead metal halide lights. A tug slowly moved an American Airlines 747 out into the desert night. It was quickly detached and the tug moved back inside the hangar.

Even 3,000 feet away the panels of the van began to vibrate as the four Rolls Royce engines of the 747 started up in sequence. The noise became even louder as the jumbo jet turned around and started to move away, the exhaust pointed in their direction. It disappeared as the American jet moved around the far side of the hangar, towards its awaiting gate.

Just before midnight, a second van approached from the direction of the main cargo terminal. The driver flashed his headlights, the signal that they were to follow. The two vehicles drove to the hangar and parked. Farouk got out and walked over to Abdul. "Wait here until I signal," he said.

Silently, he opened an unlocked side door of the hangar and went inside followed by two men who had accompanied him in the van. All the men, including Abdul, wore uniforms that Farouk had supplied, making them largely indistinguishable from one another. In a few minutes, two of Farouk's men came out the van and escorted a woman through the door and into the hangar. Then Farouk motioned for Abdul to enter the building.

In sharp contrast to the exterior, the interior of the hangar was brightly illuminated, almost blindingly so. Abdul followed Farouk across the polished concrete floor directly toward an awaiting jet. A loud buzzer sounded, the enormous doors started to slide open. As they started up the boarding stairs Abdul shouted to Farouk, "Where is Hamid?"

"Hurry, I will tell you later. Get into the plane!" Abdul obeyed, climbing the stairs and entering the aircraft, passing the official Iranian State Seal as he did so. Abdul was taken into the passenger compartment and was seated opposite the woman that he'd seen exiting the van. From his former vantage point, he'd completely missed the fact that she was handcuffed.

"But where is Hamid?"

"Quiet! No names my friend."

"But …"

"Sit!" It wasn't a request, more like an order. "To answer you simply, he's returning to safe house to wait. Now, I must go. Good luck, my friend. Allahu Akbar!"

"Thank you." One of Farouk's men followed Farouk out of the plane and closed the outside cabin door. Before the guard returned to his seat Abdul felt the airliner lurch as the tug began to move it outside. The guard removed the handcuffs from the woman's wrists. In spite of being a prisoner in an extremely vulnerable position, she had a look of defiance about her, much like Mrs. Janette Sutton.

"Thank you for removing the handcuffs. They were beginning to become uncomfortable."

From the cockpit Abdul could faintly hear, "McCarran tower, this is Iranian Air Force Flight Zero One requesting permission to taxi."

"Roger Iranian Zero One. You are cleared to taxi to runway Zero Seven Left."

Ten minutes later the roar of the engines increased as the aircraft accelerated down the runway, the wheels thumping loudly as they crossed each joint in the concrete. The frequency increased swiftly to a rumble then quieted as the jet rose into the air.

January 1, 1981

Less than an hour after departing McCarran, Iranian Zero One radioed ahead to report a problem. "Salt Lake. This is Iranian Zero One out of Las Vegas. We are requesting an alternate airfield to Salt Lake."

"Roger Zero One. What's the problem?"

"We are starting to lose fuel at an unexpected rate."

"Roger Zero One. Are you declaring an emergency?"

"Negative, Salt Lake."

"Can you divert to Reno Lake Tahoe?"

After an intentional pause the pilot said, "Negative, Salt Lake."

"The nearest airfield is Wendover, a private airfield about 30 miles northwest."

"Can you provide us with a vector to Wendover?"

"Roger, Iranian Zero One. Turn left three-three-zero. Distance 28 miles."

"Roger, Salt Lake. Turn left three-three-zero." The two Iranian pilots knew exactly where they were. There was no fuel leak or problem of any sort. The Boeing had just had a complete overhaul courtesy of the United States government. The aircraft was only losing fuel because the pilots had actuated a valve to empty some of the excess fuel from the tanks. The plane didn't need all the fuel that had been loaded on board in Las Vegas and couldn't safely land with that much excess weight. It was all a ruse to get clearance to land at Wendover.

Since the tower at Wendover was not operating, the biggest problem the two pilots faced was landing with no guidance. They had flown over the abandoned base several times during the past three days, both during the day and night, to familiarize themselves with lights and landmarks, but only in a small two-seater aircraft.

"Do you think Jaffar will be able to get the lights working properly?" asked one of the pilots.

"If he doesn't, the landing will be very difficult," said the other.

Both men sat in silence, knowing this was indeed an understatement. It would be almost impossible.

Wendover Base, Utah

With the exception of the small town of West Wendover, there were very few lights or landmarks in this secluded corner of Utah. The airfield location was chosen for its isolation and this evening it was pitch black among the seemingly endless expanse of millions of acres.

"Sameed! I want you to help Abbas with the lights. We need them on in the next hour."

"Yes, Jaffar."

"What is taking you so long. You've been at this for hours?"

"We are working with antiques. Most of these lights have not been used for many years. At one time there were three runways and three sets of lights. Many modifications have been made over the years. We have not been able to get lights working on any of them."

"No! You must get lights working on only one. We cannot land a plane on two of the runways, they are broken up too much. You must turn on the lights only on the one upon which we landed our jet last fall."

"But, Excellency! We are having problems. For many weeks you have asked us to stay out of sight, not be noticed."

"You must get those lights on. We must help those pilots get that plane to a safe landing. I want you and the men to get them on, as well as any other lights on buildings."

"But, Excellency ..."

"Enough, Sameed! We've now got just fifty-five minutes. I don't want that plane to have any problems trying to land." Sameed ran off to continue the search for tools and equipment.

Sameed, Abbas and every other available man had been searching for additional electrical panels and circuit panels. None were found. With just twelve minutes until the plane was due to arrive, Sameed went to the corner office to tell Jaffar they had failed.

"Don't tell me that!" Jaffar was red-faced, screaming at Sameed. "You and your men have had all day to find them. Surely someone must know where they are! Maybe someone who built this place. Someone who works for the government!"

A light went on in Jaffar's head.

"That's it! Someone who works for the government must know! The man who sold me this place, that real estate agent." Jaffar went into his desk drawer to rummage for the name and number.

"Here it is. Tony Barnetson." Jaffar dialed the number that he'd been given, Tony's direct line. Jaffar wondered if this is what Tony had in mind when he'd said, "Call me any time of the day or night." The year was not yet an hour old.

Las Vegas, Nevada

The party was in full swing. The loud music thundered from the massive floor speakers that sat in each corner of the room. It seemed as though the bass would tear the condo down around the partiers.

The room was filled wall-to-wall with men and women who were almost all well past a state of inebriation. They had been watching the festivities of the Ninth Annual Dick Clark New Year's Eve Special from the Big Apple. All of them counted down the seconds as the red ball descended, bringing in the year 1981.

Tony Barnetson was fortunate to have heard his telephone ring at all because anyone trying to carry on a conversation amid the ruckus had to do so by yelling. For a moment he thought about ignoring it since he was pretty drunk, but he picked it up anyway. "Hello!" He yelled into the cordless phone.

Jaffar could hear the cacophony of noise in the background. He winced and pulled his ear away from the receiver; Tony's greeting physically hurt his ear in its intensity. "Mr. Barnetson, this is Jaffar."

Tony could barely hear anything through the phone, "Who?"

Jaffar yelled his answer into the phone, "It's Jaffar."

"Hold on. I can't hear you very well." He walked down the hallway of the posh suite, towards the bedrooms. Without knocking he entered one, closing the door behind him. From somewhere in the darkness, a woman said, "Hey, who is it? We were here first!"

"Just a minute while I take this call, lady." Tony put his ear to the phone once more. "Hello! This is Tony. Who is this?"

"This is Mr. Hodgeson, Jaffar Hodgeson."

"Yes, Jaffar. What can I do for you?" Tony wasn't so drunk that he didn't remember one of his best clients of the past year. He was, after all, using some of the commission he earned on the deal with Jaffar for this party tonight—booze and cocaine were on the house.

"I need to know where the runway light controls are right away," Jaffar said, clearly panicked.

"The runway lights? What do you need them for?"

"I have a plane coming in for a landing in about ten minutes. I've got to turn those lights on. Where are they controlled from?"

"From the tower of course."

"Of course!" Without even saying 'thank you' Jaffar hung up the phone in Tony's ear.

"Asshole!" Tony reached for the door handle to let himself out, but before he could leave, a hand reached out and pulled him back into the room. The light on the nightstand was suddenly switched on and the sight of two naked women greeted Tony.

"Come and join us."

Tony knew one of the girls. Her name was Candace. She'd never given him any indication that she was a switch-hitter. Tony looked from one girl to the other, then to the partially consumed lines of cocaine on the nightstand. "Oh, what the hell." He began to unbutton his shirt, but was stopped by Candace's friend, Charlene. Tony took advantage of the moment to reach over and lock the door. "We don't want any interruptions do we?" All three laughed.

Wendover, Utah

"Sameed, quickly! You and your men drive to the tower. The switches are there! Hurry!"

"Yes, Jaffar at once."

Twenty miles southwest of the field, it was clear to the pilots that they were flying into a sea of black. The Iranian jet dropped flaps and throttled back slightly to reduce airspeed in a last-ditch attempt to give Jaffar and his men as much time as possible to get the lights working. Even as they slowed, the jet ate up the interval between them at almost three miles a minute. They had at most eight minutes of flying time left, then they would be on their own. Fortunately the weather was cooperating, with clear skies and good visibility.

Only five minutes left and still no lights! The men looked at each other and then stared out the windscreen into the blackness, as if to will the lights on. Suddenly, "There. There's the runway!" They could see the airfield light up like a dazzling jewel in the black desert. "He's done it. Praise be to Allah!"

The plane settled smoothly onto the runway, which was covered in a light dusting of snow. The white powder was kicked up by the wake of the aircraft, white funnels trailed from the tips of both wings. Just after one o'clock on New Year's Day, the Boeing was guided into the hangar by a small column of trucks and cars. The doors were closed and the lights around the airfield were all hurriedly turned out. As the sounds of the engines faded, the outside world was once more a dark and quiet place, with the wind just barely audible in the vicinity of the hangar.

— Chapter 20 —

Wendover, Utah

All the men gathered in the hangar to stare at the newest arrival. "Someone quickly get the stairs in place." Jaffar shouted, a wide grin on his face, "Come on, quickly!"

The stair was pushed gently against the fuselage of the Iranian jet and the cabin door opened. Abdul looked down at the crowd that had gathered at the foot of the stairs. A loud cheer erupted from the men. Abdul smiled back. He walked slowly down the stairs to join the crowd, just happy to be on solid ground again. Almost everyone continued to stare up at the twin Boeing jets, which now were parked wingtip to wingtip.

It didn't take long for the grin to disappear from Jaffar's face. "I want you men to get the covers removed from the engine in preparation to remove it. It has to be cool enough to work on."

A moment later they were joined by the two pilots, followed immediately by a woman, who was blindfolded and handcuffed, led by two men in United Parcel uniforms. At the bottom of the stairs one the guards demanded, "Who is in charge here?"

"I am!" Jaffar stepped forward and embraced the stranger. He knew better than Abdul not to identify himself and simply said, "Hello, my brother. You look well." The room was filled with murmurs. No one had moved yet to work on the engine.

Jaffar looked at Abdul. "I want you to take our guest to her quarters. Building number twelve I think. I will go with you." He turned to look at the rest of the men. He clapped his hands loudly together. "The rest of you get to work on the airplane."

"Yes, Excellency!" The handcuffed woman was loaded into one of the company pickup trucks and driven in silence away from the hangar.

When they arrived at building twelve, Abdul unlocked the padlock and the door to the modified storage building was opened. "What is it? Who is it?" Mrs. Sutton was sitting upright on the bed. She'd been awakened earlier by the sound of an aircraft landing nearby. She could tell by the unmistakable sound of four engines that it was a jet and for a brief moment she thought she was back in Everett, at Boeing field.

"Mrs. Sutton, I'm sorry to disturb you at this late hour."

"Jaffar? What is it?" Janette Sutton thought immediately of her husband, remembering the incident last November. "Is Joe alright?"

"Yes, Mrs. Sutton. Your husband is fine. We've brought someone to keep you company ... How do you say it?" After a short pause, "Oh yes, we've brought you a roommate."

"A roommate? I don't understand."

Abdul unlocked the handcuffs and roughly pushed the newcomer into the center of the room.

"Mrs. Janette Sutton. I would like to introduce to you your new roommate, the former Empress Farah of Iran, wife of the dead Shah." The two men turned quickly and exited the room, leaving the two stunned women alone to get acquainted.

On the ride back to the hangar Jaffar said, "It's good to have you back, Abdul. This part of the mission has been a success." It was obvious by looking at Abdul that he had many questions.

"It's good to be back here, Jaffar. What is this about the Iranian? Is he really your brother?"

"He's my younger half-brother. He was born to my step-mother, several years after my own mother was murdered."

"How did he ...?"

"Enough talk for now my friend. We can continue this tomorrow. There is much work to do."

In the hangar, Sameed and Abbas were beginning to work on the number two engine on Jaffar's aircraft. They had wasted away the previous day searching unsuccessfully for the switches to activate the runway marker lights. If it had not been for the phone call to Tony, the outcome may not have been as favorable for Jaffar.

They took some time to study the manual for the correct procedure for the removal of the Pratt and Whitney engine. Joe Sutton was alongside to assist. He was more familiar with this aircraft than almost anyone else on the planet. Jaffar and Abdul walked across the hangar, past the aircraft.

"Sameed! What are you doing just sitting around? I need this plane back in the air today."

"But, Excellency, we need time to learn the way to take the engine out and put the other one in. It's very hard."

"That's what Mr. Sutton is here for. How long will this take?"

"The book says six hours. But Excellency, we are all very tired."

"I don't care to hear excuses. You needed an engine and I got you a bloody engine. Now do it." Jaffar looked at his watch. "You have until noon!"

"That's only ten hours and fifteen minutes. The other engine is still too hot to work on."

"Alright get two hours of sleep and then start working, but my deadline still stands."

"Why, Excellency? What is so important about this that you can't wait for a day or two?" This came from Abdul.

"The longer this aircraft sits here at Wendover, the more risk there is that someone is going to come and look for it. They might already be doing just that. It must be back in the air today."

"Yes, Excellency."

Just before nine o'clock Sameed and Abbas had the damaged Pratt and Whitney disconnected and lowered down out of its nacelle. The work had gone quickly despite their lack of sleep. Mr. Sutton continued to amaze both Sameed and Abbas with his stamina and drive. He was older than their combined ages but could still out-work both men. Even Abdul had pitched in to try to help.

While Sutton was over working on the engine on the Iranian jet, Abbas and Sameed discussed things. "What do you think Jaffar is going to do with the old man after he's finished?"

"I don't know. Kill him and his wife I think."

"You know, Sameed, that fate awaits us both. Jaffar is far from pleased with me and I think that once we finish with our jobs, our fate will be the same as theirs."

"What? No! We have worked hard. You know this."

"Maybe, but I have a plan. During our searches of the many buildings I have found some places where we can hide."

"Hide. What do you mean?"

"I mean *hide*. Maybe until we can think of what to do."

"But Abbas, how long can we stay in this place? What about food and water? Blankets, what about blankets? It's still very cold outside."

"Don't worry, Sameed, I have taken much food and water there over the last weeks, ever since Jaffar let me out of my prison. I will not let him kill me."

"He will if we don't finish this plane today. It may get us back in his grace once more." They wheeled the cradle that held the old engine off to one side of the hangar, out of the way. They repositioned it under the wing of the second jet.

Four hours later the hangar doors were opened once more. It was a warm winter day with the temperature hovering at a balmy fifty degrees, thanks to a high pressure system from the west. Jaffar's plane had been rolled out onto the concrete apron, the sun glinting off of its freshly painted skin. Jaffar stood next to Abdul and Sameed, looking over the aircraft. He was pleased that the jet, his jet, was now whole once again. Arrangements had been made for several thousand gallons of jet fuel to be delivered and loaded aboard the jet. From the west, the sound of a small jet could be heard. Three pairs of eyes scanned the clear sky. "There's our ride back to Las Vegas," said Jaffar.

Jeff Davies guided the Executive Air Lear 55 to a perfect landing. He loved flying the newest addition to the companies' fleet of aircraft. Since the Lear was new when acquired, Jeff considered it to be almost his own personal jet. He'd already had almost 400 hours in it.

Jeff exited down the five steps of the sleek little jet. "Good afternoon Mr. Hodgeson. It's good to see you again."

"It's good to see you as well. Thanks for coming on such short notice."

"It's my pleasure." Pleasure had nothing to do with it. Jaffar had wired him $10,000 a few days earlier. As soon as the bonus money was in his account he'd arranged with his company to use the jet. "Are you ready to go?"

"As soon as we get some equipment loaded," said Jaffar.

Sameed and Abdul loaded the remote station onto the Lear. It was designed to fit into a small plane, so getting it through the cabin door was no problem. While this was being done Jeff took a moment to check out the two jets on the ground. He'd spotted the Boeing 720 on his approach to Wendover. It was hard to miss, the sun gleaming off the white fuselage with it green and red stripes, one above and one below the windows.

But then Jeff did a double-take. He knew a little bit of Arabic because he'd studied international relations in university. When he focused on the stripes, he suddenly realized that they weren't stripes at all, but were instead a stylized version of the words Allahu Akbar (God is Great) repeated over and over, from the cockpit windows, down the entire length of the fuselage.

"I thought you were going to keep the jet for yourself, for your company jet?" he asked Jaffar.

"Oh, it's not my jet. I'm just servicing it for some associates." Jeff was fairly sure he was lying; had already noticed the unusual wear pattern on the tire of the front landing gear. It was the same pattern that he'd seen on the jet when it was parked at Mile High Aviation the previous summer. Jeff managed to sneak a peek inside the hangar and spotted the other jet inside. A quick look was all he needed. He noticed the empty engine nacelle and recalled the problems Jaffar's Boeing 720 had had during the trip to this airfield. *That's funny. Why would he lie?*

His curiosity piqued, he took a longer look at both planes. They were more than just similar; they were almost identical right down to the registration number on the vertical stabilizer. *Now that's too fucking weird.*

"Jeff! Are you ready?"

"I'll be right there." He sprinted past the parked 720 to his Lear.

There was a short delay while Jaffar and Sameed boarded the small jet. Jeff pulled the boarding stairs up after them and was just closing the door when the first engine on the Boeing spooled up. Jeff pulled back on the control column and the Lear lifted smoothly into the clear Utah sky. He banked left and circled Wendover. He watched the jet with the four working turbofans take off below him. He waited until the bigger jet passed him on the way to its cruising altitude then pushed the throttles forward and matched speed and course with the Boeing. Then he took up a position a mile behind and slightly above the jet. The two jets headed southwest at thirty-one thousand feet; conditions were perfect with clear skies.

"Alright Sameed, it's time to test out Mr. Sutton's remote controls."

Sameed switched the dial to the prearranged frequency and flipped the power switch to the 'on' position. The remote station came to life with a quiet hum. A mile and a half away, an amber light lit up on the instrument panel of the Boeing 720. A second later an adjacent green light came on, indicating that both sending and receiving units were linked and operational.

The Iranian pilot gingerly held the controls, not quite ready to relinquish full control. A moment later Sameed began to move his controls and watched as the jet slowly banked in the desired direction. Following Mr. Sutton's instructions, Sameed manipulated the controls carefully, banking the plane several times to the left and right. The pilots on board watched with both fascination and anxiety, as the jet was controlled remotely from the smaller jet, as if by magic.

Jeff, who was unaware of what was happening in the cabin of his airplane, watched in bewilderment as the Boeing 720 banked left and right, then climbed slightly and then descended. He watched as the jet accelerated and decelerated. The sequence was repeated several more times. Jeff switched to the radio frequency of the large jet and was greeted by static. The operation of the unit had the effect of blocking out all normal communications, a consequence Mr. Sutton had expected. It was specifically designed into the unit. Only one channel would work.

Maybe they are having some instrument problems, Jeff thought. For a second he considered accelerating ahead and trying to make visual contact with the pilot. He reset the radio to the previous frequency and then switched the intercom on. "Jaffar, can you come up to the cabin please?"

"Yes, Jeff what is it?"

"The pilot seems to be having problems with his controls, and I can't contact him on one hundred nineteen-point-nine Megahertz."

"What do you mean?"

"For the last ten minutes he's been banking left and right, climbing and descending, accelerating and then decelerating. It's totally weird." The word weird had been more prevalent in Jeff's vocabulary as of late.

"The pilots are probably just testing their controls. They had been having some issues with them before landing at Wendover."

"Oh, that explains it." Jaffar returned to the passenger compartment and closed the cockpit door behind him, leaving Jeff to wonder what was going on.

Bullshit, Jeff said to himself. *What pilot in his right mind would take off with flight control problems?* Then as suddenly as it had started, the 720 stopped its acrobatics and maintained smooth, controlled level flight, as if nothing had happened at all.

Now, that's too fucking weird! He thought about reporting what he'd seen, but he was being too well-paid to rock the boat so he decided to keep his mouth shut.

One hundred and fifteen miles out of Las Vegas, the secondary radar at McCarran International picked up two radar returns from the aircraft. It was New Year's Day and traffic was light. As the two jets moved closer to Las Vegas they entered the primary control area for air traffic control at the normally busy airport. The two aircraft were so close that the two blips were almost on top of one another.

Controller Sam Cooper was one of two air traffic controllers on duty. "Oh shit," he said under his breath. "McCarran Control to inbound aircraft bearing one-four-eight degrees at one-zero-zero miles, please squawk ident."

The Iranian pilot pushed the Ident button on his transponder and the blip bloomed on the radar display at ATC. "Thank you. Confirm your destination."

"This is Iranian Air Force Zero One Boeing 720, at three-one-thousand bound for McCarran."

"Roger Zero One. Be advised of traffic to your left. Turn right 20 degrees immediately and reduce altitude to 18,000 feet."

Sam was relieved to see that after a few moments the two radar returns gradually separated. "McCarran Control to inbound aircraft, bearing one-four-eight degrees at nine-zero miles. Squawk ident."

The radar blip brightened on the controller's screen. "Thank you. Confirm your destination."

"This is Executive Air Lear 55 Lima Tango Five Two inbound for McCarran."

"Roger Executive Five Two. Be advised of traffic in your area off to your right. Turn left to bearing one-six-five degrees. You are cleared into McCarran, runway two six."

"Roger, McCarran."

The rest of the flight was uneventful for both crews. Fourteen hours after Iranian Air Force Flight Zero One had departed, its counterfeit double rolled into the American Airways hanger. After shutting down the aircraft's systems, the two Iranian pilots disembarked the aircraft. They were two of only a select few who knew the truth about the jet.

A few minutes later, Jeff Davies taxied the Executive Airways jet to the South Terminal, and stopped adjacent to Executive's Las Vegas servicing hangar. Jaffar had hastily arranged to sublet warehouse space nearby, in which some of the remaining work on his jet would be carried out. In addition Jaffar was also arranging for the jet to be moved from its regular home in the American Airlines hanger to another hangar where work could proceed unimpeded and unnoticed. This was made easier by the fact that American Airlines were more than happy to have some of their limited hangar space back. All this was handled by Behrouz Kholm of the Iran consulate's media affairs office, the same official who had arranged the flight to Wendover with the Empress Farah aboard.

Jeff and Jaffar disembarked the Lear and walked into Executive's offices. Hamid was waiting there for Jaffar. While Jeff went to the counter to arrange to have the Lear prepared for the short hop back to Sacramento, Jaffar took Hamid and Sameed aside. "I want you to unload our remote control unit from the Lear. Put it into the truck and drive it over to the warehouse."

"Yes, Excellency!"

"You must be very careful with it. If you damage it in the least, I will hold you responsible." Hamid and Sameed looked at each other; both knew they would take extra care handling the remote control unit. Any damage, however slight, would probably cost them their lives.

Jaffar was certain that both men understood. He could tell by the looks on their faces. "I will be over in a few minutes," he said.

Hamid backed the truck through the open door of the warehouse, Sameed verbally guiding him while he steadied the vital electronic control in the Chevy's cargo box. "You are good, Hamid," he said.

While the unit was being unloaded, Jaffar walked around the empty warehouse. His footfalls echoed off the unfinished walls and ceiling of the space. He watched as the two men gently lowered the unit to concrete floor.

"Hamid I want you and Sameed to stay here overnight and return to Wendover tomorrow. I have arranged for a delivery in the morning."

"Yes, Excellency."

"I am returning to Sacramento this afternoon. I will be back out to Utah in a few weeks. Make sure that our guests are comfortable there."

Jaffar walked across the tarmac, back towards Executive's hangar, leaving his men to stare after him. For the first time in many months Jaffar was optimistic about the chances for the successful outcome of the operation.

"Jaffar is a donkey's rectum," Hamid said softly after he was gone.

Sameed was surprised at the outburst, but laughed anyway. "Be careful my friend. Many have died for less."

"He didn't even make certain that we had food or water. Anyway he cannot hear me." Hamid closed the door and locked it. "We will take turns sleeping on the seat of the truck." Both men knew that it would be a long night.

Camp Pendleton, California

Jack and Donny sat with the rest of their squad in the large situation room to discuss the aftermath of the raid on the base. Many people in the group were still sporting wounds to various parts of their bodies.

"Gentleman!" Lieutenant General Roy stood before a large scale map of the base. "I do not need to tell you how surprised and disappointed I am with the results of the incursion onto my base this a.m." The map told the story with some help from the long list of casualties. "What started out as a small screw-up at the gate, quickly turned into a real cluster-fuck!" He looked over at Colonel Hart, and then directly at Private Jacobson. "Any comments?"

"Sir! Sergeant Riggs and I were caught completely off guard."

"That pretty well sums it up. You both let your guard down and a couple of beach bums in a van managed to get onto the base and take control of a large portion of it." He let those words sink in for a few seconds. "What about you, Sergeant?"

"Sir. I looked at the woman passenger and saw the clothing. I thought they were just a couple of civilians on the way to the beach. I failed to see the threat." He lied. Riggs had been involved in planning the operation from the beginning.

"That much is certain, Sergeant." The room was filled with murmurs as General Roy sat down and Colonel Hart stood up to take his place.

"Gentlemen, that will be enough!" Hart said. "We are not here to assign blame as much as to see where we can improve base security. With that, I will turn this discussion over to the mastermind of this little exercise."

Still dressed in his Hawaiian shirt, Jack stood up. "First I would like to introduce all of you to Lieutenant Michelle Hough." He looked over at Riggs and Jacobson. "Some of you will remember her as the woman in the passenger seat."

Both men rubbed their chests and winced, the areas around the impacts were brilliant red and swollen. "That hurt like hell!" This was from Jacobson.

"You're lucky the Lieutenant was just firing paintballs, Private." Jack was sure Jacobson was understating his case. The Rossman Model MP5 was accurate to over one hundred feet, with a muzzle velocity more than two times that of the recreational Co2 guns available to the general public. They certainly packed a hell of a wallop.

The critiquing of the exercise continued for the rest of the day. Many important lessons had been painfully learned or relearned. Measures could now be taken to address the last of the shortcomings of base security, lessons which could and would most certainly be passed on to other base commanders. After all was said and done the exercise was deemed a success.

Lieutenant General Roy and Colonel Hart sat back during most of the meeting. The general was again very impressed with Jack and Donny as they critiqued the exercise. The operation had, unfortunately, gone exactly as Jack had presented it to the two of them just two days before. But what impressed Lieutenant General Roy the most was the ease of leadership of both men.

"I would say that they are ready both physically and mentally for your new unit, Colonel," he said to Hart.

"Thank you, General. I would have to agree." The colonel of course, hadn't had any doubt of the outcome from the very beginning.

Sacramento, California

The day's flying over, Jeff was preparing to part ways with this most generous of employers.

"Thank you, Mr. Hodgeson. It's been a pleasure doing business with you once again. Don't hesitate to call if you need me."

"I will need you sometime in March. Towards the end of the month, I think."

"Same arrangements?"

"Yes, Jeff. The very same arrangements."

Jeff didn't know it, but the arrangements were definitely not going to be the same. Not by a long shot. Jeff shook Jaffar's hand and watched him as he strolled towards the waiting taxi, then he turned around, logbook in hand, and headed into the office to fill out the last of the paperwork, smiling as he did so.

January 2, 1981

Just before nine o'clock, Tom Anderson, the driver for Lucky Strike Delivery, rolled through the gate and onto the concrete expanse that was McCarran field. He quickly spotted the right building, thanks to the directions given by the security guard at the gate.

The hammering on the metal overhead door reverberated through the nearly empty warehouse. Hamid and Sameed were startled awake as the thunderous noise echoed through the space, momentarily disoriented by the unfamiliar surroundings.

Hamid quickly climbed out of the truck and crossed the floor. "Alright! We are coming!" Hamid yelled in an effort to stop the offending noise. He unlatched the door and pulled on the chain. The driver of the delivery truck stood there, looking very annoyed.

"What took you so long, Bud?"

Not wanting to admit that they were sleeping, Hamid replied, "We were busy in the office."

The driver looked inside at the empty space. "I'll bet!" He thrust a clipboard at Hamid. "So who gets the bad news?"

"What do you mean, bad news?"

Tom thought, *Christ! Dumb fucking ragheads* but instead said, "You know, a signature on the weigh bill for the delivery."

"That would be me." Hamid signed the form beside the indicated 'X' then handed it back to the driver.

Tom quickly looked over the forms. Satisfied, he said, "Where do you want this stuff?"

"Along that wall."

Tom used the Hiab crane at the front of the flatbed to first unload a small, motorized pallet jack. He was anxious to finish as quickly as possible. He lowered all of the pallets to the ground then effortlessly maneuvered them into position. In less than half an hour Tom Anderson was on his way, leaving Hamid and Sameed alone with their potentially deadly cargo.

Hamid closed the door and started examining the blue steel barrels. Each of them had a large warning label below the company name: Pacific Northwest Farm Supply, Yakima, Washington.

"Sameed! Let's get going. We have a long drive ahead of us."

Wendover, Utah

Mrs. Sutton sat on the only chair in small room, while the Empress Farah sat on the edge of the bed. The door suddenly opened and Abdul motioned for Janette to join him outside. This was now a normal part of her daily routine, but she quickly realized that 'normal' was not the case this day. One of the guards was standing next to the pickup as usual, but today he carried a menacing-looking AK-47 assault rifle.

This new development completely unnerved Janette Sutton. The last time she had seen a guard with an automatic rifle was when Joe had taken her to Playa Del Carmen on a holiday. Outside all the banks in the town, an armed guard stood.

"What's going on?" she asked nervously.

"I'm taking you to visit your husband, just as I have done for the three months."

"Why does that man have a gun?"

"Don't worry! It's not for you. He is here to stop the Iranian Queen from trying to escape."

"She's not the Queen, she's the Empress."

"Yes, of course. Now come with me!" As Janette stepped out of her now-shared room, Abdul took her elbow then turned around to take one last look inside and derisively spit at their royal visitor.

"Ha!" He closed the door and locked it.

Janette hurried into the hangar, almost running as she did so. Joe was at his workbench, examining a part while Abbas looked on. Another guard stood nearby, also armed with an assault rifle. When she reached her husband she embraced him. "Joe! I'm so glad to see you!"

She held him so tightly Joe was uncertain if all his ribs were still intact. "What's wrong Janette?"

His wife looked around, first at Abdul, then at Abbas and then finally at the guard, "I can't say for sure."

During their many years together Joe could count the times on one hand that his wife had been tongue-tied, at a loss for words. "I've never known you to not say what was on your mind, Mrs. Sutton." Joe looked over at Abdul. It was then that he noticed the second armed guard. Maybe his wife did have cause for alarm.

"Are you worried about the men with the guns?"

"Yes, I am. They seem to be everywhere."

Joe knew his wife was frightened of guns, but was sure that she must be exaggerating about them being everywhere. "I will talk to Jaffar when I see him," he said. He wasn't aware that Jaffar had returned to Sacramento, leaving Abdul in charge.

"I need to talk to you, Joe!" said Janette softly.

"All right! Let's go over there." He motioned towards the Boeing jet in the middle of the hangar. "You can talk to me while I take a look at the number two engine nacelle."

"What?"

As Joe peered up into the empty space of the nacelle, examining each wire and line leading into it with his flashlight, he said, "Okay, honey. What's up?"

"What's up? What do you mean, 'Okay, honey. What's up?' What's wrong with you Joe?"

"Nothing is wrong with me!"

"Joe, look around, for God's sake. Those men over there have guns. In case you have forgotten they have kidnapped us and threatened our families. We are prisoners here!" Joe just kept working. She added, "As of tonight, now they have another!"

"Who?"

"Last night, Abdul and Jaffar brought Empress Farah, the wife of the late Shah of Iran, to my cell."

"What?" For a moment Joe Sutton stopped poking around the empty engine compartment of the jet. "The Empress of Iran?"

"Yes, Joe! It's obvious to me that that only two of us are being kept here against our will, and if you'd stop playing around with your Goddamn airplanes for a minute, you'd realize it too!" Janette Sutton turned and walked away.

As she passed Abdul, she demanded, "Take me back to my cell!"

Sacramento, California - January 6, 1981

Giti hurried to get Sina ready for school—the first day back in the new year. "Come on Sina, let's hurry. You don't want to be late."

"I'm coming! I can't find my new book and I want to show Matthew."

"You can show it to him tomorrow."

Jaffar entered the kitchen just as Giti was stuffing the last item into Sina's already bulging backpack. "What is all this? Are you running away from home Sina?" Jaffar laughed.

"Come on, Sina. Out to the car."

"I can drive him, Giti. I've got to go into town for an hour or so. I can drop him off on the way."

"Thank you, Jaffar that would be great. I can finish the rest of the chores before you get back." Giti added hopefully, "Maybe we can spend some quality time together before I go back to work tomorrow. Perhaps we can go for out lunch?"

A quiet lunch sounded good to Jaffar. "All right. I will not be long."

"Sina! Don't forget to put your lunch into the fridge when you get to school." She gave Sina a kiss on the cheek.

"Bye, Mom."

Giti had been finding it hard lately to juggle her job and duties at home, especially since the pregnancy was making her tired. For the past four or five months, with Jaffar away so often, it seemed that everything had been left up to her. It was a welcome surprise when Jaffar offered to help by driving Sina to school.

During the past two weeks she'd managed to catch up on almost all her housework; in fact today there was just a couple of loads of laundry to do, mostly belonging to Jaffar.

In the master bedroom, armed with a basket of clean laundry, Giti put fresh sheets on the bed, then started hanging up Jaffar's freshly-ironed shirts. She would not have noticed the manila envelope on the shelf, except for one unlucky occurrence; the hanger from one of the last shirts she was putting in the closet caught the corner of it and dragged it off the shelf. Before Giti could catch it, it fell to the floor.

"Oh, damn!" Giti bent down to pick it up. She glanced at the front. "Sunwest Properties Limited? What's this?"

Normally Giti would have simply put it back on the shelf but, not recognizing the company name as a normal part of Jaffar's business, curiosity got the better of her so she looked closer. The envelope was from Utah Power and Light.

"My God! He's got another woman in Utah. That's why he hasn't been home much!" She nervously opened the envelope and read its contents. It was a bill for utilities in the amount of $1,251.09.

"What? That is a huge bill!"

Thinking she had misread the amount, Giti looked again. It was stamped "PAID – October 14, 1980." Now she stood on her tip-toes, trying to look at the spot where the envelope had been. There was Jaffar's briefcase, underneath which were several other large, thick manila envelopes. All were addressed to Sunwest Properties, at a post office box right here in Sacramento.

Giti sat on the bed, unsure if she should open and examine the contents of the envelopes. Jaffar had always been adamant that she was not to interfere in his business dealings. However, in light of his long absences and what she'd just found, Giti felt compelled to investigate further. An hour later she was still engrossed, reading and rereading the documents that were spread around her on the bed. She didn't hear the front door open and close and so was taken by surprise when Jaffar said, "What's going on in here?"

Giti practically leapt from the bed, papers flying in all directions, frightened half out of her wits. She looked at Jaffar, her face suddenly pale. "Nothing." The word just barely escaped her lips, in a hoarse croak.

"What do you mean, nothing?" Jaffar looked at the correspondence that covered the bed everywhere except where Giti had been sitting. From across the room, Jaffar didn't grasp the significance of the papers, but that changed as he stepped closer. Giti recoiled as he did so.

"These are my things. This is my property," Jaffar said coldly.

"Yes! Speaking of property, what's all this?" Giti grabbed a handful of papers off the bed. "You have trucks, tools, even an old airport."

"That's my business, not yours!" Jaffar shouted.

Giti was too angry to back down. All the months of loneliness and frustration came suddenly boiling to the surface. "It *is* my business, Jaffar. I'm your wife. Christ almighty! You even have a Goddamn airplane! You're living some strange life without me and I don't know what it is! I have a right to ask. What man needs an airport and an airplane? What are you doing out there in Utah anyway? What is so top secret that you can't share it with your own wife?"

She was crying now, betrayed and angry. "Who is this stranger who is my husband? Are you doing something illegal? Are you smuggling drugs?" she sobbed.

"That's enough!" Without thinking, Jaffar lashed out at Giti with his fist, striking her as hard as he'd hit anyone in his life. The blow landed squarely on the side of her face and her eyes rolled up into her head. Jaffar was certain he felt her jawbone break the instant before she flew backwards, summersaulting over the bed to hit the wall then sliding down it to lay motionless in a heap on the floor, at the foot of the bed.

His reaction had been one of pure rage, blind and uncontrollable—a man possessed. Upon seeing his pregnant wife lying still on the carpet, however, her face contorted, a stream of blood seeping from her nostrils, reason began to take hold.

"Giti! My God, what have I done?" He rushed to her and crouched down. She was so still, it frightened him. He nervously put his finger against her neck to feel her pulse. He could feel none. He began to panic, feeling his own heart race, his own pulse quicken. He checked Giti's once again, but he could still not find it.

For several minutes Jaffar did nothing. He didn't know what to do; but then, like any wild animal, his survival instincts kicked in. Not only did his heartbeat accelerate, but his mind began to race. He was afraid of the authorities, to be sure, but Jaffar was even more afraid of what his associates overseas would do to him if he failed to carry out the plans they had all worked on for so long.

He knew he had to leave Sacramento—now. There was only one thing to do. Jaffar reached up and pulled down the briefcase from the shelf, put it on the bed and opened it. He quickly scooped up all the papers from the bed and shoved them into the briefcase. All the shirts that Giti had lovingly ironed and hung up were next. These were hastily stuffed into a small suitcase, along with a few pairs of pants.

He grabbed the briefcase and suitcase by their handles and took a last look around the room. He tried to avert his eyes when they passed over where Giti lay. Then he turned and left, not even bothering to switch off the light. With the luggage tucked away in the trunk of his car, Jaffar backed the car out of the driveway and drove away as calmly as he could, knowing that in all likelihood he would never see this house or street again.

Just before one o'clock, as Jaffar drove east along I-80, from the backseat of the car Sina happily read aloud "Welcome to Nevada." He was amazed that he was actually leaving California for the first time.

Jaffar was surprised how easy it had been to get Sina out of school. *Those foolish Americans, so trusting*, he thought as he drove. He had to put as much distance between himself and Zinfandel Drive as possible.

"Wow! I can't wait until Mom comes to join us!" Sina exclaimed happily.

"Of course, Sina. That will be good." In an effort to change the subject he said, "Let's get something to eat for lunch. There's a McDonald's in Reno."

"Okay," Sina said innocently.

— Chapter 21 —

January 7, 1981 - Sacramento, California

Fatemah drove slowly between the rows of parked cars. The leaves had long since fallen, leaving bare branches stretching overhead towards the opposite sides of the street, forming a latticework tunnel.

Even before turning into the driveway, Fatemah noticed something was amiss. There were no cars parked in the driveway; normally at least one would be there. She parked the car and went up the porch steps to ring the doorbell. There was no answer. *Strange*, she thought. Normally, Sina would have practically bowled her over in his haste to get to her car—on the rare occasion she managed to make it out of the car, much less up the steps to ring the doorbell. *Perhaps I am mixed up!* Fatemah was almost certain that it was her turn to drive the two of them to work.

She returned home and was surprised to see the Giti wasn't at her and Zafar's house either. She expected that if somehow they had both got their wires crossed they may have driven past one another, so the next logical step was to assume that Giti was at Sina's elementary school. However, at the school Fatemah found the last of the students reluctantly filing into their classrooms and no sign of her nephew or her sister-in-law.

She was at a loss as to where they could be. She looked at her watch. It was ten minutes to nine. *Oh my! I'll be late for work.* She drove off, fully expecting Giti to be at work when she got there.

Wendover, Utah

Jaffar and Sina had arrived at the airfield the night before, both exhausted, but for far different reasons: Jaffar was now a fugitive—having fled across two state lines—and was by now almost certainly wanted by the FBI. Sina was just tired; tired of looking out the car window at the monotonous, grey brown landscape; tired of trying to pretend his stepfather was fun and nice.

Jaffar couldn't help but be irritated by the boy; he had lost count of the number of times Sina had asked the age-old question, "Are we there yet?" He did recall, however, the exact number of times Sina had asked him, "When is my Mom coming?"

"Soon," was all he could reply.

Immediately after arriving unexpectedly at the front gate at Wendover, Jaffar quickly and quietly instructed Abdul to have all the guards to put their rifles away. "I don't want to frighten the child needlessly." That would come soon enough, of that Jaffar was certain.

As they walked into the hangar, Sina was in the middle of asking for the umpteenth time, "When is my Mom ..." But then his jaw dropped as he saw the jet sitting quietly in the middle of the hangar floor, gleaming under the lights. "Wow!"

"You remember last summer, when you and I took your little plane to the school playground? Well Sina, this is my little plane."

"Is it really?" Then he added, "But it's not little, it's huge!" Sina bolted toward the aircraft, without even bothering to wait for either a reply or permission.

"Yes, Sina, it is." He'd hoped Sina would do exactly what he'd done. It would get the boy's mind off his mother. Jaffar wondered, however, if the same could be said for him. He kept trying to block the image of Giti crumpled on the floor out of his mind.

That night as Jaffar lay on his bed, he glanced over at Sina who had only moments before fallen asleep on a cot in the room. Since his youth Jaffar had broken the law countless times. He had been, either directly or indirectly, responsible for the murder of hundreds—even thousands—of innocent people. But even with such a history, Jaffar could not recall ever feeling as he did now. Here he was, in a foreign country without a home, with a huge task to accomplish and his life on the line if he failed. And what had he done? He had killed the one beautiful thing he had and now a lonely little boy was going to grow up without a mother. For the first time in his life, Jaffar not only felt afraid, he felt guilty. He slept poorly that night. He wished he could change what he had done.

The next morning, Jaffar watched as Sina, with arms out like an airplane, ran as fast as he could, down the hall and into the hangar, making noises like a jet engine on full after-burner as he did so. This time he even asked permission from Jaffar as he made a bee-line for the jet. Jaffar couldn't help smiling at the boy's excitement.

Abdul was beside him moments later. "Abdul, how are our guests doing?" Jaffar asked when he saw him.

"Good, Excellency! There are no problems," he said, adding, "Mr. Sutton thinks he has found the problem with the old motor."

Although Jaffar thought this was a complete waste of time, he realized quickly that fixing the old engine would keep Sutton occupied—maybe even until Jaffar could figure out how to deal him, not to mention the two women. This was something that had suddenly become a great deal more complicated in his mind.

"Try to keep him away from the boy as much as possible," Jaffar said, "And no more visits from Mrs. Sutton." All Sina would need right now would be to get attached to people who may not be around for much longer.

Sacramento, California

"She must be somewhere! She's not here." Zafar was almost shouting at his wife. "I don't know where she is! When did you see her last?"

"There's no need to shout, Zafar. I looked at home. I looked at her house. I even drove past the school."

"Yes! But you didn't go into the house or the school?"

"No, I didn't. I didn't think I needed to!" As each minute passed their level of concern rose exponentially. It was almost at the panic stage.

When Fatemah had arrived at work she'd noticed the stall where Giti normally parked her car was empty. That Giti wasn't there was confirmed when she entered the building. That's when she called Zafar from out of the warehouse.

"I want you to call the school and see if Sina is in class," instructed Zafar. "If he is not, maybe they can tell you where he is." Zafar was hoping this was nothing more than a simple miscommunication of some sort. "Maybe Giti tried to call you last night while you were on the phone."

"She would have called us today!"

Zafar knew she was right, but he didn't say so.

Fatemah dialed the phone and Gladys Hopkins pushed the button to answer the waiting caller, switching off the public address system as she did so. "M.B Sanford Elementary School, good morning! No Mrs. Roshtti, Sina hasn't come into school today," Gladys said.

"Are you certain?"

"Yes, I know for a fact. I was just handed the class lists from this morning and Sina was among the students who were absent." After a short pause, "It looks like Sina was absent from school yesterday afternoon as well."

"Do you know why?"

"I don't, but I will check with Mrs. Cassidy and see if she can tell me. I will call you back shortly."

"If you can't get an answer from the school, maybe we should call the police," Zafar said as Fatemah hung up.

"Really Zafar, is that necessary?" she asked. Somehow she already knew the answer.

More than two hours had passed since Fatemah had first parked in Giti's driveway. The call she and Zafar made to the police fell on deaf ears. The desk sergeant, although sympathetic, said, "I'm sorry, we can't investigate every time a father takes a child out of school. We simply do not have the manpower."

Zafar had never had any love for Jaffar. "If something has happened to her and it's his fault, I will kill him," he said darkly, "I've never trusted him. Not once since I first saw him! I'm going to check on her, Fatemah. Something is wrong."

The two of them left the business under the care of the senior secretary, who promised to call if anything happened or if Giti walked in the door, and they drove over to Zinfandel Drive. They pulled up to Giti's house and got out of the car.

Even though Reza had been gone for more than two years, Zafar wasn't willing to separate himself from his brother's legacy and the sister-in-law he adored. He would see this through, Jaffar or no Jaffar. And if there was something not right, that man would pay. Zafar unlocked the front door to his brother's house.

When they stepped inside, both he and Fatemah were immediately aware of how quiet the house was, eerily quiet. As they closed the door, they could just make out the faint hum from the refrigerator coming from the kitchen. There were still no cars in the driveway.

"Giti?" called Fatemah.

Neither expected an answer. Fatemah called once more, but there was only silence. Zafar went to check downstairs and Fatemah headed down the hallway. There was a light on in the master bedroom. Zafar was almost at the bottom of the stairs when he heard his wife scream. Using the handrail for leverage he launched himself up the stairs towards the main floor, faster than he ever thought possible. "What is it? Where are you?"

"I'm in Giti's room. Come quickly!"

Entering the last door off the hallway, Zafar found his wife kneeling down at the foot of the bed. "What is it?"

As he got closer, Zafar could see around his wife; Giti was lying on the floor, her face half-covered by a horrific bruise, the surrounding skin a garish yellow.

"Oh good God, is she …" Zafar could not bring himself to finish the sentence.

"I don't know. Call an ambulance! Hurry!" It was Fatemah's turn to shout at her husband, even if it was out of just plain panic. Fatemah was shaking uncontrollably as she held Giti's limp hand in her own.

In spite of her shock and fear, Fatemah managed to remember the small amount of first aid she'd been taught many years earlier. It took a determined effort for Fatemah to detect either a pulse or respiration as both were extremely weak, but there was some relief when she found out Giti was still alive. She desperately wanted to move her to somewhere more comfortable, only a few feet away, but somewhere in that small amount of training she remembered that moving people when they were injured was not the best thing to do. She was limited to monitoring Giti's weak vital signs as best she could as she waited for an ambulance to arrive.

"The ambulance is on the way, as are the police," said Zafar. Fatemah had resisted the idea of calling the police, but could not argue now with the fact that they were dealing with a situation that was far more serious than they had previously thought.

"Where's our little Sina, Fatemah?"

"I don't know. With Jaffar, that's what the school said." Until a few moments ago, they had both hoped that all three were together and alright. Now Zafar felt a cold ball of fear settle inside his stomach.

The ambulance arriving and the first aid that was administered to Giti was a blur. Zafar didn't return to himself until he sat, dazed and devastated and watched the ambulance accelerate down the street, lights flashing, siren wailing, on its way to Mercy Hospital. The two most important women in his life were in the back, one just barely alive. And his nephew was in the care of a madman.

He had to take care of the police report; he'd been asked to come down to the station at his convenience to talk to the attending officer. Officer Bob Grant had responded to the call and he was polite and kind to Zafar as they worked through the details of what had potentially happened, but after gathering all the facts from the medics about Giti, and from the school about Sina, in the end the officer said to Zafar, "I'm sorry Mr. Roshtti, but there is just not enough probable cause to take this investigation any further at this time."

"But you saw Giti's injuries. She did not get those on her own!"

"Right now, I can't say what the caused her injuries. She may have simply tripped and hit her head on the closet door frame."

"What about my nephew? What about Sina?"

"This may be nothing more than an accident and the boy's father ..."

"Stepfather! He's not his father. His father died two years ago."

"I'm sorry to hear that," Officer Grant said sympathetically, but he didn't change his position. "The boy's *stepfather*, then, may have had a legitimate reason for taking your nephew out of school. And Giti's injuries may simply be a coincidence."

"Coincidence!" Zafar was trying to stay calm. "I'm telling you, this is no coincidence. You have to do something!"

"We have to wait until Mrs. Roshtti regains consciousness, or until Sina and his stepfather return from what he told the school was business trip. I'm sorry, Mr. Roshtti."

Wendover, Utah

"Abdul! Where the hell are Sameed and Abbas?" Jaffar yelled. "I want one of them to accompany you to Las Vegas."

"I asked the men. No one has seen them for many days."

"Days? Days? How many days," Jaffar screamed.

"I do not remember. About the time the other jet left here. Before you returned with the boy."

"But that was ...? The guards, what were they doing?" Jaffar could not even fathom what the answer to that was.

"You ordered all of us inside the buildings. The guards have had little to do but keep watch over the old couple and the Iranian Queen."

"They can't have gone far on foot. Where would they go?" All Jaffar could hope that his missing men would not get stopped by the police and questioned. A gust of wind howled by the window.

"Maybe they have died out there in this cold, God-forsaken place," Abdul muttered

"We can only hope. I have enough problems on my hands! Inshallah!"

Washington, D.C. - January 19, 1981

United Airlines Flight 1966 touched down at Dulles International Airport in Washington just before 4:30 p.m. local time. Jack and Donny walked down the jet-way and into the terminal, following the signs that directed them to the luggage carousel.

Before five o'clock, they were standing in front of the domestic terminal under a large metal and glass canopy that protected them from the elements. "I never figured I would be back to D.C. and this damned snow. At least not so soon," Donny said as he looked out at the long line of cabs creeping through the six inches of slush that covered the roadway.

"I still remember the snowfalls we had in Wisconsin when we were kids. It didn't seem to bother you then, Don!"

"Like you said Jack, we were kids." Donny turned up his collar to ward off the chill, as Jack hailed a cab. A yellow cab moved toward them, unintentionally sending a wave of slush over the edge of the sidewalk. Unaware passers-by got an abrupt, cold welcome to D.C. and, as the cabbie got out to help Jack and Don, he was met with curses from some very unhappy people. "I'm sorry," was all he could say as he helped load their luggage. Once inside the cab he asked, "Where to?"

"The Hotel Carrington, on Eleventh please."

January 20, 1981

At eight o'clock sharp, Jack and Donny exited the third-floor elevator at NATA headquarters, having already passed through four levels of security including a recently installed retina scan. This was only the fifth time Jack had been to the recently completed facility.

"Good morning, Colonel," they said in unison when they exited the elevator to find their commanding officer waiting for them.

"Donny, Jack! How's the Harrington Hotel?"

"Fine Sir! It's a big day in Washington today."

"Bigger than you know! Have a seat." Jack and Donny sat down opposite Kip Holmes and Michelle.

"Good morning," Michelle said then winked at Don. Don blew her a kiss.

"What's up?" Jack asked.

"Michelle pulled this off DIANA yesterday," he said, handing them each a typed sheet of paper. "This is one of the reasons I had come on such short notice." The colonel gave them a minute to each scan the documents which were from a CIA operative in Tehran.

"So it seems like several groups of hostages have been seen being moved about city ..." Don said.

"Yes, it would seem so. As you all know they have been kept in small groups to defeat any more attempts at rescue," the colonel said.

"This indicates they are being taken to one place. For release or for execution, that's the question," Jack mused.

"I don't think the Ayatollah wants to screw with Ronald Reagan too much. My money is on release, Jack."

"And what's this about a planned attack here on U.S. soil?" Jack said, scanning another paper.

"I wish we had more bodies on the ground in Tehran to flesh this one out because I can't confirm anything. But that's the word. We got screwed when those bastards took over the Embassy in Tehran—we only have a handful of operatives over there now."

"Islamic Hamas!" exclaimed Don. "Isn't that the group that our friends Al-Kubesi and Harraj belong to?"

"Yes, Donny, one and the same. You've got a good memory," the colonel said. He continued, "You and Jack were looking into his finances here in the States last year, weren't you?"

Jack remembered what a shit-storm that activity had caused, "We didn't mean to step on any toes, Colonel."

"I know you didn't, Jack. I spent weeks on the phone to Vegas trying to get that Detective off your back. He was persistent. I also spent a bunch of time trying to get Captain Nichols to calm you down and get you to back off."

"I remember, Colonel!" Jack could still recall the lecture Nichols had given him. "But what ever happened to the Detective?"

The colonel smiled. "If I tell you, I'll have to kill you," he said. "But let's just say he got an early retirement package at the hands of his boss. Truthfully, he's happier. He's a golfer. He moved to Palm Springs with the money from his buy-out."

Jack was happy to hear that. The guy was a pest, but at least he cared about solving cases. He'd probably make a good private investigator. He wondered if he should look him up and try to sell him his business now that NATA was his full-time gig.

"So," the colonel continued, "You both remember that Abdul Al-Kubesi was the Chief of Police in Al Qa'im?"

"Was?"

"They had to find a replacement. Another guy is running the show over there now. It seems our boy Al-Kubesi just up and vanished, sometime in the last twelve months or so. He's wanted by the FBI here, for the murder of Mohammed Hussan. You remember that guy, Jack?"

"Of course I remember! He was one of the two brothers who were tailing me that T-boned that police cruiser. One brother was killed."

"Al-Kubesi allegedly stabbed Mohammed in Las Vegas then fled back to Sacramento. The last record of him is a photo taken by a security camera in the international departures lounge at Sacramento International, on twenty-nine February, 1980."

"What about Harraj?"

"We have nothing concrete on him, mostly just rumors about him. If our information is correct, he's the money man—or at least the middleman—for the Islamic Hamas Movement."

"I gave Captain Ken Nichols a ledger we found in Mohammed Hussan's apartment. It indicated holdings north of $100 million, but nothing about the source of the cash," Jack said.

"Well it might be significant, but officially he has done nothing illegal since arriving here in the U.S." said Hart. "Even in Al-Qa'im he keeps a low profile, always having one of his cronies—mostly his Chief of Police it would seem—do the dirty work for him. I guess you guys are aware that he's in Sacramento and married to Giti Roshtti, the woman who won the case against PSA when her husband died in that horrific crash a few years ago?"

Jack felt his stomach flip. This was where the whole thing had started. He'd been hired to find her … so a terrorist could marry her. He felt anger in the pit of his stomach. Such a lovely woman deserved better. Don saw him pale and clapped him on the back. When Jack looked at him, he said softly, "Not your fault, buddy."

Hart looked confused. "What's that?" he asked. Don gave him a brief history of how the two of them had crossed paths with Hussan in the first place.

"Then somehow this woman is a key," Hart mused. "We need to talk to her. If Harraj is at the top of that Hamas outfit, then he can't have got there without bloodying his hands along the way."

"No doubt!" Don said as Jack sat in his chair mentally kicking himself.

"But as I've said," Hart continued, "We don't have proof tying him to any killings. Hamas has taken credit for dozens of bombings and assassinations over the last several years, but Jaffar Harraj has always distanced himself. He's a very shrewd operator. Al-Kubesi, on the other hand, has kept his hands in deep shit and we know he's been in and out of the U.S. at least two times in the last three years. We know this partly from what you," he indicated Jack and Donny, "have said. And the rest of what we know was filled in by Kip."

Kip spoke up. "I've been to Al-Qa'im personally, looking into these two. Jaffar has some nice digs there. You should see them—just like some mansion in Beverly Hills. He hasn't been seen there for quite some time, though. In addition, it seems that Harraj and Al-Kubesi always travel together using a variety of top-notch forged passports and other identification."

"How good are these forgeries, Kip?"

"They are the very best money can buy. Look here!" Kip produced four U.S. passports, all with his picture in them. "Which one is the real government-issued, U.S. passport for Mr. John H. Leslie, from Rockville Maryland?" he asked. John H. Leslie was the alias he used when he was overseas on government business.

The four of them examined the passports carefully and after a few moments, Donny, Michelle and Colonel Hart all selected the one they thought was real, but Jack sat for another minute and scratched his head before saying confidently. "They are all fakes."

Kip smiled. "How did you know?" He produced his real passport from a folder in front of him.

"I didn't know for certain, but I just figured that if you could get three close to perfect forgeries, why not four? By the way what did they cost you?"

"I got them from one of the guys Harraj uses for all his documents, from a little shop in Bagdad. I paid the guy a thousand dollars."

"We should get this guy to issue our Government IDs!" Don laughed.

"Not funny, Donny!" said Hart. Michelle and Jack laughed anyway.

Sacramento, California

For the past eight weeks, Zafar and Fatemah had been at Giti's bedside each day, rubbing her hands and talking to her. The nurses assured them both that Giti could hear their words, even if she couldn't respond.

Giti's exterior wounds and the bruising Jaffar had caused had almost totally disappeared—and even her jaw had mended nicely—but her internal injuries remained. Zafar and Fatemah had difficulty understanding the medical jargon, works like 'subdural hematoma' and 'brain bleed' were some of the easier ones; but what was more difficult still was watching Giti and hoping she'd be whole when she woke. That was torture for both of them.

The visits from the detectives were down to a trickle; there were no new leads and the case had been down-graded to a missing persons case. This had resulted in a furor at the desk of Detective Colin Bursil—Zafar had been red-faced, yelling at the detective, "What do you mean just a missing persons case? My nephew has been taken by force and my sister-in-law is in hospital in a coma! Her unborn child is dead! This is murder!" But his words fell on apparently deaf ears.

However, only a result of Zafar's constant pleading was an additional detective put on the file, making a total of three men trying to find out why his sister-in-law had been left for dead and his nephew had disappeared. When Zafar pressed for a larger team, however, it was always the same story, "I'm sorry Mr. Roshtti, there's nothing more that we can do. We have limited manpower and a city full of unsolved cases. We're doing what we can!"

The police were no closer to finding Sina and that snake Jaffar than they had been eight weeks ago and it was making Zafar crazy. He had to do something.

March 2, 1981

Television crews gathered inside the conference room at Mercy Hospital, cameras pointed at the front of the room. In the centre was a podium festooned with microphones from KXTV, CBS-13 and several other stations. All were preparing to go live, streaming through the thousands of feet of cable snaking outside to their respective broadcast trucks in the parking lot.

The news conference that was about to take place had been largely due to Zafar's efforts. He had inundated the press with his sister-in-law's story and eventually got word out that Giti Roshtti was the famous lady who had won her wrongful death suit against PSA two years previous. This ignited a press storm; not only was she pretty, but she was a public figure, a single mother, a woman who had fought an injustice and won. Suddenly, her story was interesting. As well, it seemed she might have unsuspectingly married a possible terrorist. As a Middle Eastern man, Jaffar was suspect anyway. The fact that he'd taken her son made him downright evil.

Just before ten o'clock, the chief surgeon and one of his colleagues filed into the room and took their places at the podium. They were followed by Zafar and Fatemah Roshtti, as well as several FBI agents. All took seats at tables on each side of the podium.

At ten o'clock the chief surgeon looked over the audience of reporters and began the news conference. "Good morning ladies and gentlemen. My name is Dr. Mark Matishak. I am the Chief Surgeon here at Mercy Hospital and

I have some news about one of patients here." He stopped and took a sip from a glass of water next to him. "This news has been a long time coming, almost two months in fact. But finally, I'm pleased to announce that our patient, Mrs. Giti Roshtti, has emerged from her coma."

The group of reporters let out a cheer. Many had been expecting bad news.

"I'm afraid, however, that the news is not all good. I'm going to turn the microphone over to Mrs. Roshtti's attending physician."

He stepped aside and a petite woman with a head of curly brown hair and a long, elegant nose toke the microphone from him.

"Hello. My name is Dr. Jasmine Leslie and I'm head of the Neurology Department here at Mercy Hospital. As Dr. Matishak has told you, Mrs. Roshtti is out of her coma, which lasted 52 days. Some of you reported last month that Mrs. Roshtti was several months pregnant. I can confirm that fact now, but I am sorry to report the infant was lost due to complications arising from Mrs. Roshtti's injuries and her subsequent coma. The infant male died in utero and was removed by Caesarean section so the mother's life could be saved."

There was a collective sigh of disappointment then every reporter in the room raised their hands, with one shouting out, "What is the Federal Bureau of Investigation doing here?"

"I'm afraid they are going to have to answer that. I cannot comment on anything other than Mrs. Roshtti's medical condition."

"Where is her son?"

"Are you referring to her unborn, infant son?"

"No! Her other son!"

"Once again I cannot comment on matters other than medical ones." As the questions about Sina continued, the physicians relinquished the microphone to the FBI agents with some relief. Special Agent in Charge Anthony Edwards stepped to microphone and introduced himself. He then pointed to the reporter in the audience who had asked the Doctor about Sina.

"Yes?" he said.

"Can you tell us about Mrs. Roshtti's other son?"

"First let me start by stating that Mrs. Roshtti arrived here at the hospital, severely injured, on January seventh of this year. Her injuries were the result of an assault. This fact was finally confirmed in a very short interview we were allowed to conduct with her last evening."

"But ..."

"Let me finish! Please!" After a short pause, Edwards continued, "Giti's husband, Jaffar Harraj, and her son Sina, are still missing. Harraj is Sina's stepfather. Those of you familiar with the Roshtti name are probably aware that Mrs. Roshtti's first husband, the boy's father, died in a plane crash two years ago. Mr. Harraj and Sina have been missing since the incident at the Roshtti household in January that resulted in Mrs. Roshtti's injuries and the loss of her unborn child. The whereabouts of Mr. Harraj and Sina Roshtti are still unknown at this time."

"What about the assault? Can you tell us what took place?'

"As I've explained, our interview with Giti Roshtti was short. Due to her weakened state, both mental and physical, we were not able to have the access to Mrs. Roshtti that we would have liked to have had."

"When do you think you can see her again to resolve some of these questions?"

"That is entirely up to the doctors and Mrs. Roshtti herself. Thank you!"

Wendover, Utah - March 8, 1981

For more than two months, Jaffar remained holed up at the deserted Army Air Force base, certain that any moment the FBI and their hostage rescue team would be storming the front gate. He had not stepped foot outside the base since he'd arrived with Sina two months earlier. He was afraid to go out in public—even masquerading as Jaffar Hodgeson. He was sure his likeness was on wanted posters all over the country.

Indeed, the FBI had at first issued a 'Be On The Lookout' (BOLO) order for him, but they had very little information to go on. Giti was still in a coma at Mercy Hospital in Sacramento, unable to speak or shed any light on the investigation.

Abdul now handled all the trips outside the base for supplies, always using cash and never going to the same place twice in a row. Jaffar still had men to feed, along with the Suttons, the Empress and, of course, Sina.

Besides Jaffar, Hamid and Abdul were the only two who knew the complete scope of the mission in America. They also knew the deadline was only days away. With Jaffar in hiding, Abdul and Hamid stepped up to handle all the face-to-face dealings and Hamid took care of the technical aspect of the mission. The final preparations in Las Vegas had all been taken care of, via telephone calls to Behrous Kholm.

It was Jaffar's intention that the base appear once again to be deserted so the guards had been pulled back to the interior of the buildings, along with all the Sunwest Properties vehicles. Even the signage had been removed. The only activity that continued was the daily trips to attend to the needs of Mrs. Sutton and the Empress Farrah, the latter of whom had taken a liking to Sina.

Jaffar was unhappy about the situation he now found himself in. When he'd first purchased this base, the idea of owning an airplane and an airport had been exhilarating. Now, after his abrupt run from Sacramento with the boy, Jaffar found this windswept grassland and its old concrete buildings to be nothing but a million-acre prison, surrounded by ten-foot-high perimeter fences topped with rusty barbed wire. It felt forlorn and he felt trapped.

Out of habit Jaffar he watched the nightly news as he'd done for so many years at his home in Al Qa'im. The only station he could get with any clarity was KUTV, the CBS affiliate in Salt Lake City; all the others were simply audio accompanied by a screen of electronic 'snow'.

Tonight the newsman informed him that, "… in breaking news, police in Ogden are investigating the possible disappearance of more than 500 pounds of high explosives from the Bedrock Sand and Gravel Company. The owner of the company, who didn't want to appear on camera, said he cannot confirm the theft and he suspects it might just be a simple case of sloppy bookkeeping. Officials from the Bureau of Alcohol, Tobacco, Firearms and Explosives discovered the eleven boxes of explosive were unaccounted for during a routine check. In other news ..."

"Well at least something has gone right!" Jaffar smiled.

"And in international news, the Empress Farah, wife of the former Shah of Iran who was kidnapped almost a month ago, has not yet been found. The incident has international ramifications and the United States is considering implementing stricter protocols around international flights, given that she was last seen on her own Iranian jet …"

Jaffar's stomach sank as he felt walls close in around him.

— Chapter 22 —

March 10, 1981 - Las Vegas, Nevada

At McCarran International Airport, though its livery told a different story, the Boeing 720 belonging to Jaffar sat waiting for her passengers and cargo to be loaded so she could take her final journey.

It was fitting that she was so prepared; in spite of the release of the American hostages from Tehran in January, tensions between the United States and Iran had not eased—if anything they had increased. Stories of the inhumane treatment by their captors had surfaced, angering many citizens around the U.S.

Jaffar was edgy; he wanted the mission to succeed and could not take a chance that his jet would be damaged in any way. The guards assigned to the hangar were the same guards who had delivered the empress to Wendover months previous and security was tight. The hangar itself was far enough away from the runways and other traffic that it didn't attract attention. As well, all of its windows were obscured, making observation of the interior and the jet impossible, and all the doors were double bolted. Only three people had keys; Jaffar, Abdul and Jaffar's half-brother, Bijan.

A quarter of a mile away from the hangar, Abdul, Bijan and two others worked on the final preparation of the jet's cargo. Pallets of empty steel pails sat on the floor, delivered the previous day by from Global Industries. The 150 pails completed the list of items Jaffar needed.

Abdul hated the workspace he found himself in. The Quonset hut was dimly lit and the curved metal roof seemed to absorb the heat from the day, turning the building into an oven—a full 30 degrees hotter than outside. They could not open the doors to get a breeze to flow through; Jaffar had been most insistent on this. To thwart nosy visitors, even the filthy windows had been left dirty to keep outsiders from seeing in. Unfortunately, the dirt also kept most of the light out.

The building had been chosen for the sake of security; it was away from the main activity of the airport, yet close enough to the old hangar that housed the Boeing that they could keep an eye on the plane.

Abdul wasn't used to hard labor. The last time he had done any strenuous activity was when he had killed Mohammed and hidden his lifeless body in the wash almost a year earlier. The four men were soaked in sweat from the hard work and oppressive heat.

At night, the temperature dropped rapidly to below freezing, much like it did in the desert near Al Qa'im, the cold night air sucking the heat from the building as the sun went down. Having long ago grown accustomed to the comforts of his life as chief of police in that small and distant town, there was no happy medium for Abdul. "I hate this place!" he said to whoever would listen.

Bijan Harraj had used several types of explosives over the years, dynamite and plastic mostly. If you had the right connections and the right amount of money, it was easy to obtain any type of explosive in the Middle East—from TNT to C4—all stolen from the hundreds of military bases in the region. This was the first time Bijan had mixed such a large amount of ammonium nitrate and nitro methane, though. These two things were not readily available in Iraq.

Bijan supervised the other men while they added the proper portions of the fertilizer and nitro methane fuel to each of the black pails arranged on one side of the warehouse. Following explicit instructions, one-half inch diameter holes were drilled through the lids of ten pails. This was where the charges would go.

Abdul opened a cardboard box from Biafo Industries in Islamabad, Pakistan. He then gently placed a few of the sausage-shaped Tovex charges into the pail, completely surrounding a small ten-pound acetylene bottle, which had been placed in first. The acetylene, when ignited, would increase the fireball and the shattering effect of the explosion.

Then three of the Tovex sausages were wired to three leads. These leads would further be wired to three separate firing circuits prior to the jet's take-off. Finally, the holes in the lids were lined with grommets to prevent any sharp edges fraying the leads. They were then sealed with quick-drying, black latex caulking so that to the casual observer, they looked like normal pails.

A further 90 pails were filled with the ammonium nitrate and nitro methane mix, the ratio carefully monitored by Bijan. A thick, continuous bead of caulking was applied to the top edge of them and the lever lock lids were put on and snapped into place. This created an airtight seal, preventing the nitro methane from degrading, evaporating or bleeding off, which might lessen the explosion.

The remaining 50 empty pails were filled with a mixture of the ammonium nitrate fertilizer and a half gallon of diesel fuel.

In addition to the dangerous task of mixing and filling the pails, each pail had to be placed individually on a scale, weighed and numbered. Then the information was recorded in a ledger. This job was particularly difficult, as all four men—after working for hours in the poorly lit and ventilated room—had developed severe headaches. Ventilating the space, would have required opening a door or window and inviting discovery.

They managed though, and finally the pallets were reloaded with the pails and they were shrink-wrapped. Only then did Bijan allowed the door to be opened a few inches to vent the space to the great relief of the men inside.

With fresh air finally filling the space, cleanup commenced. All literature and labels on the outside of the empty nitro methane containers was peeled off; the empty cardboard boxes that had contained the Tovex were broken down; and all that was left was a trip to the onsite recycling plant that serviced McCarran International.

Finally, the Quonset building was closed up and locked, once more giving the look of a derelict structure. This time however, it now contained enough high explosives to level a good portion of the surrounding airport.

Upon completion of the work, Bijan permitted himself, Abdul and the other men to return to Jaffar's small, rented warehouse that served as sleeping quarters for the men. There were cots and the office had been converted to a makeshift kitchen, with a hot plate and a kettle. To Abdul, today this place seemed like Jannah—his Heaven.

Sacramento, California - March 16, 1981

Over the past two weeks Giti had made some good progress and was well enough to be discharged from Mercy Hospital. The only concern left was her lack of memory.

"Like I explained to Officer Grant, I don't remember a fight in the bedroom and I don't remember who hit me." Giti continued, "I also don't remember a man named Jaffar and I don't remember a son." Detective Bursil could not think of any more questions to ask. He exhaled loudly.

"Do you remember telling us that a man hit you?"

"Yes! But that's all I know! At least it's all I think I know." Giti threw her hands to her face and began to cry. Fatemah went to her and consoled her; soon the sobbing stopped and Giti lifted her head.

"But you do remember Zafar and me, don't you Giti?" Giti smiled as she wasn't sure about much, but something inside her told her that the couple was indeed family.

"Yes! I think so." The two faces were reflected in many photographs throughout the home, and yes, there was something familiar about them. Giti smiled again.

"For the last week you have shown me pictures of my family and a man named Reza." Giti stopped for a moment, "Also a man who was my husband, Jaffer something?"

"Yes, you were married to him," the detective said sourly. He was getting frustrated.

Fatemah gave him a dirty look. It had the instant effect of stopping him from going further. He looked over at his partner, frustrated and also ashamed. "Let's go, Colin. I think we have as much as we are going to get today."

Zafar showed the two men to the front door. He followed them as they walked down the front stairs and watched as they continued out to the street. The two detectives walked past the solitary TV reporter that still maintained a vigil on the street. Zafar walked back into the house, to hear the voices of his wife and his sister-in-law.

"Why do you and Zafar call me Giti?"

Fatemah looked puzzled, "Because Giti, that's your name, dear."

"Well from now on I want you to call me Donya!"

Fatemah couldn't think of anything to say, except simply, "Alright, Donya."

Zafar looked at his watch as he entered the living room, "I don't know about you ladies, but I'm starving." The hour was late and all three had not eaten since lunchtime.

"Yes, I am hungry and I'm sure Giti—I mean Donya—should eat as well! The doctors said you must keep up your strength; it's all part of getting better."

"But, will I, Fatemah? Will I get better?" It was a question that they had been unable to answer, for weeks.

That night as Giti crawled into bed, she immediately felt drowsy thanks to a couple of tablets the doctor had prescribed for her. Just before falling asleep, she thought about the bottle Fatemah had taken the pills from. The bottle had said: *For Giti Roshtti, prescribed by Dr. Zack Phillips, take two tablets at bedtime, DO NOT mix with alcohol.* Then the blackness of sleep took over.

Although Giti went quickly into a deep sleep, her mind was awash with images, a kaleidoscope of images. Images of photographs, like the ones on her mantel of people she knew that somehow she had a connection to; images of faces, like the faces of the two detectives who had visited often over the last weeks, along with faces of several FBI agents. These men all seemed to be shouting questions at her, "Who? What? When? Where? Why?"

If someone had been in the room with Giti, they would have seen her hands gesticulate, her feet twitch and her legs move. They would have seen the minute changes of expression on her face as the movie which had been her life played before her eyes, the reel of images unfolding in her mind's eye as the night turned to morning. Sometimes the images were high definition, but most of the time she saw her dreams as if a finger had smeared Vaseline across her eyes, the images foggy and surreal.

Sometime after midnight, the thrashing of her legs and arms stopped and Giti fell into a very deep sleep once more. This lasted but a few short hours; soon the images began surfacing again from her subconscious. Her respiration increased and her bedclothes and sheets were soon soaked through with an uncomfortable sweat. The flood of images moved faster and faster through her brain ... over and over ...

There was a wedding under brilliant sunshine, laughter, a little boy, an airliner upside down, falling from the sky like a wounded bird ... a son, her son ... *I have a son!*

"Sina! Sina!" Giti shouted as she stared toward the window, now just barely awake. "Sina!" Giti got up and ran to the window, staring out at the dark, deserted street; even the lone TV reporter had given up and gone home for the night.

Light from the hallway flooded the room as Fatemah and Zafar ran quickly to her. "What is it Giti … I mean Donya? What's wrong?"

"Where's my poor Sina? And where the hell is that Goddamned Jaffar?" In spite of her shocking appearance and words of rage, both Zafar and Fatemah smiled.

Giti looked at her sister-in-law, puzzled. "Fatemah, what's with the name Donya?" Zafar and Fatemah both smiled again.

"You wanted to be called that and we did so because we wanted you to be happy … so you would remember your life and what has happened … and you do!" exclaimed Fatemah happily.

"Answer my question!" demanded Giti. "Where is my son?"

Zafar said it as kindly as he could. "We don't know where they are."

"What?"

"No one has seen them since Jaffar took Sina from the school."

Giti walked over to the dresser, stared at her reflection in the mirror with her eyes wide with disbelief and shock. Her hand went to her jaw and she stroked her newly lumpy visage. Then her eyes went cold. "He did this to me. Jaffar hit me! And he has taken my son!"

Zafar had never seen her so angry. "Do you want us to call the police?"

"No," she said firmly. "Not right now. Let's talk first. I need to know how to deal with this." She was white with worry for Sina and Fatemah gathered her in an embrace.

The three of them talked for over an hour—not as long as Giti wanted, and Fatemah insisted on putting her to bed before she was ready—but long enough to fill in the gaps missing from Giti's memory as well as to fill her in on what had happened during the last two months when she had been hospitalized. When Giti had finished asking questions, however, the two most important ones still remained unanswered.

"Where are Sina and Jaffar? Is my son alive?"

March 17, 1981

"Good morning Fatemah. Where's Zafar?" said Giti as Fatemah let her into the house.

Fatemah marveled; it was like a light switch had been thrown and a circuit had closed. The old Giti was climbing back to the light. She was almost normal, except for the sadness around her eyes as she worried about her missing son.

"It's Tuesday morning. He's at work. I told him he should go." Fatemah recalled the reluctance with which Zafar had done so. It wasn't until she used the words 'girl talk' that he relented. Both knew that Giti was holding something back, that her reluctance to talk was no longer a case of a failed memory. Over a plate of eggs and toast, the discussion from the night before resumed.

"I'm so scared Fatemah! What if he has harmed Sina?"

"You need to speak to the police!"

"But if I do, I may seal Sina's fate! I don't know what to do!"

"But you know where he is, or at least you have an idea." Fatemah could tell by Giti's reluctance to look at her.

This morning Giti had quietly gone through her closet, the one she had shared with Jaffar. She vaguely recalled paper, lots of paper, and how angry Jaffar had been to see her going through it. The secret to finding Sina was in those papers—but he had taken them all. She was desperate to find anything, but the closet revealed nothing, not a single shred of evidence. She turned her attention to the nightstands. The one on Jaffar's side of the bed was empty of clues. Then she looked down to see a dust bunny trapped between the nightstand and the bed post.

My God look at this place. It's been months since I've cleaned. Suddenly the thought occurred to her to look under the bed. Something was there in the darkness, it was difficult to see what exactly … a scrap of paper.

Giti got down on her stomach. It was a letter, one Jaffar had missed. It had been under the bed since January seventh, not even three feet from her still form as she lay unconscious for nearly a whole day—a day she had barely survived.

Washington, D.C.

Michelle walked into the conference room, papers in hand, "Happy Saint Patrick's Day you guys!"

Donny and Jack looked up to see her dressed in a green wool sweater and skirt, a huge smile on her face. Noticing the sheaf of papers in her hand, Don asked, "What's up Michelle? Did the White House approve a bill to have the Potomac dyed green today?"

"Better than that. I just got this through from the FBI in Sacramento. DIANA spit it out, not five minutes ago."

Jack did a quick scan of the first two pages. This morning the FBI had issued an arrest warrant for Jaffar Hamid Harraj. He was no longer a missing person; he now wanted for kidnapping the son of Giti Roshtti.

"Bingo! It seems like Mr. Harraj is up to no good right here in the good old U.S. of A." Jack sat and thought for a few seconds, "Don, let's go down to see the Colonel. It looks like you and I could be headed west."

Less than five minutes later Jack and Donny sat opposite the colonel in his third floor office. While they waited for Michelle and Kip to join them, Jack scanned the papers Michelle had handed him minutes earlier. Don glanced out the office window at DuPont Circle. The traffic was light and he noticed that the clouds were clearing. "Looks like good weather for today's parade along Constitution Avenue."

The colonel looked down at the tree-lined circular street below. It was a view that would have been the envy of many others, but one that Colonel Hart rarely let himself enjoy. "It sure does Don!" Kip and Michelle arrived seconds later and took their seats.

"Before we begin this afternoon's briefing," Hart said, "What do you have Jack, that prompted you to ask this meeting be moved up an hour?" Jack handed the two pages to the Colonel who read them slowly, digesting the information. Then, as if he could read Jack's mind, he said, "So you want to go out there and see what you can dig up on our old friend Harraj?"

"How did you know?"

"As my mother used to say to me when I was a boy, I can read you like a book!" The colonel smiled. "I guess we could spare you and Donny for a few days, but let's get some other business taken care of first."

"Right!"

There were a few things on the table to discuss besides Harraj. An incident on 12th January at the San Juan Air National Guard base in Puerto Rico, where eleven men disguised as soldiers placed explosives on several aircraft and destroyed some of them was high on the list. It prompted a discussion about security.

"We have all seen what a small lapse in security can do," the colonel said, thinking of the way Jack and Michelle had duped the trainees at Coronado.

"They had the base under surveillance for some time and knew the routine," Michelle said. "But their surveillance was sloppy and did not go completely unnoticed. It seems some civilians living nearby recognized several of the perpetrators."

"That's right, Michelle," said Hart. "And they have arrested the man responsible for the raid, a Juan Carlos Rivera, but the ring-leader and head of the Boricua Popular Army, Filiberto Rios, escaped."

"He was ex-FBI, wasn't he?" Jack asked.

"Yes, and he claimed responsibility for the 1978 bombings of several small power stations in the San Juan area," Michelle said.

"What else do you have?" asked Hart.

Kip read the latest report from the CIA. "I have the latest of several reports about an Islamic extremist group calling itself Komando Jihad."

"Any specifics?"

"Nothing rock solid, but they have evidence this group is planning an attack on an airliner or airport in the next week or ten days." Nothing about this job was ever 100 percent.

"Let's hope your source can dig up some more facts," Hart said gruffly.

Colonel Hart was not angry, just frustrated by the lack of human intelligence in many spots around the globe. The CIA, with its budget that far outpaced his, still had issues with the lack of 'boots on the ground'.

"If that is all, then we will continue this discussion tomorrow morning," he concluded. Then he added, "Jack! Can you and Don remain for a moment?"

Sacramento, California - March 18, 1981

It had been well over two years since Jack had first driven down Zinfandel Drive. The trees were in bloom, unlike in Washington, D.C. where the trees were still bare. The Cherry Blossom Festival was still a few weeks away.

That earlier time had been in the autumn of 1978, and the trees had been brilliant colors, oranges and reds. The street had also been a chaotic mess of TV trucks and reporters; this time the street was quiet.

Jack and Donny walked up the front stairs and the front door opened before either of them could knock. They were greeted by Zafar. "I was just about to tell you two to go away, but you aren't police are you? In fact you look familiar."

"We were here for Reza's funeral a couple of years ago. I'm Jack Coward and this is Don Zeigler."

"Won't you two come in?" This time the invitation was accepted.

In the small front room, Giti and Fatemah were sitting on the couch. Introductions were made, "Giti, Fatemah—you two remember these gentlemen? They are the ones who saved me from the news reporter after Reza died. This is Jack and this is Don," Zafar said, indicating each man. Then, "These two lovely ladies are my wife Fatemah and my sister-in-law, Giti." Everyone shook hands.

No introductions were needed from Jack's point of view. He was very familiar with both women, especially Giti, albeit from pictures taken by Don through a telephoto lens.

"Won't you sit down! Would you like some tea or coffee?" Fatemah asked.

"I would love a cup of coffee, Fatemah," said Don.

"Nothing for me thanks!" Jack was sure he would spill it. He was a little nervous about this whole matter and not completely sure how to proceed. Though they had clearance from the FBI, he now had to face the white lie he and Don had told years ago … that they were friends of Reza's. He may even have to admit that he had been hired to find her by the very man who had hurt her!

"The FBI telephoned me a little while ago and said that two men would coming from Washington," said Zafar.

"That would be Donny and I." Jack continued, "We work for newly formed federal investigation agency."

Giti was confused, "I thought the FBI was handling this investigation? What agency do you work for?"

Jack tried to dodge it. "We are here regarding your husband, Jaffar. We understand he is missing."

Knowing how difficult this was on Giti, Zafar responded to Jack. "Yes, along with my nephew Sina. They have not been seen since January."

"We know the FBI has been on the case, but they haven't had any real leads," Giti said.

"Is there anything you can remember, anything you may have not told the police or the FBI, something that might help us find them?" Jack asked gently.

Giti looked him in the eye, "Who did you say you work for?"

Jack sighed. She was no pushover. "We are from the National Anti-Terrorism Agency," he said.

She gasped. "Do you think my husband is a terrorist?" she asked as Fatemah and Zafar stared with wide eyes at Jack and Don.

"Possibly," said Jack. There was no way to sugar-coat this.

Zafar recovered first. "Giti did find a utility bill from the State of Utah. No—it was from Utah Power or something ..."

"It was from Utah Power and Light," Giti said. "It was for a property in Utah, but it was addressed to Jaffar Hodgeson, here in Sacramento, to a post office box."

"Giti, can you tell us what kind of property it was for ... was it for a house or apartment?"

"No! No! Nothing like that! Oh my God ..." she said as she connected the dots, "It was for an airport, a real airport!"

Don and Jack's eyebrows both shot up. "This bill, can we see it?"

"I don't have it! Only the envelope! Jaffar took those papers with him. But I'm sure that is where he and Sina are!"

"Those papers were addressed to Jaffar Hodgeson?"

"Yes!"

Fatemah entered with a tray piled high with a variety of desserts as well as coffee and tea.

"Here you are," she said. "Are you sure you wouldn't like some coffee or cake? A tea perhaps?" She looked at Jack.

"A tea would be fine, thank you," he relented.

"I'm sure my little Sina is there, but I'm afraid Jaffar will hurt him! That's why I never told the police about it." Giti began to cry, but quickly regained her composure.

"Don't worry, Giti," Jack said. It was out of character for him to touch others, but without thinking he put one hand on her arm to comfort her. "I'm certain Don and I can get him back."

For a moment, their eyes met and Jack felt a shiver down his spine. There was something haunting about this woman. From the first time he'd seen her, he'd felt it. Quickly he looked away.

Half an hour later, as they walked to the car Jack said to Don, "Looks like there is a hell of a lot more to this than meets the eye!"

"Yes! If the information about the airport is correct, then we may have a lot more to worry about than a simple kidnapping."

March 19, 1981

Jack, Don, Michelle and Kip were back at headquarters in Washington. They were meeting to discuss what Jack and Don had learned in Sacramento.

"Kip! What does our little electronic marvel DIANA have to say about one Jaffar Hodgeson?" Michelle asked.

"Well let's see... Jaffar Hamid Harraj, A.K.A. Jaffar Hodgeson—that much we knew. Owner of Sunwest Properties, the company that owns a large portion of Wendover Air Force base in Utah. He has one aircraft, a Boeing 720, purchased last year from a company called Mile High Aviation."

"So, everything that Giti Roshtti told us checks out!" Jack said. "Has anyone contacted the owner of Mile High Aviation?"

"Kip and I were there last year," Michelle said. "Fred Carlson, the owner of Mile High was murdered around the time of that purchase!"

"That's too much of a coincidence!" said Don.

"Yes, but there's no evidence to tie Jaffar or anyone else to the crime," Michelle said. "The local police just think it was just a robbery gone bad."

"As I recall, both these places are out in the middle of nowhere, out in the desert!" Jack said.

"I know, robbery doesn't seem likely," Michelle mused.

"The Colonel wants us out there to do reconnaissance on Wendover." Michelle said. "I've already arranged flights to Salt Lake City. We will need a place that's a little more local to Wendover as a staging point."

"Any reason for Salt Lake? As I recall, that's over a hundred miles away."

"We need to check out a local rock quarry in Ogden, you remember that bulletin from the ATF about missing explosives a few weeks back?"

"Are you thinking that perhaps it has something to with Jaffar?"

"I'm not sure! Probably it's just another one of your coincidences, Jack."

"You guys know I don't believe in coincidences!" He laughed. He knew they didn't either.

It seemed the visit to Giti Roshtti was the beginning of uncovering a real hornet's nest.

Ogden, Utah - March 20, 1981

"So you say that 500 pounds of Tovex is missing?" Jack asked Brian Croft, owner-operator of Bedrock Sand and Gravel Company. Croft had been grilled by both FBI and ATF agents alike and was tired of the parade of federal agents who had descended on his place of business. The ATF had threatened to close his business down permanently.

"Look I'm tired! I've answered questions until I'm blue in the face."

"Perhaps you could answer just a few more questions for us? It won't take long." Michelle smiled and that seemed to calm Mr. Croft down somewhat.

"Okay! Ask away!"

"Thank you."

"Now, about the 500 pounds of explosives ..."

"Actually it was 550 pounds," Croft said.

"So, 550 pounds of explosive are missing. Are you sure it wasn't used in a shoot and not recorded properly?"

"As I've already told the people at the ATF, no! It was a theft. I'm certain of that!"

"In 1979, 50 pounds went missing, didn't it?" Jack had read the ATF report about that.

"It was theft, both then and now. I record every ounce of explosive I use." Jack nodded, he had also looked over audits done by both the FBI and the ATF. Mr. Croft had kept remarkable records over the years.

He asked, "Are you sure you haven't forgotten something? Any scrap of memory you have might tell us something."

"No! Nothing."

Jack handed Croft his card. "If you remember something, please give me a call. There's an answering machine. Leave a message if I'm not in."

"I will." Croft watched as Jack and Michelle got back into their rental car and headed back across the gravel parking lot towards the gate. They stopped the car and waited. A minute later a man dressed in a business suit approached them. He spoke to Jack through the open driver's side window then got in. Jack began reversing back towards the office.

"Christ Almighty! What now?" Croft asked. A minute later all three agents stood at his desk.

"Donny here was canvassing the neighborhood businesses. One of them said they seem to recall a couple of trucks in the area around the time of the theft. Normally they wouldn't have taken notice, but on occasion these two trucks stopped and watched your place for over an hour."

"That's right! I seem to recall a couple of pickup trucks driving into the yard and turning around. They did it twice in the days just before the theft."

"Can you describe these trucks?"

"No! Just ordinary Chevy pickups, but there were signs on each door."

"Can you remember what the signs said?"

"No! But the trucks were both the same color, a light yellow."

"Is that all?"

"Yes! I haven't see the trucks since. I would have noticed, we don't get much traffic out here, especially since you feds shut down my whole operation!"

"Thank you, Mr. Croft. Keep in touch if you remember anything else."

"I will."

As they made the 35-minute drive back to Salt Lake City and their hotel, all three had questions going through their minds. But the ride remained a quiet one, except for the sound of the tires on the pavement, interrupted by the occasional passing of an oncoming car. The silence was finally broken by Michelle, who said to no one in particular, "Maybe our next stop will prove more fruitful. I wonder what we're going to find there?"

Wendover, Utah - March 21, 1981

The moon was now a day past full, hidden behind high, thin cirrus clouds. This cast an eerie glow over the entire landscape. With the headlights off, Jack drove slowly along the north perimeter fence of Wendover Air Force

Base and past the front gate. Donny and Michelle were in the back seat wearing night vision goggles, focusing on the airport while Jack did his best to focus on the road.

At the northwest corner of the airfield, Jack made a left and followed the road south for a few hundred yards. He stopped and made a U-turn then drove the four wheel drive Jeep into the sand off the left side of the road, just inside the Nevada border which was only a few dozen yards away.

The Jeep was hidden amongst the scrub, in line with the south side of the concrete apron which ran in front of all of the main hangars. It was no wonder that General Leslie Groves had chosen this airfield to train his top secret atomic bomb air crews on, for it was truly isolated.

The wind came from the northwest. Jack, Donny and Michelle lay hidden from view behind a small berm as they focused their night vision goggles on the main hangars and other buildings. There were no vehicles, nor were there any lights. The base, for all intents and purposes, looked deserted.

"I thought it would be a bit warmer," Don said. "After all, today is the first day of spring." Donny pulled the zipper of his jacket up the last quarter of an inch, in an effort to trap more warm air close to his body.

"A month from now it will be about ten degrees warmer here. But I know what you are saying." Michelle repeated Don's actions. The infrared technology of the goggles relied not on light amplification, but on heat sources.

Jack said, "I can see very little! All the structures just show ambient heat radiation from the sun, no warm bodies. Looks like no one is home." They knew that this was not the case, however.

"Let's change location," suggested Don. The three removed their goggles and headed south down the west perimeter road. There were tire tracks in and out of the main gate, but it was difficult to tell exactly how old they were—but they did verify human presence.

A few minutes later, Don said, "This should be good here." He'd spotted a place where water had eroded a small gully under the fences. The gap was big enough for them to crawl under without much effort. They were now on the northwest corner of Wendover Airfield, a cold, unwelcoming and seemingly deserted place.

"Where to, Jack?" Don asked softly.

"Let's check out the operations building, then the tower."

They passed by the first large squadron hangar and in less than ten minutes, the trio arrived at the 'tee' shaped, two-story operations building.

As they circumnavigated the aging structure, they heard no sounds apart from the wind and the cracking of the flaking white paint, knocked loose as they hugged the exterior seeking maximum concealment. They quickly and quietly checked each door and window for signs of entry. There were none.

"I think we should check out the tower," Jack whispered.

"Do you want me here on the ground for cover, Jack?" Don asked. Normally that would be the case, as anyone in the tower would be trapped above if discovered, their only escape route blocked.

"No, Donny! I want three sets of eyes up in the tower, it should provide a really good vantage point from which to survey things." Then Jack added, "Besides, this place looks deserted. I think we'll be okay."

In the tower, their perch, fifty feet above the ground, did in fact provide an excellent view of their surroundings, as it had done for aircraft controllers in decades past. Unfortunately, *they* had not gone unobserved in the stillness of the high desert. Their conversation had been picked out of the sound of the wind by other men who also sought to hide.

After descending the metal stairs, Jack, Donny and Michelle moved fast towards the Enola Gay hangar, using the smaller buildings and the squadron hangars along the way as cover. During World War II, these hangars had housed P51 and P47 fighters; now the structures were dilapidated, empty buildings. The only buildings that remained seemingly intact were the enlisted men's quarters, the operations building and the large Enola Gay hangar, which was in front of them.

They walked cautiously and quietly along the concrete apron in front of the buildings, their rubber soles muffling their footfalls. Jack was just about to step forward out of the shadow of the last small building, when the relative silence of the Wendover base was broken by a loud rattle as the large door of the hangar began to slide open.

They froze in place, breathing as quietly as they could. There was no light from inside the hangar to cast a glow onto the ground so they hastily put their goggles on again and saw a pickup pull out of the dark space and into the faint moonlight. It was light colored, with a magnetic sign on each door. Michelle whispered, "Doesn't that look like one of the trucks Mr. Croft described yesterday?"

"It sure does," Jack whispered back. They watched as the truck moved away in the darkness toward the smaller buildings in the distance, all the while the driver not turning on the lights.

"You were right, Don," Jack said. "Looks like someone is home after all, but they don't want anyone to know it!"

Because the area around the hangar was flat terrain, it was unsuitable for observation. Jack decided he needed a different vantage point. "You two are going to have to stay put for now, I'm going to try and get to the northwest corner of the hangar," he told Don and Michelle.

"Be careful, Jack," Michelle said quietly.

Jack didn't have to be told. "Don't worry about me. You two just stay out of sight and try to keep me covered from here."

With that, Jack made a beeline for the largest building on the entire base, the one that had housed the B-29 that dropped the atomic bomb on Hiroshima in 1945. It was the safest choice; the entire exterior of the building was covered by a layer of rust so the sheet metal would not reflect light—or Jack's shadow.

"As long as the moon stays behind those clouds, he'll be okay, Michelle. There's not enough light for him to be seen without night vision goggles," Don assured her.

"I know! But, I still don't like it."

"Jack can take care of himself."

Jack's surveillance risk was rewarded a few minutes later when the sound of an engine was heard in the distance, growing louder as it approached. The truck was back. It made a right hand turn and came to a halt in front of the immense hangar doors, not 100 feet from Jack. The driver signaled with a short honk of the horn and the large center panel moved on its overhead track, revealing a brightly lit interior. But instead of opening just enough for the truck to enter, however, the panel kept going, soon slipping behind a second, third and fourth panel, leaving a gaping opening 80 feet wide that revealed the interior of the hangar.

"Why are the doors open like this?" A man ran towards the door, waving his arms, shouting, "Hamid! What's going on?"

"I'm sorry, Excellency! But the door control on the wall is still broken and this remote is not working!"

Jaffar Hamid Harraj stood with his hands on his hips, silhouetted by the lit interior of the hangar. In the background was a four-engine Boeing jet. "You idiot! I told you to get that fixed." Jaffar turned towards another man. "You! Get those overhead lights off! Now!" The man ran toward the electrical panel and doused the large flood lights.

Donny and Michelle had removed their night vision equipment as soon as the interior lights began to illuminate the tarmac in front of the hangar. They had ample time to look at the huge space inside the hangar. Donny could only guess, but he figured they were looking at upwards of 100,000 square feet of floor area with offices along the north and south walls, hidden behind doors.

Minutes later, the cranky remote unit was repaired, the pickup was driven inside and the doors closed once again. From his vantage point, Jack heard Jaffar shouting inside the building, issuing a command that men be dispatched to check outside, "You two and you, go with Atash, check outside! Don't forget to take your weapons with you this time!"

Jack did not pause for one second. He moved quickly away from the hangar to rejoin Donny and Michelle. No sooner had he crouched down, when the man-size door, not ten feet from where he had been hiding, opened and four armed men stepped outside.

"You two go that way, we will go this way," one man said, indicating direction to his comrades.

With their night vision goggles on, they could clearly see that all four men were armed with Kalashnikov assault rifles. "What are we going to do, Jack?" Michelle whispered.

"I don't know about you two, but I had a pretty good look inside that hangar. My infrared scope of the south wall offices showed only four others inside, not counting the two guys in the truck, and the four we already could see in the main part of the hangar."

"So, we are looking at … what … ten Tangos, including Jaffar himself?" Don asked.

Jack nodded.

"Any sign of the boy?"

"Nope."

They watched two of the security detail glumly walking the in front of the hangar, half-heartedly searching.

"Look at those two. They don't seem too interested in their duties do they?" Jack asked.

Donny and Michelle watched as the two men finished their slow traverse of the front of the hangar and turned left, disappearing from sight. "No they sure don't. Their rifles were carried down at their sides."

Michelle's eyes were slightly better than the men's. She added, "I didn't notice any large magazines in either weapon, just small clips—and neither man's fingers were anywhere near their triggers."

"I'm sure I heard Jaffar reminding all four of those guys to take their weapons with them this time." Jack thought for a second then said, "I would like to wait until tomorrow to get a few more bodies here, but my gut says we go in right now!"

He looked at his companions in the dark. This option had been discussed with Colonel Hart, but Jack was cautioned to do so only if he felt the situation warranted it. "We can take the four in the security detail without too much trouble," he said. "That would cut the odds almost in half. I don't think they are expecting trouble."

Their Sig Sauer P226 pistols were fitted with the latest noise suppression hardware. This weapon was the newest available to special forces, though it was not yet available to U.S. troops in general. In addition each of them carried an M249 automatic rifle.

"Also, I bet that our friend Jaffar won't want to get his hands dirty … he won't come out shooting," said Don wryly.

"Let's do it," Michelle said.

"Okay! Don, you and Michelle take the two as they come around the corner, and I'll take the other two as they come back at us from the left." Pumped on adrenaline, Don and Michelle nodded.

Jack watched as the pair of guards went around the rear of the hangar. He quickened his pace so he could arrive at the corner before his targets did, aware that the pair he had been following might just meet up with the other two and do an about-face.

He stopped just shy of the corner and waited. He was sure the time for his targets to arrive had come and gone. For an instant he worried that they might be on their way to Donny and Michelle's position. They would be expecting only two men. This could be bad.

Then he risked a quick glance around the corner and relaxed. All four men stood in a circle, unarmed, their rifles leaning against the side of the hangar. Each had their hands cupped around a glowing cigarette, unsuspectingly taking a break—and ruining whatever night vision they might have had.

Jack had a few options. He could wait until they were through smoking and they had split up to continue their rounds and go ahead as he and Don and Michelle had planned, or he could attack now while they were unarmed and unsuspecting … but to do so he would have to quietly cross 150 feet of concrete, unobserved. Not a good option Jack, he said to himself.

The best option was to wait for Donny and Michelle to come looking for their quarry. He didn't have to wait long; on the far side of the hangar he could see Don's smiling face through his goggles. Don signaled for him to wait at his corner of the building. Both men knew that if they engaged the four guards at the rear of the building they would be in each other's line of fire.

It seemed like the smoke break was taking an eternity. Finally the four guards reluctantly picked up their rifles and each pair continued on their rounds. Jack backed around the corner and waited for his two guards to appear. As they did, he shot them both dead, a single round through each heart.

On the south side of the building Donny did the same seconds later.

"What now, Don?" Michelle asked him. That question was answered a minute later when Jack came around the corner carrying a bundle of clothes.

"Here, Donny, put on the jacket. I will help you with the head gear in a minute." He continued, "Michelle help me get the jacket and head scarf off one of these two gentlemen."

As she bent down to do so, Michelle got a whiff of the two dead men, "I don't think I can do this Jack! These guys smell like they haven't bathed in months." It was probably true.

"I know, but it's better than getting shot. Their outfits might buy us a few critical minutes!"

Michelle did as asked and tried not to gag.

They quietly opened the side door of the hangar and took a peep into the dimly-lit interior. It would provide ample cover, even without the element of surprise. "We walk in like we own the place and find our two main targets.

Jaffar and Sina are to be taken alive at all costs; any armed hostiles will be dealt with as the situation dictates. Eliminate them if you have to."

"Donny, you walk down the north side of the hangar and clear the office and work spaces. Michelle and I will do the same on the opposite side. Let's go!"

The three entered the hangar and split up. Jack took care of the two men focused on repairing the door mechanism while Michelle started to check the offices one by one. She stopped when she heard voices in the office ahead. There were three men there, two had accents and one did not.

"I would like to know why you did not do as I asked, Mr. Sutton?"

"But, I did Jaffar! I have done all the things you asked me to and more."

"Then tell me why the door controls are still not fixed? I asked you weeks ago to do this and tonight the door wide stayed open." Jaffar looked over at the guard. "I could have you shot!"

"Please! I just want to go home to my family and see my wife again!"

"So you shall. Your work here is finished." Jaffar and the guard turned and started out of the office. A butt of a rifle struck the guard from behind. Jaffar looked down at the unconscious guard, startled. Before he could yell out, a hand covered his mouth and he was forced by one of his guards, to back up against the wall. Something isn't right, he thought as he stared at the man in front of him.

"Where is the boy, Jaffar?" the man whispered. Jaffar's eyes grew wide. This man shouldn't be here, couldn't be here. He should have disappeared months ago.

"You! But it can't be!"

"Yes, Jaffar! It's me, your old pal, the private detective. Now for the last time, where's the boy?"

"Sina is down the hall in the last office on the right. I haven't touched a hair on his head." Michelle hurried down to the office, where she found Sina fast asleep in bed.

"Order your men to surrender!"

This was done and four unarmed men emerged from the upstairs mezzanine and quietly gave themselves up.

Michelle returned from down the aisle after deciding to let Sina sleep. "Jack, the boy is safe and sound down the way, fast asleep. I think we should just leave him there for the time being."

"Okay! But once Donny makes sure the rest of the hangar is secure, I want you to go back and watch over him."

The main lights were turned on and everyone was herded into a single group. Jack had kept the casualties to a minimum; the only ones killed had been the four outside guards.

"Now, let's see what's what and who's who," Jack said. All of them knew Jaffar, but the man with whom he had been arguing was a mystery.

"Who are you, sir?"

"My name is Joe Sutton. My wife and I were kidnapped and have been held here for almost six months."

"Why?"

"I worked for Boeing in Seattle all my life and Jaffar, here, forced me to work on this aircraft and another."

"Jack, I recognize this aircraft from the markings. I know who it belongs to!" Michelle said excitedly.

"Who?"

Suddenly someone yelled, "Put your guns down!" It was Sameed. Having seen the three NATA agents in the control tower, he'd decided it was time to quit hiding. Maybe when this was over he would actually be able to go home to Iraq if he acted now and pleased Jaffar. Maybe he wasn't going to die after all!

In Sameed's right hand was a nasty-looking knife with a curved blade, which was pressed against the skin of Mrs. Janette Sutton's neck. Tears were streaming down her face. Beside Sameed, Abbas stood holding a fully automatic AK-47 assault rifle, with a curved thirty-round clip. It was trained on another handcuffed female prisoner. Both women were crying and shaking with fear. Jack had no choice. "Put down your weapons," he instructed Don and Michelle. Then, to Sameed and Abbas, he said, "Please! Don't hurt the ladies!"

— Chapter 23 —

March 21, 1981 - Wendover, Utah

"Good job, Sameed! Your timing is excellent, if somewhat of a surprise ... You men, relieve these infidels of their weapons!" commanded Jaffar.

In a few short minutes Jack, Donny and Michelle had been stripped of all weapons and lined up against the wall, their hands tied behind their backs. This time they were guarded by two very alert, armed guards.

"Where have you and Abbas been?"

"I have been … we have been hiding in the control building. You know, the one where the landing lights are made to work from."

"But, why, Sameed?"

"We thought we had made you angry, disappointed."

"No! This is not true. You have done well." Indeed, the two had snatched victory from the jaws of defeat. "I want you to take Mrs. Sutton and our special guest back to their quarters and then return here at once."

"Yes, Jaffar."

Janette Sutton and the empress were escorted into one of the pickups by an armed guard, the hangar door was opened just enough for the truck to leave and the prisoners were driven away.

"Jack! Do you know who that was?" Michelle asked.

"No idea! Who?"

A rifle butt landed in Jack's mid-section, causing him to double over and fall to the floor. He barely had time to see it coming, much less to prepare himself for it.

"Quiet! No talking."

Jack lay on the concrete floor, gasping, trying to catch his breath.

"That will be enough, Farouk!" Jaffar smiled as he spoke. He'd wanted bad things to happen to this private detective for a very long time, but now he had other plans for him.

"Abbas, take the woman and put her in with the boy." Jaffar smiled, "And make sure once more that she has no more weapons on her." His meaning was clear and Don jumped to Michelle's defense.

"Leave her alone!" This time it was Donny's turn to receive a rifle butt to the stomach. In an instant he collapsed to the concrete, close to his friend.

"Take her away, and put a guard outside her door!"

Ten minutes later, Sameed and the guard returned from the storage building.

"Now, Mr. Private Detective, you and this other gentleman are going to take a drive. I do not want the least bit of trouble from you."

"Donny and I are not fond of drives." For that Jack received another blow to the mid-section.

"If there is any trouble from you, or my men are not back in 15 minutes, I will shoot the boy and the woman, just as you shot my four guards earlier."

"You don't seem too upset about that!" Jack somehow wasn't surprised.

Jaffar leaned closer to Jack and whispered, "Their usefulness was finished anyway, you only moved up their deaths by a day or two." The he laughed. "Remember, 15 minutes, starting right now!"

Jack was placed in the lead vehicle and Donny was placed in the second pickup. There would be no tricks.

March 24, 1981

Jack and Donny had been given no food or water since they'd been thrown into the cold, dark empty building. Both men were dehydrated and weak. Under their shirts, they sported huge black and yellow bruises. After almost 36 hours, the door to their prison opened. The sudden change in light caused both men to squint. "Out! Now!'

Both Donny and Jack struggled to get to their feet. They could not afford another attack from a rifle butt, "I said out!"

"We are coming," Jack said to the guard, hoping to preempt any such attack. When they stepped out of the building, black hoods were immediately placed over both their heads and they were led over to a pickup, where they were made to lie face-down in the truck's box. Both their stomachs hurt. The truck moved away.

"Where do you think they are taking us, Jack?" whispered Don.

"I have no idea, but I don't think it's to a firing squad."

"Yeah, I know! Our pal Jaffar does seem to have a real cruel streak in him, doesn't he?"

"You're not kidding!"

The Sunwest Properties truck drove slowly around the airport, down one runway, and then down the other. For fifteen minutes they repeated the process, slowing down, turning, reversing—all in an effort to disorient the two prisoners.

Finally the truck stopped in front of storage building number twelve. It had been vacated earlier that morning by Mrs. Sutton and the Empress Farah. Jack and Donny were helped out of the truck and led through the door. Their bindings were cut and they were ordered to the far side of the room, away from the door. "There will a guard outside the door. Do not try anything," warned their captors.

The heavy door was slammed shut and was bolted and locked from the outside.

After a few seconds, Jack's eyes adjusted to the dim lighting. "Look Don! Food and water!" Jack was a bit surprised; a few minutes earlier he thought perhaps their fate was either to die of starvation or thirst. "Also, we have a wood stove!"

Things were indeed looking up. They each had a small drink of water and Donny picked up a slice of bread. "What if this stuff is poisoned?"

"Not much we can do about it! Besides, if Jaffar wanted us dead, we'd already have been shot. No! He has something more sinister up his sleeve for us." Both men began to eat.

After a few minutes Don said, "You know, Jack, if we'd got here earlier we'd have had some female company!"

"What the hell are you talking about?" Jack took a whiff. All he could smell was himself and his over-ripe partner. "How can you smell anything?"

"Really, Jack! I tell you, there were women here sometime this morning. I can smell their scent."

Jack thought for a second. If anybody could smell a woman, it would be Donny. "Well, you old hound dog. You are not going to have any female company for a while so you can help me get a fire going in the stove. At least that will keep us warm."

Donny handed Jack a couple of the smallest pieces of wood that were stacked beside the stove, "I wonder where Michelle is?" he said morosely.

"I'm sure she's okay, buddy. Like I said, Jaffar wants us for something, I'm just not sure what!"

With a fire burning in the antique, cast-iron stove, the small wooden structure turned almost cozy. Jack and Donny started to examine their prison for a means of escape. Although the building was going on fifty years old, it was still structurally sound. Unfortunately, the improvements made by Jaffar's men had made it even more so.

"Well, let's see what we can find inside that may help us!" Jack said.

A thorough search of their prison turned up some surprising finds. Laid out on the bed, reassembled after being searched from top to bottom, were two knives from a set of cutlery, a ball point pen and, last of all, a small file. One of the knives—which had perhaps once been able to cut through a good steak when it was first purchased—could now easily filet a sockeye salmon … or even a man's throat.

Don was still searching in the desk, feeling around to make sure he didn't miss anything hidden in the corners. "Did you find anything in the desk?" Jack asked.

"A book. It appears to be a diary of sorts." Donny opened it. The words were definitely written in a feminine hand. He began reading and said to Jack, "Seems the former tenant here was Mrs. Sutton. She and her husband were on vacation last fall and were kidnapped by Jaffar."

"That's guy in the hangar."

"Yep!" Donny read further entries, written faithfully everyday—and with hope as well. This was a chronicle of Janette Sutton's imprisonment as well as her husband's—as best she knew it—since they had been separated the whole time.

For almost half an hour Don read quietly while Jack rested on the bed. His bruised stomach still hurt, but he was in a better frame of mind. He heard a noise outside and alerted Don.

"Listen! Does that sound like a truck? Quick! Hide the stuff." There were voices speaking Farsi outside the building and soon the door to their jail was opened once more.

"Back away from the door," Farouk yelled. Donny joined Jack on the bed. A box of food and a few jugs of water were placed on the floor, just inside the door. The guard with the Kalashnikov kept the weapon trained on the Americans. A second armed man stood behind a woman. A moment later, the women was forced to enter, prompted by the business end of the Kalashnikov. "Join your new friends!" a man said harshly.

The door was once again closed and bolted. Jack heard the truck drive off, leaving the trio alone.

"Mrs. Sutton, I presume!" Jack said, recognizing the woman he'd seen two nights previous with a knife pressed against her throat.

"You are correct, young man."

Jack and Donny stood up. "My name is Jack Coward and this man here is my friend, Don Zeigler. We are from the National Anti-Terrorist Agency, in D.C."

"I'm sorry, I've never heard of it."

"I'm not surprised. We are fairly new, and we don't advertise."

Jack motioned for Janette to sit down on the bed. "Can you tell us what's going on here? What's happening in the hangar?"

"Yes! First thing this morning, Farah and I were taken from here to the hangar."

"Farah?" Jack asked.

"Yes, the former Empress of Iran!" said Janette.

Don and Jack looked at each other, shocked. "What's she doing here?" Jack asked Don.

He just shrugged. "This gets weirder and weirder," he said. Mrs. Sutton had no answer, so she continued her story.

"Joe has been working on that plane in the hangar for months and I don't know why he's doing it. It breaks my heart that he's helping those animals! He acts like he's brain- washed!"

"It happens sometimes. It's called Stockholm Syndrome. Remember Patty Hearst and the Symbionese Liberation Army back in 1974? She ended up joining that little band of radicals," Jack said.

"I think he is trying to protect *you*," Don assured her, "Maybe he's afraid of you getting hurt!"

Suddenly Janette suddenly noticed the diary on the desk. For a moment she looked afraid.

"I'm sorry Mrs. Sutton, we read your diary. We were looking for things we could use to help us escape."

"Then you found our knives, the ones Farah and I were making to try and escape?"

"Yes," Jack said. Then he rubbed his chin, deep in thought. "What would Jaffar want with the Empress of Iran?" he asked.

"I don't know, but she told me they kidnapped her *and* her plane!" Janette said.

Jack sat back down on the single bed, brow furrowed as he tried to puzzle it out. Don and Janette sat down beside him, waiting.

Meanwhile, Jaffar was preparing his men and vehicles for the long drive to Las Vegas. There was only enough room for nine people in the three pickup trucks, but all their gear could go in the back.

"The Americans must have come here somehow. I'm sure they did not walk!" Jaffar yelled at his men. He pointed at two of them. "You two men search along the road to the west." He pointed at two more. "You two take the north side. Look off the road. That is the most likely place!"

"Yes, Excellency."

"And try not to be seen as you do it! We still need two more uninterrupted hours here!"

"Yes, Excellency."

It only took an hour to find Jack's rented four wheel drive Jeep. "The keys were still in it," one of Jaffar's men shouted triumphantly as they arrived back at the hangar.

"I want you to search the vehicle from top to bottom, from front to back. I do not want any more surprises. Mr. Jack Coward and his two companions have been enough trouble," Jaffar instructed. Then he thought about ridding himself of the troublesome trio. Simply killing them isn't enough, I want them to suffer for the trouble they have caused me, he thought to himself.

The men searched the truck and placed all the items they found in front of Jaffar.

"What do we have here?" Jaffar asked as he examined the weapons, ammo and IDs Jack, Donny and Michelle had stashed in the jeep. He was surprised to find that the private detective he had hired in 1978 was now someone he had to fear.

"The National Anti-Terrorist Agency!" He exclaimed, shocked. Then he examined the other two wallets. Immediately he rounded up his men. "We have run out of time. Everyone get to the trucks in ten minutes or you will be left behind!" he yelled. He was pretty sure the FBI wanted him for kidnapping; now it seemed he was wanted by other federal agencies who understood his terrorist ties. It was time to put the plan into action, ready or not.

All of Jaffar's men, with the exception of the two guarding Sina, Joe Sutton, Michelle and Farah, assembled in the main hangar. "I see all of you have finished shaving. Your faces can have nothing but close-cut beards. You will now dress in the clothes I have provided for you," Jaffar instructed, then "... and all of you will remove and discard your head scarves!"

There was a murmur of discontent; to do so would be dishonorable in the eyes of Allah. Jaffar nipped it in the bud. "There will no discussion about this! You will wear the hats provided. Your heads will still be covered, but you must blend in as much as possible."

In preparation for flight, over the past few weeks Jaffar had obtained, at great cost, fake IDs for all the men, including driver's licenses and other forged papers, such as a Brinks guard ID for one and a UCLA faculty member document for another.

"You have been given used wallets, with your new identities in each of them," he announced to his men. "Each of you must now assume your new roles. For the next stage of the operation to be successful, we cannot afford for you to be caught or for our hostage to be taken alive. If you are stopped by police you cannot talk. The IDs you have should get you past most scrutiny. There most likely won't be any trouble. Allahu Akbar!"

"Allahu Akbar!" the guards yelled in return.

By noon, two pairs of vehicles were heading south on U.S. Interstate 93, separated by ten minutes and several miles. They left behind a nearly-empty airfield; only a pair of men who had been given the unenviable task of guarding Jack, Donny and Mrs. Sutton remained. These men were not particularly happy about their task; the job was now even more difficult because they no longer had a means of transportation at their disposal. To bring the prisoners food and water, they now had to complete a round trip from the hangar to the storage building and back, carrying supplies, by foot.

It was well into the evening when the armed guards pounded on the door and ordered them to step back. They brought enough food and water to last for a few days then locked the door and left. When their footfalls died away, Jack said, "Donny, did you hear that?"

"I didn't hear anything!"

"Exactly, Don! Janette, do the guards always come in a truck?" Jack remembered the guards doing so, the night they arrived on the base.

"Yes! They come at least once a day, usually in the evenings … unless I get to visit Joe."

"These guys didn't have a truck. I think they were on foot."

"That's right Jack! I don't recall hearing a truck!"

"I bet that they've bugged out, leaving just these two guards." Jack and Don smiled at each other. Janette looked hopeful. Maybe this was their chance! All that day they had probed the building for weakness and once again had failed to find one. The only way out was the door—but two armed men would surely try to stop them. They had to get past them … but how?

Mrs. Sutton stood close to the wood stove, rubbing her hands together in an effort to warm up. "Every time those guards come and open the door, it takes forever to heat this darned place up again!" she complained. Jack looked at her, his face suddenly clearly displaying a 'eureka' thought.

"Mrs. Sutton, you're a genius! I could kiss you!" he said.

"What?"

"The stove! That's our way of here."

"What? Do you want to burn the place down, Jack?"

"No, Janette! Quite the opposite, in fact. I want to stop putting wood on the fire."

"Why? What good will that do?"

Jack looked thoughtfully over at Donny. "Don, what do you think that stove weighs?"

"I'd guess 250, maybe 300 pounds?"

"I bet it weighs all of that, probably more," Jack said. "Don't you think it would make an excellent battering ram?"

"It sure would Jack!" Donny walked over to the stove. He knew exactly what his friend had in mind. He put his hands near the top. "It's way too hot to move now though."

Las Vegas, Nevada - March 25, 1981

Bijan and Abdul had spent four long days moving the pallets of pails from the Quonset building to the hangar. It had been a slow process, because each load had to be unwrapped and transported then pail-by-pail carried up a flight of stairs and gingerly placed in its assigned seat. All of this was done according to a diagram each of them had and the process had to be exact; every pail had a label on its lid, and, depending on its contents, was placed in a certain seat.

After each pail was placed, it was secured to the seat back by several wrappings of grey duct tape. The curved shape of the seat backs and the round pails made this the easiest part of the job; the task of lifting the heavy pails one at a time up the stairs and navigating the plane's narrow aisles was most difficult. Abdul had lost almost 30 pounds over the last several weeks and was the fittest he'd been in many years.

When all 150 pails were aboard, the last thing to do—prior to actually arming the bombs—was to connect all the leads to the three firing circuits. There were primary and secondary circuits; if the first one failed, there was a backup. There was also another backup hooked up to an altimeter.

Jaffar unlocked the side door of the hangar and walked over to the jet, his jet. The stacks of empty pallets along the wall gave him an indication of the progress that had been made by Abdul and Jaffar's half-brother. As he looked up at the gleaming aircraft he felt a slight twinge of regret. It would be shame to see such a beautiful machine destroyed—after all it had cost him several million dollars.

But as quickly as that thought came, it was gone, replaced by one of victory. One more day and this would all be over … and if everything went well he would be safely out of the country with millions in the bank—because no one was going to be alive who would know the whereabouts of Jaffar Hodgeson.

Wendover, Utah

"It's getting cold in here!"

"I'm sorry Mrs. Sutton, but it can't be helped." Jack and Don both offered their jackets and both were refused once again.

"I shouldn't complain. At least I had a warm bed to sleep on last night. You poor dears were on the floor, with no blankets or anything."

The stove was as cold as it was going to get unless they wanted to take the risk of being discovered in mid-plan. At some point the guards were coming back to check on them and they needed to be prepared.

"Let's do this," Jack said to Don. "We'll start by getting those screws out of the flue." Using one of the knives, Don removed the screws and the section of pipe between the stove and the ceiling. Then Jack and Don strained as they lifted the stove to move it into position. Dirt and soot flowed out of the roof vent and covered the pair from head to toe, leaving them looking like a pair of raccoons. It would have prompted a laugh from all three, except for the situation. They had been wise enough to hold their breath and close their eyes.

Then, "One! Two! Three!" they yelled in unison and with perfect timing they moved step by step towards the door, about a dozen feet. They looked at each other, braced themselves and then counted again—and let the stove fly, with explosive results. The cast iron projectile hit the door just below mid-height and ripped it and its heavy frame completely from the rest of the wall, clean and neat. The sound of the heavy cast iron stove striking the concrete was incredibly loud, almost like a cannon volley. It seemed to echo off the nearby hills.

"That might bring the guards in a big hurry!" gasped Janette.

"I doubt it, but just in case, Mrs. Sutton, I want you and Donny to high-tail it out of here, now. Head north! Try to find a gap in the fence. Scale it, if you have to!"

"Just a minute, let me get my diary."

"You can come back for that later! Now get going, both of you."

"What are you going to do, Jack?" Donny almost didn't want to know. He could guess, even before Jack opened his mouth.

"I can disarm the guards! If there's a working phone, I will get word to Colonel Hart."

Don nodded. "I will try to get to the Jeep, get Janette to safety and alert the local authorities. There are a couple of small towns nearby, that's where we're headed," he said. Jack did not have to remind Donny about not coming in with guns blazing and sirens on.

"Good Luck, Jack!" Don said as he guided Mrs. Sutton away toward the north fence. The fast-approaching dusk would mask their escape—and Jack's as well.

A short while later, Jack was in the hangar talking on the phone inside the small office that was once Jaffar's. "I'm still in Wendover, Colonel. Right now I'm standing over two sorry-looking assholes, who are the last of Jaffar's group remaining here."

"I was about to send a posse out to look for you, Jack! Where are Donny and Michelle?"

There were many more questions than answers at this point.

Las Vegas, Nevada

Jaffar made the long-awaited phone call to Executive Air, "Jeff Davies please."

"Hold on, I'll see if he's still here," said a woman's cheerful voice.

A minute later, Jeff came to the telephone, "Hello!" Jeff sounded out of breath.

"Jeff. This is Jaffar Hodgeson. I am calling to remind you of our flight tomorrow."

Jeff paused before speaking. "Uh, I was going to call you. I'm afraid I have to cancel, Mr. Hodgeson," he said. He had been unwilling to make that call, knowing it would cost him a cool ten grand. "I've just come from the maintenance hangar and the Lear 55 is down for the count!"

"Down for the count? What does that mean?"

"It will not be flight-worthy for the remainder of the week," Jeff said. Then he went on to explain that there was no other aircraft available. "Every other aircraft we have is committed," he said.

"What? This cannot be!"

"I'm afraid it is."

"I need you to make that flight tomorrow!"

"I can't. I haven't a single aircraft I can use."

"Can you borrow a jet?" Jaffar was going to suggest that Jeff steal a jet. "I am desperate!"

I wonder how desperate? Jeff thought to himself. "I will make some calls, maybe I can get you a ride. I will call you back."

Jaffar needed that airplane. He could not depend on his own pilots to do the job.

March 26, 1981

In the very wee hours of the morning, Jaffar's telephone rang. It was Jeff with mixed news. "I have found you a Lear that I can pilot."

"That's great news!"

"The lease rate is rather steep."

"How steep?"

"Ferguson wants $50,000 cash, and of course I will need my ten."

"So, $60,000!" Jaffar knew it was robbery, but he really didn't have much choice. "Alright!"

"I will see you tomorrow."

"No! That's today, Jeff! It's already today!"

"Right! Seven sharp." Jeff yawned as he hung up the telephone.

The light of the yellow morning sun filled room 313 of Arizona Charlie's Boulder Casino Hotel. This room was specifically chosen, along with the one next door, so the men could kneel on their prayer mats and face Mecca if they chose to do so. This luxury was something not available to them inside the huge metal and concrete hangar where they had all spent the last several months.

Farouk had already performed the Fajr prayer at five o'clock and was just finishing the sunrise prayer. In bed, Sina slept in a drug-induced slumber; a low dose of Valium had been administered to the boy as the months of separation from his mother had created an anxiety in him that could not be talked away. The door was doubled-locked and Farouk was a light sleeper, his pistol never too far from his side.

Next door, in room 315, Akmed had just finished his morning prayer ritual. Empress Farah was his charge, but she was not drugged and instead was bound and gagged and laying on the bed. Neither she nor Sina would be travelling to the airport today; they were Jaffar's insurance in case anything went wrong.

At McCarran Airport, Joe and Michelle were not held under such luxurious conditions. For the second night in a row they had been forced to sleep on the cold, concrete hangar floor with only a blanket for warmth. In spite of this each had managed a few hours' sleep.

The side door opened and a cold blast of wind swept across the concrete, waking Michelle as surely as a bucket of cold water. Jaffar entered, followed by his half-brother, Abdul and one of the guards. The door was locked behind them and all four men walked up the stairs and into the aircraft that towered above where Joe and Michelle lay.

A moment later Michelle heard the unmistakable sound of a suppressed pistol being fired; the sound echoed lightly in the hangar. Jaffar, Bijan and Abdul exited the airliner and then the hangar building. Joe had managed to sleep through the whole thing.

This deadly procession was repeated several times until all of the guards who had travelled from Wendover to McCarran were now dead, a single .22 caliber bullet to the back of each head as they prayed for the success of the mission. They now occupied the remaining seats, not containing explosives, each covered by a simple white sheet.

After the last guard was executed, Abdul stood over Joe with a pistol in his hand. Joe was aroused from his stupor by the toe of Abdul's boot. Michelle was already standing up and he wearily got to his feet beside her. "What's going on?" he asked blearily.

Bijan jabbed his pistol into Michelle's ribs, "You! Get into the plane."

There was nothing she could do except obey; neither she nor Joe were in a position to fight back. She was frightened, but Jack had said he thought they'd all be dead by now if there was no purpose for them, so with this in mind, she retained some hope for her life. That changed the instant she stepped through the door and into the aircraft. The minute she saw the pails and the wires leading into them, she knew she was on a flying bomb. She gasped quietly. This was bad.

Bijan seated her in one of the rear-facing jump seats, where a flight attendant would normally sit. The bonds behind her back were checked once more then both she and Joe were further tied to the seat frame below.

Abdul looked at his watch, "Bijan, don't forget you have a flight to New York in an hour. Sameed and I will finish this." Bijan turned and hurried from the aircraft.

Seated by Michelle and tied the same, Joe Sutton was surprisingly calm. Once they were alone, Michelle looked over at him and was amazed at how calm he was. "Joe! Why aren't you scared. I'm shaking like a leaf!"

"Michelle, as I've told my wife time and time again over the last six months, these men don't scare me. It's what they are doing that scares me." After a moment he continued, "The last time I was scared for my life was the 25th of June, 1951." He closed his eyes and for an instant his mind went back almost 30 years. "The Korean War was only a day into its second year. I was flying a sortie over North Korea, in an F-86 Sabre. Another USAF pilot in a P-51 Mustang was in a dog-fight with two Mig-15s. I managed to shoot down both and save the pilot, but I was shot down by a third Mig-15, three miles north of Kaeson."

"What happened?"

"It wasn't very pleasant. I was a prisoner of war for over two years. I figured every day was going to be my last."

"But, you made it through. It must have been awful."

"Like I said, these bastards don't scare me much."

"But, Joe! What about the explosives?" Michelle added, "And the pilots?"

"If we can somehow get loose, I've got a plan to deal with one problem … if you can help me with the other."

Their conversation was interrupted as the two pilots entered the aircraft, followed by Jaffar.

"Speak of the devil!" Michelle mouthed to Joe.

Jaffar poked his head around the corner and said sarcastically, "I hope you two are comfortable. Enjoy the ride!" He laughed as he entered the cockpit to give the two pilots last-minute instructions.

Sameed had the remote unit powered up in the hangar. He switched it on. The amber light on the instrument panel of the jet once again lit up. A second later, the jet's unit was synchronized with the remote. The pilot gave the thumbs up to indicate that the appropriate lights were on and Sameed powered down the remote and prepared to load it aboard the borrowed Lear.

Ely, Nevada

"Kip what do you have for us?" Jack asked over the phone. Kip had been in the office since just after midnight—ever since Colonel Hart had received the call from Jack. Mrs. Sutton was now safely in hands of the FBI and the two guards Jack had apprehended were tucked away in a jail cell—but not answering any questions.

"Well, Jack, so far I've managed to dig up leases for some hangar space Jaffar has at McCarran International, as well as warehouse space he has nearby."

"Donny and I are stopped in Ely, Nevada for gas. We're about three hours from Las Vegas." He checked his watch. "We should be there about nine-thirty."

"What do you want me to tell the natives?"

"Nothing! We just want to go in nice and quiet-like. Check out things first."

"Yeah, I know. You've got four friendlies to worry about."

"Yes! That and all sorts of collateral damage. Jaffar has no compunction about killing."

"Check in with airport security when you get there. They will steer you in the right direction."

"How's Mrs. Sutton doing?"

"She's doing okay. She's one tough lady. Her family is on the way to Salt Lake as we speak."

"That's great Kip! We will talk in a few hours."

Las Vegas, Nevada

Jeff Davies and Charlie Ferguson arrived exactly on time thought Jeff looked like he'd been dragged through hell. He'd managed to get four hours of sleep and it didn't meet the FAA minimum for sleep prior to a flight duty period, but he would lie and fudge his flight log—anything to collect his ten grand.

Charlie, on the other hand, was somewhat more awake and chipper. He was expecting a hefty payday today. He drove and Jeff tried to nap. Jaffar was waiting for them when they arrived.

"Good morning, Mr. Hodgeson," Jeff greeted him.

"Good morning, Jeff." They shook hands, "And you must be the fellow with the airplane?" asked Jaffar.

"Yes, sir! The name's Charles Ferguson, but first things first."

"Ah! Of course." Jaffar handed Charlie a cheap-looking, but new briefcase, purchased just this morning from a gift shop in the main terminal. Ferguson opened the case and saw six bundles of hundred dollar bills, one hundred bills to a bundle.

Satisfied that Jaffar had kept his end of the bargain, Charlie handed Jeff the briefcase and looked at his watch. "Jeff, go and get the plane. She should be all fueled up and ready to go." He threw Jeff the keys to his car.

"Mr. Ferguson! Do you think you can give me hand carrying some equipment from the hangar?"

"Sure thing, Mr. Hodgeson!"

The main door closed behind Charlie with a thud. He looked up at the Iranian jet, recognizing it. "Hey! What the hell's going on here?"

His brain never registered the sound of the silenced pistol discharging behind his head, or the impact of the bullet as it entered his skull. The bullet fragments ricocheted around the inside of Charlie's cranium, shredding his brain and killing him instantly. Quickly his body was wrapped in a sheet and loaded aboard the Boeing then Jaffar helped Sameed ready the remote unit. It would be loaded once the Lear jet taxied to front of the hangar.

The hangar doors were fully opened for the first time in many weeks and the pushback tug was allowed to tow the B720 out for refueling. It would have a full fuel load when it left Las Vegas.

The aircraft provided by Ferguson Aircraft wasn't as new as the one Jeff was used to flying, nor was it quite as well-appointed. However, the cockpit controls were identical and Jeff was as at home in it as he'd been in the Executive Airlines jet. The Lear stopped in front of the open hangar doors, dwarfed by the huge, empty cavernous building.

"Where's Charlie?"

Jaffar shook his head. "I'm not sure, Jeff. He said he wasn't feeling well. He thought he might be getting a migraine."

"Where did he go?"

"He may have gone to the main building to get some aspirin but by the look of him I'm pretty sure that he won't be flying today."

"Kind of the way I feel. Like death warmed over!" Jeff laughed.

"Exactly, Jeff!"

They loaded the remote control unit, secured it in place, and waited for the Boeing refueling to be completed. Finally, at 8:35 a.m., the Boeing 720 sat at the west end of the taxiway, awaiting instructions from the tower.

McCarran ATC: Iranian Zero One, be advised. Traffic inbound runway two five left, at twelve miles. You are cleared onto runway two five left, for immediate departure.

Iranian Zero One: Roger, McCarran.

The pilot of Iranian Zero One advanced his four throttles and the aircraft started its takeoff roll down the concrete runway. Once it reached the takeoff speed, the pilot pulled back on the yoke and the aircraft lifted itself into the clear Las Vegas sky.

Jeff sat in the cockpit, a sense of awe filling him as he watched the beautiful white jet climb away. To Jeff there was still something almost magical about anything bigger than a sparrow taking flight, much less 150 tons of metal climbing into the sky.

After a Southwest Airlines 737 from Los Angeles landed, Jeff taxied out and took his place at the end of the runway. He could see the Iranian jet climbing quickly eastward to its cruising altitude.

Just before nine o'clock, Jack and Donny arrived at McCarran. They were escorted by security to the two warehouses and finally to the deserted hangar where Jaffar had been only hours before.

It had taken them a little longer to get there than they had hoped; earlier that morning, the Professional Air Traffic Controllers Organization (PATCO), had set up a picket line at the main entrances to McCarran as part of a rotating, but illegal, one-day job action program meant to focus attention on the ever-worsening conditions in control towers across the nation. The result was that traffic was snarled at the main gate and also along Wayne Newton Boulevard, as taxi drivers sympathetic to PATCO refused to shuttle their fares to and from terminals through the picket line. Jack and Donny had been still two miles from the gate when Jaffar's jet lifted off.

"Not much here!" Jack said when they got into the hangar. He could see the rubber scuff marks on the concrete from the tricycle landing gear of the big jet, but he had no idea how old they were.

Donny, however, spotted the trail of blood from the side door to the middle of the hangar. "Looks like blood over here, Jack!" he said as he bent over and touched one of the larger drops. He rubbed the blood between his fingers. It had begun to congeal, but was not dry.

"How old, Don?"

"Oh! I'd say about two or three hours. It's not quite dry." There was fear in his eyes and Jack knew he was thinking of Michelle. Both men looked at the end of the blood trail. It did not lead outside. Donny spotted the stairs against the far wall. A similar set of blood drops went right down the middle.

"By the shape of the drops I'd say they are going up, wouldn't you Donny?"

"Yeah! That would be my guess!"

"Whoever it was went out this way," Jack said. Both of them looked out of the open hangar doors.

— Chapter 24 —

Over Southwest Utah

Jaffar occupied the copilot's seat of the smaller jet. He scanned ahead to locate his Boeing. The weather had remained clear and he could easily locate the aircraft; it trailed four faint exhaust plumes, as it moved over Utah.

"Jeff, could you show me how to speak to the pilots of that aircraft ahead?"

This request was completely unnecessary, as Jaffar had spent many weeks familiarizing himself with the dual Collins communications systems, the autopilot, as well as all of the other controls of the Lear. Further, Jaffar had had some training with multi-engine, propeller-driven aircraft earlier in his life. However, his intention was to be able to land the aircraft using visual flight rules if Jeff became incapacitated, uncooperative, or worse.

"Sure thing!" Jeff said. "This readout here is the frequency," he pointed out. "It's controlled by this dial here." Jeff continued to point to various places on the instrument panel on the pilot's side, and Jaffar followed along on the right side of the jet. "As you can see, the readout is set to one 132.4 megahertz, so we can talk to the tower at McCarran. The normal aviation frequencies to speak to ATC towers are from one 118 to 137 megahertz."

"I understand!"

"But after all is said and done, you still need to know which frequency they are on to have a conversation. Do you remember walkie-talkies when you were a kid?"

"Yes," was all Jaffar said and he keyed the microphone. "Iranian Zero One this is November Seven Two Alpha X-ray. Switch to 141 megahertz."

"Roger Seven Two Alpha X-ray."

Jaffar reached up like a veteran, turned the knob and changed the digital display, it stopped at 141 megahertz. He keyed the microphone once again and spoke in Farsi, "How are our guests doing?"

"They are just where you left them."

"Good! Check on them every 15 minutes! I do not want any problems now. We are mere hours away from success. I will call again in two hours. Jaffar out!"

Now, that is too fucking weird, Jeff thought. He didn't know what that was all about, but he was beginning to realize that whatever Jaffar's intentions were, they were much more sinister than he'd first thought. *You don't give rides to guys at ten grand a pop for nothing!* Suddenly, Jeff felt the hair stand up on the back of his neck. *Why the two identical airplanes?* He continued to think ... *and now this guy handles the radio like a pro! What the fuck is going on here?*

Las Vegas, Nevada

"That hangar space was arranged by Mr. Behrouz Kholm of the Iranian Consulate's Media Affairs Office up in Ottawa. We have other information indicating that the hangar, as well as the warehouse and Quonset buildings, were rented and paid for by Mr. Jaffar Hodgeson, also known as Jaffar Hamid Harraj," Jack said. He was at the McCarran Airport, speaking to Doug Watts, manager of the airport.

"Why does that name ring a bell?"

"He's wanted for kidnapping by the FBI. He is on the run with his stepson and we're sure he's responsible for at least three more kidnappings, perhaps more."

"What does that have to do with the Iranian Air Force jet that was in the hangar?"

"I don't know. Can you tell me the destination of the jet?"

Before Doug Watts could answer, one of the airport's canine units arrived along with Chris Roberts, McCarran's security chief.

"Sorry to interrupt, Doug! This is one of our canine units. This is Officer Cathy Jamieson and her dog, Storm."

Jack looked down, to see a beautiful golden retriever sitting obediently at Jamieson's left side.

"What's up Mr. Roberts?" asked Doug.

"I'd better let Officer Jamieson explain, sir."

Jamieson smiled and it appeared as if the dog did as well. "This morning, after my shift ended, I tried to leave by the main gate as usual, but there's a PATCO picket line set up. So I turned around."

Oh, no, Doug thought, *now the canine units are going to stop crossing the picket line. What a screw up! I have an airport to run!*

Jamieson continued, "I headed for the west gate, you know the small one, reserved just for maintenance vehicles?"

"Yes, I know the one." Doug didn't know where this was going and gave his head of security a look.

"Anyway, as I was driving past one of the old Quonset buildings, Storm lets out a bark, and then nothing, so I kept on driving. Then when I passed by that big old hangar, today the doors were open, and Storm just went ape-shit ... if you'll pardon the expression, sir!"

Doug Watts knew how good his canine sniffer units were. "So Storm got a hit near that old warehouse and then perhaps something at the hangar as well?"

"Yes, sir!"

"What happened next?"

"I stopped the car and got Storm out and on her lead. She made a beeline for that hangar. I had to let her go—I thought she'd pull my arm out of its socket. She stood at the bottom of the boarding stairs that were along one wall and sat down. I called security on my radio and here I am."

Security Chief Roberts spoke up confidently, "We've got the whole place cordoned off, as well as the Quonset building. If there's anything to be found we'll do so!"

"What about the warehouse?" Jack asked.

"This Jaffar character had a warehouse here as well?" Doug Watts asked.

"Yes!" said Chris Roberts. "It was some distance away from the hangar and the Quonset building, though. But I will send my men out there also," he assured his boss.

"No! Please!" Jack interrupted. He hadn't meant to shout. He continued in a calmer voice. "Donny and I will handle it, if you don't mind. I still don't know if there are hostages in there. But we need someone to come along with a set of keys so we can quietly gain access to the building without having to break down any doors."

"I can go with you," Roberts said. "After that, we will all meet up over at the hangar."

"Ms. Jamieson, could you and Storm remain here for a bit and then come along over there with me?" Roberts asked.

"Of course! Storm and I are anxious to find out what's going on!"

"So are we, Ms. Jamieson! So are we!"

Somewhere Over Eastern Utah

Joe and Michelle heard the door to the cockpit open. The copilot stepped into the aisle to check on his hostages. He looked down and forced them both to lean forward. After satisfying himself that their ropes were secure, he returned to the cockpit without uttering a single word.

"A real Chatty Cathy, isn't he!" Michelle said sarcastically.

"Just keep working on your ropes, Michelle," Joe admonished. Since the moment the jet aircraft had started to move, Michelle and Joe had both been fighting to free themselves by rubbing their ropes back and forth against the seat frame. Joe remembered that one of the minor assembly line defects in the 707 and the 720 were that these frames were not always ground completely smooth after welding. Though he could not feel with his fingers to see if this was the case with this aircraft, there was a good chance of it.

"How long do you think it was since that goon came to visit us?" Joe asked quietly.

To some people it may have seemed like a lifetime, to others in their predicament, mere heartbeats. "Maybe twenty minutes, maybe a bit less!" Michelle was fairly sure.

"We'll be able to tell when he makes his next visit."

The motion of sawing up and down and side to side was beginning to take a toll on Michelle. She could only move a small amount and, besides giving her muscle cramps, she was also starting to sweat profusely, her T-shirt soaking through. But despite her wrists and arms aching from the effort, she continued to work her bonds. Her skin glistened as her body fought to cool itself.

Joe looked over at her, and, seeing the results of her struggle, asked, "Michelle. How are you doing?"

"What do you mean Joe? With these ropes? Or are you worried about me?"

"Both!"

"I'm almost there with the ropes. I think with a couple more minutes of work I'll be able to free myself."

"What about *you*? How are you holding up?"

"I'm doing okay. Just scared about what's going to happen!" she said.

"Do you think you can cry?" Joe asked unexpectedly.

"What?"

"When our friend from the cockpit comes back, do you think you can cry? With real tears?"

"Joe! I'm a woman! I can cry at the drop of a hat if I want. Why?"

"If he sees you in kind of a hysterical state, looking the way you do, with tears flowing down your cheeks, it will throw him right off his game."

"I get it! He'll think he's won, that you and I are too afraid to act, that we realize our situation is futile."

"Exactly! I'm hoping he might not even check your ropes."

Joe knew about women. He'd been married to good one for over 35 years. He knew men as well—from the very good to the very bad. Colonel Kim Tubong from the North Korean POW camp had definitely been evil. Through the bars of his cage, Joe had watched the nightly line of young South Korean girls and women who were paraded into his quarters then raped and killed, many buried in the area around the camp, never to see their families again. Like Tubong, those two men in the cockpit were in the latter category of men—along with the evil men they followed. Joe had noticed the look in the eyes of the copilot as he'd checked Michelle's bindings a short time ago. He'd seen that look before.

"So if I'm going to cry, what about you? What's the plan?"

"I'm sorry, Michelle! I'm going to sit here, like a weak old man and do absolutely nothing!"

Michelle knew what Joe Sutton meant—that they would just have to bide their time and wait for the right opportunity.

Las Vegas, Nevada

Security Chief Roberts had over one thousand keys in his possession, but only five master keys gave him unfettered access to every single building at McCarran Airport, from the small shed where the Floor Dry was kept, all the way up to, and including, the doors to the largest hangar.

Roberts silently and smoothly tried the first two keys in the lock of the warehouse. He was successful with the third. The deadbolt slid back into the door with just a quiet click. He stood aside for the NATA agents to enter.

Jack and Donny both had their sidearms unholstered, ready to engage any hostiles who might be inside. Jack turned the door handle and opened the door a crack, just enough to reveal that the rear of the warehouse space was not only dimly lit, but was also quiet. Jack motioned for Chief Roberts to remain where he was and the two armed NATA agents entered, closing the door behind them.

The room gave the appearance of a makeshift dormitory, with eight cots lined up neatly in two rows. Light came only from the front office portion of the warehouse. There was a musty odor of sweat permeating the space. Jack motioned to Donny and they quickly and quietly crossed the concrete floor toward the front of the unit. It was soon clear the warehouse was no longer occupied. They felt free to speak aloud.

"Don! Can you smell that? It's some kind of chemical smell!"

"Yeah! It's very faint. Almost like the smell a few days after ordinance is expended on the battlefield!"

"That's it! But, like you say, very faint." Jack flipped the switch to turn on the lights. "Go let the chief in and let's see what we can find."

When Chief Roberts entered the vacated warehouse space he could hardly believe his eyes. The space reminded him of some refugee camp you might see on the evening news. He stood there with his mouth agape. "What the hell's going on here?"

"I don't know, but Jack and I can both smell traces of what we believe is ammonium nitrate. Can you get Storm and her handler over here to have a look?"

"Jamieson's busy at the Quonset building. I will see who else is available." Jack could see the look of concern on the face of the security chief and was quite sure he'd grasped the gravity of the situation. Jack and Donny continued their search of the office while the chief called in another canine sniffer unit.

In the office space at the front of the warehouse they found a refrigerator with food inside. The cupboards, where one would normally have found stationary or other office supplies, were full of canned goods. The front windows and door glass had been coated with a thin, translucent white-wash of paint so that daylight was still able to penetrate while hiding the activities inside. The coat closet was stacked with a dozen prayer mats. It was clear to both Jack and Donny that this dormitory hadn't just been used for a few days, but for weeks or even months. It was also apparent that few, if any, hostages were ever here.

"A canine unit will be here in five minutes," Chief Roberts announced, still astounded that this had been going on under his nose for what appeared to be many weeks. "I'm a loss, gentlemen!" he said, clearly frustrated. The hangar buildings were enough of a problem, but now they'd found evidence of explosives in both the hangar and Quonset buildings. He could feel a headache coming on, and he was sure it was going to be a doozey.

Minutes later, Watts arrived at what was turning out to be a third potential crime scene, or worse, a terrorist lair. "What have we got Roberts?"

"I don't know for sure, Mr. Watts. These boys from NATA seem to feel that there's been some possible presence of explosives inside."

"Let's have a look!" They opened the door and walked into the warehouse. Watts stopped in his tracks and stood there, looking from one wall of the space to the other.

"Christ Almighty! What's going on here Roberts? I've got two buildings on the property that the canine units are all over and now this, this..." He couldn't find the words.

"I know, sir! It looks like some kind of camp. These boys seem pretty sure that they can smell explosives."

"All I can smell is body odor!"

Jack and Donny were both certain about their suspicions. "We were both overseas some years back, in 'Nam … that's a smell you never forget."

Watts looked at two men with a new respect, "I never went to 'Nam myself. Just heard stories."

A car pulled up outside and shortly after a dog could be heard barking outside the door. Chief Roberts opened the door and another sniffer dog entered, followed by its handler.

"Gentlemen, this is Officer Lodewijk."

"Hello," Jack and Donny said in unison.

"These men are from NATA," Roberts said. Lodewijk greeted them.

"This is Tulsa," she said, indicating her dog.

Officer Vickie Lodewijk, who had been with her canine partner for over three years, could tell from the way her dog was acting that this space was definitely a hit. She let Tulsa off her lead.

"Tulsa! Search!"

The dog immediately went to work, investigating the warehouse from side to side in a very methodical, organized routine. Tulsa was particularly interested in two of the cots.

"These men told the chief they can smell a trace of explosives," Watts said to Lodewijk, but he seemed to still be skeptical.

Lodewijk said, "Tulsa will let us know for sure. It looks like she already zeroed in on a couple of the beds." Lodewijk went over to the Belgian Shepherd, reattached her lead and then escorted the dog to the front office area of the warehouse.

"Tulsa! Search!" she said again. Even though there was a plastic garbage can in the corner, full of used paper plates and scrapes of moldy food that would have distracted any other dog, Tulsa ignored them and a moment later sat down in front of the closet and let out a single bark. Lodewijk opened the closet and Tulsa's sensitive nose scanned the stack of prayer mats. She let out another small bark and sat down.

"Good girl!" said Lodewijk.

Lodewijk led her four-legged partner to the rear of the warehouse and asked the dog to search there as well. Tulsa obediently did another complete search, stopping once more at the two cots, where again she sat down and let out a quiet bark, as she'd done in the kitchen. All of this took less than five minutes. The four men who witnessed the exercise were impressed by her skill.

"Good girl, Tulsa! Good girl!" Lodewijk said. She walked over and faced her audience. "I can say without hesitation that you gentlemen were correct about the explosives. Tulsa got hits on two of the beds and the front closet in the office, or should I say kitchen."

"Thank you, Officer Lodewijk! That was quite a show," Jack said.

"Chief Roberts! Do you need me to assist at the other two locations or can I return to the main terminal to finish my shift?" Lodewijk asked.

"I think that will be all for now. Just go back on your regular patrol duties."

"Thank you, sir!" The pretty, blonde officer turned and headed towards the door, her team-mate following along, wagging her tail as she went.

"We have a major problem here!"

"Yes, Director Watts! I would say we do," Roberts said, still dumbfounded at what had been discovered this day.

"Chief Roberts! I want a squad of officers here now and I want this place gone over with a fine-toothed comb! I want you to find every scrap of evidence there is to find. Anything that can tell us what went on, what's going on here and why this has gone on under the radar for what appears to be weeks!"

"But ..." Roberts began.

"No excuses! I want a verbal report in my office within an hour. Do I make myself clear? Jobs are on the line here, Roberts!"

"Yes, sir!" The head of security turned and rushed out the door.

More than jobs were on the line—much more, as Jack and Donny well-knew.

After composing himself, Director Watts ran his hand through his thinning hair and exhaled slowly. "Now, agents! Let's go over what we know. Maybe you can give me the lowdown on this Jaffar character. Apart from being a kidnapper, what can you tell me?"

"I think we should talk on the way back to your office. I'm going to give Colonel Hart a call. We have a serious situation here! We can give you a rundown on what we know, up to this point," Jack said. Director Watts agreed. If this situation was in fact as bad as it looked, he was happy to have the two men from NATA on board. *I'll be lucky to keep my job if this goes too far south,* he thought.

In the Air Over The Utah-Colorado Border

"He should be coming out any minute now," Joe said, not looking at Michelle. "Let's put on a good show for him, shall we?" Joe Sutton had no idea whether this, or any part of his plan, would work. For this initial part, he was counting on good, old-fashioned human nature … and he wasn't sure if it would work on these hard, inhumane men.

As if on cue, the door to the cockpit opened a moment later and the Arab—whom Joe had dubbed 'Mr. Personality'—entered the main cabin. Almost immediately, Michelle had the required tears flowing nicely down each cheek.

"Please! Please! I'm begging you, don't kill me," Michelle pleaded with her captor. It was a performance worthy of an Oscar, or at least a nomination. "I'll do *anything*!"

The young, bearded Arab looked down at Joe with contempt. When he looked at Michelle, he smiled. He then returned to the cockpit, exactly as Joe had predicted.

"He's just trying to work up the courage to act out what's on his mind," he said softly to Michelle.

Michelle had also seen the look on the man's face. Even if he didn't speak any English, he could see the desperation and defeat on both her and Joe's face. She immediately resumed work, trying to free herself from her ropes.

In a matter of minutes she was no longer tied to the seat. With her wrists still bound, she managed to get her hands in front of her, then, using her teeth she tore at the damp ropes. They finally slid over her sweat-slickened skin, allowing her complete freedom of movement for the first time in days. Her aching muscles could finally relax.

"We don't have much time, Michelle!" The reminder was unnecessary; Michelle worked quickly to free Joe. With what they'd figured was one-third of their allotted time already expired, Joe was now also free.

"Let's start by searching the bodies of the dead guards. They might have weapons we can use." It would have been a matter of divine providence, but it was not to be. Aside from some useless ammunition, the only real weapon was a Swiss Army knife with a two-and-a-half inch blade. Not much to work with when literally bringing a knife to a gunfight.

"Back to plan A," Joe said.

Timing was critical to Joe's plan. If the copilot should make an early entrance, then they would have to fight him and then also perhaps fight their way into the cockpit and since they were clearly out-armed, this was not appealing. They had to work fast.

While Joe had not understood that the Boeing jet was being turned into a bomb—at least until he stepped inside it with a semi-automatic pistol pressed against his spine and saw the explosives on board—during half a year of imprisonment when he'd been forced to work on the aircraft, he'd understood clearly that his kidnappers were dangerous men. And he'd suspected he might be on this plane one day, so he'd hidden assorted tools in and around the rear galley, claiming to have misplaced them. He was glad he had done so; it might save his and Michelle's life.

Joe rolled the movable galley unit away from the cabin wall, certain that the sound of the four jet turbines would mask any sound. Underneath were the breakers; he flipped them off to eliminate the possibility of a short circuit or even electrocution, then opened the door to the warming oven, removed the inside panel and began removing and rerouting the insulated wiring within.

"This would be a lot easier if I had my standard wiring service kit on hand!" he grumbled.

"I still don't understand what you are doing, Joe!"

"This aircraft has a three-phase, four-wire system, either 115 volts or 200 volts, depending on where in the system you are working, and how many wires you happen to be working with."

Michelle remembered some of this from her air force days when she had been on maintenance duty. "What do you intend to do with all the wires and this other stuff?" she asked.

"I'm going to give our friends here the shock treatment!" Joe nodded towards the cockpit door, one hundred feet away. "Please bring me the service trolley and start disassembling the frame."

"Okay!" They would have to work quickly and quietly and be aware of the time.

The light-weight frame of the trolley wasn't stout enough to be used as a club and was made to be taken apart with no tools which made it ideal for Joe's plan. In ten minutes he had a tinkered-together contraption assembled and hidden away under a sheet covering one of Jaffar's dead guards.

Michelle returned to her seat, slipped her significantly loosened bonds back around her wrists and Joe used some of the ropes from his side of the seat frame to once again secure her in position. This was perhaps the most dangerous part of Joe's plan, as Joe had no bindings on at all—only the small knife in his hands, behind his back. However, if things went as planned, the guard would give Joe only a cursory glance, his carnal desires overriding his sense of caution. Joe was hoping the copilot would ignore him and concentrate on Michelle. If not, Joe was in for the fight of his life and could not expect any help from Michelle. He would have only the briefest moment of surprise on his side, either way.

Las Vegas, Nevada

Jack, Don, Watts and Roberts gathered in Watts' office for the second time that morning. Roberts had just given Watts his report of the findings at the crime scenes. The meager physical evidence from the latest one was spread on the director's desk and consisted of just a few food-stained gas and grocery receipts.

"Not much to go on," said Colonel Hart who, with Kip Holmes, was listening via speaker phone from Washington, D.C. It was noon there.

"Jack! Milt and I and a few others have pulled an all-nighter here," Kip chimed in. "We want this bastard as much as you do. What about the aircraft?"

"There was an aircraft here belonging to the Iranian Air Force. The former Shah and his wife used it as their own personal airplane until his death last summer. Now she uses it," Jack said. "She was kidnapped by Jaffar and held at Wendover, according to Mrs. Sutton. Clearly Jaffar has taken her, our agent Michelle Hough, Mr. Sutton and possibly Giti Roshtti's son, Sina, as hostages."

"Do you think they could be on the aircraft?" asked the colonel.

"It's definitely a possibility, sir." Jack paused and scratched his head. Something had been nagging at Jack, for the better part of two days.

"Are you there, Jack?" asked the colonel.

"Yup. I just thought of something," Jack replied. He turned to Director Watts and asked, "Do you have a photograph of the aircraft?"

"Yeah, sure," said Watts. From a file cabinet, he pulled a glossy color photograph of the Iranian jet and handed it to Jack.

Excitedly, Jack showed it to Don. "Look at this, Don. That's the plane we saw at the hangar in Wendover yesterday!"

"It sure is!"

"You boys are mistaken!" said Watts. "That plane has been here, at McCarran, for the last several months—in that hangar!"

"I'm afraid you're mistaken, sir. Don and I both saw it yesterday at Wendover! It only had three engines, but otherwise it was complete. We saw it just as sure as you're standing in front of me now!" Jack said, somewhat annoyed at having his words doubted.

"But, that can't be, I tell you!"

"Unless …" Jack said.

"Unless what, Jack?"

"Oh my God! Mrs. Sutton told me the Empress Farah said she had been kidnapped *on her own plane!* What if Jaffar had a second jet, a doppelganger—you know, a twin!"

"Why would he need a second aircraft?" asked Watts.

"One plane only had three engines … that's why!" exclaimed Don. "He needed the Iranian jet for parts! The empress was just icing on *that* cake!"

"Shit!" Jack said, "That's what Michelle was trying to tell me the other day in the hangar at Wendover! She said she recognized that plane."

"You say the jet is heading for the east coast?" Don asked, "Where exactly?"

"They filed a flight plan for JFK. The flight is exactly on course, at last report." Watts looked at his watch. "They should be over the Rockies about now."

"Kip, what's happening in New York today?" Jack asked anxiously.

"Damn, Jack! Right at the top of the list is President Reagan giving a speech at a dinner honoring Anwar Sadat and Manachem Begin, at the U.N. General Assembly this afternoon. Jimmy Carter is also expected to attend … and the Empress of Iran is expected too!"

All of a sudden Kip exclaimed excitedly over the phone, "Don! Did you say that the plane in Wendover only had three engines?

"Yes, Kip, one of them was one missing."

"Hold on! Give me two minutes!" In less time that, Kip returned to the phone out of breath. "Yeah! Here it is. Last September the owner of Mile High Aviation was murdered in an apparent burglary gone bad."

"I hear a big 'but' coming," said Jack.

"Michelle and I went out there to check out Mile High," said Kip. "They had sold six Boeing jets to the Iraqis the week before we arrived. Michelle and I checked everything out—even where these aircraft had been parked. She could tell that seven jets had been parked there and though they were long gone, one of them had an engine that was about to pack it in. It was leaking. We took photos.

"Was it the inboard engine on the left wing?"

"Yes, Jack! As a matter of fact it was! How did you know?"

"That's the engine that was missing from the jet at Wendover!"

"So, gentlemen," said the colonel. "To sum things up, we have an aircraft en route to New York where President Reagan is giving an address to the United Nations. It's probably loaded with explosives and it's carrying an unknown number of hostages."

"Yes, Colonel, that appears to be what we are dealing with," said Jack calmly. He couldn't believe how this situation had escalated and he suddenly had a clear picture of Giti in his mind. He was surprised by the level of emotion he felt; he had been directly responsible for leading this animal to her. When this was over, he vowed to find the woman and explain himself.

The colonel said, "That aircraft cannot be allowed to reach New York city."

"But Colonel! Michelle might be on that plane!" Don protested.

"We don't know that for certain, Don. And I can't operate on 'maybes'. I'm sorry, Donny. Kip get in touch with NORAD!"

East of the Rocky Mountains

"Before you go to the main cabin to visit the American whore, I will need to use the washroom, Davood."

"Of course, Majeed. I've got the aircraft."

Michelle and Joe watched the captain as he returned to the cockpit. He avoided looking at Joe, his focus was on Michelle. He had a smile on his face as he looked her up and down. Both Americans knew what was coming next.

As Captain Najafeed shut the door to the cockpit he said, "Don't take too long with her. Jaffar will be calling in less than a half an hour and I don't think it would be wise if he should find out one of us buggering some whore when he should be flying the aircraft!" All the same, the captain smiled, "Go have your fun with her."

The copilot left the cockpit and closed the door. He stood and looked at the hostages and then slapped Joe viciously on the side of the head—but, thankfully, he did not bother to check his ropes, just as Joe had hoped. Anxious to get to his prize, he pulled out a knife and cut Michelle free then he jerked her to her feet and roughly dragged her toward the rear of the aircraft, where things were a bit more private.

"Get undressed," he told her, waving the knife in her face. She began to unbutton her shirt, exposing herself from the waist up. "Take your pants off! Now!" he demanded as he began to undress. Michelle slowly begin to comply. "Hurry up, you stupid bitch!" he yelled.

That was Joe's signal. He got up from the jump seat and slowly made his way aft, creeping forward, watching the action at the rear of the passenger cabin as he did so. When Joe reached the seat where he'd squirreled away his device, he knelt down and carefully searched under the sheet. *Where is it?* Joe thought anxiously—just before his right hand touched the cold aluminum body of the mechanism.

The copilot stepped out of his pants and exposed his now-swollen member. For a moment, Michelle thought she was going to hurl. *Suck it up girl, you've got play your part,* she thought. For some reason—perhaps he'd heard the faint movements of Joe Sutton behind him, or perhaps had caught the slightest glimpse of movement in his peripheral vision—the copilot began to turn his head.

"Oh no, big boy! Bring that monster over here!" Michelle adlibbed, then she tore off her bra, exposing her breasts.

His eyes narrowed like a predator's as he ogled her. His attention was once again fully focused on what he was about to do and he advanced slowly towards her. "You are a whore, just like we talked about!" he said, taunting her.

He was less than two feet away from Michelle when Joe's cattle prod discharged two hundred volts directly into his left butt cheek, causing his heart to go into uncontrolled fibrillation. He didn't even have a chance to cry out in pain; instead he went rigid and lost consciousness. Where the two points had contacted his skin, second degree burns were immediately apparent.

With the body of would-be rapist sprawled at her feet, Michelle breathed a sigh of relief and said, "God, Joe! I was just about to kick the filthy bastard in the balls. I'm sure glad your little device worked."

"*Our* little device, Michelle. It worked like a charm, didn't it?" Joe had been pretty certain it would, he just hadn't been sure about how *well* it would work. He had a big grin on his face.

Michelle began to dress. "Well, I guess this bra is shot!" she said and, for the first time in ages, she laughed.

"Oh, I don't know, I can fix almost anything!" Joe said. This time they both laughed.

"What are we going to about lover boy here?" Michelle asked.

"Is he alive? If not, we don't have to worry, do we?"

Michelle reached down to feel for a pulse. "It's faint, but it's there. Breathing is shallow as well."

"Doesn't look too good for him. All the same I've got some left over electrical wire. Let's tie his hands securely behind his back and stuff a rag in his mouth."

"Then what?"

"We'll just leave him where he is and when his friend comes to look for him we can give him the same treatment, or we can stick a gun in his face and *then* shock him." Michelle nodded. Joe added, "But I don't like the idea of using a gun in the aircraft. A sudden cabin decompression would be disastrous."

"Agreed," said Michelle. As ex-Air Force, she was very aware of the risks.

Suddenly Joe said, "Watch out, Michelle! Don't move!"

"Oh!" She looked down to see her right elbow only inches away from the business end of their device, which was propped against the wall.

"I gotta watch that," she said.

The intercom suddenly crackled to life, "Davood! It's time for you to return to the cockpit."

"Michelle! Forget the electrical wire for binding our friend. You know what to do!"

Joe quickly returned to his seat and Michelle undid her shirt about halfway down and sat down next to the unconscious copilot. She intentionally mussed her hair into a tangled mess and once again began to cry. The plan was essentially the same as before, except this time Michelle would be armed with the pistol provided by the inert Iranian on the floor.

"Davood! Stop what you are doing and return to the cockpit at once!" There obviously wasn't any response.

The cockpit door opened seconds later and Captain Najafeed strode into the passenger compartment. He turned to Joe and just as the copilot had done, gave Joe a hard backhand. "Oh! Please don't!" Joe didn't resist—couldn't resist.

At the aft end of the aircraft and could see the bare legs of his copilot sticking out into the aisle. "Stupid fool!" He hurried down the aisle, to wake up his second in command so that they could get back to the business of flying the jet.

Sweet Jesus! He's gone and left the cockpit. Now no one is up there, was all Joe could think.

The captain stood over Davood and nudged him with the toe of his shoe. "Come on Davood, it's time to wake up!" There was no response. He looked over at Michelle and then gave his copilot a good kick, one hard enough to wake him up for sure.

"What's wrong with him? What have you done?"

"Nothing! Nothing at all! He was fucking me and all of a sudden he rolled over and grabbed his chest. I think he had a heart attack. "Oh my God!" Michelle stood up, as if to get herself away from the man on the floor. "Is he dead?"

Just as Michelle had done, the aircraft commander bent down to feel for a pulse. It was still very faint, just as it had been minutes earlier. He began to get up and a smile crossed his lips. He looked over at Michelle just in time to see the butt of her pistol arcing through the air. He barely had time to flinch before it smashed his left temple.

"That one's for Joe!" Michelle said.

Joe Sutton arrived mere seconds later, cattle prod in hand. "Back away my dear!" Joe drained the remaining charge into the unconscious body of the captain. "That's for Michelle and my wife! Asshole!"

The result of being electrocuted was much direr for the first officer than it had been for his accomplice. He died within a few minutes.

Joe took no time to gloat. He knew what was at stake. "Michelle! Right now you've got to get to the cockpit and fly this aircraft. He's left no one at the controls!"

"We knew he would. What an idiot!"

"I'm going to get these two trussed up nice and tight so they won't be any more trouble and then I'm going to get to work deactivating these explosives, if I can."

Michelle collected the captain's weapon and headed forward. She settled into the left seat of the aircraft and placed the headphones over her ears. The cockpit was familiar to her—it was very similar to the KC-135 tankers she'd flown over the Atlantic Ocean during her military service. The tension from the last few days began to fade a bit; at last she felt she finally had some kind of control over things.

Out of the corner of her left eye, movement caught her attention. A General Dynamics F-16D Fighting Falcon, fully armed with AIM-9 Sidewinder missiles was less than 100 feet off her left wing. His wingman was most likely off to the right, about a mile or so to the rear.

The pilot pointed at the side of his helmet with his gloved hand. Michelle made direct eye contact, knowing that the pilot wanted radio contact. She shook her head in the affirmative and pointed at her headset then immediately keyed the cabin intercom.

"Joe!" she called. "You'd better get up here as soon as you are finished with our two friends. We've got company!" She then switched to the emergency Guard channel of 121.5 Mhz.

"Iranian Flight Zero One!" said the fighter pilot. "This is Iwo Jima One. I am an armed air defense fighter. How do you read?"

"This is Iran Flight Zero One on Emergency Guard Channel. I read you loud and clear. Over!" said Michelle.

"You are warned not to proceed to New York city or approach any other populated center, unless instructed by myself to do so! If you try to do this, I am authorized to use lethal force! Do you understand? Over."

"Iwo Jima Flight I understand. Our situation has changed since departure. This is former Lieutenant Michelle Hough of the United States Air Force. We have two tangos down and are now in command of this aircraft. Over."

"Where were you stationed Lieutenant?"

"I flew out of Griffiss, with the 41st! Over."

"Roger Iranian Zero One! Please stand by."

While Michelle waited for the pilot of Iwo Jima Flight to get back to her with further instructions she looked over the instruments. Everything looked good; the aircraft was in good shape. She looked out the forward window of the aircraft and could see nothing but favorable weather ahead. Michelle relaxed a bit more.

But suddenly, on the instrument panel to the far right, in front of where the copilot would sit, a bright amber light flashed, quickly followed by a green one.

What the hell? wondered Michelle.

Before Michelle could react, the steering yoke jerked to the right and the Boeing 720 banked and started to descend towards the Kansas countryside far below.

"Iranian Flight Zero One! What's happening? Why are you deviating from your flight path without authorization?"

"Iwo Jima Flight! I suddenly have no control of the aircraft. I repeat. I have lost use of my flight controls, for an unknown reason."

She stared wide-eyed at the yoke. This was worse than she thought.

— Chapter 25 —

"Joe! Get up here on the double! We're in real trouble!" she called through the intercom to Joe.

Michelle glanced at the altimeter. With this rate of descent, a fiery explosive crash was all she could envision. "No," she screamed at the windscreen. They had come too far, had fought too hard to give up now. She pulled on the steering yoke as hard as she could. The column moved ever so slightly in the direction she wished, but the effort of freeing herself all morning had taken its toll. Her forearms and biceps ached.

The cockpit door opened and Joe practically fell forward into the cockpit. He quickly took his seat and buckled in. The first thing his eyes focused on were the two lights illuminated on the instrument panel.

"Son of a bitch!"

"What's going on, Joe? Besides the obvious?"

"Jaffar has control of the aircraft!"

"What?"

"Jaffar has control of this aircraft!"

"Help me pull us out this dive! I can't do it alone!" Michelle screeched as the plane started to nose down. The controls responded, but not nearly as quickly as Michelle wanted. "Now! What's this about Jaffar?"

"Jaffar had me build him a remote control unit so that he or someone else could control this plane via line of sight from another aircraft."

"What kind of aircraft?"

"A business jet, like a Lear. Something with enough legs to keep up with this aircraft."

"Iwo Jima Flight leader. Can you locate a Lear jet, a business jet, somewhere in the vicinity? That is our bandit, over!"

"Iranian Zero One. Roger, Lieutenant. We passed a Lear just before intercepting you! What's your situation? Over."

"Iwo Jima Flight. I will pass you over to my copilot. He can explain the situation more easily that I can. I have an aircraft to fly. Over."

"Roger Iranian Zero One. We are standing by."

Joe put on the copilot's headset and keyed the microphone. "Iwo Jima Flight. This is Joe Sutton. I was chief design engineer at Boeing Company in Seattle. I'm sorry I don't have more time to reminisce with you fighter pukes, but you kids had better listen up. My wife and I were kidnapped last fall, I was forced to modify this jet and its controls by an individual who now occupies that Lear!"

Joe looked over at Michelle. It was clear she was having difficulties and could not be expected to maintain minimal control of the aircraft.

"They can, and are, controlling this aircraft. It is imperative that the Lear be diverted out of range! Over."

"Roger, Iranian Zero One. Stand by, sir."

Moments later, the side windscreen of the Lear piloted by Jeff Davies was filled by the shape of the fighter as it suddenly appeared beside the aircraft. Exactly as he had done with Michelle minutes earlier, the pilot made contact with Jeff.

"November 72 Alpha X-ray, this is Iwo Jima Flight One One calling you on Emergency Guard channel. How do you read over?"

"Iwo Jima Flight. I read you loud and clear. Over!"

"November 72 Alpha X-ray. Are you, or is someone on board your aircraft, interfering with the controls of the Boeing 720 off to the east, distance three miles? Over."

"Iwo Jima Flight. I can confirm that such a person is on board. Over."

"November 72 Alpha X-ray. I am equipped with both missiles and guns and am authorized to use lethal force. Do you understand?"

"Iwo Jima Flight One One. I understand."

"November 72 Alpha X-ray. Come to a heading of two-eight-three degrees and lower and lock your landing gear into place. Do you understand? Over."

"Iwo Jima Flight One One. I am lowering and locking my landing gear and commencing requested turn to heading two-eight-three degrees now! Over."

"Roger, November 72 Alpha X-ray. Your destination is Buckley Air Force base in Aurora, Colorado. Do not! I Repeat! Do not deviate from this heading, unless ordered to do so by myself or my wingman. If you do, you will be fired upon without warning. How do you copy?"

"This is November 72 Alpha X-ray. I copy and will comply! Over."

"November 72 Alpha X-ray. My Two Flight will escort you towards Buckley. You will be met by a flight of two F-Sixteens from the One Hundred and Twentieth Air National Guard. You will then follow their instructions as you would do mine. That flight will intercept you in eight minutes. Over."

"Iwo Jima Flight One One. I read you loud and clear. I will standby on Guard channel. Over."

"Roger, November 72 Alpha X-ray."

"What are doing, Jeff?" Jaffar burst into the cockpit, alerted by the sound of the landing gear coming down.

"I am changing course, as instructed by an Air Defense F-Sixteen fighter."

"They were bothering the Boeing. What are they bothering us for?"

"They are not bothering us Mr. Hodgeson! They are threatening to blow out of the fucking sky if we don't comply."

"Why did you turn us away from my jet?"

"Again! That F-Sixteen out there can blow us out of the sky with either guns or missiles, and he can do so from miles away. I don't feel like dying today! Do you?"

"You're right, Jeff. You made the right call."

"You're dammed right I did!"

Sameed stuck his head into the small cockpit of the Lear, "Jaffar! I have lost contact with your plane."

Jaffar knew what that meant. His flying bomb would never reach New York city. President Reagan would congratulate Begin and Sadat for their treachery. All three would live, along with every one of the other infidels in the United Nations.

"I just hope we were close enough to arm the two bombs before we had to turn away!" he said with resignation.

"I'm sure we were Jaffar."

Jaffar smiled.

What the fuck? Jeff thought. He finally came to the full realization that Jaffar was some kind of deranged maniac, a sociopath. After the events of that morning, things were now crystal clear to Jeff. *He's got bombs on board that jet!* This day just had gone from very bad, to worse.

"I'm going to take a nap, Jeff!" said Jaffar.

A nap? Jeff just looked at him. Clearly this was not a time to nap. He supposed Jaffar was really just finding an excuse to keep an eye on him, or else why was he not returning to the main cabin?

Jaffar sat in the right-hand cockpit seat and closed his eyes. He felt down but he was not defeated yet. Mixed in with regrets about missed chances and the failure to carry out his carefully-crafted plan for Hamas was the thought that there was still a chance he could escape. Hamas would be angry at him for failing, but he could cut and run if he was careful and fast. *At least I have my millions. If I can escape the police when we land* … Jaffar smiled and drifted off into a light sleep.

For almost half a minute, Jeff sat in the captain's seat, in control of the aircraft, unsure how to proceed. *How can I warn the military about the bombs on the Boeing without alerting Jaffar?* If he waited until they landed the Lear, it might be too late! Beside him, Jaffar dozed or at least pretended to doze. Jeff didn't want to take a chance on the latter.

"Iwo Jima Flight One One. This is Iranian Zero One. Over"

"Iranian Flight Zero One. I read you. Over."

"Iwo Jima Flight. How long before we contact second Air Defense flight? Over."

"Is this guy dense or what?" the pilot of the small fighter thought. "November 72 Alpha X-ray. They should rendezvous with us in less than four mikes. Over."

"Roger, Iwo Jima One One. I am on Guard channel standing by."

"God! I hope this works." Jeff keyed the microphone and released it. He keyed the microphone once more and released it, "M-A-Y-D-A-Y--M-A-Y-D-A-Y--T-H-I-S--I-S--N-7-2-A-X--T-H-E-R-E--I-S--A--B-O-M-B--O-N--B-O-A-R-D--B-O-E-I-N-G--7-2-0----I--R-E-P-E-A-T--M-A-Y-D-A-Y--M-A-Y-D-A-Y--" Jeff repeated the message five more times, until he fingers ached then repeated it once more.

In his F-16D, Captain Paul Halloran switched his radio to the preset frequency for his base at Buckley. "Iwo Jima Flight One One to Cuckoo's Nest. How do you read? Over."

"Iwo Jima Flight. We read you loud and clear. Over."

"Cuckoo's Nest. Can you monitor Guard channel. I'm not sure but I think someone is transmitting in Morse code. I would suggest you turn volume to maximum so it will be more clear. I will stand by on this RF (radio frequency). Over.

"Iwo Jima Flight. This is Cuckoo's Nest. We read you loud and clear and are affirmative on request to monitor Guard channel. We are switching RF. Please stand by."

After a few minutes it was clear the noises from the Lear weren't just static or random noise; it was a message.

"Cuckoo's Nest to Iwo Jima Flight. That is affirmative on message. But why the need for Morse Code? Why not just transmit in the clear? Over."

"Maybe the pilot of November 72 Alpha X-ray is not our bandit. Maybe someone else in the aircraft is monitoring his transmissions. Over."

"Or perhaps sitting in the copilot's seat. Over."

"Iwo Jima Flight. Vipers from the One Hundred and Twentieth should be forming up with you in one minute. Over."

"Roger, Cuckoo's Nest! I have a visual on Whiskey Flight. Over."

"Iwo Jima Flight One One. Hand November 72 Alpha X-ray over to them and rejoin your flight. Over."

"Roger. Over and out!"

The air defense flight from the One Hundred and Twentieth positioned themselves on either side of the Lear jet. "November 72 Alpha X-ray. This is Whiskey Juliet Flight One One on Guard. How do you read? Over."

"Whiskey Juliet Flight One One. I read you loud and clear. Over."

"November 72 Alpha X-ray. You will form up on my aircraft and follow me into Buckley. My wingman is off to the right and is authorized to shoot you down. Do not deviate from your course! Do you understand? Over."

"Roger, Whiskey Juliet Flight! I read you loud and clear." Jeff was developing a headache. *God, this day just keeps getting better and better!* His temples pounded. It felt like every time his heart beat and forced blood into his arteries, his headache got that much more intense.

I wonder if this is how Charlie felt when he got sick this morning when we were dropping off the Lear to Jaffar? he wondered. This was the first time Jeff had taken the time to review the strange conversation he'd had with Jaffar outside the hangar. *I hope Charlie's okay! What if Jaffar had him killed?* Jeff looked over at Jaffar, resting comfortably in his seat. *No that's just my imagination running away with itself.* Then he realized that with this individual, anything was possible.

Over Central Kansas

"Iwo Jima Flight leader to Iranian Flight Zero One. Over."

"Iwo Jima Flight. This is Iranian Flight Zero One. I read you. Over."

"Iranian Flight Zero One can you tweak your RF? Over."

"Iwo Jima Flight. This is Iranian Flight Zero One. We will tweak RF down three. Over."

"Iranian Flight Zero One. Since we were on Guard I wasn't sure, but the walls could have ears and I could not communicate in the clear. Over."

Joe Sutton keyed on his microphone. "Iwo Jima Flight. Let's cut the crap! In case your air bosses aren't aware, we are in deep shit over here. We've had a major fur-ball inside the aircraft and don't have the time to piss around! Over."

"Iranian Flight. What exactly is your present situation? Over."

"Iwo Jima. We once again have complete control of the aircraft. All controls are responding normally. In the passenger cabin we have several dead tangos, including the former captain of this flight. More importantly we have 150 barrels of what I suspect are explosives throughout the cabin where passengers would normally sit. I have started to render them inactive but I have not, I repeat, not completed this task. Over."

"Iranian Flight Zero One. Standby one minute. Over."

Michelle had clearly heard the sharp intake of breath on the other end of the radio when Joe had given him the news. "Iwo Jima Flight. We are standing by. Over."

"I bet he's chatting up to base right now about the good news you just gave him. I'm sure Jaffar didn't announce to the folks at McCarran that he had an aircraft full of explosives."

"I'm pretty sure this will cause all those people at his base and at NORAD some consternation."

"Yes! I'm sure they didn't expect a 120-ton bomb flying above over the U.S. when they got up this morning."

"I wonder what their reaction to that news will be?"

"I can tell you for certain, Joe, that we will not be allowed to put this aircraft down anywhere near a big city."

"I'm sure you are right. On the other hand, they could always shoot us down over a sparsely populated area and be done with it. Just kidding!"

"Not the way I want to buy the farm, Joe. Besides, why waste a $600,000 missile?"

One minute turned into two and two turned into three. After five long minutes Joe and Michelle finally heard, "Iranian Flight Zero One. Sorry for the delay."

"Iwo Jima Flight. What's the scoop? Over"

"Iranian Flight Zero One. You have become, how shall I say, 'persona non grata' at every airport within range. Over."

"Iwo Jima Flight. So what are we supposed to do? Fly around up here in an orbit above some God-forsaken landscape until we are bingo fuel? Please advise! Over."

"Iranian Flight Zero One. Change course to two-two-five degrees. Over."

"Iwo Jima. Roger. We are making the turn to two-two-five degrees as requested. Over."

"Iranian Flight Zero One. I'm sorry, Lieutenant Hough. Over."

Both Michelle and Joe knew where this course change would take them. They were being herded towards New Mexico, where they would be placed in a race track orbit, exactly as Michelle had predicted.

"It sucks to be us, Joe," Michelle said, tears starting to show. It was no act this time. There was no Oscar to be awarded.

"Buck it up, Lieutenant Hough. That's an order! I left the air force with the rank of Captain, so I outrank you in both braid and years. The problem with you youngsters today is that you give up too God-dammed easy!"

"Yes, sir!"

"What's our gas situation?" Joe could have looked on the instrument panel to see for himself very easily, but it gave Michelle something to focus on.

"We are looking at 60 percent fuel on board."

"Right! Until we have expended every single drop of fuel and those four Pratt & Whitney turbofans out there are just sucking air, you have an aircraft to fly."

"Yes, Joe! Yes, sir!"

Joe was feeling the same emotions as Michelle, but couldn't give into despair. They had worked too hard, fought too hard and cheated death more than once today, against all odds. Perhaps they could do it once more! Michelle was less than half his age; she had a lot of life to live. He couldn't really blame her for her fear.

"You are one of the bravest people I have ever met in my entire life," he said to her. "I'm sure there is a way out of this. We've just got to figure it out, that's all."

"Yes, Joe."

"I'm going to finish what I started in the main cabin! We are not done yet, Michelle."

Buckley Air Force Base, Colorado

The Lear taxied to the end of the ramp closest to the flight operations building. The stairs were lowered and the occupants were ordered to disembark the aircraft. The men from the main cabin exited first. Sameed walked out, followed by Abbas, Abdul and finally the last two of Jaffar's guards. Fifteen feet away, four armed U.S. Air Force guards waited. "Halt! You men in the cockpit. Come out now!"

"We are coming! Don't shoot!" Jeff stood at the top of the stairs. Jaffar was right behind him. Jaffar threw two bundles of loose one hundred dollar bills, into the air. The slight breeze, scattered the money all around.

The four air force guards were momentarily distracted and Jaffar pushed Jeff Davies ahead of him and down the stairs onto the tarmac, a pistol pressed roughly into his ribs. This was the cue for Jaffar's guards to lung forward and engage the air force personnel, allowing Jeff and Jaffar to escape.

It worked—Jaffar jabbed Jeff with the gun and the two of them ran as a shootout ensued which left Abbas and the two guards dead and Abdul injured. Only Sameed survived the melee unscathed.

"That was my money, Jaffar!" Jeff yelled angrily as they ran.

"Don't worry, Jeff. You still have $40,000 left," said Jaffar.

A unoccupied armoured Humvee idled at a nearby curb. "There! Jump into that truck. That's our ticket out of here!" yelled Jaffar. Momentarily disoriented by the claxon horns that had started blaring, Jeff panicked.

"Sorry, Jaffar! You jump into that truck. I'm staying put!" Jeff argued.

"As you wish!" Jaffar pointed the pistol at Jeff and squeezed the trigger then jumped into the Humvee and was soon headed for the perimeter fence surrounding the base, leaving Jeff on the ground bleeding from the right side of his abdomen.

He clutched at his side, to try and stem the flow of blood. "Man down! Get a corpsman over here on the double!" he heard someone yell. "Hold on there. An ambulance is on the way."

"Two remote bombs on board jet," Jeff said, then everything faded to black as he lost consciousness.

Back near the Lear, Abdul lay bleeding on the ground. He'd been shot in both legs by the Air Force guards. He was conscious, but the former Chief of Police of Al Qa'im was out of the fight. The bodies of Abbas and the two guards were placed into the rear of a truck and taken to the base morgue. Sameed was hand-cuffed and escorted to a detention cell.

The blaring claxons stopped and soon the only evidence that anything was out of the ordinary was a civilian aircraft parked on the apron and a damaged fence. Of course there was still the matter of the stolen Humvee and a base commander with a whole lot of questions.

Colonel Dale Graham sat down at the table in the interrogation room. Across from him, Sameed was shackled to the cross-bar at the bottom of the table, his hands free from handcuffs. A hastily prepared after-action report lay on the table between them. In the time between the shootout and present, Sameed had been given a hot shower and some fresh clothes. This was more for the colonel's benefit than anything else, but it might also serve as an enticement for cooperation. Colonel Graham opened the file and quickly scanned its contents. "Now, Sameed. That's your name is it not?"

"Yes! I am Sameed."

"Well, Sameed. I can tell you, as Base Commander, the lightest possible charges will be brought against you if you cooperate and answer my questions. I see that the Sergeant," he indicated his colleague in the corner, "has already read you your Miranda rights. You understand that you don't have to answer my questions without a lawyer present?"

"I want to answer."

"That would certainly make it easier," said the colonel. "First of all, why did you attack my men? Three men died for nothing out there!" Luckily, none of the colonel's men had died. If any of them had been killed, the conversation wouldn't have such a calm, rational tone to it.

"I did not attack your men. It was Jaffar's idea. He needed a distraction while he escaped. He was going to kill us all."

"I know. You stood back—that is the reason my men did not shoot you. So you say this Jaffar person needed a diversion?"

"Yes! Jaffar was going to kill us if we didn't do what he said!"

"What can you tell us about Jaffar? What was he doing in the skies above the United States?"

"He has an airplane with bombs on board! He was going to blow up that U.N. building, in New York."

The colonel quickly went into crisis mode as he immediately understood that there was much more to this than he had at first thought. He was going to have to record these proceedings and get other agencies involved.

"We're going to have to call the feds on this one," he told his sergeant. "Get Washington on the line, will you?"

Over Colorado-New Mexico Border

"Okay, Michelle! Every one of the wires to those barrel bombs has been removed," Joe said as he sat down in his seat.

"That's good news, for once."

"Do you think it will make any difference to NORAD or anyone else?"

"All we can do is ask!" Michelle keyed the microphone once more, "Iwo Jima Flight. This is Iranian Zero One. Over."

"Iranian Zero One. What is your current condition? Over."

"Iwo Jima Flight. Joe has neutralized all the explosives on board. We have all barrel bombs deactivated! Over."

"Iranian Zero One. Stand by."

Now all they could do was wait. "God Joe, I'm tired."

Michelle looked like shit, but Joe wasn't going to tell her that. "You're doing great, Lieutenant," he said. Joe still needed her to focus on the job at hand. "If you want, I could fly the aircraft for a while, and you can catch some zees."

Although she was very tempted, Michelle knew that if she went to sleep now, she'd be far worse off in an hour or two. "I haven't slept much since the three of us attacked that base," Michelle said. She had to stop and think about when it was. "Was that two days ago, or was it three?" she said, more to herself than to Joe.

All of a sudden a light clicked on for Joe.

"That's it!" he said. It was so obvious he was amazed he hadn't thought about it sooner. "We can land back at Wendover. The place is deserted. Surely they can't refuse us permission to land there!"

"You're right, Joe! And don't call me Shirley!" Michelle laughed. "It's from *Airplane*. I'll tell you later."

"Oh yeah! I saw the ads on T.V." Joe keyed the microphone. "Iwo Jima Flight. This is Iranian Flight Zero One on Guard. Over." There was no reply.

"Iwo Jima Flight. This is Iranian Flight Zero One on Guard. Over."

"Iranian Flight Zero One. This is Iwo Jima Flight. I read you. Over."

"Iwo Jima Flight. We request diversion to Wendover Base. Over."

"Iranian Zero One. Say again last transmission. Over."

"Iwo Jima Flight. Request diversion to Wendover Base, Utah. Over"

"Iranian Flight Zero One. Will pass along request. Stand by."

"That's our best bet, Joe!"

"It's our only bet, by the look of things."

In the fighter jet, Iwo Jima Flight, Captain Halloran was almost as frustrated with the situation as Joe and Michelle, except it wasn't him facing a life and death situation with every radio transmission and depressed microphone button.

"Iwo Jima Flight. This is Crystal Mountain. How do you read? Over."

Oh, oh! Right to the big boss. This can't be good, Halloran thought. "Crystal Mountain. This is Iwo Jima Flight. I read you loud and clear. Over."

"Iwo Jima Flight. Permission for diversion to Wendover is granted. I repeat, affirmative for Iranian flight course change to Wendover. Over."

"Crystal Mountain. I read you loud and clear. Can you provide tactical navigation to Wendover? Over." He was grinning what his wingman would certainly call a big, shit-eating grin. He couldn't wait to tell them.

"Iranian Flight Zero one. You are cleared for course change to Wendover. Come to new heading of three three-zero degrees and form on my wing. Distance to Wendover base is just over 600 nautical."

"Iwo Jima Flight. You just made our week. Commencing turn."

"Now, lieutenant. Tell me about this *Airplane* movie," Joe said after letting out a deep breath he hadn't realized he was holding.

"The first funny thing is the auto-pilot, George—they call the auto-pilot Otto and he's a blowup doll that the stewardess has to inflate by giving him a blow job ..." Joe started to laugh and the sense of relief it gave Michelle almost made her cry.

Buckley Air Force Base, Colorado

"Captain! They found the Humvee."

"Where?" asked the base commander angrily.

"In the long term parking at Stapleton, sir."

"Get a team over there ASAP!" the captain yelled, then he picked up the phone and punched up the number for his boss's office. "Colonel Graham, Captain Phillips here! They found our Humvee, sir! Over in the long term lot at Stapleton."

"Get on the blower! I want every jet out of there stopped and searched. I want flight operations over there shut down to all traffic immediately!"

"I was just about to do that, sir! Someone is sure going to get their panties in a bunch over this!"

"Yeah I know, Bert! But I want this bastard caught ASAP! No one is going to fly jets over our country on the way to bomb the God-dammed United Nations and get away with it. Not on my watch." The line went dead.

Phillips punched another line and made the call to the manager of flight operations at Stapleton to give him the good news.

North on I-25, Colorado

The defroster in the brand new Monte Carlo worked extremely well, keeping the windshield clear and the interior warm and toasty. There was no need to wear the winter coat he'd hastily purchased in an airport shop; it lay beside Jaffar on the bench seat. If he could make it to the Wyoming border, he was sure he could make good his escape. It was only 90 miles or so. Denver was a big place and Jaffar was confident it would take authorities hours, if not days, to find the Hummer. Even if the authorities found the vehicle right away, finding one person out of the 50,000 who used the Stapleton airport daily would take some time; he would be long gone by the time they realized he wasn't on a plane.

He smiled and stepped on the gas.

Stapleton Airport's managing director looked out at the fast-approaching storm. A shift to the south in the jet stream over Canada had turned what appeared this morning to be a rather pleasant spring day into something certainly less appealing. However, he was sure his crews and equipment could keep up with any snow accumulations; only four inches was forecast. The telephone rang, startling him. *Cripes!* he thought.

He picked up. "Director Banks here," he said. "Hello, Captain Phillips. How can I be of service?" His mouth fell open when he heard what he was to do. "Right away," he said. It was of importance to national security that he act immediately.

Within minutes of the call, the flight information display system changed all flight status from 'On Time,' 'Delayed' or 'Boarding,' to 'Cancelled'. All inbound flights were diverted to Salt Lake City or other airports nearby. Stapleton International was locked down, a temporary prison for all inside.

A squad of Air National Guardsmen were stationed at each gate around the airport. They were all armed, with orders to search every vehicle coming or going in and out of Stapleton and a dozen different agencies across the United States had been alerted, including NATA. A photograph of Jaffar Hamid Harraj appeared quickly on the FBI's most wanted list, though there was no mention of the flying bomb Jaffar had created. The travelling public was only told that they were being searched because of a kidnapping.

On televisions scattered about the airport, a CBS reporter announced, "A UCLA professor was detained by police in New York City today for trying to disrupt today's dinner at the United Nations. In other news a severe spring storm ..."

One hundred miles north of Stapleton, Jaffar turned west onto the now-familiar Interstate Route 80 that would take him to Salt Lake City. The falling snow slowed his progress only slightly and was actually an advantage, as traffic was light. Jaffar was comfortable with the driving conditions; he'd learned to drive in snowy England.

As he sped down the highway, he revisited the events of the day, wondering how it had all gone so wrong. It had started so well, but quickly turned into a disaster with the arrival of the fighter jets in the skies over Kansas. This wasn't a possibility Jaffar had counted on. But all was not lost; if Sameed had managed to arm the bombs on board his jet as he'd been instructed then perhaps there was still a chance the jet would be shot down over a city or would run out of fuel and crash somewhere where a lot of infidels would be killed and then all his hard work would not be a complete waste. He smiled. One could only hope.

It was late afternoon and dusk was closing in rapidly when his headlights illuminated the sign that read, Welcome To Utah. The next sign was the mileage sign, just inside the state border.

Maybe I should stay in Salk Lake City tonight! It's only eighty miles, Jaffar thought. He was tired, his day had been a roller-coaster, to say the least. He decided against it. He would stop for gas and something to eat only. His instinct to flee, to put as much distance between himself and Denver as possible, was overwhelming. The snow continued to fall. It was growing a bit worse.

Over Southeastern Utah

The Iranian aircraft and her two smaller escorts had just passed the point exactly halfway between Mexican Hat and Bluff, Utah. They were exactly on course for Wendover.

"Iwo Jima Flight to Iranian Flight Zero One. Over."

"Iwo Jima Flight. We read you. Over."

"Iranian Flight Zero One. Cuckoo's Nest has informed me of bombs on board your aircraft. Do you copy?"

"Iwo Jima Flight. We copy. That is affirmative. We have bombs on board, but they are all deactivated. I repeat all bombs on board have all been deactivated. Over"

"Iranian Flight Zero One. I have authorization to read you this message received by Crystal Mountain Command. Over"

"Go ahead with message, Iwo Jima Flight."

"Iwo Jima Flight One One. Lear landed at Buckley AFB. Jaffar Harraj escaped. His men have activated two bombs by remote control, before your intercept. I repeat, before your intercept. Over."

"Iwo Jima flight. Where are the bombs located? Over."

"Iranian Flight Zero One. Unknown at this time. Please continue to Wendover Base with present course and speed. Over." Halloran wished there was more to say, wished he could do more to help those two pilots who were less than 100 feet away. All he could do was increase separation as instructed, in case the unthinkable happened.

— Chapter 26 —

Over Southeastern Utah

"Iwo Jima flight. Message received and understood. Continuing on to Wendover. Will standby."

Joe was already unfastening his seat belt, heading aft.

"This day just doesn't seem to end, does it Joe?"

"I'm going to search this aircraft from fore to aft, from top to bottom and from side to side. I will find those two bombs Michelle, you can count on it." No one alive knew the Boeing as well as Joe Sutton. He was going to search every nook and cranny of the jet.

"I'm looking at that storm off to our northeast, Michelle. It looks to be moving into Colorado." *Keep her mind on the job, Joe,* he thought. "We should be on the ground before it hits. We'll be in Wendover in less than an hour."

Las Vegas, Nevada

Every airport in the country had closed its doors to the Iranian jet, and Jack, Don, Kip and Colonel Hart were worried for Michelle. But the safety of the public was at stake. There was nothing the men could do but wait tensely for good news. Finally, it came.

"Colonel! Word has it our jet has diverted to Wendover. Is that true?" Jack asked excitedly over the phone.

"Yes!" Hart said. "It certainly seems incredible, but it is true." Positive Jack was about to ask if he and Donny could catch the next flight to Salt Lake City, he added, "And before you ask, I'm afraid the answer is 'no'! And you can't drive either," he added for good measure.

"Yes, sir!" Don and Jack replied as one. But they were itching to go. "What can Donny and I do, Colonel?" Jack asked.

"Just sit tight! There is team of FBI Agents due to leave Salt Lake shortly. They will take custody of the aircraft when it lands, along with any of Jaffar's men. Michelle and Joe will travel with some of them back to Salt Lake City."

"Okay! Let us know if and when we can be of any help," Don said, clearly worried.

Salt Lake City, Utah

Jaffar sat in the driver's seat watching the cylindrical digits on the gas pump spin. It reminded him of the one-armed bandits in Las Vegas. He was enjoying the sandwich he'd purchased next door at the cafe and even the tea tasted acceptable. His mood was improving. Under the steel, wood and fiberglass canopy that covered the pump islands, he was protected from the elements, he was warm and he felt safe.

"That will be $18 even, sir!" Jaffar handed the attendant a $20 bill.

"Keep the change!" he said. Then he watched the fellow hurry back inside, out of the storm's wrath.

The snow, which had both increased and decreased over the last 20 miles, was increasing again. Jaffar thought he was on its leading edge and that perhaps he could outrace it as he drove west toward Nevada. To the west was freedom; to the east, was nothing but capture and imprisonment—maybe death. His choice was clear.

Over Central Utah

"I've got one," Joe announced as he entered the cockpit. He had found a very simple timing-detonator mechanism on one of bombs. Thankfully, the most complicated part of it had been the receiving unit. "I could put this together from components at Radio Shack," he said with disdain.

"We're halfway home!" Michelle told him excitedly.

"Where are we, really?" Joe smiled.

"We are 35 minutes out of Wendover, just about to begin our descent."

"I'll keep looking for the other one."

"And I will keep flying the aircraft!"

They weren't out of the woods yet, but Joe could sense the improved mood of his pilot.

The first bomb had been hidden in the aft, port-side lavatory, in the cabinet below the sink. Joe had also found the body of Charlie Ferguson stuffed in the water closet, wrapped in a sheet. Because Jaffar hadn't placed Charlie's body under a sheet in the main cabin, as he'd done with all the guards, Joe was curious, and so he gave the washroom an extra-thorough search.

He looked in all the overhead compartments and storage bins. He searched through all the galley equipment—even the ones that he'd taken apart—just to be certain. The only places that remained to be searched were the seats. The bomb had to be under or inside one of the seat cushions. At least he hoped so; if the bomb was in the cargo hold they might be FUBAR'd (fucked up beyond all repair).

Starting at the front of the cabin, he got on his hands and knees and examined the bottom of every seat, thinking, *I'm getting too old for this!* His knees were aching, but he pressed on. Soon he was at row 14.

Finally, in row 30, Joe saw a faint red glow reflecting off the walls of the fuselage, just above the floor.

"That's it!" he exclaimed out loud. The bomb was located exactly over the main center fuel tank. Even a small device exploded there would have catastrophic results.

Joe gently pulled the device clear of the seat and went to work disarming it then rushed into the cockpit, "I've got them! I've got them!" he shouted.

"That's great, Joe!" Michelle said, relieved. "Now fasten yourself in! We are 20 miles out and at Angels six point five (sixty-five hundred feet) and on final."

"I found a guy stuffed into the rear lav along with the first bomb."

"Who is he, Joe? Another one of Jaffar's men?"

"I doubt it very much! But he was killed execution style, one shot to the back of the head, just like all rest."

Michelle nodded, then keyed her mic.

"Iranian Flight Zero One. Looking good. Over."

"Iwo Jima Flight. I'm on final for Runway 30 at Wendover. Over."

"Roger Iranian Zero One. You are in the groove and lined up. My Dash Two reports that runway is clear. Over."

Michelle and Joe could see the runway in the distance. There wasn't going to be a friendly voice from the ATC, or help from an instrument landing system. They would have to fly using visual flight rules and depend on some help from Iwo Jima Flight.

"Iranian Flight you are at Cherubs eight (eight hundred feet) and looking good."

They flew over the south perimeter fence of Wendover. "Iranian Flight. You are at Cherubs two and in the groove."

Michelle could see the end of the runway coming up fast, she concentrated on a spot about a football field length away from the end.

"Iranian Flight you are at 50 feet and looking good."

Michelle set the Boeing down 200 feet from the south end of the runway. She applied the reverse thrusters and Joe activated the spoilers. The big jet slowed down and they soon taxied onto the main flight apron at Wendover.

"Iranian Flight Zero One. Good job Lieutenant! We are RTB. Over."

"Iwo Jima Flight. Thanks for not turning us into a smoking hole Captain Halloran! Over."

"Iranian Flight. The beers are on you and Captain Sutton, our place. Over."

"Iwo Jima Flight One. That's a big affirmative, Captain. Over and out!"

Back to the matter at hand, Michelle said, "Joe, where do you want me to park this mother?"

"Over near the hangar at the end." It was the same one from which the jet had left almost three full months earlier. "I don't want to leave it out in the open—you know, outside. Once we bail out, we are going to have a hell of a time getting back in without a ladder. And I sure don't want to leave it with a door we can't secure and explosive devices inside. I'm also concerned about the bodies."

That would mean only one thing. Joe would have to lower himself to the ground somehow and open the main hangar door. The drop was almost eleven feet. If he held onto the lower lip of the door opening, the drop was about six.

They opened the forward, outside cabin door and Joe latched it into the open position. A blast of ice-cold air swirled into the cabin, ripping at his clothes. "God! That's cold!" he said. Then he took the bull by the horns and lowered himself down. Gripping the lower door frame, he steeled himself for the drop. The best he could hope for was not to twist or break an ankle on the tarmac.

A sheriff's car from Tooele County appeared suddenly in front of the left wing of the Boeing. A county sheriff got out and lumbered toward the jet and the older man.

"I see you got her down safe," he shouted at Joe, so he could be heard over the still turning turbofans.

"What?" Joe lost his grip on the door frame and fell to the concrete. He landed on his feet, then fell onto his ass. And then Joe stood up, uninjured.

"Christ Almighty! You scared the shit outta me!" Joe said, but he was glad to see the big law enforcement officer just the same.

"Sorry! Been waiting for half the afternoon for you all to get here! I'm Roy Hazelton, the sheriff around here."

"My name's Joe Sutton and that young lady in the pilot's seat is Michelle Hough. I was just heading to open the hangar doors."

"No can do! The Feds have it locked up tight as drum and they've taken the keys! No one gets in or out. It's a crime scene."

"Look Sheriff! We've got an aircraft with almost a dozen dead bodies on board and the seats are full of explosives. I'm not going to let all of that sit out here. We've got to secure this aircraft. Believe me, I don't want to spend a minute more here than I have to—I was held here against my will for six months! But I need to see to this before anything else."

"That was *you* that was held here? Then I guess you do know what you're talking about. I'm with you on this. I've got a crowbar in the trunk!" In five minutes they had the hangar door open and the jet tucked safely inside, right back alongside its twin.

"Lord Almighty! What was going on in here?" The sheriff had not had the opportunity to inspect the inside of the hangar before.

"Can you help me get the stairs up to the cabin door?" Joe called to him.

"Okay, Joe!" The four engines began to spool down and Joe threw a wheel chock around the forward landing gear tire. They rolled the stair into place and Michelle stepped down onto the hangar floor.

Then she threw her arms around Joe. "Thank God," she said.

The skies over Wendover turned dark as banks of thick clouds moved in from the northeast, trying to obscure the fast-setting sun. The temperature started dropping rapidly and snow began to fall; dusk was soon to follow.

"Let's get that door closed!" Joe said to the sheriff.

"Yes!" Michelle stood there in her thin shirt, shivering, "That's a great idea. Maybe we can get this place warmed up." She walked away, trying to find a jacket, anything to cut the chill a bit.

Soon the massive hangar door was closed and Joe had the huge natural gas heaters near the ceiling turned on. "It should climb to over fifty in short order," he said.

Michelle returned wrapped in the only thing she could find—a coarse wool blanket. "This is all I could find," she said. "Here, I brought one for you Joe!"

"Thanks, Michelle!" Joe took his and walked over to his workbench where he cut a hole in the center of the blanket. He stuck his head through the hole. "There! Instant poncho! I guess you didn't find any food in your travels did you?"

"No! Didn't look." Both Michelle and Joe suddenly became aware of how thirsty and hungry each of them was. Neither of them had eaten since the day before.

"You won't find anything here!" the sheriff said. "The FBI hauled it outta here this morning, evidence, they said." Then, after a short pause he added, "Where are my manners? I can go out and grab you something from West Wendover. There's a Burger King there." He looked at his watch, "Or there's the Salt Flats Cafe! It's still open and the food's pretty good!"

"Anything, would be great!" Michelle said. She was still shivering.

"I'll check with them FBI boys while I'm gone and see what's keeping them! They should have been here hours ago!" He headed out the door and into the storm.

Las Vegas, Nevada

"Bad news, Jack! There's a storm moving into the area. It wasn't supposed to move so far to the southwest. Now there's no way the FBI can get from Salt Lake City to Wendover tonight. The roads are getting worse and soon traffic will be at a standstill," Hart said somberly.

"You did say the jet landed safely?" Jack queried.

"Yes, Jack! They beat the storm front by half an hour. NORAD reported them on the ground at Wendover. Their pilot described the landing as a perfect VFR touchdown. Joe and Michelle are both safe and sound.

Wendover Base, Utah

When he arrived back with burgers, fries and milkshakes, Sheriff Hazelton could see two sets of vehicle tracks in the snow ahead of him as he drove across the airfield. That's funny! Maybe those FBI boys made it here after all, he thought.

On high cop alert, he followed the tracks east like a old coon dog and as soon as he rounded the corner to park in front of the hangar, he spotted the Monte Carlo. *That sure ain't no FBI vehicle,* he said to himself.

He pulled in, stopped beside the Chevrolet and shut his motor off. The area was plunged into darkness once more as his headlights cut out. He called for backup on the radio, but he knew they would be quite a while arriving on scene. The bags of food and tray of drinks were left on the bench seat.

He got out, closed his door quietly and stepped over to the Chevy. It was still warm as he knew it would be. He noticed a fresh set of shoe prints heading directly for the man door at the side of the hangar. *One set! An uninvited guest?*

Sheriff Hazelton stood for a moment outside the door. The door did not shut properly and the bright, overhead lights cast a sliver of gold across the snow. He could hear voices inside. He unholstered his weapon and stepped quietly through the door. The voices grew louder.

"So, young lady, I see my plane has landed safe and sound! That is most unfortunate!" Jaffar had been shocked to see his aircraft parked beside the Shah's jet. For an instant he was sure he was hallucinating. But when he saw Michelle, he knew it was for real.

The sheriff watched Jaffar—notorious kidnapper and wanted man—level his pistol at Michelle. She was shocked and angry. "What the fuck are you doing here?" she demanded.

He just smiled. "This is last place anyone is going to look for me, at least for now. But enough chit chat! Where is my crew and where is that old man?"

"Over here! I'm right here Jaffar!" said Joe.

"Where are my men?"

"They are dead! They got sick on the plane. One of them cut us loose before he died, but they looked like they both had heart attacks!" Joe said as sincerely as he could.

"Both of them?"

Joe stepped over to stand beside Michelle. He had a grin on his face. "Yeah! Both of them."

"What's so funny, old man?"

"Nothing! It's just that every one of your men are dead and you are all alone now."

"You're wrong, old man! I've still got the boy!" Jaffar looked down the barrel of the pistol at Joe. "Now it's time for you to join my men!"

"Drop it," the Sheriff shouted, leveling his gun at Jaffar.

Jaffar began to turn, ready to shoot the sheriff.

"Not this time," Joe said as he stepped forward and smashed Jaffar on the right shoulder with the biggest wrench he could hide beneath his makeshift poncho. Almost at that same instant, a thunderous report filled the hangar and Joe looked to see Jaffar falling to the floor, a hole in his left shoulder area from the sheriff's bullet and pool of blood was starting to spread beneath him.

"Is everyone okay?" asked the sheriff.

"Yes! We are both fine." It was a miracle that the only one who had been shot was Jaffar.

"Quickly! Get some clean rags, anything to stop the bleeding!" said Joe.

"What?!"

"You heard me, Lieutenant! Get something to stem the flow!"

"Yes, sir!"

Michelle gathered up anything that she could find that was suitable to use for first aid. "Why are you doing this, Joe?"

"I want this son of a bitch to pay for what he's done!" Joe said. "And I want my wife back!" He looked down at Jaffar. "Don't die on me, you son of a bitch!"

Las Vegas, Nevada - March 27, 1981

Jack had lost count of how many times during the night he'd wanted to disobey the colonel, roust Donny out of bed and drive back to Wendover.

Donny had only a few hours of sleep as well. He'd had similar thoughts and was even willing to go it alone if need be.

He'd actually left once. As dawn broke and he heard Jack stir, he whispered, "I made it out as far as the Coke machine in the lobby, Jack."

"Yeah, I know. I heard you leave."

"What? You didn't try to stop me?"

"Nope! I figured that common sense would prevail. Besides the roads are still pretty shitty!"

The roads from Crystal Springs all the way north into Wyoming had picked up a foot of snow and were almost impassable. Highway maintenance crews were only just starting to clear them for travel.

"There wasn't a lot we could accomplish last night. Let's go downstairs and grab some breakfast. From there we can head over to McCarran and give the Colonel a call."

The loud growl from Donny stomach, seemed to support that decision. They both laughed. "I guess all three of us are in agreement!" Don said.

McCarran International

"I was wondering when you boys were going to show up." McCarran's Director Watts was in a far better mood than he'd been the previous day, in spite of having to deal with the overflow of aircraft from several closed airports during the evening. "How was your room?"

"Fine, thank you for providing it!"

"It was the least we could do. We here at McCarran owe you two fellows and your Agency a great deal of thanks. There would be nothing but a big smoking hole at the United Nations if it wasn't for you."

"Nobody can know about this, Director," Jack said solemnly.

"What?" Director Watts was very confused.

"Nobody can know about the plane, the bombs. Nobody can know about us! NATA doesn't exist as far as the public is concerned."

"I understand!" He didn't, really, but he respected Jack and Don and he knew how to keep a secret.

"Thanks for the clothes by the way," Don said, eyeing the rather ill-fitting McCarran Security uniforms he and Jack wore. They were all Chief Roberts had on hand on such short notice but they were a far cry better than the soiled clothes both men had on the previous day.

"You two clean up quite well," Watts said. "By the way, I have your Colonel on the phone."

As he had 24 hours earlier, Colonel Hart was listening in via speaker-phone from Washington. "Good morning Jack, Donny! I heard a snippet of the conversation when you two were coming into the office. Director Watts, you and anyone under your command are not to reveal what they witnessed yesterday and today, under orders of the National Security Advisor. Documents are being prepared that you and your staff must sign."

"Yes, sir!" Watts said.

"Any news, Colonel?" Donny asked worriedly, thinking of Michelle.

"Yes! I have good news, I have great news and I have bad news."

"Give it to us, Colonel," Don ordered. Then he added contritely, "Please, in that order, sir."

"I told you they landed safe and sound at Wendover. They got your doppelganger back in the hangar right beside the Shah's plane. That's the good news."

"It's great news to us!"

"To everyone, Don! But even greater news is that someone showed up just hours later!"

"Who?" Donny asked.

"Jaffar!" Jack said quickly.

"That's right, Jack! How did you know?"

"Go back to where you started from. Who would look there, right! Denver is what … half a day's drive?"

"You're quick, Jack," said the colonel.

"So, what's the bad news?" All three men were praying that neither Michelle, Joe nor anyone else had fallen victim to that bastard, Jaffar.

"Jaffar was shot! He might not make it."

"That's bad news?" This was from Director Watts.

Both Donny and Jack knew that it was bad news. "Has he said where her son is?" Jack asked, feeling cold creep up his spine.

"No, he's not conscious yet. But Mrs. Roshtti will want to know about him. Why don't you give her a call, Jack?"

"Yes, sir," Jack said. "I will call you back."

When he hung up from the colonel, Jack waited a few minutes to collect his thoughts and figure out what to say. Then he picked up the telephone and dialed the number in Sacramento from memory. The sound of the Roshtti household telephone ringing was like London's Big Ben, ticking in Jack's ear.

"Hello?" Giti answered.

"Hello! Mrs. Roshtti. Jack Coward here. I'm calling you from Las Vegas."

"Any news?" she asked anxiously.

"Yes and no, Mrs. Roshtti," Jack said.

"Please, Mr. Coward. Call me Giti! And tell me what you know."

"We have Jaffar. He has been captured," Jack said hesitantly, "but we don't have Sina. Not yet, at least. We will make him tell us where he is, I promise you that."

Giti stifled as sob and Jack felt his heart reach out to hers. No mother should have to suffer as she had. On a whim he said, "Giti … is there anything you can tell that might give me a clue, anything at all?"

Giti hesitated. "I don't want to sound like a crazy woman, Jack. But I have this feeling. And I had a very strange dream the other night, very early in the morning. In my dream, I got a phone call from my Sina. He sounded so strange in this dream."

Jack felt the hair on his arms rise. He was a logical man, but there was something about her sing-song voice as she remembered her dream that made him want to believe her words, to milk them for truth. He had learned that sometimes a woman's intuition could be real.

"What did he say in this dream?" he asked, trying to draw her out.

"I'm sorry Mr. Coward, this so stupid. It was just a dream!"

"No! No! Go ahead tell me what Sina told you."

"He told me he was tired."

"What else did he say in this dream?"

"This will sound strange, but he told me 'I can see a red horse running, Mommy'. Then he hung up. When I woke up, the telephone cord was wrapped around the lamp base and was hanging down to the floor. The phone was beeping because it was off the hook. I have no memory of picking it up, though. Please don't think I'm crazy. It was just a dream."

"Mrs. Roshtti … Giti … I don't think you are crazy and I am happy that you felt comfortable enough to tell me of this. I think it might be helpful.

But I don't want you to get too excited. I have an idea though, so I have to go. And Giti? I promise I will call you back soon."

After he hung up, Jack grinned hugely. "Donny! I think I know where Sina is!"

It didn't take long for the SWAT team from the Las Vegas Police department to quickly and quietly evacuate every room—with the exception of adjoining rooms 313 and 315— of Arizona Charlie's Boulder Casino Hotel complex. While guests were being escorted out, a search of the hotel's registration and some intense conversations with the manager and staff confirmed that these two rooms were almost definitely where the hostages were being held.

"Yes! We have brought their meals to them for almost a week, by room service. Some of my staff have seen a little boy asleep on the bed. They told us he was ill and seeing a specialist in Las Vegas! We had no reason to doubt them."

"That's room 313, right?"

"Yes!"

"What about the other room? Room 315?"

"No! No one has seen the inside of that room for almost a week. We drop off the room service trolley and then pick it up empty later on."

Across the street, two SWAT sharp-shooters lay prone on the roof of the Turf Hotel.

"Team two here! We are in position," they radioed in.

Two other teams had taken up positions in the adjacent rooms, one in room 311 and another in room 317. They opened their blinds completely, bracketing and highlighting the target rooms.

"Team two! Do you have a visual on teams three and four?"

"That is affirmative, team leader!"

"What about targets, team two?"

"Negative!"

Jack was with team three in room 311; Donny was three doors down in room 317 with team four. Jack looked at his watch, it was almost noon. He was hoping that SWAT wouldn't have to go busting in.

Inside the rooms, to observe the proper prayer schedules, both Farouk and Akmed had placed their mats on the floor, just in time for the Dhuhr prayer the minute before noon. Neither had heard from Jaffar, nor had they heard of an airliner crashing into the U.N. It was clear Jaffar had failed and would not be issuing anymore instructions.

Only a few more tasks to perform, Farouk said to himself. *Now we must kill the hostages.*

The men opened their blinds at approximately the same time which startled the sniper teams for an instant.

"Team leader! This is team two! We have a visual into both rooms at this time!

"Roger, team two!"

"Do we have permission to engage?"

"That's affirmative, team two."

When Farouk and Akmed finished their midday prayer, they stood erect. They didn't even notice when a star-shaped defect appeared in each window in front of them and a silenced supersonic round found the center of each man's forehead, killing each of them instantly.

"Targets are down! I repeat targets are down!"

Two battering rams smashed through two doors within seconds of one another. Jack rushed into room 313, pistol drawn. Donny did the same next door. Jack bent down and picked up Sina, who had slept blissfully through the whole thing. He carried him out the door and down the hall toward the lobby and the waiting ambulance.

"Come on Sina. Let's go and give your Mom a call, shall we?" Sina's head was on Jack's shoulder. Sina stirred slightly, "Okay, Daddy!" It was obvious Sina was still drugged, dreaming about Reza.

Jack looked in wonder at the red horse logo of the Turf Hotel across the street, as he delivered the sleeping boy to the ambulance attendants.

— Epilogue —

Edwards Air Force Base, California - December 1, 1984

Jaffar's jet sat on the tarmac of Edwards Air force Base. For the last four years, it had been in the care of the FAA, its fate uncertain. It was now painted in its final livery, under the National Aeronautics and Space Administration. More than a dozen technicians moved in, out and around the aircraft, making last minute adjustments to instruments and controls. Today would be the very last flight for the Boeing 720. Today would be a unique flight experiment called Controlled Impact Demonstration, or CID.

On the eastern edge of Rodgers dry lake bed at Edwards Air Force Base, a special gravel runway had been constructed for today. It featured several short, vertical steel posts that had been concreted into the ground. These posts were wing cutters, meant to slice open the wings and breach the fuel tanks in those wings. The purpose of the test was to look at how a promising fuel additive, used for suppressing fire, acted in a real world crash landing scenario. This morning the jet had been filled with just over 76,000 pounds of Jet-A fuel containing this fuel additive.

In the passenger cabin, the tourist class seats no longer had five gallon pails of various explosive mixtures in them; instead each had a sophisticated crash test dummy loaded with sensors. As well, there were cameras mounted throughout the aircraft, ready to transmit the event to screens and recorders at NASA's Dryden Flight Research Centre, located at Edwards.

Both front cockpit seats were empty, however, and the camera feed from the cockpit would not go to Dryden; instead, it was on a separate channel being fed strictly to a room which would record and televise the event for a very select audience.

Twenty minutes before takeoff, all activity around the jet came to a halt. The technicians had made their final checks and everything was ready to go. The last two technicians closed up some of the access hatches on the belly of the fuselage, gave each other the thumbs up and joined their companions in the van, which then moved off.

The NASA Flight Director, George Kreuzkamp, arrived and entered the aircraft for his final check. A moment later, he stood at the top of the stairs, raised his hand and waved, signaling the all-clear. Before he reached the bottom step, a light-grey, unmarked van with U.S. Government plates stopped nearby. Two men got out.

"Good luck, gentlemen," Director Kreuzkamp said. Followed by, "Don't forget to lock the door on your way out!"

"We won't, sir," Jack replied. He watched the NASA official drive off. "Okay, Donny we're clear."

They had 15 minutes to accomplish their task, as the plane was leaving with or without them. From the two rear seats, two men were taken from the van. Both were in handcuffs and wearing black hoods. They were escorted up the stairs and led a short distance to the left then the handcuffs were removed. Then the two men were each, in turn, gently made to sit in their seats and their forearms and legs were then bound to the seats with straps. Only then were their hoods removed and only then did Jaffar Hamid Harraj realize he was in the left-hand pilot's seat of his old jet while Abdul Salam Al-Kubesi occupied the copilot's seat.

Jaffar recognized the plane immediately. "What is going on here? Why are we on my plane?"

"This is no longer your plane," Jack explained gently. "It was forfeited to the United States government a long time ago."

"You! You two!" Jaffar gasped.

"Yes, Jaffar, it's us two."

"What's happening?"

"What's happening Jaffar, is that we have bestowed a special honor on you and your pal here. You are now part of a NASA experiment."

"What? What kind of experiment, we are not astronauts!"

"Oh! Nothing like that my friend." Jack continued, "You can see in front of you that the steering yoke for the elevators and ailerons have both been removed."

"How will we steer the plane?"

"You won't Jaffar, these two cameras and your little box contraption will!'

"What!"

"Yep! You made all of this possible Jaffar and you've got a front row seat!"

"Where are we going?" Abdul finally asked.

"Well, well Abdul! I didn't think we were going hear anything from you," Jack said. Then he explained, "This jet is loaded with over thirty-eight tons of special jet fuel. You and Jaffar will go for a little ride and NASA will monitor the plane as part of a test. The cabin is full of some very sensitive CTDs, some big, some small. NASA wants to see how they hold up during the experiment."

Abdul didn't have the good sense to ask what a CTD was. He seemed to relax considerably. Jaffar on the other hand was curious, "What is a CTD, Mr. Private Detective?" he sneered.

Jack leaned over and whispered in his ear, too softly for Abdul to hear, "CTD is short for crash test dummy!"

Jaffar's eyes grew wide with sudden comprehension and he began to scream "No! You can't do this to us! Show us a little ..." Jaffar tried to think of the right word or words, "… a little mercy, a little sympathy!"

"Sympathy! Sympathy?" Jack almost spat out the words. "Sympathy like you were going to show those hundreds of innocent people at the United Nations or New York City? Sympathy?" Jack continued, "Did you show sympathy for Lorena Salvador, the pretty young woman you strangled to death with your bare hands at the print shop! Did you show sympathy for Mr. and Mrs. Sutton, the wife and husband you kidnapped? Or for the Empress? Or …" and at this Jack moved in close to Jaffar's face, his fury clear, "… did you show sympathy for Giti, your wife … the woman you raped and almost beat to death? Or the baby she lost? Or your stepson, Sina who you kidnapped and drugged and were totally prepared to kill?"

Jaffar gulped. Jack turned to Abdul.

"And you, Abdul. Did you show sympathy to that family of thirteen you murdered simply because their father delivered a fucking package a few hours late? If you're looking for sympathy, you'll find it between 'shit' and 'syphilis' in the dictionary … and you'll get none from us. If I was you two, I'd start to pray. You've both got about fifteen or twenty minutes to live."

"If you do this, you are no better than me, Jack Coward," Jaffar said coldly ... but there was genuine fear in his voice. Jack stopped for a moment as he heard engine number one start to spool up. It was almost time to go.

"I will always be better than you," he said.

"No! Please! Please!" Both men started to struggle frantically against their bonds. Their cries for help were soon drowned out by the engine noise as Jack and Donny made their way outside, closing the forward cabin door as promised. They hurried down the stairs then moved the steps back so the jet could safely get under way.

Once Jack and Donny were in the van and moving away from the jet, Jack radioed to the range safety officer that he was clear. The Boeing made a normal takeoff with a left hand turn and climbed to 2,300 feet altitude. Its controller maintained a race track course for two orbits, to make sure everything was functioning properly. Everything was perfect. The last orbit was directly in line, with the centerline of the new gravel runway. The okay was given by Director Kreuzkamp to begin the descent.

In the viewing room were six television screens. The feed from the remote cameras in the Boeing 720's cockpit was being viewed exclusively by eight men: Colonel Hart, Jack, Donny, Zafar, the assistant directors of both the CIA and the National Security Agency—the latter of whom had had the pleasure of interrogating and hosting Jaffar and Abdul for the last 44 months—the assistant to the Secretary of State and finally, Mohammed Al Shazir, the oxen-driver who'd put up with Abdul's abuse in Al Qa'im years earlier and who now occupied Jaffar's former home. He was there at the special request of Colonel Hart.

Jaffar had been declared missing and dead three years earlier, leaving all his material goods to his wife. Giti had no desire to live in Iraq and was certain she would have no use for the home in Al Qa'im, no matter how lovely it was.

Following Jaffar's detainment, NATA had sent Kip to Iraq to investigate Jaffar's relationship to Islamic Hamas and one day he got stuck in traffic behind Mohammed Al Shazir and his oxen. He got out to talk with the man and discovered the variety of abuses he and others in Al Qa'im had endured under Abdul's reign of terror as chief of police. He further discovered that Mohammed Al Shazir held evening lesson groups for children who wanted to learn to read and write. He asked if he had need of a building for a school and Mohammed said he had prayed to Allah for just such a thing. When Giti heard the story, she immediately signed Jaffar's house over to him, along with a trust fund to cover upkeep and school supplies in perpetuity.

Now, as a group, the men watched as the aircraft started its descent in line with the short runway. The landing gear was not lowered for this landing; in fact it was locked in the retracted position.

The aircraft descended on a shallow glide slope of about four degrees, and exterior views of the plane were provided by two chase cameras on each side of the 720. If everything went well, the aircraft would land with its wings level, exactly lined up with the runway centerline. This would allow the fuselage to remain intact while the wings were sliced open by the steel wing cutters on each side.

This however, was not to be. Somehow, during the last moments of the flight, either Jaffar Abdul had managed to loosen the straps on their feet. In a desperate attempt to escape, one of them stepped on the rudder pedal—on purpose or accidentally, no one would ever know. The aircraft suddenly began to drift off course at less than 170 feet above the dry lake bed. The ground controller tried in vain in correct the deviation, but as the aircraft neared the ground, the left wing contacted it short of the cutters. The nose of the aircraft started to yaw to the left as it slid on the gravel runway. It was sideways at about 45 degrees when one of the wing cutters destroyed the inboard engine on the right wing, causing a huge fuel leak that erupted in flames.

In its final seconds the Boeing 720 continued to swing to the left until it was almost completely sideways, causing the damaged right wing to break off and fold over. Soon, the fuselage was engulfed in a massive fireball, fed by the leaking fuel. It took more than an hour to extinguish the blaze.

Colonel Hart was tasked with the job of securing the recording of the grim events that had unfolded on the television screens. The bodies of Jaffar and Abdul were quickly and quietly returned to Al Qa'im. There, they were buried in an unmarked grave on Jaffar's former property, transported to their graves by an oxen-drawn cart, courtesy of Mohammed Al Shazir.

La Paz, Baja California Sur - December 2, 1984

It had been an easy flight. Jack and Donny had left immediately after the demise of the 720 and the deaths of Jaffar and Abdul. After checking into their hotel, the two men went to see their old friend, Captain Miguel. The last time they had seen him was in 1980, before the unpleasant business with Jaffar. Before an unmanned jet loaded with explosives threatened America.

But while much had changed for Jack and Don, four years later, Miguel's life was much the same. They found him where they expected him to be, onboard his boat—but the warm smile they associated with him was absent; instead, he was somewhat upset. He was looking over at a brand new boat, moored cock-eyed, right beside his own.

"Hola, Captain Miguel!" called out Donny.

"Hola." He still looked unhappy—until he recognized Jack and Don. Then he broke out into a huge smile, " Señor Jack! Señor Donny! Hola!" He gave each man a vigorous handshake.

"What's the matter, Miguel? You don't look very pleased," Jack asked.

"Look there! Some rich gringo has tied up too close to me, there in no way around. No respect! I can't get out to go fishing today." Miguel added, "I will have to try and track down the owner, it will take most of the day."

Jack heard music playing, as if right on cue. "Oh, I don't know about that amigo, I think the owner is coming along right about now."

Along the pier, three women appeared, one of them carrying a huge, new boom box. They were followed by three boys, two very small and one a teenager. The music grew louder as they approached and Miguel immediately recognized the dark-haired woman. It was his wife, Esmeralda—but she was keeping company with strangers and carrying a stereo he did not recognize. The song it was playing was *Please Don't Let Me Be Misunderstood*, the Santa Esmeralda version. Miguel felt he was indeed misunderstanding something. But he didn't want to question his wife in front of all these people.

He hopped onto the dock to greet her and she smiled then turned down the volume on the boom box. "It is a new CD player, Miguel," she said, still smiling. "It is ours."

Miguel's eyes widened. This was a luxury his family could not afford. Esmeralda placed the ghetto blaster on the pier then just stood there and smiled.

"Miguel," Don said, stifling a grin, "It seems your lovely wife has already met my wife Michelle and my son, Don Junior."

A towheaded three-year-old boy smiled joyfully at Miguel. "I want to catch a fish please," he said.

"So big, this boy," said Miguel. Don's son was already the size of a five-year-old.

"He won't stop eating," said Michelle. "He's just like his dad."

Miguel turned to look at Jack, who was standing proudly beside a petite, dark-haired woman whose grace and beauty were equal to that of his own wife, Esmeralda. The two children beside her were dark like their mother, but the youngest had Jack's cheekbones and chin. He looked to be about the same age as Don's child, if a little smaller.

"Senor Jack ..." Miguel gestured to the boy, "Is this yours?" he asked, smiling from ear to ear.

"Yes," Jack said proudly. "This is my wife, Giti, and these are my two sons, Sina and John." Sina extended his hand to Miguel and his little brother copied him. Miguel shook each child's hand in turn.

"Such fine young men," he said. Giti smiled and patted little John's head.

Jack had not expected a romance to blossom with Giti. It was true that she had captivated him from the first time he'd seen her, but he'd also been aware that the circumstances under which they'd met might make him seem to be the one at fault for her meeting, and ultimately marrying, Jaffar.

However, shortly after Jaffar was captured and officially declared 'missing' by the U.S. government, Jack decided to stop by to deliver the news to Giti in person. He didn't know what reaction to expect; in his opinion, Jaffar deserved every bad thing that happened to him. But women are softer. He was afraid she would break down and blame him—after all, she had been married to the man. Maybe she loved him still.

When he arrived on her doorstep, she invited him in for coffee and, after he delivered the news that Jaffar was missing, she was stoic. All she said was, "Good. I will never forgive the man who took my son from me. And I will always love the man who brought him back."

Her eyes were so intense and she looked at him with such sweetness that Jack decided he'd better get it over with. He remembered that day—the day he told her about being hired by Mohammed to find her for Jaffar—as more terrifying to him than being wounded in 'Nam. But he knew he had to come clean and so, impulsively, he told her the whole story—leaving out the part about the plane bomb.

He did mention, however, that Jaffar had stolen Reza's idea for a remote control jet and had planned to use the technology for profit. He wanted her to know that Reza had come up with something wonderful and that she should be proud of him.

From there, things just blossomed. Giti said it was because of the shopping cart he had helped her with the day he had followed her to the mall.

"You are here to help me, Jack Coward," she announced as she took his hand in marriage, "and I know that you always will be."

With their full-time NATA jobs and respective entries into family life, neither Jack nor Don had had an opportunity to thank Miguel for what ultimately was his role in saving countless lives ... if he had not taken them to the best place to fish for roosterfish, Jack would not have been on television, Detective Strohman wouldn't have noticed him and Colonel Hart wouldn't have contacted him. If these things hadn't happened, the world would be a different place right now—and that was why they were back in La Paz; to thank him.

"Señor Jack, can you tell me about the owner of this boat?" Miguel asked, gesturing to the boat with annoyance. He did not want to let another good day's fishing go by. Esmeralda removed a set of shiny new keys from her pocket and jingled them at him, smiling.

"Miguel, you are the proud owner of that brand-new, 35-foot Phoenix Sport-fish with twin Volvo diesel engines and a 10-foot beam," Jack said. He and Don had arranged for its delivery early this morning—all Miguel had to do was pack his fishing gear on board.

Esmeralda started to cry. "She is a beautiful boat for my husband."

Miguel stood there, speechless, tears of joy welling in his eyes. Jack took the keys from Esmeralda and handed them to him. "Well Captain Miguel, what do you say? The ladies have agreed to stay at the hotel while we five gentlemen go after some roosterfish."

"Yay! Roosterfish!" was the chorus from the two youngest. Jack was sure all three boys imagined they would be fishing for male chickens with gills.